GREAT RUSSIAN SHORT STORIES

GREAT
RUSSIAN SHORT STORIES

Edited by

Stephen Graham

———

LIVERIGHT
PUBLISHING CORPORATION
New York

Copyright © 1959 by Ernest Benn Limited

Reprinted in a Liveright paperbound edition 1975

ISBN 0 87140 105 3 (Paper Edition)
ISBN 0 87140 615 2 (Cloth Edition)

ALL RIGHTS RESERVED
Published simultaneously in Canada
by George J. McLeod Limited, Toronto

Printed in the United States of America
1 2 3 4 5 6 7 8 9

PREFACE

IN THIS comprehensive collection are to be found some of the finest stories in world literature: "The Pistol-Shot" by Pushkin, "The Cloak" by Gogol, "The Grand Inquisitor" by Dostoievsky, "Dushechka" by Chekov. Other remarkable stories by celebrated writers are—"The Herald of the Beast" by Sologub, "Psyche" by Kuprin, "The Marble Bust" by Brusof, "Twenty-six and One" by Gorky and "His Majesty, Kneeb Piter Komondor" by Boris Pilniak, a very original study of Peter the Great.

Many of the stories here collected were not available in English and were specially translated for this anthology. That is true of this long short story of Pilniak's which was issued as a booklet in Soviet Russia. Another work which was specially translated is Apukhtine's "The Archive of Countess D——" which is a curiosity. The two stories by Ertel have a unique value as they can be found in English only in this volume. Alexander Ertel, a friend of Tolstoy, was the father of the brilliant translator from the Russian Natalie Duddington. Other stories which appeared here first are the two from Bunin, Nobel Prize winner in 1935. Bunin who died in 1957 may be reckoned the greatest Russian emigre writer.

Kuprin who, before he died, made his peace with the U.S.S.R. excelled as a writer of short stories. His "Psyche" was translated for this volume as were also the tales of Garshin and Chirikof and "The Sentry" by Leskov. "Death and the Soldier" by the folklorist Afanasief, "How Hassan Lost his Trousers" by Doroshevitch once a literary idol, "The Three Girdles" by Zhukovsky and "An Evening of Culture" probably the most amusing piece which Michael

Zoschenko composed before he was stopped making fun of Soviet institutions.

Zoschenko who may be called the Chekof of post-revolutionary Russia was required to "alter course" and during the last ten years of his life began to write such humourless stories as "The Inglorious End", being a propagandist view of the last days of Kerensky. His name was removed from the 2nd edition of the Soviet Encyclopaedia. Curiously enough much space in that work is given to Bunin and his stories appear to have been published in the U.S.S.R. The official view of the short story is that it ought to be in the nature of a brochure encouraging the Stakhanovites or glorifying the achievements of the Communist state. It was characteristic that Romanof was deflected from his intimate studies of individual men and women to describe the automobile factories at Gorky. Kataef, a Lenin prize-winner, had nevertheless to rewrite his unique war story to meet the requirements of the Party. Realism is *out*.

All the same the cult of the short story still flourishes. There are many magazines to publish them and the circulation is four-fold what it was. Reading Chekhof and Kuprin aloud used to be a feature of student parties but now they have many stories coming over on the radio or adapted for television. What is new has preference but the great writers of the past are not neglected. With a few exceptions all the stories printed in this anthology are available in the original Russian and can be read in cheap re-prints or at the university libraries.

No such collection as *Great Russian Short Stories* exists in Russia and is perhaps not necessary. But for British and American readers it has a special value as it covers the whole range of Russian writers and contains a number of stories not available in English translation in any other publication.

STEPHEN GRAHAM

CONTENTS

CONTENTS

ACKNOWLEDGMENTS

Messrs. Constable & Co.: "Rhea Silvia" and "The Marble Bust" by Valery Brusof; "Tempting Providence," "The Song and the Dance" and "Mechanical Justice" by Kuprin; "Turandina," "The Herald of the Beast," "Adventures of a Cobble-stone" and "Equality" by Fedor Sologub.

Mrs. Constance Garnett and Messrs. Heinemann: "The Grand Inquisitor" and "A Gentle Spirit" by Dostoievsky.

Hodder & Stoughton, Ltd.: "The Little Angel" by Leonide Andreyef.

Jarrolds, Ltd.: "Twenty-six and One" by Maxim Gorky.

Alfred A. Knopf, Ltd.: "The Life and Adventures of Matvey Pavlitchenko" by Isaac Babel.

Mr. and Mrs. Aylmer Maude and the Oxford University Press: "Where Love is, God is" and "The Three Hermits" by Tolstoy in the World's Classics edition.

Thomas Nelson & Sons, Ltd.: "Father Sergius" by Tolstoy.

Messrs. Scribner: "The Song of Love Triumphant" and "The Dream" by Turgenief: "On the Way" and "Rothschild's Fiddle" by Chekhov.

Ivan Bunin: "Never-ending Spring" and "Sunstroke."

Also to Mrs. Natalie Duddington, Mrs. Rosa Graham, Mrs. Helen Matheson, Mr. Roman Sagovsky and Mr. Leonide Zarine, who have translated certain stories specially for this anthology.

S. G.

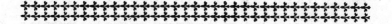

GREAT RUSSIAN SHORT STORIES

✢✢

VASSILY ZHUKOVSKY

(1783–1852)

✢✢

THE THREE GIRDLES

A RUSSIAN FAIRY STORY

(Translated by LEONIDE ZARINE)

D U R I N G the reign of the great prince Vladimir there lived in a lonely hut on the banks of the Dnieper not far from Kief three orphan girls called Peresveta, Miroslava and Ludmila. They were great friends. Peresveta and Miroslava were as beautiful as a spring day, people referred to them as the blushing roses, and because of this they had become somewhat conceited. Ludmila was not a beauty, nobody praised her, and the friends she so dearly loved told her every day: "Ludmila, poor Ludmila, you will never marry, no one will fall in love with you, you are neither beautiful nor rich." The good Ludmila in the simplicity of her heart believed them and was not sad. "They speak the truth; I shall never marry, but what does it matter? I shall love Peresveta and Miroslava more than anything else in the world and will be loved by them. What happiness can I want more?" So thought the simple Ludmila and her pure heart was content. She reached her fifteenth year. But no extravagant desire excited her innocent heart; to

love her friends, to tend the flowers, to sing her songs as a
tender bird, such were the pleasures of the good Ludmila.

One day the three friends were walking along the river
bank gathering flowers. Peresveta and Miroslava were
braiding their hair and Ludmila was helping them, for herself she thought it unbecoming to think of self-adornment.
Suddenly they saw on the river bank an old woman in deep
slumber; the sun poured down on her scanty grey locks. Peresveta and Miroslava began to joke. "Sister," said one, "what
do you think of this beauty? She is better-looking than you,
Miroslava!" "And than you, Peresveta! A buttercup could
hardly surpass the yellowness of those wrinkled cheeks!"
"And her nose, Peresveta, how modestly it curves down to
her chin; and to tell the truth, the chin curves up in answer."
"They grew together, sister!" During this conversation they
both laughed continuously. "Ah, sisters," said the quiet
Ludmila, "you ought not to make fun of this old woman.
What has she done to you? If she is old it is not her fault.
You also will be old in your turn, so why laugh at the defects
which you will not be able to avoid? To laugh at old people
is, above all, to laugh at one's self. Be considerate, or perhaps I should say be merciful. See how the sun scorches the
head of this poor woman. Let us break down some of the
birch branches and make a shelter round her so that her
sleep may be quiet and safe. When she awakens she will
bless us, pray for us, and my dear mother used to tell me
that heaven always fulfils the prayers of old women and
beggars." Peresveta and Miroslava felt that they had done
wrong and they joined with Ludmila in breaking down
branches and making a shelter round the head of the sleeper.
She soon awoke and was amazed to find herself in the shade.
She began to look round and saw before her the three girls.
"I thank you, kind strangers," said she; "come nearer. I
should like to give you a token of my gratitude. Here are
three girdles—you can each choose the one which you like
the best and which you think will best suit your appear-

ance." The old woman placed three girdles on the grass; two were extremely rich, emblazoned with large pearls and diamonds, the third was a pure white ribbon embroidered with violets. Peresveta and Miroslava seized the pearls and diamonds, Ludmila took the white ribbon. "I thank you," said she to the old woman. "This simple ornament is most suitable for me. Peresveta and Miroslava are beautiful, they must also have beautiful finery, something quite simple and modest is suitable for me." "You are quite right, my friend," said the old woman, putting the girdle round Ludmila; "never, for the richest treasure in the world, take off this ribbon; do not believe people who say it does not suit you, guard against the temptations of pride; if you lose this girdle you will lose the happiness which goes with it." Ludmila kissed the old woman and promised never to give the ribbon to anyone. The old woman disappeared. Peresveta and Miroslava had not heard her words, they had been so busy examining with delight their pearls and diamonds that they had scarcely had time to utter a word of thanks. Hand in hand they ran towards their hut. Ludmila, observing that they had some secret between themselves, followed in the distance. "Is it not true," said Miroslava at last to Ludmila, "that this queer old woman made you an extremely rich present?" "Not rich, but one which pleases me very much, I do not like display." "But why did she not treat you the same as us?" "I never thought about it. I am more pleased to have what people give to me than I could be by what they refuse." "See how our diamonds glisten." "Look how white my ribbon is." "And you are not envious?" "Can one be envious of those one loves? I am pleased that you are happy." "You are a good girl, Ludmila. Stay at home and we will go to Kief to buy new dresses; those we have are too poor to wear with these jewelled girdles. For one pearl we can buy a dozen of the richest dresses." Peresveta and Miroslava went to Kief; Ludmila remained at home to water the flowers and to feed her little birds.

Towards evening Peresveta and Miroslava returned to the hut with a large supply of rich clothing. "There is important news," they told Ludmila; "the young prince Sviatoslav, son of the great prince Vladimir, brave and as handsome as a spring day, is about to choose a bride. Numerous beauties, daughters of noblemen and even of ordinary country people, are assembling in Kief from the distant Russian towns and villages. Who is there to prevent us from seeking the hand of the handsome Sviatoslav? God made us beautiful and the good old woman presented us with riches. Miroslava and I want to go to live in Kief; thanks to our precious girdles we can appear with honour and distinction before the people. We have decided to go to-morrow, and you, dear Ludmila, may follow us. You will be able to look after our home and to see the magnificent ceremony of the election of the bride." "I will willingly comply with your wishes, sisters," answered Ludmila with a happy smile. "I will do all in my power to serve you; your pleasure makes all my happiness. Try to win the handsome prince and I will pray that his heart may be turned towards you."

It was no sooner said than done. The friends went the following morning to Kief. Miroslava and Peresveta gave themselves out to be the daughters of a rich burgomaster of Novgorod. Their name was entered by a court official in the list of those desirous of presenting themselves at the election before Prince Sviatoslav. Ludmila did not appear anywhere. She prayed for the happiness of her friends, sewed their dresses, strung their necklaces, covered their corsages with gold braid and diamonds, forgetting herself and living for them.

At last came the great day of the election. Towards evening the palace of the great prince Vladimir was illuminated with thousands of lanterns; the great room which was to be used for the ceremony was covered in rich crimson velvet; the seats on which the beauties of Kief and other parts were to sit were covered with gold-embroidered silks, and for the great prince Vladimir and Prince Sviatoslav was prepared a dais on which stood two thrones of ivory inlaid with gold. In the street which led to the royal palace thronged a multitude of people. At last the drums sounded and a beautiful spectacle appeared—hundreds of beauties, blooming like the roses of spring, went in pairs through the throngs of people towards the palace of the great prince; each had a servant in attendance; Ludmila accompanied Peresveta and Miroslava. Ludmila was attired in a white dress and was wearing her girdle. Her fair hair was plaited and braided with ordinary ribbon. She approached the palace of the great prince Vladimir fearfully, sat behind her friends, and with a secret and timid premonition gazed on the door through which the great prince and his son would enter. For a long time there was a great silence in the chamber. Suddenly military music began to play, the doors opened and the courtiers and valiant knights entered in pairs, the courtiers attired in rich gold-brocaded robes and the knights in splendid armour, with golden mail and glistening helmets with white plumes. They took up their positions on both sides of the throne. The martial music ceased and tender flutes could be heard; all eyes turned on the open doors. Suddenly the great prince Vladimir appeared, clad in rich princely garments and leading by the hand the young prince Sviatoslav, simply dressed, bareheaded, his fair locks flowing on his shoulders, charming and blooming with youth. On his cheeks he wore a blush like a spring rose, his dark eyes surrounded with thick lashes shone with tender flames, his bearing was supple and graceful, all his movements were regal and pleasing. Ah, Ludmila, poor Ludmila, what took place in your heart when you gazed on the beautiful youth? "Why am I not beautiful and rich?" thought she, sighing, and lowering her eyes, her bosom heaving more strongly than before. But soon, against her will, she raised her eyes and again looked on the charming prince who stood alone in the centre of the chamber, charming as an angel in this body of men. . . . But how did she feel? Her whole heart was in a turmoil . . . her eyes met those of the handsome Sviatoslav. . . . Oh, Heavens, he was approaching her! Miroslava and Peresveta stood up, thinking that the choice must fall on one of them. . . . Sviatoslav gave his hand to Ludmila. "Here she is," said he, "here is she who has appeared to my heart in life and in my dreams by night; I give to her my hand and my heart." Ludmila could not believe her ears; she went pale, trembled and blushed. Sviatoslav approached with his chosen one to the great prince Vladimir, then seated her at his side on a throne of ivory inlaid with gold. A murmur could be heard in the chamber. "What a choice," whispered the offended beauties as they looked upon Ludmila in her simple dress of white and her modest beauty. Peresveta and Miroslava were out of their minds with rage and envy. "Who could have thought such a thing?" they were saying to each other, "to prefer Ludmila to us. What blindness!" The men also gazed at Ludmila, but their feelings were different. "How charming she is," exclaimed both old and young; "what becoming modesty, what an innocent heart, what a tender, sweet soul shows itself on her face, already as pleasant as a sweet flower!" Ludmila could not understand the tender feeling which filled her heart. She did not dare look upon the handsome prince, and her charming confusion made her more beautiful. Sviatoslav pressed her hand and encouraged her with the fire of his look.

But the great prince Vladimir began to speak, and everything was silent. "My son," said he to the handsome Sviatoslav, "your choice pleases my fatherly heart, but beauty is not the only quality in a wife, I want it to be combined with more real qualities and gifts. The bride whom you have chosen surpasses all the others with charm of looks, let us see how they compare in gifts and intelligence." Ludmila went pale when she heard the words of the great prince Vladimir. "Ah," exclaimed she, "I have never studied anything! This momentary glory will only serve to prove my ignorance to the whole world. Let me go, O great prince Vladimir; I did not come here to contest with others, more deserving, for the happiness for which I was not destined. I came to enjoy the pleasure of my dear friends. Let me go; my fate is to hide in a poor hut, to look after the flowers and to be content with my low station, not to aspire to a gorgeous throne." The great prince looked with a benevolent smile on the modest Ludmila and ordered her to remain in her place. Harps were brought in. Each beauty in her turn sang songs in honour of brave knights or of tender love; each tried to render in music the feelings Prince Sviatoslav inspired in their hearts. At last the turn of Ludmila came; she went pale and trembled, but then someone unseen whispered in her ear: "Take heart, Ludmila, my protecting glances are upon you. Sing the song which your mother taught you, you do not yet know with what gifts nature has blessed you." Ludmila recognised the voice of the fairy, the old woman who had given the girdle to her. She went forward and seated herself at the harp. O wonder of wonders! Her fingers flew lightly over the strings, her voice had the purity and clarity of a nightingale; it flowed into the heart producing a sweet delight, filling it with reverie and languid meditation. Ludmila sang the song which her dear mother had sung when she lulled her in the cradle.

"Rose, dear spring flow'r,
　　Hide thou in the shade
Of a leafy bow'r,
　　Trusting not the rays—
Sweetest tender flow'r—
　　Of the scorching sun."
So the golden butterfly
　　Whispered to the rose.

But this simple warning
　　The rose would not take
All shadows scorning,
　　For her pride's sake.

"The bright sun in duty
  Gives to me its rays;
Why, with my great beauty,
  Should I shun his gaze?"

Senseless in its pride,
  The boastful flower,
Soon was sorely tried
  In the noontide hour.
The rose soon was tired,
  Drooped its splendid head,
Soon its petals withered
  And its perfume fled.

So, beauteous lady,
  In your noon-day bower,
Think of the heyday
  Of the haughty flower!
Like a simple lily,
  Bloom in modesty,
In your simple innocence—
  Like a lily be.

Destiny for you will bear
  A very modest fate.
Joy for you is there,
  O most charming maid,
In the woods in innocence,
  A brooklet is streaming,
Past banks of flowers and scents
  Tenderly gleaming.

Ludmila ended her song, but her voice was still resounding in the hearts of her hearers. The young prince in his inexpressible delight pressed her to his heart. "No, you cannot be a mortal, you are an angel descended from heaven to make Sviatoslav happy!" "Ah, me," said poor Ludmila, "I myself cannot understand it, some sort of spell must have been cast upon you to blind your vision; you think I am beautiful, but it is not so. I never was beautiful. You wish to raise me to the throne, Sviatoslav, but I was born for the fields, for a poor unknown hut." The music began to play again and dancing started. The rivals of Ludmila delighted the onlookers with their agreeable gestures, their lightness, their quickness, but Ludmila, again encouraged by the voice of the fairy, eclipsed them all with the charm of simplicity; in all her movements there was something charming, modesty combined with refreshing gaiety; innocence and pleasure showed in her eyes. The onlookers could not take their eyes from her. The music stopped. . . . Ludmila with lowered eyes and flushed cheeks seated herself in her place. She did not dare to show her pleasure, did not dare to glance at the handsome Sviatoslav.

Midnight was already long past. The great prince Vladimir took Sviatoslav by the hand and they left the chamber, followed by the courtiers and knights. The beauties departed, but the selection was not at an end, it was to be held for three consecutive nights. Ludmila was given an apartment in the palace and many ladies to wait on her. She remained alone in deep meditation, with her new, until now unknown, feelings and with the vision of the charming Sviatoslav in her heart.

And leaving for a time Ludmila we will think of her two friends, Peresveta and Miroslava. "Could we have imagined this?" said Miroslava to Peresveta when they returned home. "To prefer Ludmila to us. They must be blind, the thing is impossible. What do you think, Peresveta? Is there some secret talisman hidden in the girdle which the old fairy gave to her? How could she leave Ludmila out, having been so generous to us? Her simple girdle is certainly more precious than ours, covered though they are with pearls and diamonds. Did you notice how it shone on her last evening?" "That is so, Miroslava, you are quite right; Ludmila has a talisman of which she does not realise the price—we must get it. Then we will see whether she will surpass us with her beauty."

On the following day, early in the morning, Peresveta and Miroslava entered the apartment of Ludmila. She embraced them and kissed them with delight, blushing as they poured on her their insincere congratulations. "Dear friends, I am amazed at the honours which were showered upon me

yesterday," said the modest Ludmila; "I cannot understand
how they came to prefer me, the poor plain Ludmila, to you
who are so beautiful and rich and deserving of every preference." "Good Ludmila," replied Miroslava, "what is strange
to you seems quite natural to us. We are not envious, but
are quite pleased to see your happiness. It is time to open
your eyes. You must think no longer that you are not
beautiful. God has blessed you with a charming face. Out
of our love for you we called you ugly; praise would have
spoiled your innocent heart. But pretence is no longer of
use and it is time, dear Ludmila, that you should know that
you surpass all other women in beauty, kindness and gifts."
"But, my sisters, are you not making fun of me?" "Ah, my
friend, how can you think such a thing? we are speaking
the real truth. But let us offer you a little friendly advice,
there are two important faults which are preventing you
from putting the gifts which nature gave you to the best
advantage: you are too modest and too careless in your
attire. To-night we are all to be presented again to the great
prince Vladimir and his son Sviatoslav. We hear that a
beauty has arrived in Kief, of such perfect fairness and so
well dressed that you must take care lest she steals from you
the love of the handsome Sviatoslav. Do dress with the
utmost magnificence, wear clothing so gorgeous that it will
correspond with your looks. We have brought several robes
for you to choose from; put on the one which you think best
and we will be delighted at your conquest."

Miroslava and Peresveta spread before the eyes of Ludmila
several gorgeous robes. A new feeling took shape in the
heart of the innocent girl; she imagined herself to be the
first beauty in the whole of Russia, and blushed as she
glanced at her simple and poor attire. She tried the robes on
one after the other and chose the most elaborate, wishing to
put on a rich girdle over the white ribbon which she had
received as a gift from the old woman, but unfortunately
the girdle was too small. Miroslava and Peresveta persuaded

her to sacrifice the poor ribbon and to wear a gorgeous pearl girdle. Ludmila wavered, but at last gave way to their demands and gave the white ribbon to Peresveta. "What a graceful and charming form," exclaimed the two friends. "This new-comer has arrived in Kief only to make the triumph of our Ludmila more pronounced. Now we must go, dear friend, but we shall meet again this evening in the palace of the great prince Vladimir." They parted. Ludmila admired herself in her new rich attire, posed before the mirror, tried on the pearl girdle, and the white ribbon was quite forgotten. Ah, Ludmila, you are busy now with your beauty like a vain worldly charmer, you admire yourself before the mirror, whereas in the old days you gazed into the clear stream to admire its purity, its gentle ripple and the pebbles glistening in its bed!

At last the desired moment arrived. The beauties, the courtiers and the knights flowed into the chamber of the palace of the great prince Vladimir. The handsome Sviato-slav with pulsing heart looked towards the door through which Ludmila must enter. The sound of flutes was heard and Ludmila, covered in a white shawl and surrounded by richly-dressed attendants, entered. Sviatoslav flew towards her. With impatient hands he tore from her head the white shawl. What a change! He could not recognise Ludmila. "What do I see?" exclaimed the astonished prince. "Who are you, stranger, and where is my Ludmila?" "I am Ludmila; can it be that you do not recognise me, Sviatoslav the beautiful?" "You!—Ludmila? That cannot be, it is an untruth!" A whisper of displeasure could be heard in the chamber—nobody could recognise Ludmila. Sviatoslav step-ped aside, he gazed with disturbed eyes among the crowd of beauties for the girl who had conquered his heart, but the great prince Vladimir raised his hand and everything again was silent. "You say you are Ludmila," he said to the trembling and sorrowful girl; "I believe your words; I believe that it is possible that your beauty could change in a day, but your gifts must be unchangeable. Take the harp, be seated and sing to us the song which you sang yesterday." Ludmila, somewhat cheered, approached the harp. Oh, the miracle! Her fingers were immovable, her voice wild and discordant. The great prince Vladimir rose from his throne in anger and ordered the poor Ludmila to depart. "The selection is deferred until to-morrow evening!"

What happened to the poor, unfortunate, good-hearted Ludmila? She cried, suffered in despair, longed for her hopeless love. Where was her previous happiness; the previous tranquillity of her innocent heart? The orphan was bathed in tears. She left Kief and hastened to hide in the poor hut on the banks of the clear stream under the shadow of the leafy birches where she had spent her childhood. "Why, why did I ever leave you, my quiet hut?" thought Ludmila, passing through the grove near the well-known winding path. She approached the hut and saw a light burning within. She was afraid and did not know whether to enter or not. At last she decided, opened the door, and behold! in her hut sat her friend, the old fairy. Ludmila was dumb with astonishment, for some time she did not say a word, then she came to herself and wept bitterly. "Ah," said she to the old woman, "you are the cause of my misfortune. Why with your charm did you raise me yesterday to a throne for which I had not sought, of which I had not even dreamed? And why now, when hope has blinded my soul, when the love produced by you in my heart has become more precious than all the honours of a throne, have I suddenly lost everything? Why am I covered with shame, and by whom? By you, to whom I never did harm but sought rather to do good, without hoping for reward! Ah, why did you tempt the eyes of Sviatoslav the beautiful, why did you put a hopeless love in my heart? What shall I do now, so hopeless, in my lonely hut? The beautiful place in which I was born and where I passed my youth will now seem a prison. My heart is within the walls of Kief; I shall never forget what I have lost after possessing it for one brief moment. What worldly happiness can replace the tender looks which Sviatoslav cast on me, filling my heart which was before so tranquil and so gay? Ah, my fragrant flowers, you will fade; who will tend you? Dear, sweet singing birds, you will no longer come to my hut; who will bring you grain and re-echo your sweet song? I will sit in the wide road looking towards Kief and sending to it my heart. What have I done, fairy, to bring on myself your displeasure?" "Hear what I have to say, good Ludmila," answered the fairy; "it is easy for me to explain. I loved you from the first glance, and as a token of my gratitude I gave to you a magic girdle which has the power to beautify any woman. The girl who possesses it triumphs over all her rivals, has all the charms, all the gifts; but without it the charms and the gifts lose their power, people who have been astonished discontinue to like them. Why then, Ludmila, did you not keep the treasure which I gave to you? Why did you exchange the girdle of modesty for that of vanity? Having lost the talisman which gave to you your triumph, you lost the charms which went with it, your lover himself could not recognise you in your new attire." "Ah," exclaimed Ludmila, "my poor, miserable fate, I am myself to blame for everything. I have deprived myself of happiness. I shall never enjoy again the old times. The gaiety has flown from my heart, my previous pleasures have run away; I shall never cease weeping, another will take possession of the heart of Sviatoslav the beautiful." Ludmila buried her face in her hands and sobbed bitterly. "Console yourself, my friend," said the fairy with a gentle smile, taking her by the hand, "you were deceived by your inexperience and by the deceit of your envious friends, Miroslava and Peresveta, but you are innocent in your heart. I return to you your lost girdle. I followed unseen behind Peresveta and Miroslava when they left you with their spoils. They had a terrible quarrel, each wanted the girdle, but neither took possession of it, for

I took it away. I now return it to the only one who is deserving of it by her goodness and modesty." Ludmila covered the hand of her good fairy in kisses; the fairy wiped away her tears, kissed her rosy cheeks and encircled her with the ribbon.

Suddenly, at the command of the fairy, the roof of the hut opened and before the eyes of the astonished Ludmila appeared a magnificent chariot to which were harnessed two stags with silvery fur and golden antlers; instead of the ugly old woman appeared a young girl of unsurpassable beauty clad in a magic robe with a belt of white on which glistened in gold the signs of the zodiac. Dobrada, as the fairy was named, seated Ludmila in the chariot, the stags unfolded their golden wings, and in less than a second the chariot was outside the walls of Kief. The fairy conducted Ludmila to a secluded chamber and forbade her to leave until evening, blessed her and disappeared.

Evening came. Ludmila, clad very simply and wearing her white girdle, entered the chamber of the palace of the great prince Vladimir and seated herself in her old place behind Peresveta and Miroslava. They did not see her and were laughing among themselves at her stupid credulity, talking to each other of their own vain hopes. But Ludmila forgot their existence, her eyes only saw Sviatoslav. He was seated on his throne of ivory inlaid with gold, near the great prince Vladimir, full of thought, his head resting on his hand. He did not trouble to give a single glance to the beauties who surrounded him, his heart yearned only for Ludmila, her charming image floated before him, an enchanting vision of departed delights. Suddenly, oh joy, he saw her in the place in which she had first appeared, in the same simple dress, directing on him her gaze with a soulful tender love. "Oh, Ludmila!" he exclaimed, and threw himself on his knees before her. "Long live the charming Ludmila!" shouted the courtiers and the knights in one voice. Sviatoslav, beside himself with delight, pressed his charming bride elect to his heart, and she, with lowered eyes and burning cheeks, seemed an angel of beauty and innocence; he approached with her the throne of the great prince Vladimir and seated her on his right. Peresveta and Miroslava went pale with rage. Music began to be played, and everyone had again to give place to Ludmila in the art of dancing and singing. Again she eclipsed her rivals, who, with the exception of Peresveta and Miroslava, agreed to accept her as the victor and were even pleased with her conquest, so strong was the charm of her modest beauty, her good-heartedness and innocence. Suddenly there resounded through the chamber a piercing shriek. What was it? Terrible serpents with distended jaws, with sharp fangs and burning eyes, were encircling Peresveta and Miroslava in the place where their pearl and diamond girdles had been. Ludmila hastened to their assistance, hoping to save them from the sting of these monsters, but her efforts were in vain. The onlookers were frozen with terror. Suddenly there sounded a soft singing accompanied by the music of magic strings; a pleasant perfume of roses and violets was diffused in the air and the fairy Dobrada appeared, surrounded by a pink radiance. Ludmila threw herself on her knees before her. "Save Peresveta and Miroslava," she asked entreatingly. "Good Ludmila," answered the fairy, "I will forgive them because of my love of you. The serpents which encircle them are the poisonous serpents of self-love and envy. Touch them with your white ribbon and they will disappear." Ludmila did the bidding of the fairy and the serpents disappeared. Peresveta and Miroslava embraced their forgiving friend; they avowed their sincere friendship, and within them awoke a genuine love for the one whom a moment before they had hated and sought to destroy.

The great prince Vladimir gave his blessing to his son and the girl. "Oh, Sviatoslav," said the charming bride, pointing towards the fairy Dobrada, "there is my benefactress, there is the one to whom I am indebted for your love. Ah, only three days ago I was just Ludmila, a simple girl, but now. . . . No, I should never have been noticed by Sviatoslav the beautiful if the bountiful Dobrada had not beautified me with the magic of those gifts which nature had not given to me. So, Sviatoslav, in this girdle all my beauty and talents are combined."

This modest confession made Ludmila more beautiful than ever in the eyes of Sviatoslav. "My friend," said Dobrada, "keep this girdle, the precious gift of my friendship; nothing can make a woman more beautiful, be she in a poor hut or in a royal palace. Wearing it you will be adored by your husband, your friends and your subjects, adored until the end of your days." Dobrada disappeared. Is it necessary to say what followed? Is it possible to imagine that Sviatoslav was not happy in the possession of Ludmila?

ALEXANDER PUSHKIN

(1799–1837)

✢✢

(I)

THE PISTOL-SHOT

I

W E were quartered at ——. The daily routine of an officer
in the army is not unknown. Drills and the riding-school in
the morning, dinner at the commandant's quarters or in
a Jewish eating-house, and cards and punch in the evening,
constitute the day's work. There was no society at ——, nor
were there any marriageable girls; we used to meet at each
other's rooms, where only men in uniform were to be seen.

One civilian, however, was admitted within our circle.
He might have reached the age of five-and-thirty, and we
therefore looked upon him as being greatly our senior in
years. His large experience secured to him a certain amount
of deference, and his usual moroseness, his stern and sarcastic
disposition, exercised a powerful influence over our youthful imaginations. His past career seemed shrouded in
mystery. Though bearing a foreign name, he was apparently a Russian. He had served at one time in the Hussars,
and had even been fortunate in professional advancement;
none of us knew the reason why he had retired from the
service and taken up his abode in this wretched neighbourhood where he lived penuriously and yet extravagantly: he
invariably went out on foot, and he was always seen in a
black surtout the worse for wear, but at the same time he
kept open house for all the officers of our regiment. Truth
to tell, two or three dishes, cooked by an old pensioner,

constituted his dinner, but, on the other hand, champagne flowed at his table. His circumstances and his income were unknown, and none of us presumed to ask any questions about either. His only books were works connected with the military service, and some novels which he willingly lent, never asking to have them returned, but neither did he give back those which he had borrowed. His chief pastime consisted in pistol practice. The walls of his apartment were well riddled and perforated like a honeycomb. A valuable collection of pistols formed the only luxury of his humble habitation. The degree of perfection he had attained in this art was inconceivable; and had he required to shoot at a pear on anyone's head, not one of our fellows would have hesitated to offer himself. Our conversation often touched on the subject of duelling. Silvio (as I shall name him) never joined in it; and when asked whether he had ever had occasion to fight, would answer dryly that he had; but he entered upon no details, and it was evident that these and similar questions were distasteful to him. We concluded that the recollection of some unfortunate victim to this dreadful accomplishment troubled his conscience, the idea of cowardice never, even suggesting itself. There are people whose exterior alone suffices to disarm such suspicions. An unexpected occurrence disconcerted us all.

Some ten of us were one day dining with Silvio. We drank as usual,—that is, excessively,—and after dinner we endeavoured to prevail upon our host to be the banker in a game of faro. For some time he persisted in declining, for he seldom played, but at length he ordered the cards to be brought, threw fifty ducats on the table, and commenced to deal. We all took our places and the game began. Silvio was wont to keep the strictest silence upon such occasions, never discussing or explaining anything. If the punter chanced to make a mistake, he either paid up the balance immediately or noted the surplus. We were already aware of this, and therefore never interfered. But of our number there was a young officer who had lately joined. He took part in the game, and in a fit of absent-mindedness scored one point too many. Silvio took up the chalk and rectified the score, as was his custom. The officer, thinking he was mistaken, began to explain matters. Silvio continued dealing in silence. The officer, losing patience, rubbed out what to him appeared unnecessary. Silvio, taking up the chalk, again marked the score. The officer, excited with wine, and by the game and the laughter of his comrades, imagined himself cruelly offended, and in his passion he lifted a metal candlestick off the table and threw it at Silvio, who had barely time to avoid the blow. We felt confused. Silvio rose, and with fire in his eyes said: "Please to walk out, sir, and thank your stars that this has happened under my roof."

We did not doubt the consequences, and we looked upon our new comrade as a dead man. He walked out, declaring himself ready to answer for the affront in such manner as the banker might elect. The game was continued for a few moments longer, but feeling how little our host's thoughts were in it, we left, one by one, and repaired to our quarters, discussing the possibility of a speedy vacancy.

When we met in the riding-school on the following day, we immediately inquired of each other if our poor ensign was still alive. When he himself appeared, we greeted him, putting the same question! He replied that he had heard nothing of Silvio as yet. This surprised us. We went to Silvio and found him in the yard, sending bullet after bullet into an ace of cards, which he had fixed to the gate. He received us as usual, and did not allude to the event of the preceding evening. Three days elapsed, and the ensign still lived. We asked in astonishment: "Can it be possible that Silvio will not fight?" Silvio did not fight. A very slight explanation satisfied him, and peace was restored.

Such conduct might have injured him excessively in the estimation of youth. The want of pluck is what young men excuse least, for they generally consider it the highest of human virtues—one that covers a multitude of sins! However, little by little, all was forgotten, and Silvio regained his former influence.

I alone could not become reconciled to him. Being naturally of a romantic turn of mind, I had, more than anybody, attached myself to the man whose very existence was an enigma, and who appeared to me to be the hero of some mysterious drama. He liked me, at least it was with me alone that he laid aside his usual cutting, ill-natured observations, and that he conversed upon various subjects with perfect good-nature and rare pleasantness. But I could not, subsequently to that unfortunate evening, rid myself of the idea that his honour had been tarnished, and that it was his own doing that the stain had not been removed. This thought prevented my feeling towards him as I had hitherto done, and I felt ashamed to look upon him. Silvio was far too clever and too shrewd not to notice this and not to divine the cause. He appeared hurt, and I fancied that I had more than once detected a wish on his part to come to an understanding with me; but I avoided each opportunity, and Silvio withdrew. Thereafter, I only met him in the presence of my comrades, and our former intimacy came to an end.

The busy inhabitants of a capital can have no conception of the various excitements so familiar to those who live in small towns or in villages—for example, the looking-out for the periodical post-day; on Tuesdays and Fridays our regimental office was crowded with officers; some expecting remittances, some letters, and some newspapers. Letters and parcels were opened on the spot, news communicated, and the office presented the most animated appearance. Silvio's letters were addressed under cover to our regiment, and he was therefore usually present. Upon one of these occasions a letter was handed to him, the seal of which he broke with a look of the greatest impatience. His eyes brightened up as he perused it. The officers were themselves too much engaged to notice anything. "Gentlemen," said Silvio, "circumstances require me to leave without delay; I go this night, and hope you will not refuse to dine with me for the last time. I expect you also," he continued, turning to me; "I expect you without fail." With these words he hastened out, and we shortly dispersed, having agreed to meet at Silvio's.

I arrived at the appointed hour, and found nearly the whole of my brother-officers. Silvio's movables were all packed, and little remained but the bare and battered walls. We sat down to dinner; our host was in high spirits, and his cheerfulness was soon shared by us; the corks flew incessantly, our glasses frothed and sparkled unceasingly, and we wished the traveller with all possible sincerity God-speed, and every blessing. It was already late when we rose. While the caps were being sorted, Silvio, bidding everyone "good-bye," took me by the hand and detained me just as I was upon the point of leaving. "I must speak to you," said he in a low voice. I remained.

The guests had left; being alone, we sat opposite each other, and silently began to smoke our pipes. Silvio was careworn, and there were no longer any traces of his affected cheerfulness. The pallor of his sombre face, his sparkling eyes, and the dense smoke issuing from his mouth gave him a truly demoniacal look. Several minutes passed away, and Silvio broke silence.

"We may perhaps never meet again," said he; "I wish to have an explanation with you before we part. You must have noticed how little I value the opinion of the world, but I like you, and I feel that it would prey upon me were I to leave an unjust impression respecting myself on your mind."

He stopped and began to refill his emptied pipe; I remained silent with lowered eyes.

"You thought it strange," he continued, "that I did not demand satisfaction from that tipsy fool R——. You will doubtless own that, the right to choose weapons being mine, his life was in my hands, my own being almost beyond the reach of danger. I might ascribe this forgiveness to pure generosity, but I will not deceive you. Had it been in my power to punish R—— without risking my own life in the least degree, I would by no means have let him off."

I looked at Silvio in some surprise, and was completely taken aback by such a confession. Silvio went on:

"That's just it. I have no right to imperil my life. I received a box on the ear six years ago, and my enemy still lives."

My curiosity was thoroughly awakened. "You did not fight him?" asked I. "Circumstances probably parted you?"

"I did fight him," answered Silvio; "and here is the memorial of our duel."

Silvio rose and took out of a hat-box a red cap, ornamented with a gold tassel and braid (what the French would call *bonnet de police*); he put it on; it had a hole about an inch from its edge.

"You know," continued Silvio, "that I served in the —— Hussars. My disposition is known to you. I am accustomed to take the lead, but in my early days it was a passion. At that time practical jokes were in fashion, and I was the greatest scamp in the whole army. We prided ourselves upon our drinking powers: I outdid the famous B——,[1] whom D—— D—— has sung. Duels took place constantly in our regiment. I took a part in all of them, either as a witness or as a principal. My comrades idolised me, and the regimental commanders, who were constantly changing, looked upon me as an unavoidable evil.

"I was thus quietly (that is, turbulently) enjoying my popularity, when there joined us a wealthy youth, a member of a well-known family (I do not wish to mention names). Never in my life have I met such a favoured child of fortune! Imagine to yourself youth, talent, good looks, the most

[1]A cavalry officer whose drinking powers and bravery have been immortalised by the poet, Denis Davidoff (time of Alexander I).—Tr.

exuberant cheerfulness, the most undaunted courage, a high-sounding name, wealth to which he knew no bounds, and you will form some idea of the impression his presence produced among us. My pre-eminence received a check. Dazzled by my reputation, he would have sought my friendship, but I received him coldly, and he turned from me without any show of regret. I began to hate him. His success in our regiment and in the society of ladies threw me into complete despair. I sought opportunities for a quarrel, but my epigrams were answered by epigrams, which always seemed to me more unexpected and more stinging than my own; they were, of course, immeasurably more lively. He was facetious; I was vicious. At last, upon the occasion of a ball given by a Polish gentleman, seeing that he was the object of attention of all the ladies, and especially of the hostess herself, who was an ally of mine, I whispered to him some grossly rude remark. He warmed up, and gave me a box on the ear. We flew to our swords. The ladies fainted; we were separated, but that same night we drove off to fight a duel.

"The day was breaking. I stood at the appointed spot, attended by my two seconds. I awaited with inexpressible impatience the arrival of my opponent. The sun had already risen, and its rays were gathering heat. I observed him in the distance. He was on foot, in uniform, wearing his sword, and accompanied by one second. We walked on to meet him. He approached, holding in his hand his cap, which was full of cherries. Our seconds proceeded to measure twelve paces. I was to have fired first, but my rage was so great that I could not rely upon the steadiness of my hand, and to gain time I conceded to him the first shot. My opponent would not consent to this. It was decided that we should draw lots; he, with his usual good luck, won the toss. He aimed, and his ball went through my cap. It was now my turn. His life was in my hands at last. I looked eagerly at him, trying to detect even a shadow of uneasiness. He stood covered by my pistol, selecting the ripest cherries out of his cap, and spitting out the stones, which nearly reached me as they fell. His coolness exasperated me. What is the use, thought I, of depriving him of his life when he values it so little? A wicked thought flitted across my mind. I dropped the pistol. 'You are not thinking of death now,' said I; 'you prefer to enjoy your breakfast; I do not wish to disturb you!' 'You do not disturb me in the least,' replied he, 'please to fire away; but, by the way, that is just as you please; your fire remains with you: I am always ready and at your service!' I turned to the seconds, declaring that I did not intend to proceed at present, and thus our meeting ended.

"I quitted the service, and retired to this place. But not a day has since passed without a thought of vengeance. Now my time has come. . . ."

Silvio drew out of his pocket the letter he had that morning received, and handed it to me. Somebody (probably the person entrusted with the care of his business matters) wrote word to him from Moscow that a *certain individual* was soon about to be united in lawful wedlock to a young and beautiful girl.

"You guess," said Silvio, "who is meant by this *certain individual*. I go to Moscow. We shall see whether he will meet death as coolly on the eve of his marriage as he once awaited it at his meal of cherries!"

Silvio rose at these words, threw his cap upon the floor, and paced the room to and fro like a tiger in his cage. I had listened to him in silence; strange and conflicting feelings had taken possession of me.

The servant walked in and reported the horses ready. Silvio pressed my hand warmly; we embraced each other. He took his place in the *telega*,[1] wherein lay two boxes, one containing his pistols, the other his necessaries. We bade each other good-bye once more, and the horses were off.

[1] Country cart.—Tr.

II

Several years had elapsed, and my private affairs neces-
sitated my settling in a poverty-stricken little village in the
district of N——. Though occupied with the duties of landlord, I could not help silently sighing after my former
rackety and restless existence. I found it so difficult to get
accustomed to spend the long dismal spring and winter
evenings in such complete seclusion. By chatting with the
mayor, or going over new buildings in progress, I managed
somehow to drag through the day, up to the dinner-hour;
but I literally knew not what to do with myself at dusk. I
had read the limited number of books which I had found
on the bookshelves or in the lumber-room until I knew them
by heart. All the stories which the housekeeper Kirilovna
knew had been told me over and over again. I grew weary
of listening to the peasant women's songs, and I might have
had recourse to sweet liqueurs but that they made my head
ache; and I confess that I feared I might become a drunkard,
of which I saw a number of instances in our district.

I had no near neighbours, if I except two or three of those
wretched fellows whose conversation consisted chiefly of
hiccoughs and sighs. Solitude was more endurable At last
I decided upon going to bed as early as possible, and upon
dining as late as possible; in this way I contrived to shorten
the evenings and add to the length of the days, which I
spent in useful occupations.

Four versts from me lay a very valuable estate belonging
to the Countess B——; it was occupied by the agent only;
the countess had visited it but once, and that in the first
year of her marriage, when she had not stayed over a month.
During the second year of my seclusion, rumours were
current that the countess and her husband were coming to
spend the summer. They really did arrive at about the
beginning of June.

The appearance of a well-to-do neighbour is an important

event to rustics. Landlords and tenants speak of it for two months previously and for three years subsequently. I confess that, so far as I was concerned, the presence of a young and beautiful neighbour seemed a matter of considerable importance to me. I burned with impatience to see her, and betook myself, therefore, after dinner, the first Sunday subsequently to their arrival, to pay my respects to their excellencies, as their nearest neighbour and most devoted of servants.

A footman showed me into the count's library and went to announce me. The spacious apartment was furnished with the greatest possible luxury; the walls were lined with bookcases, each of which was surmounted by a bronze bust; over the marble chimney-place was placed a large mirror; the floor was covered with green cloth and spread with carpets. Having lost all habits of luxury in my poor retreat, and having long since ceased to be familiar with the effects produced by the riches of others, I became timid, and awaited the count with a certain trepidation, like a provincial petitioner expecting the approach of a minister. The doors opened, and a handsome man of two-and-thirty came in. The count approached me with frankness and friendliness. I endeavoured to muster courage and to explain the object of my call; but he anticipated me. We sat down. His easy and agreeable conversation soon dispelled my awkward shyness; I had already assumed my usual manner, when suddenly the countess entered, and my perturbation became greater than before. She was beautiful indeed. The count introduced me; I wished to seem to be at my ease, but the more I tried the more awkward did I feel. My new acquaintances, wishing to give me time to recover, and to feel myself more at home, conversed together, dispensing with all etiquette, thus treating me like an old friend. I had risen from my seat in the meanwhile, and was pacing the room inspecting the books and pictures. I am no judge of paintings, but one there was which specially attracted my attention. It represented a landscape in Switzerland, but I was struck, not by the beauty of the artist's touch, but because it was perforated by two bullets, one hole being just above the other.

"This is a good shot," said I, turning to the count.

"Yes," said he; "a very remarkable shot. Do you shoot well?" he went on.

"Pretty well," I replied, overjoyed that the conversation had turned upon a subject of interest. "I mean I could not miss a card at thirty paces; of course, when I know the pistols."

"Indeed," said the countess, with a look of great attention; "and you, my dear, could you hit a card at thirty paces?"

"Some day," answered the count, "we shall try. I was not a bad shot in my time, but it is now four years since I held a pistol."

"Oh," remarked I, "that being the case, I do not mind betting that your Excellency will not be able to hit a card at twenty paces even: pistol shooting requires daily practice. I know this by experience. I used to be considered one of the best shots in my regiment. It so happened once that I had not touched a pistol for a whole month: my own were undergoing repair, and, will your Excellency believe it, when I took to shooting again, I missed a bottle four successive times at twenty paces. Our riding-master, a sharp, amusing fellow, happening to be present, cried out: 'I say, old boy, thou canst not lift thy hand against the bottle, eh?' No, your Excellency, it is a practice that ought not to be neglected, if one does not wish to become rusty at it. The best shot I ever happened to come across practised every day, and would fire at least three times before dinner. This was a rule with him, as was his glass of vodka."

The count and countess appeared pleased at my having become talkative.

"And what kind of a shot was he?" asked the count.

"Of that sort, your Excellency, that if he happened to see a fly on the wall. . . . You are smiling, countess. But it is true, indeed . . . when he chanced to see a fly, he would call out, 'Kooska, my pistols!' Kooska brings him a loaded pistol. Bang! and there is the fly flattened to the wall!"

"That was wonderful," said the count. "What was his name?"

"Silvio, your Excellency."

"Silvio!" exclaimed he, jumping up; "you knew Silvio?"

"Knew him? Of course, your Excellency. We were friends; he was considered by the regiment as being quite one of ourselves; but it is now five years since I heard anything of him. Your Excellency appears also to have known him."

"I knew him—knew him very well. Did he ever relate a very strange occurrence to you?"

"Your Excellency cannot possibly mean a box on the ear, which some young scamp gave him at a ball?"

"And did he name that scamp to you?"

"No, your Excellency, he did not; but—your Excellency," continued I, the truth beginning to dawn upon me—"I beg your pardon—I was not aware—can it be yourself?"

"I myself," answered the count, with an exceedingly perturbed countenance, "and the perforated picture is the reminiscence of our last meeting."

"Oh! pray, dear," said the countess, "pray do not speak of it. I dread hearing the story."

"No," replied he, "I shall relate the whole of it. He knows how I offended his friend, let him now also know how Silvio took his revenge."

The count bade me be seated, and I listened with the liveliest curiosity to the following recital.

"I was married five years ago. The first month, the *honeymoon*, was spent in this village. It is to this house that I am indebted for the happiest, as also for one of the saddest moments of my life.

"We were out riding one evening; my wife's horse became

unmanageable; she got frightened, gave me the bridle, set out homewards on foot. I saw upon entering the stable-yard a travelling *telega*, and was informed that a gentleman, who had refused to give his name, and had simply said that he had some business to transact, was waiting for me in the library. I entered this room, and in the twilight saw a man covered with dust and wearing a long beard. He was standing by the fireplace. I approached him, trying to recall to mind his features. 'Thou dost not recognise me, count,' said he, with trembling voice. 'Silvio!' exclaimed I; and I confess I felt my hair stand on end! 'Yes, it is I,' he continued, 'the shot remains with me; I have come to discharge my pistol; art thou ready?' The pistol protruded out of his side-pocket. I measured twelve paces, and stood there, in that corner, begging him to fire quickly, before my wife returned. He hesitated, he asked for lights. Candles were brought in. I shut the door, gave orders that no one should come in, and again begged him to fire. He took out his pistol, and proceeded to take aim. . . . One dreadful minute passed. Silvio let his arm drop. 'I regret,' said he, 'that my pistol is not loaded with cherry-stones. . . . The bullet is heavy. This appears to me not a duel, but murder: I am not accustomed to aim at an unarmed man: let us begin anew, let us draw lots who is to have the first fire.'

"My head swam. . . . I suppose I was not consenting. . . . At last another pistol was loaded; two bits of paper were rolled up; he placed them in the cap I had once shot through; I again drew the winning number. 'Thou art devilish lucky, count,' said he, with an ironical smile I can never forget. I do not understand what possessed me, and by what means he forced me to it . . . but I fired—and hit that picture there."

The count pointed to the perforated picture; his face was crimson, the countess had become whiter than her handkerchief; I could not suppress an exclamation.

"I fired," the count went on: "and, thank God, missed.

Then Silvio . . ." (he looked really dreadful at that moment) "Silvio aimed at me. Suddenly the doors opened, Masha[1] rushed in, and with a scream threw herself on my neck. Her presence restored to me all my courage. 'Darling!' said I, 'don't you see that we are joking? How frightened you are! Go and take a glass of water and come back to us; I shall introduce an old friend and comrade to you.' Masha still doubted. 'Tell me, is what my husband says true?' said she, turning to the sombre Silvio, 'is it true that you are both in fun?' 'He is always in fun, countess,' replied Silvio. 'Once upon a time he gave me a box on the ear, in fun; in fun, he shot through this cap; in fun, he just now missed me; now I have a fancy to be in fun also!' So saying, he was about to take aim . . . before her! Masha threw herself at his feet. 'Get up, Masha, for shame!' I exclaimed, enraged; 'and you, sir, will you cease jesting at a poor woman? Are you, or are you not, going to fire?' 'I am not going to,' answered Silvio, 'I am content. I have seen your hesitation, your timidity. I made you fire at me. I am satisfied. You will remember me. I leave you to your conscience!' Here he was about to take his departure, but stopping in the doorway, he looked at the perforated picture, fired his pistol at it, almost without aiming, and disappeared. My wife had fainted; the servants dared not stop him, and looked at him with terror; he walked out, called the *yamstchik*,[2] and drove off before I had even time to recover myself."

The count concluded. Thus did I learn the ending of a story which had so interested me at its commencement. I did not again meet its hero. It was said that at the time of the revolt under Alexander Ypsilanti, Silvio commanded a detachment of the Heterae, and was killed in the combat before Skulleni.

[1]The pet name for Maria.—Tr.   [2]A driver of post-horses.—Tr.

(II)

THE POST-MASTER

I s there anybody who has not cursed the post-masters, who has not abused them? Is there anybody who has not demanded of them the fatal book in an angry moment, so as to enter therein the unavailing complaint against delays, incivility and inexactitude? Is there anybody who does not look upon them as being the scum of the human race, like the clerks under the late administration, or at least like the Muromsky brigands?[1] Let us, however, be just; let us realise the position, and perhaps we shall judge them with some leniency. What is a post-master? The veritable martyr of the fourteenth grade, whose rank serves only to save him from blows, and not even that at all times. (I appeal to the conscience of my readers.) What is the duty of these dictators, as Prince Viazemsky humorously styles them? Is it not in truth hard labour? No rest day or night. It is the post-master that the traveller assails irritated by the accumulated vexations of a tiresome journey. Is the weather atrocious; are the roads in a bad state; is the driver dogged; do the horses refuse to go?—the fault is surely the post-master's. On entering his poor dwelling, the wayfarer looks upon him as upon a foe; the post-master may consider himself fortunate if he succeeds in ridding himself of his uninvited guest; but should there be no horses? Heavens! what abuse, what threats! He is about in the rain and sleet, and in storms takes refuge in the lobby, so as to escape, were it but for a moment, the complaints and assaults of the irritated travellers. A general arrives: the trembling post-master gives his two last *troikas*, including the courier's. The general is off, without uttering so much as "Thank you." Five minutes later—bells!

---

[1] *Murom*, a territory in the Government of Vladimir, where robbers formerly infested the woods.—TR.

—and a State messenger throws his order for horses on the table! Let us examine these matters closely, and our hearts will commiserate rather than fill with indignation. A few words more. In the course of twenty years, I have travelled through Russia in all directions; I know almost all the post roads, and I am acquainted with several generations of drivers; there are few post-masters unknown to me by sight, and few with whom I have not had some intercourse. I hope to publish at no distant period some interesting notes made during my travels; I shall here merely observe, that the post-masters as a class are most falsely represented. These much-calumniated post-masters are in a general way quiet people, naturally obliging, sociably inclined, unassuming, and not over money-loving. From their conversation (which travellers do wrong to scorn) one may learn much that is interesting and instructive. I must own, that so far as I myself am concerned, I much prefer it to the tall talk of some employé of the sixth grade, travelling on the service of the Crown.

It will be easily guessed that I have some friends among this respectable class of men. Indeed, the memory of one of them is precious to me. Circumstances had once brought us together, and it is of him I now intend to speak to my kind readers.

In May, 1816, I happened to be travelling through the Government of ——, on a road which is now in disuse. My rank was insignificant; I changed carriages at every stage, paying post-rates for two horses. Consequently, the post-masters did not treat me with any distinction, and I often had to obtain by force what should have been mine by right. Young and impetuous, I used to vent my indignation on the post-masters for their meanness and obsequiousness, especially when the *troika* to which I had a right was given to some person of high rank. In the same way it took me some time to get accustomed to being passed over by a discriminating serf at the Governor's dinner-table. To-day, both these matters appear to me to be in the order of things. Indeed, what would become of us if the one very convenient maxim, *Rank honours rank*, were superseded by this other, *Intellect honours intellect?* What differences of opinion would arise; and upon whom would dependents wait first? But to return to my tale.

The day was hot. A few drops of rain fell at three versts from the station, but it soon began to pour, and I got wet through. On arrival, my first care was to change my clothes as quickly as possible, my second to order tea.

"Here, Dunia!" shouted the post-master, "get the *samovar* ready, and run and fetch some cream."

At these words, a girl of about fourteen appeared from behind the partition, and ran into the lobby. I was struck by her beauty.

"Is that thy daughter?" asked I of the post-master.

"Yes, it is," answered he, with an air of satisfied pride; "she is so sensible and so quick, and quite takes after her poor mother."

Here he began to copy my order for horses, whilst I amused myself looking at the prints which ornamented the walls of his humble but tidy dwelling. They represented the story of the Prodigal Son: in the first, a venerable old man, in night-cap and dressing-gown, says good-bye to a restless youth, who hastily accepts his blessing and a bag of money. In the next, the dissipated conduct of the young man is portrayed in glaring colours: he is sitting at a table, surrounded by false friends and shameless women. Further on, the ruined youth, in a tattered shirt and cocked hat, is seen feeding swine and sharing their meal: his face expresses deep sorrow and repentance. His return to his father is last represented: the good old man, in the very same night-cap and dressing-gown, rushes to meet him; the prodigal son is on his knees; in the background, the cook is slaying the fatted calf, and the elder brother is inquiring of the servants the reason for so much rejoicing. Under each of these pictures I read appropriate verses in German. All this has remained impressed on my memory, as have also the pots of balsam, the bed with coloured curtains, and the other objects which then surrounded me. I fancy I still see the host himself, a fresh and good-natured-looking man of about fifty, wearing a long green coat, with three medals suspended by faded ribbons.

I had scarcely settled with my old driver when Dunia returned with the *samovar*. The little coquette had at a second glance noticed the impression she had made on me; she dropped her large blue eyes; I entered into conversation with her; she answered without the slightest timidity, like a girl accustomed to the ways of the world. I offered a glass of punch to her father, gave Dunia a cup of tea, and we three conversed as if we had always known each other.

The horses had long been ready, but I was unwilling to part with the post-master and his little daughter. At last I bade them Good-bye; the father wished me a prosperous journey, and the daughter accompanied me to the carriage. I stopped in the lobby and asked leave to kiss her: Dunia consented. I can remember having given many kisses "since I first took to that occupation," but none has left such lasting, such pleasant recollections.

Several years passed by, and circumstances led me to the same places by the same roads. I remembered the old post-master's daughter, and rejoiced at the prospect of seeing her again. "But," thought I, "the old post-master has perhaps been removed. Dunia is probably married." The possibility of the death of the one or of the other also crossed my mind, and I neared the station of —— with melancholy apprehensions. The horses stopped at the little post-house. On entering the room, I at once recognised the pictures representing the history of the Prodigal Son; the table and bed stood in their old places, but there were now no flowers on the sills, and everything showed symptoms of decay and neglect. The post-master was sleeping under his sheep-skin coat; my arrival awoke him; he raised himself. It was Sampson Virin, indeed; but how he had aged! Whilst he was arranging the papers to copy my order for horses, I looked at his grey hairs, at the deep wrinkles on a long-unshaven face, on his bent form, and could not help wondering how it was possible that three or four years had changed him, hale as he used to be, into a feeble old man.

"Dost thou recognise me?" asked I; "we are old friends."

"Maybe," answered he, gruffly, "this is the high-road, many travellers have halted here."

"Is thy Dunia well?" I continued.

The old man frowned. "God knows," answered he.

"Then she is married, I suppose," said I.

The old man feigned not to hear me, and continued reading my official order for post-horses in a whisper. I ceased interrogating him, and asked for some tea. A feeling of curiosity disquieted me, and I was hoping that some punch would loosen the tongue of my old acquaintance.

I was not mistaken; the old man did not refuse the proffered glass. I observed that the rum was dispelling his moroseness. He became talkative at the second glass, remembered, or pretended to remember me, and I learned from him the story, which at that time interested and touched me deeply.

"And so you knew my Dunia?" he began. "Who did not know her? Oh! Dunia, Dunia! what a girl she was. All who came here praised her; never a word of complaint. Ladies sometimes used to give her a kerchief or a pair of ear-rings. Travellers would stop purposely, as it were, to dine or to sup; but, in truth, only to look at my Dunia a little longer. The gentlemen, however choleric, would calm down in her presence and talk kindly to me. Will you believe it, sir? Courtiers, State messengers, used to converse with her for half an hour at a time. She kept the house; she cleaned up, she got things ready, she used to find time for everything. And I, old fool that I am, could not admire her sufficiently, could not appreciate her enough!

Did I not love my Dunia? did not I pet my child? Was not her life happiness itself? But no, one cannot flee misfortunes; what is ordained must come to pass." Here he recounted his troubles in detail. Three years had passed since one winter evening, whilst the post-master was ruling out a new book, and his daughter was working at a new dress behind the partition, a *troika* pulled up, and a traveller, wearing a Circassian cap and military cloak, and wrapped in a shawl, entered the room, calling for horses. All the relays were out. At this piece of intelligence the traveller was about to raise his voice and his stick, but Dunia, accustomed to such scenes, ran out, and softly addressing the stranger, asked him whether he would be pleased to take some refreshment! Dunia's appearance produced its usual effect. The traveller's anger passed off; he consented to wait for the horses, and ordered supper. Upon taking off his wet rough cap, undoing his shawl, and throwing off his cloak, the traveller turned out to be a slight young Hussar, with a small black moustache. He made himself at home, and conversed gaily with the post-master and his daughter. Supper was served. Horses had in the meanwhile returned, and the post-master ordered their being put to without even being fed; but on re-entering the room, he found the young man lying on a bench, almost insensible: he had suddenly felt faint, his head ached, and he could not possibly proceed on his journey. What was to be done? The post-master gave up his bed to him, and it was decided that the doctor at S—— should be sent for, should the patient not feel better in the morning.

The next day the Hussar was worse. His servant rode off to the town for the doctor. Dunia bound his head with a handkerchief steeped in vinegar, and sat down at her work by his bedside. In the post-master's presence, the patient groaned and scarcely spoke; but he managed nevertheless to empty two cups of coffee, and, still groaning, to order his dinner. Dunia never left him. He was constantly calling for something to drink, and Dunia would hold up a mug of lemonade, which she had herself prepared. The patient would wet his lips, and whenever he returned the mug, his feeble hand pressed Dunia's in token of gratitude. The doctor arrived towards noon. He felt the patient's pulse, had some conversation with him in German, and declared in Russian that all he required was rest, and that in a couple of days he would be able to resume his journey. The Hussar handed him twenty-five roubles as his fee, and invited him to dinner. The doctor accepted; they ate with good appetites, drank a bottle of wine, and parted perfectly satisfied with each other.

Another day passed, and the Hussar was quite himself again. He was exceedingly cheerful, joking incessantly, now with Dunia, then with the post-master, whistling all sorts of tunes, copying their orders for horses into the post-book, and he contrived to ingratiate himself so much with the good-natured post-master that he felt sorry to part with his amiable host when the third morning arrived. It was a Sunday. Dunia was preparing to go to Mass. The Hussar's carriage drove up. He took leave of the post-master, having rewarded him liberally for his board and hospitality; he also bid Dunia good-bye, and offered to drive her as far as the church, which was situated at the further end of the village. Dunia looked perplexed. "What art thou afraid of?" asked her father; "his Excellency is not a wolf, and will not eat thee;. take a drive as far as the church." Dunia took her seat in the carriage next to the Hussar, the servant jumped into the rumble, the driver whistled, and the horses were off.

The poor post-master was not able to understand how he, of his own accord, should have allowed Dunia to drive off with the Hussar; how he could have been blinded to such an extent, and what could have possessed him. Half an hour had not elapsed when his heart already ached, and he felt so much anxiety, that he could contain himself no longer, and accordingly strode off to the church. On reaching it, he saw that the people were already dispersing, but Dunia was neither within the enclosure nor yet at the porch. He hurriedly entered the church; the priest was emerging from behind the altar; the clerk was extinguishing the candles; two old women were still praying in a corner; but no Dunia was to be seen. The poor father could scarcely make up his mind to ask the clerk whether she had been at Mass. The clerk answered that she had not. The post-master returned home, neither dead nor alive. One hope remained. Dunia might possibly, young and thoughtless as she was, have taken it into her head to go on to the next station where her godmother lived. He awaited in a desperate state of agitation the return of the *troika* which had carried them off. No driver returned. At last towards evening he appeared, but alone and tipsy, with the devastating news that Dunia had eloped with the Hussar.

The disaster was too much for the old man; he immediately took to the bed where the young deceiver had lain only the day before. And he now conjectured, after pondering over all the late circumstances, that the illness had been feigned. The poor father then contracted scarlet fever; he was removed to the town of S——, and another post-master was temporarily appointed to replace him. The medical man who had seen the Hussar attended him also. He assured him that the young man was in perfect health, and that he had, even when he visited him, a suspicion of his wicked intentions, but had observed silence for fear of chastisement. Whether what the German said was true, or whether he only wished to make a boast of his foresight, he did not minister any consolation to the poor sufferer. Scarcely had he recovered from his illness than the post-master at once applied to the post-master at S—— for two months' leave of absence, and without saying a word respecting his intentions, set out on foot in search of his daughter. He knew by his papers that the cavalry Captain Minsky

was going from Smolensk to St. Petersburg. The man who
had driven him had said, that though she appeared to go
willingly, Dunia had cried the whole way. "It is just
possible," thought the post-master, "that I may bring home
my little lost sheep." He arrived at St. Petersburg with this
idea, and stopping at the Ismailoffsky Barracks, put up at
the quarters of a retired sub-officer, an old comrade, and
commenced his search. He soon learnt that Minsky was at
St. Petersburg, staying at Demuth's inn. The post-master
decided upon going to him.

He appeared at his door early the following morning, and
asked to be announced as an old soldier who wished to see
his Excellency. The military servant, who was cleaning a
boot on a last, declared that his master was asleep, and that
he saw no one before eleven o'clock. The post-master went
away and returned at the appointed hour. Minsky himself
came to him, in his dressing-gown and a red smoking cap.
"What is it thou wantest, my friend?" he asked. The old
man's heart beat fast, tears gushed to his eyes, and he could
only utter in a trembling voice: "Your Excellency!—for
God's sake do me the favour!"—Minsky threw a quick glance
at him, bridled up, took him by the hand, led him into his
study, and closed the door. "Your Excellency!" the old
man continued, "what is fallen is lost; give me back my poor
Dunia. You have trifled sufficiently with her; do not ruin
her uselessly." "What is done cannot be undone," said the
young man in extreme confusion. "I am guilty before thee
and ready to ask thy forgiveness; but do not imagine I can
abandon Dunia; she will be happy, I give thee my word
for it. What dost thou want her for? She loves me, she is
no longer accustomed to her former mode of living. Neither
of you will be able to forget the past." Here he slipped
something into the old man's sleeve, opened the door, and
the post-master found himself in the street, he scarcely knew
how.

For a long time he stood motionless; at last he noticed a

roll of paper in the cuff of his sleeve; he drew it out, and unrolled several bank-notes of the value of five and ten roubles each. Tears came to his eyes again—tears of indignation! He crushed the notes, threw them from him, trampled them underfoot, and walked away. Having proceeded a few paces, he stopped, reflected, and retraced his steps—but no bank-notes were there. A well-dressed young man on seeing him rushed up to a *droshky*, into which he hastily threw himself and shouted out: "Go on!" The post-master did not follow him. He had made up his mind to return home, but he wished to see his poor Dunia once again before leaving. With this end in view he returned to Minsky two days later; but the soldier-servant roughly told him that his master received no one, and pushing him out of the hall, slammed the door in his face. The post-master waited, and still waited, and then went his way.

He was walking along the *Letéynaya* that same evening, having listened to a *Te Deum* at the church of *Vseh Skarbiast-chech*. A smart *droshky* suddenly dashed past him and he recognised Minsky. The *droshky* stopped at the entrance of a three-storied house, and the Hussar ran up the steps. A happy thought flashed across the post-master. He turned back, and approaching the coachman, "Whose horse is this, my friend?" asked he; "not Minsky's?"—"Yes, Minsky's," answered the coachman: "what dost thou want?"—"Why, this; thy master ordered me to take a note to his Dunia, and I have forgotten where his Dunia lives."—"It is here she lives, on the second floor. Thou art too late with thy note, my friend, he is with her himself now." "No matter," said the post-master, with a violent beating of the heart; "thanks for directing me; I shall know how to manage my business."

The doors were closed; he rang. For several seconds he stood in uneasy expectation. The key rustled; the doors were opened. "Does Aodotia Samsónovna live here?" asked he. "Yes," answered the young servant. "What dost thou want her for?" The post-master, without saying a word, entered the ante-room. "You cannot come in, you cannot come in," shouted the girl after him. "Aodotia Samsónovna has visitors." But the post-master walked on without heeding her. The first two rooms were dark, there were lights in the third. He approached the open door and stopped; Minsky was seated thoughtfully in this richly furnished apartment. Dunia, dressed in all the luxury of fashion, was sitting on the arm of his easy-chair, like a horsewoman in her English saddle, looking tenderly down upon Minsky, and twisting his dark curls with her jewelled fingers. Poor post-master! Never had he seen his daughter looking so beautiful! He could not help admiring her. "Who is there?" asked she, without raising her head. He remained silent. Not receiving any reply, Dunia looked up—and uttering a cry, fell to the floor. The alarmed Minsky rushed to raise her, but on becoming aware of the old post-master's presence, he left Dunia and approached him, quivering with rage. "What dost thou want?" said he, clenching his teeth. "Why dost thou track me as if I were a brigand? Dost thou want to murder me? Be off!" And seizing the old man by the collar, with a strong arm he pushed him down the stairs.

The old man returned to his rooms. His friend advised him to lodge a complaint; but the post-master, having reflected awhile, waved his hand, and decided upon giving it up. Two days later he left St. Petersburg and returned direct to his station, where he resumed his duties. "This is now the third year that I live without Dunia, and I have neither heard from her nor have I seen her. God knows whether she is alive or dead. Anything may happen. She is neither the first nor the last who has been enticed away by a scampish wayfarer, and who has first been cared for and then deserted. There are plenty of these young simpletons in St. Petersburg, who are to-day in satins and velvet, and to-morrow you see them sweeping the streets in degraded misery. When the thought crosses me that Dunia may be ruining herself in the same manner, one sins involuntarily, and wishes she were in the grave."

Such was the story of my friend the old post-master—a story more than once interrupted by tears, which he picturesquely wiped away with his coat-tails, like zealous Terentich in Dmitrieff's beautiful ballad. Those tears were partly induced by the punch, of which he emptied five glasses during his recital; but be that as it may, they touched me deeply. Having taken my leave, it was long before I could forget the old post-master, and long did I think of poor Dunia.

Lately again, on passing through —— I recollected my friend. I learned that the station which he had superintended had been abolished. To my inquiry, "Is the old post-master alive?" I could obtain no satisfactory answer. I made up my mind to visit the familiar locality, and, hiring a private conveyance, I left for the village of N——.

It was autumn. Grey clouds obscured the sky; a cold wind swept over the harvested fields, carrying before it the red and yellow leaves that lay in its course. I entered the village at sunset and stopped before the little post-house. A fat old woman came into the lobby (where poor Dunia had once kissed me), and replied to my inquiries by saying that the old post-master had been dead about a year, that a brewer was settled in his house, and that she herself was the brewer's wife. I began to regret my useless drive and the seven roubles I had profitlessly expended.

"What did he die of?" I inquired of the brewer's wife.

"Drink, sir," answered she.

"And where is he buried?"

"Behind the enclosure, next to his wife."

"Could anybody conduct me to the grave?"

"Why not? Here, Vanka, leave off pulling the cat about. Take this gentleman to the churchyard and show him the post-master's grave."

At these words a ragged, red-haired lad, who was blind of one eye, ran up to me, and set out as my guide.

"Didst thou know the dead man?" I asked him by the way.

"How was I not to know him? He taught me how to make reed whistles. Many a time have we shouted after him when on his way from the public-house (God rest his soul!), ' Daddy, daddy, give us some nuts!' And he would then throw nuts at us. He always played with us."

"And do travellers ever talk of him?"

"There are few travellers now. The assessor may occasionally turn in this way, but it is not the dead he cares for. In the summer, a lady actually did drive by, and she did ask after the post-master, and went to see his grave."

"What lady?" asked I, with curiosity.

"A beautiful lady," answered the lad: "she drove a coach and six horses, with three little gentlemen, a wet-nurse and a black pug-dog, and when told that the old post-master had died, she began to cry, and said to the children, 'Sit you here quietly whilst I go to the churchyard.' Well, I offered to show her the way. But the lady said, 'I know the road myself,' and she gave me five kopecks in silver—such a lady!"

We arrived at the cemetery, a bare place, with nothing to mark its limits, strewn with wooden crosses, with not a tree to shade it. Never in my life had I seen such a melancholy graveyard.

"This is the grave of the old post-master," said the boy, jumping on a mound of earth, over which a black cross with a copper image was placed.

"And the lady came here?" asked I.

"Yes," answered Vanka. "I looked at her from a distance. She threw herself down here, and so she lay a long time. Then she went into the village, called the priest, gave him some money, and drove away; and to me she gave five kopecks in silver—a splendid lady!"

I also gave the lad five kopecks, and no longer regretted my journey, or the seven roubles I had spent.

NICHOLAS GOGOL

(1809–1852)

✠✠

(I)

THE CLOAK

(Translated by Isabel F. Hapgood)

I N the department of—— But it is better not to name the department. There is nothing more irritable than all kinds of departments, regiments, courts of justice, and, in a word, every branch of public service. Each separate man nowadays thinks all society insulted in his person. They say that, quite recently, a complaint was received from a justice of the peace, in which he plainly demonstrated that all the imperial institutions were going to the dogs, and that his sacred name was being taken in vain, and in proof he appended to the complaint a huge volume of some romantic composition, in which the justice of the peace appears about once in every ten lines, sometimes in a drunken condition. Therefore, in order to avoid all unpleasantness, it will be better for us to designate the department in question as *a certain department*. So, *in a certain department* serves *a certain tchinovnik* (official)—not a very prominent official, it must be allowed—short of stature, somewhat pock-marked, rather red-haired, rather blind, judging from appearances, with a small bald spot on his forehead, with wrinkles on his cheeks, with a complexion of the sort called sanguine. . . . How could he help it? The Petersburg climate was responsible for that. As for his *tchin* (rank)—for with us the rank must be stated first of all—he was what is called a perpetual titular councillor, over which, as is well known, some writers make merry and crack their jokes, as they have the praiseworthy custom of attacking those who cannot bite back.

His family name was Bashmatchkin. It is evident from the name, that it originated in *bashmak* (shoe); but when, at what time, and in what manner, is not known. His father and grandfather, and even his brother-in-law, and all the Bashmatchkins, always wore boots, and only had new heels two or three times a year. His name was Akakiy Akakievitch. It may strike the reader as rather singular and far-fetched; but he may feel assured that it was by no means far-fetched, and that the circumstances were such that it would have been impossible to give him any other name; and this was how it came about. Akakiy Akakievitch was born, if my memory fails me not, towards night on the 23rd of March. His late mother, the wife of a *tchinovnik*, and a very fine woman, made all due arrangements for having the child baptised. His mother was lying on the bed opposite the door; on her right stood the godfather, a most estimable man, Ivan Ivanovitch Eroshkin, who served as presiding officer of the senate; and the godmother, the wife of an officer of the quarter, a woman of rare virtues, Anna Semenovna Byelobrushkova. They offered the mother her choice of three names—Mokiya, Sossiya, or that the child should be called after the martyr Khozdadat. "No," pronounced the blessed woman, "all those names are poor." In order to please her they opened the calendar at another place: three more names appeared— Triphiliy, Dula and Varakhasiy. "This is a judgment," said the old woman. "What names! I truly never heard the like. Varadat or Varukh might have been borne, but not Triphiliy and Varakhasiy!" They turned another page—Pavsikakhiy and Vakhtisiy. "Now I see," said the old woman, "that it is plainly fate. And if that's the case, it will be better to name him after his father. His father's name was Akakiy, so let his son's be also Akakiy." In this manner he became Akakiy Akakievitch. They christened the child, whereat he wept, and made a grimace, as though he foresaw that he was to be a titular councillor. In this manner did it all come about. We have mentioned it in order that the reader might see for himself that it happened quite as a case of necessity, and that it was utterly impossible to give him any other name. When and how he entered the department, and who appointed him, no one could remember. However much the directors and chiefs of all kinds were changed, he was always to be seen in the same place, the same attitude, the same occupation—the same official for letters; so that afterwards it was affirmed that he had been born in undress uniform with a bald spot on his head. No respect was shown him in the department. The janitor not only did not rise from his seat when he passed, but never even glanced at him, as if only a fly had flown through the reception-room. His superiors treated him in a coolly despotic manner. Some assistant chief would thrust a paper under his nose without so much as saying, "Copy," or, "Here's a nice, interesting matter," or anything else agreeable, as is customary in well-bred service. And he took it, looking only at the paper, and not observing who handed it to him, or whether he had the right to do so: he simply took it, and set about copying it. The young officials laughed at and made fun of him, so far as their official wit permitted; recounted there in his presence various stories concocted about him and about his landlady, an old woman of seventy; they said that she beat him; asked him when the wedding was to be; and strewed bits of paper over his head, calling them snow. But Akakiy Akakievitch answered not a word, as though there had been no one before him. It even had no effect upon his employment: amid all these molestations he never made a single mistake in a letter. But if the joking became utterly intolerable, as when they jogged his hand, and prevented his attending to his work, he would exclaim, "Leave me alone! Why do you insult me?" And there was something strange in the words and the voice in which they were uttered. There was in it a something which moved to pity; so that one young man, lately entered, who, taking pattern by the others, had permitted himself to make sport of him, suddenly stopped short, as though all had undergone a transformation before him, and presented itself in a different aspect. Some unseen force repelled him from the comrades whose acquaintance he had made on the supposition that they were well-bred and polite men. And long afterwards, in his gayest moments, there came to his mind the little official with the bald forehead, with the heart-rending words "Leave me alone. Why do you insult me?" And in these penetrating words, other words resounded— "I am thy brother." And the poor young man covered his face with his hand; and many a time afterwards, in the course of his life, he shuddered at seeing how much inhumanity there is in man, how much savage coarseness is concealed in delicate, refined worldliness, and, O God! even in that man whom the world acknowledges as honourable and noble.

It would be difficult to find another man who lived so entirely for his duties. It is saying but little to say that he served with zeal: no, he served with love. In that copying he saw a varied and agreeable world. Enjoyment was written on his face; some letters were favourites with him; and when he encountered them, he became unlike himself; he smiled and winked, and assisted with his lips, so that it seemed as though each letter might be read in his face as his pen traced it. If his pay had been in proportion to his zeal he would perhaps, to his own surprise, have been made even a councillor of state. But he served, as his companions, the wits, put it, like a buckle in a button-hole.

Moreover, it is impossible to say that no attention was paid to him. One director, being a kindly man, and desirous of rewarding him for his long service, ordered him to be given something more important than mere copying; namely, he was ordered to make a report of an already concluded affair, to another court: the matter consisted simply in changing the heading, and altering a few words from the first to the third person. This caused him so much toil that he was all in a perspiration, rubbed his forehead, and finally said, "No, give me rather something to copy." After that they let him copy on for ever. Outside this copying it appeared that nothing existed for him. He thought not at all of his clothes: his undress uniform was not green, but a sort of rusty-meal colour. The collar was narrow, low, so that his neck, in spite of the fact that it was not long, seemed inordinately long as it emerged from that collar, like the necks of plaster cats which wag their heads, and are carried about upon the heads of scores of Russian foreigners. And something was always sticking to his uniform—either a piece of hay or some trifle. Moreover, he had a peculiar knack, as he walked in the street, of arriving beneath a window when all kind of rubbish was being flung out of it; hence he always bore about on his hat melon and water-melon rinds, and other such stuff. Never once in his life did he give heed to what was going on every day in the street; while it is well known that his young brother official, extending the range of his bold glance, gets so that he can see when anyone's trouser-straps drop down upon the opposite side-walk, which always calls forth a malicious smile upon his face. But Akakiy Akakievitch, if he looked at anything, saw in all things the clear, even strokes of his written lines; and only when a horse thrust his muzzle, from some unknown quarter, over his shoulder, and sent a whole gust of wind down his neck from his nostrils, did he observe that he was not in the middle of a line, but in the middle of the street.

On arriving at home, he sat down at once at the table, supped his cabbage-soup quickly, and ate a bit of beef with onions, never noticing their taste, ate it all with flies and anything else which the Lord sent at the moment. On observing that his stomach began to puff out, he rose from the table, took out a little vial with ink, and copied papers which he had brought home. If there happened to be none, he took copies for himself, for his own gratification, especially if the paper was noteworthy, not on account of its beautiful style, but of its being addressed to some new or distinguished person.

Even at the hour when the grey Petersburg sky had quite disappeared, and all the world of *tchinovniks* had eaten or dined each as he could, in accordance with the salary he received, and his own fancy; when all were resting from the departmental jar of pens running to and fro, their own and other people's indispensable occupations, and all the work that an uneasy man makes willingly for himself, rather than what is necessary; when *tchinovniks* hasten to dedicate to pleasure the time which is left to them—one bolder than the rest goes to the theatre; another, into the streets, devoting it to the inspection of some bonnets; one wastes his evening in compliments to some pretty girl, the star of a small official circle; one—and this is the most common case of all—goes to his comrades on the fourth or third floor, to two small rooms with an ante-room or kitchen, and some pretensions to fashion, a lamp or some other trifle which has cost many a sacrifice of dinner or excursion—in a word, even at the hour when all *tchinovniks* disperse among the contracted quarters of their friends to play at whist, as they sip their tea from glasses with a kopek's worth of sugar, draw smoke through long pipes, relating at times some bits of gossip which a Russian man can never, under any circumstances, refrain from, or even, where there is nothing to say, recounting everlasting anecdotes about the commandant whom they had sent to inform that the tails of the horses on the Falconet Monument had been cut off—in a word, even when all strive to divert themselves, Akakiy Akakievitch yielded to no diversion. No one could ever say that he had seen him at any sort of an evening party. Having written to his heart's content, he lay down to sleep, smiling at the thought of the coming day—and of what God might send him to copy on the morrow. Thus flowed on the peaceful life of the man, who, with a salary of four hundred roubles, understood how to be content with his fate; and thus it would have continued to flow on, perhaps, to extreme old age, were there not various ills sown along the path of life for titular councillors as well as for private, actual, court and every other species of councillor, even for those who never give any advice or take any themselves.

There exists in St. Petersburg a powerful foe of all who receive four hundred roubles a year, or thereabouts. This foe is no other than our Northern cold, although it is said to be very wholesome. At nine o'clock in the morning, at the very hour when the streets are filled with men bound for the departments, it begins to bestow such powerful and piercing nips on all noses impartially, that the poor officials really do not know what to do with them. At the hour when the foreheads of even those who occupy exalted positions ache with the cold, and tears start to their eyes, the poor titular councillors are sometimes unprotected. Their only salvation lies in walking as quickly as possible, in their thin little cloaks, five or six streets, and then warming their feet well in the porter room, and so thawing all those talents and qualifications for official service which have become frozen on the way. Akakiy Akakievitch had felt for some time that his back and shoulders suffered with peculiar poignancy, in spite of the fact that he always tried to get to the office with all possible speed. He finally wondered whether the fault did not lie in his cloak. He examined it thoroughly at home, and discovered that in two places, namely, on the back and shoulders, it had become thin as mosquito-netting: the cloth was worn to such a degree that he could see through it, and the lining had fallen into pieces. You must know that Akakiy Akakievitch's cloak served as an object of ridicule to the *tchinovniks:* they even deprived it of the noble name of cloak, and called it a *capote* (a woman's cloak). In fact, it was of singular make: its collar diminished year by year, but served to patch its other parts. The patching did not exhibit great skill on the part of the tailor, and made it, in fact, baggy and ugly. Seeing how the matter stood, Akakiy

Akakievitch decided that it would be necessary to
cloak to Petrovitch, the tailor, who lived somewher
fourth floor up a dark staircase, and who, in spite
having but one eye, and pock-marks all over his face, h ..ed
himself with considerable success in repairing the trousers and
coats of officials and others; that is to say, when he was sober,
and not nursing some other scheme in his head. It is not
necessary to say much about this tailor; but as it is the
custom to have the character of each personage in a novel
clearly defined, there is nothing to be done; so here is
Petrovitch the tailor. At first he was called only Grigoriy,
and was some gentleman's serf: he began to call himself
Petrovitch from the time when he received his free papers,
and began to drink heavily on all holidays, at first on the
great ones, and then on all Church festivals without dis-
crimination whenever a cross stood in the calendar. On this
point he was faithful to ancestral custom; and, quarrelling
with his wife, he called her a low female and a German. As
we have stumbled upon his wife, it will be necessary to say a
word or two about her; but unfortunately little is known of
her beyond the fact that Petrovitch has a wife, who wears a
cap and a dress; but she cannot lay claim to beauty, it seems
—at least, no one but the soldiers of the guard, as they pulled
their moustaches, and uttered some peculiar sound, even
looked under her cap when they met her.

  Ascending the staircase which led to Petrovitch—which, to
do it justice, was all soaked in water (dish-water) and penetrated with the smell of spirits which affects the eyes, and is
an inevitable adjunct to all dark stairways in Petersburg
houses—ascending the stairs, Akakiy Akakievitch pondered
how much Petrovitch would ask, and mentally resolved not
to give more than two roubles. The door was open; for the
mistress, in cooking some fish, had raised such a smoke in the
kitchen that not even the beetles were visible. Akakiy
Akakievitch passed through the kitchen unperceived even by
the housewife, and at length reached a room where he beheld

Petrovitch seated on a large, unpainted table, with his legs tucked under him like a Turkish pasha. His feet were bare, after the fashion of tailors as they sit at work, and the first thing which arrested the eye was his thumb, very well known to Akakiy Akakievitch, with a deformed nail thick and strong as a turtle's shell. On Petrovitch's neck hung a skein of silk and thread, and upon his knees lay some old garment. He had been trying for three minutes to thread his needle, unsuccessfully, and so was very angry with the darkness, and even with the thread, growling in a low voice, "It won't go through, the barbarian! you pricked me, you rascal!" Akakiy Akakievitch was displeased at arriving at the precise moment when Petrovitch was angry: he liked to order something of Petrovitch when the latter was a little down-hearted, or, as his wife expressed it, "When he had settled himself with brandy, the one-eyed devil!"

Under such circumstances, Petrovitch generally came down in his price very readily, and came to an understanding, and even bowed and returned thanks. Afterwards, to be sure, his wife came, complaining that her husband was drunk, and so had set his price too low: but, if only a ten-kopek piece were added, then the matter was settled. But now it appeared that Petrovitch was in a sober condition, and therefore rough, taciturn, and inclined to demand, Satan only knows what price. Akakiy Akakievitch felt this, and would gladly have beat a retreat, as the saying goes; but he was in for it. Petrovitch screwed up his one eye very intently at him; and Akakiy Akakievitch involuntarily said, "How do you do, Petrovitch?"

"I wish you a good-morning, sir," said Petrovitch, and squinted at Akakiy Akakievitch's hands, wishing to see what sort of booty he had brought.

"Ah! . . . to you, Petrovitch, this——" It must be known that Akakiy Akakievitch expressed himself chiefly by prepositions, adverbs, and by such scraps of phrases as had no meaning whatever. But if the matter was a very difficult one, then he had a habit of never completing his sentences; so that quite frequently, having begun his phrase with the words, "This, in fact, is quite . . ." there was no more of it, and he forgot himself, thinking that he had already finished it.

"What is it?" asked Petrovitch, and with his one eye scanned his whole uniform, beginning with the collar down to the cuffs, the back, the tails and button-holes, all of which were very well known to him, because they were his own handiwork. Such is the habit of tailors: it is the first thing they do when a customer enters.

"But I—here, this, Petrovitch . . . a cloak, cloth . . . here you see, everywhere, in different places, it is quite strong . . . it is a little dusty and looks old, but it is new, only here in one place it is a little . . . on the back, and here on one of the shoulders it is a little . . . do you see? this is all. And a little work . . ."

Petrovitch took the mantle, spread it out to begin with, on the table, looked long at it, shook his head, put out his hand to the window-sill after his snuff-box, adorned with the portrait of some general—just what general is unknown, for the place where the face belonged had been rubbed through by the finger, and a square bit of paper had been pasted on. Having taken a pinch of snuff, Petrovitch spread the cloak out on his hands, and inspected it against the light, and again shook his head: then he turned it lining upwards, and shook his head once more; again he removed the general-adorned cover with its bit of pasted paper, and having stuffed his nose with snuff, covered and put away the snuff-box, and said, finally, "No, it is impossible to mend it; it's a miserable garment!"

Akakiy Akakievitch's heart sank at these words.

"Why is it impossible, Petrovitch?" he said, almost in the pleading voice of a child: "all that ails it is, that it is worn on the shoulders. You must have some pieces . . ."

"Yes, patches could be found, patches are easily found," said Petrovitch, "but there's nothing to sew them to. The thing is completely rotten: if you touch a needle to it—see, it will give way."

"Let it give way, and you can put on another patch at once."

"But there is nothing to put the patches on: there's no use in strengthening it; it is very far gone. It's lucky that it's cloth; for, if the wind were to blow, it would fly away."

"Well, strengthen it again. Now this, in fact . . ."

"No," said Petrovitch, decisively, "there is nothing to be done with it. It's a thoroughly bad job. You'd better, when the cold winter weather comes on, make yourself some putties out of it, because stockings are not warm. The Germans invented them in order to make more money." (Petrovitch loved, on occasion, to give a fling at the Germans.) "But it is plain that you must have a new cloak."

At the word *new* all grew dark before Akakiy Akakievitch's eyes, and everything in the room began to whirl round. The only thing he saw clearly was the general with the paper face on Petrovitch's snuff-box cover. "How a new one?" said he, as if still in a dream. "Why, I have no money for that."

"Yes, a new one," said Petrovitch, with barbarous composure.

"Well, if it came to a new one, how, it . . ."

"You mean how much would it cost?"

"Yes."

"Well, you would have to lay out a hundred and fifty or more," said Petrovitch, and pursed up his lips significantly. He greatly liked powerful effects, liked to stun utterly and suddenly, and then to glance sideways to see what face the stunned person would put on the matter.

"A hundred and fifty roubles for a cloak!" shrieked Akakiy Akakievitch—shrieked perhaps for the first time in his life, for his voice had always been distinguished for its softness.

"Yes, sir," said Petrovitch, "for any sort of a cloak. If you have marten fur on the collar, or a silk-lined hood, it will mount up to two hundred."

"Petrovitch, please," said Akakiy Akakievitch in a beseeching tone, not hearing, and not trying to hear, Petrovitch's words, and all his "effects," "some repairs, in order that it may wear yet a little longer."

"No, then it would be a waste of labour and money," said Petrovitch; and Akakiy Akakievitch went away after these words, utterly discouraged. But Petrovitch stood long after his departure with significantly compressed lips, and not betaking himself to his work, satisfied that he would not be dropped and an artistic tailor employed.

Akakiy Akakievitch went out into the street as if in a dream. "Such an affair!" he said to himself: "I did not think it had come to . . ." And then after a pause he added, "Well, so it is! see what it has come to at last! and I never imagined that it was so!" Then followed a long silence, after which he exclaimed, "Well, so it is! See what already exactly, nothing unexpected that . . . it would be nothing . . . what a circumstance!" So saying, instead of going home, he went in exactly the opposite direction without himself suspecting it. On the way, a chimney-sweep brought his dirty side up against him, and blackened his whole shoulder: a whole hatful of rubbish landed on him from the top of a house which was building. He observed it not; and afterwards, when he ran into a sentry, who, having planted his halberd beside him, was shaking some snuff from his box into his horny hand—only then did he recover himself a little, and that because the sentry said, "Why are you thrusting yourself into a man's very face? Haven't you the pavement?" This caused him to look about him and turn towards home. There only he finally began to collect his thoughts, and to survey his position in its clear and actual light, and to argue with himself, not brokenly, but sensibly and frankly, as with a reasonable friend, with whom one can discuss very private and personal matters. "No," said Akakiy Akakievitch, "it is impossible to reason with Petrovitch now: he is that . . . evidently his wife has been beating him. I'd better go to him

Sunday morning; after Saturday night he will be a little cross-eyed and sleepy, for he will have to get drunk, and his wife won't give him any money; and at such a time a ten-kopek piece in his hand will—he will become more fit to reason with, and then the cloak, and that . . ." Thus argued Akakiy Akakievitch with himself, regained his courage, and waited until the first Sunday, when, seeing from afar that Petrovitch's wife had gone out of the house, he went straight to him. Petrovitch's eye was very much askew, in fact, after Saturday, his head drooped, and he was very sleepy; but for all that, as soon as he knew what the question was, it seemed as though Satan jogged his memory. "Impossible," said he; "please to order a new one." Thereupon Akakiy Akakievitch handed over the ten-kopek piece. "Thank you, sir, I will drink your good health," said Petrovitch, "but as for the cloak, don't trouble yourself about it; it is good for nothing. I will make you a new coat famously, so let us settle about it now."

Akakiy Akakievitch was still for mending it, but Petrovitch would not hear of it, and said, "I shall certainly make you a new one, and please depend upon it that I shall do my best. It may even be, as the fashion goes, that the collar can be fastened by silver hooks under a clasp."

Then Akakiy Akakievitch saw that it was impossible to get along without a new cloak, and his spirit sank utterly. How, in fact, was it to be accomplished? Where was the money to come from? He might, to be sure, depend in part upon his present at Christmas; but that money had long been doled out and allotted beforehand. He must have some new trousers, and pay a debt of long standing to the shoemaker for putting new tops to his old boots, and he must order three shirts from the seamstress, and a couple of pieces of linen which it is impossible to mention in print; in a word, all his money must be spent; and even if the director should be so kind as to order forty-five roubles instead of forty, or even fifty, it would be a mere nothing, and a mere drop in the

ocean towards the capital necessary for a cloak: although
he knew that Petrovitch was wrong-headed enough to blurt
out some outrageous price, Satan only knows what, so that
his own wife could not refrain from exclaiming, "Have you
lost your senses, you fool?" At one time he would not work
at any price, and now it was quite likely that he had asked a
price which it was not worth. Although he knew that Petrovitch would undertake to make it for eighty roubles, still,
where was he to get the eighty roubles? He might possibly
manage half; yes, and half of that might be procured: but
where was the other half to come from? But the reader must
first be told where the first half came from. Akakiy Akakievitch had a habit of putting, for every rouble he spent, a
copeck into a small box, fastened with lock and key, and
with a hole in the top for the reception of money. At the
end of each half-year he counted over the heap of coppers
and changed it into small silver coins. This he continued for
a long time, and thus, in the course of some years, the sum
proved to amount to over forty roubles. Thus he had one-
half in hand; but where to get the other half? where to get
another forty roubles. Akakiy Akakievitch thought and
thought, and decided that it would be necessary to curtail his
ordinary expenses, for the space of one year, at least—to
dispense with tea in the evening; to burn no candle and, if
there was anything which he must do, to go into his landlady's room and work by her light; when he went into the
street he must walk as lightly as possible, and as cautiously,
upon the stone and flagging, almost upon tip-toe, in order
not to wear out his heels in too short a time; he must give
the laundress as little to wash as possible; and in order not
to wear out his clothes, he must take them off as soon as he
got home, and wear only his cotton dressing-gown, which
had been long and carefully saved.

To tell the truth, it was a little hard for him at first to
accustom himself to these deprivations; but he got used to
them at length, after a fashion, and all went smoothly—he

even got used to being hungry in the evening; but he made up for it by treating himself in spirit, bearing ever in mind the thought of his future cloak. From that time forth his existence seemed to become, in some way, fuller, as if he were married, as if some other man lived in him, as if he were not alone, and some charming friend had consented to go along life's path with him—and the friend was no other than that cloak, with thick wadding and a strong lining incapable of wearing out. He became more lively, and his character even became firmer, like that of a man who has made up his mind and set himself a goal. From his face and gait doubt and indecision—in short, all hesitating and wavering traits—disappeared of themselves. Fire gleamed in his eyes, occasionally the boldest and most daring ideas flitted through his mind; why not, in fact, have marten fur on the collar? The thought of this nearly made him absent-minded. Once, in copying a letter, he nearly made a mistake, so that he exclaimed almost aloud, "Ugh!" and crossed himself. Once in the course of each month, he had a conference with Petrovitch on the subject of the coat—where it would be better to buy the cloth, and the colour, and the price—and he always returned home satisfied, though troubled, reflecting that the time would come at last when it could all be bought, and then the cloak could be made. The matter progressed more briskly than he had expected. Far beyond all his hopes, the director appointed neither forty nor forty-five roubles for Akakiy Akakievitch's share, but sixty. Did he suspect that Akakiy Akakievitch needed a cloak, or did it merely happen so? at all events, twenty extra roubles were by this means provided. This circumstance hastened matters. Only two or three months more of hunger—and Akakiy Akakievitch had accumulated about eighty roubles. His heart, generally so quiet, began to beat. On the first possible day he visited the shops in company with Petrovitch. They purchased some very good cloth—and reasonably, for they had been considering the matter for six months, and rarely did a month

pass without their visiting the shops to inquire prices, and
Petrovitch said himself that no better cloth could be had.
For lining they selected a cotton stuff, but so firm and thick
that Petrovitch declared it to be better than silk, and even
prettier and more glossy. They did not buy the marten fur,
because it was dear, in fact, but in its stead they picked out
the very best of cat-skin which could be found in the shop,
and which might be taken for marten at a distance.

Petrovitch worked at the cloak two whole weeks, for there
was a great deal of quilting, otherwise it would have been
done sooner. Petrovitch charged twelve roubles for his work
—it could not possibly be done for less; it was all sewed with
silk, in small double seams; and Petrovitch went over each
seam afterwards with his own teeth, stamping in various
patterns. It was—it is difficult to say precisely on what day,
but it was probably the most glorious day in Akakiy Akakievitch's life when Petrovitch at length brought home the
cloak. He brought it in the morning, before the hour when
it was necessary to go to the department. Never did a cloak
arrive so exactly in the nick of time; for the severe cold had
set in, and it seemed to threaten increase. Petrovitch presented himself with the coat, as befits a good tailor. On his
countenance was a significant expression, such as Akakiy
Akakievitch had never beheld there. He seemed sensible to
the fullest extent that he had done no small deed, and that
a gulf had suddenly appeared, separating tailors who only
put in linings and make repairs from those who make new
things. He took the cloak out of the linen towel in which
he had brought it. (The towel was fresh from the laundress:
he now removed it, and put it in his pocket to use as handkerchief.) Taking out the cloak, he gazed proudly at it, held it
with both hands, and flung it very skilfully over the shoulders
of Akakiy Akakievitch; then he pulled it and fitted it down
behind with his hand; then he draped it around Akakiy
Akakievitch without buttoning it. Akakiy Akakievitch, as a
man advanced in life, wished to try the sleeves. Petrovitch

helped him on with them, and it turned out that the sleeves were satisfactory also. In short, the cloak appeared to be perfect, and just in season. Petrovitch did not neglect the opportunity to observe that it was only because he lived in a narrow street, and had no sign-board, and because he had known Akakiy Akakievitch so long, that he had made it so cheaply; but, if he had been on the Nevsky Prospect he would have charged seventy-five roubles for the making alone. Akakiy Akakievitch did not care to argue this point with Petrovitch, and he was afraid of the large sums with which Petrovitch was fond of raising the dust. He paid him, thanked him, and set out at once in his new cloak for the department. Petrovitch followed him, and, pausing in the street, gazed long at the cloak in the distance, and went to one side expressly to run through a crooked alley and emerge again into the street to gaze once more upon the cloak from another point, namely, directly in front.

Meantime Akakiy Akakievitch went on with every sense in holiday mood. He was conscious every second of the time that he had a new cloak on his shoulders; and several times he laughed with internal satisfaction. In fact, there were two advantages—one was its warmth, the other its beauty. He saw nothing of the road, and suddenly found himself at the department. He threw off his cloak in the ante-room, looked it over well, and confided it to the especial care of the janitor. It is impossible to say just how everyone in the department knew at once that Akakiy Akakievitch had a new cloak, and that the "mantel" no longer existed. All rushed at the same moment into the ante-room, to inspect Akakiy Akakievitch's new cloak. They began to congratulate him, and to say pleasant things to him, so that he began at first to smile, and then he grew ashamed. When all surrounded him, and began to say that the new cloak must be "christened," and that he must give a whole evening at least to it, Akakiy Akakievitch lost his head completely, knew not where he stood, what to answer, and how to get out of it. He stood blushing all over

for several minutes, and was on the point of assuring them
with great simplicity that it was not a new cloak, that it was
so-and-so, that it was the old cloak. At length one of the
tchinovniks, some assistant chief probably, in order to show
that he was not at all proud, and on good terms with his
inferiors, said, "So be it; I will give the party instead of
Akakiy Akakievitch; I invite you all to tea with me to-night;
it happens quite apropos, as it is my name-day." The officials
naturally at once offered the assistant chief their congratulations and accepted the invitation with pleasure. Akakiy
Akakievitch would have declined; but all declared that it was
discourteous, that it was simply a sin and a shame, and that
he could not possibly refuse. Besides, the idea became
pleasant to him when he recollected that he should thereby
have a chance to wear his new cloak in the evening also.
That whole day was truly a most triumphant festival day for
Akakiy Akakievitch. He returned home in the most happy
frame of mind, threw off his cloak, and hung it carefully on
the wall, admiring afresh the cloth and the lining; and then
he brought out his old, worn-out cloak for comparison. He
looked at it and laughed, so vast was the difference. And
long after dinner he laughed again, when the condition of
the mantle recurred to his mind. He dined gaily, and after
dinner wrote nothing, no papers even, but took his ease for
a while on the bed, until it got dark. Then he dressed himself
luxuriously, put on his cloak, and stepped out into the street.
Where the host lived, unfortunately we cannot say: our
memory begins to fail us badly; and everything in St. Petersburg, all the houses and the streets, have run together, and
become so mixed up in our mind that it is very difficult to
produce anything thence in proper form. At all events, this
much is certain, that the *tchinovnik* lived in the best part of the
city, and therefore it must have been anything but near to
Akakiy Akakievitch. Akakiy Akakievitch was first obliged to
traverse a sort of wilderness of deserted, dimly-lighted streets;
but in proportion as he approached the *tchinovnik's* quarter of

the city, the streets became more lively, more populous, and more brilliantly illuminated. Pedestrians began to appear; handsomely dressed ladies were more frequently encountered; the men had otter collars; peasant cabmen in their grate-like sledges with brass-topped nails became rarer; on the other hand, more and more coachmen in red velvet caps, with lacquered sleighs and bear-skin robes, began to appear; carriages with decorated coach-boxes flew swiftly through the streets, their wheels scrunching the snow. Akakiy Akakievitch gazed upon all this as upon a novelty. He had not been in the streets of an evening for years. He halted out of curiosity before the lighted window of a shop, to look at a picture representing a handsome woman, who had thrown off her shoe, thereby baring her whole foot in a very pretty way; and behind her the head of a man with side-whiskers and a handsome moustache peeped from the door of another room. Akakiy Akakievitch shook his head and laughed, and then went on his way. Why did he laugh? Because he had met with a thing utterly unknown, but for which everyone cherishes, nevertheless, some sort of feeling; or else he thought, like many officials, as follows: "Well, those French! What is to be said? If they like anything of that sort, then, in fact, that . . ." But possibly he did not think that.

For it is impossible to enter a man's mind and know all that he thinks. At length he reached the house in which the assistant chief lodged. The assistant chief lived in fine style: on the staircase burned a lantern; his apartment was on the second floor. On entering the vestibule, Akakiy Akakievitch beheld a whole row of overshoes on the floor. Amid them, in the centre of the room, stood a samovar, humming and emitting clouds of steam. On the walls hung all sorts of coats and cloaks, among which there were even some with beaver collars or velvet facings. Beyond the wall the buzz of conversation was audible, which became clear and loud when the servant came out with a trayful of empty glasses, cream-jugs and sugar-bowls. It was evident that the *tchinovniks* had

arrived long before, and had already finished their first glass
of tea. Akakiy Akakievitch, having hung up his own cloak,
entered the room; and before him all at once appeared
lights, officials, pipes, card-tables; and he was surprised by a
sound of rapid conversation rising from all the tables, and
the noise of moving chairs. He halted very awkwardly in the
middle of the room, wondering, and trying to decide what he
ought to do. But they had seen him; they received him with
a shout, and all went out at once into the ante-room, and
took another look at his cloak. Akakiy Akakievitch, somewhat confused, was open-hearted, and could not refrain from
rejoicing when he saw how they praised his cloak. Then, of
course, they all dropped him and his cloak, and returned, as
was proper, to the tables set out for whist. All this—the
noise, talk and throng of people—was rather wonderful to
Akakiy Akakievitch. He simply did not know where he
stood, or where to put his hands, his feet, and his whole body.
Finally, he sat down by the players, looked at the cards,
gazed at the face of one and another, and after a while began
to gape, and to feel that it was wearisome—the more so as
the hour was already long past when he usually went to bed.
He wanted to take leave of the host; but they would not let
him go, saying that he must drink a glass of champagne, in
honour of his new garment, without fail. In the course of an
hour, supper was served, consisting of vegetable salad, cold
veal, pastry, confectioner's pies and champagne. They made
Akakiy Akakievitch drink two glasses of champagne, after
which he felt that the room grew livelier; still, he could not
forget that it was twelve o'clock, and that he should have
been at home long ago. In order that the host might not
think of some excuse for detaining him, he went out of the
room quietly, sought out in the ante-room his cloak, which,
to his sorrow, he found lying on the floor, brushed it, picked
off every speck, put it on his shoulders, and descended the
stairs to the street. In the street all was still bright. Some
petty shops, those permanent clubs of servants and all sorts of

people, were open; others were shut, but, nevertheless, showed a streak of light the whole length of the door-crack, indicating that they were not yet free of company, and that probably domestics both male and female were finishing their stories and conversations, leaving their masters in complete ignorance as to their whereabouts.. Akakiy Akakievitch went on in a happy frame of mind: he even started to run, without knowing why, after some lady, who flew past like a flash of lightning, and whose whole body was endowed with an extraordinary amount of movement. But he stopped short, and went on very quietly as before, wondering whence he had got that gait. Soon there opened before him those deserted streets, which are not cheerful in the daytime, not to mention the evening. Now they were even more dim and lonely: the lanterns began to grow rarer—oil, evidently, had been less liberally supplied; then came wooden houses and fences; not a soul anywhere; only the snow sparkled in the streets, and mournfully darkled the low-roofed cabins with their closed shutters. He approached the place where the street crossed an endless square with barely visible houses on its farther side, and which seemed a fearful desert.

Afar, God knows where, a tiny spark glimmered, from some sentry-box, which seemed to stand on the edge of the world. Akakiy Akakievitch's cheerfulness diminished at this point in a marked degree. He entered the square, not without an involuntarily sensation of fear, as though his heart warned him of some evil. He glanced back and on both sides—it was like a sea about him. "No, it is better not to look," he thought, and went on, closing his eyes; and when he opened them, to see whether he was near the end of the square, he suddenly beheld standing just before his very nose some bearded individuals—of just what sort he could not make out. All grew dark before his eyes, and his breast throbbed.

"But of course the cloak is mine!" said one of them in a loud voice, seizing hold of the collar. Akakiy Akakievitch was about to shout *watch*, when the second man thrust a fist into his mouth, about the size of a *tchinovnik's* head, muttering, "Now scream!"

Akakiy Akakievitch felt them take off his cloak and give him a push with a knee; he fell headlong upon the snow, and felt no more. In a few minutes he recovered consciousness and rose to his feet; but no one was there. He felt that it was cold in the square, and that his cloak was gone; he began to shout, but his voice did not appear to reach to the outskirts of the square. In despair, but without ceasing to shout, he started on a run through the square, straight towards the sentry-box beside which stood the watchman, leaning on his halberd, and apparently curious to know what devil of a man was running towards him from afar and shouting. Akakiy Akakievitch ran up to him, and began in a sobbing voice to shout that he was asleep, and attended to nothing, and did not see when a man was robbed. The watchman replied that he had seen no one; that he had seen two men stop him in the middle of the square, and supposed that they were friends of his; and that, instead of scolding in vain, he had better go to the captain on the morrow, so that the captain might investigate as to who had stolen the cloak. Akakiy Akakievitch ran home in complete disorder; his hair, which grew very thinly upon his temples and the back of his head, was entirely disarranged; his side and breast, and all his trousers, were covered with snow. The old woman, mistress of his lodgings, hearing a terrible knocking, sprang hastily from her bed, and, with a shoe on one foot only, ran to open the door, pressing the sleeve of her chemise to her bosom out of modesty; but when she had opened it she fell back on beholding Akakiy Akakievitch in such a state. When he told the matter, she clasped her hands, and said that he must go straight to the superintendent, for the captain would turn up his nose, promise well, and drop the matter there; the very best thing to do would be to go to the superintendent; that he knew her, because Finnish Anna, her former cook, was now nurse at the superintendent's; that she often saw him passing the house; and that he was at church every Sunday, praying, but at the same time gazing cheerfully at everybody; and that he must be a good man, judging from all appearances. Having listened to this opinion, Akakiy Akakievitch betook himself sadly to his chamber, and how he spent the night there, anyone can imagine who can put himself in another's place. Early in the morning he presented himself at the superintendent's; but they told him that he was asleep; he went again at ten, and was again informed that he was asleep; he went at eleven o'clock, and they said, "The superintendent is not at home"; at dinner time, and the clerks in the ante-room would not admit him on any terms, and insisted upon knowing his business, and what brought him, and how it had come about. So that at last, for once in his life, Akakiy Akakievitch felt an inclination to show some spirit, and said curtly that he must see the superintendent in person; that they should not presume to refuse him entrance; that he came from the department of justice, and, when he complained of them, they would see. The clerks dared make no reply to this, and one of them went to call the superintendent. The superintendent listened to the extremely strange story of the theft of the cloak. Instead of directing his attention to the principal points of the matter, he began to question Akakiy Akakievitch. Why did he return so late? Was he in the habit of going, or had he been, to any disorderly house? So that Akakiy Akakievitch got thoroughly confused, and left him without knowing whether the affair of his cloak was in proper train or not. All that day he never went near the office (for the first time in his life). The next day he made his appearance, very pale, and in his old mantle, which had become even more shabby. The news of the robbery of the cloak touched many; although there were officials present who never omitted an opportunity, even the present, to ridicule Akakiy Akakievitch. They decided to take up a collection for him on the spot; but it turned out a mere trifle; for the *tchinovniks* had already spent a great deal in

subscribing for the director's portrait, and for some book, at
the suggestion of the head of that division, who was a friend
of the author; and so the sum was trifling. One, moved by
pity, resolved to help Akakiy Akakievitch with some good
advice at least, and told him that he ought not to go to the
captain, for although it might happen that the police-captain,
wishing to win the approval of his superior officers, might
hunt up the cloak by some means, still, the cloak would
remain in the possession of the police if he did not offer legal
proof that it belonged to him; the best thing for him to do
would be to apply to a certain *prominent personage*, that this
prominent personage, by entering into relations with the proper
persons, could greatly expedite the matter. As there was
nothing else to be done, Akakiy Akakievitch decided to go to
the *prominent personage*. What was the official position of the
prominent personage remains unknown to this day. The reader
must know that the *prominent personage* had but recently
become a *prominent personage*, but that up to that time he had
been an insignificant person. Moreover, his present position
was not considered prominent in comparison with others
more prominent. But there is always a circle of people to
whom what is magnificent in the eyes of others is always
important enough. Moreover, he strove to increase his
importance by many devices; namely, he managed to have
the inferior officials meet him on the staircase when he
entered upon his service; no one was to presume to come
directly to him, but the strictest etiquette must be observed;
the "Collegiate Recorder" must announce to the government
secretary, the government secretary to the titular councillor,
or whatever other man was proper, and the business came
before him in this manner. In Holy Russia all is thus con-
taminated with the love of imitation: each man imitates and
copies his superior. They even say that a certain titular
councillor, when promoted to the head of some little separate
court-room, immediately partitioned off a private room for
himself, called it the *Audience Chamber*, and posted at the door

a lackey with red collar and braid, who grasped the handle of the door and opened to all comers; though the audience chamber would hardly hold an ordinary writing-table.

The manners and customs of the *prominent personage* were grand and imposing, but rather exaggerated. The main foundation of his system was strictness. "Strictness, strictness, and always strictness!" he generally said, and at the last word he looked significantly into the face of the person to whom he spoke. But there was no necessity for this, for the half-score of *tchinovniks* who formed the entire force of the mechanism of the office were properly afraid without it: on catching sight of him afar off, they left their work and waited, drawn up in line, until their chief had passed through the room. His ordinary converse with his inferiors smacked of sternness, and consisted chiefly of three phrases: "How dare you?" "Do you know to whom you are talking?" "Do you realise who stands before you?" Otherwise he was a very kind-hearted man, good to his comrades, and ready to oblige; but the rank of general threw him completely off his balance. On receiving that rank he became confused, as it were, lost his way, and never knew what to do. If he chanced to be with his equals, he was still a very nice kind of man— a very good fellow in many respects, and not stupid; but just the moment that he happened to be in the society of people but one rank lower than himself, he was simply incomprehensible; he became silent; and his situation aroused sympathy, the more so, as he felt himself that he might have made an incomparably better use of the time. In his eyes there was sometimes visible a desire to join some interesting conversation and circle; but he was held back by the thought, Would it not be a very great condescension on his part? Would it not be familiar? and would he not thereby lose his importance? And in consequence of such reflections, he remained ever in the same dumb state, uttering only occasionally a few monosyllabic sounds, and thereby earning the name of the most tiresome of men. To this *prominent per-*

sonage our Akakiy Akakievitch presented himself, and that at
the most unfavourable time, very inopportune for himself,
though opportune for the *prominent personage*. The *prominent
personage* was in his cabinet, conversing very very gaily with a
recently arrived old acquaintance of his childhood, whom he
had not seen for several years. At such a time it was
announced to him that a person named Bashmatchkin had
come. He asked abruptly, "Who is he?" "Some *tchinovnik*,"
they told him. "Ah, he can wait! this is no time," said the
important man. It must be remarked here that the important
man lied outrageously: he had said all he had to say to his
friend long before; and the conversation had been inter-
spersed for some time with very long pauses, during which
they merely slapped each other on the leg and said, "You
think so, Ivan Abramovitch!" "Just so, Stepan Varlamo-
vitch!" Nevertheless, he ordered that the *tchinovnik* should
wait, in order to show his friend—a man who had not been
in the service for a long time, but had lived at home in the
country—how long *tchinovniks* had to wait in his ante-room.
  At length, having talked himself completely out, and more
than that, having had his fill of pauses, and smoked a cigar
in a very comfortable arm-chair with reclining back, he
suddenly seemed to recollect, and told the secretary, who
stood by the door with papers of reports, "Yes, it seems indeed
that there is a *tchinovnik* standing there. Tell him that he may
come in." On perceiving Akakiy Akakievitch's modest mien,
and his worn undress uniform, he turned abruptly to him and
said, "What do you want?" in a curt, hard voice, which he
had practised in his room in private, and before the looking-
glass, for a whole week before receiving his present rank.
Akakiy Akakievitch, who already felt betimes the proper
amount of fear, became somewhat confused; and, as well as
he could, as well as his tongue would permit, he explained
with a rather more frequent addition than usual of the word
that, that his cloak was quite new, and had been stolen in the
most inhuman manner; that he had applied to him in order

that he might, in some way, by his intermediation, that . . . he might enter into correspondence with the chief superintendent of police and find the cloak. For some inexplicable reason this conduct seemed familiar to the general. "What, my dear sir!" he said abruptly, "don't you know etiquette? Where have you come to? Don't you know how matters are managed? You should first have entered a complaint about this at the court: it would have gone to the head of the department, to the chief of the division, then it would have been handed over to the secretary, and the secretary would have given it to me. . . ."

"But, your Excellency," said Akakiy Akakievitch, trying to collect his small handful of wits, and conscious at the same time that he was perspiring terribly, "I, your Excellency, presumed to trouble you, because secretaries that . . . are an untrustworthy race. . . ."

"What, what, what!" said the important personage. "Where did you get such courage? Where did you get such ideas? What impudence towards their chiefs and superiors has spread among the young generation!" The *prominent personage* apparently had not observed that Akakiy Akakievitch was already in the neighbourhood of fifty. If he could be called a young man, then it must have been in comparison with someone who was seventy. "Do you know to whom you speak? Do you realise who stands before you? do you realise it? I ask you!" Then he stamped his foot, and raised his voice to such a pitch that it would have frightened even a bolder man than Akakiy Akakievitch. Akakiy Akakievitch's senses failed him; he staggered, trembled in every limb, and could not stand; if the porters had not run in to support him he would have fallen to the floor. They carried him out insensible. But the *prominent personage*, gratified that the effect should have surpassed his expectations, and quite intoxicated with the thought that his word could even deprive a man of his senses, glanced sideways at his friend in order to see how he looked upon this, and perceived, not without

satisfaction, that his friend was in a most undecided frame
of mind and even beginning, on his side, to feel a trifle
frightened.

Akakiy Akakievitch could not remember how he descended the stairs and stepped into the street. He felt neither
his hands nor feet. Never in his life had he been so rated by
any general, let alone a strange one. He went on through the
snow-storm, which was howling through the streets, with his
mouth wide open, slipping off the pavement; the wind, in
Petersburg fashion, flew upon him from all quarters, and
through every cross-street. In a twinkling it had blown a
quinsy into his throat, and he reached home unable to utter
a word: his throat was all swollen, and he lay down on his
bed. Such an effect a severe talking-to can have sometimes!
The next day a violent fever made its appearance. Thanks to
the generous assistance of the Petersburg climate, the malady
progressed more rapidly than could have been expected;
and when the doctor arrived, he found, on feeling his pulse,
that there was nothing to be done except to prescribe a
fomentation, merely that the sick man might not be left
without the beneficent aid of medicine; but, at the same time,
he predicted his end in another thirty-six hours. After this
he turned to the landlady and said, "And as for you, my
dear, don't waste your time upon him: order his pine-coffin
now, for an oak one will be too expensive for him." Did
Akakiy Akakievitch hear these fatal words? and, if he heard
them, did they produce any overwhelming effect upon him?
Did he lament the bitterness of his life? We know not; for he
continued in a raving, feverish condition. Visions incessantly appeared to him, each stranger than the other: now
he saw Petrovitch, and ordered him to make a cloak, with
some traps for robbers, who seemed to him to be always under
the bed, and he cried, every moment, to the landlady to pull
one robber from under his coverlet: then he inquired why his
old mantle hung before him when he had a new cloak; then
he fancied that he was standing before the general, listen-

ing to a thorough scolding, and saying, "Forgive, your
Excellency!" but at last he began to curse, uttering the most
horrible words, so that his aged landlady crossed herself,
never in her life having heard anything of the kind from
him—the more so, as these words followed directly after the
words *your Excellency*. Later, he talked utter nonsense, of
which nothing could be understood: all that was evident, was
that his incoherent words and thought centred ever in one
thing—his cloak.

At last poor Akakiy Akakievitch breathed his last. They
sealed up neither his room nor his effects, because, in the first
place, there were no heirs, and, in the second, there was very
little inheritance; namely, a bunch of goose-quills, a quire of
white official paper, three pairs of socks, two or three buttons
which had burst off his trousers, and the mantle already
known to the reader. To whom all this fell, God knows. I
confess that the person who told this tale took no interest in
the matter. They carried Akakiy Akakievitch out, and buried
him. And St. Petersburg was left without Akakiy Akakievitch, as though he had never lived there. A being disappeared, and was hidden, who was protected by none, dear
to none, interesting to none, who never even attracted to
himself the attention of an observer of nature, who omits no
opportunity of thrusting a pin through a common fly and
examining it under the microscope—a being who bore
meekly the jibes of the department, and went to his grave
without having done one unusual deed, but to whom nevertheless, at the close of his life, appeared a bright visitant in
the form of a cloak, which momentarily cheered his poor life,
and upon whom, thereafter, an intolerable misfortune descended, just as it descends upon the heads of the mighty of
this world! . . . Several days after his death, the porter was
sent from the department to his lodgings with an order for
him to present himself immediately, the chief commands it;
but the porter had to return unsuccessful, with the answer
that he could not come; and to the question, Why? he

explained in the words, "Well, because he is already dead! he was buried four days ago." In this manner did they hear of Akakiy Akakievitch's death at the department, and the next day a new and much larger *tchinovnik* sat in his place, forming his letters by no means upright, but more inclined and slantwise.

But who could have imagined that this was not the end of Akakiy Akakievitch, that he was destined to raise a commotion after death, as if in compensation for his utterly insignificant life? But so it happened, and our poor story unexpectedly gains a fantastic ending.

A rumour suddenly spread throughout St. Petersburg that a ghost had taken to appearing on the Kalinkin Bridge, and far beyond, at night, in the form of a *tchinovnik* seeking a stolen cloak, and that, under the pretext of its being the stolen cloak, he dragged every one's cloak from his shoulders without regard to rank or calling—cat-skin, beaver, wadded, fox, bear, raccoon coats; in a word, every sort of fur and skin which men adopted for their covering. One of the department employees saw the dead man with his own eyes, and immediately recognised in him Akakiy Akakievitch: nevertheless, this inspired him with such terror that he started to run with all his might, and therefore could not examine thoroughly, and only saw how he threatened him from afar with his finger. Constant complaints poured in from all quarters, that the backs and shoulders, not only of titular, but even of court councillors, were entirely exposed to the dangers of a cold on account of the frequent dragging off of their cloaks. Arrangements were made by the police to catch the corpse at any cost, alive or dead, and punish him as an example to others, in the most severe manner; and in this they nearly succeeded, for a policeman on guard in Kirushkin Alley caught the corpse by the collar on the very scene of his evil deeds, for attempting to pull off the frieze cloak of some retired musician who had blown the flute in his day. Having seized him by the collar, he summoned, with a shout, two of his comrades, whom he enjoined to hold him fast while he himself felt for a moment in his boot, in order to draw thence his snuff-box, to refresh his six times for ever frozen nose; but the snuff was of a sort which even a corpse could not endure. The policeman had no sooner succeeded, having closed his right nostril with a finger, in holding half a handful up to the left, than the corpse sneezed so violently that he completely filled the eyes of all three. While they raised their fists to wipe them, the dead man vanished utterly, so that they positively did not know whether they had actually had him in their hands at all. Thereafter the watchmen conceived such a terror of dead men that they were afraid even to seize the living, and only screamed from a distance, "Hey, there! go your way!" and the dead *tchinovnik* began to appear even beyond the Kalinkin Bridge, causing no little terror to all timid people.

But we have totally neglected that *certain prominent personage* who may really be considered as the cause of the fantastic turn taken by this true history. First of all, justice compels us to say, that after the departure of poor, thoroughly anni-hilated Akakiy Akakievitch, he felt something like remorse. Suffering was unpleasant to him: his heart was accessible to many good impulses, in spite of the fact that his rank very often prevented his showing his true self. As soon as his friend had left his cabinet he began to think about poor Akakiy Akakievitch. And from that day forth, poor Akakiy Akakievitch, who could not bear up under an official reprimand, recurred to his mind almost every day. The thought of the latter troubled him to such an extent that, a week later, he even resolved to send an official to him, to learn whether he really could assist him; and when it was reported to him that Akakiy Akakievitch had died suddenly of fever, he was startled, listening to the reproaches of his conscience, and was out of sorts for the whole day. Wishing to divert his mind in some way, and forget the disagreeable impression, he set out that evening for one of his friend's houses, where he found quite a large party assembled; and, what was better, nearly every one was of the same rank, so that he need not feel in the least embarrassed. This had a marvellous effect upon his mental state. He expanded, made himself agreeable in conversation, charming: in short, he passed a delightful evening. After supper he drank a couple of glasses of champagne—not a bad recipe for cheerfulness, as everyone knows. The champagne inclined him to various out-of-the-way adventures; and, in particular, he determined not to go home but to go to see a certain well-known lady, Carolina Ivanovna, a lady, it appears, of German extraction, with whom he felt on a very friendly footing. It must be mentioned that the *prominent personage* was no longer a young man, but a good husband and respected father of a family. Two sons, one of whom was already in the service, and a good-looking, sixteen-year-old daughter, with a rather *retroussée* but pretty little nose, came every morning to kiss his hand, and say, "*Bon jour*, papa." His wife, a still fresh and good-looking woman, first gave him her hand to kiss, and then, reversing the procedure, kissed his. But the *prominent personage*, though perfectly satisfied in his domestic relations, considered it stylish to have a friend in another quarter of the city. This friend was hardly prettier or younger than his wife, but there are such puzzles in the world, and it is not our place to judge them. So the important personage descended the stairs, stepped into his sleigh, and said to the coachman, "To Carolina Ivanovna's," and, wrapping himself luxuriously in his warm cloak, found himself in that delightful position than which a Russian can conceive nothing better, which is, when you think of nothing yourself, yet the thoughts creep into your mind of their own accord, each more agreeable than the other, giving you no trouble to drive them away or seek them. Fully satisfied, he slightly recalled all the sly points of the evening just passed, and all the *mots* which had made the small circle laugh: many of them he repeated in a low voice, and found them quite as funny as before; and therefore it is not surprising that he should laugh heartily at them. Occasionally, however, he was hindered by gusts of wind, which, coming suddenly, God knows whence or why, cut his face, flinging in it lumps of snow, filling out his cloak-collar like a sail and suddenly blowing it over his head with supernatural force, and thus causing him constant trouble to disentangle himself. Suddenly the important personage felt someone clutch him very firmly by the collar. Turning round, he perceived a man of short stature in an old, worn uniform, and recognised, not without terror, Akakiy Akakie-vitch. The *tchinovnik's* face was white as snow, and looked just like a corpse's. But the horror of the important personage transcended all bounds when he saw the dead man's mouth open, and, with a terrible odour of the grave, utter the follow-ing remarks: "Ah, here you are at last! I have you, that . . . by the collar! I need your cloak; you took no trouble about mine, but reprimanded me; now give up your own." The pallid *prominent personage* nearly died. Brave as he was in the office, and in the presence of inferiors generally, and although, at the sight of his manly form and appearance, everyone said, "Ugh! how much character he has!" yet, at this crisis, he, like many possessed of an heroic exterior, experienced such terror that, not without cause, he began to fear an attack of illness. He flung his cloak hastily from his shoulders and shouted to his coachman in an unnatural voice, "Home, at full speed!" The coachman, hearing the tone which is generally employed at critical moments, and even accompanied by something much more tangible, drew his head down between his shoulders in case of an emergency, flourished his knout, and flew on like an arrow. In a little more than six minutes the *prominent personage* was at the entrance of his own house. Pale, thoroughly scared, and cloakless, he went home instead of to Karolina Ivanovna's, got to his apartment after some fashion, and passed the night in the direst distress, so that the next morning over their tea his daughter said plainly, "You are very pale to-day, papa."

But papa remained silent, and said not a word to anyone of what had happened to him, where he had been, or where he had intended to go. This occurrence made a deep impression upon him. He even began to say less frequently to the under-officials, "How dare you? do you realise who stands before you?" and, if he did utter the words, it was after first having learned the bearings of the matter. But the most noteworthy point was that from that day the apparition of the dead *tchinovnik* quite ceased to be seen; evidently the general's cloak just fitted his shoulders; at all events, no more instances of his dragging cloaks from people's shoulders were heard of. But many active and apprehensive persons could by no means reassure themselves, and asserted that the dead *tchinovnik* still showed himself in distant parts of the city. And, in fact, one watchman in Kolomna saw with his own eyes the apparition come from behind a house; but being rather weak of body, so much so, that once upon a time an ordinary full-grown pig running out of a private house knocked him off his legs, to the great amusement of the surrounding *izvoshtchiks* (public coachmen), from whom he demanded a kopeck apiece for snuff, as damages—being weak, he dared not arrest him, but followed him in the dark, until, at length, the apparition looked round, paused, and inquired, "What do you want?" and showed such a fist as you never see on living men. The watchman said: "It's of no consequence," and turned about instantly. But the apparition was much too tall, wore huge moustaches, and, directing its steps apparently towards the Obrikof Bridge, disappeared in the darkness of the night.

(II)

THE NIGHT OF CHRISTMAS EVE

A Legend of Little Russia

T H E last day before Christmas had just closed. A bright winter night had come on, stars had appeared, and the moon rose majestically in the heavens to shine upon good men and the whole of the world, so that they might gaily sing carols and hymns in praise of the nativity of Christ. The frost had grown more severe than during the day; but, to make up for this, everything had become so still that the crisping of the snow under-foot might be heard nearly half a verst round. As yet there was not a single group of young peasants to be seen under the windows of the cottages; the moon alone peeped stealthily in at them, as if inviting the maidens, who were decking themselves, to make haste and have a run on the crisp snow. Suddenly, out of the chimney of one of the cottages, volumes of smoke ascended in clouds towards the heavens, and in the midst of those clouds rose, on a besom, a witch.

If at that time the magistrate of Sorochinsk[1] had happened to pass in his carriage, drawn by three horses, his head covered by a lancer cap with sheepskin trimming, and wrapped in his great cloak, covered with blue cloth and lined with black sheepskin, and with his tightly plaited lash, which he uses for making the driver drive faster—if this worthy gentleman had happened to pass at that time, no doubt he would have seen the witch, because there is no witch who could glide away without his seeing her. He knows to a certainty how many sucking pigs each swine brings forth in each cottage, how much linen lies in each box, and what each one has pawned in the brandy-shop out of his clothes

---

[1] Chief town of a district in the government of Poltava.

or his household furniture. But the magistrate of Sorochinsk happened *not* to pass; and then, what has he to do with those out of his jurisdiction? he has his own circuit. And the witch by this time had risen so high that she only looked like a little dark spot up above; but wherever that spot went, one star after another disappeared from heaven. In a short time the witch had got a whole sleeveful of them. Some three or four only remained shining. On a sudden, from the opposite side, appeared another spot, which went on growing, spreading, and soon became no longer a spot. A short-sighted man, had he put, not only spectacles, but even the wheels of a britzka on his nose, would never have been able to make out what it was. In front, it was just like a German;[1] a narrow snout, incessantly turning on every side, and smelling about, ended like those of our pigs, in a small, round, flattened end; its legs were so thin, that had the village elder got no better, he would have broken them to pieces in the first squatting-dance. But, as if to make amends for these deficiencies, it might have been taken, viewed from behind, for the provincial advocate, so much was its long pointed tail like the skirt of our dress-coats. And yet, a look at the goat's beard under its snout, at the small horns sticking out of its head, and at the whole of its figure, which was no whiter than that of a chimney-sweep, would have sufficed to make anyone guess that it was neither a German nor a provincial advocate, but the devil in person, to whom only one night more was left for walking about the world and tempting good men to sin. On the morrow, at the first stroke of the church bell, he was to run, with his tail between his legs, back to his quarters. The devil then, and the devil it was, stole warily to the moon, and stretched out his hand to get hold of it; but at the very same moment he drew it hastily back again, as if he had burnt it, shook his foot, sucked his fingers, ran round on the

---

[1] Every foreigner, whatever may be his station, used to be called a German by Russian peasants. A dress coat was often sufficient to procure this name for its wearer.

other side, sprang at the moon once more, and once more drew his hand away. Still, notwithstanding his being baffled, the cunning devil did not desist from his mischievous designs. Dashing desperately forwards, he grasped the moon with both hands, and, making wry faces and blowing hard, he threw it from one hand to the other, like a peasant who has taken a live coal in his hand to light his pipe. At last, he hastily hid it in his pocket, and went on his way as if nothing had happened.

At Dikanka,[1] nobody suspected that the devil had stolen the moon. It is true that the village scribe, coming out of the brandy-shop on all fours, saw how the moon, without any apparent reason, danced in the sky, and took his oath of it before the whole village, but the distrustful villagers shook their heads, and even laughed at him. And now, what was the reason that the devil had decided on such an unlawful step? Simply this: he knew very well that the rich Cossack Choop[2] was invited to an evening party at the parish clerk's, where he was to meet the elder, also a relation of the clerk, who was in the archbishop's chapel, and who wore a blue coat and had a most sonorous *basso profondo*, the Cossack Sverbygooze, and some other acquaintances; where there would be for supper, not only the *kootia*,[3] but also a *varenookha*,[4] as well as corn-brandy, flavoured with saffron, and divers other dainties. He knew that in the meantime Choop's daughter, the belle of the village, would remain at home; and he knew, moreover, that to this daughter would come the blacksmith, a lad of athletic strength, whom the devil

[1] A village in the government of Poltava, in which Gogol placed the scene of most of his folk stories.

[2] Almost every family name in Little Russia has some meaning; the name of *Choop* means the tuft of hair growing on the crown of the head, which was alone left to grow by the Little Russians; they uniformly shaved the occiput and temples; in Great or Middle Russia, peasants, on the contrary, let the hair grow on these parts. Now there is not much difference in headdress.

[3] *Kootia* is a dish of boiled rice and plums, eaten by Russians on Christmas Eve.

[4] *Varenookha* is corn-brandy boiled with fruit and spice.

held in greater aversion than even the sermons of Father Kondrat. When the blacksmith had no work on hand he used to practise painting, and had acquired the reputation of being the best painter in the whole district. Even the centurion[1] had expressly sent for him to Poltava, for the purpose of painting the wooden palisade round his house. All the tureens out of which the Cossacks of Dikanka ate their *borsch* were adorned with the paintings of the blacksmith. He was a man of great piety, and often painted images of the saints; even now, some of them may be seen in the village church; but his masterpiece was a painting on the right side of the church-door; in it he had represented the Apostle Peter, at the Day of Judgment, with the keys in his hand, driving an evil spirit out of hell; the terrified devil, apprehending his ruin, rushed hither and thither, and the sinners, freed from their imprisonment, pursued and thrashed him with scourges, logs of wood, and anything that came to hand. All the time that the blacksmith was busy with this picture, and was painting it on a great board, the devil used all his endeavours to spoil it; he pushed his hand, raised the ashes out of the forge, and spread them over the painting; but, notwithstanding all this, the work was finished, the board was brought to the church, and fixed in the wall of the porch. From that time the devil vowed vengeance on the blacksmith. He had only one night left to roam about the world, but even in that night he sought to play some evil trick upon the blacksmith. For this reason he had resolved to steal the moon, for he knew that old Choop was lazy above all things, not quick to stir his feet; that the road to the clerk's was long, and went across back lanes, next to mills, along the churchyard, and over the top of a precipice; and though the *varenookha* and the saffron brandy might have got the better of Choop's laziness on a moonlight night, yet, in such darkness, it would be difficult to suppose that anything could

[1] A rank in irregular troops, corresponding to that of captain in the army.

prevail on him to get down from his oven[1] and quit his cottage. And the blacksmith, who had long been at variance with Choop, would not on any account, in spite even of his strength, visit his daughter in his presence.

So stood events: hardly had the devil hidden the moon in his pocket, when all at once it grew so dark that many could not have found their way to the brandy-shop, still less to the clerk's. The witch, finding herself suddenly in darkness, shrieked aloud. The devil coming near her, took her hand, and began to whisper to her those same things which are usually whispered to all womankind.

How oddly things go on in this world of ours! Everyone who lives in it endeavours to copy and ape his neighbour. Of yore there was nobody at Mirgorod[2] but the judge and the mayor, who in winter wore fur cloaks covered with cloth; all their subordinates went in plain uncovered *tooloops*;[3] and now, only see, the deputy, as well as the undercashier, wear new cloaks of black sheep fur covered with cloth. Two years ago, the village scribe and the town clerk bought blue nankeen, for which they paid full sixty kopecks the *arsheen*. The sexton, too, has found it necessary to have nankeen trousers for the summer, and a striped woollen waistcoat. In short, there is no one who does not try to cut a figure. When will the time come when men will desist from vanity? One may wager that many will be astonished at finding the devil making love. The most provoking part of it is, to think that really he fancies himself a beau, when the fact is, that he has such a phiz that one is ashamed to look at it—such a phiz that, as one of my friends says, it is the abomination of abominations; and yet he, too, ventures to make love!

But it grew so dark in the sky, and under the sky, that there

---

[1] The ovens of the peasants' cottages are built in the shape of furnaces, with a place on the top which is reserved for sleeping.

[2] Chief town of a district in the government of Poltava.

[3] Long coats made of sheepskins, with the fur worn inside. They are used in Russia by common people.

was no possibility of further seeing what passed between the devil and the witch.

"So thou sayest, kinsman, that thou hast not yet been in the clerk's new abode?" said the Cossack Choop, stepping out of his cottage, to a tall meagre peasant in a short *tooloop*, with a well-grown beard, which it was evident had remained at least a fortnight untouched by the piece of scythe which the peasants use instead of a razor.[1] "There will be a good drinking party," continued Choop, endeavouring to smile at these words, "only we must not be too late;" and with this, Choop drew still closer his belt, which was tightly girded round his *tooloop*, pulled his cap over his eyes, and grasped more firmly his whip, the terror of importunate dogs; but looking up, remained fixed to the spot. "What the devil! look, kinsman!"

"What now?" uttered the kinsman, also lifting up his head.

"What now? Why, where is the moon gone?"

"Ah! sure enough, gone she is."

"Yes, that she is!" said Choop, somewhat cross at the equanimity of the kinsman, "and it's all the same to thee."

"And how could I help it?"

"That must be the trick of some evil spirit," continued Choop, rubbing his moustaches with his sleeve. "Wretched dog, may he find no glass of brandy in the morning! Just as if it were to laugh at us; and I was purposely looking out of window as I was sitting in the room; such a splendid night; so light, the snow shining so brightly in the moonlight; everything to be seen as if by day; and now we have hardly crossed the threshold, and behold it is as dark as blindness!"

And Choop continued a long time in the same strain, moaning and groaning, and thinking all the while what was to be done. He greatly wished to have a gossip about all sorts of nonsense at the clerk's lodgings, where, he felt quite sure, were already assembled the elder, the newly-arrived *basso profondo*, as well as the tar-maker Nikita, who went every

---

[1] Little Russians shave beard and whiskers, leaving only their moustaches.

fortnight to Poltava on business, and who told such funny stories that his hearers used to laugh till they were obliged to hold their belts. Choop even saw, in his mind's eye, the *varenookha* brought forth upon the table. All this was most enticing, it is true; but then the darkness of the night put him in mind of the laziness which is so very dear to every Cossack. Would it not be well now to lie upon the oven, with his feet drawn up to his body, quietly enjoying a pipe, and listening through a delightful drowsiness to the songs and carols of the gay lads and maidens who would come in crowds under the windows? Were Choop alone, there is no doubt he would have preferred the latter; but to go in company would not be so tedious or so frightful after all, be the night ever so dark; besides, he did not choose to appear to another either lazy or timorous; so, putting an end to his grumbling, he once more turned to the kinsman. "Well, kinsman; so the moon is gone?"

"She is."

"Really, it is very strange! Give me a pinch of thy snuff. Beautiful snuff it is; where dost thou buy it, kinsman?"

"I should like to know what is so beautiful in it," answered the kinsman, shutting his snuff-box, made of birch bark and adorned with different designs pricked on it; "it would not make an old hen sneeze."

"I remember," continued Choop in the same strain, "the defunct pot-house keeper, Zoozooha, once brought me some snuff from Niegen.[1] That was what I call snuff—capital snuff! Well, kinsman, what are we to do? The night is dark."

"Well, I am ready to remain at home," answered the kinsman, taking hold of the handle of the door.

Had not the kinsman spoken thus, Choop would certainly have remained at home; but now, there was something which prompted him to do quite the contrary. "No, kinsman; we will go; go we must;" and whilst saying this, he was already cross with himself for having thus spoken. He

[1] Chief town of a district in the government of Chernigoff.

was much displeased at having to walk so far on such a night, and yet he felt gratified at having had his own way, and having gone contrary to the advice he had received. The kinsman, without the least expression of discontent on his face, like a man perfectly indifferent to sitting at home or to taking a walk, looked round, scratched his shoulder with the handle of his cudgel, and away went the two kinsmen.

Let us now take a glance at what Choop's beautiful daughter was about when left alone. Oxana has not yet completed her seventeenth year, and already all the people of Dikanka, nay, even the people beyond it, talk of nothing but her beauty. The young men are unanimous in their decision, and have proclaimed her the most beautiful girl that ever was, or ever can be, in the village. Oxana knows this well, and hears everything that is said about her, and she is, of course, as capricious as a beauty knows how to be. Had she been born to wear a lady's elegant dress, instead of a simple peasant's petticoat and apron, she would doubtless have proved so fine a lady that no maid could have remained in her service. The lads followed her in crowds; but she used to put their patience to such trials, that they all ended by leaving her to herself, and taking up with other girls, not so spoiled as she was. The blacksmith was the only one who did not desist from his love suit, but continued it, notwithstanding her ill-treatment, in which he had no less share than the others.

When her father was gone, Oxana remained for a long time ornamenting herself, and coquetting before a small looking-glass, framed in tin. She could not tire of admiring her own likeness in the glass. "Why do men talk so much about my being so pretty?" said she, absently, merely for the sake of gossiping aloud. "Nonsense; there is nothing pretty in me." But the mirror, reflecting her fresh, animated, childish features, with brilliant dark eyes, and a smile most inexpressibly bewitching, proved quite the contrary. "Unless," continued the beauty, holding up the mirror, "maybe, my black eye-brows and my dark eyes are so pretty that no prettier are to be found in the world; as for this little snub nose of mine, and my cheeks and my lips, what is there pretty in them? or, are my tresses so very beautiful? Oh! one might be frightened at them in the dark; they seem like so many serpents twining round my head. No, I see very well that I am not at all beautiful!" And then, on a sudden, holding the looking-glass a little further off, "No," she exclaimed, exultingly, "no, I really am pretty! and how pretty! how beautiful! What joy shall I bring to him whose wife I am to be! How delighted will my husband be to look at me! He will forget all other thoughts in his love for me! He will smother me with kisses."

"A strange girl, indeed," muttered the blacksmith, who had in the meantime entered the room, "and no small share of vanity has she got! There she stands for the last hour, looking at herself in the glass, and cannot leave off, and moreover praises herself aloud."

"Yes, indeed, lads! is anyone of you a match for me?" continued the pretty flirt; "look at me, how gracefully I walk; my bodice is embroidered with red silk, and what ribbons I have got for my hair! You have never seen any to be compared with them! All this my father has bought on purpose, that I may marry the smartest fellow that ever was born!" and so saying, she laughingly turned round and saw the blacksmith. She uttered a cry and put on a severe look, standing erect before him. The blacksmith was quite abashed. It would be difficult to specify the expression of the strange girl's somewhat sunburnt face; there was a degree of severity in it, and, in this same severity, somewhat of raillery at the blacksmith's bashfulness, as well as a little vexation, which spread an almost imperceptible blush over her features. All this was so complicated, and became her so admirably well, that the best thing to have done would have been to give her thousands and thousands of kisses.

"Why didst thou come hither?" she began. "Dost thou wish me to take up the shovel and drive thee from the house? Oh! you, all of you, know well how to insinuate yourselves into our company! You scent out in no time when the father has turned his back on the house. Oh! I know you well! Is my box finished?"

"It will be ready, dear heart of mine—it will be ready after the festival. Couldst thou but know how much trouble it has cost me—two whole nights I worked on it. Sure enough, thou wilt find no such box anywhere, not even belonging to a priest's wife. The iron I used for binding it! I did not use the like even for the centurion's dog-cart. And then, the painting of it! Wert thou to go on thy white feet round all the district, thou wouldst not find such another painting. The whole of the box will sparkle with red and blue flowers. It will be a delight to look upon. Be not angry with me. Allow me—be it only to speak to thee—nay, even to look on thee."

"Who means to forbid it? Speak and look," and she sat down on the bench, threw one more glance at the glass, and began to adjust the plaits on her head, looked at her neck, at her new bodice, embroidered with silk, and a scarcely visible expression of self-content played over her lips and cheeks and brightened her eyes.

"Allow me to sit down beside thee," said the blacksmith.

"Be seated," answered Oxana, preserving the same expression about her mouth and in her looks.

"Beautiful Oxana! Nobody will ever have done looking at thee—let me kiss thee!" exclaimed the blacksmith, recovering his presence of mind, and drawing her towards him, endeavoured to snatch a kiss; her cheek was already quite close to the blacksmith's lips, when Oxana sprang aside and pushed him back. "What wilt thou want next? When he has got honey, he wants a spoon too. Away with thee! thy hands are harder than iron, and thou smellest of smoke thyself; I really think thou hast besmeared me with thy soot." She then took the mirror and once more began to adorn herself.

"She does not care for me," thought the blacksmith, hanging down his head. "Everything is but play to her, and I am here like a fool standing before her, and never taking my eyes off her. Charming girl. What would I not do only to know what is passing in her heart. Whom does she love? But no, she cares for no one, she is fond only of herself, she delights in the sufferings she causes to my own poor self, and my grief prevents me from thinking of anything else, and I love her as nobody in the world ever loved or is likely to love."

"Is it true that thy mother is a witch?" asked Oxana, laughing; and the blacksmith felt as if everything within him laughed too, as if that laugh had found an echo in his heart and in all his veins; and at the same time he felt provoked at having no right to cover her pretty laughing face with kisses.

"What do I care about my mother! Thou art my mother, my father—all that I hold precious in the world! Should the Tsar send for me to his presence and say to me, 'Blacksmith Vakoola, ask of me whatever I have best in my realm—I'll give it all to thee; I'll order to have made for thee a golden smithy, where thou shalt forge with silver hammers.' 'I'll none of it,' would I answer the Tsar. 'I'll have no precious stones, no golden smithy, no, not even the whole of thy realm—give me only my Oxana!'"

"Now, only see what a man thou art! But my father has got another idea in his head; thou'lt see if he does not marry thy mother!"[1] said Oxana with an arch smile. "But what can it mean? Why haven't the girls come—it is high time for our carol. I am getting dull."

"Never mind about them, my beauty!"

"But, of course, I do mind; they will bring some lads with them, and then, how merry we shall be! I can fancy all the droll stories that will be told!"

"So thou art merry with them?"

[1] This, according to the laws of the Greek Church, would prevent their children from intermarrying.

"Of course, merrier than with thee. Ah! there is somebody knocking at the door; it must be the girls and the lads!"

"Why need I stay any longer?" thought the blacksmith. "She laughs at me; she cares no more about me than about a rust-eaten horseshoe. But, be it so. I will at least give no one an opportunity to laugh at me. Let me only mark who it is she prefers to me. I'll teach him how to——"

His meditation was cut short by a loud knocking at the door, and a harsh, "Open the door," rendered still harsher by the frost.

"Be quiet, I'll go and open it myself," said the blacksmith, stepping into the passage with the firm intention of giving vent to his wrath by breaking the bones of the first man who should come in his way.

The frost increased, and it became so cold that the devil went hopping from one hoof to the other, and blowing his fingers to warm his benumbed hands. And, of course, he could not feel otherwise than quite frozen; all day long he did nothing but saunter about hell, where, as everybody knows, it is by no means so cold as in our winter air; and where, with his cap on his head, and standing before a furnace as if really a cook, he felt as much pleasure in roasting sinners as a peasant's wife feels at frying sausages for Christmas. The witch, though warmly clad, felt cold too, so lifting up her arms, and putting one foot before the other, just as if she were skating, without moving a limb, she slid down as if from a sloping ice mountain right into the chimney. The devil followed her example; but as the devil is swifter than any boot-wearing beau, it is not at all astonishing that at the very entrance of the chimney he went down upon the shoulders of the witch, and both slipped down together into a wide oven, with pots all round it. The lady traveller first of all noiselessly opened the oven-door a little, to see if her son Vakoola had not brought home some party of friends; but there being nobody in the room, and only some sacks lying in the middle of it on the floor, she crept out of the oven, took off her warm coat, put her dress in order, and was quite tidy in no time, so that nobody could ever possibly have suspected her of having ridden on a besom a minute before.

The mother of the blacksmith Vakoola was about forty; she was neither handsome nor plain; indeed it is difficult to be handsome at that age. Yet, she knew well how to make herself pleasant to the aged Cossacks (who, by the bye, did not care much about a handsome face); many went to call upon her, the elder, Ossip Nikiphorovitch the clerk (of course when his wife was from home), the Cossack Kornius Choop, the Cossack Kassian Sverbygooze. At all events this must be said for her, she perfectly well understood how to manage them; none of them ever suspected for a moment that he had a rival. Was a pious peasant going home from church on some holiday; or was a Cossack, in bad weather, on his way to the vodka-shop; what should prevent him from paying Solokha a visit, to eat some greasy curd dumplings with sour cream, and to have a gossip with the talkative and good-natured mistress of the cottage? And the Cossack made a long circuit on his way to the vodka-shop, and called it "just looking in as he passed." When Solokha went to church on a holiday, she always wore a gay-coloured petticoat, with another short blue one over it, adorned with two gold braids, sewed on behind it in the shape of two curly moustaches. When she took her place at the right side of the church, the clerk was sure to cough and wink at her; the elder twirled his moustaches, twisted his crown-lock of hair round his ear, and said to his neighbour, "A splendid woman! a devilish fine woman!" Solokha nodded to everyone, and everyone thought that Solokha nodded to him alone. But those who liked to pry into other people's business, noticed that Solokha exerted the utmost of her civility towards the Cossack Choop.

Choop was a widower; eight ricks of corn stood always

before his cottage; two strong bulls used to put their heads
out of their wattled shed, gaze up and down the street, and
bellow every time they caught a glimpse of their cousin a cow,
or their uncle the stout ox; the bearded goat climbed up to
the very roof, and bleated from thence in a key as shrill as
that of the mayor, and teased the turkeys which were
proudly walking in the yard, and turned his back as soon
as he saw his inveterate enemies, the urchins, who used to
laugh at his beard. In Choop's boxes there was plenty of
linen, many warm coats, and many old-fashioned dresses
bound with gold braid; for his late wife had been a dashing
woman. Every year there was a couple of beds planted with
tobacco in his kitchen-garden, which was, besides, well
provided with poppies, cabbages and sunflowers. All this,
Solokha thought, would suit very well if united to her own
household; she was already mentally regulating the management of this property when it should pass into her hands;
and so she went on increasing in kindness towards old Choop.
At the same time, to prevent her son Vakoola from making
an impression on Choop's daughter, and getting the whole
of the property (in which case she was sure of not being
allowed to interfere with anything), she had recourse to the
usual means of all women of her age—she took every opportunity to make Choop quarrel with the blacksmith. These
very artifices were perhaps the cause that it came to be
rumoured amongst the old women (particularly when they
happened to take a drop too much at some gay party) that
Solokha was positively a witch; that young Kiziakaloopenko
had seen on her back a tail no bigger than a common
spindle; that on the last Thursday but one she ran across the
road in the shape of a black kitten; that once there had
come to the priest a hog, which crowed like a cock, put on
Father Kondrat's hat, and then ran away. It so happened
that as the old women were discussing this point, there came
by Tymish Korostiavoï, the herdsman. He could not help
telling how, last summer, just before St. Peter's fast, as he laid

himself down for sleep in his shed, and had put some straw
under his head, with his own eyes he beheld the witch, with
her hair unplaited and nothing on but her shift, come and
milk her cows; how he was so bewitched that he could not
move any of his limbs; how she came to him and greased his
lips with some nasty stuff, so that he could not help spitting
all the next day. And yet all these stories seem of a somewhat
doubtful character, because there is nobody but the magistrate of Sorochinsk who can distinguish a witch. This was
the reason why all the chief Cossacks waved their hands on
hearing such stories. "Mere nonsense, stupid hags!" was
their usual answer.

Having come out of the oven and put herself to rights,
Solokha, like a good housewife, began to arrange and put
everything in its place; but she did not touch the sacks:
"Vakoola had brought them in—he might take them out
again." In the meantime the devil, as he was coming down
the chimney, caught a glimpse of Choop, who, arm in arm
with his kinsman, was already a long way off from his cottage.
Instantly, the devil flew out of the chimney, ran across the
way, and began to break asunder the heaps of frozen snow
which were lying all around. Then began a snow-storm.
The air was all whitened with snow-flakes. The snow went
rushing backwards and forwards, and threatened to cover,
as it were with a net, the eyes, mouth and ears of the pedestrians. Then the devil flew into the chimney once more,
quite sure that both kinsmen would retrace their steps to
Choop's house, who would find there the blacksmith, and
give him so sound a thrashing that the latter would never
again have the strength to take a brush in his hand and paint
offensive caricatures.

As soon as the snow-storm began, and the wind blew sharply
in his eyes, Choop felt some remorse, and, pulling his cap
over his very eyes, he began to abuse himself, the devil and
his own kinsman. Yet his vexation was but assumed; the

snow-storm was rather welcome to Choop. The distance they had still to go before reaching the dwelling of the clerk was eight times as long as that which they had already gone; so they turned back. They now had the wind behind them; but nothing could be seen through the whirling snow.

"Stop, kinsman, it seems to me that we have lost our way," said Choop, after having gone a little distance. "There is not a single cottage to be seen! Ah! what a storm it is! Go a little on that side, kinsman, and see if thou canst not find the road; and I will seek it on this side. Who but the devil would ever have persuaded anyone to leave the house in such a storm! Don't forget, kinsman, to call me when thou findest the road. Eh! what a lot of snow the devil has sent into my eyes!"

But the road was not to be found. The kinsman, in his long boots, started off on one side, and, after having rambled backwards and forwards, ended by finding his way right into the vodka-shop. He was so glad of it that he forgot everything else, and, after shaking off the snow, stepped into the passage without once thinking about his kinsman who had remained in the snow. Choop in the meantime fancied he had found out the road; he stopped and began to shout with all the strength of his lungs, but seeing that his kinsman did not come, he decided on proceeding alone.

In a short time he saw his cottage. Great heaps of snow lay around it and covered its roof. Rubbing his hands, which were numbed by the frost, he began to knock at the door, and in a loud tone ordered his daughter to open it.

"What dost thou want?" roughly demanded the blacksmith, stepping out.

Choop, on recognising the blacksmith's voice, stepped a little aside. "No, surely this is not my cottage," said he to himself; "the blacksmith would not come to my cottage. And yet—now I look at it again, it cannot be his. Whose, then, can it be? Ah! how came I not to know it at once! it is the cottage of lame Levchenko, who has lately married a young wife; his is the only one like mine. That is the reason why it seemed so strange to me that I got home so soon. But, let me see, why is the blacksmith here? Levchenko, as far as I know, is now sitting at the clerk's. Eh! he! he! he! the blacksmith comes to see his young wife! That's what it is! Well, now I see it all!"

"Who art thou? and what hast thou to do lurking about this door?" asked the blacksmith, in a still harsher voice, and coming nearer.

"No," thought Choop, "I'll not tell him who I am; he might beat me, the cursed fellow!" and then, changing his voice, answered, "My good man, I come here in order to amuse you by singing carols beneath your window."

"Go to the devil with thy carols!" angrily cried Vakoola. "What dost thou wait for? didst thou hear me? begone, directly."

Choop himself had already the same prudent intention; but he felt cross at being obliged to obey the blacksmith's command. Some evil spirit seemed to prompt him to say something unpleasant to Vakoola.

"What makes thee shout in that way?" asked he in the same assumed voice; "my intention is to sing a carol, and that is all."

"Ah! words are not sufficient for thee!" and immediately after, Choop felt a heavy blow upon his shoulders.

"Now, I see, thou art getting quarrelsome!" said Choop, retreating a few paces.

"Begone, begone!" exclaimed the blacksmith, striking again.

"What now!" exclaimed Choop, in a voice which expressed at the same time pain, anger, and fear. "I see thou quarrellest in good earnest, and strikest hard."

"Begone, begone!" again exclaimed the blacksmith, and shut the door violently.

"Look, what a bully!" said Choop, once more alone in the street. "But thou hadst better not come near me! There's a man for you! giving thyself such airs, too! Dost thou think there is no one to bring thee to reason? I *will* go, my dear fellow, and to the police-officer will I go. I'll teach thee who I am! I care not for thy being blacksmith and painter. However, I must see to my back and shoulders: I think there are bruises on them. The devil's son strikes hard, it seems. It is a pity it's so cold, I cannot take off my fur coat. Stay a while, confounded blacksmith; may the devil break thy bones and thy smithy too! Take thy time—I will make thee dance, cursed squabbler! But, now I think of it, if he is not at home, Solokha must be alone. Hem! her dwelling is not far from here; shall I go? At this time nobody will trouble us. Perhaps I may. Ah! that cursed blacksmith, how he has beaten me!"

And Choop, rubbing his back, went in another direction. The pleasure which was in store for him in meeting Solokha diverted his thoughts from his pain, and made him quite insensible to the snow and ice, which, notwithstanding the whistling of the wind, might be heard crackling under his feet. Sometimes a half-benignant smile brightened his face, and his beard and moustaches were whitened over by snow with the same rapidity as that displayed by a barber who has tyrannically got hold of the nose of his victim. But for the snow which danced backwards and forwards before the eyes, Choop might have been seen a long time, stopping now and then to rub his back, muttering, "How painfully that cursed blacksmith has beaten me!" and then proceeding on his way.

At the time when the dashing gentleman, with a tail and a goat's beard, flew out of the chimney, and then into the chimney again, the pouch which hung by a shoulder-belt at his side, and in which he had hidden the stolen moon, in some way or other caught in something in the oven, flew open, and the moon, availing herself of the opportunity, mounted through the chinmey of Solokha's cottage and rose majestically in the sky. It grew light all at once; the storm subsided; the snow-covered fields seemed all covered with silver, set with crystal stars; even the frost seemed to have grown milder; crowds of lads and lasses made their appearance with sacks upon their shoulders; songs resounded, and but few cottagers were without a band of carollers. How beautifully the moon shines! It would be difficult to describe the charm one feels in sauntering on such a night among the troops of maidens who laugh and sing, and of lads who are ready to adopt every trick and invention suggested by the gay and smiling night. The tightly-belted fur coat is warm; the frost makes one's cheeks tingle more sharply; and the Cunning One, himself, seems, from behind your back, to urge you to all kinds of frolics. A crowd of maidens, with sacks, pushed their way into Choop's cottage, surrounded Oxana, and bewildered the blacksmith by their shouts, their laughter, and their stories. Everyone was in haste to tell something new to the beauty; some unloaded their sacks, and boasted of the quantity of loaves, sausages and curd dumplings which they had already received in reward for their carolling. Oxana seemed to be all pleasure and joy, went on chattering, first with one, then with another, and never for a moment ceased laughing. The blacksmith looked with anger and envy at her joy, and cursed the carolling, notwithstanding his having been mad about it himself in former times.

"Odarka," said the joyful beauty, turning to one of the girls, "thou hast got on new boots! Ah! how beautiful they are! all ornamented with gold too! Thou art happy, Odarka, to have a suitor who can make thee such presents; I have nobody who would give me such pretty boots!"

"Don't grieve about boots, my incomparable Oxana!" chimed in the blacksmith; "I will bring thee such boots as few ladies wear."

"Thou?" said Oxana, throwing a quick disdainful glance at him. "We shall see where thou wilt get such boots as will suit my foot, unless thou bringest me the very boots which the Tsarina wears!"

"Just see what she has taken a fancy to now!" shouted the group of laughing girls.

"Yes!" haughtily continued the beauty, "I call all of you to witness, that if the blacksmith Vakoola brings me the very boots which the Tsarina wears, I pledge him my word instantly to marry him."

The maidens led away the capricious belle.

"Laugh on, laugh on!" said the blacksmith, stepping out after them. "I myself laugh at my own folly. It is in vain that I think over and over again, where have I left my wits? She does not love me—well, God be with her! Is Oxana the only woman in all the world? Thanks be to God! there are many handsome maidens in the village besides Oxana. Yes, indeed, what is Oxana? No good housewife will ever be made out of her; she only understands how to deck herself. No, truly, it is high time for me to leave off making a fool of myself." And yet at the very moment when he came to this resolution, the blacksmith saw before his eyes the laughing face of Oxana, teasing him with the words—"Bring me, blacksmith, the Tsarina's own boots, and I will marry thee!" He was all agitation, and his every thought was bent on Oxana alone.

The carolling groups of lads on one side, of maidens on the other, passed rapidly from street to street. But the blacksmith went on his way without noticing anything, and without taking any part in the rejoicings, in which, till now, he had delighted above all others.

The devil had, in the meanwhile, quickly reached the utmost limits of tenderness in his conversation with Solokha; he kissed her hand with nearly the same look as the magistrate used when making love to the priest's wife; he pressed his hand upon his heart, sighed, and told her that if she did not choose to consider his passion, and meet it with due return, he had made up his mind to throw himself into the water, and send his soul right down to hell. But Solokha was not so cruel—the more so, as the devil, it is well known, was in league with her. Moreover, she liked to have someone to flirt with, and rarely remained alone. This evening she expected to be without any visitor, on account of all the chief inhabitants of the village being invited to the clerk's house. And yet quite the contrary happened. Hardly had the devil set forth his demand, when the voice of the stout elder was heard. Solokha ran to open the door, and the quick devil crept into one of the sacks that were lying on the floor. The elder, after having shaken off the snow from his cap, and drunk a cup of vodka which Solokha presented to him, told her that he had not gone to the clerk's on account of the snow-storm, and that, having seen a light in her cottage, he had come to pass the evening with her. The elder had just done speaking when there was a knock at the door, and the clerk's voice was heard from without. "Hide me wherever thou wilt," whispered the elder; "I should not like to meet the clerk." Solokha could not at first conceive where so stout a visitor might possibly be hidden; at last she thought the biggest charcoal sack would be fit for the purpose; she threw the charcoal into a tub, and the sack being empty, in went the stout elder, moustaches, head, cap and all. Presently the clerk made his appearance, giving way to a short dry cough, and rubbing his hands together. He told her how none of his guests had come, and how he was heartily glad of it, as it had given him the opportunity of taking a walk to her abode, in spite of the snow-storm. After this he came a step nearer to her, coughed once more, laughed, touched her bare plump arm with his fingers, and said in a sly, and at the same time a pleased voice, "What have you got here, most magnificent Solokha?" after which words he jumped back a few steps.

"How, what? Ossip Nikiphorovitch! it is my arm!" answered Solokha.

"Hem! Your arm! he! he! he!" smirked the clerk, greatly rejoiced at his beginning, and he took a turn in the room.

"And what is this, dearest Solokha?" said he, with the same expression, again coming to her, gently touching her throat, and once more springing back.

"As if you cannot see for yourself, Ossip Nikiphorovitch!" answered Solokha, "it is my throat and my necklace on it."

"Hem! Your necklace upon your throat! he! he! he!" and again he walked up and down the room, rubbing his hands.

"And what have you here, unequalled Solokha?"

We know not what the clerk's long fingers would now have touched, if just at that moment he had not heard a knock at the door, and, at the same time, the voice of the Cossack Choop.

"Heavens! what an unwelcome visitor!" said the clerk in a fright, "whatever will happen if a person of my character is met here! If it should reach the ears of Father Kondrat!" But, in fact, the clerk's real anxiety was of quite a different description; above all things he dreaded lest his wife should be acquainted with his visit to Solokha; and he had good reason to dread her, for her powerful hand had already made his thick plait[1] a very thin one. "In Heaven's name, most virtuous Solokha!" said he, trembling all over; "your goodness, as the Scripture saith, in St. Luke, chapter the thir—thir—there *is* somebody knocking, decidedly there is somebody knocking at the door! In Heaven's name let me hide somewhere!"

Solokha threw the charcoal out of another sack into the tub, and in crept the clerk, who, being by no means corpulent, sat down at the very bottom of it, so that there would have

---

[1] Village clerks in Russia used to have their hair plaited. Many priests, not allowed by the custom of the land to cut their hair short, wore it, for convenience' sake, plaited when at home and only loosened it during the performance of the duties of their office. This is still the case.

been room enough to put more than half a sackful of charcoal on top of him.

"Good-evening, Solokha," said Choop, stepping into the room. "Thou didst not perhaps expect me, didst thou? Certainly not; may be I hindered thee," continued Choop, putting on a gay knowing look, which expressed at once that his lazy brain was at work, and that he was on the point of saying some sharp and sportive witticism. "Maybe thou wert already engaged in flirting with somebody! Maybe thou hast already hidden someone? Is it so?" said he; and delighted at his own wit, Choop gave way to a hearty laugh, inwardly exulting at the thought that he was the only one who enjoyed the favours of Solokha. "Well now, Solokha, give me a glass of vodka; I think the abominable frost has frozen my throat! What a night for a Christmas Eve! As it began snowing, Solokha—just listen, Solokha—as it began snowing —eh! I cannot move my hands; impossible to unbutton my coat! Well, as it began snowing——"

"Open!" cried someone in the street, at the same time giving a thump at the door.

"Somebody is knocking at the door!" said Choop, stopping in his speech.

"Open!" cried the voice, still louder.

"'Tis the blacksmith!" said Choop, taking his cap; "listen, Solokha!—put me wherever thou wilt! on no account in the world would I meet that confounded lad! Devil's son! I wish he had a blister as big as a haycock under each eye."

Solokha was so frightened that she rushed backwards and forwards in the room, and quite unconscious of what she did, shoved Choop into the same sack where the clerk was already sitting. The poor clerk had to restrain his cough and his sighs when the weighty Cossack sat down almost on his head, and placed his boots, covered with frozen snow, just on his temples.

The blacksmith came in, without saying a word, without

taking off his cap, and threw himself on the bench. It was easy to see that he was in a very bad temper. Just as Solokha shut the door after him, she heard another tap under the window. It was the Cossack Sverbygooze. As to this one, he decidedly could never have been hidden in a sack, for no sack large enough could ever have been found. In person he was even stouter than the elder, and as to height, he was even taller than Choop's kinsman. So Solokha went with him into the kitchen garden, in order to hear whatever he had to say to her.

The blacksmith looked vacantly round the room, listening at times to the songs of the carolling parties. His eyes rested at last on the sacks: "Why do these sacks lie here? They ought to have been taken away long ago. This stupid love has made quite a fool of me; to-morrow is a festival, and the room is still full of rubbish. I will clear it away into the smithy!" And the blacksmith went to the enormous sacks, tied them as tightly as he could, and would have lifted them on his shoulders; but it was evident that his thoughts were far away, otherwise he could not have helped hearing how Choop hissed when the cord with which the sack was tied twisted his hair, and how the stout elder began to hiccup very distinctly. "Shall I never get this silly Oxana out of my head?" mused the blacksmith; "I will not think of her; and yet, in spite of myself, I think of her, and of her alone. How is it that thoughts come into one's head against one's own will? What, the devil! Why the sacks appear to have grown heavier than they were; it seems as if there was something else besides charcoal! What a fool I am! have I forgotten that everything seems to me heavier than it used to be? Some time ago, with one hand I could bend and unbend a copper coin, or a horse-shoe; and now, I cannot lift a few sacks of charcoal; soon every breath of wind will blow me off my legs. No," cried he, after having remained silent for a while, and coming to himself again, "shall it be said that I am a woman? No one shall have the laugh against me; had

I ten such sacks, I would lift them all at once." And, accordingly, he threw the sacks upon his shoulders, although two strong men could hardly have lifted them. "I will take this little one, too," continued he, taking hold of the little one, at the bottom of which was coiled up the devil. "I think I put my instruments into it"; and thus saying, he went out of the cottage, whistling the tune:

"No wife I'll have to bother me."

Songs and shouts grew louder and louder in the streets; the crowds of strolling people were increased by those who came in from the neighbouring villages; the lads gave way to their frolics and sports. Often amongst the Christmas carols might be heard a gay song, just improvised by some young Cossack. Hearty laughter rewarded the improviser. The little windows of the cottages flew open, and from them was thrown a sausage or a piece of pie, by the thin hand of some old woman or some aged peasant, who alone remained indoors. The booty was eagerly caught in the sacks of the young people. In one place, the lads formed a ring to surround a group of maidens; nothing was heard but shouts and screams; one was throwing a snowball, another was endeavouring to get hold of a sack crammed with Christmas donations. In another place, the girls caught hold of some youth, or put something in his way, and down he fell with his sack. It seemed as if the whole of the night would pass away in these festivities. And the night, as if on purpose, shone so brilliantly; the gleam of the snow made the beams of the moon still whiter.

The blacksmith with his sacks stopped suddenly. He fancied he heard the voice and the sonorous laughter of Oxana in the midst of a group of maidens. It thrilled through his whole frame; he threw the sacks on the ground with so much force that the clerk, sitting at the bottom of one of them, groaned with pain, and the elder hiccupped aloud; then, keeping only the little sack upon his shoulders, the blacksmith joined a company of lads who followed close after a group of maidens, amongst whom he thought he had heard Oxana's voice.

"Yes, indeed; there she is! standing like a queen, her dark eyes sparkling with pleasure! There is a handsome youth speaking with her; his speech seems very amusing, for she is laughing; but does she not always laugh?" Without knowing why he did it and as if against his will, the blacksmith pushed his way through the crowd, and stood beside her.

"Ah! Vakoola, here art thou; a good evening to thee!" said the belle, with the very smile which drove Vakoola quite mad. "Well, hast thou received much? Eh! what a small sack! And didst thou get the boots that the Tsarina wears? Get those boots and I'll marry thee!" and away she ran laughing with the crowd.

The blacksmith remained riveted to the spot. "No, I cannot; I have not the strength to endure it any longer," said he at last. "But, Heavens! why is she so beautiful? Her looks, her voice, all, all about her makes my blood boil! No, I cannot get the better of it; it is time to put an end to this. Let my soul perish! I'll go and drown myself, and then all will be over." He dashed forwards with hurried steps, overtook the group, approached Oxana, and said to her in a resolute voice: "Farewell, Oxana! Take whatever bridegroom thou pleasest; make a fool of whom thou wilt; as for me, thou shalt never more meet me in this world!" The beauty seemed astonished, and was about to speak, but the blacksmith waved his hand and ran away.

"Whither away, Vakoola?" cried the lads, seeing him run. "Farewell, brothers," answered the blacksmith. "God grant that we may meet in another world; but in this we meet no more! Fare you well! keep a kind remembrance of me. Pray Father Kondrat to say a mass for my sinful soul. Ask him forgiveness that I did not, on account of worldly cares, paint the tapers for the church. Everything that is found in my big box I give to the Church; farewell!"—and thus saying, the blacksmith went on running, with his sack on his back.

"He has gone mad!" said the lads. "Poor lost soul!" piously ejaculated an old woman who happened to pass by; "I'll go and tell about the blacksmith having hanged himself."

Vakoola, after having run for some time along the streets, stopped to take breath. "Well, where am I running?" thought he; "is really all lost?—I'll try one thing more; I'll go to the fat Patzuck, the Zaporozhian. They say he knows every devil, and has the power of doing everything he wishes; I'll go to him; 'tis the same thing for the perdition of my soul." At this, the devil, who had long remained quiet and motionless, could not refrain from giving vent to his joy by leaping in the sack. But the blacksmith, thinking he had caught the sack with his hand, and thus occasioned the movement himself, gave a hard blow on the sack with his fist, and after shaking it about on his shoulders, went off to the fat Patzuck.

This fat Patzuck had indeed once been a Zaporozhian. Nobody, however, knew whether he had been turned out of that warlike community, or whether he had fled from it of his own accord. He had already been for some ten, nay, it might even be for some fifteen years, settled at Dikanka. At first, he had lived as best suited a Zaporozhian; working at nothing, sleeping three-quarters of the day, eating not less than would satisfy six harvest-men, and drinking almost a whole pailful at once. It must be allowed that there was plenty of room for food and drink in Patzuck; for, though he was not very tall, he tolerably made up for it in bulk. Moreover, the trousers he wore were so wide, that long as might be the strides he took in walking, his feet were never seen at all, and he might have been taken for a wine cask moving along the streets. This may have been the reason for giving him the nickname of "Fatty." A few weeks had hardly passed since his arrival in the village, when it came to be known that he was a wizard. If anyone happened to fall ill, he called Patzuck directly; and Patzuck had only to mutter a few words to put an end to the illness at once. Had any hungry Cossack swallowed a fish-bone, Patzuck knew how to give him right skilfully a slap on the back, so that the fish-bone went where it ought to go without causing any pain to the Cossack's throat. Latterly, Patzuck was scarcely ever seen out of doors. This was perhaps caused by laziness, and perhaps, also, because to get through the door was a task which with every year grew more and more difficult for him. So the villagers were obliged to repair to his own lodgings whenever they wanted to consult him. The blacksmith opened the door, not without some fear. He saw Patzuck sitting on the floor after the Turkish fashion. Before him was a tub on which stood a tureen full of lumps of dough cooked in grease. The tureen was put, as if intentionally, on a level with his mouth. Without moving a single finger, he bent his head a little towards the tureen, and sipped the gravy, catching the lumps of dough with his teeth. "Well," thought Vakoola to himself, "this fellow is still lazier than Choop; Choop at least eats with a spoon, but this one does not even raise his hand!" Patzuck seemed to be busily engaged with his meal, for he took not the slightest notice of the entrance of the blacksmith, who, as soon as he crossed the threshold, made a low bow.

"I am come to thy worship, Patzuck!" said Vakoola, bowing once more. The fat Patzuck lifted his head and went on eating the lumps of dough.

"They say that thou art—I beg thy pardon," said the blacksmith, endeavouring to compose himself, "I do not say it to offend thee—that thou hast the devil among thy friends"; and in saying these words Vakoola was already afraid he had spoken too much to the point, and had not sufficiently softened the hard words he had used, and that Patzuck would throw at his head both the tub and the tureen; he even stepped a little on one side and covered his face with his sleeve, to prevent it from being sprinkled by the gravy.

But Patzuck looked up and continued sipping.

The encouraged blacksmith resolved to proceed:—"I am come to thee, Patzuck; God grant thee plenty of everything, and bread in good *proportion!*" The blacksmith knew how to put in a fashionable word sometimes; it was a talent he had acquired during his stay at Poltava, when he painted the centurion's palisade. "I am on the point of endangering the salvation of my sinful soul! nothing in this world can serve me! Come what will, I am resolved to seek the help of the devil. Well, Patzuck," said he, seeing that the other remained silent, "what am I to do?"

"If thou wantest the devil, go to the devil!" answered Patzuck, not giving him a single look, and going on with his meal.

"I am come to thee for this very reason," returned the blacksmith with a bow; "besides thyself, methinks there is hardly anybody in the world who knows how to go to the devil."

Patzuck, without saying a word, ate up all that remained on the dish. "Please, good man, do not refuse me!" urged the blacksmith. "And if there be any want of pork, or sausages, or buckwheat, or even linen or millet, or anything else—why, we know how honest folk manage these things. I shall not be stingy. Only do tell me, if it be only by a hint, how to find the way to the devil."

"He who has got the devil on his back has no great way to go to him," said Patzuck quietly, without changing his position.

Vakoola fixed his eyes upon him as if searching for the meaning of these words on his face. "What does he mean?" thought he, and opened his mouth as if to swallow his first word. But Patzuck kept silence. Here Vakoola noticed that there was no longer either tub or tureen before him, but

instead of them there stood upon the floor two wooden pots,
the one full of curd dumplings, the other full of sour cream.
Involuntarily his thoughts and his eyes became riveted to
these pots. "Well, now," thought he, "how will Patzuck eat
the dumplings? He will not bend down to catch them like
the bits of dough, and, moreover, it is impossible; for they
ought to be first dipped into the cream." This thought had
hardly crossed the mind of Vakoola, when Patzuck opened
his mouth, looked at the dumplings, and then opened it still
wider. Immediately, a dumpling jumped out of the pot,
dipped itself into the cream, turned over on the other side,
and went right into Patzuck's mouth. Patzuck ate it, once
more opened his mouth, and in went another dumpling in
the same way. All Patzuck had to do was to chew and to
swallow them. "That is wondrous indeed," thought the
blacksmith, and astonishment made him also open his
mouth; but he felt directly, that a dumpling jumped into it
also, and that his lips were already smeared with cream; he
pushed it away, and after having wiped his lips, began to
think about the marvels that happen in the world and the
wonders one may work with the help of the devil; at the
same time he felt more than ever convinced that Patzuck
alone could help him. "I will beg of him still more earnestly
to explain to me—but, what do I see? to-day is a fast, and he
is eating dumplings, and dumplings are not food for fast
days![1] What a fool I am! staying here and giving way to
temptation! Away, away," and the pious blacksmith ran
with all speed out of the cottage. The devil, who remained
all the while sitting in the sack, and already rejoiced at the
glorious victim he had entrapped, could not endure to see
him get free from his clutches. As soon as the blacksmith left
the sack a little loose, he sprang out of it and sat upon the
blacksmith's neck.

[1] Russians are much more severe in their fasts than Catholics, eating no
milk or eggs. Some even go so far as to eat no fish and no hot dishes,
restricting their food to cold boiled vegetables and bread.

Vakoola felt a cold shudder run through all his frame; his courage gave way, his face grew pale, he knew not what to do; he was already on the point of making the sign of the cross; but the devil, bending his dog's muzzle to his right ear, whispered: "Here I am, I, thy friend; I will do everything for a comrade and a friend such as thou! I'll give thee as much money as thou canst wish for!" squeaked he in his left ear. "No later than this very day Oxana shall be ours!" continued he, turning his muzzle once more to the right ear.

The blacksmith stood considering. "Well," said he, at length, "on this condition I am ready to be thine."

The devil clapped his hands and began to indulge his joy by springing about on the blacksmith's neck. "Now, I've caught him!" thought he to himself. "Now, I'll take my revenge upon thee, my dear fellow, for all thy paintings and all thy tales about devils! What will my fellows say when they come to know that the most pious man in the village is in my power?" and the devil laughed heartily at the thought of how he would tease all the long-tailed breed in hell, and how the lame devil, who was reputed the most cunning of them all for his tricks, would feel provoked.

"Well, Vakoola!" squeaked he, while he continued sitting on Vakoola's neck, as if fearing the blacksmith should escape; "thou knowest well that nothing can be done without contract."

"I am ready," said the blacksmith. "I've heard that it is the custom with you to write it in blood; well, stop, let me take a nail out of my pocket"—and putting his hand behind him, he suddenly seized the devil by his tail.

"Look, what fun!" cried the devil, laughing. "Well, let me alone now, there's enough of play!"

"Stop, my dear fellow!" cried the blacksmith, "What wilt thou say now?" and he made the sign of the cross. The devil grew as docile as a lamb. "Stop," continued the blacksmith, drawing him by the tail down to the ground; "I will teach thee how to make good men and upright Christians sin;" and the blacksmith sprang on his back, and once more raised his hand to make the sign of the cross.

"Have mercy upon me, Vakoola!" groaned the devil in a lamentable voice; "I am ready to do whatever thou wilt, only do not make the dread sign of the cross on me!"

"Ah! that is the strain thou singest now, cursed German that thou art! I know now what to do! Take me a ride on thy back directly, and harkee! a pretty ride must I have!"

"Whither?" gasped the mournful devil.

"To St. Petersburg, straightway to the Tsarina!" and the blacksmith thought he should faint with terror as he felt himself rising up in the air.

Oxana remained a long time pondering over the strange speech of the blacksmith. Something within her told her that she had behaved with too much cruelty towards him. "What if he should indeed resort to some frightful decision! May not such a thing be expected! He may, perhaps, fall in love with some other girl, and, out of spite, proclaim *her* to be the belle of the village! No, that he would not do, he is too much in love with me! I am so handsome! For none will he ever leave me. He is only joking; he only feigns. Ten minutes will not pass, ere he returns to look at me. I am indeed too harsh towards him. Why not let him have a kiss? just as if it were against my will; that to a certainty would make him quite delighted!" and the flighty belle began once more to sport with her friends. "Stop," said one of them, "the blacksmith has left his sacks behind; just see what enormous sacks too! His luck has been better than ours; methinks he has got whole quarters of mutton, and sausages, and loaves without number. Plenty indeed; one might feed upon the whole of next fortnight."

"Are these the blacksmith's sacks?" asked Oxana; "let us take them into my cottage just to see what he has got in them." All laughingly agreed to her proposal.

"But we shall never be able to lift them!" cried the girls, trying to move the sacks.

"Stay a bit," said Oxana; "come with me to fetch a sledge, and we'll drag them home on it."

The whole party ran to fetch a sledge.

The prisoners were far from pleased at sitting in the sacks, notwithstanding that the clerk had succeeded in poking a big hole with his finger. Had there been nobody near, he would perhaps have found the means of making his escape; but he could not endure the thought of creeping out of the sack before a whole crowd, and of being laughed at by everyone, so he resolved to await the event, giving only now and then a suppressed groan under the impolite boots of Choop. Choop had no less a desire to be set free, feeling that there was something lying under him, which was excessively inconvenient to sit upon. But on hearing his daughter's decision he remained quiet and no longer felt inclined to creep out, considering that he would have certainly some hundred, or perhaps even two hundred steps to walk to get to his dwelling; that upon creeping out, he would have his sheepskin coat to button, his belt to buckle—what a trouble! and last of all, that he had left his cap behind him at Solokha's. So he thought it better to wait till the maidens drew him home on a sledge.

The event, however, proved to be quite contrary to his expectations; at the same time that the maidens ran to bring the sledge, Choop's kinsman left the vodka-shop, very cross and dejected. The mistress of the shop would on no account give him credit; he had resolved to wait until some kindhearted Cossack should step in and offer him a glass of vodka; but, as if purposely, all the Cossacks remained at home, and as became good Christians, ate *kootia* with their families. Thinking about the corruption of manners, and about the Jewish mistress of the shop having a wooden heart, the kinsman went straight to the sacks and stopped in amazement. "What sacks are these? somebody has left them on the road," said he, looking round. "There must be pork for a certainty in them! Who can it be? who has had the good luck to get so many donations? Were there nothing more than buckwheat cakes and millet-biscuits—why, that would be well enough! But supposing there were only loaves, well, they are welcome too! The Jewess gives a glass of vodka for every loaf. I had better bring them out of the way at once, lest anybody should see them!" and he lifted on his shoulders the sack in which sat Choop and the clerk, but feeling it to be too heavy, "No," said he, "I could not carry it home alone. Now, here comes, as if purposely, the weaver, Shapoovalenko! Good-evening, Ostap!"

"Good-evening," said the weaver, stopping.

"Where art thou going?"

"I am walking without any purpose, just where my legs carry me."

"Well, my good man, help me to carry off these sacks; some caroller has left them here in the midst of the road. We will divide the booty between us."

"And what is there in the sacks? rolls or loaves?"

"Plenty of everything, I should think." And both hastily snatched sticks out of a palisade, laid one of the sacks upon them, and carried it away on their shoulders.

"Where shall we carry it? to the vodka-shop?" asked the weaver, leading the way.

"I thought, too, of carrying it there; but the vile Jewess will not give us credit; she will think we have stolen it somewhere, the more so that I have just left her shop. We had better carry it to my cottage. Nobody will interfere with us; my wife is not at home."

"Art thou sure that she is not at home?" asked the weaver warily.

"Thank Heaven, I am not yet out of my mind," answered the kinsman. "What should I do there if she were at home? I expect she will wander about all night with the rest of the women."

"Who is there?" cried the kinsman's wife, hearing the noise which the two friends made in coming into the passage with the sack.

The kinsman was quite aghast.

"What now?" muttered the weaver, letting his arms drop.

The kinsman's wife was one of those treasures which are often found in this good world of ours. Like her husband, she scarcely ever remained at home, but went all day long fawning among wealthy, gossiping old women; paid them different compliments, ate their donations with great appetite, and beat her husband only in the morning, because it was the only time that she saw him. Their cottage was even older than the trousers of the village scribe. Many holes in the roof remained uncovered and without thatch; of the palisade round the house, few sticks existed, for no one who was going out ever took with him a stick to drive away the dogs, but went round by the kinsman's kitchen garden and got one out of his palisade. Sometimes no fire was lighted in the cottage for three days together. Everything which the affectionate wife succeeded in obtaining from kind people was hidden by her as far as possible out of the reach of her husband; and if he had got anything which he had not had the time to sell at the vodka-shop, she invariably snatched it from him. However meek the kinsman's temper might be, he did not like to yield to her at once; for which reason, he generally left the house with black eyes, and his dear better-half went moaning to tell stories to the old women about the ill conduct of her husband, and the blows she had received at his hands.

Now, it is easy to understand the displeasure of the weaver and the kinsman at her sudden appearance. Putting the sack on the ground, they took up a position of defence in front of it, and covered it with the wide skirts of their coats; but it was already too late. The kinsman's wife, although her old eyes had grown dim, saw the sack at once. "That's good," she

said, with the countenance of a hawk at the sight of its prey;
"that's good of you to have collected so much. That's the
way good people always behave! But it cannot be! I think
you must have stolen it somewhere; show me directly what
you have got there!—show me the sack directly! Do you
hear me?"

"May the bald devil show it to thee! we will not," answered
the kinsman, assuming an air of dogged resolution.

"Why should we?" said the weaver; "the sack is ours, not
thine."

"Thou shalt show it to me, thou good-for-nothing drunkard,"
said she, giving the tall kinsman a blow under his chin, and
pushing her way to the sack. The kinsman and the weaver,
however, stood her attack courageously, and drove her back;
but had hardly time to recover themselves, when the woman
darted once more into the passage, this time with a poker
in her hand. In no time she gave a cut over her husband's
fingers, another on the weaver's hand, and stood beside the
sack.

"Why did we let her go?" said the weaver, coming to his
senses.

"Why did we indeed? and why didst thou?" said the
kinsman.

"Your poker seems to be an iron one!" said the weaver,
after keeping silent for a while, and scratching his back.
"My wife bought one at the fair last year; well, hers is not to
be compared—does not hurt at all."

The triumphant dame, in the meanwhile, set her candle on
the floor, opened the sack, and looked into it.

But her old eyes, which had so quickly caught sight of the
sack, for this time deceived her. "Why, here lies a whole
boar!" cried she, clapping her hands with delight.

"A boar, a whole boar! dost hear?" said the weaver, giving
the kinsman a push. "And thou alone art to blame."

"What's to be done?" muttered the kinsman, shrugging his
shoulders.

"How, what? why are we standing here quietly? we must have the sack back again! Come!"

"Away, away with thee! it is our boar!" cried the weaver, advancing.

"Away, away with thee, she-devil! it is not thy property," said the kinsman.

The old hag once more took up the poker, but at the same moment Choop stepped out of the sack, and stood in the middle of the passage stretching his limbs like a man just awake from a long sleep.

The kinsman's wife shrieked in terror, while the others opened their mouths in amazement.

"What did she say, then, the old fool—that it was a boar?"

"It's not a boar!" said the kinsman, straining his eyes.

"Just see, what a man someone has thrown into the sack," said the weaver, stepping back in a fright. "They may say what they will—the evil spirit must have lent his hand to the work; the man could never have gone through a window."

"'Tis my kinsman," cried the kinsman, after having looked at Choop.

"And who else should it be, then?" said Choop, laughing. "Was it not a capital trick of mine? And you thought of eating me like pork? Well, I'll give you good news: there is something lying at the bottom of the sack; if it be not a boar, it must be a sucking-pig, or something of the sort. All the time there was something moving under me."

The weaver and the kinsman rushed to the sack, the wife caught hold of it on the other side, and the fight would have been renewed, had not the clerk, who saw no escape left, crept out of the sack.

The kinsman's wife, quite stupefied, let go the clerk's leg, which she had taken told of in order to drag him out of the sack.

"There's another one!" cried the weaver with terror; "the

devil knows what happens now in the world—it's enough to send one mad. No more sausages or loaves—men are thrown into the sacks."

"'Tis the devil!" muttered Choop, more astonished than anyone. "Well, now, Solokha!—and to put the clerk in a sack too! That is why I saw her room all full of sacks. Now, I have it: she has got two men in each of them; and I thought that I was the only one. Well now, Solokha!"

The maidens were somewhat astonished at finding only one sack left. "There is nothing to be done; we must content ourselves with this one," said Oxana. They all went at once to the sack, and succeeded in lifting it upon the sledge. The elder resolved to keep quiet, considering that if he cried out, and asked them to undo the sack, and let him out, the stupid girls would run away, fearing they had got the devil in the sack, and he would be left in the street till the next morning. Meanwhile, the maidens, with one accord, taking one another by the hand, flew like the wind with the sledge over the crisp snow. Many of them, for fun, sat down upon the sledge; some went right upon the elder's head. But he was determined to bear everything. At last they reached Oxana's house, opened the doors of the passage and of the room, and with shouts of laughter brought in the sack. "Let us see what we have got here," cried they, and hastily began to undo the sack. At this juncture, the hiccups of the elder (which had not ceased for a moment all the time he had been sitting in the sack) increased to such a degree that he could not refrain from giving vent to them in the loudest key. "Ah! there is somebody in the sack!" shrieked the maidens, and they darted in a fright towards the door.

"What does this mean?" said Choop, stepping in. "Where are you rushing, like mad things?"

"Ah! father," answered Oxana, "there is somebody sitting in the sack!"

"In what sack? Where did you get this sack from?"

"The blacksmith threw it down in the middle of the road," was the answer.

"I thought as much!" muttered Choop. "Well, what are you afraid of, then? Let us see. Well, my good man (excuse me for not calling thee by thy Christian and surname), please to make thy way out of the sack."

The elder came out.

"Lord have mercy upon us!" cried the maidens.

"The elder was in too!" thought Choop to himself, looking at him from head to foot, as if not trusting his eyes. "There now! Eh!" and he could say no more. The elder felt no less confused, and he knew not what to say. "It seems to be rather cold out of doors?" asked he, turning to Choop.

"Yes! the frost is rather severe," answered Choop. "Do tell me, what dost thou use to black thy boots with: tallow or tar?" He did not at all wish to put this question; he intended to ask—How didst thou come to be in this sack? but he knew not himself how it was that his tongue asked quite another question.

"I prefer tar," answered the elder. "Well, good-bye, Choop," said he, and putting his cap on, he stepped out of the room.

"What a fool I was to ask him what he uses to black his boots with," muttered Choop, looking at the door out of which the elder had just gone. "Well, Solokha! To put such a man into a sack! May the devil take her; and I, fool that I was—but where is that infernal sack?"

"I threw it into the corner," said Oxana, "there is nothing more in it."

"I know these tricks well! Nothing in it, indeed! Give it me directly; there must be one more! Shake it well. Is there nobody? Abominable woman! And yet to look at her one would think she must be a saint, that she never had a sin——"

But let us leave Choop giving vent to his anger, and return

to the blacksmith; the more so as time is running away, and by the clock it must be near nine.

At first, Vakoola could not help feeling afraid at rising to such a height that he could distinguish nothing upon the earth, and at coming so near the moon, that if he had not bent down, he would certainly have touched it with his cap. Yet, after a time, he recovered his presence of mind, and began to laugh at the devil. All was bright in the sky. A light silvery mist covered the transparent air. Everything was distinctly visible; and the blacksmith even noticed how a wizard flew past him, sitting in a pot; how some stars, gathered in a group, played at blind man's buff; how a whole swarm of spirits were whirling about in the distance; how a devil who danced in the moonbeam, seeing him riding, took off his cap and made him a bow; how there was a besom flying, on which, apparently, a witch had just taken a ride. They met many other things; and all, on seeing the blacksmith, stopped for a moment to look at him, and then continued their flight far away. The blacksmith went on flying, and suddenly he saw St. Petersburg all in a blaze. (There must have been an illumination that day.) Flying past the town gate, the devil changed into a horse, and the blacksmith saw himself riding a high-stepping steed, in the middle of the street. "Good heavens! What a noise, what a clatter, what a blaze!" On either side rose houses, several stories high; from every quarter the clatter of horses' hoofs, and of wheels arose, like thunder; at every step arose tall houses, as if starting from beneath the ground; bridges quivered under flying carriages; the coachmen shouted; the snow crisped under thousands of sledges rushing in every direction; pedestrians kept the wall of the houses along the footpath, all studded with flaring pots of fire, and their gigantic shadows danced upon the walls, losing themselves amongst the chimneys and on the roofs. The blacksmith looked with amazement on every side. It seemed to him as if all the houses looked at him with their innumerable fire-eyes. He saw such a number of gentlemen wearing fur cloaks covered with cloth, that he no longer knew to which of them he ought to take off his cap. "Gracious Lord! What a number of nobility one sees here!" thought the blacksmith; "I suppose everyone here, who goes in a fur cloak, can be no less than a magistrate! and as for the persons who sit in those wonderful carts with glasses, they must be, if not the chiefs of the town, certainly commissaries, and, maybe, of a still higher rank!"

Here, the devil put an end to his reflections, by asking if he was to bring him right before the Tsarina? "No, I should be too afraid to go at once," answered the blacksmith; "but I know there must be some Zaporozhians here, who passed through Dikanka last autumn on their way to Petersburg. They were going on business to the Tsarina. Let us have their advice. Now, devil, get into my pocket, and bring me to those Zaporozhians." In less than a minute the devil grew so thin and so small that he had no trouble in getting into the pocket, and in the twinkling of an eye, Vakoola (himself, he knew not how) ascended a staircase, opened a door and fell a little back, struck by the rich furniture of a spacious room. Yet he felt a little more at ease when he recognised the same Zaporozhians who had passed through Dikanka. They were sitting upon silk-covered sofas, with their tar-besmeared boots tucked under them, and were smoking the strongest tobacco fibres.

"Good-evening, God help you, your worships!" said the blacksmith, coming nearer, and he made a low bow, almost touching the ground with his forehead.

"Who is that?" asked a Zaporozhian, who sat near Vakoola, of another who was sitting farther off.

"Do you not recognise me at once?" said Vakoola; "I am the blacksmith, Vakoola! Last autumn, as you passed through Dikanka, you remained nearly two days at my cottage. God grant you good health, and many happy years! It was I who put a new iron tyre round one of the forewheels of your vehicle."

"Ah!" said the same Zaporozhian, "it is the blacksmith who paints so well. Good-evening, countryman, what didst thou come for?"

"Only just to look about. They say——"

"Well, my good fellow," said the Zaporozhian, assuming a grand air, and trying to speak with the high Russian accent, "what dost thou think of the town? Is it large?"

The blacksmith was no less desirous to show that he also understood good manners. We have already seen that he knew something of fashionable language. "The site is quite considerable," answered he very composedly. "The houses are enormously big, the paintings they are adorned with are thoroughly important. Some of the houses are to an extremity ornamented with gold letters. No one can say a word to the contrary: the proportion is marvellous!" The Zaporozhians, hearing the blacksmith so familiar with fine language, drew a conclusion very much to his advantage.

"We will have a chat with thee presently, my dear fellow. Now, we must go at once to the Tsarina."

"To the Tsarina? Be kind, your worships, take me with you!"

"Take thee with us?" said the Zaporozhian, with an expression such as a tutor would assume towards a boy four years old, who begs to ride on a real, live, great horse. "What hast thou to do there? No, it cannot be," and his features took an important look. "My dear fellow, we have to speak to the Tsarina on business."

"Do take me," urged the blacksmith. "Beg!" whispered he to the devil, striking his pocket with his fist. Scarcely had he done so, when another Zaporozhian said, "Well, come, comrades, we will take him."

"Well, then, let him come!" said the others.

"Put on such a dress as ours, then."

The blacksmith hastily donned a green dress, when the

door opened, and a man, in a coat all ornamented with silver braid, came in and said it was time to start.

Once more was the blacksmith overwhelmed with astonishment, as he rolled along in an enormous carriage, hung on springs, lofty houses seeming to run away on both sides of him, and the pavement to roll of its own accord under the feet of the horses.

"Gracious Lord! what a glare," thought the blacksmith to himself. "We have no such light at Dikanka, even during the day." The Zaporozhians entered, stepped into a magnificent hall, and went up a brilliantly lighted staircase. "What a staircase!" thought the blacksmith; "it is a pity to walk upon it. What ornaments! And they say that fairytales are so many lies; they are plain truth! My heavens! what a balustrade! what workmanship! The iron alone must have cost not less than some fifty roubles!"

Having ascended the staircase, the Zaporozhians passed through the first hall. Warily did the blacksmith follow them, fearing at every step to slip on the waxed floor. They passed three more saloons, and the blacksmith had not yet recovered from his astonishment. Coming into a fourth, he could not refrain from stopping before a picture which hung on the wall. It represented the Holy Virgin, with the Infant Jesus in her arms. "What a picture! what beautiful painting!" thought he. "She seems to speak, she seems to be alive! And the Holy Infant! there, he stretches out his little hands! there, it laughs, the poor babe! And what colours! Good heavens! what colours! I should think there was no ochre used in the painting, certainly nothing but ultramarine and lake! And what a brilliant blue! Capital workmanship! The background must have been done with white lead! And yet," he continued, stepping to the door and taking the handle in his hand, "however beautiful these paintings may be, this brass handle is still more worthy of admiration; what neat work! I should think all this must have been made by German blacksmiths at the most exorbitant prices." . . .

The blacksmith might have gone on for a long time with his reflections, had not the attendant in the braid-covered dress given him a push, telling him not to remain behind the others. The Zaporozhians passed two rooms more, and stopped. Some generals, in gold-embroidered uniforms, were waiting there. The Zaporozhians bowed in every direction, and stood in a group. A minute afterwards there entered, attended by a numerous suite, a man of majestic stature, rather stout, dressed in the hetman's uniform and yellow boots. His hair was uncombed; one of his eyes had a small cataract on it; his face wore an expression of stately pride; his every movement gave proof that he was accustomed to command. All the generals, who before his arrival were strutting about somewhat haughtily in their gold-embroidered uniforms, came bustling towards him with profound bows, seeming to watch every one of his words, nay, of his movements, that they might run and see his desires fulfilled. The hetman did not pay any attention to all this, scarcely nodding his head, and went straight to the Zaporozhians.

They bowed to him with one accord till their brows touched the ground.

"Are all of you here?" asked he, in a somewhat drawling voice, with a slight nasal twang.

"Yes, father, every one of us is here," answered the Zaporozhains, bowing once more.

"Remember to speak just as I taught you."

"We will, father, we will!"

"Is it the Tsar?" asked the blacksmith of one of the Zaporozhians.

"The Tsar! a great deal more; it is Potemkin himself!" was the answer.

Voices were heard in the adjoining room, and the blacksmith knew not where to turn his eyes, when he saw a multitude of ladies enter, dressed in silk gowns with long trains, and courtiers in gold-embroidered coats and bag-wigs. He was dazzled with the glitter of gold, silver, and precious stones. The Zaporozhians fell with one accord on their knees, and cried with one voice, "Mother, have mercy upon us!" The blacksmith, too, followed their example, and stretched himself full length on the floor.

"Rise up!" was heard above their heads, in a commanding yet soft voice. Some of the courtiers officiously hastened to push the Zaporozhians forward.

"We will not arise, mother; we will die rather than arise!" cried the Zaporozhians.

Potemkin bit his lips. At last he came himself, and whispered imperatively to one of them. They arose. Then only did the blacksmith venture to raise his eyes, and saw before him a lady, not tall, somewhat stout, with powdered hair, blue eyes, and that majestic, smiling air which conquered everyone, and could be the attribute only of a sovereign lady.

"His Highness[1] promised to make me acquainted to-day with a people under my dominion whom I have not yet seen," said the blue-eyed lady, looking with curiosity at the Zaporozhians. "Are you satisfied with the manner in which you are provided for here?" asked she, coming nearer.

"Thank thee, mother! Provisions are good, though mutton is not quite so fine here as at home; but why should one be so very particular about it?"

Potemkin frowned at hearing them speak in quite a different manner from what he had told them to do.

One of the Zaporozhians stepped out from the group, and, in a dignified manner, began the following speech:—
"Mother, have mercy upon us! What have we, thy faithful people, done to deserve thine anger? Have we ever given assistance to the miscreant Tartars? Did we ever help the Turks in anything? Have we betrayed thee in our acts, nay, even in our thoughts? Wherefore, then, art thou ungracious towards us? At first they told us thou hadst ordered fortresses

[1]Potemkin was created by Catherine II Prince of Tauride, with the title of Highness, an honour rarely bestowed in Russia.

to be raised against us; then we were told thou wouldst make regular regiments of us; now, we hear of new evils coming on us. In what were the Zaporozhians ever in fault with regard to thee? Was it in bringing thy army across Perekop? or in helping thy generals to get the better of the Crimean Tartars?"

Potemkin remained silent, and, with an unconcerned air, was brushing the diamonds which sparkled on his fingers.

"What do you ask for, then?" demanded Catherine, in a solicitous tone of voice.

The Zaporozhians looked knowingly at one another.

"Now's the time! the Tsarina asks what we want!" thought the blacksmith, and suddenly down he went on his knees. "Imperial Majesty! Do not show me thy anger, show me thy mercy! Let me know (and let not my question bring the wrath of thy Majesty's worship upon me!) of what stuff are made the boots that thou wearest on thy feet? I think there is no bootmaker in any country in the world who ever will be able to make such pretty ones. Gracious Lord! if ever my wife had such boots to wear!"

The empress laughed; the courtiers laughed too. Potemkin frowned and smiled at the same time. The Zaporozhians pushed the blacksmith, thinking he had gone mad.

"Stand up!" said the empress, kindly. "If thou wishest to have such shoes, thy wish may be easily fulfilled. Let him have directly my richest gold-embroidered shoes. This artlessness pleases me exceedingly." Then, turning towards a gentleman with a round pale face, who stood a little apart from the rest, and whose plain dress, with mother-of-pearl buttons, showed at once that he was not a courtier, "There you have," continued she, "a subject worthy of your witty pen."

"Your Imperial Majesty is too gracious! It would require a pen no less able than that of a Lafontaine!" answered, with a bow, the gentleman in the plain dress.

"Upon my honour! I tell you I am still under the impres-

sion of your '*Brigadier*.'[1] You read exceedingly well!"
Then, speaking once more to the Zaporoghians, she said, "I
was told that you never married at your Siecha?"

"How could that be, mother? Thou knowest well, by thyself, that no man could ever do without a woman," answered
the same Zaporozhian who had conversed with the blacksmith; and the blacksmith was astonished to hear one so well
acquainted with polished language speak to the Tsarina, as
if on purpose, in the coarsest accent used among peasants.

"A cunning people," thought he to himself; "he does it
certainly for some reason."

"We are no monks," continued the speaker, "we are sinful
men. Every one of us is as much inclined to forbidden fruit
as a good Christian can be. There are not a few among us
who have wives, only their wives do not live in the Siecha.
Many have their wives in Poland; others have wives in
Ukraine; there are some, too, who have wives in Turkey."

At this moment the shoes were brought to the blacksmith.

"Gracious Lord! what ornaments!" cried he, overpowered
with joy, grasping the shoes. "Imperial Majesty! if thou dost
wear such shoes upon thy feet (and thy Honour, I dare say,
does use them even for walking in the snow and the mud),
what, then, must thy feet be like?—whiter than sugar, at the
least, I should think!"

The empress, who really had charming feet of an exquisite
shape, could not refrain from smiling at such a compliment
from a simple-minded blacksmith, who, notwithstanding his
sunburnt features, must have been accounted a handsome
lad in his Zaporozhian dress.

The blacksmith, encouraged by the condescension of the
Tsarina, was already on the point of asking her some questions about all sorts of things, whether it was true that

[1] The author alluded to is Von Wiessen, who, in his writings (particularly
in two comedies, the *Brigadier*, and the *Young Nobleman without Employment*), ridiculed the then prevailing fashion amongst the Russian nobility
of despising national and blindly following foreign (particularly French)
customs.

sovereigns fed upon nothing but honey and lard, and so on;
but feeling the Zaporozhians pull the skirts of his coat, he
resolved to keep silent; and when the empress turned to the
older Cossacks, and began to ask them about their way of
living, and their manners, in the Siecha, he stepped a little
back, bent his head towards his pocket, and said in a low
voice: "Quick, carry me hence, away!" and in no time he
had left the town gate far behind.

"He is drowned! I'll swear to it, he's drowned! May I never
leave this spot alive if he is not drowned!" said the fat
weaver's wife, standing in the middle of the street, amidst a
group of the villagers' wives.

"Then I am a liar? Did I ever steal anything? Did I ever
cast an evil eye upon anyone, that I am no longer worthy of
belief?" shrieked a hag wearing a Cossack's dress, and with
a violet-coloured nose, brandishing her hands in the most
violent manner. "May I never have another drink of water
if old Pereperchenko's wife did not see with her own eyes how
that the blacksmith has hanged himself!"

"The blacksmith hanged himself? what is this I hear?"
said the elder, stepping out of Choop's cottage; and he
pushed his way nearer to the talking women.

"Say rather, mayest thou never wish to drink vodka again,
old drunkard!" answered the weaver's wife. "One must be
as mad as thou art to hang one's self. He is drowned!
drowned in the ice-hole! This I know as well as that thou
just now didst come from the vodka-shop!"

"Shameless creature! what meanest thou to reproach me
with?" angrily retorted the hag with the violet-coloured nose,
"thou hadst better hold thy tongue, good-for-nothing woman
Don't I know that the clerk comes every evening to thee?"

The weaver's wife became red in the face. "What does the
clerk do? to whom does the clerk come? What lie art thou
telling?"

"The clerk?" cried, in shrill voice, the clerk's wife, who,

dressed in a hare-skin cloak covered with blue nankeen, pushed her way towards the quarrelling ones; "I will let you know about the clerk! Who is talking here about the clerk?"

"There is she to whom the clerk pays his visits!" said the violet-nosed woman, pointing to the weaver's wife.

"So, thou art the witch," continued the clerk's wife, stepping nearer the weaver's wife; "thou art the witch who sends him out of his senses and gives him a charmed beverage in order to bewitch him?"

"Wilt thou leave me alone, she-devil!" cried the weaver's wife, drawing back.

"Cursed witch! Mayest thou never see thy children again, good-for-nothing woman!" and the clerk's wife spat right into the eyes of the weaver's wife.

The weaver's wife wished to return her the same compliment, but instead of that, spat on the unshaven beard of the elder, who had come near the squabblers in order to hear what was going on. "Ah! nasty creature!" cried the elder, wiping his face with his skirt, and lifting his whip. This motion made them all fly in different directions, scolding the whole time. "The abominable creature!" continued the elder, still wiping his beard. "So the blacksmith is drowned! Gracious Heaven! and such a capital painter! and what strong knives, and sickles, and ploughshares he used to forge! How strong he was himself!

"Yes," continued he, meditatively, "there are few such men in our village! That was the reason of the poor fellow's ill-temper, which I noticed while I was sitting in that confounded sack! So much for the blacksmith! He was here, and now nothing is left of him! And I was thinking of letting him shoe my speckled mare," . . . and, full of such Christian thoughts, the elder slowly went to his cottage.

Oxana was very downcast at hearing the news; she did not put any faith in the evidence of Pereperchenko's wife, or in the gossiping of the women. She knew the blacksmith to be too pious to venture on letting his soul perish. But what if indeed he had left the village with the resolve never to return? And scarcely could there be found anywhere such an accomplished lad as the blacksmith. And he loved her so intensely! He had endured her caprices longer than anyone else. All the night long, the belle turned beneath her cover-let, from right to left, and from left to right, and could not go to sleep. Now she scolded herself almost aloud, throwing herself into the most bewitching attitudes, which the dark-ness of the night hid even from herself; then, in silence, she resolved to think no more of anything and still continued thinking, and was burning with fever; and in the morning she was quite in love with the blacksmith.

Choop was neither grieved nor rejoiced at the fate of Vakoola; all his ideas had concentrated themselves into one: he could not for a moment forget Solokha's want of faith; and even when asleep, ceased not to abuse her.

The morning came; the church was crowded even before daylight. The elderly women, in their white linen veils, their flowing robes, and long jackets made of white cloth, piously made the sign of the cross, standing close to the entrance of the church. The Cossacks' wives, in green and yellow bodices, and some of them even in blue dresses, with gold braidings behind, stood a little before them. The girls endeavoured to get still nearer to the altar, and displayed whole shopfuls of ribbons on their heads, and of necklaces, little crosses, and silver coins on their necks. But right in front stood the Cossacks and the peasants, with their moustaches, their crown-tufts, their thick necks and their freshly-shaven chins, dressed for the most part in cloaks with hoods, from beneath which were seen white, and sometimes blue coats. On every face, wherever one looked, one might see it was a holiday. The elder already licked his lips at the idea of breaking his fast with a sausage. The girls were thinking about the pleasure of running about with the lads, and sliding upon the ice. The old women muttered their prayers more zeal-ously than ever. The whole church resounded with the thumps which the Cossack Sverbygooze gave with his forehead against the floor as he prostrated himself.

Oxana alone was out of sorts. She said her prayers, and yet could not pray. Her heart was besieged by so many different feelings, one more mournful than the other, one more perplexing than the other, that the greatest dejection appeared upon her features, and tears moistened her eyes. None of the girls could understand the reason of her state, and none would have suspected its being occasioned by the blacksmith. And yet Oxana was not the only one who noticed his absence; the whole congregation remarked that there lacked something to the fullness of the festival. Moreover, the clerk, during his journey in the sack, had got a bad cold, and his cracked voice was hardly audible. The newly-arrived chanter had a deep bass indeed. But at all events it would have been much better if the blacksmith had been there, as he had so fine a voice, and knew how to chant the tunes which were used at Poltava; and besides, he was churchwarden.

The matins were said. The liturgy had also been brought to a close. Well, what had indeed happened to the blacksmith?

The devil, with the blacksmith on his back, had flown with still greater speed during the remainder of the night. Vakoola soon reached his cottage. At the very moment he heard the crow of a cock. "Whither away?" cried he, seeing the devil in the act of sneaking off; and he caught him by his tail. "Wait a bit, my dear fellow; I have not done with thee; thou must get thy reward!" and, taking a stick, he gave him three blows across his back, so that the poor devil took to his heels, exactly as a peasant might do who had just been punished by a police officer. So, the enemy of mankind, instead of cheating, seducing, or leading anybody into foolishness, was made a fool of himself. After this, Vakoola went into the passage, buried himself in the hay, and slept till noon.

When he awoke, he was alarmed at seeing the sun high in the heavens. "I have missed matins and liturgy!" and the pious blacksmith fell into mournful thoughts, and decided that the sleep which had prevented him from going to church on such a festival was certainly a punishment inflicted by God for his sinful intention of killing himself. But he soon quieted his mind by resolving to confess no later than next week, and from that very day to make fifty genuflexions during his prayers for a whole year. Then he went into the room, but nobody was there; Solokha had not yet returned home. He cautiously drew the shoes from his breast pocket, and once more admired their beautiful workmanship, and marvelled at the events of the preceding night. Then he washed, and dressed himself as fine as he could, putting on the same suit of clothes which he had got from the Zaporozhians, took out of his box a new cap with a blue crown and a trimming of black sheepskin, which had never been worn since he bought it in Poltava; he took out also a new belt, of divers brilliant colours; wrapped up these with a scourge, in a handkerchief, and went straight to Choop's cottage.

Choop opened wide his eyes as he saw the blacksmith enter his room. He knew not at what most to marvel, whether at the blacksmith being once more alive, or at his having ventured to come into his house, or at his being dressed so finely, like a Zaporozhian; but he was still more astonished when he saw Vakoola undo his handkerchief, and set before him an entirely new cap, and such a belt as had never before been seen in the village; and when Vakoola fell at his knees, saying in a deprecating voice: "Father, have mercy on me! do not be angry with me! There, take this scourge, whip me as much as thou wilt! I give myself up. I acknowledge all my trespasses. Whip me, but put away thine anger! The more so that thou and my late father were like two brothers, and shared bread, and salt, and brandy together."

Choop could not help feeling inwardly pleased at seeing at

his feet the blacksmith, the very same blacksmith who would not concede a step to anyone in the village, and who bent copper coins between his fingers as if they were so many buckwheat fritters. To make himself still more important, Choop took the scourge, gave three strokes with it upon the blacksmith's back, and then said: "Well, that will do! Stand up! Attend to men older than thyself. I forget all that has taken place between us. Now, speak out, what dost thou want?"

"Father, let me have Oxana!"

Choop remained thinking for a while; he looked at the cap —he looked at the belt; the cap was beautiful—the belt not less so; he remembered the bad faith of Solokha, and said, in a resolute voice, "Well, send me thy marriage sponsors."

"Ah!" shrieked Oxana, stepping across the threshold; and she stared at him with a look of joy and astonishment.

"Look at the boots I have brought thee!" said Vakoola; "they are the very boots which the Tsarina wears."

"No, no, I do not want the boots!" said Oxana, and she waved her hands, never taking her eyes off him; "it will do without the boots." She could speak no more, and her face turned all crimson.

The blacksmith came nearer, and took her hand. The belle cast down her eyes. Never yet had she been so marvellously handsome; the exulting blacksmith gently stole a kiss, and her face flushed still redder, and she looked still prettier.

As the late archbishop happened to pass on a journey through Dikanka, he greatly commended the spot on which that village stands, and driving down the street, stopped his carriage before a new cottage. "Whose cottage is this, so highly painted?" asked his Eminence of a handsome woman who was standing before the gate, with an infant in her arms.

"It is the blacksmith Vakoola's cottage!" answered Oxana, for she it was, making him a deep curtsy.

"Very good painting, indeed! Capital painting!" said the

Right Eminent, looking at the door and the windows. And, in truth, every window was surrounded by a stripe of red paint; and the door was painted all over with Cossacks on horseback, with pipes in their mouths. But the archbishop bestowed still more praises on Vakoola, when he was made acquainted with the blacksmith's having performed public penance, and with his having painted, at his own expense, the whole of the church choir, green, with red flowers running over it. But Vakoola had done still more: he had painted the devil in hell, upon the wall which is to your left when you step into the church. This devil had such an odious face that no one could refrain from spitting, as they passed by. The women, as soon as their children began to cry, brought them to this picture and said, "Look! is he not an odious creature?" and the children stopped their tears, looked sideways at the picture, and clung more closely to their mother's bosom.

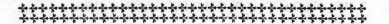

IVAN TURGENIEF

(1818–1883)

✢✢

(I)

THE SONG OF LOVE TRIUMPHANT

(Translated by Isabel F. Hapgood)

Wage du zu irren und zu traümen!
Schiller.

Dedicated to the Memory of Gustave Flaubert

The following is what I read in an Italian manuscript:

I

About the middle of the sixteenth century there dwelt in Ferrara—(it was then flourishing under the sceptre of its magnificent dukes, the patrons of the arts and of poetry)—there dwelt two young men, named Fabio and Muzio. Of the same age and nearly related, they were almost never separated; a sincere friendship had united them since their early childhood, and a similarity of fate had strengthened this bond. Both belonged to ancient families; both were wealthy, independent, and without family; the tastes and inclinations of both were similar. Muzio occupied himself with music, Fabio with painting. All Ferrara was proud of them as the finest ornaments of the Court, of society, and of the city. But in personal appearance they did not resemble each other, although both were distinguished for their stately, youthful beauty. Fabio was the taller of the two, white of complexion, with ruddy-gold hair, and had blue eyes. Muzio, on the contrary, had a swarthy face, black hair, and in his dark brown eyes there was not that merry gleam, on his lips not that cordial smile, which Fabio had; his thick eyebrows overhung his narrow eyelids, while Fabio's golden brows rose in slender arches on his pure, smooth forehead. Muzio was less animated in conversation also; nevertheless, both friends were equally favoured by the ladies; for not in vain were they models of knightly courtesy and lavishness.

At one and the same time with them there dwelt in Ferrara a maiden named Valeria. She was considered one of the greatest beauties in the city, although she was to be seen only very rarely, as she led a retired life and left her house only to go to church;—and on great festivals for a walk. She lived with her mother, a nobly born but not wealthy widow, who had no other children. Valeria inspired in everyone whom she met a feeling of involuntary amazement and of equally involuntary tender respect: so modest was her mien, so little aware was she, to all appearance, of the full force of her charms. Some persons, it is true, thought her rather pale; the glance of her eyes, which were almost always lowered, expressed a certain shyness and even timidity; her lips smiled rarely, and then but slightly; hardly ever did anyone hear her voice. But a rumour was in circulation to the effect that it was very beautiful, and that, locking herself in her chamber, early in the morning, while everything in the city was still sleeping, she loved to warble ancient ballads to the strains of a lute, upon which she herself played. Despite the pallor of her face, Valeria was in blooming health; and even the old people, as they looked on her, could not refrain from thinking: "Oh, how happy will be that young man for whom this bud still folded in its petals, still untouched and virgin, shall at last unfold itself!"

II

Fabio and Muzio beheld Valeria for the first time at a sumptuous popular festival, got up at the command of the

Duke of Ferrara, Ercole, son of the famous Lucrezia Borgia, in honour of some distinguished personages who had arrived from Paris on the invitation of the Duchess, the daughter of Louis XII, King of France. Side by side with her mother sat Valeria in the centre of an elegant tribune, erected after drawings by Palladius on the principal square of Ferrara for the most honourable ladies of the city. Both Fabio and Muzio fell passionately in love with her that day; and as they concealed nothing from each other, each speedily learned what was going on in his comrade's heart. They agreed between themselves that they would both try to make close acquaintance with Valeria, and if she should deign to choose either one of them the other should submit without a murmur to her decision.

Several weeks later, thanks to the fine reputation which they rightfully enjoyed, they succeeded in penetrating into the not easily accessible house of the widow; she gave them permission to visit her. From that time forth they were able to see Valeria almost every day and to converse with her; and with every day the flame kindled in the hearts of both young men blazed more and more vigorously. But Valeria displayed no preference for either of them, although their presence evidently pleased her. With Muzio she occupied herself with music; but she chatted more with Fabio: she was less shy with him. At last they decided to learn their fate definitely, and sent to Valeria a letter wherein they asked her to explain herself and say on whom she was prepared to bestow her hand. Valeria showed this letter to her mother, and informed her that she was content to remain unmarried; but if her mother thought it was time for her to marry, she would wed the man of her mother's choice. The honourable widow shed a few tears at the thought of parting from her beloved child; but there was no reason for rejecting the suitors: she considered them both equally worthy of her daughter's hand. But as she secretly preferred Fabio, and suspected that he was more to Valeria's taste also, she fixed upon him. On the following day Fabio learned of his happiness: and all that was left to Muzio was to keep his word and submit.

This he did; but he was not able to be a witness to the triumph of his friend, his rival. He immediately sold the greater part of his property, and collecting a few thousand ducats, he set off on a long journey to the Orient. On taking leave of Fabio he said to him that he would not return until he should feel that the last traces of passion in him had vanished. It was painful for Fabio to part from the friend of his childhood and his youth . . . but the joyful anticipation of approaching bliss speedily swallowed up all other sentiments and he surrendered himself completely to the transports of happy love.

He soon married Valeria, and only then did he learn the full value of the treasure which it had fallen to his lot to possess. He had a very beautiful villa at a short distance from Ferrara; he removed thither with his wife and her mother. A bright time then began for them. Wedded life displayed in a new and captivating light all Valeria's perfections. Fabio became a remarkable artist—no longer a mere amateur, but a master. Valeria's mother rejoiced and returned thanks to God as she gazed at the happy pair. Four years flew by unnoticed like a blissful dream. One thing alone was lacking to the young married couple, one thing caused them grief: they had no children . . . but hope had not deserted them. Toward the end of the fourth year a great, and this time a genuine grief, visited them: Valeria's mother died, after an illness of a few days.

Valeria shed many tears; for a long time she could not reconcile herself to her loss. But another year passed; life once more asserted its rights and flowed on in its former channel. And, lo! one fine summer evening, without having forewarned any one, Muzio returned to Ferrara.

III

During the whole five years which had elapsed since his departure, no one had known anything about him. All rumours concerning him had died out, exactly as though he had vanished from the face of the earth. When Fabio met his friend on one of the streets in Ferrara he came near crying out aloud, first from fright, then from joy, and immediately invited him to his villa. There, in the garden, was a spacious, detached pavilion; he suggested that his friend should settle down in that pavilion. Muzio gladly accepted, and that same day removed thither with his servant, a dumb Malay—dumb but not deaf, and even, judging from the vivacity of his glance, a very intelligent man. . . . His tongue had been cut out. Muzio had brought with him scores of chests filled with divers precious things which he had collected during his prolonged wanderings. Valeria was delighted at Muzio's return; and he greeted her in a cheerfully friendly but composed manner. From everything it was obvious that he had kept the promise made to Fabio. In the course of the day he succeeded in installing himself in his pavilion; with the aid of his Malay he set out the rarities he had brought—rugs, silken tissues, garments of velvet and brocade, weapons, cups, dishes, and beakers adorned with enamel, articles of gold and silver set with pearls and turquoises, carved caskets of amber and ivory, faceted flasks, spices, perfumes, pelts of wild beasts, the feathers of unknown birds, and a multitude of other objects, the very use of which seemed mysterious and incomprehensible. Among the number of all these precious things there was one rich pearl necklace which Muzio had received from the Shah of Persia for a certain great and mysterious service; he asked Valeria's permission to place this necklace on her neck with his own hand; it seemed to her heavy, and as though endowed with a strange sort of warmth . . . it fairly adhered to the skin. Toward evening, after dinner,

as they sat on the terrace of the villa, in the shade of ole-
anders and laurels, Muzio began to narrate his adventures.
He told of the distant lands which he had seen, of mountains higher than the clouds, of rivers like unto seas; he
told of vast buildings and temples, of trees thousands of
years old, of rainbow-hued flowers and birds; he enumer-
ated the cities and peoples he had visited . . . (their very
names exhaled something magical). All the Orient was
familiar to Muzio: he had traversed Persia and Arabia,
where the horses are more noble and beautiful than all
other living creatures; he had penetrated the depths of
India, where is a race of people resembling magnificent
plants; he had attained to the confines of China and Tibet,
where a living god, the Dalai Lama by name, dwells upon
earth in the form of a speechless man with narrow eyes.
Marvellous were his tales! Fabio and Valeria listened to
him as though enchanted.

In point of fact, Muzio's features had undergone but little
change: swarthy from childhood, his face had grown still
darker—had been burned beneath the rays of a more
brilliant sun; his eyes seemed more deeply set than of yore,
that was all; but the expression of that face had become
different: concentrated, grave, it did not grow animated
even when he alluded to the dangers to which he had been
subjected by night in the forests, deafened by the roar of
tigers, by day on deserted roads where fanatics lie in wait
for travellers and strangle them in honour of an iron goddess
who demands human blood. And Muzio's voice had grown
more quiet and even; the movements of his hands, of his
whole body, had lost the flourishing ease which is peculiar
to the Italian race.

With the aid of his servant, the obsequiously alert Malay,
he showed his host and hostess several tricks which he had
been taught by the Brahmins of India. Thus, for example,
having preliminarily concealed himself behind a curtain,
he suddenly appeared sitting in the air, with his legs doubled

up beneath him, resting the tips of his fingers lightly on a bamboo rod set upright, which not a little amazed and even alarmed Fabio and Valeria. . . . "Can it be that he is a magician?" the thought occurred to her. But when he set to calling out tame snakes from a covered basket by whistling on a small flute—when, wriggling their fangs, their dark, flat heads made their appearance from beneath the motley stuff, Valeria became frightened and begged Muzio to hide away those horrors as quickly as possible.

At supper Muzio regaled his friends with wine of Shiraz from a round flask with a long neck; extremely fragrant and thick, of a golden hue, with greenish lights, it sparkled mysteriously when poured into the tiny jasper cups. In taste it did not resemble European wines: it was very sweet and spicy; and, quaffed slowly, in small sips, it produced in all the limbs a sensation of agreeable drowsiness. Muzio made Fabio and Valeria drink a cup apiece, and drank one himself. Bending over her cup, he whispered something and shook his fingers. Valeria noticed this; but as there was something strange and unprecedented in all Muzio's ways in general, and in all his habits, she merely thought: "I wonder if he has not accepted in India some new faith, or whether they have such customs there?"—Then, after a brief pause, she asked him: "Had he continued to occupy himself with music during the time of his journeys?" In reply Muzio ordered the Malay to bring him his Indian violin. It resembled those of the present day, only, instead of four strings it had three; a bluish snake-skin was stretched across its top, and the slender bow of reed was semicircular in form, and on its very tip glittered a pointed diamond.

Muzio first played several melancholy airs—which were, according to his assertion, popular ballads—strange and even savage to the Italian ear; the sound of the metallic strings was plaintive and feeble. But when Muzio began the last song, that same sound suddenly strengthened, quivered powerfully and resonantly; the passionate melody

poured forth from beneath the broadly-handled bow—
poured forth with beautiful undulations, like the snake which
had covered the top of the violin with its skin; and with
so much fire, with so much triumphant joy did this song
beam and blaze that both Fabio and Valeria felt a tremor
at their hearts, and the tears started to their eyes . . . while
Muzio, with his head bent down-and pressed against his
violin, with pallid cheeks, and brows contracted into one
line, seemed still more concentrated and serious than ever,
and the diamond at the tip of the bow scattered ray-like
sparks in its flight, as though it also were kindled with the
fire of that wondrous song. And when Muzio had finished
and, still holding the violin tightly pressed between his
chin and his shoulder, dropped his hand which held the
bow—"What is that? What hast thou been playing to us?"
Fabio exclaimed. Valeria uttered not a word, but her whole
being seemed to repeat her husband's question. Muzio laid
the violin on the table, and lightly shaking back his hair,
said, with a courteous smile: "That? That melody . . . that
song I heard once on the island of Ceylon. That song is
known there, among the people, as the song of happy,
triumphant love."

"Repeat it," whispered Fabio.

"No; it is impossible to repeat it," replied Muzio. "And
it is late now. Signora Valeria ought to rest; and it is high
time for me also. . . . I am weary."

All day long Muzio had treated Valeria in a respectfully
simple manner, like a friend of long standing; but as he
took leave he pressed her hand very hard, jamming his
fingers into her palm, staring so intently into her face the
while that she, although she did not raise her eyelids, felt
conscious of that glance on her suddenly flushing cheeks.
She said nothing to Muzio, but drew away her hand, and
when he was gone she stared at the door through which he
had made his exit. She recalled how, in former years also,
she had been afraid of him . . . and now she was perplexed.

Muzio went off to his pavilion; the husband and wife withdrew to their bed-chamber.

IV

Valeria did not soon fall asleep; her blood was surging softly and languidly, and there was a faint ringing in her head . . . from that strange wine, as she supposed, and, possibly, also from Muzio's tales, from his violin playing.
. . . Toward morning she fell asleep at last, and had a remarkable dream.

It seems to her that she enters a spacious room with a low, vaulted ceiling. . . . She has never seen such a room in her life. All the walls are set with small blue tiles bearing golden patterns; slender carved pillars of alabaster support the marble vault; this vault and the pillars seem semi-transparent. . . . A pale, rose-coloured light penetrates the room from all directions, illuminating all the objects mysteriously and monotonously; cushions of gold brocade lie on a narrow rug in the very middle of the floor, which is as smooth as a mirror. In the corners, barely visible, two tall incense-burners, representing monstrous animals, are smoking; there are no windows anywhere; the door, screened by a velvet drapery, looms silently black in a niche of the wall. And suddenly this curtain softly slips aside, moves away . . . and Muzio enters. He bows, opens his arms, smiles. . . . His harsh arms encircle Valeria's waist; his dry lips have set her burning all over. . . . She falls prone on the cushions. . . .

.   .   .   .   .   .

Moaning with fright, Valeria awoke after long efforts. Still not comprehending where she is and what is the matter with her, she half raises herself up in bed and looks about her. . . . A shudder runs through her whole body. . . . Fabio is lying beside her. He is asleep; but his face, in the light of the round, clear moon, is as pale as that of a corpse . . .

it is more melancholy than the face of a corpse. Valeria
awoke her husband—and no sooner had he cast a glance
at her than he exclaimed: "What is the matter with
thee?"

"I have seen . . . I have seen a dreadful dream," she
whispered, still trembling. . . .

But at that moment, from the direction of the pavilion,
strong sounds were wafted to them—and both Fabio and
Valeria recognised the melody which Muzio had played to
them, calling it the Song of Love Triumphant.—Fabio cast
a glance of surprise at Valeria. . . . She closed her eyes, and
turned away—and both, holding their breath, listened to
the song to the end. When the last sound died away the
moon went behind a cloud, it suddenly grew dark in the
room. . . . The husband and wife dropped their heads on
their pillows, without exchanging a word, and neither of
them noticed when the other fell asleep.

V

On the following morning Muzio came to breakfast; he
seemed pleased, and greeted Valeria merrily. She answered
him with confusion—scrutinised him closely, and was startled
by that pleased, merry face, those piercing and curious eyes.
Muzio was about to begin his stories again . . . but Fabio
stopped him at the first word.

"Evidently thou wert not able to sleep in a new place?
My wife and I heard thee playing the song of last night."

"Yes? Did you hear it?" said Muzio. "I did play it, in
fact; but I had been asleep before that, and I had even had
a remarkable dream."

Valeria pricked up her ears.—"What sort of a dream?"
inquired Fabio.

"I seemed," replied Muzio, without taking his eyes from
Valeria, "to see myself enter a spacious apartment with a
vaulted ceiling, decorated in Oriental style. Carved pillars

supported the vault; the walls were covered with tiles, and although there were no windows nor candles, yet the whole room was filled with a rosy light, just as though it had all been built of transparent stone. In the corners Chinese incense-burners were smoking; on the floor lay cushions of brocade, along a narrow rug. I entered through a door hung with a curtain, and from another door directly opposite a woman whom I had once loved made her appearance. And she seemed to me so beautiful that I became all aflame with my love of days gone by . . ."

Muzio broke off significantly. Valeria sat motionless, only paling slowly . . . and her breathing grew more profound.

"Then," pursued Muzio, "I woke up and played that song."

"But who was the woman?" said Fabio.

"Who was she? The wife of an East Indian. I met her in the city of Delhi. . . . She is no longer among the living. She is dead."

"And her husband?" asked Fabio, without himself knowing why he did so.

"Her husband is dead also, they say. I soon lost sight of them."

"Strange!" remarked Fabio. "My wife also had a remarkable dream last night—which she did not relate to me," added Fabio.

But at this point Valeria rose and left the room. Immediately after breakfast Muzio also went away, asserting that he was obliged to go to Ferrara on business, and that he should not return before evening.

VI

Several weeks before Muzio's return Fabio had begun a portrait of his wife, depicting her with the attributes of Saint Cecilia. He had made noteworthy progress in his art; the famous Luini, the pupil of Leonardo da Vinci, had come to him in Ferrara, and aiding him with his own advice, had also imparted to him the precepts of his great master. The portrait was almost finished; it only remained for him to complete the face by a few strokes of the brush, and then Fabio might feel justly proud of his work.

When Muzio departed to Ferrara, Fabio betook himself to his studio, where Valeria was generally awaiting him; but he did not find her there; he called to her—she did not respond. A secret uneasiness took possession of Fabio; he set out in quest of her. She was not in the house; Fabio ran into the garden—and there, in one of the most remote alleys, he descried Valeria. With head bowed upon her breast, and hands clasped on her knees, she was sitting on a bench, and behind her, standing out against the dark green of a cypress, a marble satyr, with face distorted in a malicious smile, was applying his pointed lips to his reed-pipes. Valeria was visibly delighted at her husband's appearance, and in reply to his anxious queries she said that she had a slight headache, but that it was of no consequence, and that she was ready for the sitting. Fabio conducted her to his studio, posed her, and took up his brush; but, to his great vexation, he could not possibly finish the face as he would have liked. And that not because it was somewhat pale and seemed fatigued . . . no; but he did not find in it that day the pure, holy expression which he so greatly loved in it, and which had suggested to him the idea of representing Valeria in the form of Saint Cecilia. At last he flung aside his brush, told his wife that he was not in the mood, that it would do her good to lie down for a while, as she was not feeling quite well, to judge by her looks—and turned his easel so that the portrait faced the wall. Valeria agreed with him that she ought to rest, and repeating her complaint of headache, she retired to her chamber.

Fabio remained in the studio. He felt a strange agitation which was incomprehensible even to himself. Muzio's sojourn under his roof, a sojourn which he, Fabio, had himself invited, embarrassed him. And it was not that he was jealous . . . was it possible to be jealous of Valeria?—but in his friend he did not recognise his former comrade. All that foreign, strange, new element which Muzio had brought with him from those distant lands—and which, apparently, had entered into his very flesh and blood—all those magical processes, songs, strange beverages, that dumb Malay, even the spicy odour which emanated from Muzio's garments, from his hair, his breath—all this inspired in Fabio a feeling akin to distrust, nay, even to timidity. And why did that Malay, when serving at table, gaze upon him, Fabio, with such disagreeable intentness? Really, one might suppose that he understood Italian. Muzio had said concerning him, that that Malay, in paying the penalty with his tongue, had made a great sacrifice, and in compensation now possessed great power. What power? And how could he have acquired it at the cost of his tongue? All this was very strange! Very incomprehensible!

Fabio went to his wife in her chamber; she was lying on the bed fully dressed, but was not asleep. On hearing his footsteps she started, then rejoiced again to see him, as she had done in the garden. Fabio sat down by the bed, took Valeria's hand, and after a brief pause, he asked her, "What was that remarkable dream which had frightened her during the past night? And had it been in the nature of that dream which Muzio had related?"

Valeria blushed and said hastily—"Oh, no! no! I saw . . . some sort of a monster, which tried to rend me."

"A monster? In the form of a man?" inquired Fabio.

"No, a wild beast . . . a wild beast!" And Valeria turned away and hid her flaming face in the pillows. Fabio held his wife's hand for a while longer; silently he raised it to his lips, and withdrew.

The husband and wife passed a dreary day. It seemed as though something dark were hanging over their heads . . . but what it was they could not tell. They wanted to be

together, as though some danger were menacing them; but
what to say to each other they did not know. Fabio made
an effort to work at the portrait, to read Ariosto, whose
poem, which had recently made its appearance in Ferrara,
was already famous throughout Italy; but he could do
nothing. . . . Late in the evening, just in time for supper,
Muzio returned.

VII

He appeared calm and contented—but related few stories;
he chiefly interrogated Fabio concerning their mutual
acquaintances of former days, the German campaign, the
Emperor Charles; he spoke of his desire to go to Rome, to
have a look at the new Pope. Again he offered Valeria wine
of Shiraz—and in reply to her refusal he said, as though to
himself, "It is not necessary now."

On returning with his wife to their bedroom Fabio speedily
fell asleep . . . and waking an hour later was able to convince
himself that no one shared his couch: Valeria was not with
him. He hastily rose, and at the selfsame moment he beheld
his wife, in her night-dress, enter the room from the garden.
The moon was shining brightly, although not long before a
light shower had passed over.—With widely-opened eyes,
and an expression of secret terror on her impassive face,
Valeria approached the bed, and fumbling for it with her
hands, which were outstretched in front of her, she lay down
hurriedly and in silence. Fabio asked her a question, but
she made no reply; she seemed to be asleep. He touched
her, and felt rain-drops on her clothing, on her hair, and
grains of sand on the soles of her bare feet. Then he sprang
up and rushed into the garden through the half-open door.
The moonlight, brilliant to harshness, inundated all objects.
Fabio looked about him and descried on the sand of the
path traces of two pairs of feet; one pair was bare; and those
tracks led to an arbour covered with jasmine, which stood
apart, between the pavilion and the house. He stopped

short in perplexity; and lo! suddenly the notes of that song which he had heard on the preceding night again rang forth! Fabio shuddered, and rushed into the pavilion. . . . Muzio was standing in the middle of the room, playing on his violin. Fabio darted to him.

"Thou hast been in the garden, thou hast been out, thy clothing is damp with rain."

"No . . . I do not know . . . I do not think . . . that I have been out of doors . . ." replied Muzio, in broken accents, as though astonished at Fabio's advent, and at his agitation.

Fabio grasped him by the arm. "And why art thou playing that melody again? Hast thou had another dream?"

Muzio glanced at Fabio with the same surprise as before, and made no answer.

"Come, answer me!"

> The moon is steel, like a circular shield . . .
> The river gleams like a snake . . .
> The friend is awake, the enemy sleeps—
> The hawk seizes the chicken in his claws . . .
> Help!"

mumbled Muzio, in a singsong, as though in a state of unconsciousness.

Fabio retreated a couple of paces, fixed his eyes on Muzio, meditated for a space . . . and returned to his house, to the bed-chamber.

With her head inclined upon her shoulder, and her arms helplessly outstretched, Valeria was sleeping heavily. He did not speedily succeed in waking her . . . but as soon as she saw him she flung herself on his neck, and embraced him convulsively; her whole body was quivering.

"What aileth thee, my dear one, what aileth thee?" said Fabio repeatedly, striving to soothe her.

But she continued to lie as in a swoon on his breast. "Ah, what dreadful visions I see!" she whispered, pressing her face against him.

Fabio attempted to question her . . . but she merely trembled. . . .

The window-panes were reddening with the first gleams of dawn when, at last, she fell asleep in his arms.

VIII

On the following day Muzio disappeared early in the morning, and Valeria informed her husband that she intended to betake herself to the neighbouring monastery, where dwelt her spiritual father—an aged and stately monk, in whom she cherished unbounded confidence. To Fabio's questions she replied that she desired to alleviate by confession her soul, which was oppressed with the impressions of the last few days. As he gazed at Valeria's sunken visage, as he listened to her faint voice, Fabio himself approved of her plan: venerable Father Lorenzo might be able to give her useful advice, disperse her doubts. . . . Under the protection of four escorts, Valeria set out for the monastery, but Fabio remained at home; and while awaiting the return of his wife, he roamed about the garden, trying to understand what had happened to her, and feeling the unremitting terror and wrath and pain of indefinite suspicions. . . . More than once he entered the pavilion; but Muzio had not returned, and the Malay stared at Fabio like a statue, with an obsequious inclination of his head, and a far-away grin—at least, so it seemed to Fabio—a far-away grin on his bronze countenance.

In the meantime Valeria had narrated everything in confession to her confessor, being less ashamed than frightened. The confessor listened to her attentively, blessed her, absolved her from her involuntary sins, but thought to himself: "Magic, diabolical witchcraft . . . things cannot be left in this condition" . . . and accompanied Valeria to her villa, ostensibly for the purpose of definitely calming and comforting her.

At the sight of the confessor Fabio was somewhat startled; but the experienced old man had already thought out beforehand how he ought to proceed. On being left alone with Fabio, he did not, of course, betray the secrets of the confessional; but he advised him to banish from his house, if that were possible, his invited guest who, by his tales, songs, and his whole conduct, had upset Valeria's imagination. Moreover, in the old man's opinion, Muzio had not been firm in the faith in days gone by, as he now recalled to mind; and after having sojourned so long in regions not illuminated by the light of Christianity, he might have brought thence the infection of false doctrines; he might even have dabbled in magic; and therefore, although old friendship did assert its rights, still wise caution pointed to parting as indispensable.

Fabio thoroughly agreed with the venerable monk. Valeria even beamed all over when her husband communicated to her her confessor's counsel; and accompanied by the good wishes of both husband and wife, and provided with rich gifts for the monastery and the poor, Father Lorenzo wended his way home.

Fabio had intended to have an explanation with Muzio directly after supper, but his strange guest did not return to supper. Then Fabio decided to defer the interview with Muzio until the following day, and husband and wife withdrew to their bed-chamber.

IX

Valeria speedily fell asleep; but Fabio could not get to sleep. In the nocturnal silence all that he had seen, all that he had felt, presented itself to him in a still more vivid manner; with still greater persistence did he ask himself questions, to which, as before, he found no answer. Was Muzio really a magician? And had he already poisoned Valeria? She was ill . . . but with what malady? While he

was engrossed in painful meditations, with his head propped
on his hand and restraining his hot breathing, the moon
again rose in the cloudless sky; and together with its rays,
through the semi-transparent window-panes, in the direction of the pavilion, there began to stream in—or did Fabio
merely imagine it?—there began to stream in a breath
resembling a faint, perfumed current of air. . . . Now an
importunate, passionate whisper began to make itself heard
. . . and at that same moment he noticed that Valeria was
beginning to stir slightly. He started, gazed; she rose, thrust
first one foot, then the other from the bed, and, like a som-
nambulist, with her dull eyes strained straight ahead, and
her arms extended before her, she advanced toward the
door into the garden! Fabio instantly sprang through the
other door of the bedroom, and briskly running round
the corner of the house, he closed the one which led into the
garden. . . . He had barely succeeded in grasping the handle
when he felt someone trying to open the door from within,
throwing their force against it . . . more and more strongly
. . . then frightened moans resounded.

"But Muzio cannot have returned from the town, surely,"
flashed through Fabio's head, and he darted into the
pavilion. . . .
What did he behold?
Coming to meet him, along the path brilliantly flooded
with the radiance of the moonlight, also with arms outstretched and lifeless eyes staring widely—was Muzio. . . .
Fabio ran up to him, but the other, without noticing him,
walked on, advancing with measured steps, and his impassive
face was smiling in the moonlight like the face of the Malay.
Fabio tried to call him by name . . . but at that moment
he heard a window bang in the house behind him. . . .
He glanced round. . . .
In fact, the window of the bedroom was open from top to
bottom, and with one foot thrust across the sill stood Valeria

in the window . . . and her arms seemed to be seeking Muzio, her whole being was drawn toward him.

Unspeakable wrath flooded Fabio's breast in a suddenly-invading torrent.—"Accursed sorcerer!" he yelled fiercely, and seizing Muzio by the throat with one hand, he fumbled with the other for the dagger in his belt, and buried its blade to the hilt in his side.

Muzio uttered a piercing shriek, and pressing the palm of his hand to the wound, fled, stumbling, back to the pavilion. . . . But at that same instant when Fabio stabbed him, Valeria uttered an equally piercing shriek and fell to the ground like one mowed down.

Fabio rushed to her, raised her up, carried her to the bed, spoke to her. . . .

For a long time she lay motionless; but at last she opened her eyes, heaved a deep sigh, convulsively and joyously, like a person who has just been saved from inevitable death —caught sight of her husband and, encircling his neck with her arms, pressed herself to his breast.

"Thou, thou, it is thou," she stammered. Gradually the clasp of her arms relaxed, her head sank backward, and whispering, with a blissful smile—"Thank God, all is over . . . But how weary I am!"—she fell into a profound but not heavy slumber.

X

Fabio sank down beside her bed, and never taking his eyes from her pale, emaciated, but already tranquil face, he began to reflect upon what had taken place . . . and also upon how he ought to proceed now. What was he to do? If he had slain Muzio—and when he recalled how deeply the blade of his dagger had penetrated he could not doubt that he had done so—then it was impossible to conceal the fact. He must bring it to the knowledge of the Duke, of the judges . . . but how was he to explain, how was he to narrate such an incomprehensible affair? He, Fabio, had

slain in his own house his relative, his best friend! People
would ask, "What for? For what cause? . . ." But what if
Muzio were not slain?—Fabio had not the strength to remain any longer in uncertainty, and having made sure that
Valeria was asleep, he cautiously rose from his arm-chair,
left the house, and directed his steps toward the pavilion.
All was silent in it; only in one window was a light visible.
With sinking heart he opened the outer door (a trace of
bloody fingers still clung to it, and on the sand of the path
drops of blood made black patches), traversed the first dark
chamber . . . and halted on the threshold, petrified with
astonishment.

In the centre of the room, on a Persian rug, with a brocade
cushion under his head, covered with a wide scarlet shawl
with black figures, lay Muzio, with all his limbs stiffly extended. His face, yellow as wax, with closed eyes and lids
which had become blue, was turned toward the ceiling, and
no breath was to be detected: he seemed to be dead. At his
feet, also enveloped in a scarlet shawl, knelt the Malay. He
held in his left hand a branch of some unfamiliar plant,
resembling a fern, and bending slightly forward, he was
gazing at his master, never taking his eyes from him. A
small torch, thrust into the floor, burned with a greenish
flame, and was the only light in the room. Its flame did not
flicker nor smoke.

The Malay did not stir at Fabio's entrance, but merely
darted a glance at him and turned his eyes again upon
Muzio. From time to time he raised himself a little, and
lowered the branch, waving it through the air—and his
dumb lips slowly parted and moved, as though uttering
inaudible words. Between Muzio and the Malay there lay
upon the floor the dagger with which Fabio had stabbed his
friend. The Malay smote the blood-stained blade with his
bough. One minute passed . . . then another. Fabio approached the Malay, and bending toward him, he said in a
low voice: "Is he dead?" The Malay bowed his head, and

disengaging his right hand from beneath the shawl, pointed imperiously to the door. Fabio was about to repeat his question, but the imperious hand repeated its gesture, and Fabio left the room, raging and marvelling but submitting.

He found Valeria asleep, as before, with a still more tranquil face. He did not undress, but seated himself by the window, propped his head on his hand, and again became immersed in thought. The rising sun found him still in the same place. Valeria had not wakened.

XI

Fabio was intending to wait until she should awake, and then go to Ferrara—when suddenly someone tapped lightly at the door of the bedroom. Fabio went out and beheld before him his aged major-domo, Antonio.

"Signor," began the old man, "the Malay has just informed us that Signor Muzio is ailing and desires to remove with all his effects to the town; and therefore he requests that you will furnish him with the aid of some persons to pack his things—and that you will send, about dinner-time, both pack- and saddle-horses and a few men as guard. Do you permit?"

"Did the Malay tell thee that?" inquired Fabio. "In what manner? For he is dumb."

"Here, signor, is a paper on which he wrote all this in our language, very correctly."

"And Muzio is ill, sayest thou?"

"Yes, very ill, and he cannot be seen."

"Has not a physician been sent for?"

"No; the Malay would not allow it."

"And was it the Malay who wrote this for thee?"

"Yes, it was he."

Fabio was silent for a space.

"Very well, take the necessary measures," he said at last.

Antonio withdrew.

Fabio stared after his servant in perplexity.—"So he was not killed?" he thought . . . and he did not know whether to rejoice or to grieve. "He is ill?" But a few hours ago he had beheld him a corpse!

Fabio returned to Valeria. She was awake, and raised her head. The husband and wife exchanged a long, significant look.

"Is he already dead?" said Valeria suddenly.

Fabio shuddered.

"What . . . he is not?—Didst thou. . . . Has he gone away?" she went on.

Fabio's heart was relieved. "Not yet; but he is going away to-day."

"And I shall never, never see him again?"

"Never."

"And those visions will not be repeated?"

"No."

Valeria heaved another sigh of relief; a blissful smile again made its appearance on her lips. She put out both hands to her husband.

"And we shall never speak of him, never, hearest thou, my dear one. And I shall not leave this room until he is gone. But now do thou send me my serving-women . . . and stay: take that thing!"—she pointed to a pearl necklace which lay on the night-stand, the necklace which Muzio had given her—"and throw it immediately into our deep well. Embrace me—I am thy Valeria—and do not come to me until . . . that man is gone."

Fabio took the necklace—its pearls seemed to have grown dim—and fulfilled his wife's behest. Then he began to roam about the garden, gazing from a distance at the pavilion, around which the bustle of packing was already beginning. Men were carrying out chests, lading horses . . . but the Malay was not among them. An irresistible feeling drew Fabio to gaze once more on what was going on in the pavilion. He recalled the fact that in its rear façade there was a secret door through which one might penetrate to the interior of the chamber where Muzio had been lying that morning. He stole up to that door, found it unlocked, and pushing aside the folds of a heavy curtain, darted in an irresolute glance.

XII

Muzio was no longer lying on the rug. Dressed in travelling attire, he was sitting in an arm-chair, but appeared as much of a corpse as at Fabio's first visit. The petrified head had fallen against the back of the chair, the hands lay flat, motionless, and yellow on the knees. His breast did not heave. Round about the chair, on the floor strewn with dried herbs, stood several flat cups filled with a dark liquid which gave off a strong, almost suffocating odour—the odour of musk. Around each cup was coiled a small, copper-coloured serpent, which gleamed here and there with golden spots; and directly in front of Muzio, a couple of paces distant from him, rose up the tall figure of the Malay, clothed in a motley-hued mantle of brocade, girt about with a tiger's tail, with a tall cap in the form of a horned tiara on his head.

But he was not motionless: now he made devout obeisances and seemed to be praying, again he drew himself up to his full height, even stood on tiptoe; now he threw his hands apart in broad and measured sweep, now he waved them urgently in the direction of Muzio, and seemed to be menacing or commanding with them, as he contracted his brows in a frown and stamped his foot. All these movements evidently cost him great effort, and even caused him suffering: he breathed heavily, the sweat streamed from his face. Suddenly he stood stock-still on one spot, and inhaling the air into his lungs and scowling, he stretched forward, then drew toward him his clenched fists, as though he were holding reins in them . . . and to Fabio's indescribable horror,

Muzio's head slowly separated itself from the back of the chair and reached out after the Malay's hands. . . . The Malay dropped his hands, and Muzio's head again sank heavily backward; the Malay repeated his gestures, and the obedient head repeated them after him. The dark liquid in the cups began to seethe with a faint sound; the very cups themselves emitted a faint tinkling, and the copper snakes began to move around each of them in undulating motion. Then the Malay advanced a pace, and elevating his eyebrows very high and opening his eyes until they were of huge size, he nodded his head at Muzio . . . and the eyelids of the corpse began to flutter, parted unevenly, and from beneath them the pupils, dull as lead, revealed themselves. With proud triumph and joy—a joy that was almost malicious —beamed the face of the Malay; he opened his lips widely, and from the very depths of his throat a prolonged roar wrested itself with an effort. . . . Muzio's lips parted also, and a faint groan trembled on them in reply to that inhuman sound.

But at this point Fabio could endure it no longer: he fancied that he was witnessing some devilish incantations! He also uttered a shriek and started off at a run homeward, without looking behind him—homeward as fast as he could go, praying and crossing himself as he ran.

XIII

Three hours later Antonio presented himself before him with the report that everything was ready, all the things were packed, and Signor Muzio was preparing to depart. Without uttering a word in answer to his servant, Fabio stepped out on the terrace, whence the pavilion was visible. Several pack-horses were grouped in front of it; at the porch itself a powerful black stallion, with a roomy saddle adapted for two riders, was drawn up. There also stood the servants with bared heads and the armed escort. The door of the pavilion opened and, supported by the Malay, Muzio made his appearance. His face was deathlike, and his arms hung down like those of a corpse—but he walked . . . yes! he put one foot before the other, and once mounted on the horse, he held himself upright, and got hold of the reins by fumbling. The Malay thrust his feet into the stirrups, sprang up behind him on the saddle, encircled his waist with his arm, and the whole procession set out. The horses proceeded at a walk, and when they made the turn in front of the house, Fabio fancied that on Muzio's dark countenance two small white patches gleamed. . . . Could it be that he had turned his eyes that way? The Malay alone saluted him . . . mockingly, but as usual.

Did Valeria see all this? The shutters of her windows were closed . . . but perhaps she was standing behind them.

XIV

At dinner-time she entered the dining-room, and was very quiet and affectionate; but she still complained of being weary. Yet there was no agitation about her, nor any of her former constant surprise and secret fear; and when, on the day after Muzio's departure, Fabio again set about her portrait, he found in her features that pure expression, the temporary eclipse of which had so disturbed him . . . and his brush flew lightly and confidently over the canvas.

Husband and wife began to live their life as of yore. Muzio had vanished for them as though he had never existed. And both Fabio and Valeria seemed to have entered into a compact not to recall him by a single sound, not to inquire about his further fate; and it remained a mystery for all others as well. Muzio really did vanish, as though he had sunk through the earth. One day Fabio thought himself bound to relate to Valeria precisely what had occurred on that fateful night . . . but she, probably divining his intention, held her breath, and her eyes narrowed as though she was anticipating a blow. . . . And Fabio understood her: he did not deal her that blow.

One fine autumnal day Fabio was putting the finishing touches to the picture of his Cecilia; Valeria was sitting at the organ, and her fingers were wandering over the keys. . . . Suddenly, contrary to her own volition, from beneath her fingers rang out that Song of Love Triumphant which Muzio had once played—and at that same instant, for the first time since her marriage, she felt within her the palpitation of a new, germinating life. . . . Valeria started and stopped short. . . .

What was the meaning of this? Could it be. . . .

With this word the manuscript came to an end.

(II)

THE DREAM

(Translated by ISABEL F. HAPGOOD)

I

I w A s living with my mother at the time, in a small seaport town. I was just turned seventeen, and my mother was only thirty-five; she had married very young. When my father died I was only seven years old; but I remembered him well. My mother was a short, fair-haired woman, with a charming, but permanently sad face, a quiet, languid voice, and timid movements. In her youth she had borne the reputation of a beauty, and as long as she lived she remained attractive and pretty. I have never beheld more profound, tender and melancholy eyes. I adored her, and she loved me. . . . But our life was not cheerful; it seemed as though some mysterious, incurable and undeserved sorrow were constantly sapping the root of her existence. This sorrow could not be explained by grief for my father alone, great as that was, passionately as my mother had loved him, sacredly as she cherished his memory. . . . No! there was something else hidden there which I did not understand, but which I felt—felt confusedly and strongly as soon as I looked at those quiet, impassive eyes, at those very beautiful but also impassive lips, which were not bitterly compressed, but seemed to have congealed for good and all.

I have said that my mother loved me; but there were moments when she spurned me, when my presence was burdensome, intolerable to her. At such times she felt, as it were, an involuntary aversion for me—and was terrified afterward, reproaching herself with tears and clasping me to her heart. I attributed these momentary fits of hostility to her shattered health, to her unhappiness. . . . These hostile sentiments might have been evoked, it is true, in a certain measure, by some strange outbursts, which were incomprehensible even to me myself, of wicked and criminal feelings which occasionally arose in me. . . .

But these outbursts did not coincide with the moments of repulsion. My mother constantly wore black, as though she were in mourning. We lived on a rather grand scale, although we associated with no one.

II

My mother concentrated upon me all her thoughts and cares. Her life was merged in my life. Such relations between parents and children are not always good for the children . . . they are more apt to be injurious. Moreover, I was my mother's only child . . . and only children generally develop irregularly. In rearing them the parents do not think of themselves so much as they do of them. . . . That is not practical. I did not get spoiled, and did not grow obstinate (both these things happen with only children), but my nerves were unstrung before their time; in addition to which I was of rather feeble health—I took after my mother, to whom I also bore a great facial resemblance. I shunned the society of lads of my own age; in general, I was shy of people; I even talked very little with my mother. I was fonder of reading than of anything else, and of walking alone—and dreaming, dreaming! What my dreams were about it would be difficult to say. It sometimes seemed to me as though I were standing before a half-open door behind which were concealed hidden secrets—standing and waiting, and swooning with longing—yet not crossing the threshold; and always meditating as to what there was yonder ahead of me—and always waiting and longing . . . or falling into slumber. If the poetic vein had throbbed in me I should, in all probability, have taken to writing verses; if I had felt an inclination to religious devoutness I might have become a monk; but there was nothing of the sort about me, and I continued to dream—and to wait.

III

I have just mentioned that I sometimes fell asleep under the inspiration of obscure thoughts and reveries. On the whole, I slept a great deal, and dreams played a prominent part in my life; I beheld visions almost every night. I did not forget them, I attributed to them significance, I regarded them as prophetic, I strove to divine their secret import. Some of them were repeated from time to time, which always seemed to me wonderful and strange. I was particularly perturbed by one dream. It seems to me that I am walking along a narrow, badly-paved street in an ancient town, between many-storied houses of stone, with sharp-pointed roofs. I am seeking my father, who is not dead, but is, for some reason, hiding from us, and is living in one of those houses. And so I enter a low, dark gate, traverse a long courtyard encumbered with beams and planks, and finally make my way into a small chamber with two circular windows. In the middle of the room stands my father, clad in a dressing-gown and smoking a pipe. He does not in the least resemble my real father: he is tall, thin, black-haired, he has a hooked nose, surly, piercing eyes; in appearance he is about forty years of age. He is displeased because I have hunted him up; and I also am not in the least delighted at the meeting—and I stand still, in perplexity. He turns away slightly, begins to mutter something and to pace to and fro with short steps. . . . Then he retreats a little, without ceasing to mutter, and keeps constantly casting glances behind him, over his shoulder; the room widens out and vanishes in a fog. . . . I suddenly grow terrified at the thought that I am losing my father again. I rush after him—but I no longer see him, and can only hear his angry, bear-like growl. . . . My heart sinks within me. I wake up, and for a long time cannot get to sleep again. . . . All the following day I think about that dream and, of course, am unable to arrive at any conclusion.

IV

The month of June had come. The town in which my mother and I lived became remarkably animated at that season. A multitude of vessels arrived at the wharves, a multitude of new faces presented themselves on the streets. I loved at such times to stroll along the quay, past the coffee-houses and inns, to scan the varied faces of the sailors and other people who sat under the canvas awnings, at little white tables with pewter tankards filled with beer.

One day, as I was passing in front of a coffee-house, I caught sight of a man who immediately engrossed my entire attention. Clad in a long black coat of peasant cut, with a straw hat pulled down over his eyes, he was sitting motion-less, with his arms folded on his chest. Thin rings of black hair descended to his very nose; his thin lips gripped the stem of a short pipe. This man seemed so familiar to me, every feature of his swarthy, yellow face, his whole figure, were so indubitably stamped on my memory, that I could not do otherwise than halt before him, could not help putting to myself the question: "Who is this man? Where have I seen him?" He probably felt my intent stare, for he turned his black, piercing eyes upon me. . . . I involuntarily uttered a cry of surprise. . . .

This man was the father whom I had sought out, whom I had beheld in my dream!

There was no possibility of making a mistake—the resemblance was too striking. Even the long-skirted coat, which enveloped his gaunt limbs, reminded me, in colour and form, of the dressing-gown in which my father had presented himself to me.

"Am not I dreaming?" I thought to myself. . . . "No. . . . It is daylight now, a crowd is roaring round me, the sun is shining brightly in the blue sky, and I have before me, not a phantom, but a living man."

I stepped up to an empty table, ordered myself a tankard of beer and a newspaper, and seated myself at a short distance from this mysterious being.

V

Placing the sheets of the newspaper on a level with my face, I continued to devour the stranger with my eyes. He hardly stirred, and only raised his drooping head a little from time to time. He was evidently waiting for someone. I gazed and gazed. . . . Sometimes it seemed to me that I had invented the whole thing, that in reality there was no resemblance whatever, that I had yielded to the semi-involuntary deception of the imagination . . . but "he" would suddenly turn a little on his chair, raise his hand slightly, and again I almost cried aloud, again I beheld before me my "nocturnal" father! At last he noticed my importunate attention, and, first with surprise, then with vexation, he glanced in my direction, started to rise, and knocked down a small cane which he had leaned against the table. I instantly sprang to my feet, picked it up and handed it to him. My heart was beating violently.

He smiled in a constrained way, thanked me, and putting his face close to my face, he elevated his eyebrows and parted his lips a little, as though something had struck him.

"You are very polite, young man," he suddenly began, in a dry, sharp, snuffling voice. "That is a rarity nowadays. Allow me to congratulate you. You have been well brought up."

I do not remember precisely what answer I made to him; but the conversation between us was started. I learned that he was a fellow-countryman of mine, that he had recently returned from America, where he had lived many years, and whither he was intending to return shortly. He said his name was Baron . . . I did not catch the name well. He, like my "nocturnal" father, wound up each of his remarks with an indistinct, inward growl. He wanted to know my name. . . . On hearing it he again showed signs of surprise. Then he asked me if I had been living long in that town, and with whom? I answered him that I lived with my mother.

"And your father?"

"My father died long ago."

He inquired my mother's Christian name, and immediately burst into an awkward laugh—and then excused himself, saying that he had that American habit, and that altogether he was a good deal of an eccentric. Then he asked where we lived. I told him.

VI

The agitation which had seized upon me at the beginning of our conversation had gradually subsided; I thought our intimacy rather strange—that was all. I did not like the smile with which the baron questioned me; neither did I like the expression of his eyes when he fairly stabbed them into me. . . . There was about them something rapacious and condescending . . . something which inspired dread. I had not seen those eyes in my dream. The baron had a strange face! It was pallid, fatigued and, at the same time, youthful in appearance, but with a disagreeable youthfulness! Neither had my "nocturnal" father that deep scar, which intersected his whole forehead in a slanting direction, and which I did not notice until I moved closer to him.

Before I had had time to impart to the baron the name of the street and the number of the house where we lived, a tall negro, wrapped up in a cloak to his very eyes, approached him from behind and tapped him softly on the shoulder. The baron turned round, said: "Aha! At last!" and nodding lightly to me, entered the coffee-house with the negro. I remained under the awning. I wished to wait until the baron should come out again, not so much for the sake of entering again into conversation with him (I really did not know what topic I could start with), as for the purpose of again verifying my first impression.—But half an hour passed; an hour passed. . . . The baron did not make his appearance. I entered the coffee-house, I made the circuit of all the rooms—but nowhere did I see either the baron or the negro. . . . Both of them must have taken their departure through the back door.

My head had begun to ache a little, and with the object of refreshing myself I set out along the seashore to the extensive park outside the town, which had been laid out ten years previously. After having strolled for a couple of hours in the shade of the huge oaks and plantain trees, I returned home.

VII

Our maid-servant flew to meet me, all tremulous with agitation, as soon as I made my appearance in the ante-room. I immediately divined, from the expression of her face, that something unpleasant had occurred in our house during my absence. And, in fact, I learned that half an hour before a frightful shriek had rung out from my mother's bedroom. When the maid rushed in she found her on the floor in a swoon which lasted for several minutes. My mother had recovered consciousness at last, but had been obliged to go to bed, and wore a strange, frightened aspect; she had not uttered a word, she had not replied to questions —she had done nothing but glance around her and tremble. The servant had sent the gardener for a doctor. The doctor had come and had prescribed a soothing potion, but my mother had refused to say anything to him either. The gardener asserted that a few moments after the shriek had rung out from my mother's room he had seen a strange man run hastily across the flower-plots of the garden to the street gate. (We lived in a one-story house, whose windows looked out upon a fairly large garden.) The gardener had not been able to get a good look at the man's face; but the latter was gaunt, and wore a straw hat and a long-skirted coat. . . . "The baron's costume!" immediately flashed into my head. The gardener had been unable to overtake him; moreover, he had been summoned, without delay, to the house and despatched for the doctor.

I went to my mother's room; she was lying in bed, whiter than the pillow on which her head rested. . . . At sight of me she smiled faintly and put out her hand to me. I sat down by her side, and began to question her; at first she persistently parried my questions; but at last she confessed that she had seen something which had frightened her greatly.

"Did someone enter here?" I asked.

"No," she answered hastily, "no one entered, but it seemed to me . . . I thought I saw . . . a vision. . . ."

She ceased speaking and covered her eyes with her hand. I was on the point of communicating to her what I had heard from the gardener—and my meeting with the baron also, by the way . . . but, for some reason or other, the words died on my lips.

Nevertheless I did bring myself to remark to my mother that visions do not manifest themselves in the daylight. . . .

"Stop," she whispered, "please stop; do not torture me now. Some day thou shalt know. . . ." Again she relapsed into silence. Her hands were cold, and her pulse beat fast and unevenly. I gave her a dose of her medicine and stepped a little to one side, in order not to disturb her.

She did not rise all day. She lay motionless and quiet, only sighing deeply from time to time, and opening her eyes in a timorous fashion.—Everyone in the house was perplexed.

VIII

Toward night a slight fever made its appearance, and my mother sent me away. I did not go to my own chamber, however, but lay down in the adjoining room on the divan. Every quarter of an hour I rose, approached the door on tiptoe, and listened. . . . Everything remained silent—but my mother hardly slept at all that night. When I went into her room early in the morning her face appeared to me to be swollen, and her eyes were shining with an unnatural brilliancy. In the course of the day she became a little easier, but toward evening the fever increased again.

Up to that time she had maintained an obstinate silence, but now she suddenly began to talk in a hurried, spasmodic voice. She was not delirious, there was sense in her words, but there was no coherency in them. Not long before midnight she raised herself up in bed with a convulsive movement (I was sitting beside her), and with the same hurried voice she began to narrate to me, continually drinking water in gulps from a glass, feebly flourishing her hands, and not once looking at me the while. . . . At times she paused, exerted an effort over herself, and went on again. . . . All this was strange, as though she were doing it in her sleep, as though she herself were not present, but as though some other person were speaking with her lips, or making her speak.

IX

"Listen to what I have to tell thee," she began. "Thou art no longer a young boy; thou must know all. I had a good friend. . . . She married a man whom she loved with all her heart, and she was happy with her husband. But during the first year of their married life they both went to the capital to spend a few weeks and enjoy themselves. They stopped at a good hotel and went out a great deal to theatres and assemblies. My friend was very far from homely; everyone noticed her, all the young men paid court to her; but among them was one in particular . . . an officer. He followed her unremittingly, and wherever she went she beheld his black, wicked eyes. He did not make her acquaintance, and did not speak to her even once; he merely kept staring at her in a very strange, insolent way. All the pleasures of the capital were poisoned by his presence. She began to urge her husband to depart as speedily as possible, and they had fully made up their minds to the journey. One day her husband went off to the club; some officers—officers who belonged to the same regiment as this man—had invited him to play cards. . . . For the first time she was left alone. Her husband did not return for a long time; she dismissed her maid and went to bed. . . . And suddenly a great dread came upon her, so that she even turned cold all over and began to tremble. It seemed to her that she heard a faint tapping on the other side of the wall—like the noise a dog makes when scratching—and she began to stare at that wall.

In the corner burned a shrine-lamp; the chamber was all
hung with silken stuff. . . . Suddenly something began to
move at that point, rose, opened. . . . And straight out of
the wall, all black and long, stepped forth that dreadful
man with the wicked eyes!

"She tried to scream and could not. She was benumbed
with fright. He advanced briskly toward her, like a rapacious
wild beast, flung something over her head, something stifling,
heavy and white. . . . What happened afterward I do not
remember. . . . I do not remember! It was like death, like
murder. . . . When that terrible fog dispersed at last—when
I . . . my friend recovered her senses, there was no one in
the room. Again—and for a long time—she was incapable
of crying out, but she did shriek at last . . . then again everything grew confused. . . .

"Then she beheld by her side her husband, who had been
detained at the club until two o'clock. . . . His face was distorted beyond recognition. He began to question her, but
she said nothing. . . . Then she fell ill. . . . But I remember
that when she was left alone in the room she examined that
place in the wall. . . . Under the silken hangings there proved
to be a secret door. And her wedding-ring had disappeared
from her hand. This ring was of an unusual shape. Upon
it seven tiny golden stars alternated with seven tiny silver
stars; it was an ancient family heirloom. Her husband
asked her what had become of her ring; she could make no
reply. Her husband thought that she had dropped it somewhere, hunted everywhere for it, but nowhere could he find
it. Gloom descended upon him, he decided to return home
as speedily as possible, and as soon as the doctor permitted
they quitted the capital. . . . But imagine! On the very day
of their departure they suddenly encountered, on the street,
a litter. . . . In that litter lay a man who had just been killed
with a cleft skull!—and just imagine! that man was that
same dreadful nocturnal visitor with the wicked eyes. . . .
He had been killed over a game of cards!

"Then my friend went away to the country, and became a mother for the first time . . . and lived several years with her husband. He never learned anything about that matter, and what could she say? She herself knew nothing. But her former happiness had vanished. Darkness had invaded their life—and that darkness was never dispelled. . . . They had no other children either before or after . . . but that son. . . ."

My mother began to tremble all over, and covered her face with her hands.

"But tell me now," she went on, with redoubled force, "whether my friend was in any way to blame? With what could she reproach herself? She was punished, but had not she the right to declare, in the presence of God Himself, that the punishment which overtook her was unjust? Then why can the past present itself to her, after the lapse of so many years, in so frightful an aspect, as though she were a sinner tortured by the gnawings of conscience? Macbeth slew Banquo, so it is not to be wondered at that he should have visions . . . but I . . ."

But my mother's speech became so entangled and confused that I ceased to understand her. . . . I no longer had any doubt that she was raving in delirium.

X

Anyone can easily understand what a shattering effect my mother's narration produced upon me! I had divined, at her very first word, that she was speaking of herself, and not of any acquaintance of hers; her slip of the tongue only confirmed me in my surmise. So it really was my father whom I had sought out in my dream, whom I had beheld when wide awake! He had not been killed, as my mother had supposed, but merely wounded. . . . And he had come to her, and had fled, affrighted by her fright. Everything suddenly became clear to me; the feeling of involuntary repugnance for me which sometimes awoke in my mother,. and her constant sadness, and our isolated life. . . . I remember that my head reeled, and I clutched at it with both hands, as though desirous of holding it firmly in its place. But one thought had become riveted in it like a nail. I made up my mind, without fail, at any cost, to find that man again! Why? With what object?—I did not account to myself for that; but to find him . . . to find him—that had become for me a question of life or death!

On the following morning my mother regained her composure at last . . . the fever passed off . . . she fell asleep. Committing her to the care of our landlord and landlady and the servants, I set out on my quest.

XI

First of all, as a matter of course, I betook myself to the coffee-house where I had met the baron; but in the coffee-house no one knew him or had even noticed him: he was a chance visitor. The proprietors had noticed the negro—his figure had been too striking to escape notice; but who he was, where he stayed, no one knew either. Leaving my address, in case of an emergency, at the coffee-house, I began to walk about the streets and the water-front of the town, the wharves, the boulevards; I looked into all the public institutions, and nowhere did I find anyone who resembled either the baron or his companion. . . . As I had not caught the baron's name, I was deprived of the possibility of appealing to the police; but I privately gave two or three guardians of public order to understand (they gazed at me in surprise, it is true, and did not entirely believe me) that I would lavishly reward their zeal if they should be successful in coming upon the traces of those two individuals, whose personal appearance I tried to describe as minutely as possible.

Having strolled about in this manner until dinner-time, I

returned home thoroughly worn out. My mother had got out of bed; but with her habitual melancholy there was mingled a new element, a sort of pensive perplexity, which cut me to the heart like a knife. I sat with her all the evening. We said hardly anything; she laid out her game of patience, I silently looked at her cards. She did not refer by a single word to her story, or to what had happened the day before. It was as though we had both entered into a compact not to touch upon those strange and terrifying occurrences. . . . . She appeared to be vexed with herself and ashamed of what had involuntarily burst from her; but perhaps she did not remember very clearly what she had said in her semi-fevered delirium, and hoped that I would spare her. . . . And, in fact, I did spare her, and she was conscious of it; as on the preceding day she avoided meeting my eyes.

A frightful storm had suddenly sprung up out of doors. The wind howled and tore in wild gusts, the window-panes rattled and quivered; despairing shrieks and groans were borne through the air, as though something on high had broken loose and were flying with mad weeping over the shaking houses. Just before dawn I lost myself in a doze . . . when suddenly it seemed to me as though someone had entered my room and called me, had uttered my name, not in a loud, but in a decided voice. I raised my head and saw no one; but, strange to relate! I not only was not frightened —I was delighted; there suddenly arose within me the conviction that now I should, without fail, attain my end. I hastily dressed myself and left the house.

XII

The storm had subsided . . . but its last flutterings could still be felt. It was early; there were no people in the streets; in many places fragments of chimneys, tiles, boards of fences which had been rent asunder, the broken boughs of trees, lay strewn upon the ground. . . . "What happened at sea last night?" I involuntarily thought at the sight of the traces left behind by the storm. I started to go to the port, but my feet bore me in another direction, as though in obedience to an irresistible attraction. Before ten minutes had passed I found myself in a quarter of the town which I had never yet visited. I was walking, not fast, but without stopping, step by step, with a strange sensation at my heart; I was expecting something remarkable, impossible, and, at the same time, I was convinced that that impossible thing would come to pass.

XIII

And lo, it came to pass, that remarkable, that unexpected thing! Twenty paces in front of me I suddenly beheld that same negro who had spoken to the baron in my presence at the coffee-house! Enveloped in the same cloak which I had then noticed on him, he seemed to have popped up out of the earth, and with his back turned toward me was walking with brisk strides along the narrow pavement of the crooked alley! I immediately dashed in pursuit of him, but he re-doubled his gait, although he did not glance behind him, and suddenly made an abrupt turn around the corner of a projecting house. I rushed to that corner and turned it as quickly as the negro had done. . . . Marvellous to relate! Before me stretched a long, narrow, and perfectly empty street; the morning mist filled it with its dim, leaden light—but my gaze penetrated to its very extremity. I could count all its buildings . . . and not a single living being was anywhere astir! The tall negro in the cloak had vanished as suddenly as he had appeared! I was amazed . . . but only for a moment. Another feeling immediately took pos-session of me; that street which stretched out before my eyes, all dumb and dead, as it were—I recognised it! It was the street of my dream. I trembled and shivered—the morning was so chilly—and instantly, without the slightest wavering, with a certain terror of confidence, I went onward.

I began to seek with my eyes. . . . Yes, there it is, yonder, on the right, with a corner projecting on the pavement— yonder is the house of my dream, yonder is the ancient gate with the stone scrolls on each side. . . . The house is not circular, it is true, but square . . . but that is a matter of no importance. . . . I knock at the gate, I knock once, twice, thrice, ever more and more loudly. . . . The gate opens slowly, with a heavy screech, as though yawning. In front of me stands a young serving-maid with a dishevelled head and sleepy eyes. She has evidently just waked up.

"Does the baron live here?" I inquire, as I run a swift glance over the deep, narrow courtyard. . . . It is there; it is all there . . . there are the planks which I had seen in my dream.

"No," the maid answers me, "the baron does not live here."

"What dost thou mean by that? It is impossible!"

"He is not here now. He went away yesterday."

"Whither?"

"To America."

"To America!" I involuntarily repeated. "But he is coming back?"

The maid looked suspiciously at me.

"I don't know. Perhaps he will not come back at all."

"But has he been living here long?"

"No, not long; about a week. Now he is not here at all."

"But what was the family name of that baron?"

The maid-servant stared at me.

"Don't you know his name? We simply called him the baron. Hey, there! Piótr!" she cried, perceiving that I was pushing my way in—"come hither: some stranger or other is asking all sorts of questions."

From the house there presented itself the shambling figure of a robust labourer.

"What's the matter? What's wanted?" he inquired in a hoarse voice—and having listened to me with a surly mien, he repeated what the maid-servant had said.

"But who does live here?" I said.

"Our master."

"And who is he?"

"A carpenter. They are all carpenters in this street."

"Can he be seen?"

"Impossible now, he is asleep."

"And cannot I go into the house?"

"No; go your way."

"Well, and can I see your master a little later?"

"Why not? Certainly. He can always be seen. . . . That's his business as a dealer. Only, go your way now. See how early it is."

"Well, and how about that negro?" I suddenly asked.

The labourer stared in amazement, first at me, than at the maid-servant.

"What negro?" he said at last. "Go away, sir. You can come back later. Talk with the master."

I went out into the street. The gate was instantly banged behind me, heavily and sharply, without squeaking this time.

I took good note of the street and house and went away, but not home. I felt something in the nature of disenchantment. Everything which had happened to me was so strange, so remarkable—and yet, how stupidly it had been ended! I had been convinced that I should behold in that house the room which was familiar to me—and in the middle of it my father, the baron, in a dressing-gown and with a pipe. . . . And instead of that, the master of the house was a carpenter, and one might visit him as much as one pleased —and order furniture of him if one wished!

But my father had gone to America! And what was left for me to do now? . . . Tell my mother everything, or conceal for ever the very memory of that meeting? I was absolutely unable to reconcile myself to the thought that such a

senseless, such a commonplace ending should be tacked on
to such a supernatural, mysterious beginning!

I did not wish to return home, and walked straight ahead,
following my nose, out of the town.

XIV

I walked along with drooping head, without a thought,
almost without sensation, but wholly engrossed in myself.
A measured, dull and angry roar drew me out of my torpor.
I raised my head: it was the sea roaring and booming fifty
paces from me. Greatly agitated by the nocturnal storm, the
sea was a mass of white-caps to the very horizon, and steep
crests of long breakers were rolling in regularly and breaking
on the flat shore. I approached it, and walked along the
very line left by the ebb and flow on the yellow, ribbed
sand, strewn with fragments of trailing seawrack, bits of
shells, serpent-like ribbons of eel-grass. Sharp-winged gulls
with pitiful cry, borne on the wind from the distant aerial
depths, soared white as snow against the grey, cloudy sky,
swooped down abruptly, and as though skipping from wave
to wave, departed again and vanished like silvery flecks in
the strips of swirling foam. Some of them, I noticed, circled
persistently around a large isolated boulder which rose
aloft in the midst of the monotonous expanse of sandy shores.
Coarse seaweed grew in uneven tufts on one side of the
rock; and at the point where its tangled stems emerged from
the yellow salt-marsh, there was something black, and long,
and arched, and not very large. . . . I began to look intently.
. . . Some dark object was lying there—lying motionless
beside the stone. . . . That object became constantly clearer
and more distinct the nearer I approached. . . .

I was only thirty paces from the rock now. . . .

Why, that was the outline of a human body! It was a
corpse; it was a drowned man, cast up by the sea! I went
clear up to the rock.

It was the corpse of the baron, my father! I stopped short, as though rooted to the spot. Then only did I understand that ever since daybreak I had been guided by some unknown forces—that I was in their power—and for the space of several minutes there was nothing in my soul save the ceaseless crashing of the sea, and a dumb terror in the presence of the Fate which held me in its grip. . . .

XV

He was lying on his back, bent a little to one side, with his left arm thrown above his head . . . the right was turned under his bent body. The sticky slime had sucked in the tips of his feet, shod in tall sailor's boots; the short blue pea-jacket, all impregnated with sea-salt, had not unbuttoned; a red scarf encircled his neck in a hard knot. The swarthy face, turned skyward, seemed to be laughing; from beneath the upturned upper lip small close-set teeth were visible; the dim pupils of the half-closed eyes were hardly to be distinguished from the darkened whites; covered with bubbles of foam, the dirt-encrusted hair spread out over the ground and laid bare the smooth forehead with the purplish line of the scar; the narrow nose rose up like a sharp, white streak between the sunken cheeks. The storm of the past night had done its work. . . . He had not beheld America! The man who had insulted my mother, who had marred her life, my father—yes! my father, I could cherish no doubt as to that—lay stretched out helpless in the mud at my feet. I experienced a sense of satisfied vengeance, and compassion, and repulsion, and terror most of all . . . of twofold terror: terror of what I had seen, and of what had come to pass. That evil, that criminal element of which I have already spoken, those incomprehensible spasms rose up within me . . . stifled me.

"Aha!" I thought to myself: "so that is why I am what I am. . . . That is where blood tells!" I stood beside the corpse and gazed and waited, to see whether those dead pupils would not stir, whether those benumbed lips would not quiver. No! everything was motionless; the very sea-weed, among which the surf had cast him, seemed to have congealed; even the gulls had flown away—there was not a fragment anywhere, not a plank or any broken rigging. There was emptiness everywhere . . . only he—and I—and the foaming sea in the distance. I cast a glance behind me; the same emptiness was there; a chain of hillocks on the horizon . . . that was all!

I dreaded to leave that unfortunate man in that loneliness, in the ooze of the shore, to be devoured by fishes and birds; an inward voice told me that I ought to hunt up some men and call them thither, if not to aid—that was out of the question—at least for the purpose of laying him out, of bearing him beneath an inhabited roof. . . . But indescribable terror suddenly took possession of me. It seemed to me as though that dead man knew that I had come thither, that he himself had arranged that last meeting—it even seemed as though I could hear that dull, familiar muttering. . . . I ran off to one side . . . looked behind me once more. . . . Something shining caught my eye; it brought me to a standstill. It was a golden hoop on the outstretched hand of the corpse. . . . I recognised my mother's wedding-ring. I remember how I forced myself to return, to go close, to bend down. . . . I remember the sticky touch of the cold fingers, I remember how I panted and puckered up my eyes and gnashed my teeth, as I tugged persistently at the ring. . . .

At last I got it off—and I fled—fled away, in headlong flight—and something darted after me, and overtook me and caught me.

XVI

Everything which I had gone through and endured was, probably, written on my face when I returned home. My mother suddenly rose upright as soon as I entered her room, and gazed at me with such insistent inquiry that, after having unsuccessfully attempted to explain myself, I ended by silently handing her the ring. She turned frightfully pale, her eyes opened unusually wide and turned dim like *his*. She uttered a faint cry, seized the ring, reeled, fell upon my breast, and fairly swooned there, with her head thrown back and devouring me with those wide, mad eyes. I encircled her waist with both arms, and standing still on one spot, never stirring, I slowly narrated everything, without the slightest reservation, to her, in a quiet voice: my dream and the meeting, and everything, everything. . . . She heard me out to the end, only her breast heaved more and more strongly, and her eyes suddenly grew more animated and drooped. Then she put the ring on her fourth finger, and, retreating a little, began to get out a mantilla and a hat. I asked where she was going. She raised a surprised glance to me and tried to answer, but her voice failed her. She shuddered several times, rubbed her hands, as though endeavouring to warm herself, and at last she said: "Let us go at once thither."

"Whither, mother dear?"

"Where he is lying. . . . I want to see. . . . I want to know. . . . I shall identify. . . ."

I tried to persuade her not to go; but she was almost in hysterics. I understood that it was impossible to oppose her desire, and we set out.

XVII

And lo, again I am walking over the sand of the dunes, but I am no longer alone, I am walking arm in arm with my mother. The sea has retreated, has gone still further away; it is quieting down; but even its diminished roar is menacing and ominous. Here, at last, the solitary rock has shown itself ahead of us—and there is the seaweed. I look intently, I strive to distinguish that rounded object lying on the ground—but I see nothing. We approach closer. I involuntarily retard my steps. But where is that black, motionless thing? Only the stalks of the seaweed stand out darkly against the sand, which is already dry. . . . We go to the very rock. . . . The corpse is nowhere to be seen, and only on the spot where it had lain there still remains a depression, and one can make out where the arms and legs lay. . . . Round about the seaweed seems tousled, and the traces of one man's footsteps are discernible; they go across the down, then disappear on reaching the flinty ridge.

My mother and I exchange glances and are ourselves frightened at what we read on our own faces. . . .

Can he have got up of himself and gone away?

"But surely thou didst behold him dead?" she asks in a whisper.

I can only nod my head. Three hours have not elapsed since I stumbled upon the baron's body. . . . Someone had discovered it and carried it away. I must find out who had done it, and what had become of him.

But first of all I must attend to my mother.

XVIII

While she was on her way to the fatal spot she was in a fever, but she controlled herself. The disappearance of the corpse had startled her as the crowning misfortune. She was stupefied. I feared for her reason. With great difficulty I got her home. I put her to bed again; again I called the doctor to her; but as soon as my mother partly recovered her senses she at once demanded that I should instantly set out in search of "that man." I obeyed. But, despite all possible measures, I discovered nothing. I went several times to the police-office, I visited all the villages in the neighbourhood, I inserted several advertisements in the newspapers, I made inquiries in every direction—all in vain! It is true that I did hear that a drowned man had been found at one of the hamlets on the seashore. . . . I immediately hastened thither, but he was already buried, and from all the tokens he did not resemble the baron. I found out on what ship he had sailed for America. At first everyone was positive that that ship had perished during the tempest; but several months afterward, rumours began to circulate to the effect that it had been seen at anchor in the harbour of New York. Not knowing what to do, I set about hunting up the negro whom I had seen. I offered him, through the newspapers, a very considerable sum of money, if he would present himself at our house. A tall negro in a cloak actually did come to the house in my absence. . . . But after questioning the servant-maid, he suddenly went away and returned no more.

And thus the trace of my . . . my father grew cold; thus did it vanish irrevocably in the mute gloom. My mother and I never spoke of him. Only, one day, I remember that she expressed surprise at my never having alluded before to my strange dream; and then she added: "Of course, it really . . ." and did not finish her sentence.

My mother was ill for a long time, and after her convalescence our former relations were not re-established. She felt awkward in my presence until the day of her death. . . . Precisely that, awkward. And there was no way of helping her in her grief. Everything becomes smoothed down, the memories of the most tragic family events gradually lose their force and venom; but if a feeling of awkwardness has been set up between two closely connected persons, it is impossible to extirpate it!

I have never again had that dream which had been wont so to disturb me; I no longer "search for" my father; but it has sometimes seemed to me—and it seems so to me to this day—that in my sleep I hear distant shrieks, unintermittent, melancholy plaints; they resound somewhere behind a lofty wall, across which it is impossible to clamber;

they rend my heart—and I am utterly unable to comprehend what it is: whether it is a living man groaning, or whether I hear the wild, prolonged roar of the troubled sea. And now it passes once more into that beast-like growl —and I awake with sadness and terror in my soul.

(III)

BEZHIN MEADOW

I t was a beautiful July day, one of those days seen only in settled fine weather. Immediately after daybreak the sky is perfectly serene; the dawn does not come forth in a vast glare of light, but with a modest vermeil tint; the sun does not seem to be of fire or of red-hot iron, as in the dog-days, nor of a dark purple—a sure sign of storms—but its rays are soft and clear; it appears to shine from behind a thin veil of pearly whiteness; its beams are invigorating; it seems to be bathed in light vapours called forth by itself from the joyful earth. The colour of the horizon is light, and of a pale lilac; the same everywhere and throughout the day. Nowhere can the least cloud omening bad weather be seen, except, perhaps, some thin clouds in light blue strips, descending in the far distance, and carrying with them a light rain hardly perceptible. In the evening the light clouds disappear; the last of them fall down on the eastern horizon in rose-tinted flakes, opposite to the setting sun; while above the spot where the sun has sunk in untroubled glory—as calmly as it rose in the morning— a purple light dwells for a few minutes in the heavens, and the evening star comes out, but with a doubting face, and with a soft and still uncertain light. On such days all colours are soft and clear without being brilliant; everything is impressed with a modest pathos. The heat is, however, sometimes powerful, and the sloping fields send out a light sort of mist; but the low winds dissipate the accumulated heat, and one may see on the roads and on the fallow land high white columns of whirling dust--a certain symptom of settled fair weather. The pure dry air breathes by fits odours of wormwood, rye and buckwheat. No moistness prevails in the atmosphere till after midnight. Such are the days which the labourer sighs for in the time of harvest.

It was on a day of this kind that I was shooting partridges in the district of Tchensk, which forms a part of the government of Tula. I was very successful; my game-bag was so crammed that the belt pained my shoulder very much, and weighed heavily on my chest. The stars were beginning to come out, and in the still luminous atmosphere mists began to gather and to spread over the landscape, which might not be unattended with danger, especially as I was exhausted by a day's hard shooting. I therefore decided on immediately returning to my shooting-box. I crossed with long strides an immense track of ground covered with bushes and copse-wood, climbed a little hill, and expected to see from it the plain I had so often crossed, the little wood on the right, and the village church in the distance, but, to my great disappointment, a part of the country completely unknown to me met my view. Below me stretched a narrow plain; right before me rose, like a wall, a thick grove of aspens. I stopped in astonishment: "Ah!" thought I, "I have lost my way; I must have kept too much to the left." I descended the hill quickly. Arrived at the foot of it, I felt myself surrounded by a malignant humid vapour, such as is perceived in old vaults. The tall thick grass that grew at the bottom of the valley was covered with a shroud of whitish vapour, resembling a lake of milky water; it would have been imprudent to cross it. I turned to the left, and skirted the aspen thicket. By this time the bats were wheeling in mysterious circles above the tops of the aspens, while a goshawk rose perpendicularly from the ground, without paying any attention to the motions of these birds of the night, and flew off in haste to regain its nest. "I shall soon get out of this scrape," I said to myself; "there must be a road not far from this; I must have gone a good mile out of my way."

At length I reached the end of the wood, but there still appeared no traces of any road; low tufts of some herb or other were scattered here and there in my path; I was astonished that they had not been mowed down. Beyond, but in the far distance, I thought I could perceive a boundless plain—an uninhabited desert. I stopped again: "Here is a misfortune! Where am I now?" I said aloud. I went over in my mind the track which I had pursued during the day. "Ah! yes; I see where I am now! these must be the Parakhink bushes, and that is the Sindeyef Wood. But how have I happened to lose my reckoning in this way?—it is very strange; in the meantime I must keep to the right."

I went to the right, through the bushes. Meanwhile the night was growing darker, the sky was covered with what seemed a heavy storm-cloud, the air was becoming thicker above and below; I perceived that I had reached a path very much overgrown with weeds, and difficult to travel, but still a path; of course I followed it as carefully as I could. All around me lay an unimaginable silence, broken only at infrequent intervals by the long-drawn cry of the quail. At times, too, some little night-bird, flying low and without noise, would almost strike against me, and then fly off in terrified haste. I worked my way through the bushes, and found myself on the edge of the plain. I could hardly distinguish objects at a distance; a greyish-white fog was lying along the plain; beyond, dull clouds moved about, and heaped themselves in immense moving masses. My steps sounded dully in the cold, dense atmosphere. The bleak sky was now succeeded by the deep blue of night, and the stars appeared one after the other in slow succession.

What I had taken for a wood was but a range of low hills. "Heavens! where am I?" I stopped a third time, and looked inquiringly at Diana, a white English bitch, certainly the

most intelligent of all quadrupeds. But the most intelligent
of quadrupeds, wagging her tail, and moving her eyelids
quickly, in answer to my look, knew no more than I did
about the country. I rushed on in despair. I rounded the
hill, and found myself in a valley that bore marks of
the plough. A strange feeling seized me. This valley had the
regular appearance of a pot, very wide at the mouth. At the
bottom were lying, as if they had been placed there by design,
enormous blocks of white stone—one would have said that
they were ranged there for the council-meetings of mysterious
beings. All was silent and sad in this hollow; the sky above
it appeared flat and melancholy. A feeble breath of wind
murmured plaintively among the stones. I hurried away,
and climbed a height, from which I looked round in all directions. Up to this moment I had not given up the hope of
finding my way home, but now I had to admit that I was
completely lost; and, no longer making any attempt to recognise the features of the country, I walked forward at hazard,
guiding my steps by the positions of the stars. I travelled in
this way for about half an hour, not without fatigue. I thought
I had never seen such solitudes—not a light to be seen in the
distance, not a sound in the air. One hill succeeded another;
then came boundless plains; then bushes, which seemed to
rise out of the earth, to scratch and wound my face as I proceeded. I began to think that the only course to be taken was
to look out for some tree, or some little spot carpeted with
moss, and lie down there to wait the end of this miserable
night.

I was engaged in thinking about this, when suddenly I
found myself on the brink of a frightful precipice; I had just
time to draw back. Before me I discovered an immense plain.
A broad river bounded it in an immense semicircle that
swept from the point where I was standing. The water had
the brilliancy of polished steel, and this brilliancy marked its
course; although less distinct in some places than in others.
The hill on which I was stood out in dark brown on the deep

azure of the sky, and descended almost perpendicularly right
below me, not far from the river, which seemed like a motionless mirror at the foot of the traveller. On my right rose the
smoke of two small bivouac fires, not far from each other.
Around me I could discern the shadows of people moving; at
moments I could distinguish even the curly head of some
youngster.

At last I knew where I was. The plain before me was a
prairie well known in this part of the country under the name
of Bezhin Wood. I had to give up the idea of reaching my
house, the more as I was excessively tired. I resolved to go up
to the bivouac, and wait for the morning among the people
I saw there, and whom I took to be travelling merchants. I
descended the hill without accident: but I had hardly let go
the last branch of brambles that I had taken hold of to help
me in my way down, when suddenly two large white dogs
rushed towards me, barking furiously. The clear voices of
children were audible from the fires, and two or three boys
were in a moment on the *qui vive*. . . . I replied to their
shouts. . . . They ran up to me, calling in their dogs, which
had been roused from their slumbers by the appearance of
Diana.

I was mistaken in taking the company for merchants; they
were the peasant boys of the neighbouring village watching
a *taboun*.[1] In the hot weather of the dog-days it is the custom
in our country to take the horses out at night to pasture in the
prairie; the gadflies and other insects prevent them from eating during the day. It is capital fun for the young villagers
to drive the horses to the prairie before nightfall, and bring
them back in the morning safe and sound. Riding bare-
backed on the most spirited colts, they gallop off, laughing
and shouting, throwing their arms about, every limb alive
with joy and merriment. A brown column of fine dust follows
their track; in the distance one hears the sound of their merry
gallop; the horses run with their ears erect; while, in advance

[1] A troop of horses turned out to graze without bridles or hobbles.

of all, his tail streaming in the wind, careers some rough, powerful horse, uncombed and uncurried, with his hair twisted into uncombable knots.

Telling the children that I had lost my way, I seated myself on a large stone beside them. They asked me where I came from, and were afterwards silent, seated together at a little distance from me. I lay down about six paces from the fire, under a bush almost leafless, and began to observe the surrounding objects. Round the fire there trembled, as if just on the point of expiring, a reddish glow, standing out against the darkness. A small flickering flame shot out now and then from this circle; a thin jet of light would be thrown on the leafless branches of a wild osier, and disappear in a moment; long points of shadow flickered about the fire; and the darkness struggled with the light. At times, from the increasing obscurity, would suddenly appear the brown or white head of a horse, looking at us with an air of stupid attention, as he paused for a moment in his browsing, and then as suddenly disappear in the darkness, though we could still hear his munching and snorting. From the spot where we were it was impossible to distinguish the objects lying in deep shade, so that everything at a distance seemed covered with an impenetrable black curtain; but farther off, on the horizon, we could see long confused spots, which were no doubt forests and hills. The moonless sky, dark but pure, bent solemnly over us, visible to infinite depths. The breast rose and fell voluptuously, breathing those fresh odours—the odours of a Russian summer night. Not a sound was to be heard, except now and then, in the river that flowed near us, the splashing of large fish chasing each other, the light rattling of reeds in a bend of the bank, or the low crackling of our fires.

The children were seated round the bivouac fires, in company with the two dogs that had been so eager to attack me. It was some time before these two brave guardians could accustom themselves to my presence, and they now and then growled at me from their lairs near the fire. There were five boys—Fédia, Pavloucha, Ilyusha, Kostia, and Vania. It was from their conversation that I learned their names; and I humbly beg the reader to allow me to introduce them to my young hosts.

The first of them, the young Fédia, is a boy you would guess to be about fourteen years old. His features are delicate and regular, his hair curls naturally, his eye is brilliant, his look bold and independent, and his countenance animated by a smile, half serious, half comic. His whole appearance seems to tell you at once that he belongs to a family in good circumstances, and has come out to-night only for his own pleasure. He had on a blouse of striped calico, edged with a cord of a rustic yellow colour; above it a little *armiak*, the sleeves of which hung loose, and which was fastened round his neck. His blouse was fitted to his waist by a blue belt, from which hung a little horn comb. His boots, that reached only up to the calf, were his own boots, and not his father's.[1]

Paul or Pavlucha, the second, had black dishevelled hair, grey eyes, prominent cheek-bones, a pale complexion marked with freckles, a mouth large but regular, an enormously large head—or, to use an Orel comparison, as big as a beer-pot—and a short, thick-set figure. There was nothing, in truth, to praise in his appearance; but the young fellow pleased me much, notwithstanding, for I was attracted at once by his frank and intelligent look; and the clear tone of his voice seemed to indicate some firmness of character. His costume was not more elegant than his head-dress; it consisted of a coarse dirty blouse, with trousers patched at the knees and about the waist.

The physiognomy of the third boy, Ilyusha, was insignificant enough. His prominent mouth, weak nose and

[1]In the country, the father's boots are used by his wife and all the other members of the family—permission being first asked and received from him. Even in the capital towns of the districts, one may often see, when it rains, a troop of young village-girls in holiday dress, each with a pair of boots in her hand, or hanging on her shoulder. These are the family boots; they must not put them on when it is raining.

chin, short-sighted look, stupid and restless air, lips closed
and immovable, meeting eyebrows, his continual winking
before the fire, his flaxen hair that hung down from beneath
a cap of coarse felt, and which he was always pushing behind
his ears—all this was anything but agreeable to the observer.

He had shoes of plaited bark, with narrow strips of cloth
bound round his legs above the ankle, in the fashion of gaiters;
a triple cord was passed round his waist, and kept tight his
little frock, which was decent enough. Ilyusha and Paul
seemed both about twelve years of age.

Kostia was evidently not more than ten years old. He
interested me, however, by his pensive air and sad look;
his face was small, thin, and peaked—the lower part
tapered like the nose of a squirrel, and I could hardly distinguish his lips. What especially made a strange impression,
was his large black eyes, that shone with a melting brilliancy,
and seemed as if about to speak, although he never uttered
a word. He was little, of a delicate complexion, and poorly
clad.

The fifth boy, Vania, had escaped my notice at first;
he was lying on the ground, rolled up in a square mat,
and very seldom did he put out his little curled head from
beneath this covering. This child could hardly be more than
seven years old.

I lay under the bush, a little apart, observing the boys. A
pot was suspended above one of the fires; they were cooking
potatoes in it. Paul was attending to them, and, on his knees
before the fire, now and then with a splinter of wood moved
the potatoes about in the boiling water. Fédia was lying on
a slightly sloped piece of ground, leaning on his elbow, with
his *armiak* above him. Ilyusha lay beside the little Kostia, and
kept winking with an air of great attention. Kostia raised his
head a little, and seemed to look at something in the distance.
Vania remained motionless under his mat. For myself I
pretended to be asleep. Gradually the boys resumed their
conversation.

At first they chatted about this or that, of to-morrow's work, of this or that horse. Fédia turned suddenly to Ilyusha, and, resuming a conversation probably interrupted by my appearance, he said to him:

"You say that you have seen the *domovoï?*"[1]

"No, I have never seen him, nor has anybody," answered Ilyusha, in a feeble and trembling voice, that corresponded perfectly with the expression of his features; "but I have heard him, and I am not the only one that has heard him."

"And where does he stay when he comes to you?" asked Paul.

"In the tub-house—the place where they put the tubs, opposite the mill-wheel, near the wall in the paper-manu-factory."

"Oh! you work in the factory, do you?"

"Yes; my brother and little Avdéa, and I work a little with the glazers."

"Oh! so you are work-people."

"Well! but how did you hear the *domovoï?*" asked Fédia.

"I'll tell you how: there were my brother Avdéa, and Fédor Mikhéïtch, and Ivan Kosoï, and Ivan from Red Hills, and Ivan Sukhorukof, and some more boys, all working together that day; we were just going to separate in the evening, it was very late, when the foreman said to us—'You must come back to-morrow early; there is a great deal of work to do. Why go away at all, my boys? You had better remain here. . . .' So we remained and slept together in the tub-house. We had just lain down, when Avdéa said to us—'What if we should have a visit from the *domóvoï!*' . . . The moment Avdéa spoke we heard above our heads a curious sound; we were on the lower story, and the sound was right above us; then we heard it on the wheel; it tramped and groaned, the planks bent and creaked; the *domovoï* passed again above our

[1] The *domovoï-dukh* is the familiar spirit of the house, like the Scottish Brownie.

heads, and then the water grumbled and groaned, and struck against the wheel; the wheel turned . . . and yet the foreman had fastened it carefully before he went to bed. But the wheel turned a good many times, and then stopped, and the water did not push against it any more; the *domovoï* was at the door above us; then it came down the ladder . . . slowly, for it is heavy; the steps of the ladder creaked under it. . . . Then it was just behind our door . . . what is it waiting there for? We looked . . . the door opened wide. We were half-dead with fear; we still looked . . . nothing at all! And then we saw near a tub a spoon moving about with a string tied to it. It raised itself up, then dived into a tub; then marched along through the air by itself, sometimes moving up and down, just as if somebody was cleaning it, then it was put back into its place. After that, near another tub, a hook was broken off, and, a moment after, it was replaced. At last it was as if somebody had returned to the door, and began coughing and bleating like a sheep, making such a noise. . . . We had all crawled together into a heap—one on the other, like bags of lead. Oh! we had a jolly fright, I can tell you."

"What made the *domovoï* cough in that way?" asked Paul.

"I don't know; perhaps the damp . . ."

After some moments of silence, Fédia said, "Are the potatoes ready?"

Paul tried one: "No, not yet." Then, turning quickly towards the river, he added, "How he leapt! did you hear? It must have been a pike." Then looking into the sky: "Look, look, a shooting star!"

"Boys," said Kostia in his weak voice, "listen, till I tell you what my aunt told me the other day."

"Very well, we are listening," said Fédia, with a patronising air.

"You all know Gavrilo, the carpenter of the further village?"

"Yes, yes . . . well?"

"Do you know why he is so melancholy—why he never speaks to anybody? I'll tell you why. He went out one day, my aunt told me, to gather nuts; he gathered a great many, but he lost his way in the wood. . . . He went on and on, God knows where; he stopped, looked about him, thought, then walked and walked on . . . but no, he could not find his way, and night was come. He seated himself under a tree: 'Well,' he said, 'I shall wait here for daylight.' He wrapped himself up and fell asleep. He was in a deep sleep when he heard a voice calling, 'Gavrilo! Gavrilo!' He rubbed his eyes, looked . . . there was nothing. He goes to sleep again, and again he heard somebody calling him. He looks about him, more attentively . . . and at last he sees before him, on a branch, a *roussalka*[1] laughing and laughing till it almost burst. . . . The moon was shining very clearly, and the will-o'-the-wisp himself was shining like the moon; and the *roussalka* was very white—white and glittering as if it were all of silver. It saw that poor Gavrilo was half dead with fear; and it laughed and laughed, and called him through its hand in this way. . . . Gavrilo rose, and was going, just imagine it, to approach the *roussalka*, when, God be thanked, he changed his mind, and began to seek for his baptismal cross with both hands, but it was very difficult to find! Ah! boys, he said himself that his hand felt like stone, and his fingers were quite stiff. . . . But at last he brought out his cross, and placed it on his blouse, in the middle of his breast. The *roussalka* didn't laugh any more . . . it began to cry . . . and to shed tears. It wiped its face with its green hair—as green as grass. Gavrilo, not so much frightened now, looked at it for a long time, and then said to it, 'Eh! green leaf, you can speak, can you? Come, tell me what you are weeping for.' The *roussalka* answered, 'Dear little man, you should not, you should not have touched your cross; you would have lived with me till the end of the world; but I weep, and I must suffer a great deal; but I shall not suffer alone, you will suffer

[1] A wood fairy.

too, you will, till time ends.' And Gavrilo saw it sink and disappear . . . and he understood that very moment how he was to find his way out of the wood; he was at the edge of it in two minutes. . . . Since that night, he has never been merry, he has never felt any pleasure in living."

"Cursed *roussalka*!" said Fédia, after a minute's silent reflection; "but how does it happen that vermin like that can hurt the soul of a Christian? for he did not obey it; he did not yield to it."

"It is quite the same; besides, it is true," answered Kostia . . . "and Gavrilo said that the voice of the *roussalka* was sad and mournful like a frog's."

"And it was your aunt that told you all that?" said Fédia.

"Yes, I was in bed, but I was listening; I did not lose a single word."

"It is very curious. But what makes him so sad now? Did he touch it? He must have pleased the cursed thing, since it called him."

"Yes, he pleased it! . . . You know it wanted to tickle him; that is what it wanted; that is what the *roussalkas* do."

"But can there be any *roussalkas* here?" said Fédia.

"No," answered Kostia; "here, it is an open part of the country . . . and besides, there is the river."

All reflected in silence. Suddenly, in the distance, sounded a long cry of sorrow and anguish—one of those voices of the night, those indefinable and inconceivable sounds which are born of silence itself, which rise, seem to hang somewhere in the air, and then die slowly away. You listen; it seems nothing, and yet a sound has struck upon your ear. At this time it was as if, far away on the horizon, someone had shouted, and then in the forest another had answered in a thin short burst of laughter; and a feeble hissing sound seemed to fly along on the surface of the river.

The boys looked at each other. . . . They shuddered.

"The cross protect us!" murmured Ilia.

"Ah! boys," cried Paul, "are you not afraid? . . . But, come, let us see whether the potatoes are ready."

Four little heads bent above the pot, and they began to devour the smoking potatoes. Ivan alone did not move.

"Well! won't you have any?" said Paul. But he would not even draw his arms out of the folds of his mat.

The pot was not long in being emptied.

"Do you know, boys," said Ilyusha, "what happened at Barnabitzis near us?"

"Beside the old wall?" said Fédia.

"Yes, yes, at the old deserted wall. . . . An abominable place! all surrounded with hollows, and ravines, and grottoes . . . and great numbers of snakes."

"Well! what happened there? tell us."

"Perhaps you don't know, Fédia, that there is a man buried there—a man who was drowned a long time ago, when the pond was deep. The body was buried on the bank. The grave is not very easily found, but there is still a little rising to be seen on the earth. Well, listen. The steward sent for the huntsman Ermil some days ago, and ordered him to go to the post—it is always Ermil that is sent to the post. He has not à single dog to train, not even a dog to himself; they all died; not one of them could live with him or near him. A pretty huntsman, isn't he? So Ermil went to the post; and when he got to town he stayed there a little; and he had a good deal in his head when he mounted his horse to go back to the village. Night came on; but afterwards it became very clear, for it was full moon, and Ermil had reached, though he did not know very well how, the old wall; he had to pass this nasty place. He went on without hesitation; he arrived at the grave of the drowned man; he looked at it, and saw lying upon it a pretty lamb with nice white curled wool. The little animal began to walk up and down on the grave. The huntsman Ermil is a good-hearted man; he thought that it would lose itself if it stayed in this evil place, so he got down from his horse and took it up. The lamb was perfectly quiet in his arms. Ermil approached his horse, but he backed, and kicked, and flung, and snorted, and neighed, and shook his head; but Ermil soon brought him to reason. So he remounted, and went along with the pretty lamb on the saddle before him. Ermil looked at the lamb, and it looked at him straight in the face. This seemed very strange to Ermil, whose memory was a little confused, but who, for all that, could not remember that he had ever heard of sheep looking in this way, straight into people's faces. But he settled with himself that this was a peculiar case. He paid no more attention to it; he caressed it; and, quite pleased to find the wool so soft, he said to the lamb, 'Byasha! byasha!' and then the lamb immediately showed his teeth, and said the same, 'Byasha! byasha! . . .' "

The boy had not finished these two last words when the dogs leaped up together, and, bounding off at a furious rate, disappeared in the darkness. All the boys were at once on the alert; even Vania came out from beneath his matting. Paul, shouting at the top of his voice, rushed after the dogs, whose barkings were every minute becoming more and more distant. I heard the mad and disordered galloping of the terrified *taboun*. Paul redoubled his shouts of encouragement to the dogs: "Grey, Grey! Blackie! seize 'em! seize 'em!" A few moments after, the barkings ceased; the last shouts of Paul were but faintly heard in the distance. This silence continued for fully a quarter of an hour; the boys looked at each other with an expression of uncertainty. . . . At last we heard the gallop of a horse that stopped suddenly just at our feet, and Paul, by the help of the mane, vaulted to the ground. The two dogs also bounded into the illuminated circle, where they lay down with their deep red tongues lolling out.

"What was it? What did you see?" cried the boys.

"Nothing," replied Paul, signing with his arm a dismissal to his horse. "The dogs came upon the trace of some beast or other; I think it was a wolf, but I could not see in the dark," he added coolly, and then began to breathe hard.

I could not help admiring this little fellow, he looked so handsome at this moment, plain as he was. His countenance, animated by his rapid run, was full of different emotions, and shone with resolution and intrepidity. Without even a stick in his hand, in the dark, though he believed that some danger was near, he had run without hesitation against a wolf, perhaps several. . . . I thought, while I looked at him standing before the fire, so calm, so modest, "What a charming boy!"

"And were there any wolves, eh?" said the chicken-hearted Kostia.

"There are always some wolves in the fields in the nighttime," answered Paul negligently, "but they are not troublesome except in winter."

And he took his old seat near the fire. While arranging himself at his ease on the ground, one of his arms happened to fall on the back of one of the dogs, which, happy in this accidental caress, cast at Paul a look of proud gratitude, and remained thus for a long time without turning his head, tired as he was with his long chase.

Vania, the youngest of the party, rolled himself up in his matting again.

"Ah! Ilyusha, what were you talking about? you remember," said Fédia, who, as the son of a rich peasant, thought himself entitled to be entertained with stories. He spoke very little himself, as if he wished to guard his acknowledged dignity. "You stopped when the dogs leaped up. . . . Yes, yes, it was about a haunted place near your house."

"Barnabitzi? Ah! spirits have been seen there too. More than once they have seen the dead squire walking there. They say he goes in a long coat; he stalks along, sighs and looks on the ground, God knows for what. One night, Father Trofim met him, and said to him, 'Little father Ivan Ivanitch, what are you looking for on the ground?'"

"What! Trofim dared to speak to him!" said Fédia, astonished.

"Yes, he spoke to him."

"Well, he is a famous old fellow is old Trofim. And what did the dead man say?"

"'I am looking for the magic herb,' said the spirit, in a dull, hollow voice. Yes, he said the magic herb. 'And what do you want with the sorcerer's herb when you are dead, little father Ivan Ivanitch?' 'The earth is choking me, I am suffocating below it,' said the dead man. . . . 'I must get out of that, Trofim.'"

"An odd old fellow," said Fédia—"dead and wants air! I suppose he did not live long enough."

"It is astonishing," said Kostia; "I thought that nobody could see the dead except on Roditelskaïa Saturday."[1]

"One can see the dead at any time," answered Ilyusha confidently, who, so far as I observed, was best acquainted with the village traditions. "Only, when Roditelskaïa Saturday comes, you can see the people who are marked for death, and all these people must die before the year ends. You have only to go and seat yourself on the steps in front of the church, and look, without moving an inch, straight before you. If you do that, you will see everybody whose turn is come to die. Old Ouliana went last year and sat on the steps."

"Ah! and did she see anybody?" asked Kostia eagerly.

"Well, at first she sat a long time—a very long time—motionless, looking, listening, but without seeing or hearing anybody . . . only she thought she heard a dog barking and howling strangely from somewhere, it seemed to her from the bottom of a vault. . . . At last, a little boy in a blouse passed her on the path; she saw him, and following him attentively with her eye, she recognised him; it was Ivashka Fedosief."

"Little Ivan, who died last spring?"

"Yes, it was he. He was walking with his head down, so she

[1]The day on which the Russians celebrate the memory of their deceased relations.

did not know who he was at first . . . but she knew him after he passed her. Some time after him, a woman passed slowly. Ouliana knew her at once, I mean she recognised herself; it was herself, Ouliana, that was walking on the path."

"What! it was herself that was walking below, and herself that she saw?" said Fédia.

"Yes, herself; what of it?"

"Well, but she is not dead yet."

"But the year is not ended yet. Come to-morrow to our village and look at her; her soul and body hardly hold together."

The boys were silent. Paul threw a handful of dry wood on the fire; the branches falling raised myriads of sparks, then began to blacken, twisted, cracked, emitted jets of grey smoke, with here and there peaks of lighted gas that gradually grew larger and mixed together, and then the whole mass broke into flame, sending up a fierce, red, roaring blaze, mixed with showers of sparks. A dove flew out of the darkness right to the crest of the flame, round which it flew three times, and then disappeared, clapping its wings loudly.

"Ah!" said Paul, "there is a dove that has lost its way home; it will fly about till it finds a safe place to wait in until morning comes."

"But, tell me, Paul . . . mayn't it be," said Kostia, "the soul of a good man going up to heaven, eh?"

"Perhaps . . . perhaps it may," answered Paul, throwing another handful of branches on the other fire.

"Paul," said Fédia, who never liked any interruption to the stories he was enjoying, "tell me, if you please, whether you saw at Chalachof, the . . . what we saw, the . . . eclipse, I think they call it."

"Oh! . . . when the sun is covered with black! I know . . . yes, yes, we saw it."

"You were terribly frightened, surely?"

"Yes, and not we poor peasants only. Our *barin* had told us himself beforehand that he was going to see the—the eclipse

. . . and the moment he saw the night coming in place of the day, he was very much afraid himself, they say. There is an old woman in his kitchen; when she saw the night coming at that time, she thought that there would not be any more cooking at all; so she took pots, and bowls, and dishes, and saucepans and pitched them all into the big oven, muttering, 'Nobody has any need to eat on the day of judgment.' And the vegetables and the meal too followed the pots and pans. And in all the village they said that white wolves were going to cover the whole earth, and with the help of the birds of prey eat up all the men and women, and that we should first see *Trichka*."[1]

"Well, but what is this *Trichka?*" asked Kostia.

"Don't you know?" said Ilyusha with warmth; "you are a famous blockhead, not to know who *Trichka* is! What do the people of your village do when they are all sitting together? they are as dumb as the seats they sit on, I suppose. *Trichka!* he's a wonderful man who will come to our villages some day. And how is he a wonderful man? Why, nobody ever will be able to catch him, or to hurt him; the whole baptised world would like to seize him, and they will come out of their yards with pitchforks and cudgels, and chains and cords, and try to catch him and chain him, and trample him underfoot; but he will make them all squint, so that they will strike, and kick, and seize each other, while they fancy they are hurting him. Do you know now? Ah! but that is not all; he will let them put him in prison; well, they will guard him and keep him always in sight; he will ask a little water to drink—they will bring him some in a wooden bowl, and then he will shrivel up in the air and plunge into the bowl . . . and you may look for him as long as you like! They will load him with irons— he gives himself a little shake, and all the rings lie broken about him. This *Trichka*, I tell you, will run through all the hamlets, and villages, and towns: he is a shrewd fellow; he will make a fool of all good Christians, and yet make

[1]Peasant nickname for Antichrist.

everybody like him. There will not be any use trying to injure him. . . . Yes, yes, he'll be a cunning, astonishing fellow."

"It is quite true," replied Paul, without animation or haste, "it is quite true; it is the very same *Trichka* that our people are expecting. The old people said, 'If the eclipse takes place that the *barins* talk about, *Trichka* will make his appearance for certain.' The eclipse commenced; all the people came out of their houses, and spread themselves in the street, on the roads, and in the fields. They waited to see it. At our village the ground is high, and we can see a great distance all round us. . . . Not an eye was closed. . . . Then, all of a sudden, not far from the further village, on the path over the hill, there appeared, and then began to descend the hill, a strangely-shaped man, with an astonishing head. . . . We all looked and looked, and everybody began to cry, 'Ohi! ohi! ohi! *Trichka! Trichka!*' and they rushed away in fright in every direction. Our *starosta*[1] leaped into a ditch; his wife ran and crept below the carriage-gate, crying as if she were possessed, and frightening even her own yard-dog out of his wits; he broke his chain, bolted into the garden, over the gate, and ran for the wood. And Kuzka's father ran among the oats, lay down, and began to imitate, as well as he could, the cry of the quail. 'The enemy of souls,' thought he, 'the angry devil, will never think of laying hold of a poor corn-bird.' So they were all terrified almost to death. . . . Just fancy, the man that was coming to the village, just as much frightened as the rest, was Vavill, our cooper. He had gone to the town to buy a big pail bound with iron hoops, and he had put it on his head for convenience' sake."

The five boys laughed at the adventure, and then remained a moment perfectly silent, as one may often notice when people are conversing in the open air. I looked round on every side; over the wide prairie the night reigned silent and solemn; to the freshness of advanced evening had succeeded

[1] The representative head of the village.

the healthy and pleasant coolness of midnight—its reign was to continue over the country for several hours longer; we had still some time to wait for the first rose-tints of the dawn, the first signs of the awakening of nature. The moon would not rise for some hours yet. The countless golden stars of heaven seemed to be running a race with each other, as if they had a rendezvous in the Milky Way, and while looking at them I seemed to feel vaguely under me the rapid incessant revolution of the earth. . . . A sudden, piercing, mournful cry rose twice above the river; some minutes after, the same cry was repeated, but farther off.

Kostia shuddered.

"What is it?" he said.

"It is the heron," answered Paul, very quietly.

"The heron? the heron? . . . But, Paul, what was I told yesterday evening? . . . that . . . but perhaps you know yourself, Paul."

"What are you talking about? Come, tell us."

"Well, you know, I was going from Kamennaïa-Grad to Chachkino; I went along our hazel-wood, and then I took the road by the low meadow, you know, down at the place where the meadow borders on the sharp turn of the river. . . . You remember that there is just beside it a *boutchilo*,[1] and a large part of the *boutchilo* is changed into reed-marshes? well, I was passing this *boutchilo*, when I heard not far from me cries of 'Ouh! ouh! ouh! ohi!' They were so sad, so mournful. . . . Oh, my God! brothers, my heart was at my throat, and my legs could hardly carry me. It was late; the voice always followed me; ah! I wept so sore, I wept till I thought I had shed all the tears in my head. Tell me, boys, what do you think it could have been?"

"About a year ago," said Paul, "some thieves drowned the field-watchman Akim there; perhaps it was his soul shrieking."

[1] A *boutchilo* is a deep pool of water left after the inundation of a river.

"Ah! I did not know that the thieves had drowned poor Akim there; if I had known, I should not have been so much frightened."

"Besides, I must tell you," added Paul, "I have heard people say that there are little frogs whose cry very much resembles the cries of a human being in great pain and sorrow."

"Frogs? no, Paul; it was not frogs: what frogs do you mean? . . ."

The heron again flung its peculiar cry above the river.

"There is another, now," said Kostia, involuntarily; "it must be the cry of the *leshie*."[1]

"The *leshie* doesn't cry; it is dumb," said Ilyusha immediately; "it does nothing but strike one hand against the other, and clack with its tongue."

"I suppose you have seen it, eh?" asked the self-important Fédia in a tone of raillery.

"No, I never saw it, comrade, and God preserve me from ever seeing it! but other people have. Only the other day, the spirit met one of our moujiks at the edge of the wood; he pushed him and pushed him towards the thicket; the moujik had to go round the field ten times, always trying to keep away from the thicket, but he could not get to his cottage till the sun rose, and he was dreadfully knocked up, I can tell you."

"And he saw the *leshie?*"

"Yes! he says that the *leshie* is very tall and very brown, always covered from head to foot in the bark of a tree, and that one can never get a fair look at him because he always keeps out of the moon's light, but he keeps looking at you and winking. . . ."

"Oh, horrible!" cried Fédia, shuddering and shrugging his shoulders.

"What I can't understand," said Paul, "is that such vermin can breed and continue on the earth as they do."

[1] The *leshie* is the evil spirit of the woods.

"Hush! don't say anything ill about him; take care, he will hear you; he is dumb, but he is not deaf," said Ilyusha, "and he is very revengeful."

After a few minutes' meditation on the necessity of not irritating the wood-goblin, little Vania cried, "O! brothers! look, look! . . . (The first movement of all was to shudder); look at the stars of the good God! they are like great swarms of bees."

Speaking thus, he drew his fresh little face out of his covering, and leaning on his elbow, fixed his bright gaze on the starry sky. His four wise friends, following his example, raised their innocent faces to the sublime vault, and I remarked with pleasure that it was with reluctance they turned them again towards the ground. But as all contemplation has an end, Fédia, the son of the rich peasant, said to the little Ivan:

"What news of your sister Anyuta; is she well?"

"Yes," answered Vania, "she is well."

"Ask her, then, why she does not come to see us."

"I don't know what keeps herrr," answered Vania, who had a strong burr.

"Well, tell her to come."

"Yes, I will tell herrr."

"Tell her I have something nice for her."

"And me, will you give me something too?"

"Yes, you too."

Little Van sighed, and then said, "No, not to me, I don't want anything; give what you were going to give me, give it to her. She is such a good, good sister." And his head fell softly on the ground again.

Paul rose, and took up in his left hand the empty pot.

"Where are you going?" asked Fédia.

"To the river for water, I am thirsty."

The dogs rose with him, and followed Paul to the river.

"Take care, Paul, and not fall into the river," cried Ilyusha.

"Why should he fall into the water?" said Fédia, "there is no fear of that."

"No fear! no fear! How do you know? Perhaps when he is leaning over and drawing water . . . the *vodianoï*[1] will seize him by the arms and pull him in. And then the people will say, 'He fell in, poor fellow! he fell into the water.' He fell in! it is very easily said. . . . Ah! did you hear? something moved over there among the bushes."

They all listened. The bushes and reeds rustled.

"And is it true," said Kostia, "that Akulina, the poor idiot, has been so since ever she fell into the water?"

"Yes, yes. Isn't she frightful just now? Well, they say she was once a beauty. It was the *vodianoï* that disfigured her and spoiled her. He did not expect they would draw her out so soon . . . but he had time, for all that, to twist and deform her as you see."

I have myself met this Akulina many times. The poor wretch is covered with rags, frightfully lean, with a face as black as coal, haggard eyes, teeth always gnashing. She will stand a long time in one place, no matter where, stamping with her feet on the ground, crossing her bony arms over her breast, and shifting from one leg to the other like a ferocious beast in a confined cage.

"They say," resumed Kostia, "that Akulina threw hersel into the water because her lover deceived her."

"Quite true."

"And do you remember Vasia?" added Kostia in a sad tone.

"What Vasia do you mean?" said Fédia.

"Oh! the one that was drowned—drowned in this river. How handsome he was! how handsome! And Feclista, his mother, loved him so much! Do you know that she felt . . . that she always felt that Vasia would come to his death by the water. Sometimes Vasia went with the rest of us boys, in the summer-time, to bathe in the river; and Feclista, every time, kept

[1] The *Vodianoï*, from *voda*, water, the water-spirit.

trembling in such a way. All the other women, without thinking there was any danger, would pass quite tranquilly with
their tubs to the washing-place; but Feclista always set her
tub on the ground, and cried out to Vasia, 'Come out of the
water, my little darling, come out, come here, come, my
lamb, come!' How he drowned himself, God knows. He was
one day playing on the bank, his mother was not there; she
was turning the hay in the meadow. All of a sudden she began
to feel uneasy, she ran to the river, she looked about her, she
saw bubbles mounting to the top of the water, and Vasia's
cap floating . . . floating. . . . Since that day Feclista
has not been in her right mind. She goes to the place and
stretches herself on the ground, and sings a little song, the
song that Vasia was always singing, it is *that* she sings, and
then she weeps and weeps—God ought to have pity on
her."

"Here is Pavlucha coming back," said Fédia.

Paul rejoined his friends; he brought back the pot full.
He was very silent at first, and then I heard him murmuring:

"Ah! dear comrades, it is a dreadful thing . . ."

"What is it? What is the matter with you?" said Kostia
impetuously.

"I heard in the river the soft voice of Vasia . . ."

The little circle shuddered.

"What do you say? eh? what?" said Kostia, in a wondering
tone of voice.

"God is my witness; when I leaned down over the water, I
heard just from the bottom of the river the voice of Vasia
calling to me, 'Pavlucha, Pavlucha, come here, come
here!' I drew back quickly; and for all that, you see I have
brought back my pot full of fresh clear water."

"Oh! Lord God, Lord God! have mercy on us!" said the
four boys, crossing themselves; and Paul, after them, crossed
himself still more solemnly.

"It must have been the *vodianoï* that called you, Paul; it

was the *vodianoï*," said Fédia; "and imagine, just a minute ago, we were talking of poor Vasia."

"It is . . . a . . . bad omen . . . a . . . bad omen, that," said Ilyusha in a voice broken by emotion.

"Well, what must be will be! God preserve us!" said Paul resolutely, seating himself near the fire. "Nobody can escape from his fate."

The boys sat still as if petrified; Paul's words had produced a profound impression on them. . . . They began to arrange themselves round the fire, and disposed themselves at last to sleep.

"What is that?" said Kostia, raising his eyes.

Paul listened: "Snipe," said he, "that whistling, . . . yes, it is a flight of snipe."

"And where are they going to?"

"They are going to the country where there is no winter."

"What! is there any country so very unfortunate?"

"Oh yes! a warm country."

"Far away?"

"Far, far away; away over the warm seas." Kostia sighed, and an instant afterwards his eyes closed.

Three hours had passed since I joined the boys and began to listen to their chat. Tired as I was, I felt that I could listen to them three hours more: but the silence remained unbroken. The moon appeared; I did not remark her presence at first, she was so thin and pale. But this night, like all the nights of this season, was not the less magnificent that it wanted the light of the moon. By this time many of the stars had neared the dim horizon, after leaving the sublime elevation they had reached under the mighty vault. Everything was silent in the air and on the earth, as the first hours after midnight always are; a deep and motionless sleep spread over all. The air seemed less impregnated with odours, and a faint moistness wandered in the lower regions of the atmosphere. . . . The nights of summer are not long. The fires slept with the tired fancies of the little boys. The dogs took advantage of the

silence of our party; the horses, so far as I could perceive by
the feeble and uncertain light of the stars, were lying their
whole length upon the meadow. My eyelids began to grow
heavy . . . and . . . in one moment I fell asleep.

A fresh, light breeze breathed on my face. I opened my
eyes. . . . The darkness was disappearing: it was not yet
the purple dawn; but the day was breaking. The landscape
was becoming visible across the shifting darkness. The
greyish-white sky began to grow clearer and more cool and
blue; the stars shed an uncertain light, like diamonds below
gauze, and disappeared; the earth sent up clouds of mist, the
leaves began to stir softly; from somewhere, I knew not where,
sounds came to me, I could not say what sounds—of voices
doubtless—the first voices of the life that still slumbered; a
faint breeze—the morning breeze, passed wanderingly, capriciously, lightly over the earth. My body saluted it with a
light voluptuous shiver. . . . I rose quickly and went up to
the boys; they were sleeping soundly beside the white ashes
of their dead fires; Paul alone rose, sat up and looked
at me.

I bade him good-bye, looked at him for a moment, then bade
him good-bye again. I then turned to go home along the
river, whose course was marked by white mists. I had hardly
travelled two versts, when all around me, on the wide prairie
glistening with dew, on the green hills, from thicket to thicket,
and from copse to copse; farther off, too, on the dusty roads,
on the bushes bepearled and rainbowed with tears, on the
river that was shining out of a deeper and deeper blue under
the breaking mist—the dawning day threw up its rays of fiery
purple, and then poured forth floods of fresh and resplendent
golden light. . . . A stirring, an awakening, a breathing
full of joy and hope—and all living nature burst into voice
and song; everywhere large stirring drops of dew displayed
their thousand varied lights. . . . From the distance, pure,
clear, distinct, as if bathed in the freshness of the morning,
came the sounds of the village church-bell; and almost

immediately after galloped up behind me the whole *taboun* of Bezhin Meadow, driven by the boys.

I am sorry to be obliged to add to this narrative, already perhaps too long, that Paul died in the course of the year. But he was not drowned; he was killed by a fall from a horse. I am sorry, he was a delightful child.

ALEXANDER AFANASIEF

(1826–1871)

❖❖

DEATH AND THE SOLDIER

(Translated by Rosa Graham)

T H E R E was once a soldier who served for twenty-five years on end, and never got his discharge—never.

He began to turn things over in his mind and wonder at fate.

"What's the meaning of this?" said he. "I've served God and the great Tsar for twenty-five years; I've never been brought up for punishment—I've got a clean sheet—and yet they don't give me my discharge. I think I'll just run off as far as my legs will carry me."

He thought and thought, and at last he ran away. He journeyed a whole day, and the next, and on the third day he met the Lord.

And the Lord asked him:

"Where are you going—on service?"

"O Lord, I've served truly and faithfully for twenty-five years and I see they're not giving me my discharge—and so now I'm running away as far as I can go."

"Oh, well, since you've served twenty-five years faithfully and truly, you may step up to Paradise and enter the kingdom of heaven."

So the soldier comes into heaven, sees there ineffable bliss, and thinks to himself, "Ah, that's the way to live!" But as soon as he began to move about and to walk in the heavenly places, he went up to the holy fathers and asked them:

"Isn't there anyone here who sells tobacco?"

"What sort of tobacco do you expect to find here? You're

not in the army now! This is Paradise—the kingdom of heaven."

The soldier was silent.

He walked on and walked on, all about the heavenly places, and once more approached the holy fathers and asked:

"Isn't there any place round about here where they sell wine?"

"Oh, you, you think you're still in the army! How could there be any wine here?"

"But how can it possibly be heaven—with no tobacco and no wine?" said the soldier, and he left Paradise straightway, and went out.

He walked and he walked about on earth, and at last he ran up against the Lord and said: "What sort of a place was that Paradise you sent me to? Why, there is neither tobacco nor wine there!"

"Well, just turn to the left," answered the Lord, "you'll find everything there."

So the soldier turned to the left and went along the road. An unclean spirit was running along there, and said to him: "What are you looking for, Mr. Soldier?"

"Let's find a place where we can sit, and then we can talk," said the soldier.

So the soldier was taken into the hot place.

"And have you got tobacco here?" asked he of the unclean spirit.

"Oh yes, soldier."

"And wine?"

"Yes, wine too."

"Well, give me some of everything!" So the unclean spirits gave him a pipe and tobacco and a square bottle half full of pepper brandy.

The soldier drank and walked about and smoked his pipe and became very joyful.

"Ah, this is really Paradise, such a Paradise!"

But after he'd walked about a little, he found so many devils crowding round him on all sides that he felt sick.

What could he do? A fanciful idea came into his mind—he would measure off a *sazhen*; he made himself a yard-stick and began to measure.

Then a devil rushed up to him and said:

"What are you doing, soldier?"

"Are you blind? Can't you see? I'm going to build a monastery."

The devil runs off to his grandfather and says: "Just look, grandfather, the soldier wants to build a monastery here."

The grandfather jumped up at once and ran to the soldier.

"What are you doing there?" says he.

"Don't you see?" answered the soldier. "I'm going to build a monastery."

Grandfather was terribly frightened, and he at once ran straight to God.

"O Lord, what kind of soldier have you sent us here? He wants to build us a monastery."

"Well, what's it to do with me? Why do you take people of that kind?"

"Take him back again, Lord, out of here!"

"But how can I take him back? He himself wanted to go there!"

"Alas!" moaned grandfather, "what can we poor things do with him?"

"You go and take the skin off one of your little devils, make a drum of it, and sound the alarm: he'll go out at once."

So grandfather went back, caught one of the little devils, and took his skin and made a drum of it.

"Now just be on the watch," said he to the devils, "and as soon as the soldier runs out from the hot place, close the doors at once and shut them up as tight as tight, so that he can't any way break in again."

The grandfather went outside the gate and sounded the alarm, and the soldier, as soon as he heard the bar-a-ban-ban of the drum, dashed out of hell at a run, as if he were crazy, frightening all the devils as he went, and flew out of the gate.

And as soon as he was out, slam went the gate, and they shut it up as tight as tight.

The soldier looked all around. He could see no one, and he didn't hear the alarm any longer, so he went back and began to knock at the door.

"Open quickly," he yelled at the top of his voice. "If you don't, I'll burst the door in."

"Oh no, you won't, brother," said the devils. "You can go off where you like. We're not going to let you in again; we're stronger than you are."

The soldier bowed his head and wandered off whither his eyes led him. He walked and walked until he met the Lord.

"Where are you going, soldier?"

"I don't know myself."

"Well, where shall I put you? I sent you to heaven and you didn't like it! I sent you to hell and you couldn't live there."

"O Lord, let me stand at your gates as a sentry."

"Well, stand there!"

So God stood the soldier at the gates of Paradise and commanded him:

"See that no one comes in."

"I obey. You can't teach an old soldier anything."

So he stands on sentry and lets no one through.

Then Death comes along.

"Who goes there?"

"Death."

"Where going?"

"To God."

"What for?"

"To ask him who I've got to kill next."

"You wait a minute. I'll go and ask him."

"Lord, Death has come. Whom do you want him to kill next?"

"Tell him for the next three years to kill only old people."

The soldier thought to himself: "That means that my old father and mother will die, if you please—they're old people, you see."

So he went back and said to Death:

"You're to go into the forest, and for three years you are to kill the very oldest oaks there."

Death wept and cried: "For what reason is the Lord angry with me, that he sends me to cut down the oaks?"

And he wandered away into the forests, and for three years he cut down the very oldest oak trees; and when the time came round, he returned once more to God for his orders.

"Why do you come trapesing here again?" asks the soldier.

"I come for orders—to know whom the Lord commands me to kill."

"Wait a minute. I'll go and ask him."

So the soldier goes to the Lord again and asks:

"Death has come again, Lord, and wants to know whom he shall kill."

"Tell him to kill the young people for three years."

The soldier thought to himself: "That means he will be killing my young brothers. So he went out and said to Death:

"Go back to the forests and destroy young oak trees for three years. That's what the Lord has ordered."

"What makes the Lord so angry with me?" wept Death; and he went off again into the forests, and for three years he destroyed young oak trees, and as soon as the time was up, he came back to God, hardly able to drag his feet along.

"Where are you going?" asks the soldier.

"To God—for my orders—whom he wants me to kill."

"Wait a minute. I'll go and ask him."

So he went once more to God and said: "Lord, Death has come. Whom do you want him to kill?"

"Tell him for three years to kill young children."

The soldier thought to himself: "My brothers have some little children: that means that Death will slay them."

So he went back and said to Death. "Go back again to those same forests, and for three whole years destroy the smallest oaks you can find."

"Why does God torment me so?" wept Death; and he went off to the forests, and for three years he destroyed the very tiniest of young oak trees, and so the time passed away, and he went back again to God, hardly able to drag his legs along.

"Now, even if I have to fight that soldier, I'll go myself to the Lord, and ask him why for nine years he has been punishing me!"

The soldier saw Death coming, and called out to him:

"Where are you going?"

Death was silent and began to climb up the steps. But the soldier took him by the scruff of the neck and wouldn't let him come in.

And they made such a rumpus that the Lord heard it and came out.

"What's all this?" he asked.

Death fell at his feet.

"Lord, why are you so angry with me? I have been suffering all these nine years, and struggling in the forests. For three years I cut down the old oak trees; for three years I cut down the young oak trees; and for three years I destroyed the tiniest oak saplings . . . I can hardly drag my feet along."

"That's all your doing," said the Lord to the soldier.

"I'm sorry, Lord," said the soldier.

"Then go away from here," said the Lord, "and carry Death for nine years on your shoulders."

So Death sat on the soldier's back, and off they went together.

The soldier couldn't help himself—he had to carry Death on his back, and he carried him and carried him until he got tired. And he pulled out his horn snuff-box and began to sniff at it. Death saw that the soldier was smelling at something, and said to him: "Soldier, let me smell the snuff too!"

"Well, here you are; crawl down off my back into the box, and you can smell it as much as you like."

"Well, open the box!"

So the soldier opened his snuff-box; and as soon as Death had crawled into it, at that very minute he shut up the box with Death inside it, and stuffed it into the top of one of his boots.

And then he returned to his old post and stood on sentry again.

When the Lord saw him, he asked: "And where's Death?"

"He's with me."

"Where—with you?"

"Here he is, in the top of my boot!"

"Well, show him to me!"

"Oh no, Lord; I'm not going to show him to you, because he mustn't come out for nine years. It's no joke to carry Death on your back for nine years; he's no light weight!"

"Show him to me, and I'll forgive you!"

So the soldier pulled the snuff-box out of the top of his boot, and as soon as he opened it, Death at once jumped on to his shoulder.

"Come down off of that, since you hadn't the sense to stick up there when you were put," said the Lord.

Death came down.

"And now you can kill the soldier," said the Lord; and he went off, God knows where.

"Well, soldier!" said Death to him. "You heard what was said. The Lord has given me orders to kill you."

"What about it?" said the soldier. "One's got to die some time or other; only give me time to get ready for it."

"All right. You can do that."

So the soldier put on clean linen and dragged in a coffin.

"Are you ready?" asked Death.

"Quite ready."

"Well, lie down in the coffin."

So the soldier lay down in the coffin, on his stomach.

"No, not like that," said Death.

"Well, how?" asked the soldier, and turned on to his side.

"No, not like that at all. It wouldn't be right for you to die lying like that."

So he turned and lay on his other side.

"Oh dear, what a person you are, truly; don't you really know how people die? Haven't you ever seen? Get up, and I'll show you."

The soldier jumped up out of the coffin, and Death lay down in his place. Then the soldier grabbed hold of the coffin-lid, put it quickly on top of the coffin and fastened it on with iron hoops. In a moment he had lifted it on to his shoulder and carried it down to the river.

He carried it down to the river, and then returned to his former post and stood on sentry.

The Lord saw him and asked him: "And where's Death?"

"Oh, I've put him into the river."

The Lord looked in that direction, and saw, far away, Death swimming in the water.

And the Lord helped him out on to dry land.

"Why didn't you kill the soldier?" he asked.

"He's so artful, one can't do anything with him."

"Don't you have any more talk with him; just go and kill him at once!"

Some say that Death then went and killed the soldier, but others think he tricked Death again, and that he lived for a long while still in the world and only just lately died.

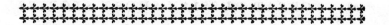

FEDOR DOSTOIEVSKY

(1828–1881)

✠

(I)

THE GRAND INQUISITOR

(Translated by Constance Garnett)

"Fifteen centuries have passed since He promised to come in His glory, fifteen centuries since His prophet wrote, 'Behold, I come quickly;' 'Of that day and that hour knoweth no man, neither the Son, but the Father,' as He Himself predicted on earth. But humanity awaits Him with the same faith and with the same love. Oh, with greater faith, for it is fifteen centuries since man has ceased to see signs from Heaven.

> No signs from Heaven come to-day
> To add to what the heart doth say.

There was nothing left but faith in what the heart doth say. It is true there were many miracles in those days. There were saints who performed miraculous cures; some holy people, according to their biographies, were visited by the Queen of Heaven herself. But the devil did not slumber, and doubts were already arising among men of the truth of these miracles. And just then there appeared in the north of Germany a terrible new heresy. 'A huge star like to a torch' (that is, to a church) 'fell on the sources of the waters and they became bitter.' These heretics began blasphemously denying miracles. But those who remained faithful were all the more ardent in their faith. The tears of humanity rose up to Him as before, awaited His coming, loved Him, hoped for

227

Him, yearned to suffer and die for Him as before. And so many ages mankind had prayed with faith and fervour, 'O Lord our God, hasten Thy coming,' so many ages called upon Him, that in His infinite mercy He deigned to come down to His servants. Before that day He had come down, He had visited some holy men, martyrs and hermits, as is written in their 'Lives.' Among us, Tyutchev, with absolute faith in the truth of his words, bore witness that

> Bearing the Cross, in slavish dress
> Weary and worn, the Heavenly King
> Our mother, Russia, came to bless,
> And through our land went wandering.

And that veritably was so, I assure you.

"And behold, He deigned to appear for a moment to the people, to the tortured, suffering people, sunk in iniquity, but loving Him like children. My story is laid in Spain, in Seville, in the most terrible time of the Inquisition, when fires were lighted every day to the glory of God, and 'in the splendid *auto-da-fé* the wicked heretics were burnt.' Oh, of course, this was not the coming in which He will appear according to His promise at the end of time in all His heavenly glory, and which will be sudden 'as lightning flashes from east to west.' No, He visited His children only for a moment, and there where the flames were crackling round the heretics. In His infinite mercy He came once more among men in that human shape in which He walked among men for three years fifteen centuries ago. He came down to the 'hot pavements' of the southern town in which on the day before almost a hundred heretics had, *ad majorem gloriam Dei,* been burnt by the cardinal, the Grand Inquisitor, in a magnificent *auto-da-fé,* in the presence of the king, the court, the knights, the cardinals, the most charming ladies of the court, and the whole population of Seville.

"He came softly, unobserved, and yet, strange to say, every one recognised Him. That might be one of the best passages in the poem. I mean, why they recognised Him. The people are irresistibly drawn to Him, they surround Him, they flock about Him, follow Him. He moves silently in their midst with a gentle smile of infinite compassion. The sun of love burns in His heart, light and power shine from His eyes, and their radiance, shed on the people, stirs their hearts with responsive love. He holds out His hands to them, blesses them, and a healing virtue comes from contact with Him, even with His garments. An old man in the crowd, blind from childhood, cries out, 'O Lord, heal me and I shall see Thee!' and, as it were, scales fall from his eyes and the blind man sees Him. The crowd weeps and kisses the earth under His feet. Children throw flowers before Him, sing, and cry hosannah. 'It is He! it is He!' all repeat. 'It must be He, it can be no one but Him!' He stops at the steps of the Seville cathedral at the moment when the weeping mourners are bringing in a little open white coffin. In it lies a child of seven, the only daughter of a prominent citizen. The dead child lies hidden in flowers. 'He will raise your child,' the crowd shouts to the weeping mother. The priest, coming to meet the coffin, looks perplexed, and frowns, but the mother of the dead child throws herself at His feet with a wail. 'If it is Thou, raise my child!' she cries, holding out her hands to Him. The procession halts, the coffin is laid on the steps at His feet. He looks with compassion, and His lips once more softly pronounce, 'Maiden, arise!' and the maiden arises. The little girl sits up in the coffin and looks round, smiling with wide-open wondering eyes, holding a bunch of white roses they had put in her hand.

"There are cries, sobs, confusion among the people, and at that moment the cardinal himself, the Grand Inquisitor, passes by the cathedral. He is an old man, almost ninety, tall and erect, with a withered face and sunken eyes, in which there is still a gleam of light. He is not dressed in his gorgeous cardinal's robes, as he was the day before, when he was burning the enemies of the Roman Church—at that moment he was wearing his coarse, old, monk's cassock. At a distance behind him come his gloomy assistants and slaves and the 'holy guard.' He stops at the sight of the crowd and watches it from a distance. He sees everything; he sees them set the coffin down at His feet, sees the child rise up, and his face darkens. He knits his thick grey brows and his eyes gleam with a sinister fire. He holds out his finger and bids the guards take Him. And such is his power, so completely are the people cowed into submission and trembling obedience to him, that the crowd immediately make way for the guards, and in the midst of deathlike silence they lay hands on Him and lead Him away. The crowd instantly bows down to the earth, like one man, before the old inquisitor. He blesses the people in silence and passes on. The guards lead their prisoner to the close, gloomy, vaulted prison in the ancient palace of the Holy Inquisition and shut Him in. The day passes and is followed by the dark, burning, 'breathless' night of Seville. The air is 'fragrant with laurel and lemon.' In the pitch darkness the iron door of the prison is suddenly opened and the Grand Inquisitor himself comes in with a light in his hand. He is alone; the door is closed at once behind him. He stands in the doorway and for a minute or two gazes into His face. At last he goes up slowly, sets the light on the table and speaks.

" 'Is it Thou? Thou?' but receiving no answer, he adds at once: 'Don't answer, be silent. What canst Thou say, indeed? I know too well what Thou wouldst say. And Thou hast no right to add anything to what Thou hast said of old. Why, then, art Thou come to hinder us? For Thou hast come to hinder us, and Thou knowest that. But dost Thou know what will be to-morrow? I know not who Thou art and care not to know whether it is Thou or only a semblance of Him, but to-morrow I shall condemn Thee and burn Thee at the stake as the worst of heretics. And the very people who have to-day kissed Thy feet, to-morrow at the faintest sign from me will rush to heap up the embers of Thy fire. Knowest Thou that? Yes, maybe Thou knowest it,' he added, with thoughtful penetration, never for a moment taking his eyes off the Prisoner."

"I don't quite understand, Ivan. What does it mean?" Alyosha, who had been listening in silence, said with a smile. "Is it simply a wild fantasy, or a mistake on the part of the old man—some impossible *qui pro quo?*"

"Take it as the last," said Ivan, laughing, "if you are so corrupted by modern realism and can't stand anything fantastic. If you like it to be a case of mistaken identity, let it be so. It is true," he went on, laughing, "the old man was ninety, and he might well be crazy over his set idea. He might have been struck by the appearance of the Prisoner. It might, in fact, be simply his ravings, the delusion of an old man of ninety, over-excited by the *auto-da-fe* of a hundred heretics the day before. But does it matter to us, after all, whether it was a mistake of identity or a wild fantasy? All that matters is that the old man should speak out, should speak openly of what he has thought in silence for ninety years."

"And the Prisoner too is silent? Does He look at him and not say a word?"

"That's inevitable in any case," Ivan laughed again. "The old man has told Him He hasn't the right to add anything to what He has said of old. One may say it is the most fundamental feature of Roman Catholicism, in my opinion at least. 'All has been given by Thee to the Pope,' they say, 'and all, therefore, is still in the Pope's hands, and there is no need for Thee to come now at all. Thou must not meddle for the time, at least.' That's how they speak and write too—the Jesuits, at any rate. I have read it myself in the works of their theologians. 'Hast Thou the right to reveal to us one of the mysteries of that world from which Thou hast come?' my old man asks Him, and answers the question for Him. 'No, Thou hast not; that Thou mayest not add to what has been said of old, and mayest not take from men the freedom which Thou didst exalt when Thou wast on earth. Whatsoever Thou

revealest anew will encroach on men's freedom of faith; for it
will be manifest as a miracle, and the freedom of their faith
was dearer to Thee than anything in those days of fifteen
hundred years ago. Didst Thou not often say then, "I will
make you free"? But now Thou hast seen these "free" men,'
the old man adds suddenly, with a pensive smile. 'Yes, we've
paid dearly for it,' he goes on, looking sternly at Him, 'but
at last we have completed that work in Thy name. For
fifteen centuries we have been wrestling with Thy freedom,
but now it is ended and over for good. Dost Thou not believe
that it's over for good? Thou lookest meekly at me and
deignest not even to be wroth with me. But let me tell Thee
that now, to-day, people are more persuaded than ever that
they have perfect freedom, yet they have brought their freedom to us and laid it humbly at our feet. But that has been
our doing. Was this what Thou didst? Was this Thy
freedom?' "

"I don't understand again," Alyosha broke in. "Is he ironical, is he jesting?"

"Not a bit of it! He claims it as a merit for himself and his
Church that at last they have vanquished freedom and have
done so to make men happy. 'For now' (he is speaking of the
Inquisition, of course) 'for the first time it has become possible to think of the happiness of men. Man was created
rebel; and how can rebels be happy? Thou wast warned,' he
says to Him, 'Thou hast had no lack of admonitions and
warnings, but Thou didst not listen to those warnings; Thou
didst reject the only way by which men might be made
happy. But, fortunately, departing Thou didst hand on the
work to us. Thou hast promised, Thou hast established by
Thy word, Thou hast given to us the right to bind and to
unbind, and now, of course, Thou canst not think of taking it
away. Why, then, hast Thou come to hinder us?' "

"And what's the meaning of 'no lack of admonitions and
warnings'?" asked Alyosha.

"Why, that's the chief part of what the old man must say.

" 'The wise and dread Spirit, the spirit of self-destruction and non-existence,' the old man goes on, 'the great spirit talked with Thee in the wilderness, and we are told in the books that he "tempted" Thee. Is that so? And could anything truer be said than what he revealed to Thee in three questions and what Thou didst reject, and what in the books is called "the temptation"? And yet if there has ever been on earth a real stupendous miracle, it took place on that day, on the day of the three temptations. The statement of those three questions was itself the miracle. If it were possible to imagine simply for the sake of argument that those three questions of the dread spirit had perished utterly from the books, and that we had to restore them and to invent them anew, and to do so had gathered together all the wise men of the earth—rulers, chief priests, learned men, philosophers, poets—and had set them the task to invent three questions, such as would not only fit the occasion, but express in three words, three human phrases, the whole future history of the world and of humanity—dost Thou believe that all the wisdom of the earth united could have invented anything in depth and force equal to the three questions which were actually put to Thee then by the wise and mighty spirit in the wilderness? From those questions alone, from the miracle of their statement, we can see that we have here to do not with the fleeting human intelligence, but with the absolute and eternal. For in those three questions the whole subsequent history of mankind is, as it were, brought together into one whole, and foretold, and in them are united all the unsolved historical contradictions of human nature. At the time it could not be so clear, since the future was unknown; but now that fifteen hundred years have passed, we see that everything in those three questions was so justly divined and foretold, and has been so truly fulfilled, that nothing can be added to them or taken from them.

" 'Judge Thyself who was right—Thou or he who questioned Thee then. Remember the first question; its meaning, in other words, was this: "Thou wouldst go into the world, and art going with empty hands, with some promise of freedom which men in their simplicity and their natural unruliness cannot even understand, which they fear and dread—for nothing has ever been more insupportable for a man and a human society than freedom. But seest Thou these stones in this parched and barren wilderness? Turn them into bread, and mankind will run after Thee like a flock of sheep, grateful and obedient, though for ever trembling, lest Thou withdraw Thy hand and deny them Thy bread." But Thou wouldst not deprive man of freedom and didst reject the offer, thinking, What is that freedom worth if obedience is bought with bread? Thou didst reply that man lives not by bread alone. But dost Thou know that for the sake of that earthly bread the spirit of the earth will rise up against Thee, and will strive with Thee and overcome Thee, and all will follow him, crying, "Who can compare with this beast? He has given us fire from heaven!" Dost Thou know that the ages will pass, and humanity will proclaim by the lips of their sages that there is no crime, and therefore no sin; there is only hunger? "Feed men, and then ask of them virtue!" that's what they'll write on the banner which they will raise against Thee, and with which they will destroy Thy temple. Where Thy temple stood will rise a new building; the terrible tower of Babel will be built again, and though, like the one of old, it will not be finished, yet Thou mightest have prevented that new tower and have cut short the sufferings of men for a thousand years; for they will come back to us after a thousand years of agony with their tower. They will seek us again, hidden underground in the catacombs, for we shall be again persecuted and tortured. They will find us and cry to us, "Feed us, for those who have promised us fire from heaven haven't given it!" And then we shall finish building their tower, for he finishes the building who feeds them. And we alone shall feed them in Thy name, declaring falsely that it is in Thy name. Oh, never, never can they feed themselves without us! No science will give them bread so long as they remain free. In the end they will lay their freedom at our feet, and say to us, "Make us your slaves, but feed us." They will understand themselves, at last, that freedom and bread enough for all are inconceivable together, for never, never will they be able to share between them! They will be convinced, too, that they can never be free, for they are weak, vicious, worthless and rebellious. Thou didst promise them the bread of Heaven, but, I repeat again, can it compare with earthly bread in the eyes of the weak, ever-sinful and ignoble race of men? And if for the sake of the bread of Heaven thousands and tens of thousands shall follow Thee, what is to become of the millions and tens of thousands of millions of creatures who will not have the strength to forego the earthly bread for the sake of the heavenly? Or dost Thou care only for the tens of thousands of the great and strong, while the millions, numerous as the sands of the sea, who are weak but love Thee, must exist only for the sake of the great and strong? No, we care for the weak too. They are sinful and rebellious, but in the end they, too, will become obedient. They will marvel at us and look on us as gods, because we are ready to endure the freedom which they have found so dreadful and to rule over them—so awful it will seem to them to be free. But we shall tell them that we are Thy servants and rule them in Thy name. We shall deceive them again, for we will not let Thee come to us again. That deception will be our suffering, for we shall be forced to lie.

" 'This is the significance of the first question in the wilderness, and this is what Thou hast rejected for the sake of that freedom which Thou hast exalted above everything. Yet in this question lies hid the great secret of the world. Choosing "bread" Thou wouldst have satisfied the universal and everlasting craving of humanity—to find someone to worship. So long as man remains free he strives for nothing so incessantly and so painfully as to find someone to worship. But man seeks to worship what is established beyond dispute, so that all men would agree at once to worship it. For these pitiful creatures are concerned not only to find what one or the other can worship, but to find something that all would believe in and worship; what is essential is that all may be *together* in it. This craving for *community* of worship is the chief misery of every man and of all humanity from the beginning of time. For the sake of common worship they've slain each other with the sword. They have set up gods and challenged one another: "Put away your gods and come and worship ours, or we will kill you and your gods!" And so it will be to the end of the world, even when gods disappear from the earth; they will fall down before idols just the same. Thou didst know, Thou couldst not but have known, this fundamental secret of human nature, but Thou didst reject the one infallible banner which was offered Thee to make all men bow down to Thee alone—the banner of earthly bread; and Thou hast rejected it for the sake of freedom and the bread of Heaven. Behold what Thou didst further. And all again in the name of freedom! I tell Thee that man is tormented by no greater anxiety than to find someone quickly to whom he can hand over that gift of freedom with which the ill-fated creature is born. But only one who can appease their conscience can take over their freedom. In bread there was offered Thee an invincible banner; give bread, and man will worship Thee, for nothing is more certain than bread. But if someone else gains possession of his conscience—oh! then he will cast away Thy bread and follow after him who has ensnared his conscience. In that Thou wast right. For the secret of man's being is not only to live but to have something to live for. Without a stable conception of the object of life, man would not consent to go on living, and would rather destroy himself than remain on earth, though he had bread in abundance. That is true. But what happened? Instead of taking men's freedom from them, Thou didst make it greater than ever! Didst Thou forget that man prefers peace, and even death, to freedom of choice in the knowledge of good and evil? Nothing is more seductive for man than his freedom of conscience, but nothing is a greater cause of suffering. And behold, instead of giving a firm foundation for setting the conscience of man at rest for ever, Thou didst choose all that is exceptional, vague and enigmatic; Thou didst choose what is utterly beyond the strength of men, acting as though Thou didst not love them at all—Thou who didst come to give Thy life for them! Instead of taking possession of man's freedom, Thou didst increase it, and burdened the spiritual kingdom of mankind with its sufferings for ever. Thou didst desire man's free love, that He should follow Thee freely, enticed and taken captive by Thee. In place of the rigid ancient law, man must hereafter with free heart decide for himself what is good and what is evil, having only Thy image before him as his guide. But didst Thou not know that he would at last reject even Thy image and Thy truth, if he is weighed down with the fearful burden of free choice? They will cry aloud at last that the truth is not in Thee, for they could not have been left in greater confusion and suffering than Thou hast caused, laying upon them so many cares and unanswerable problems.

" 'So that, in truth, Thou didst Thyself lay the foundation for the destruction of Thy kingdom, and no one is more to blame for it. Yet what was offered Thee? There are three powers, three powers alone, able to conquer and to hold captive for ever the conscience of these impotent rebels for their happiness—those forces are miracle, mystery and authority. Thou hast rejected all three and hast set the example for doing so. When the wise and dread spirit set Thee on the pinnacle of the temple and said to Thee, "If Thou wouldst know whether Thou art the Son of God, then cast Thyself down, for it is written: The angels shall hold him up lest he fall and bruise himself; and Thou shalt know then whether Thou art the Son of God and shalt prove then how great is Thy faith in Thy Father." But Thou didst refuse and wouldst not cast Thyself down. Oh! of course, Thou didst proudly and well, like God; but the weak, unruly race of men, are they gods? Oh, Thou didst know then that in taking one step, in making one movement to cast Thyself down, Thou wouldst be tempting God and have lost Thy faith in Him, and wouldst have been dashed to pieces against that Earth which Thou didst come to save. And the wise spirit that tempted Thee would have rejoiced. But I ask again, Are there many like Thee? And couldst Thou believe for one moment that men, too, could face such a temptation? Is the nature of men such that they can reject miracle, and at the great moments of their life, the moments of their deepest, most agonising spiritual difficulties, cling only to the free verdict of the heart? Oh, Thou didst know that Thy deed would be recorded in books, would be handed down to remote times and the utmost ends of the earth, and Thou didst hope that man, following Thee, would cling to God and not ask for a miracle. But Thou didst not know that when man rejects miracle he rejects God too; for man seeks not so much God as the miraculous. And as man cannot bear to be without the miraculous, he will create new miracles of his own for himself, and will worship deeds of sorcery and witchcraft, though he might be a hundred times over a rebel, heretic and infidel. Thou didst not come down from the Cross when they shouted to Thee, mocking and reviling Thee, "Come down from the cross and we will believe that Thou art He." Thou didst not come down, for again Thou wouldst not enslave man by a miracle, and didst crave faith given freely, not based on miracle. Thou didst crave for free love and not the base raptures of the slave before the might that has overawed him for ever. But Thou didst think too highly of men therein, for they are slaves, of course, though rebellious by nature. Look round and judge; fifteen centuries have passed, look upon them. Whom hast Thou raised up to Thyself? I swear, man is weaker and baser by nature than Thou hast believed him. Can he, can he do what Thou didst? By showing him so much respect, Thou didst, as it were, cease to feel for him, for Thou didst ask far too much from him—Thou who hast loved him more than Thyself! Respecting him less, Thou wouldst have asked less of him. That would have been more like love, for his burden would have been lighter. He is weak and vile. What though he is everywhere now rebelling against our power, and proud of his rebellion? It is the pride of a child and a schoolboy. They are little children rioting and barring out the teacher at school. But their childish delight will end; it will cost them dear. They will cast down temples and drench the earth with blood. But they will see at last, the foolish children, that, though they are rebels, they are impotent rebels, unable to keep up their own rebellion. Bathed in their foolish tears, they will recognise at last that He who created them rebels must have meant to mock at them. They will say this in despair, and their utterance will be a blasphemy which will make them more unhappy still, for man's nature cannot bear blasphemy, and in the end always avenges it on itself. And so unrest, confusion and unhappiness—that is the present lot of men after Thou didst bear so much for their freedom! Thy great prophet tells in vision and in image that he saw all those who took part in the first resurrection and that there were of each tribe twelve thousand. But if there were so many of them, they must have been not men, but gods. They had borne Thy cross, they had endured scores of years in the barren, hungry wilderness, living upon locusts and roots— and Thou mayest indeed point with pride at those children of freedom, of free love, of free and splendid sacrifice for Thy name. But remember that they were only some thousands; and what of the rest? And how are the other weak ones to blame, because they could not endure what the strong have endured? How is the weak soul to blame that it is unable to receive such terrible gifts? Canst Thou have simply come to the elect and for the elect? But if so, it is a mystery and we cannot understand it. And if it is a mystery, we too have a right to preach a mystery, and to teach them that it's not the free judgment of their hearts, not love that matters, but a mystery which they must follow blindly, even against their conscience. So we have done. We have corrected Thy work and have founded it upon *miracle, mystery and authority*. And men rejoiced that they were again led like sheep, and that the terrible gift that had brought them such suffering, was, at last, lifted from their hearts. Were we right teaching them this? Speak! Did we not love mankind, so meekly acknowledging their feebleness, lovingly lightening their burden, and permitting their weak nature even sin with our sanction? Why hast Thou come now to hinder us? And why dost Thou look silently and searchingly at me with Thy mild eyes? Be angry. I don't want Thy love, for I love Thee not. And what use is it for me to hide anything from Thee? Don't I know to Whom I am speaking? All that I can say is known to Thee already. And is it for me to conceal from Thee our mystery? Perhaps it is Thy will to hear it from my lips. Listen, then. We are not working with Thee, but with *him*— that is our mystery. It's long—eight centuries—since we have been on *his* side and not on Thine. Just eight centuries ago, we took from him what Thou didst reject with scorn, that last gift he offered Thee, showing Thee all the kingdoms of the earth. We took from him Rome and the sword of Cæsar, and proclaimed ourselves sole rulers of the earth, though hitherto we have not been able to complete our work. But whose fault is that? Oh, the work is only beginning, but it has begun. It has long to await completion and the earth has yet much to suffer, but we shall triumph and shall be Cæsars, and then we shall plan the universal happiness of man. But Thou mightest have taken even then the sword of Cæsar. Why didst Thou reject that last gift? Hadst Thou accepted that last counsel of the mighty spirit, Thou wouldst have accomplished all that man seeks on earth—that is, someone to worship, someone to keep his conscience, and some means of uniting all in one unanimous and harmonious ant-heap, for the craving for universal unity is the third and last angu.'sh of men. Mankind as a whole has always striven to organise a universal state. There have been many great nations with great histories, but the more highly they were developed the more unhappy they were, for they felt more acutely than other people the craving for world-wide union. The great conquerors, Timours and Genghis-Khans, whirled like hurricanes over the face of the earth, striving to subdue its people, and they too were but the unconscious expression of the same craving for universal unity. Hadst Thou taken the world and Cæsar's purple, Thou wouldst have founded the universal state and have given universal peace. For who can rule men if not he who holds their conscience and their bread in his hands? We have taken the sword of Cæsar, and in taking it, of course, have rejected Thee and followed *him*. Oh, ages are yet to come of the confusion of free thought, of their science and cannibalism. For having begun to build their tower of Babel without us, they will end, of course, with cannibalism. But then the beast will crawl to us and lick our feet and spatter them with tears of blood. And we shall sit upon the beast and raise the cup, and on it will be written, "Mystery." But then, and only then, the reign of peace and happiness will come for men. Thou art proud of Thine elect, but Thou hast only the elect, while we give rest to all. And besides, how many of those elect, those mighty ones, who could become elect, have grown weary waiting for Thee, and have transferred and will transfer the powers of their spirit and the warmth of their heart to the other camp, and end by raising their *free* banner against Thee? Thou didst Thyself lift up that banner. But with us all will be happy and will no more rebel nor destroy one another as under Thy freedom. Oh, we shall persuade them that they will only become free when they renounce their freedom to us and submit to us. And shall we be right or shall we be lying? They will be convinced that we are right, for they will remember the horrors of slavery and confusion to which Thy freedom

brought them. Freedom, free thought and science, will lead
them into such straits and will bring them face to face with
such marvels and insoluble mysteries, that some of them, the
fierce and rebellious, will destroy themselves; others, rebellious but weak, will destroy one another; while the rest,
weak and unhappy, will crawl fawning to our feet and whine
to us: "Yes, you were right, you alone possess His mystery,
and we come back to you ; save us from ourselves!"

" 'Receiving bread from us, they will see clearly that we
take the bread made by their hands from them, to give it to
them, without any miracle. They will see that we do not
change the stones to bread, but in truth they will be more
thankful for taking it from our hands than for the bread
itself! For they will remember only too well that in old days,
without our help, even the bread they made turned to stones
in their hands, while since they have come back to us, the
very stones have turned to bread in their hands. Too, too
well will they know the value of complete submission! And
until men know that, they will be unhappy. Who is most tc
blame for their not knowing it? Speak! Who scattered the
flock and sent it astray on unknown paths? But the flock will
come together again and will submit once more, and then it
will be once for all. Then we shall give them the quiet,
humble happiness of weak creatures such as they are by
nature. Oh, we shall persuade them at last not to be proud,
for Thou didst lift them up and thereby taught them to be
proud. We shall show them that they are weak, that they
are only pitiful children, but that childlike happiness is the
sweetest of all. They will become timid and will look to us
and huddle close to us in fear, as chicks to the hen. They will
marvel at us and will be awe-stricken before us, and will be
proud at our being so powerful and clever, that we have been
able to subdue such a turbulent flock of thousands of millions.
They will tremble impotently before our wrath, their minds
will grow fearful, they will be quick to shed tears like women
and children, but they will be just as ready at a sign from us

to pass to laughter and rejoicing, to happy mirth and childish song. Yes, we shall set them to work, but in their leisure hours we shall make their life like a child's game, with children's songs and innocent dance. Oh, we shall allow them even sin; they are weak and helpless, and they will love us like children because we allow them to sin. We shall tell them that every sin will be expiated, if it is done with our permission, that we allow them to sin because we love them, and the punishment for these sins we take upon ourselves. And we shall take it upon ourselves, and they will adore us as their saviours who have taken on themselves their sins before God. And they will have no secrets from us. We shall allow or forbid them to live with their wives and mistresses, to have or not to have children—according to whether they have been obedient or disobedient—and they will submit to us gladly and cheerfully. The most painful secrets of their conscience, all, all they will bring to us, and we shall have an answer for all. And they will be glad to believe our answer, for it will save them from the great anxiety and terrible agony they endure at present in making a free decision for themselves. And all will be happy, all the millions of creatures except the hundred thousand who rule over them. For only we, who guard the mystery, shall be unhappy. There will be thousands of millions of happy babes, and a hundred thousand sufferers who have taken upon themselves the curse of the knowledge of good and evil. Peacefully they will die, peacefully they will expire in Thy name, and beyond the grave they will find nothing but death. But we shall keep the secret, and for their happiness we shall allure them with the reward of heaven and eternity. Though if there were anything in the other world, it certainly would not be for such as they. It is prophesied that Thou wilt come again in victory, Thou wilt come with Thy chosen, the proud and strong, but we will say that they have only saved themselves, but we have saved all. We are told that the harlot who sits upon the beast, and holds in her hands the *mystery*, shall be put to shame, that the weak will rise up again, and will rend her royal purple and will strip naked her loathsome body. But then I will stand up and point out to Thee the thousand millions of happy children who have known no sin. And we who have taken their sins upon us for their happiness will stand up before Thee and say: "Judge us if Thou canst and darest." Know that I fear Thee not. Know that I too have been in the wilderness, I too have lived on roots and locusts, I too prized the freedom with which Thou hast blessed men, and I too was striving to stand among Thy elect, among the strong and powerful, thirsting "to make up the number." But I awakened and would not serve madness. I turned back and I joined the ranks of those *who have corrected Thy work*. I left the proud and went back to the humble, for the happiness of the humble. What I say to Thee will come to pass, and our dominion will be built up. I repeat, to-morrow Thou shalt see that obedient flock who at a sign from me will hasten to heap up the hot cinders about the pile on which I shall burn Thee for coming to hinder us. For if anyone has ever deserved our fires, it is Thou. To-morrow I shall burn Thee. Dixi.'

"When the Inquisitor ceased speaking he waited some time for his Prisoner to answer him. His silence weighed down upon him. He saw that the Prisoner had listened intently all the time, looking gently in his face and evidently not wishing to reply. The old man longed for Him to say something, however bitter and terrible. But He suddenly approached the old man in silence and softly kissed him on his bloodless aged lips. That was all His answer. The old man shuddered. His lips moved. He went to the door, opened it, and said to Him: 'Go, and come no more . . . come not at all, never, never!' And he led Him out into the dark alleys of the town. The Prisoner went away."

(II)

A GENTLE SPIRIT

(Translated by Constance Garnett)

Part I

I

O h, while she is still here, it is still all right; I go up and look at her every minute; but to-morrow they will take her away —and how shall I be left alone? Now she is on the table in the drawing-room—they put two card-tables together; the coffin will be here to-morrow—white, pure white "gros de Naples"—but that's not it. . . .

I keep walking about, trying to explain it to myself. I have been trying for the last six hours to get it clear, but still I can't think of it all as a whole.

The fact is, I walk to and fro, and to and fro.

This is how it was. I will simply tell it in order. (Order!)

Gentlemen, I am far from being a literary man and you will see that; but no matter. I'll tell it as I understand it myself. The horror of it for me is that I understand it all!

It was, if you care to know, that is, to take it from the beginning, that she used to come to me simply to pawn things, to pay for advertising in the *Voice* to the effect that a governess was quite willing to travel, to give lessons at home, and so on, and so on. That was at the very beginning, and I, of course, made no difference between her and the others: "She comes," I thought, "like anyone else," and so on.

But afterwards I began to see a difference. She was such a slender, fair little thing, rather tall, always a little awkward with me, as though embarrassed.   (I fancy she was the same with all strangers, and in her eyes, of course, I was exactly like anybody else—that is, not as a pawnbroker but as a man.)

As soon as she received the money she would turn round at once and go away. And always in silence. Other women argue so, entreat, haggle for me to give them more; this one did not ask for more. . . .

I believe I am muddling it up.

Yes; I was struck first of all by the things she brought; poor little silver-gilt earrings, a trashy little locket, things not worth sixpence. She knew herself that they were worth next to nothing, but I could see from her face that they were treasures to her, and I found out afterwards as a fact that they were all that was left her belonging to her father and mother.

Only once I allowed myself to scoff at her things. You see I never allow myself to behave like that. I keep up a gentlemanly tone with my clients; few words, politeness and severity. "Severity, severity!"

But once she ventured to bring her last rag, that is, literally the remains of an old hareskin jacket, and I could not resist saying something by way of a joke. My goodness! but she flared up! Her eyes were large, blue and dreamy, but—how they blazed. But she did not drop one word; picking up her "rags" she walked out.

It was then for the first time I noticed her *particularly*, and thought something of the kind about her—that is, something of a particular kind. Yes, I remember another impression that summed up everything. It was that she was terribly young, so young that she looked just fourteen. And yet she was within three months of sixteen. I didn't mean that, though, that wasn't what summed it all up. Next day she came again. I found out later that she had been to Dobronravov's and to Mozer's with that jacket, but they take nothing but gold and would have nothing to say to it. I once took some stones from her (rubbishy little ones) and, thinking it over afterwards, I wondered: I, too, only lend on gold and silver, yet from her I accepted stones. That was my second thought about her then; that I remember. That time, that is, when she came from Mozer's, she brought an amber cigar-holder. It was a connoisseur's article, not bad, but, again, of no value to us, because we only deal in gold. As it was the day after her "mutiny," I received her sternly. Sternness with me takes the form of dryness. As I gave her two roubles, however, I could not resist saying, with a certain irritation, "I only do it for *you*, of course; Mozer wouldn't take such a thing."

The words "for *you*" I emphasised particularly, and with a particular implication.

I was spiteful. She flushed up again when she heard that "for you," but she did not say a word, she did not throw down the money, she took it—that is poverty! But how hotly she flushed! I saw I had stung her. And when she had gone out, I suddenly asked myself whether my triumph over her was worth two roubles. He! He!! He!!! I remember I put that question to myself twice over, "Was it worth it? was it worth it?"

And, laughing, I inwardly answered it in the affirmative. And I felt very much elated. But that was not an evil feeling; I said it with design, with a motive; I wanted to test her, because certain ideas with regard to her had suddenly come into my mind. That was the third thing I thought particularly about her. . . . Well, it was from that time it all began. Of course, I tried at once to find out all her circumstances indirectly, and awaited her coming with a special impatience. I had a presentment that she would come soon. When she came, I entered into effable conversation with her, speaking with unusual politeness. I have not been badly brought up and have manners. H'm. It was then I guessed that she was soft-hearted and gentle.

The gentle and soft-hearted do not resist long, and though they are by no means very ready to reveal themselves, they do not know how to escape from a conversation; they are niggardly in their answers, but they do answer, and the more readily the longer you go on. Only, on your side you must not flag, if you want them to talk. I need hardly say that she did not explain anything to me then. About the *Voice* and all that I found out afterwards. She was at that time spending her last farthing on advertising, haughtily at first, of course. "A governess prepared to travel and will send terms on application," but later on: "willing to do anything, to teach, to be a companion, to be a housekeeper, to wait on an invalid, plain sewing, and so on, and so on," the usual thing! Of course, all this was added to the advertisement a bit at a time, and finally, when she was reduced to despair, it came to: "without salary in return for board." No, she could not find a situation. I made up my mind then to test her for the last time. I suddenly took up the *Voice* of the day and showed her an advertisement. "A young person, without friends and relations, seeks a situation as a governess to young children, preferably in the family of middle-aged widower. Might be a comfort in the home."

"Look here how this lady has advertised this morning, and by the evening she will certainly have found a situation. That's the way to advertise."

Again she flushed crimson and her eyes blazed, she turned round and went straight out. I was very much pleased, though by that time I felt sure of everything and had no apprehensions; nobody will take her cigar-holders, I thought. Besides, she has got rid of them all. And so it was; two days later, she came in again, such a pale little creature, all agitation—I saw that something had happened to her at home, and something really bad. I will explain directly what had happened, but now I only want to recall how I did something *chic*, and rose in her opinion. I suddenly decided to do it. The fact is she was pawning the ikon (she had brought herself to pawn it!) Ah, listen! listen! This is the beginning now, I've been in a muddle. You see, I want to recall all this, every detail, every little point. I want to bring them all together and look at them as a whole and—I cannot. . . . It's these little things, these little things. . . . It was an ikon of the Madonna. A Madonna with the Babe, an old-fashioned, homely one, and the setting was silver-gilt, worth —well, six roubles, perhaps. I could see the ikon was precious to her; she was pawning it whole, not taking it out of the setting. I said to her:

"You had better take it out of the setting, and take the ikon home; for it's not the thing to pawn."

"Why, are you forbidden to take them?"

"No, it's not that we are forbidden, but you might, perhaps, yourself . . ."

"Well, take it out."

"I tell you what. I will not take it out, but I'll set it here in the shrine with the other ikons," I said, on reflection. "Under the little lamp" (I always had the lamp burning as soon as the shop was opened), "and you simply take ten roubles."

"Don't give me ten roubles. I only want five; I shall certainly redeem it."

"You don't want ten? The ikon's worth it," I added, noticing that her eyes flashed again.

She was silent. I brought out five roubles.

"Don't despise anyone; I've been in such straits myself; and worse too, and that you see me here in this business . . . is owing to what I've been through in the past. . . ."

"You're revenging yourself on the world? Yes?" she interrupted suddenly with rather sarcastic mockery, which, however, was to a great extent innocent (that is, it was general, because certainly at that time she did not distinguish me from others, so that she said it almost without malice).

"Ah," thought I; "so that's what you're like. You've got character; you belong to the new movement.

"You see!" I remarked at once, half-jestingly, half-mysteriously, "I am part of that part of the Whole that seeks to do ill, but does good. . . ."

Quickly and with great curiosity, in which, however, there was something very childlike, she looked at me.

"Stay . . . what's that idea? Where does it come from? I've heard it somewhere. . . ."

"Don't rack your brains. In those words Mephistopheles introduces himself to Faust. Have you read *Faust?* "

"Not . . . not attentively."

"That is, you have not read it at all. You must read it. But I see an ironical look in your face again. Please don't imagine that I've so little taste to try to use Mephistopheles to commend myself to you and grace the rôle of pawnbroker. A pawnbroker will still be a pawnbroker. We know."

"You're so strange . . . I didn't mean to say anything of that sort."

She meant to say, "I didn't expect to find you were an educated man"; but she didn't say it; I knew, though, that she thought that. I had pleased her very much.

"You see," I observed, "one may do good in any calling— I'm not speaking of myself, of course. Let us grant that I'm doing nothing but harm, yet . . ."

"Of course, one can do good in every position," she said, glancing at me with a rapid, profound look. "Yes, in any position," she added suddenly.

Oh, I remember, I remember all those moments! And I want to add, too, that when such young creatures, such sweet young creatures, want to say something so clever and profound, they show at once so truthfully and naïvely in their faces, "Here I am saying something clever and profound now"—and that is not from vanity, as it is with anyone like me; but one sees that she appreciates it awfully herself, and believes in it, and thinks a lot of it, and imagines that you think a lot of all that, just as she does. Oh, truthfulness! it's by that they conquer us. How exquisite it was in her!

I remember it, I have forgotten nothing! As soon as she had gone, I made up my mind. That same day I made my last investigations, and found out every detail of her position at the moment; every detail of her past I had learned already from Lukerya, at that time a servant in the family, whom I had bribed a few days before. This position was so awful that I can't understand how she could laugh as she had done that day and feel interest in the words of Mephistopheles, when she was in such horrible straits. But—that's youth! That is just what I thought about her at the time with pride and joy, for, you know, there's a greatness of soul in it—to be able to say, "Though I am on the edge of the abyss, yet Goethe's grand words are radiant with light." Youth always has some greatness of soul, if it's only a spark, and that distorted. Though it's of her I am speaking, of her alone. And, above all, I looked upon her then as *mine* and did not doubt of my power. You know that's a voluptuous idea when you feel no doubt of it.

But what is the matter with me? If I go on like this, when shall I put it all together and look at it as a whole? I must make haste, make haste—that is not what matters, oh, my God!

II

The "details" I learned about her I will tell in one word: her father and mother were dead, they had died three years before, and she had been left with two disreputable aunts: though it is saying too little to call them disreputable. One aunt was a widow with a large family (six children, one smaller than another), the other a horrid old maid. Both were horrid. Her father was in the service, but only as a copying clerk, and was only a gentleman by courtesy; in fact, everything was in my favour. I came as though from a higher world; I was anyway a retired lieutenant of a brilliant regiment, a gentleman by birth, independent and all the rest of it, and as for my pawnbroker's shop, her aunts could only have looked on that with respect. She had been living in slavery at her aunts' for those three years: yet she had managed to pass an examination somewhere—she managed to pass it, she wrung the time for it, weighed down as she was by the pitiless burden of daily drudgery, and she proved something in the way of striving for what was higher and better on her part. Why, what made me want to marry her? Never mind me, though; of that later on. . . . As though that mattered! She taught her aunt's children; she made their clothes; and towards the end not only washed the clothes, but, with her weak chest, even scrubbed the floors. To put it plainly, they used to beat her, and taunt her with eating their bread. It ended by their scheming to sell her. Tfoo! I omit the filthy details. She told me all about it afterwards.

All this had been watched for a whole year by a neighbour, a fat shopkeeper, and not a humble one, but the owner of two grocers' shops. He had ill-treated two wives and now he was looking for a third, and so he cast his eye on her. "She's a quiet one," he thought; "she's grown up in poverty, and I am marrying for the sake of my motherless children."

He really had children. He began trying to make the match and negotiating with the aunts. He was fifty years old, besides. She was aghast with horror. It was then she began coming so often to advertise in the *Voice*. At last she began begging the aunts to give her just a little time to think it over. They granted her that little time, but would not let her have more; they were always at her: "We don't know where to turn to find food for ourselves, without an extra mouth to feed."

I had found all this out already, and the same day, after what had happened in the morning, I made up my mind. That evening the shopkeeper came, bringing with him a pound of sweets from the shop; she was sitting with him, and I called Lukerya out of the kitchen and told her to go and whisper to her that I was at the gate and wanted to say something to her without delay. I felt pleased with myself. And altogether I felt awfully pleased all that day.

On the spot, at the gate, in the presence of Lukerya, before she had recovered from her amazement at my sending for her, I informed her that I should look upon it as an honour and happiness . . . telling her, in the next place, not to be surprised

at the manner of my declaration and at my speaking at the
gate, saying that I was a straightforward man and had
learned the position of affairs. And I was not lying when I
said I was straightforward. Well, hang it all, I did not only
speak with propriety—that is, showing I was a man of decent
breeding, but I spoke with originality, and that was the chief
thing. After all, is there any harm in admitting it? I want to
judge myself and am judging myself. I must speak *pro* and
contra, and I do. I remembered afterwards with enjoyment,
though it was stupid, that I frankly declared, without the
least embarrassment, that, in the first place, I was not
particularly talented, not particularly intelligent, perhaps
not particularly good-natured, rather a cheap egoist (I remember that expression, I thought of it on the way and was
pleased with it), and that very probably there was a great
deal that was disagreeable in me in other respects. All this
was said with a special sort of pride—we all know how that
sort of thing is said. Of course, I had good taste enough not
to proceed to enlarge on my virtues after honourably enu-
merating my defects, not to say, "To make up for that I have
this and that and the other." I saw that she was still horribly
frightened, but I softened nothing; on the contrary, seeing
she was frightened I purposely exaggerated. I told her
straight out that she would have enough to eat, but that fine
clothes, theatres, balls, she would have none of, at any rate,
not till later on, when I had attained my object. This severe
tone was a positive delight to me. I added as cursorily as
possible, that in adopting such a calling—that is, in keeping
a pawnbroker's shop—I had only one object, hinting there
was a special circumstance. . . . But I really had a right to
say so: I really had such an aim and there really was such a
circumstance. Wait a minute, gentlemen; I have always been
the first to hate this pawnbroking business, but in reality,
though it is absurd to talk about oneself in such mysterious
phrases, yet, you know, I was "revenging myself on society."
I really was, I was, I was! So that her gibe that morning at

the idea of my revenging myself was unjust. That is, do you see, if I had said to her straight out in words: "Yes, I am revenging myself on society," she would have laughed as she did that morning, and it would, in fact, have been absurd. But by indirect hints, by dropping mysterious phrases, it appeared that it was possible to work upon her imagination. Besides, I had no fears then: I knew that the fat shopkeeper was anyway more repulsive to her than I was, and that I, standing at the gate, had appeared as a deliverer. I understood that, of course. Oh, what is base a man understands particularly well! But what is base? How can a man judge? Didn't I love her even then?

Wait a bit: of course, I didn't breathe a word to her of doing her a benefit; the opposite, oh, quite the opposite; I made out that it was *I* that would be under an obligation to her, not *she* to me. Indeed, I said as much—I couldn't resist saying it—and it sounded stupid, perhaps, for I noticed a shade flit across her face. But altogether I won the day completely. Wait a bit, if I am to recall all that vileness, then I will tell of that worst beastliness. As I stood there, what was stirring in my mind was, "You are tall, a good figure, educated and—speaking without conceit—good-looking." That was what was at work in my mind. I need hardly say that, on the spot, out there at the gate, she said "*yes*." But . . . but I ought to add: that out there by the gate she thought a long time before she said "*yes*." She pondered for so long that I said to her, "Well?"—and could not even refrain from asking it with a certain swagger.

"Wait a little. I'm thinking."

And her little face was so serious, so serious that even then I might have read it! And I was mortified: "Can she be choosing between me and the grocer?" I thought. Oh, I did not understand then! I did not understand anything, anything, then! I did not understand till to-day! I remember Lukerya ran after me as I was going away, stopped me on the road and said, breathlessly: "God will reward you, sir, for

taking our dear young lady; only don't speak of that to her—
she's proud."

Proud, is she! "I like proud people," I thought. Proud
people are particularly nice when . . . well, when one has no
doubt of one's power over them, eh? Oh, base, tactless man!
Oh, how pleased I was! You know, when she was standing
there at the gate, hesitating whether to say "yes" to me, and
I was wondering at it, you know, she may have had some
such thought as this: "If it is to be misery either way, isn't it
best to choose the very worst?"—that is, let the fat grocer
beat her to death when he was drunk! Eh! what do you
think—could there have been a thought like that?

And, indeed, I don't understand it now, I don't understand
it at all, even now. I have only just said that she may have
had that thought: of two evils choose the worse—that is, the
grocer. But which was the worse for her then—the grocer or
I? The grocer or the pawnbroker who quoted Goethe?
That's another question! What a question! And even that
you don't understand: the answer is lying on the table and
you call it a question! Never mind me, though. It's not a
question of me at all . . . and, by the way, what is there left for
me now—whether it's a question of me or whether it is not?
That's what I am utterly unable to answer. I had better go
to bed. My head aches. . . .

III

I could not sleep. And how should I? There is a pulse
throbbing in my head. One longs to master it all, all that
degradation. Oh, the degradation! Oh, what degradation I
dragged her out of then! Of course, she must have realised
that, she must have appreciated my action! I was pleased,
too, by various thoughts—for instance, the reflection that I
was forty-one and she was only sixteen. That fascinated
me, that feeling of inequality was very sweet, was very
sweet.

I wanted, for instance, to have a wedding *à l'anglaise*, that is, only the two of us, with just the two necessary witnesses, one of them Lukerya, and from the wedding straight to the train to Moscow (I happened to have business there, by the way), and then a fortnight at the hotel. She opposed it, she would not have it, and I had to visit her aunts and treat them with respect as though they were relations from whom I was taking her. I gave way, and all befitting respect was paid the aunts. I even made the creatures a present of a hundred roubles each and promised them more—not telling her anything about it, of course, that I might not make her feel humiliated by the lowness of her surroundings. The aunts were as soft as silk at once. There was a wrangle about the trousseau too; she had nothing, almost literally, but she did not want to have anything. I succeeded in proving to her, though, that she must have something, and I made up the trousseau, for who would have given her anything? But there, enough of me. I did, however, succeed in communicating some of my ideas to her then, so that she knew them anyway. I was in too great a hurry, perhaps. The best of it was that, from the very beginning, she rushed to meet me with love, greeted me with rapture, when I went to see her in the evening, told me in her chatter (the enchanting chatter of innocence) all about her childhood and girlhood, her old home, her father and mother. But I poured cold water upon all that at once. That was my idea. I met her enthusiasm with silence, friendly silence, of course . . . but, all the same, she could quickly see that we were different and that I was—an enigma. And being an enigma was what I made a point of most of all! Why, it was just for the sake of being an enigma, perhaps, that I have been guilty of all this stupidity. The first thing was sternness—it was with an air of sternness that I took her into my house. In fact, as I went about then feeling satisfied, I framed a complete system. Oh, it came of itself without any effort. And it could not have been otherwise. I was bound to create that system owing to one inevitable fact—why should I libel myself, indeed! The system was a genuine one, Yes, listen; if you must judge a man, better judge him knowing all about it . . . listen.

How am I to begin this? for it is very difficult. When you begin to justify yourself, then it is difficult. You see, for instance, young people despise money. I made money of importance at once; I laid special stress on money. And laid such stress on it that she became more and more silent. She opened her eyes wide, listened, gazed and said nothing. You see, the young are heroic, that is, the good among them are heroic and impulsive, but they have little tolerance; if the least thing is not quite right they are full of contempt. And if I wanted breadth, I wanted to instil breadth into her very heart, to make it part of her inmost feeling, did I not? I'll take a trivial example: how should I explain my pawnbroker's shop to a character like that? Of course, I did not speak of it directly, or it would have appeared that I was apologising, and I, so to speak, worked at it through pride; I almost spoke without words, and I am masterly at speaking without words. All my life I have spoken without words, and I have passed through whole tragedies on my own account without words. Why, I, too, have been unhappy! I was abandoned by everyone, abandoned and forgotten, and no one, no one knew it! And all at once this sixteen-year-old girl picked up details about me from vulgar people and thought she knew all about me, and, meanwhile, what was precious remained hidden in the heart! I went on being silent, with her especially I was silent, with her especially, right up to yesterday—why was I silent? Because I was proud; I wanted her to find out for herself, without my help, and not from the tales of low people; I wanted her to *divine of herself* what manner of man I was and to understand me! Taking her into my house I wanted all her respect, I wanted her to be standing before me in homage for the sake of my sufferings—and I deserved it. Oh, I have always been proud, I always wanted all or nothing! You see, it was just because

I am not one who will accept half a happiness, but always wanted all, that I was forced to act like that then: it was as much as to say, "See into me for yourself and appreciate me!" For you must see that if I had begun explaining myself to her and prompting her, ingratiating myself and asking for her respect, it would have been as good as asking for charity. . . . But . . . but why am I talking of that?

Stupid, stupid, stupid, stupid! I explained to her then, in two words, directly, ruthlessly (and I emphasise the fact that it was ruthlessly), that the heroism of youth was charming, but—not worth a farthing. Why not? Because it costs them so little, because it is not gained through life; it is, so to say, merely "first impressions of existence," but just let us see you at work! Cheap heroism is always easy, and even to sacrifice life is easy too; because it is only a case of hot blood and an overflow of energy, and there is such a longing for what is beautiful! No, take the deed of heroism that is laborious, obscure, without noise or flourish, slandered, in which there is a great deal of sacrifice and not one grain of glory—in which you, a splendid man, are made to look like a scoundrel before everyone, though you might be the most honest man in the world—you try that sort of heroism and you'll soon give it up! While I have been bearing the burden of that all my life. At first she argued—ough, how she argued!—but afterwards she began to be silent, completely silent, in fact, only opened her eyes wide as she listened, such big, big eyes, so attentive. And . . . and what is more, I suddenly saw a smile, mistrustful, silent, an evil smile. Well, it was with that smile on her face I brought her into my house. It is true that she had nowhere else to go.

IV

Which of us began it first?

Neither. It began of itself from the very first. I have said that with sternness I brought her into the house. From the

first step, however, I softened it. Before she was married it
was explained to her that she would have to take pledges and
pay out money, and she said nothing at the time (note that).
What is more, she set to work with positive zeal. Well, of
course, my lodging, my furniture all remained as before. My
lodging consisted of two rooms, a large room from which the
shop was partitioned off, and a second one, also large, our
living-room and bedroom. My furniture is scanty: even her
aunts had better things. My shrine of ikons with the lamp
was in the outer room where the shop is; in the inner room
my bookcase with a few books in and a trunk of which I keep
the key; of course, there is a bed, tables and chairs. Before
she was married I told her that one rouble a day, and not
more, was to be spent on our board—that is, on food for me,
her and Lukerya whom I had enticed to come to us. "I must
have thirty thousand in three years," said I, " and we can't
save the money if we spend more." She fell in with this, but
I raised the sum by thirty kopecks a day. It was the same with
the theatre. I told her before marriage that she would not go
to the theatre, and yet I decided once a month to go to the
theatre, and in a decent way, to the stalls. We went together.
We went three times and saw *The Hunt after Happiness*, and
Singing Birds, I believe. (Oh, what does it matter!) We went
in silence and in silence we returned. Why, why, from the
very beginning, did we take to being silent? From the very
first, you know, we had no quarrels, but always the same
silence. She was always, I remember, watching me stealthily
in those days; as soon as I noticed it I became more silent than
before. It is true that it was I who insisted on the silence, not
she. On her part there were one or two outbursts, she rushed
to embrace me; but as these outbursts were hysterical, painful, and I wanted secure happiness, with respect from her, I
received them coldly. And, indeed, I was right; each time
the outburst was followed next day by a quarrel.

Though, again, there were no quarrels, but there was silence
and—and on her side a more and more defiant air. "Re-

bellion and independence," that's what it was, only she didn't
know how to show it. Yes, that gentle creature was becoming
more and more defiant. Would you believe it, I was becoming revolting to her? I learned that. And there could be no
doubt that she was moved to frenzy at times. Think, for
instance, of her beginning to sniff at our poverty, after her
coming from such sordidness and destitution—from scrubbing
the floors! You see, there was no poverty; there was frugality,
but there was abundance of what was necessary, of linen, for
instance, and the greatest cleanliness. I always used to dream
that cleanliness in a husband attracts a wife. It was not our
poverty she was scornful of, but my supposed miserliness in
the housekeeping: "He has his objects," she seemed to say,
"he is showing his strength of will." She suddenly refused to
go to the theatre. And more and more often an ironical look.
. . . And I was more silent, more and more silent.

I could not begin justifying myself, could I? What was at
the bottom of all this was the pawnbroking business. Allow
me, I know that a woman, above all at sixteen, must be in
complete subordination to a man. Women have no originality. That—that is an axiom; even now, even now, for me
it is an axiom! What does it prove that she is lying there in
the outer room? Truth is truth, and even Mill is no use
against it! And a woman who loves, oh, a woman who
loves idealises even the vices, even the villainies of the man
she loves. He would not himself even succeed in finding such
justification for his villainies as she will find for him. That is
generous but not original. It is the lack of originality alone
that has been the ruin of women. And, I repeat, what is the
use of your pointing to that table? Why, what is there original
in her being on that table? O—O—Oh!

Listen. I was convinced of her love at that time. Why, she
used to throw herself on my neck in those days. She loved
me; that is, more accurately, she wanted to love. Yes, that's
just what it was, she wanted to love; she was trying to love,
and the point was that in this case there were no villainies for

which she had to find justification. You will say, I'm a pawnbroker; and everyone says the same. But what if I am a
pawnbroker? It follows that there must be reasons, since the
most generous of men had become a pawnbroker. You see,
gentlemen, there are ideas . . . that is, if one expresses some
ideas, utters them in words, the effect is very stupid. The
effect is to make one ashamed. For what reason? For no
reason. Because we are all wretched creatures and cannot
hear the truth, or I do not know why. I said just now, "the
most generous of men"—that is absurd, and yet that is how
it was It's the truth, that is, the absolute, absolute truth!
Yes, *I had the right* to want to make myself secure and open
that pawnbroker's shop: "You have rejected me, you—
people, I mean—you have cast me out with contemptuous
silence. My passionate yearning towards you, you have met
with insult all my life. Now I have the right to put up a wall
against you, to save up that thirty thousand roubles and end
my life somewhere in the Crimea, on the south coast, among
the mountains and vineyards, on my own estate bought with
that thirty thousand, and above everything, far away from
you all, living without malice against you, with an ideal in
my soul, with a beloved woman at my heart, and a family, if
God sends one, and—helping the inhabitants all around!'"

Of course, it is quite right that I say this to myself now, but
what could have been more stupid than describing all that
aloud to her? That was the cause of my proud silence, that's
why we sat in silence. For what could she have understood?
Sixteen years old, the earliest youth—yes, what could she
have understood of my justification, or my sufferings? Un-
deviating straightness, ignorance of life, the cheap convictions of youth, the hen-like blindness of those "noble hearts,"
and what stood for most was—the pawnbroker's shop and—
enough! (And was I a villain in the pawnbroker's shop?
Did not she see how I acted? Did I extort too much?)

Oh, how awful is truth on earth! That exquisite creature,
that gentle spirit, that heaven—she was a tyrant, she was the

insufferable tyrant and torture of my soul! I should be unfair to myself if I didn't say so! You imagine I didn't love her? Who can say that I did not love her? Do you see, it was a case of irony, the malignant irony of fate and nature! We were under a curse; the life of men in general is under a curse! (mine in particular). Of course, I understand now that I made some mistake! Something went wrong. Everything was clear, my plan was clear as daylight: "Austere and proud, asking for no moral comfort, but suffering in silence." And that was how it was. I was not lying, I was not lying! "She will see for herself, later on, that it was heroic, only that she had not known how to see it, and when, some day, she divines it, she will prize me ten times more and will abase herself in the dust and fold her hands in homage,"—that was my plan. But I forgot something or lost sight of it. There was something I failed to manage. But, enough, enough! And whose forgiveness am I to ask now? What is done is done. Be bolder, man, and have some pride. It is not your fault! . . .

Well, I will tell the truth, I am not afraid to face the truth; it was *her fault, her fault!* . . .

V

Quarrels began from her suddenly beginning to pay out loans on her own account, to price things above their worth, and even, on two occasions, she deigned to enter into a dispute about it with me. I did not agree. But then the captain's widow turned up.

This old widow brought a medallion—a present from her dead husband, a souvenir, of course. I lent her thirty roubles on it. She fell to complaining, begged me to keep the thing for her—of course, we do keep things. Well, in short, she came again to exchange it for a bracelet that was not worth eight roubles; I, of course, refused. She must have guessed something from my wife's eyes. Anyway, she came again when I was not there and my wife changed it for the medallion.

Discovering it the same day, I spoke mildly but firmly and reasonably. She was sitting on the bed, looking at the ground and tapping with her right foot on the carpet (her characteristic movement); there was an ugly smile on her lips. Then, without raising my voice in the least, I explained calmly that the money was *mine*, that I had a right to look at life with *my own eyes* and—and that when I had offered to take her into my house, I had hidden nothing from her.

She suddenly leapt up, suddenly began shaking all over and —what do you think?—she suddenly stamped her foot at me; it was a wild animal, it was a frenzy, it was the frenzy of a wild animal. I was petrified with astonishment; I had never expected such an outburst. But I did not lose my head. I made no movement even, and again, in the same calm voice, I announced plainly that from that time forth I should deprive her of the part she took in my work. She laughed in my face and walked out of the house.

The fact is, she had not the right to walk out of the house. Nowhere without me, such was the agreement before she was married. In the evening she returned; I did not utter a word.

The next day, too, she went out in the morning, and the day after again. I shut the shop and went off to her aunts. I had cut off all relations with them from the time of the wedding—I would not have them to see me, and I would not go to see them. But it turned out that she had not been with them. They listened to me with curiosity and laughed in my face: "It serves you right," they said. But I expected their laughter. At that point, then, I bought over the younger aunt, the unmarried one, for a hundred roubles, giving her twenty-five in advance. Two days later she came to me: "There's an officer called Efimovitch mixed up in this," she said; "a lieutenant who was a comrade of yours in the regiment."

I was greatly amazed. That Efimovitch had done me more harm than anyone in the regiment, and about a month ago, being a shameless fellow, he once or twice came into the shop with a pretence of pawning something, and, I remember, began laughing with my wife. I went up at the time and told him not to dare to come to me, recalling our relations; but there was no thought of anything in my head, I simply thought that he was insolent. Now the aunt suddenly informed me that she had already appointed to see him, and that the whole business had been arranged by a former friend of the aunts', the widow of a colonel, called Yulia Samsonovna. "It's to her," she said, "your wife goes now."

I will cut the story short. The business cost me three hundred roubles, but in a couple of days it had been arranged that I should stand in an adjoining room, behind closed doors, and listen to the first *rendezvous* between my wife and Efimovitch, *tête-à-tête*. Meanwhile, the evening before, a scene, brief but very memorable for me, took place between us.

She returned towards evening, sat down on the bed, looked at me sarcastically, and tapped on the carpet with her foot. Looking at her, the idea suddenly came into my mind that for the whole of the last month, or, rather, the last fortnight, her character had not been her own; one might even say that it had been the opposite of her own; she had suddenly shown herself a mutinous, aggressive creature; I cannot say shameless, but regardless of decorum and eager for trouble. She went out of her way to stir up trouble. Her gentleness hindered her, though. When a girl like that rebels, however outrageously she may behave, one can always see that she is forcing herself to do it, that she is driving herself to do it, and that it is impossible for her to master and overcome her own modesty and shamefacedness. That is why such people go such lengths at times, so that one can hardly believe one's eyes. One who is accustomed to depravity, on the contrary, always softens things, acts more disgustingly, but with a show of decorum and seemliness by which she claims to be superior to you.

"Is it true that you were turned out of the regiment because you were afraid to fight a duel?" she asked suddenly, apropos of nothing—and her eyes flashed.

"It is true that by the sentence of the officers I was asked to give up my commission, though, as a fact, I had sent in my papers before that."

"You were turned out as a coward?"

"Yes, they sentenced me as a coward. But I refused to fight a duel, not from cowardice, but because I would not submit to their tyrannical decision and send a challenge when I did not consider myself insulted. You know," I could not refrain from adding, "that to resist such tyranny and to accept the consequences meant showing far more manliness than fighting any kind of duel."

I could not resist it. I dropped this phrase, as it were, in self-defence, and that was all she wanted, this fresh humiliation for me.

She laughed maliciously.

"And is it true that for three years afterwards you wandered about the streets of Petersburg like a tramp, begging for coppers and spending your nights in billiard-rooms?"

"I even spent the night in Vyazemsky's House in the Haymarket. Yes, it is true; there was much disgrace and degradation in my life after I left the regiment, but not moral degradation, because even at the time I hated what I did more than anyone. It was only the degradation of my will and my mind, and it was only caused by the desperateness of my position. But that is over . . ."

"Oh, now you are a personage—a financier!"

A hint at the pawnbroker's shop. But by then I had succeeded in recovering my mastery of myself. I saw that she was thirsting for explanations that would be humiliating to me and—I did not give them. A customer rang the bell very opportunely, and I went out into the shop. An hour later, when she was dressed to go out, she stood still, facing me, and said:

"You didn't tell me anything about that, though, before our marriage?"

I made no answer and she went away.

And so next day I was standing in that room, the other side of the door, listening to hear how my fate was being decided, and in my pocket I had a revolver. She was dressed better than usual and sitting at the table, and Efimovitch was showing off before her. And, after all, it turned out exactly (I say it to my credit) as I had foreseen and had assumed it would, though I was not conscious of having foreseen and assumed it. I do not know whether I express myself intelligibly.

This is what happened.

I listened for a whole hour. For a whole hour I was present at a duel between a noble, lofty woman and a worldly, corrupt, dense man with a crawling soul. And how, I wondered in amazement, how could that naïve, gentle, silent girl have come to know all that? The wittiest author of a society comedy could not have created such a scene of mockery, of naïve laughter, and of the holy contempt of virtue for vice. And how brilliant her sayings, her little phrases were: what wit there was in her rapid answers, what truths in her condemnation. And, at the same time, what almost girlish simplicity. She laughed in his face at his declarations of love, at his gestures, at his proposals. Coming coarsely to the point at once, and not expecting to meet with opposition, he was utterly nonplussed. At first I might have imagined that it was simply coquetry on her part—"the coquetry of a witty though depraved creature to enhance her own value." But no, the truth shone out like the sun, and to doubt was impossible. It was only an exaggerated and impulsive hatred for me that had led her, in her inexperience, to arrange this interview, but, when it came off—her eyes were opened at once. She was simply in desperate haste to mortify me, come what might, but though she had brought herself to do something so low she could not endure unseemliness. And could she, so pure and sinless, with an ideal in her heart, have been seduced by Efimovitch or any worthless snob? On the contrary, she was only moved to laughter by him. All her goodness rose up from her soul and her indignation roused her to sarcasm. I repeat, the buffoon was completely nonplussed at last and sat frowning, scarcely answering, so much so that I began to be afraid that he might dare to insult her, from a mean desire for revenge. And I repeat again; to my credit, I listened to that scene almost without surprise. I met, as it were, nothing but what I knew well. I had gone, as it were, on purpose to meet it, believing not a word of it, not a word said against her, though I did take the revolver in my pocket —that is the truth. And could I have imagined her different? For what did I love her, for what did I prize her, for what had I married her? Oh, of course, I was quite convinced of her sinlessness. I suddenly cut short the scene by opening the door. Efimovitch leapt up. I took her by the hand and suggested she should go home with me. Efimovitch recovered himself and suddenly burst into loud peals of laughter.

"Oh, to sacred conjugal rights I offer no opposition; take her away, take her away! And you know," he shouted after me, "though no decent man could fight you, yet from respect to your lady I am at your service . . . if you are ready to risk yourself."

"Do you hear?" I said, stopping her for a second in the doorway.

After which not a word was said all the way home. I led her by the arm and she did not resist. On the contrary, she was greatly impressed, and this lasted after she got home. On reaching home she sat down in a chair and fixed her eyes upon me. She was extremely pale; though her lips were compressed ironically, yet she looked at me with solemn and austere defiance and seemed convinced in earnest, for the first minute, that I should kill her with the revolver. But I took the revolver from my pocket without a word and laid it on the table! She looked at me and at the revolver. (Note that the revolver was already an object familiar to her. I had kept one loaded ever since I opened the shop. I made up my mind when I set up the shop that I would not keep a huge dog or a strong man-servant, as Mozer does, for instance. My cook opens the doors to my visitors. But in our trade it is impossible to be without means of self-defence in case of emergency, and I kept a loaded revolver. In early days, when first she was living in my house, she took great interest in that revolver, and asked questions about it, and I even explained its construction and working; I even persuaded her once to fire at a target. Note all that.) Taking no notice of her frightened eyes, I lay down on the bed, half-undressed. I felt very much exhausted; it was by that time about eleven o'clock. She went on sitting in the same place, not stirring, for another hour. Then she put out the candle and she too, without undressing, lay down on the sofa near the wall. For the first time, she did not sleep with me—note that too. . . .

VI

Now for a terrible reminiscence. . . .

I woke up, I believe, before eight o'clock, and it was very nearly broad daylight. I woke up completely to full consciousness and opened my eyes. She was standing at the table holding the revolver in her hand. She did not see that I had woke up and was looking at her. And suddenly I saw that she had begun moving towards me with the revolver in her hand. I quickly closed my eyes and pretended to be still asleep.

She came up to the bed and stood over me. I heard everything; though a dead silence had fallen I heard that silence. All at once there was a convulsive movement and, irresistibly, against my will, I suddenly opened my eyes. She was looking straight at me, straight into my eyes, and the revolver was at my temple. Our eyes met. But we looked at each other for no more than a moment. With an effort I shut my eyes again, and at the same instant I resolved that I would not stir and would not open my eyes, whatever might be awaiting me.

It does sometimes happen that people who are sound asleep suddenly open their eyes, even raise their heads for a second and look about the room, then, a moment later, they lay their heads again on the pillow unconscious, and fall asleep without understanding anything. When, meeting her eyes and feeling the revolver on my forehead, I closed my eyes and remained motionless, as though in a deep sleep—she certainly might have supposed that I really was asleep, and that I had seen nothing, especially as it was utterly improbable that, after seeing what I had seen, I should shut my eyes again at *such* a moment.

Yes, it was improbable. But she might guess the truth all the same—that thought flashed upon my mind at once, all at the same instant. Oh, what a whirl of thoughts and sensations rushed into my mind in less than a minute! Hurrah for the electric speed of thought! In that case (so I felt), if she guessed the truth and knew that I was awake, I should crush her by my readiness to accept death, and her hand might tremble. Her determination might be shaken by a new, overwhelming impression. They say that people standing on a height have an impulse to throw themselves down. I imagine that many suicides and murders have been committed simply because the revolver has been taken in the hand. It is like a precipice, with an incline of an angle of forty-five degrees, down which you cannot help sliding, and something impels you irresistibly to pull the trigger. But the knowledge that I had seen, that I knew it all, and was waiting for death at her hands without a word, might hold her back on the incline.

The stillness was prolonged, and all at once I felt on my temple, on my hair, the cold contact of the iron. You will ask, Did I confidently expect to escape? I will answer you as

God is my judge; I had no hope of it, except one chance in a hundred. Why did I accept death? But I will ask, What use was life to me after that revolver had been raised against me by the being I adored? Besides, I knew with the whole strength of my being that there was a struggle going on between us, a fearful duel for life and death, the duel fought by the coward of yesterday, rejected by his comrades for cowardice. I knew that she knew it, if only she guessed the truth that I was not asleep.

Perhaps that was not so, perhaps I did not think that then, but yet it must have been so, even without conscious thought, because I've done nothing but think of it every hour of my life since.

But you will ask me again, Why did you not save her from such wickedness? Oh! I've asked myself that question a thousand times since—every time that, with a shiver down my back, I recall that second. But at that moment my soul was plunged in dark despair; I was lost, I myself was lost— how could I save anyone? And how do you know whether I wanted to save anyone then? How can you tell what I could be feeling then?

My mind was in a ferment, though; the seconds passed; she still stood over me—and suddenly I shuddered with hope! I quickly opened my eyes. She was no longer in the room: I got out of bed: I had conquered—and she was conquered for ever!

I went to the samovar. We always had the samovar brought into the outer room, and she always poured out the tea. I sat down at the table without a word and took a glass of tea from her. Five minutes later I looked at her. She was fearfully pale, even paler than the day before, and she looked at me. And suddenly . . . and suddenly, seeing that I was looking at her, she gave a pale smile with her pale lips, with a timid question in her eyes. "So she still doubts and is asking herself, Does he know, or doesn't he know; did he see, or didn't he?" I turned my eyes away indifferently. After tea I closed the shop, went to the market and bought an iron bedstead and a screen. Returning home, I directed that the bed should be put in the front room and shut off with a screen. It was a bed for her, but I did not say a word to her. She understood without words, through that bedstead, that I "had seen and knew all," and that all doubt was over. At night I left the revolver on the table, as I always did. At night she got into her new bed without a word: uor marriage bond was broken, "she was conquered but not forgiven." At night she began to be delirious, and in the morning she had brain-fever. She was in bed for six weeks.

PART II

I

Lukerya has just announced that she can't go on living here and that she is going away as soon as her lady is buried. I knelt down and prayed for five minutes. I wanted to pray for an hour, but I keep thinking and thinking, and always sick thoughts, and my head aches. What is the use of praying?—it's only a sin! It is strange, too, that I am not sleepy: in great, too great sorrow, after the first outbursts one is always sleepy. Men condemned to death, they say, sleep very soundly on the last night. And so it must be, it is the law of nature, otherwise their strength would not hold out. . . . I lay down on the sofa, but I did not sleep. . . .

. . . For the six weeks of her illness we were looking after her day and night—Lukerya and I together with a trained nurse whom I had engaged from the hospital. I spared no expense —in fact, I was eager to spend money for her. I called in Dr. Shreder and paid him ten roubles a visit. When she began to get better I did not show myself so much. But why am I describing it? When she got up again, she sat quietly and silently in my room at a special table, which I had bought for her, too, about that time. . . . Yes, that's the truth, we were absolutely silent; that is, we began talking afterwards, but only of the daily routine. I purposely avoided expressing myself, but I noticed that she, too, was glad not to have to say a word more than was necessary. It seemed to me that this was perfectly natural on her part: "She is too much shattered, too completely conquered, "I thought, "and I must let her forget and grow used to it." In this way we were silent, but every minute I was preparing myself for the future. I thought that she was too, and it was fearfully interesting to me to guess what she was thinking about to herself then.

I will say more: oh! of course, no one knows what I went through, moaning over her in her illness. But I stifled my moans in my own heart, even from Lukerya. I could not imagine, could not even conceive of her dying without knowing the whole truth. When she was out of danger and began to regain her health, I very quickly and completely, I remember, recovered my tranquillity. What is more, I made up my mind to *defer our future* as long as possible, and meanwhile to leave things just as they were. Yes, something strange and peculiar happened to me then, I cannot call it anything else: I had triumphed, and the mere consciousness of that was enough for me. So the whole winter passed. Oh! I was satisfied as I had never been before, and it lasted the whole winter.

You see, there had been a terrible external circumstance in my life which, up till then—that is, up to the catastrophe with my wife—had weighed upon me every day and every hour. I mean the loss of my reputation and my leaving the regiment. In two words, I was treated with tyrannical injustice. It is true my comrades did not love me because of my difficult character, and perhaps because of my absurd character, though it often happens that what is exalted, precious and of value to one, for some reason amuses the herd of one's companions. Oh, I was never liked, not even at school! I was always and everywhere disliked. Even Lukerya cannot like me. What happened in the regiment, though it was the result of their dislike to me, was in a sense accidental. I mention this because nothing is more mortifying and insufferable than to be ruined by an accident, which might have happened or not have happened, from an unfortunate accumulation of circumstances which might have passed over like a cloud. For an intelligent being it is humiliating. This was what happened.

In an interval, at a theatre, I went out to the refreshment bar. A hussar called A—— came in and began, before all the officers present and the public, loudly talking to two other hussars, telling them that Captain Bezumtsev, of our regiment, was making a disgraceful scene in the passage and was, "he believed, drunk." The conversation did not go further and, indeed, it was a mistake, for Captain Bezumtsev was not drunk and the "disgraceful scene" was not really disgraceful. The hussars began talking of something else, and the matter ended there, but next day the story reached our regiment, and then they began saying at once that I was the only officer of our regiment in the refreshment bar at the time, and that when A——, the hussar, had spoken insolently of Captain Bezumtsev, I had not gone up to A—— and stopped him by remonstrating. But on what grounds could I have done so? If he had a grudge against Bezumtsev, it was their personal affair, and why should I interfere? Meanwhile, the officers began to declare that it was not a personal affair, but that it concerned the regiment, and as I was the only officer of the regiment present, I had thereby shown all the officers and other people in the refreshment bar that there could be officers in our regiment who were not over-sensitive on the score of their own honour and the honour of their regiment. I could not agree with this view. They let me know that I could set everything right if I were willing, even now, late as it was, to demand a formal explanation from A——. I was not willing to do this, and as I was irritated I refused with pride. And thereupon I forthwith resigned my commission— that is the whole story. I left the regiment, proud but crushed in spirit. I was depressed in will and mind. Just then it was that my sister's husband in Moscow squandered all our little property and my portion of it, which was tiny enough, but the loss of it left me homeless, without a farthing. I might have taken a job in a private business, but I did not. After wearing a distinguished uniform I could not take work in a railway office. And so, if it must be shame, let it be shame; if it must be disgrace, let it be disgrace; if it must be degradation, let it be degradation (the worse it is, the better)—that was my choice. Then followed three years of gloomy memories, and even Vyazemsky's House. A year and a half ago my godmother, a wealthy old lady, died in Moscow, and to my surprise left me three thousand in her will. I thought a little and immediately decided on my course of action. I determined on setting up as a pawnbroker, without apologising to anyone: money, then a home, as far as possible from memories of the past, that was my plan. Nevertheless, the gloomy past and my ruined reputation fretted me every day, every hour. But then I married. Whether it was by chance or not I don't know. But when I brought her into my home I thought I was bringing a friend, and I needed a friend so much. But I saw clearly that the friend must be trained, schooled, even conquered. Could I have explained myself straight off to a girl of sixteen with her prejudices? How, for instance, could I, without the chance help of the horrible incident with the revolver, have made her believe I was not a coward, and that I had been unjustly accused of cowardice in the regiment? But that terrible incident came just in the nick of time. Standing the test of the revolver, I scored off all my gloomy past. And though no one knew about it, *she* knew, and for me that was everything, because she was everything for me, all the hope of the future that I cherished in my dreams! She was the one person I had prepared for myself, and I needed no one else—and here she knew everything; she knew, at any rate, that she had been in haste to join my enemies against me unjustly. That thought enchanted me.

In her eyes I could not be a scoundrel now but at most a strange person, and that thought after all that had happened was by no means displeasing to me; strangeness is not a vice— on the contrary, it sometimes attracts the feminine heart. In fact, I purposely deferred the climax: what had happened was, meanwhile, enough for my peace of mind and provided a great number of pictures and materials for my dreams. That is what is wrong, that I am a dreamer: I had enough material for my dreams, and about her,—I thought she could *wait*.

So the whole winter passed in a sort of expectation. I liked looking at her on the sly, when she was sitting at her little table. She was busy at her needlework, and sometimes in the evening she read books taken from my bookcase. The choice of books in the bookcase must have had an influence in my favour too. She hardly ever went out. Just before dusk, after dinner, I used to take her out every day for a walk. We took a constitutional, but we were not absolutely silent, as we used to be. I tried, in fact, to make a show of our not being silent, but talking harmoniously, but, as I have said already, we both avoided letting ourselves go. I did it purposely, I thought it was essential to "give her time." Of course, it was strange that almost till the end of the winter it did not once strike me that, though I loved to watch her stealthily, I had never once, all the winter, caught her glancing at me! I thought it was timidity in her. Besides, she had an air of such timid gentleness, such weakness after her illness. Yes, better to wait and—"she will come to you all at once of herself. . . ."

That thought fascinated me beyond all words. I will add one thing: sometimes, as it were purposely, I worked myself up and brought my mind and spirit to the point of believing she had injured me. And so it went on for some time. But my anger could never be very real or violent. And I felt myself as though it were only acting. And though I had broken off our marriage by buying that bedstead and screen, I could never, never look upon her as a criminal. And not that I took a frivolous view of her crime, but because I had the sense to forgive her completely, from the very first day, even before I bought the bedstead. In fact, it is strange on my part, for I am strict in moral questions. On the contrary, in my eyes she was so conquered, so humiliated, so crushed, that sometimes I felt agonies of pity for her, though sometimes the thought of her humiliation was actually pleasing to me. The thought of our inequality pleased me. . . .

I intentionally performed several acts of kindness that winter. I excused two debts, I gave one poor woman money without any pledge. And I said nothing to my wife about it, and I didn't do it in order that she should know; but the woman came herself to thank me, almost on her knees. And in that way it became public property; it seemed to me that she heard about the woman with pleasure.

But spring was coming, it was mid-April; we took out the double windows and the sun began lighting up our silent room with its bright beams. But there was, as it were, a veil before my eyes and a blindness over my mind. A fatal, terrible veil! How did it happen that the scales suddenly fell from my eyes, and I suddenly saw and understood? Was it a chance, or had the hour come, or did the ray of sunshine kindle a thought, a conjecture, in my dull mind? No, it was not a thought, not a conjecture. But a chord suddenly vibrated, a feeling that had long been dead was stirred and came to life, flooding all my darkened soul and devilish pride with light. It was as though I had suddenly leaped up from my place. And, indeed, it happened suddenly and abruptly. It happened towards evening, at five o'clock, after dinner. . . .

II

Two words first. A month ago I noticed a strange melancholy in her, not simply silence, but melancholy. That, too, I noticed suddenly. She was sitting at her work, her head bent over her sewing, and she did not see that I was looking at her. And it suddenly struck me that she had grown so delicate-looking, so thin, that her face was pale, her lips were white. All this, together with her melancholy, struck me at once. I had already heard a little dry cough, especially at night. I got up at once and went off to ask Shreder to come, saying nothing to her.

Shreder came next day. She was very much surprised and looked first at Shreder and then at me.

"But I am well," she said, with an uncertain smile.

Shreder did not examine her very carefully (these doctors are sometimes superciliously careless), he only said to me in the other room, that it was just the result of her illness, and that it wouldn't be amiss to go for a trip to the sea in the spring, or, if that were impossible, to take a cottage out of town for the summer. In fact, he said nothing except that there was weakness, or something of that sort. When Shreder had gone, she said again, looking at me very earnestly:

"I am quite well, quite well."

But as she said this she suddenly flushed, apparently from shame. Apparently it was shame. Oh! now I understand: she was ashamed that I was still *her husband*, that I was looking after her still as though I were a real husband. But at the time I did not understand and put down her blush to humility (the veil!).

And so, a month later, in April, at five o'clock on a bright sunny day, I was sitting in the shop making up my accounts. Suddenly I heard her, sitting in our room, at work at her table, begin softly, softly . . . singing. This novelty made an overwhelming impression upon me, and to this day I don't understand it. Till then I had hardly ever heard her sing, unless, perhaps, in those first days, when we were still able to be playful and practise shooting at a target. Then her voice was rather strong, resonant; though not quite true, it was very sweet and healthy. Now her little song was so faint —it was not that it was melancholy (it was some sort of ballad), but in her voice there was something jangled, broken, as though her voice were not equal to it, as though the song itself were sick. She sang in an undertone, and suddenly, as her voice rose, it broke—such a poor little voice, it broke so pitifully; she cleared her throat and again began softly, softly singing. . . .

My emotions will be ridiculed, but no one will understand why I was so moved! No, I was still not sorry for her, it was still something quite different. At the beginning, for the first minute, at any rate, I was filled with sudden perplexity and terrible amazement—a terrible and strange, painful and almost vindictive amazement: "She is singing, and before me; *has she forgotten about me?*"

Completely overwhelmed, I remained where I was, then I suddenly got up, took my hat and went out, as it were, without thinking. At least I don't know why or where I was going. Lukerya began giving me my overcoat.

"She is singing," I said to Lukerya involuntarily. She did not understand, and looked at me still without understanding; and, indeed, I was really unintelligible.

"Is it the first time she is singing?"

"No, she sometimes does sing when you are out," answered Lukerya.

I remember everything. I went downstairs, went out into the street and walked along at random. I walked to the corner and began looking into the distance. People were passing by, they pushed against me. I did not feel it. I called a cab and told the man, I don't know why, to drive to Politseysky Bridge; then suddenly changed my mind and gave him twenty kopecks.

"That's for my having troubled you," I said, with a meaningless laugh, but a sort of ecstasy was suddenly shining within me.

I returned home, quickening my steps. The poor little jangled, broken note was ringing in my heart again. My breath failed me. The veil was falling, was falling from my eyes! Since she sang before me, she had forgotten me—that is what was clear and terrible. My heart felt it. But rapture was glowing in my soul and it overcame my terror.

Oh, the irony of fate! Why, there had been nothing else, and could have been nothing else but that rapture in my soul all the winter, but where had I been myself all that winter? Had I been there together with my soul? I ran up the stairs in great haste. I don't know whether I went in timidly, I only remember that the whole floor seemed to be rocking and I felt as though I were floating on a river. I went into the room. She was sitting in the same place as before, with her head bent over her sewing, but she wasn't singing now. She looked cursorily and without interest at me; it was hardly a look, but just an habitual and indifferent movement upon somebody's coming into the room.

I went straight up and sat down beside her in a chair abruptly, as though I were mad. She looked at me quickly, seeming frightened; I took her hand, and I don't remember what I said to her—that is, tried to say, for I could not even speak properly. My voice broke and would not obey me, and I did not know what to say. I could only gasp for breath.

"Let us talk . . . you know . . . tell me something!" I muttered something stupid. Oh! how could I help being stupid? She started again and drew back in great alarm, looking at my face, but suddenly there was an expression of *stern surprise* in her eyes. Yes, surprise and *stern*. She looked at me with wide-open eyes. That sternness, that stern surprise. shattered me at once: "So you still expect love? Love?" that surprise seemed to be asking, though she said nothing. But I read it all, I read it all. Everything within me seemed quivering, and I simply fell down at her feet. She jumped up quickly, but I held her forcibly by both hands.

And I fully understood my despair—I understood it! But, would you believe it? ecstasy was surging up in my head so violently that I thought I should die. I kissed her feet in delirium and rapture. Yes, in immense, infinite rapture, and that in spite of understanding all the hopelessness of my despair. I wept, said something, but could not speak. Her alarm and amazement were followed by some uneasy misgiving, some grave question, and she looked at me strangely, wildly even; she wanted to understand something quickly and she smiled. She was horribly ashamed at my kissing her feet and she drew them back. But I kissed the place on the floor where her foot had rested. She saw it and suddenly began laughing with shame (you know how it is when people laugh with shame). She became hysterical, I saw that her hands trembled. I did not think about that, but went on muttering that I loved her, that I would not get up. "Let me kiss your dress . . . and worship you like this all my life." . . . I don't know, I don't remember—but suddenly she broke into sobs and trembled all over. A terrible fit of hysterics followed. I had frightened her.

I carried her to the bed. When the attack had passed off, sitting on the edge of the bed, with a terribly exhausted look, she took my two hands and begged me to calm myself: "Come, come, don't distress yourself, be calm!" and she began crying again. All that evening I did not leave her side. I kept telling her I should take her to Boulogne to bathe in the sea now, at once, in a fortnight; that she had such a broken voice, I had heard it that afternoon; that I would shut up the shop, that I would sell it to Dobronravov; that everything should begin afresh, and above all, Boulogne, Boulogne! She listened and was still afraid. She grew more and more afraid. But that was not what mattered most to me; what mattered most to me was the more and more irresistible longing to fall at her feet again, and again to kiss and kiss the spot where her foot had rested, and to worship her; and—"I ask nothing, nothing more of you," I kept repeating; "do not answer me, take no notice of me, only let me watch you from my corner, treat me as your dog, your thing. . . ." She was crying.

"*I thought you would let me go on like that*," suddenly broke from her unconsciously, so unconsciously that, perhaps, she did

not notice what she had said, and yet—oh, that was the most
significant, momentous phrase she uttered that evening, the
easiest for me to understand, and it stabbed my heart as
though with a knife! It explained everything to me, everything, but while she was beside me, before my eyes, I could
not help hoping and was fearfully happy. Oh, I exhausted
her fearfully that evening. I understood that, but I kept
thinking that I should alter everything directly. At last, towards night, she was utterly exhausted. I persuaded her to go
to sleep, and she fell sound alseep at once. I expected her to
be delirious, she was a little delirious, but very slightly. I
kept getting up every minute in the night and going softly in
my slippers to look at her. I wrung my hands over her, looking at that frail creature in that wretched little iron bedstead
which I had bought her for three roubles. I knelt down, but
did not dare to kiss her feet in her sleep (without her consent).
I began praying, but leapt up again. Lukerya kept watch
over me and came in and out from the kitchen. I went in to
her and told her to go to bed, and that to-morrow "things
would be quite different."

And I believed in this, blindly, madly.

Oh, I was brimming over with rapture, rapture! I was eager
for the next day. Above all, I did not believe that anything
could go wrong, in spite of the symptoms. Reason had not
altogether come back to me, though the veil had fallen from
my eyes, and for a long, long time it did not come back—
not till to-day, not till this very day! Yes, and how could it
have come back then: why, she was still alive then; why, she
was here before my eyes: "To-morrow she will wake up and
I will tell her all this, and she will see it all." That was how I
reasoned then, simply and clearly, because I was in an
ecstasy! My great idea was the trip to Boulogne. I kept
thinking for some reason that Boulogne would be everything,
that there was something final and decisive about Boulogne.
"To Boulogne, to Boulogne!" . . . I waited frantically for
the morning.

III

But you know that was only a few days ago, five days, only five days ago, last Tuesday! Yes, yes, if there had been only a little longer, if she had only waited a little—and I would have dissipated the darkness! It was not as though she had not recovered her calmness. The very next day she listened to me with a smile, in spite of her confusion. . . . All this time, all these five days, she was either confused or ashamed. She was afraid, too, very much afraid. I don't dispute it, I am not so mad as to deny it. It was terror, but how could she help being frightened? We had so long been strangers to one another, had grown so alienated from one another, and suddenly all this. . . . But I did not look at her terror. I was dazzled by the new life beginning! . . . It is true, it is undoubtedly true that I made a mistake. There were even, perhaps, many mistakes. When I woke up next day, the first thing in the morning (that was on Wednesday), I made a mistake: I suddenly made her my friend. I was in too great a hurry, too great a hurry; but a confession was necessary, inevitable—more than a confession! I did not even hide what I had hidden from myself all my life. I told her straight out that the whole winter I had been doing nothing but brood over the certainty of her love. I made clear to her that my money-lending had been simply the degradation of my will and my mind, my personal idea of self-castigation and self-exaltation. I explained to her that I really had been cowardly that time in the refreshment bar, that it was owing to my temperament, to my self-consciousness. I was impressed by the surroundings, by the theatre: I was doubtful how I should succeed and whether it would be stupid. I was not afraid of a duel, but of its being stupid . . . and afterwards I would not own it and tormented everyone and had tormented her for it, and had married her so as to torment her for it. In fact, for the most part I talked as though in delirium. She herself took my hands and made me leave off. "You are exaggerating . . . you are distressing yourself," and again there were tears, again almost hysterics! She kept begging me not to say all this, not to recall it.

I took no notice of her entreaties, or hardly noticed them: "Spring, Boulogne! There there would be sunshine, there our new sunshine," I kept saying that! I shut up the shop and transferred it to Dobronravov. I suddenly suggested to her giving all our money to the poor except the three thousand left me by my godmother, which we would spend on going to Boulogne, and then we would come back and begin a new life of real work. So we decided, for she said nothing . . . she only smiled. And I believe she smiled chiefly from delicacy, for fear of disappointing me. I saw, of course, that I was burdensome to her; don't imagine I was so stupid or egoistic as not to see it. I saw it all, all, to the smallest detail, I saw better than any one; all the hopelessness of my position stood revealed.

I told her everything about myself and about her. And about Lukerya. I told her that I had wept. . . . Oh, of course, I changed the conversation. I tried, too, not to say a word more about certain things. And, indeed, she did revive once or twice—I remember it, I remember it! Why do you say I looked at her and saw nothing? And if only *this* had not happened, everything would have come to life again. Why, only the day before yesterday, when we were talking of reading and what she had been reading that winter, she told me something herself, and laughed as she told me, recalling the scene of Gil Blas and the Archbishop of Granada. And with what sweet, childish laughter, just as in old days when we were engaged (one instant! one instant!). How glad I was! I was awfully struck, though, by the story of the Archbishop; so she had found peace of mind and happiness enough to laugh at that literary masterpiece while she was sitting there in the winter. So then she had begun to be fully at rest, and begun to believe confidently "that I should leave her *like that*. I thought you would leave me like that," those were

the words she uttered then on Tuesday! Oh, the thought of
a child of ten! And you know she believed it, she believed
that really everything would remain *like that:* she at her table
and I at mine, and we should both go on like that till we were
sixty. And all at once—I come forward, her husband, and
the husband wants love! Oh, the delusion! Oh, my blindness!

It was a mistake, too, that I looked at her with rapture; I
ought to have controlled myself; as it was, my rapture
frightened her. But, indeed, I did control myself, I did not
kiss her feet again. I never made a sign of . . . well, that I was
her husband—oh, there was no thought of that in my mind,
I only worshipped her! But, you know, I couldn't be quite
silent, I could not refrain from speaking altogether! I suddenly said to her frankly, that I enjoyed her conversation and
that I thought her incomparably more cultured and developed
than I. She flushed crimson and said in confusion that I exaggerated. Then, like a fool, I could not resist telling her how
delighted I had been when I had stood behind the door
listening to her duel, the duel of innocence with that low cad,
and how I had enjoyed her cleverness, the brilliance of her
wit, and, at the same time, her childlike simplicity. She
seemed to shudder all over, was murmuring again that I
exaggerated, but suddenly her whole face darkened, she hid
it in her hands and broke into sobs. . . . Then I could not
restrain myself; again I fell at her feet, again I began kissing
her feet, and again it ended in a fit of hysterics, just as on
Tuesday. That was yesterday evening—and—in the morning . . .

In the morning! Madman! why, that morning was to-day,
just now, only just now!

Listen and try to understand: why, when we met by the
samovar (it was after yesterday's hysterics), I was actually
struck by her calmness, that is the actual fact! And all night
I had been trembling with terror over what happened yesterday. But suddenly she came up to me and, clasping her

hands (this morning, this morning!), began telling me that she was a criminal, that she knew it, that her crime had been torturing her all the winter, was torturing her now. . . . That she appreciated my generosity. . . . "I will be your faithful wife, I will respect you. . . ."

Then I leapt up and embraced her like a madman. I kissed her, kissed her face, kissed her lips like a husband for the first time after a long separation. And why did I go out this morning, only for two hours? . . . our passports for abroad. . . . Oh, God! if only I had come back five minutes, only five minutes earlier! . . . That crowd at our gates, those eyes all fixed upon me. Oh, God!

Lukerya says (oh! I will not let Lukerya go now for anything. She knows all about it, she has been here all the winter, she will tell me everything!)—she says that when I had gone out of the house, and only about twenty minutes before I came back—she suddenly went into our room to her mistress to ask her something, I don't remember what, and saw that her ikon (that same ikon of the Mother of God) had been taken down and was standing before her on the table, and her mistress seemed to have only just been praying before it. "'What are you doing, mistress?' 'Nothing, Lukerya, run along. Wait a minute, Lukerya.' She came up and kissed me. 'Are you happy, mistress?' I said. 'Yes, Lukerya.' 'Master ought to have come to beg your pardon long ago, mistress. . . . Thank God that you are reconciled.' 'Very good, Lukerya,' she said. 'Go away, Lukerya,' and she smiled, but so strangely." So strangely that Lukerya went back ten minutes later to have a look at her.

"She was standing by the wall, close to the window; she had laid her arm against the wall, and her head was pressed on her arm, she was standing like that thinking. And she was standing so deep in thought that she did not hear me come and look at her from the other room. She seemed to be smiling—standing, thinking and smiling. I looked at her, turned softly and went out, wondering to myself, and suddenly I

heard the window opened. I went in at once to say: 'It's
fresh, mistress; mind you don't catch cold,' and suddenly I
saw she had got on the window and was standing there, her
full height, in the open window, with her back to me, holding
the ikon in her hand. My heart sank on the spot. I cried
'Mistress, mistress.' She heard, made a movement to turn
back to me, but, instead of turning back, took a step forward,
pressed the ikon to her bosom, and flung herself out of
window."

I only remember that when I went in at the gate she was
still warm. The worst of it was they were all looking at me.
At first they shouted, and then suddenly they were silent, and
then all of them moved away from me . . . and she was lying
there with the ikon. I remember, as it were, in a darkness,
that I went up to her in silence and looked at her a long
while. But all came round me and said something to me.
Lukerya was there too, but I did not see her. She says she
said something to me. I only remember that workman. He
kept shouting to me that, "Only a handful of blood came from
her mouth, a handful, a handful!" and he pointed to the
blood on a stone. I believe I touched the blood with my
finger; I smeared my finger, I looked at my finger (that I
remember) and he kept repeating: "a handful, a handful!"

"What do you mean by a handful?" I yelled with all my
might, I am told, and I lifted up my hands and rushed at him.
Oh, wild! wild! Delusion! Monstrous! Impossible!

IV

Is it not so? Is it likely? Can one really say it was possible?
What for, why did this woman die?

Oh, believe me, I understand; but why she died is still a
question. She was frightened of my love, asked herself seriously whether to accept it or not, could not bear the question
and preferred to die. I know, I know, no need to rack my
brains: she had made too many promises, she was afraid she

could not keep them—it is clear. There are circumstances about it quite awful.

For why did she die? That is still a question, after all. The question hammers, hammers at my brain. I would have left her *like that* if she had wanted to remain *like that*. She did not believe it, that's what it was! No—no. I am talking nonsense, it was not that at all. It was simply because with me she had to be honest—if she loved me, she would have had to love me altogether, and not as she would have loved the grocer. And as she was too chaste, too pure, to consent to such love as the grocer wanted, she did not want to deceive me. Did not want to deceive me with half love, counterfeiting love, or a quarter love. They are honest, too honest, that is what it is! I wanted to instil breadth of heart in her, in those days, do you remember? A strange idea.

It is awfully interesting to know: did she respect me or not? I don't know whether she despised me or not. I don't believe she did despise me. It is awfully strange: why did it never once enter my head all the winter that she despised me? I was absolutely convinced of the contrary up to that moment when she looked at me with *stern surprise*. *Stern* it was. I understood on the spot that she despised me. I understood once for all, for ever! Ah, let her, let her despise me all her life even, only let her be living! I simply can't understand how she threw herself out of window! And how could I have imagined it five minutes before? I have called Lukerya. I won't let Lukerya go now for anything!

Oh, we might still have understood each another! We had simply become terribly estranged from one another during the winter, but couldn't we have grown used to each other again? Why, why couldn't we have come together again and begun a new life again? I am generous, she was too—that was a point in common! Only a few more words, another two days—no more, and she would have understood everything.

What is most mortifying of all, is that it is chance—simply a barbarous, lagging chance. That is what is mortifying! Five minutes, only five minutes too late! Had I come five minutes earlier, the moment would have passed away like a cloud, and it would never have entered her head again. And it would have ended by her understanding it all. But now again empty rooms, and me alone. Here the pendulum is ticking; it does not care, it has no pity. . . . There is no one—that's the misery of it!

I keep walking about, I keep walking about. I know, I know, you need not tell me; it amuses you, you think it absurd that I complain of chance and those five minutes. But it is evident. Consider one thing: she did not even leave a note to say, "Blame no one for my death," as people always do. Might she not have thought Lukerya might get into trouble? "She was alone with her," might have been said, "and pushed her out." In any case she would have been taken up by the police if it had not happened that four people, from the windows, from the lodge, and from the yard, had seen her stand with the ikon in her hands and jump out of herself. But that, too, was a chance, that people were standing there and saw her. No, it was all a moment, only an irresponsible moment. A sudden impulse, a fantasy! What if she did pray before the ikon? It does not follow that she was facing death. The whole impulse lasted, perhaps, only some ten minutes; it was all decided, perhaps, while she stood against the wall with her head on her arm, smiling. The idea darted into her brain, she turned giddy and—could not resist it.

Say what you will, it was clearly misunderstanding. It would have been possible to live with me. And what if it were anæmia? Was it simply from poorness of blood, from the flagging of vital energy? She had grown tired during the winter, that was what it was.

I was too late!!!

How thin she is in her coffin, how sharp her nose has grown! Her eyelashes lie straight as arrows. And, you know, when

she fell, nothing was crushed, nothing was broken! Nothing
but that "handful of blood." A dessert spoonful, that is.
From internal injury. A strange thought: if only it were possible not to bury her? For if they take her away, then . . . oh, no,
it is almost incredible that they should take her away! I am
not mad and I am not raving—on the contrary, my mind was
never so lucid—but what shall I do when there is again no
one, only the two rooms, and me alone with the pledges?
Madness, madness, madness! I worried her to death, that is
what it is!

What are your laws to me now? What do I care for your
customs, your morals, your life, your state, your faith! Let
your judge judge me, let me be brought before your court,
let me be tried by jury, and I shall say that I admit nothing.
The judge will shout, "Be silent, officer." And I will shout to
him, "What power have you now that I will obey? Why did
blind, inert forces destroy that which was dearest of all?
What are your laws to me now? They are nothing to me."
Oh, I don't care!

She was blind, blind! She is dead, she does not hear! You
do not know with what a paradise I would have surrounded
you. There was paradise in my soul, I would have made it
blossom around you! Well, you wouldn't have loved me—so
be it, what of it? Things should still have been *like that*,
everything should have remained *like that*. You should only
have talked to me as a friend—we should have rejoiced and
laughed with joy looking at one another. And so we should
have lived. And if you had loved another—well, so be it, so
be it! You should have walked with him laughing, and I
should have watched you from the other side of the street. . . .
Oh, anything, anything, if only she would open her eyes just
once! For one instant, only one! If she would look at me
as she did this morning, when she stood before me and made
a vow to be a faithful wife! Oh, in one look she would have
understood it all!

Oh, blind force! Oh, nature! Men are alone on earth—

that is what is dreadful! "Is there a living man in the country?" cried the Russian hero. I cry the same, though I am not a hero, and no one answers my cry. They say the sun gives life to the universe. The sun is rising and—look at it, is it not dead? Everything is dead, and everywhere there are dead. Men are alone—around them is silence—that is the earth! "Men, love one another"—who said that? Whose commandment is that? The pendulum ticks callously, heartlessly: Two o'clock at night. Her little shoes are standing by the little bed, as though waiting for her. . . . No, seriously, when they take her away to-morrow, what will become of me?

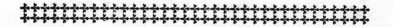

LEO TOLSTOY

(1828–1910)

(I)

FATHER SERGIUS

I

THERE happened in Petersburg during the 'forties an event which startled society.

A handsome youth, a prince, an officer in the Cuirassiers, for whom everyone had predicted the rank of aide-de-camp and a brilliant career attached to the person of Emperor Nicholas I, quitted the service. He broke with his beautiful *fiancée*, a lady-in-waiting, and a favourite of the Empress, just a fortnight before the wedding-day, and giving his small estate to his sister, retired to a monastery to become a monk.

To those who were ignorant of the hidden motives this was an extraordinary and unaccountable step; but as regards Prince Stephen Kasatsky himself, it was such a natural move that he could not conceive an alternative.

His father, a retired colonel of the Guards, died when the son was twelve. Although it was hard for his mother to let him go from her, she would not act in defiance of the wishes of her late husband, who had expressed the desire that in the event of his death the boy should be sent away and educated as a cadet. So she secured his admission to the corps.

The widow herself, with her daughter Varvara, moved to Petersburg in order to be in the same town with the boy and to take him home for his holidays. He showed brilliant capacity and extraordinary ambition, and came out first in

291

military drill, in riding, and in his studies—mathematics especially, for which he had a particular liking.

In spite of his abnormal height he was a handsome, graceful lad, and had it not been for his violent temper he would have been an altogether exemplary cadet. He never drank or indulged in any sort of dissipation, and he was particularly truthful. The fits of fury which maddened him from time to time, when he lost all control over himself and raged like a wild animal, were the only faults in his character. Once, when a cadet ragged him because of his collection of minerals, he almost threw the boy out of the window. On another occasion he rushed at an officer and struck him, it was said, for having broken his word and told a direct lie.

For this he would surely have been degraded to the rank of a common soldier if it had not been for the head of the school, who hushed up the matter and dismissed the officer.

At eighteen Kasatsky left with the rank of lieutenant, and entered an aristocratic Guard regiment. The Emperor Nicholas had known him while he was in the cadet corps, and had shown him favour while in the regiment. It was on this account that people prophesied that he would become an aide-de-camp. Kasatsky desired it greatly, although less from ambition than from passionate love for the Emperor which he had cherished since his cadet days. Each time the Emperor visited the school—and he visited it very often—as Kasatsky saw the tall figure, the broad chest, the aquiline nose above the moustache, and the close-cropped side whiskers, the military uniform, and the brisk, firm step, and heard him greeting the cadets in his strident voice, he experienced the momentary ecstasy of one who sees his well-beloved. But his passionate adoration of the Emperor was even more intense. He desired to give up something, everything, even himself, to show his infinite devotion. The Emperor Nicholas knew that he inspired such admiration, and deliberately provoked it. He played with the cadets, made them surround him, and treated them sometimes with childish simplicity, sometimes as a friend, and then again with an air of solemn grandeur.

After the incident with the officer, the Emperor, who did not allude to it, waved Kasatsky theatrically aside when the latter approached him. Then, when he was leaving, he frowned and shook his finger at the boy, saying, "Be assured that everything is known to me; but there are things I do not wish to know. Nevertheless, they are *here*," and he pointed to his heart.

When the cadets were formally received by the Emperor on leaving the school, he did not remind Kasatsky of his insubordination, but told them all, as was his custom, that they could turn to him in need, that they were to serve him and their country with loyalty, and that he would ever remain their best friend. All were touched, as usual; and Kasatsky, remembering the past, shed tears, and made a vow to serve his beloved Tsar with all his might.

When Kasatsky entered the regiment his mother and sister left Petersburg, going first to Moscow and then to their estate in the country. Kasatsky gave half his fortune to his sister. What remained was quite sufficient to support him in the expensive regiment which he had joined.

Viewed from outside, Kasatsky seemed like an ordinary brilliant young officer of the Guards making a career for himself. But within his soul there were intense and complex strivings. Although this striving, which had been going on ever since his childhood, seemed to vary in its nature, it was essentially one and the same, and had for its object that absolute perfection in every undertaking which would give him the applause and admiration of the world. Whatever it might be, accomplishments or learning, he worked to merit praise and to stand as an example to the rest. Mastering one subject, he took up another, and so obtained first place in his studies. For example, while he was still in the corps, conscious of a lack of fluency in his French, he contrived to master the language so that he knew it like his own. Then again, when he became interested in chess while still in the corps, he worked at the game till he acquired proficiency.

Apart from the chief end of life, which was in his eyes the service of the Tsar and his country, he had always some self-appointed aim; and however unimportant it might be, he pursued this with his whole soul, and lived for it until it was accomplished. But the moment it was attained another arose in its place. This passion for distinguishing himself and for pursuing an object in order to distinguish himself filled his life. So it was that after entering upon his career he set himself to acquire the utmost perfection in the knowledge of the service, and, except for his uncontrollable temper, which was sometimes the occasion of actions that were inimical to his success, he soon became a model officer.

Once during a conversation in society he realised the need of a more general education: so, setting himself to work to read books, he soon attained what he desired. Then he wanted to hold a brilliant position in aristocratic society: he learned to dance beautifully, and was presently invited to all the balls and parties in the best circles. But he was not satisfied with this: he was accustomed to being first in everything, and in this instance he was very far from that. Society at that time consisted, as I suppose it has done in every time and place, of four kinds of people—rich people who are received at Court; people who are not rich, but are born and brought up in Court circles; rich people who ape the Court; and people, neither rich nor of the Court, who copy both.

Kasatsky did not belong to the first two, but was gladly received in the last two sets. On entering society his first idea was that he must have a *liaison* with a society lady; and quite unexpectedly it soon came about. Presently, however, he realised that the circle in which he moved was not the most exclusive, and that there were higher spheres, and that, notwithstanding he was received there, he was a stranger in their midst. They were polite to him, but their manner made it plain that they had their own intimates, and that he was not one of them. Kasatsky longed to be one of them. To attain this end he must become an aide-de-camp—which he expected to be—or else he must marry into the set. He resolved upon this latter course. His choice fell upon a young girl, a beauty, belonging to the Court, and not merely to the circle he wished to move in, whose society was coveted by the most distinguished and the most firmly rooted in this circle. This was the Countess Korotkova. Kasatsky began to pay court to her purely for the sake of his career; she was uncommonly attractive, and he very soon fell in love with her. She was noticeably cool towards him at first, and then suddenly everything changed. She treated him graciously, and her mother continually invited him to the house.

Kasatsky proposed, and was accepted. He was rather astonished at the facility with which he gained his happiness, and he noticed something strange in the behaviour towards him of both mother and daughter. He was deeply in love, and love had made him blind, so he failed to realise what nearly the whole town knew—that the previous year his *fiancée* had been the favourite of the Emperor Nicholas.

Two weeks before the day arranged for the wedding Kasatsky was at Tsarskoye Selo, at the country place of his *fiancée*. It was a hot day in May. The lovers had had a walk in the garden, and were sitting on a bench in the shade of the lindens. Mary looked exceedingly pretty in her white muslin dress. She seemed the personification of love and innocence—now bending her head, now gazing at her handsome young lover, who was talking to her with great tenderness and self-restraint, as though he feared by look or gesture to offend her angelic purity. Kasatsky belonged to those men of the 'forties who do not exist nowadays, who deliberately, while condoning impurity in themselves, require in their wives the most ideal and seraphic innocence. Being prepared to find this purity in every girl of their set, they behaved accordingly. This theory, in so far as it concerned the laxity which the men permitted themselves, was certainly altogether wrong and harmful; but in its relation to the women, I think, compared with the notion of the modern young man who sees in every girl nothing but a mate or a female, there was much to be said for it. The girls, perceiving such adoration, endeavoured with more or less success to be goddesses.

Kasatsky held the views of his time, and looked with such eyes upon his sweetheart. That day he was more in love than ever, but there was nothing sensual in his feelings towards his *fiancée*. On the contrary, he regarded her with the tender adoration of something unattainable. He rose and stood at his full height before her, leaning with both hands on his sabre.

"Now for the first time I know what happiness is. And it is you—darling—who have given me that happiness," he said, smiling shyly.

He was still at that stage where endearments are not yet a habit, and it made him gasp to think of using them to such an angel.

"It is you who have made me see myself clearly. You have shown me that I am better than I thought," he added.

"I knew it long ago. That is what made me begin to love you."

The nightingales were beginning their song somewhere near and the young leaves moved in the sudden gusts of wind. He raised her hand to his lips and there were tears in his eyes.

She understood that he was thanking her for having said that she loved him. He took a few steps backwards and forwards, remaining silent, then approached her again, and sat beside her.

"You know, when I began to make love to you, it was not disinterested on my part. I wanted to get into society. And then, when I came to know you better, how little all that mattered, compared to you! Are you angry with me for that?"

She did not answer, but touched his hand. He understood that it meant "I am not angry."

"Well, you said——" he stopped. It seemed too bold to say what he intended. "You said—that you—began to love me—forgive me—I quite believe it—but there is something that troubles you and stands in the way of your feelings. What is it?"

"Yes—now or never," she thought. "He will know it anyhow. But now he will not forsake me because of it. Oh, if he should, how dreadful!" And she gazed with deep affection upon that tall, noble, powerful figure. She loved him now more than the Tsar, and were it not for Nicholas being an emperor, her choice between them would rest on Kasatsky.

"Listen," she said. "I cannot deceive you; I must tell you everything. You asked me what stood in the way. It is that I have loved before."

She again laid her hand on his with an imploring gesture.

He was silent.

"Do you want to know who it was? The Emperor."

"We all loved him. I can imagine you, a schoolgirl in the institute——"

"No. After that. It was only a passing infatuation, but I must tell you——"

"Well—what?"

"No, it was not simply——" She covered her face with her hands.

"What! You gave yourself to him?"

She was silent.

"His mistress?"

Still she did not answer.

He sprang to his feet, and pale as death, with his teeth chattering, stood before her. He now remembered how the Emperor, meeting him on the Nevsky, had congratulated him.

"O my God, what have I done? Stephen!"

"Don't touch me—don't touch me! Oh, how terrible!"

He turned and went to the house. There he met her mother.

"What's the matter with you, prince?"

She stopped, seeing his face.

The blood rushed suddenly to his head.

"You knew it! And you wanted me to shield them! Oh, if you weren't a woman——" he shouted, raising his large fist. Then he turned and ran away.

Had the lover of his *fiancée* been a private individual he would have killed him. But it was his beloved Tsar.

The next day he asked for furlough and then for his discharge. Feigning illness, he refused to see anyone, and went away to the country.

There he spent the summer putting his affairs in order. When summer was over he did not return to Petersburg, but entered a monastery with the intention of becoming a monk.

His mother wrote to dissuade him from this momentous step. He answered that he felt a vocation for God which was above all other considerations. It was only his sister, who was as proud and ambitious as himself, who understood him.

She was quite right in her estimate of his motives. His becoming a monk was only to show his contempt for all that seemed most important to the rest of the world, and had seemed so to himself while he was still an officer. He climbed to a pinnacle from which he could look down on those he had previously envied. However, contrary to his sister's opinion, this was not the only guiding motive. Mingled with his pride and his passion for ascendancy there was also a genuine religious sentiment which Varvara did not know he possessed. His sense of injury and his disappointment in Mary, whom he had thought such an angel, were so poignant that they led him to despair. His despair led where? To God, to faith, to a childish faith which had never been destroyed.

II

On the feast of the Intercession of the Virgin, Kasatsky entered the monastery, to show his superiority over all those who fancied themselves above him.

The abbot was a nobleman by birth, a learned man, and a writer. He belonged to that monastic order which hails from Wallachia, the members of which choose, and in their turn are chosen, leaders to be followed unswervingly and implicitly obeyed.

This abbot was the disciple of the famous Ambrosius, disciple of Makardix of the Leonidas, disciple of Païssy Velichkovsky.

To this abbot Kasatsky submitted himself as to the superior of his choice.

Besides the feeling of ascendancy over others which Kasatsky felt in the monastery as he had felt it in the world, he found here the joy of attaining perfection in the highest degree, inwardly as well as outwardly. As in the regiment he had rejoiced in being more than an irreproachable officer, even exceeding his duties, so as a monk his endeavour was to be perfect, industrious, abstemious, meek, and humble: and above all, pure, not only in deed but in thought; and obedient. This last quality made his life there far easier. In that much-frequented monastery there were many conditions objectionable to him, but through obedience he became reconciled to them all.

"It is not for me to reason; I have but to obey, whatever the command." On guard before the sacred relics, singing in the choir, or adding up accounts in the hostelry, all possibility of doubt was silenced by obedience to his superior. Had it not been for that, the monotony and length of the church service, the intrusion of visitors, and the inferiority of the other monks would have been extremely distasteful to him. But, as it was, he bore it all perfectly, and found it even a solace and a support.

"I don't know," he thought, "why I ought to hear the same prayers many times a day, but I know that it is necessary; and knowing this, I rejoice." His superior had told him that as food is necessary for the life of the body, so is spiritual food, such as prayers in church, necessary for maintaining the life of the spirit. He believed it, and though he found the service for which he had to rise at a very early hour a difficulty, it brought him indubitable comfort and joy. This was the result of humility and the certainty that anything done in obedience to the superior was right.

The aim of his life was neither the gradual attainment of utter subjugation of his will, nor the attainment of greater and greater humility, but the achievement of all those Christian virtues which seemed in the beginning so easy of possession.

Being not in the least half-hearted, he gave what fortune remained to him to the monastery without regret.

Humility before his inferiors, far from being difficult, was a delight to him. Even the victory over the sins of greed and lust were easy for him. The superior had especially warned him against this latter sin, but Kasatsky was glad to feel immunity from it. He was only tortured by the thought of his *fiancée*. It was not only the thought of what had been, but the vivid picture of what might have been. He could not resist recalling to himself the image of the famous mistress of the Emperor, who afterwards married and became a good wife and mother. Her husband had a high position, influence and esteem, and a good and penitent wife.

In his better hours Kasatsky was not distressed by this thought. At such times he rejoiced that these temptations were past. But there were moments when all that went to make up his present life grew dark before his mind; moments when, if he did not actually cease to believe in the foundation of his present life, he was at least unable to perceive it; when he could not discover the object of his present life; when he was overcome with recollections of the past, and, terrible to say, with regret at having abandoned the world. His only salvation in that state of mind was obedience, and work, and prayers the whole day long. He went through his usual forms at prayers—he even prayed more than was his wont—but it was lip-service, and his soul took no part. This condition would sometimes last a day, or two days, and would then pass away. But these days were hideous. Kasatsky felt that he was neither in his own hands nor God's, but subject to some outside will. All he could do at those times was to follow the advice of his superior and undertake nothing, but simply wait.

On the whole, Kasatsky lived, then, not according to his own will, but in complete obedience to his superior; and in that obedience he found peace.

Such was Kasatsky's life in his first monastery, which lasted seven years. At the end of the third year he was ordained to the priesthood, and was given the name of Sergius. The ordination was a momentous event in his inner life. He had previously experienced great comfort and spiritual uplifting at holy communions. At first, when he was himself celebrating mass, at the moment of the oblation his soul was filled with exaltation. But gradually this sense became dulled; and when on one occasion he had to celebrate mass in an hour of depression, as he sometimes had, he felt that this exaltation could not endure. The emotion eventually paled until only the habit was left.

On the whole, in the seven years of his life in the monastery Sergius began to grow weary. All that he had to learn, all that he had to attain, was done, and he had nothing more to do.

But his stupefaction only increased. During that time he heard of his mother's death and of Mary's marriage. Both events were matters of indifference to him, as all his attention and all his interest were concentrated on his inner life.

In the fourth year of his monastic experience, during which the bishop had shown him marked kindness, his superior told

him that in the event of high honours being offered to him
he should not decline. Just then monastic ambition—precisely that quality which was so disgusting to him in all the
other monks—arose within him. He was sent to a monastery
close to the capital. He would have been glad to refuse, but
his superior ordered him to accept; so he obeyed, and taking
leave of his superior, left for the other monastery.

This transfer to the monastery near the metropolis was an
important event in Sergius's life. There he encountered many
temptations, and his whole will-power was concentrated on
the struggle they entailed. In the first monastery women
were no trial to him, but in the second instance this special
temptation assumed grave dimensions, and even took definite
shape.

There was a lady known for her frivolous behaviour who
began to seek his favour. She talked to him and asked him
to call upon her. Sergius refused with severity, but was horrified at the definiteness of his desire. He was so alarmed that
he wrote to his superior. Moreover, for the sake of humiliation, he called a young novice and, conquering his shame,
confessed his weakness. He begged him to keep an eye on
him, and not let him go anywhere but to service and to do
penance.

Besides that, Sergius suffered severely on account of his
great antipathy to the abbot of this monastery, a worldly
man and clever in worldly ways, who was making a career
for himself within the Church. In spite of his most earnest
endeavours Sergius could not overcome his dislike for him.
He was submissive to him, but in his heart he criticised him
unceasingly. At last, when he had been there nearly two
years, his real sentiments burst forth.

On the feast of the Intercession of the Virgin the vesper
service was being celebrated in the church proper. There
were many visitors from the neighbourhood, and the service
was conducted by the abbot himself. Father Sergius was
standing in his usual place, and was praying; that is to say,

he was engaged in that inner combat which always occupied him during service, especially in this second monastery.

The conflict was caused by his irritation at the presence of all the fine folk, and especially the ladies. He tried not to notice what was going on around him. He could not help, however, seeing a soldier who, while conducting the better-dressed people, pushed the common crowd aside, nor noticing the ladies who pointed out the monks, often himself and another monk as well who was noted for his good looks. He tried to concentrate his mind, to see nothing but the light of the candles on the ikonostasis, the sacred images, and the priests. He tried to hear nothing but the prayers which were spoken and chanted, to feel nothing but self-oblivion in the fulfilment of his duty. This was a feeling he always experienced when he listened to prayers and anticipated the word in the prayers he had so often heard.

So he stood, crossing himself, prostrating himself, struggling with himself, now indulging in quiet condemnation, and now giving himself up to that obliteration of thought and feeling which he voluntarily induced in himself.

When the treasurer, Father Nicodemus (also a great stumbling-block in Father Sergius's way—that Father Nicodemus!), whom he couldn't help censuring for flattering and fawning on the abbot, approached him, and saluting him with a low bow that nearly bent him in two, said that the abbot requested his presence behind the holy gates, Father Sergius straightened his cassock, covered his head, and went circumspectly through the crowd.

"*Lise, regardes à droite—c'est lui,*" he heard a woman's voice say.

"*Où, où? Il n'est pas tellement beau!*"

He knew they were referring to him. As his habit was when he was tempted, he repeated, "Lead us not into temptation." Dropping his eyes and bowing his head, he walked past the lectern and the canons, who at that moment were passing in front of the ikonostasis, and went behind the holy gates by the north portal. According to custom, he crossed himself, bending double before the ikon. Then he raised his head and looked at the abbot, whom, together with someone standing beside him in brilliant array, he had already seen out of the corner of his eye.

The abbot stood against the wall in his vestments, taking his short fat hands from beneath his chasuble and folding them on his fat stomach. Fingering the braid on his chasuble, he smiled as he talked to a man wearing the uniform of a general in the Emperor's suite, with insignia and epaulettes, which Father Sergius at once recognised with his experienced military eye. This general was a former colonel in command of his regiment, who now evidently held a very high position. Father Sergius at once noticed that the abbot was fully aware of this, and was so pleased that his fat red face and his bald head gleamed with satisfaction. Father Sergius was grieved and disgusted, and all the more so when he heard from the abbot that he had only sent for him to satisfy the curiosity of the general, who wanted to see his famous "colleague," as he put it.

"I am so glad to see you in your angelic guise," said the general, holding out his hand. "I hope you have not forgotten your old comrade."

The whole thing—the abbot's red and smiling face above his white beard in evident approval of the general's words; the well-scrubbed face of the general with his self-satisfied smile, the smell of wine from the general's breath, and the smell of cigars from his whiskers—made Sergius boil.

He bowed once more before the abbot, and said, "Your Grace deigned to call me——" and he stopped, asking by the very expression of his face and eyes, "What for?"

The Abbot said, "Yes, to meet the general."

"Your Grace, I left the world to save myself from temptation," he said, pale and with quivering lips; "why, then, do you expose me to it during prayers in the house of God?"

"Go! go!" said the abbot, frowning and growing angry.

Next day Father Sergius asked forgiveness of the abbot and of the brethren for his pride. But at the same time, after a night spent in prayer, he decided that his only possible course was to leave this monastery; so he wrote a letter to his superior imploring him to grant him leave to return to his monastery. He wrote that he felt his weakness, and the impossibility of struggling alone against temptation without his help. He did penance for his sin of pride. The next post brought him a letter from the superior, who wrote that the sole cause of all his trouble was pride. The old man explained to him that his fits of anger were due to the fact that in refusing all clerical honour he humiliated himself not for the sake of God, but for the sake of his pride—merely for the sake of saying to himself: "Now, am I not a splendid fellow not to desire anything?" That was why he could not tolerate the abbot's action. "I have renounced everything for the glory of God, and here I am exhibited like a wild beast!" "If you would just give up vanity for God's glory you would be able to bear it," wrote the old man; "worldly pride is not yet dead in you. I have thought often of you, Sergius, my son. I have prayed also, and this is God's message with regard to you: Go on as you are, and submit."

At that moment tidings came that the recluse Hilary, a man of saintly life, had died in the hermitage. He had lived there for eighteen years. The abbot of that hermitage inquired whether there was not a brother who would take his place.

"Now with regard to that letter of yours," wrote the superior, "go to Father Païssy, of the T—— Monastery. I have written to him about you, and asked him to take you into Hilary's cell. I do not say you could replace Hilary, but you want solitude to stifle your pride. And may God bless you in your undertaking."

Sergius obeyed his superior, showed his letter to the abbot, and asking his permission, gave up his cell, handed all his belongings over to the monastery, and departed for the hermitage at T——.

The abbot of that hermitage, a former merchant, received Sergius calmly and quietly, and left him alone in his cell. This cell was a cave dug in a mountain, and Hilary was buried there. In a niche at the back was Hilary's grave, and in front was a place to sleep, a small table, and a shelf with ikons and books. At the entrance door, which could be closed, was another shelf. Upon that shelf food was placed once a day by a brother from the monastery.

So Father Sergius became a hermit.

III

During the Carnival in Sergius's second year of seclusion a merry company of rich people, ladies and gentlemen, from the neighbouring town made up a troika party after a meal of Carnival pancakes and wine. The company was composed of two lawyers, a wealthy landowner, an officer, and four ladies. One of the ladies was the wife of the officer; another was the wife of the landowner; the third was his sister, a young girl; the fourth was a *divorcée*, beautiful, rich, a little mad, whose ways gave rise to amazement and indignation in the town.

The night was fine, the roads smooth as a floor. They drove ten miles out of town, and then held a consultation as to whether they should turn back or go on.

"But where does this road lead?" asked Madame Makovkin, the beautiful *divorcée*.

"To T——, twelve miles farther on," said the lawyer, who was having a flirtation with Madame Makovkin.

"And beyond?"

"Then to L——, past the monastery."

"Oh, the one where Father Sergius is?"

"Yes."

"The handsome hermit—Kasatsky?"

"Yes."

"Oh, *messieurs et mesdames!* let us go in and see Kasatsky. We can rest at T—— and have a bite."

"But we shan't get home to-night?"

"We'll just spend the night at Kasatsky's then."

"Of course. There is a hostelry at the monastery, and a very good one. When I was defending Makine I stopped there."

"No, I shall spend the night at Kasatsky's!"

"Even your great power, dear lady, could not make that possible."

"Not possible? I'll bet you!"

"Good! If you spend the night at Kasatsky's I'll pay you whatever you like."

"*A discrétion!*"

"And you the same, remember."

"Agreed! Let's start."

They gave the driver some wine, and they opened a basket of pies, cakes, and wines for themselves. The ladies drew their white furs round about them. The postilions broke into a dispute as to which should go ahead, and the younger one, turning sharply round, lifted his whip-handle high up and shouted at the horses. The bells tinkled, and the runners creaked beneath the sledge; the sledge swayed and rocked a little. The outer horses trotted smoothly and briskly, with their tightly-bound tails under the gaily-decorated breech-bands. The slippery road faded away rapidly. The driver held the reins tightly.

The lawyer and the officer, who sat on the back seat, talked nonsense to Madame Makovkin's neighbour, and she herself, huddled in her furs, sat motionless and in thought.

"Eternally the same old things—the ugliness of it!—shiny red faces reeking with liquor and with tobacco, the same words, the same thoughts, for ever the same abomination. And they are all content and satisfied that it should be so. And thus they will go on till they die. But I can't—it bores me. I want something to happen that will upset and shatter the whole thing. We might at least be frozen to death, as they were at Saratov. What would these people do? How would they behave? Execrably, I suppose. Everybody would think of nothing but himself, and I no less than the rest. But I have beauty—that's something. They know it. Well, and that monk—I wonder if he really is indifferent to beauty. No; they all care for it, just like that cadet last autumn. And what a fool he was!"

"Ivan Nicolaievich," she said.

He answered, "Yes?"

"How old is he?"

"Who?"

"Why, Kasatsky."

"Over forty, I should think."

"Does he receive visitors? Does he see everybody?"

"Everybody, yes; but not always."

"Cover up my feet. Not that way—how clumsy you are! Yes, like that. But you needn't squeeze them."

Thus they came to the forest where the cell was.

She stepped out of the sledge and bade them drive on. They tried to dissuade her, but she grew irritable and commanded them to go on.

Father Sergius was now forty-nine years old. His life in solitude was very hard: not because of fasting and prayers— he endured those easily—but it was the inner struggle which he had not anticipated. There were two reasons for this struggle: his religious doubts and the temptations of desire. He thought these two were different fiends; but they were one and the same. When his doubts were gone lust was gone. But thinking these were two different devils, he fought them separately. They, however, always attacked him together.

"O my God! my God!" he cried, "why dost Thou not give me faith? There is lust, of course; but even St. Anthony and the rest had to fight that. But faith—they had that! There are moments and hours and days when I do not possess it. Why does the world exist with all its charm if it is sinful and we must renounce it? Why hast Thou created this temptation? Temptation? But isn't this temptation to renounce the joys of the world and to prepare for the life beyond, where there is nothing and where there can be nothing?" Saying this to himself, he became horrified and filled with disgust at himself. "You vile thing! And you think of being a saint!" he said.

He rose to pray. But when he began praying he saw himself as he appeared at the monastery in his vestments and all his grandeur, and he shook his head.

"No, that is not so. It is a lie. I may deceive all the world, but not myself, and not God. I am insignificant; I am pitiable"; and he pushed back the skirts of his cassock, and gazed at his thin legs in their underclothing.

Then he dropped his robe again and began to repeat his prayers, making the sign of the cross and prostrating himself.

"Will that couch be my bier?" he read; and, as if a demon whispered to him, he heard: "The solitary couch is also the coffin."

"It is a lie!" and he saw in imagination the shoulders of a widow who had been his mistress. He shook himself and went on reading. After having read the precepts he took up the Gospels. He opened the book at a passage that he had often repeated and knew by heart.

"Lord, I believe. Help thou my unbelief."

He stifled the doubts that arose. Just as one replaces an object without disturbing its balance, he carefully put his faith back into its position while it trembled at its base, and stepped back cautiously so as neither to touch it nor upset it. He again pulled himself together and regained his peace of mind; and repeating his childish prayer: "O Lord, take me, take me!" felt not only at ease, but glad and thrilled. He crossed himself and lay down to sleep on his narrow bench, putting his light summer garment under his head.

He dropped off to sleep at once. In his light slumber he heard small tinkling bells. He did not know whether he was dreaming or waking. But a knock at the door aroused him. He sat up on his couch, not trusting his senses. The knock came again. Yes, it was nearer—it was at his own door—and after it came the sound of a woman's voice.

"My God! is it true that the devil takes the form of a woman, as I have read in the lives of the saints? Yes—it is a woman's voice! So timid—so sweet—so tender!" And he spat to exorcise the devil. "No! It was only imagination!" and he went to the corner where the lectern stood, and fell on his knees, his regular and habitual motion that of itself gave him comfort and pleasure. He bowed low, his hair falling forward on his face, and pressed his bare forehead to the damp, cold floor. There was a draught from the floor. He read a psalm which, as old Father Piman had told him, would ward off the assaults of the devil. His light, slender frame started up upon its strong limbs, and he meant to go on reading his prayers. But he did not read. He involuntarily inclined his head to listen. He wanted to hear more.

All was silent. From the corner of the roof the same regular drops fell into the tub below. Without was a mist, a fog that swallowed up the snow. It was still, very still. There was a sudden rustle at the window, and a distinct voice, the same tender, timid voice, a voice that could only belong to a charming woman—

"Let me in, for Christ's sake."

All the blood rushed to his heart and settled there. He could not even sigh.

"May the Lord appear and His enemies be confounded."

"But I am not the devil!" He could not hear that the words were spoken by smiling lips. "I am not the devil. I am just a wicked woman that's lost her way, literally and figuratively." (She laughed.) "I am frozen, and I beg for shelter."

He put his face close to the window. The little ikon lamp

was reflected in the glass. He put his hands up to his face and peered between them. Fog, mist, darkness, a tree, and—at the right—she herself, a woman in thick white furs, in a fur cap, with a lovely, lovely, gentle, frightened face, two inches away, leaning towards him. Their eyes met and they recognised each other—not because they had ever seen each other before. They had never met. But in the look they exchanged they felt—and he particularly—that they knew each other, that they understood.

After that glance which they exchanged how could he entertain any further doubt that this was the devil instead of just a sweet, timid, frightened woman?

"Who are you? Why have you come?" he asked.

"Open the door, I say," she said with whimsical authority. "I tell you I've lost my way."

"But I am a monk—a hermit."

"Open the door all the same. Do you want me to freeze while you say your prayers?"

"But how——"

"I won't eat you. Let me in, for God's sake! I'm quite frozen."

She began to be really frightened, and spoke almost tearfully.

He stepped back into the room, looked at the ikon representing the Saviour with His crown of thorns—

"God help me—help me, O God!" he said, crossing himself and bowing low. Then he went to the door which opened into the little porch, and feeling for the latch, tried to unhook it. He heard steps outside. She was going from the window to the door.

"Oh!" he heard her exclaim, and he knew she had stepped into a puddle made by the dripping rain. His hands trembled, and he could not move the hook, which stuck a little.

"Well, can't you let me in? I'm quite soaked, and I'm frozen. You are only bent on saving your own soul while I freeze to death."

He jerked the door towards him in order to raise the latch, and then, unable to measure his movements, pushed it open with such violence that it struck her.

"Oh—pardon!" he said suddenly, reverting to his former tone with ladies.

She smiled, hearing that "pardon." "Oh, well, he's not so dreadful," she thought. "Never mind, it is you who must pardon me," she said, passing by him. "I would never have ventured, but such an extraordinary circumstance——"

"If you please," he said, making way for her.

He was struck by the fragrance of fine perfume that he had not smelt for many a long day.

She went through the porch into the chamber. He shut the outer door without latching it and passed into the room after her. Not only in his heart but involuntarily moving his lips he repeated unceasingly, "O Lord Jesus Christ, Son of God, have mercy on me, a sinner—have mercy on me, a sinner!"

"If you please," he said to her again.

She stood in the middle of the room, dripping, and examined him closely. Her eyes smiled.

"Forgive me for disturbing your solitude," she said, "but you must see what a position I am placed in. It all came about by our coming out for a drive from town. I made a wager that I would walk by myself from Vorobievka to town. But I lost my way. That's how I happened to find your cell." Her lies now began.

But his face confused her so that she could not proceed, so she stopped. She expected him to be quite different from the man she saw. He was not as handsome as she had imagined, but he was beautiful to her. His grey hair and beard, slightly curling, his fine, regular features, and his eyes like burning coals when he looked straight at her, impressed her profoundly. He saw that she was lying.

"Yes, very well," he said, looking at her and dropping his eyes. "Now I will go in there, and this place is at your disposal."

He took the burning lamp down from before the ikon, lit a candle, and making a low bow went out to the little niche on the other side of the partition, and she heard him begin to move something there.

"He is probably trying to shut himself up away from me," she thought, smiling. Taking off her white fur, she tried to remove her cap, but it caught in her hair and in the knitted shawl she was wearing underneath it. She had not got wet at all standing outside at the window. She said so only as a pretext to be admitted. But she had really stepped into a puddle at the door, and her left foot was wet to the ankle, and one shoe was full of water. She sat down on his bed, a bench only covered with a carpet, and began to take her shoes off. The little cell pleased her. It was about nine feet by twelve, and as clean as glass. There was nothing in it save the bench on which she sat, the book-shelf above it, and the lectern in the corner. On the door were nails where his fur coat and his cassock hung. Beside the lantern was the image of Christ with His crown of thorns, and the lamp. The room smelt strangely of oil and of earth. She liked everything, even that smell. Her wet feet were uncomfortable, the left one especially, and she took off her shoes and stockings, never ceasing to smile. She was happy not only in having achieved her object, but because she perceived that he was troubled by her presence. He, the charming, striking, strange, attractive man!

"Well, if he wasn't responsive, it doesn't matter," she said to herself. "Father Sergius! Father Sergius!—or what am I to call you?"

"What do you want?" answered a low voice.

"Please forgive me for disturbing your solitude, but really I couldn't help it. I would have fallen ill. And even now I don't know if I shan't. I'm quite wet and my feet are like ice."

"Pardon me," answered the quiet voice, "I cannot be of any assistance to you."

"I would not have come if I could have helped it. I shall only stop till dawn."

He did not answer. She heard him muttering something, probably his prayers.

"I hope you will not come in here," she said, smiling, "for I must undress to get dry."

He did not answer, continuing to read his prayers in a steady voice.

"That is a man," she thought, as she attempted to remove her wet shoe. She tugged at it in vain and felt like laughing. Almost inaudibly, she did laugh; then, knowing that he would hear, and would be moved by it, just as she wanted him to be, she laughed louder. The kind, cheerful, natural laughter did indeed affect him just as she had wished.

"I could love a man like that—such eyes, and his simple, noble face, passionate in spite of all the prayers it mutters! There's no fooling us women in that. The instant he put his face against the window-pane and saw me, he knew me and understood me. The glimmer of it was in his eyes and a seal was set upon it for ever. That instant he began to love me and to want me. Yes, he wants me," she said, finally getting off her shoe and fumbling at her stocking.

To remove those long stockings fastened with elastic she had to raise her skirts. She felt embarrassed and said, "Don't come in." But there was no answer from the other side, and she heard the same monotonous murmurs and movements.

"I suppose he's bowing down to the ground," she thought. "But that won't help him. He's thinking about me just as I'm thinking about him. He's thinking about these very feet of mine," she said, taking off the wet stockings and sitting up on the couch barefooted, with her hands clasped about her knees. She sat awhile like this, gazing pensively before her.

"It's a perfect desert here. Nobody would ever know——"

She got down, took her stockings over to the stove and hung them on the damper. It was such a quaint damper! She turned it, and then slipping quietly over to the couch she sat up there again with her feet upon it. There was absolute silence on the other side of the partition. She looked at the little watch hanging round her neck. Two o'clock. "My people will return about three." She had more than an hour before her.

"Well! am I going to sit here by myself the whole time? Nonsense! I don't like that. I'll call him at once.—Father Sergius! Father Sergius! Sergei Dimitrievich! Prince Kasatsky!"

No answer.

"I say! that's cruel. I wouldn't call you if I didn't need you. I'm ill. I don't know what's the matter," she said in a tone of suffering. "Oh! oh!" she groaned, falling back on the couch; and, strange to say, she really felt that she was getting faint, that everything ached, that she was trembling as if with fever.

"Here, listen! Help me! I don't know what's the matter with—oh! oh!"

She opened her dress, uncovering her breast, and raised her arms, bare to the elbows, above her head. "Oh, oh!"

All this time he stood on the other side of the door and prayed.

Having finished all the evening prayers, he stood motionless, fixing his eyes on the end of his nose, and praying in his heart he repeated with all his soul: "Lord Jesus Christ, Son of God, have mercy on me!"

He had heard everything. He had heard how the silk rustled when she took off her dress, how she stepped on the floor with her bare feet. He heard how she rubbed her hands and feet. He felt himself getting weak, and thought he might be lost at any moment. That was why he prayed unceasingly. His feelings must have been somewhat like those of the hero in the fairy tale who had to go on and on without ever turning back. Sergius heard and felt that the danger was there just above his head, around him, and that the only way to escape it was not to look round on it for an instant. Then suddenly the desire to see her came upon him, and at that very instant she exclaimed, "Now this is monstrous! I may die."

"Yes, I will come.—But I will go like that saint who laid one hand upon the adulteress but put the other upon burning coals."

But there were no burning coals. He looked round. The lamp! The lamp!

He put a finger over the flame and frowned, ready to endure. In the beginning it seemed to him that there was no sensation. But then of a sudden, before he had decided whether it hurt him or how much it hurt him, his face writhed, and he jerked his hand away, shaking it in the air.

"No, that I can't do."

"For God's sake, come to me! I am dying! Oh!"

"Must I be lost? No!—I'll come to you presently," he said, opening the door. And without looking at her he passed through the room to the porch where he used to chop wood. He felt about to find the block and the axe which were leaning against the wall.

"Presently!" he said, and taking the axe in his right hand, he laid the forefinger of his left hand upon the block. He raised the axe and struck at the finger below the second joint. The finger flew off more lightly than wood, and bounding up, turned over on the edge of the block and then on to the floor. Sergius heard that sound before he realised the pain; but ere he could recover his senses he felt a burning pain and the warmth of the flowing blood. He hastily pressed the end of his cassock to the maimed finger, pressed it to his hip, and going back into her room stood before the woman.

"What do you want?" he asked her in a low voice.

She looked at his pale face with its trembling cheeks and felt ashamed. She jumped up, grasped her fur, and throwing it around her shoulders tucked herself up in it.

"I was in pain—I've taken cold—I—Father Sergius—
I——"

He turned his eyes, which were shining with the quiet light
of joy, upon her, and said:

"Dear sister, why have you desired to lose your immortal
soul? Temptation must come into the world, but woe to
him by whom temptation cometh. Pray that God may
forgive us both."

She listened and looked at him. Suddenly she heard the
sound of something dripping. She looked closely and saw
that blood was dropping from his hand on to his cassock.

"What have you done to your hand?"

She remembered the sound she had heard, and seizing the
little ikon lamp, ran out to the porch. There on the floor she
saw the bloody finger.

She returned with her face paler than his, and wanted to
say something. But he went silently to his little apartment
and shut the door.

"Forgive me," she said. "How can I atone for my sin?"

"Go."

"Let me bind your wound."

"Go hence."

She dressed hurriedly and silently and sat in her furs,
waiting.

The sound of little bells reached her from outside.

"Father Sergius, forgive me."

"Go. God will forgive you."

"Father Sergius, I will change my life. Do not forsake me."

"Go."

"Forgive—and bless me!"

"In the name of the Father and of the Son and of the
Holy Ghost," she heard from behind the door. "Go."

She sobbed and went out from the cell.

The lawyer came forward to meet her.

"Well," he said, "I see I have lost. There's no help for it.
Where will you sit?"

"I don't care."

She took a seat in the sledge and did not speak a word till they reached home.

A year later she entered a convent as a novice and led a life of severe discipline under the guidance of hermit R——who wrote her letters at long intervals.

IV

Another seven years Father Sergius lived as a hermit. In the beginning he accepted a great part of what people used to bring him—tea, sugar, white bread, milk, clothes, and wood.

But as time went on he led a life of ever greater austerity. Refusing anything that could be thought superfluous, he finally accepted nothing but rye bread once a week. All that was brought to him he gave to the poor who visited him.

His entire time was spent in his cell in prayer or in conversation with visitors, whose number continually increased.

Father Sergius appeared in church only three times a year, and when it was necessary he went out to fetch water and wood.

After the episode with Madame Makovkin, the change he effected in her life, and her taking the veil, the fame of Father Sergius increased. Visitors came in greater and greater numbers, and monks came to live in his neighbourhood. A church was built there, and a hostelry. Fame, as usual, exaggerated his feats. People came from a great distance and began bringing invalids to him in the belief that he could heal them.

His first cure happened in the eighth year of his seclusion. He actually healed a boy of fourteen brought to him by his mother, who insisted on Father Sergius putting his hand on the child's head. The idea had never occurred to him that he could heal the sick. He would have regarded such a thought as a great sin of pride.

But the mother who brought the boy never ceased imploring him on her knees.

"Why wouldn't he help her son when he healed other people?" she asked, and again besought him in the name of Christ.

When Father Sergius replied that only God could heal, she said she wanted him only to lay his hands on his head and pray.

Father Sergius refused and went back to his cell. But next morning—for this happened in the autumn and the nights were already cold—coming out of his cell to fetch water, he saw the same mother with her child, the same boy of fourteen, and heard the same petitions.

Father Sergius remembered the parable of the righteous judge, and, contrary to his first instinct that he must indubitably refuse, he began to pray, and prayed until a resolve formed itself in his soul. This decision was that he must accede to the woman's request, and that her faith was sufficient to save her child. As for him, Father Sergius, he would be in that case but the worthless instrument chosen by God.

Returning to the mother, Father Sergius yielded to her request, put his hand on the boy's head, and prayed.

The mother left with her son. In a month the boy was cured, and the fame of the holy healing power of "Old Father Sergius," as he was called then, spread abroad. From that time not a week passed without sick people coming to Father Sergius.

Complying with the requests of some, he could not refuse the rest; he laid his hands on them and prayed. Many were healed, and his fame became more and more widespread.

Having thus passed seven years in the monastery and many years in the hermitage, he looked now like an old man. He had a long grey beard and his hair had grown thin.

V

Now Father Sergius had for weeks been haunted by one relentless thought, whether it was right for him to have acquiesced in a state of things not so much created by himself as by the archimandrite and the abbot.

This state of things had begun after the healing of the boy of fourteen. Since that time Sergius felt that each passing month, each week and each day, his inner life had somehow been destroyed and a merely external life had been substituted for it. It was as if he had been turned inside out. Sergius saw that he was a means of attracting visitors and patrons to the monastery, and that, therefore, the authorities of the monastery tried to arrange matters in such a way that he might be most profitable to them. For instance, he had no chance of doing any work. Everything was provided that he could require, and the only thing they asked was that he should not refuse his blessing to the visitors who came to seek it. For his convenience, days were appointed on which he should receive them. A reception-room was arranged for men; and a place was also enclosed by railings in order that the crowds of women who came to him should not overwhelm him—a place where he could bestow his blessing upon those who came.

When he was told that he was necessary to men, and that if he would follow the rule of Christ's love he could not refuse them when they desired to see him, and that his holding aloof from them would be cruel, he could not but agree.

But the more he gave himself up to such an existence the more he felt his inner life transformed into an external one. He felt the fount of living water drying up within him, and that everything he did now was performed more and more for man and less for God. Whatever he did, whether admonishing or simply blessing, or praying for the sick, or giving advice on the conduct of life, or listening to expressions of gratitude from those he had helped or healed (as they say) or instructed or advised, he could not help feeling a certain pleasure when they expressed their gratitude to him. Neither could he be indifferent to the results of his activity nor to his influence. He now thought himself a shining light. But the more he harboured that idea, the more he was conscious of the fact that the divine light of truth which had previously burned within him was flickering and dying.

"How much of what I do is done for God and how much for man?" That was the question that tormented him. Not that he could not find an answer to it, but he dared not give an answer. He felt deep down in his soul that the devil had somehow changed all his work for God into work for man. Because just as it had formerly been hard for him to be torn from solitude, now solitude itself was hard. He was often wearied with visitors, but in the bottom of his heart he enjoyed their presence and rejoiced in the praise which was heaped on him.

There came a time when he made up his mind to go away, to hide. He even thought out a plan. He got ready a peasant shirt and peasant trousers, a coat, and a cap. He explained that he wanted them to give to the poor; and he kept these clothes in his cell, thinking how he would one day put them on and cut his hair, and go away. First he would take a train and travel for about three hundred miles. Then he would get out and walk from village to village. He asked an old soldier how he tramped—if people gave alms, and whether they admitted wayfarers into their houses. The soldier told him where people were most charitable, and where they would take a wanderer in for the night; and Father Sergius decided to act on his advice. One night he even put on those clothes and was about to go. But he did not know which was best, to remain or to run away. For a time he was undecided. Then the state of indecision passed. He grew accustomed to the devil and yielded to him; and the peasant clothes only served to remind him of thoughts and feelings that were no more.

Crowds flocked to him increasingly from day to day, and he had less and less time for prayers and for renewing his spiritual strength. Sometimes, in his brighter moments, he thought he was like a place where a brook had once been. There had been a quiet stream of living water which flowed out of him and through him, he thought. That had been real life, the time when she had tempted him. He always thought with ecstasy of that night and of her who was now Mother Agnes. She had tasted of that pure water. Since then the water had hardly been given time to collect before those who were thirsty arrived in crowds, pushing one another aside, and they had trodden down the little brook until nothing but mud was left. So he thought in his clearer moments. But his ordinary state of mind was weariness and a sort of tenderness for himself because of that weariness.

It was spring, the eve of a festal day. Father Sergius celebrated vespers in the church in the cave. There were as many people as the place could hold—about twenty altogether. They all belonged to the better classes, rich merchants and such-like. Father Sergius admitted everyone to his church, but a selection was made by the monk appointed to serve him and by a man on duty who was sent to the hermitage every day from the monastery. A crowd of about eighty pilgrims, chiefly women, stood outside, waiting for Father Sergius to come out and bless them. In that part of the service, when he went to the tomb of his predecessor to bless it, he felt faint, and staggered, and would have fallen had it not been for a merchant who stood behind him and for the monk who served as deacon, who caught him.

"What is the matter with you, Father Sergius, dear Father Sergius? O God!" exclaimed a woman's voice, "he is as white as a sheet!"

But Father Sergius pulled himself together, and though still very pale, pushed aside the deacon and the merchant and resumed the prayers. Father Serafian, the deacon, and the acolytes and a lady, Sophia Ivanovna, who always lived close by the hermitage to attend on Father Sergius, begged him to bring the service to an end.

"No, there's nothing the matter," said Father Sergius, faintly smiling from beneath his moustache and continuing his prayers. "Ah, that is the way of saints," he thought.

"A holy man—an angel of God," he heard Sophia Ivanovna and the merchant who had supported him a moment before murmur.

He did not heed their entreaties, but went on with the service. Crowding one another as before, they all filed through narrow passages back into the little church, where Father Sergius completed vespers, merely curtailing the service a little. Directly after this, having pronounced the benediction on those present, he sat down outside on a little bench beneath an elm tree at the entrance to the cave. He wanted to rest—to breathe fresh air; he felt the need of it. But the moment he appeared, a crowd of people rushed to him soliciting his blessing, his advice, and his help. In the crowd was a number of women, pilgrims going from one holy place to another, from one holy man to another, ever in ecstasy before each sanctuary and before each saint.

Father Sergius knew this common, cold, irreligious, unemotional type. As for the men in the crowd, they were for the most part retired soldiers, long unaccustomed to a settled life; and most of them were poor, drunken old men who tramped from monastery to monastery merely for a living. The dull peasantry also flocked there, men and women, with their selfish requirements, seeking healing or advice in their little daily interests: how their daughters should be married, or a shop hired, or land bought, or how a woman could atone for a child she had over-lain in sleep and killed, or for a child she had borne out of wedlock.

All this was an old story to Father Sergius and did not

interest him. He knew he would hear nothing new from them. The spectacle of their faces could not arouse any religious emotion in him. But he liked to look at them as a crowd which was in need of his benediction and revered his words. This made him like the crowd, although he found them fatiguing and tiresome.

Father Serafian began to disperse the people, saying that Father Sergius was weary. But Father Sergius recollected the words of the Gospel: "Suffer the little children to come unto me, and forbid them not," and, touched at his recollection of the passage, he permitted them to approach. He rose, walked to the little railing beyond which the crowd had gathered, and began to bless them; but his answers to their questions were so faint that he was moved at hearing himself.

Despite his wish to receive them all, it was too much for him. Everything grew dark again before his eyes, and he staggered and grasped the railings. He felt the blood rushing to his head, and grew pale and then scarlet.

"I must leave the rest till to-morrow, I can do no more now," he said; and pronouncing a general benediction, returned to the bench.

The merchant supported him again, and taking him by the arm, assisted him to be seated. Voices exclaimed in the crowd:

"Father, dear father, don't forsake us. We are lost without you."

The merchant, having helped Father Sergius to the bench under the elm tree, took upon himself the duties of policeman and began energetically to disperse the crowd. It was true he spoke in a low voice so that Father Sergius could not overhear, but he spoke very decidedly and in an angry tone.

"Get away, get away, I say! He has blessed you. What else do you want? Get along, or you'll catch it. Move on there! Get along there, old woman, with your dirty rags.

Go on! Where do you think *you're* going? I told you it was finished. To-morrow's coming, but to-day he's done, I tell you!"

"Dear father! I only want to look on his dear face with my own little eyes," said an old woman.

"Little eyes indeed! You don't get in here!"

Father Sergius noticed that the merchant was doing it rather too thoroughly, and spoke to his attendant, saying the crowd was not to be turned away. He knew perfectly well that the crowd would be dispersed all the same, and he desired to remain alone and rest, but he sent his attendant with the order merely to make an impression.

"Well—well—I'm not turning them away, I'm only talking to them," answered the merchant. "They'll drive the man to death. They have no mercy. They're only thinking of themselves. No, I say! Get away! To-morrow!" and he drove them all away.

The merchant took all this trouble because he loved order and liked to turn people away and abuse them; but more because he wanted to have Father Sergius to himself. He was a widower and had an only daughter, an invalid and unmarried. He had brought her fourteen hundred miles to Father Sergius to be healed. During the two years of the girl's illness he had taken her to various cures. First to the university clinic in the principal town of the province, but this was not of much use; then to a peasant in the province of Samara, who did her a little good. Afterwards he took her to a doctor in Moscow and paid him a huge fee; but this did not help at all. Then he was told that Father Sergius wrought cures, so he brought her to him. Consequently, when he had scattered the crowd, he approached Father Sergius, and falling upon his knees without any warning, he said in a loud voice:

"Holy father! Bless my afflicted child and heal her of her sufferings. I venture to prostrate myself at your holy feet," and he put one hand on another, palms up, cup-wise. All this he did as if it were something distinctly and rigidly appointed by law and usage—as if it were the sole and precise method by which a man should request the healing of his daughter. He did it with such conviction that even Sergius felt for the moment that that was just the right way. However, he bade him rise from his knees and tell him what the trouble was. The merchant said that his daughter, a girl of twenty-two, had fallen ill two years before, after the sudden death of her mother. She just said "Ah!" as he put it, and went out of her mind. He had brought her fourteen hundred miles, and she was waiting in the hostelry till Father Sergius could receive her. She never went out by day, being afraid of the sunlight, but only after dusk.

"Is she very weak?" asked Father Sergius.

"No, she has no special weakness; but she's rather stout, and the doctor says she's neurasthenic. If you will just let me fetch her, Father Sergius, I'll be back with her in a minute. Revive, O holy father, the heart of a parent, restore his line, and save my afflicted offspring with your prayers!" and the merchant fell down on his knees again, and bending sideways with his head over his palms, which appeared to hold little heaps of something, remained like a figure in stone. Father Sergius again told him to get up, and thinking once more how trying his work was, and how patiently he bore it in spite of everything, sighed heavily. After a few moments' silence, he said: "Well, bring her to-night. I will pray over her. But now I am weary," and he closed his eyes. "I will send for you."

The merchant went away, stepping on tiptoe, which made his boots creak still louder, and Father Sergius remained alone.

Father Sergius's life was filled with Church services and with visitors; but this day was particularly difficult. In the morning an important official had come to hold a long conference with him. Then a lady came with her son. The son was a young professor, an unbeliever, and his mother, who was ardently religious and devoted to Father Sergius, brought him to Father Sergius that he might talk to him. The talk was very trying. The young man evidently did not wish to have a discussion with the monk, and just agreed with him in everything, as with an inferior. Father Sergius saw that the youth was an infidel, but that he had nevertheless a clear and tranquil conscience. The memory of the conversation was now unpleasant to him.

"Won't you eat something, Father Sergius?" asked the attendant.

"Very well—bring me something."

The attendant went to a little hut built ten paces from the cave, and Father Sergius remained alone.

The time was long past when Father Sergius lived alone, doing everything for himself, and having but a holy wafer and bread for nourishment. He had been warned long ago that he had no right to be careless of his health, and he was given wholesome meals, although of Lenten quality. He did not eat much, but more than he had done; and sometimes he even felt a pleasure in eating: the disgust and the sense of sin he had experienced before were gone.

He took some gruel, and had a cup of tea with half a roll of white bread. The attendant went away, while he remained alone on the bench under the elm tree. It was a beautiful evening in May. The leaves of the birches, the aspens, the elms, the alder bushes, and the oaks were just beginning to blossom. The alder bushes behind the elms were still in full bloom. A nightingale was singing near at hand, and two or three more in the bushes down by the river trilled and warbled. From the river came the songs of working-men, perhaps on their way home from their labours. The sun was setting behind the forest and was throwing little broken rays of light among the leaves. This side was bright green and the other side was dark. Beetles were flying about, and, colliding together, were falling to the ground. After supper Father Sergius began to repeat a prayer mentally: "O Lord

Jesus Christ, Son of God, have mercy on us," and then he read a psalm.

Suddenly, in the middle of the psalm, a sparrow flew out from a bush on the ground, and hopping along, came to him; then it flew away, frightened. He was reading a prayer that bore upon renunciation of the world, and hastened to get to the end of it in order that he might send for the merchant and his daughter. He was interested in the daughter because she offered a sort of diversion, and also because she and her father thought him a saint—a saint whose prayer was efficacious. He repudiated the idea, but in the depths of his soul he nevertheless concurred. He often wondered how he, Sergius Kasatsky, had contrived to become such an extraordinary saint and worker of miracles; but that it was a fact, he did not doubt. He could not fail to believe in the miracles he saw with his own eyes, beginning with the sick boy and ending with this last old woman who had recovered her sight through his prayers. Strange as it was, it was a fact. Accordingly the merchant's daughter interested him as a new individual that had faith in him, and besides, as an occasion of bearing witness to his healing power and to his fame.

"People come thousands of miles. Papers talk about it. The Emperor knows. All Europe knows—all godless Europe"; and then he felt ashamed of his vanity and began to pray: "God, King of heaven, Comforter, True Soul, come into—inspire me—and cleanse me from all sin, and save, O All-merciful, my soul. Cleanse me from the sin of worldly vanity that has overtaken me," he said, remembering how often he had made that prayer and how vain it had been. His prayers worked miracles for others, but as for himself God had not granted him strength to conquer this petty passion. He remembered his prayers at the commencement of his seclusion, when he asked for the grace of purity, humility, and love, and how it seemed to him at that time that God heard his prayers. He had retained his purity and had hewn off

his finger. He raised the stump of the finger with folds of
skin on it to his lips and kissed it. It seemed to him now
that at that time, when he had been filled with disgust at
his own sinfulness, he had been humble, and that he had
also possessed love. He recalled also the tender feelings with
which he had received the old drunken soldier who had
come to ask alms of him; and how he had received *her*. And
now? He asked himself whether he loved anybody; whether
he loved Sophia Ivanovna or Father Serafian; whether he
had any feeling of love for those who had come to him that
day. He asked himself if he had felt any love towards the
learned young man with whom he had held that instructive
discussion with the object only of showing off his own
intelligence and proving that he had not fallen behind in
knowledge.

He wanted love from them, and rejoiced in it, but felt no
love himself for them. Now he had neither love nor humility.
He was pleased to hear that the merchant's daughter was
twenty-two, and was anxious to know if she was good-
looking. When he inquired if she was weak, he only wanted
to know if she had feminine charm. "Is it true that I have
fallen so low?" he thought. "God help me! Restore my
strength—restore me, O God my Saviour!" and he clasped
his hands and began to pray.

The nightingales sang, a beetle flew at him and crept along
the back of his neck. He brushed it away.

"But does He exist? What if I am knocking at a house
which is locked from without. The bar is on the door, and
we can see it. Nightingales, beetles, nature, are the bar to
our understanding. That young man was perhaps right."
He began to pray aloud, and prayed long, till all these
thoughts disappeared and he became calm and firm in the
faith. He rang the bell, and told the attendant to say that
the merchant might now come with his daughter.

The merchant came, leading his daughter by the arm, and
brought her to the cell, where he left her.

The daughter was pale, with fair hair. She was very short, and had a frightened, childish face and full figure. Father Sergius remained seated on the bench at the entrance. When the girl passed him and stood near him he blessed her, feeling aghast because of the way in which he looked at her figure. As she passed by him he felt a sting. He saw by her face that she was sensual and feeble-minded. He rose and entered his cell. She was sitting on a stool waiting for him, and when he entered she rose.

"I want to go back to my papa," she said.

"Do not be afraid," he said. "Where do you feel pain?"

"I feel pain all over," she answered, and suddenly her face brightened with a smile.

"You will regain your health," he said. "Pray."

"What's the use? I've prayed. It doesn't help," and she continued smiling. "I wish you would pray and lay your ands on me. I saw you in a dream."

"How so?"

"I saw you put your hand on my chest."

She took his hand and pressed it to her breast.

"Here."

He yielded his right hand to her.

"What is your name?" he asked, his whole body shaking, and feeling that he was overcome and could not control his instinct.

"Marie. Why?"

She took his hand and kissed it, and then put her arm round his waist and pressed him.

"Marie, what are you doing?" he said. "You are a devil, Marie!"

"Oh, perhaps. Never mind."

And embracing him, she sat down at his side on the bed.

At dawn he went out of the door. Had all this really happened? Her father would come. She would tell. "She's a devil. But what have *I* done? Oh, there is the axe which I used to chop off my finger."

He took the axe and went back to the cell.

The attendant came towards him. "Do you want some wood cut? Give me the axe."

He gave him the axe, and entered the cell. She lay asleep. He looked on her with horror. Going back into the cell he put on the peasant clothes, seized the scissors, cut his hair, and then, issuing forth, took the path down the hill to the river, where he had not been for four years.

The road ran along the river. He went by it, walking till noon. Then he went into a cornfield and lay among the corn. Towards evening he approached a village, but did not enter it. He went again to the river, to a cliff.

It was early morning, half an hour before sunrise. All was grey and mournful around him, and a cold, early morning wind blew from the west.

"I must end it all. There is no God. How can I do it? Throw myself in! I can swim; I should not drown. Hang myself? Yes; just with this belt, to a branch."

This seemed so feasible and so easy that he wanted to pray, as he always did in moments of distress. But there was nothing to pray to. God was not. He dropped down on his elbow, and such a longing for sleep instantly overcame him that he couldn't hold his head up with his arm any longer. Stretching out his arm, he laid his head upon it and went to sleep. But this sleep lasted only a moment. He awoke at once, and what followed was half dream and half recollection.

He saw himself as a child in the house of his mother in the country. A carriage was approaching, and out of it stepped Uncle Nicholas Sergeivich, with a long black beard like a spade, and with him a slender girl, Pashinka, with large soft eyes and a timid, pathetic little face. This girl was taken to the place where the boys were playing, and they were forced to play with her, which was very tedious indeed. She was a silly little girl, and it ended in their making fun of her, and making her show them how she swam. She lay down on the floor and went through the motions. They laughed and turned her into ridicule; which, when she became aware of it, made her blush in patches. She looked so piteous that his conscience pricked him, and he could never forget her kind, submissive, tremulous smile. Sergius remembered how he had seen her since then. A long time ago, just before he became a monk, she had married a landowner, who had squandered all her fortune, and who beat her. She had two children, a son and a daughter. The son died when he was little, and Sergius remembered seeing her, very wretched, after that; and then again at the monastery, when she was a widow. She was still just the same; not exactly stupid, but insipid, insignificant, and piteous. She had come with her daughter and her daughter's *fiancée*. They were poor at that time, and later on he heard that she was living in a little provincial town and was almost destitute.

"Why does she come into my head?" he asked himself; but still he could not help thinking about her. "Where is she? What has become of her? Is she as unhappy as she was when she had to show us how she swam on the floor? But what's the use of my thinking of her now? My business is to put an end to myself."

Again he was afraid, and again, in order to spare himself, he began to think about her. Thus he lay a long time, thinking now of his extraordinary end, now of Pashinka. She seemed somehow the means of his salvation. At last he fell asleep, and in his dream he saw an angel, who came to him and said:

"Go to Pashinka. Find out what you have to do, and what your sin is, and what is your way of salvation."

He awoke, convinced that this was a vision from on high. He rejoiced, and resolved to do as he was told in the dream. He knew the town where she lived, three hundred miles away, so he walked to that place.

VI

Pashinka was no longer Pashinka. She had become Praskovia Mikhailovna, old, wrinkled, and shrivelled, the mother-in-law of a drunken official, Mavrikiev—a failure. She lived in the little provincial town where he had occupied his last position, and had supported the family: a daughter, a nervous, ailing husband, and five grandchildren. Her sole means of supporting them was by giving music lessons to the daughters of merchants for fifty kopecks an hour. She had sometimes four, sometimes five, lessons a day, and earned about sixty roubles a month. They all lived for the moment on that in expectation of another situation. She had sent letters to all her friends and relations, asking for a post for her son-in-law, and had also written to Sergius; but the letter had never reached him.

It was Saturday, and Praskovia Mikhailovna was kneading dough for currant bread such as the cook, a serf on her father's estate, used to make, for she wanted to give her grandchildren a treat on Sunday.

Her daughter Masha was looking after her youngest child, and the eldest boy and girl were at school. As for her husband, he had not slept that night, and was now asleep. Praskovia Mikhailovna had not slept well either, trying to appease her daughter's anger against her husband.

She saw that her son-in-law, being a weak character, could not talk or act differently, and she perceived that the reproaches of his wife availed nothing. All her energies were employed in softening these reproaches. She did not want harsh feelings and resentment to exist. Physically she could not stand a condition of ill-will. It was clear to her that bitter feelings did not mend matters, but simply made them worse. She did not think about it. Seeing anger made her suffer precisely as a bad odour or a shrill sound or a blow.

She was just showing Lucaria, the servant, how to mix the

dough when her grandson Misha, a boy six years old, with little crooked legs in darned stockings, ran into the kitchen looking frightened.

"Grandmother, a dreadful old man wants to see you!"

Lucaria looked out of the door.

"Oh, ma'am, it's a pilgrim."

Praskovia Mikhailovna wiped her thin elbows with her hands, and then her hands on her apron, and was about to go into the room to get five kopecks out of her purse, when she remembered that she had only a ten-kopecks piece, so, deciding to give bread instead, she turned to the cupboard. But then she blushed at the thought of having grudged him alms, and ordering Lucaria to cut a slice of bread, went to fetch the ten kopecks. "That serves you right," she said to herself. "Now you must give twice as much."

She gave both bread and money to the pilgrim with apologies, and in doing so she was not at all proud of her generosity. On the contrary, she was ashamed of having given so little, the man had such an imposing appearance.

In spite of having tramped three hundred miles, begging in the name of Christ, and being nearly in rags—in spite of having grown thin and weather-beaten, and having his hair cut, and wearing a peasant cap and boots—in spite, also, of his bowing with great humility—Sergius had the same impressive appearance which had attracted every one to him. Praskovia Mikhailovna did not recognise him. How could she, not having seen him for many years?

"Excuse this humble gift, father. Wouldn't you like something to eat?"

He took the bread and money, and Praskovia Mikhailovna was astonished that he did not go, but stood looking at her.

"Pashinka, I have come to you. Won't you take me in?"

His beautiful black eyes looked at her intently, imploringly, and shone, tears starting; and his lips quivered painfully under the grey moustache.

Praskovia Mikhailovna pressed her hand to her shrivelled breast, opened her mouth, and stared at the pilgrim with dilated eyes.

"It can't be possible! Steph—Sergius—Father Sergius!"

"Yes, it is I," said Sergius in a low voice. "But no longer Sergius or Father Sergius, but a great sinner, Stephen Kasatsky—a great sinner, a lost sinner. Take me in—help me."

"No, it can't be possible! Such great humility! Come." She stretched out her hand; but he did not take it, he only followed her.

But where could she lead him? They had very little space. She had a tiny little room for herself, hardly more than a closet; but even that she had given up to her daughter, and now Masha was sitting there rocking the baby to sleep.

"Please be seated here," she said to Sergius, pointing to a bench in the kitchen.

He sat down at once, and took off, with an evidently accustomed action, the straps of his wallet first from one shoulder and then from the other.

"Heavens! what humility! what an honour! And now——"

Sergius did not answer, but smiled meekly, laying his wallet on one side.

"Masha, do you know who this is?" And Praskovia Mikhailovna told her daughter in a whisper. They took the bed and the cradle out of the little room, and made it ready for Sergius.

Praskovia Mikhailovna led him in.

"Now have a rest. Excuse this humble room. I must go."

"Where?"

"I have lessons. I'm ashamed to say I teach music."

"Music! That is well. But just one thing, Praskovia Mikhailovna. I came to you with an object. Could I have a talk with you?"

"I shall be happy. Will this evening do?"

"It will. One thing more. Do not say who I am. I have only revealed myself to you. No one knows where I went, and no one need know."

"Oh, but I told my daughter——"

"Well, ask her not to tell anyone."

Sergius took off his boots and slept after a sleepless night and a forty-mile tramp.

When Praskovia Mikhailovna returned, Sergius was sitting in the little room waiting for her. He had not come out for dinner, but had some soup and gruel which Lucaria brought in to him.

"Why did you return earlier than you said?" asked Father Sergius. "May I speak to you now?"

"What have I done to deserve the happiness of having such a guest! I only missed one lesson. That can wait. I have dreamed for a long time of going to see you. I wrote to you. And now this good fortune!"

"Pashinka, please listen to what I am going to tell you, as if it were a confession—as if it were something I should say to God in the hour of death. Pashinka, I am not a holy man; I am a vile and loathsome sinner. I have gone astray through pride, and I am the vilest of the vile."

Pashinka stared at him. She believed what he said. Then, when she had quite taken it in, she touched his hand and smiled sadly, and said:

"Stevie, perhaps you exaggerate."

"No, Pashinka. I am an adulterer, a murderer, a blasphemer, a cheat."

"My God, what does he mean?" she muttered.

"But I must go on living. I, who thought I knew everything, who taught others how to live, I know nothing. I ask you to teach me."

"O Stevie, you are laughing at me. Why do you always laugh at me?"

"Very well; have it as you will that I am laughing at you.

Still, tell me how you live, and how you have lived your life."

"I? But I've lived a very bad life—the worst life possible. Now God is punishing me, and I deserve it. And I am so miserable now—so miserable!"

"And your marriage—how did you get on?"

"It was all bad. I married because I fell in love from low motives. Father didn't want me to, but I wouldn't listen to anything. I just married. And then, instead of helping my husband, I made him wretched by my jealousy, which I couldn't overcome."

"He drank, I heard."

"Well, but I didn't give him any peace. I reproached him. That's a disease. He couldn't stop it. I remember now how I took his drink away from him. We had such frightful scenes!" She looked at Kasatsky with pain in her beautiful eyes at the recollection.

Kasatsky called to mind that he had been told that her husband beat Pashinka, and looking at her thin withered neck with veins standing out behind her ears, the thin coil of hair, half grey, half auburn, he saw it all just as it happened.

"Then I was left alone with two children, and with no means."

"But you had an estate!"

"Oh, that was sold when Vasily was alive. And the money was—spent; we had to live. And I didn't know how to work—like all the young ladies of that time. I was worse than the rest—quite helpless. So we spent everything we had. I taught the children. Masha had learnt something. Then Misha fell ill when he was in the fourth class in the school, and God took him. Masha fell in love with Vania, my son-in-law. He's a good man, but very unfortunate. He's ill."

"Mother," interrupted her daughter, "take Misha. I can't be everywhere."

Praskovia Mikhailovna started, rose, and stepping quickly in her worn shoes, went out of the room and came back with a boy of two in her arms. The child was throwing himself backwards and grabbing at her shawl.

"Where was I? Yes—he had a very good post here, and such a good chief, too. But poor Vania couldn't go on, and he had to give up his position."

"What is the matter with him?"

"Neurasthenia. It's such a horrid illness. We have been to the doctor, but he ought to go away, and we can't afford it. Still, I hope it will pass. He doesn't suffer much pain, but——"

"Lucaria!" said a feeble and angry voice. "She's always sent out when I need her. Mother!"

"I'm coming," said Praskovia Mikhailovna, again interrupting her conversation. "You see, he hasn't had his dinner yet. He can't eat with us."

She went out and arranged something, and came back, wiping her thin, dark hands.

"Well, this is the way I live. I complain, and I'm not satisfied, but, thank God, all my grandchildren are such nice healthy children, and life is quite bearable. But why am I talking about myself?"

"What do you live on?"

"Why, I earn a little. How I used to hate music! and now it's so useful to me."

Her small hand lay on the chest of drawers that stood beside her where she was sitting, and she drummed exercises with her thin fingers.

"How much are you paid for your lessons?"

"Sometimes a rouble, sometimes fifty kopecks, and sometimes thirty. They are all so kind to me."

"And do your pupils get on well?" asked Kasatsky, smiling faintly with his eyes.

Praskovia Mikhailovna did not believe at first that he was asking her seriously, and looked inquiringly into his eyes.

"Some of them do," she said. "I have one very nice pupil, the butcher's daughter—such a good, kind girl. If I were a clever woman I could surely use my father's influence and get a position for my son-in-law. But it is my fault they are so badly off. I brought them to it."

"Yes, yes," said Kasatsky, dropping his head. "Well, Pashinka, and what about your attitude to the Church."

"Oh, don't speak of it! I'm so bad that way. I have neglected it so! When the children have to go, I fast and go to communion with them, but as for the rest of the time I often do not go for a month. I just send them."

"And why don't you go?"

"Well, to tell the truth"—she blushed—"I'm ashamed for Masha's sake and the children's to go in my old clothes. And I haven't anything else. Besides, I'm just lazy."

"And do you pray at home?"

"I do; but it's just a mechanical sort of praying. I know it's wrong. But I have no real religious feeling. I only know I'm wicked—that's all."

"Yes, yes. That's right, that's right!" said Kasatsky, as if in approval.

"I'm coming—I'm coming!" she called, in answer to her son-in-law, and tidying her hair, went to the other room.

This time she was absent a long while. When she returned, Kasatsky was sitting in the same position, his elbow on his knee and his head down. But his wallet was ready strapped on his back.

When she came in with a little tin lamp without a shade, he raised his beautiful, weary eyes and sighed deeply.

"I didn't tell them who you were," she began shyly. "I just said you were a pilgrim—a nobleman—and that I used to know you. Won't you come into the dining-room and have tea?"

"No."

"Then I'll bring some in to you here."

"No; I don't want anything. God bless you, Pashinka. I am going now. If you have any pity for me, don't tell anyone you have seen me. For the love of God, tell no one. I thank you. I would kneel down before you, but I know it would only make you feel awkward. Forgive me, for Christ's sake!"

"Give me your blessing."

"God bless you. Forgive me, for Christ's sake!"

He rose to go, but she restrained him, and brought him some bread and butter, which he took, and departed.

It was dark, and he had hardly passed the second house when he was lost to sight, and she only knew he was there because the dog at the priest's house was barking.

"That was the meaning of my vision. Pashinka is what I should have been, and was not. I lived for man, on the pretext of living for God; and she lives for God, imagining she lives for man! Yes; one good deed—a cup of cold water given without expectation of reward—is worth far more than all the benefits I thought I was bestowing on the world. But was there not, after all, one grain of sincere desire to serve God?" he asked himself. And the answer came: "Yes, there was; but it was so soiled, so overgrown with desire for the world's praise. No; there is no God for the man who lives for the praise of the world. I must now seek *Him*."

He walked on, just as he had made his way to Pashinka, from village to village, meeting and parting with other pilgrims, and asking for bread and a night's rest in the name of Christ. Sometimes an angry housekeeper would abuse him, sometimes a drunken peasant would revile him; but for the most part he was given food and drink, and often something to take with him. Many were favourably disposed towards him on account of his noble bearing. Some, on the other hand, seemed to enjoy the sight of a gentleman so reduced to poverty. But his gentleness vanquished all hearts.

He often found a Bible in a house where he was staying.
He would read it aloud, and the people always listened to
him, touched by what he read them, and wondering, as if
it were something new, although so familiar.

If he succeeded in helping people by his advice, or by
knowing how to read and write, or by settling a dispute, he
did not afterwards wait to see their gratitude, for he went
away directly. And little by little God began to reveal Himself within him.

One day he was walking along the road with two women
and a soldier. They were stopped by a party consisting of a
lady and gentleman in a trap drawn by a trotter, and another
gentleman and lady riding. The gentleman beside the lady
in the trap was evidently a traveller—a Frenchman—while
her husband was on horseback with his daughter.

The party stopped to show the Frenchman the pilgrims,
who, according to a superstition of the Russian peasantry,
show their superiority by tramping instead of working. They
spoke French, thinking they would not be understood.

"*Demandez-leur*," asked the Frenchman, "*s'ils sont bien sûres
de ce que leur pèlerinage est agrèable à Dieu?*" they were asked.

The old woman answered:

"Just as God wills it. Our feet have arrived at the holy
places, but we can't tell about our hearts."

They asked the soldier. He answered that he was alone in
the world, and belonged to nowhere.

They asked Kasatsky who he was.

"A servant of God."

"*Qu'est-ce qu'il dit? Il ne répond pas?*"

"*Il dit qu'il est un serviteur de Dieu.*"

"*Il doit être un fils de prêtre. Il a de la race. Avez-vous de la
petite monnaie?*"

The Frenchman had some change, and gave each of them
twenty kopecks.

"*Mais dites-leur que ce n'est pas pour les cierges que je leur donne,
mais pour qu'ils se régalent du thé.* Tea—tea," he said, with a

smile. "*Pour vous, mon vieux.*" And he patted Kasatsky on the shoulder with his gloved hand.

"Christ save you," said Kasatsky, and without putting on his hat, bent his bald head.

Kasatsky rejoiced particularly in this incident, because he had shown contempt for the world's opinion, and had done something quite trifling and easy. He accepted twenty kopecks, and gave them afterwards to a blind beggar who was a friend of his.

The less he cared for the opinion of the world the more he felt that God was with him.

For eight months Kasatsky tramped in this fashion, until at last he was arrested in a provincial town in a night-shelter where he passed the night with other pilgrims. Having no passports to show, he was taken to the police-station. When he was asked for documents to prove his identity he said he had none—that he was a servant of God. He was numbered among the tramps and sent to Siberia.

There he settled down on the estate of a rich peasant, where he still lives. He works in the vegetable garden, teaches the children to read and write, and nurses the sick.

(II)

WHERE LOVE IS, GOD IS

(Translated by Mr. and Mrs. Aylmer Maude)

I N a certain town there lived a cobbler, Martin Avdéich by name. He had a tiny room in a basement, the one window of which looked out on to the street. Through it one could only see the feet of those who passed by, but Martin recognised the people by their boots. He had lived long in the place and had many acquaintances. There was hardly a pair of boots in the neighbourhood that had not been once or twice through his hands, so he often saw his own handiwork through the window. Some he had re-soled, some patched, some stitched up, and to some he had even put fresh uppers. He had plenty to do, for he worked well, used good material, did not charge too much, and could be relied on. If he could do a job by the day required, he undertook it; if not, he told the truth and gave no false promises; so he was well known and never short of work.

Martin had always been a good man, but in his old age he began to think more about his soul and to draw nearer to God. While he still worked for a master, before he set up on his own account, his wife had died, leaving him with a three-year-old son. None of his elder children had lived, they had all died in infancy. At first Martin thought of sending his little son to his sister's in the country, but then he felt sorry to part with the boy, thinking: "It would be hard for my little Kapitón to have to grow up in a strange family, I will keep him with me."

Martin left his master and went into lodgings with his little son. But he had no luck with his children. No sooner had the boy reached an age when he could help his father and be a support as well as a joy to him, than he fell ill, and after being laid up for a week with a burning fever, died. Martin buried his son, and gave way to despair so great and overwhelming that he murmured against God. In his sorrow he prayed again and again that he too might die, reproaching God for having taken the son he loved, his only son, while he, old as he was, remained alive. After that Martin left off going to church.

One day an old man from Martin's native village, who had been a pilgrim for the last eight years, called in on his way from the Tróitsa Monastery. Martin opened his heart to him and told him of his sorrow.

"I no longer even wish to live, holy man," he said. "All I

ask of God is that I soon may die. I am now quite without hope in the world."

The old man replied: "You have no right to say such things, Martin. We cannot judge God's ways. Not our reasoning, but God's will, decides. If God willed that your son should die and you should live, it must be best so. As to your despair —that comes because you wish to live for your own happiness."

"What else should one live for?" asked Martin.

"For God, Martin," said the old man. "He gives you life, and you must live for Him. When you have learnt to live for Him, you will grieve no more, and all will seem easy to you."

Martin was silent awhile, and then asked: "But how is one to live for God?"

The old man answered: "How one may live for God has been shown us by Christ. Can you read? Then buy the Gospels and read them: there you will see how God would have you live. You have it all there."

These words sank deep into Martin's heart, and that same day he went and bought himself a Testament in large print, and began to read.

At first he meant to read only on holidays, but having once begun he found it made his heart so light that he read every day. Sometimes he was so absorbed in his reading that the oil in his lamp burnt out before he could tear himself away from the book. He continued to read every night, and the more he read the more clearly he understood what God required of him, and how he might live for God. And his heart grew lighter and lighter. Before, when he went to bed he used to lie with a heavy heart, moaning as he thought of his little Kapitón; but now he only repeated again and again: "Glory to Thee, glory to Thee, O Lord! Thy will be done!"

From that time Martin's whole life changed. Formerly, on holidays he used to go and have tea at the public-house and did not even refuse a glass or two of vodka. Sometimes, after having had a drop with a friend, he left the public-house not drunk, but rather merry, and would say foolish things: shout at a man, or abuse him. Now all that sort of thing passed away from him. His life became peaceful and joyful. He sat down to his work in the morning, and when he had finished his day's work he took the lamp down from the wall, stood it on the table, fetched his book from the shelf, opened it, and sat down to read. The more he read the better he understood and the clearer and happier he felt in his mind.

It happened once that Martin sat up late, absorbed in his book. He was reading Luke's Gospel; and in the sixth chapter he came upon the verses: "To him that smiteth thee on the one cheek offer also the other; and from him that taketh away thy cloke withhold not thy coat also. Give to every man that asketh thee; and of him that taketh away thy goods ask them not again. And as ye would that men should do to you, do ye also to them likewise."

He also read the verses where our Lord says:

"And why call ye me, Lord, Lord, and do not the things which I say? Whosoever cometh to me, and heareth my sayings, and doeth them, I will shew you to whom he is like: He is like a man which built an house, and digged deep, and laid the foundation on a rock: and when the flood arose, the stream beat vehemently upon that house, and could not shake it: for it was founded upon a rock. But he that heareth, and doeth not, is like a man that without a foundation built an house upon the earth; against which the stream did beat vehemently, and immediately it fell; and the ruin of that house was great."

When Martin read these words his soul was glad within him. He took off his spectacles and laid them on the book, and leaning his elbows on the table pondered over what he had read. He tried his own life by the standard of those words, asking himself:

"Is my house built on the rock, or on sand? If it stands on the rock, it is well. It seems easy enough while one sits here alone, and one thinks that one has done all that God commands; but as soon as I cease to be on my guard, I sin again. Still I will persevere. It brings such joy. Help me, O Lord!"

He thought all this, and was about to go to bed, but was loth to leave his book. So he went on reading the seventh chapter—about the centurion, the widow's son, and the answer to John's disciples—and he came to the part where a rich Pharisee invited the Lord to his house; and he read how the woman who was a sinner anointed His feet and washed them with her tears, and how He justified her. Coming to the forty-fourth verse, he read:

"And turning to the woman, he said unto Simon, Seest thou this woman? I entered into thine house, thou gavest me no water for my feet: but she hath wetted my feet with her tears, and wiped them with her hair. Thou gavest me no kiss; but she, since the time I came in, hath not ceased to kiss my feet. My head with oil thou didst not anoint: but she hath anointed my feet with ointment."

He read these verses and thought: "He gave no water for His feet, gave no kiss, His head with oil he did not anoint. . . ." And Martin took off his spectacles once more, laid them on his book, and pondered.

"He must have been like me, that Pharisee. He too thought only of himself—how to get a cup of tea, how to keep warm and comfortable; never a thought of his guest. He took care of himself, but for his guest he cared nothing at all. Yet who was the guest? The Lord Himself! If He came to me, should I behave like that?"

Then Martin laid his head upon both his arms and, before he was aware of it, he fell asleep.

"Martin!" he suddenly heard a voice, as if someone had breathed the word above his ear.

He started from his sleep. "Who's there?" he asked.

He turned round and looked at the door; no one was there. He called again. Then he heard quite distinctly: "Martin,

Martin! Look out into the street to-morrow, for I shall come."

Martin roused himself, rose from his chair and rubbed his eyes, but did not know whether he had heard these words in a dream or awake. He put out the lamp and lay down to sleep.

Next morning he rose before daylight, and after saying his prayers he lit the fire and prepared his cabbage soup and buck-wheat porridge. Then he lit the samovar, put on his apron, and sat down by the window to his work. As he sat working Martin thought over what had happened the night before. At times it seemed to him like a dream, and at times he thought that he had really heard the voice. "Such things have happened before now," thought he.

So he sat by the window, looking out into the street more than he worked, and whenever anyone passed in unfamiliar boots he would stoop and look up, so as to see not the feet only but the face of the passer-by as well. A house-porter passed in new felt boots; then a water-carrier. Presently an old soldier of Nicholas' reign came near the window, spade in hand. Martin knew him by his boots, which were shabby old felt ones, goloshed with leather. The old man was called Stepánich: a neighbouring tradesman kept him in his house for charity, and his duty was to help the house-porter. He began to clear away the snow before Martin's window. Martin glanced at him and then went on with his work.

"I must be growing crazy with age," said Martin, laughing at his fancy. "Stepánich comes to clear away the snow, and I must needs imagine it's Christ coming to visit me. Old dotard that I am!"

Yet after he had made a dozen stitches he felt drawn to look out of the window again. He saw that Stepánich had leaned his spade against the wall and was either resting himself or trying to get warm. The man was old and broken down, and had evidently not enough strength even to clear away the snow.

"What if I called him in and gave him some tea?" thought Martin. "The samovar is just on the boil."

He stuck his awl in its place, and rose; and putting the samovar on the table, made tea. Then he tapped the window with his fingers. Stepánich turned and came to the window. Martin beckoned to him to come in and went himself to open the door.

"Come in," he said, "and warm yourself a bit. I'm sure you must be cold."

"May God bless you!" Stepánich answered. "My bones do ache to be sure." He came in, first shaking off the snow, and lest he should leave marks on the floor he began wiping his feet, but as he did so he tottered and nearly fell.

"Don't trouble to wipe your feet," said Martin; "I'll wipe up the floor—it's all in the day's work. Come, friend, sit down and have some tea."

Filling two tumblers, he passed one to his visitor, and pouring his own out into the saucer, began to blow on it.

Stepánich emptied his glass, and turning it upside down,[1] put the remains of his piece of sugar on the top. He began to express his thanks, but it was plain that he would be glad of some more.

"Have another glass," said Martin, refilling the visitor's tumbler and his own. But while he drank his tea Martin kept looking out into the street.

"Are you expecting anyone?" asked the visitor.

"Am I expecting anyone? Well now, I'm ashamed to tell you. It isn't that I really expect anyone; but I heard something last night which I can't get out of my mind. Whether it was a vision, or only a fancy, I can't tell. You see, friend, last night I was reading the Gospel, about Christ the Lord, how He suffered and how He walked on earth. You have heard tell of it, I dare say."

[1]Turning the glass upside down was the customary way of intimating that one had had enough.

"I have heard tell of it," answered Stepánich; "but I'm an ignorant man and not able to read."

"Well, you see, I was reading of how He walked on earth. I came to that part, you know, where He went to a Pharisee who did not receive Him well. Well, friend, as I read about it, I thought how that man did not receive Christ the Lord with proper honour. Suppose such a thing could happen to such a man as myself, I thought, what would I not do to receive Him! But that man gave Him no reception at all. Well, friend, as I was thinking of this I began to doze, and as I dozed I heard someone call me by name. I got up, and thought I heard someone whispering, 'Expect me; I will come to-morrow.' This happened twice over. And to tell you the truth, it sank so into my mind that, though I am ashamed of it myself, I keep on expecting Him, the dear Lord!'"

Stepánich shook his head in silence, finished his tumbler and laid it on its side; but Martin stood it up again and refilled it for him.

"Here, drink another glass, bless you! And I was thinking, too, how He walked on earth and despised no one, but went mostly among common folk. He went with plain people, and chose His disciples from among the likes of us, from workmen like us, sinners that we are. 'He who raises himself,' He said, 'shall be humbled; and he who humbles himself shall be raised.' 'You call me Lord,' He said, 'and I will wash your feet.' 'He who would be first,' He said, 'let him be the servant of all; because,' He said, 'blessed are the poor, the humble, the meek, and the merciful.'"

Stepánich forgot his tea. He was an old man, easily moved to tears, and as he sat and listened the tears ran down his cheeks.

"Come, drink some more," said Martin. But Stepánich crossed himself, thanked him, moved away his tumbler, and rose.

"Thank you, Martin Avdéich," he said, "you have given me food and comfort both for soul and body."

"You're very welcome. Come again another time. I am glad to have a guest," said Martin.

Stepanich went away; and Martin poured out the last of the tea and drank it up. Then he put away the tea-things and sat down to his work, stitching the back seam of a boot. And as he stitched he kept looking out of the window, waiting for Christ and thinking about Him and His doings. And his head was full of Christ's sayings.

Two soldiers went by: one in Government boots, the other in boots of his own; then the master of a neighbouring house, in shining goloshes; then a baker carrying a basket. All these passed on. Then a woman came up in worsted stockings and peasant-made shoes. She passed the window, but stopped by the wall. Martin glanced up at her through the window and saw that she was a stranger, poorly dressed and with a baby in her arms. She stopped by the wall with her back to the wind, trying to wrap the baby up though she had hardly anything to wrap it in. The woman had only summer clothes on, and even they were shabby and worn. Through the window Martin heard the baby crying, and the woman trying to soothe it but unable to do so. Martin rose, and going out of the door and up the steps he called to her.

"My dear, I say, my dear!"

The woman heard and turned round.

"Why do you stand out there with the baby in the cold? Come inside. You can wrap him up better in a warm place. Come this way!"

The woman was surprised to see an old man in an apron, with spectacles on his nose, calling to her, but she followed him in.

They went down the steps, entered the little room, and the old man led her to the bed.

"There, sit down, my dear, near the stove. Warm yourself and feed the baby."

"Haven't any milk. I have eaten nothing myself since early

morning," said the woman, but still she took the baby to her breast.

Martin shook his head. He brought out a basin and some bread. Then he opened the oven door and poured some cabbage soup into the basin. He took out the porridge pot also, but the porridge was not yet ready, so he spread a cloth on the table and served only the soup and bread.

"Sit down and eat, my dear, and I'll mind the baby. Why, bless me, I've had children of my own; I know how to manage them."

The woman crossed herself, and sitting down at the table began to eat, while Martin put the baby on the bed and sat down by it. He chucked and chucked, but having no teeth he could not do it well and the baby continued to cry. Then Martin tried poking at him with his finger; he drove his finger straight at the baby's mouth and then quickly drew it back, and did this again and again. He did not let the baby take his finger in his mouth, because it was all black with cobbler's wax. But the baby first grew quiet watching the finger, and then began to laugh. And Martin felt quite pleased.

The woman sat eating and talking, and told him who she was, and where she had been.

"I'm a soldier's wife," said she. "They sent my husband somewhere, far away, eight months ago, and I have heard nothing of him since. I had a place as cook till my baby was born, but then they would not keep me with a child. For three months now I have been struggling, unable to find a place, and I've had to sell all I had for food. I tried to go as a wet-nurse, but no one would have me; they said I was too starved-looking and thin. Now I have just been to see a tradesman's wife (a woman from our village is in service with her), and she has promised to take me. I thought it was all settled at last, but she tells me not to come till next week. It is far to her place, and I am fagged out, and baby is quite starved, poor mite. Fortunately our landlady has pity on us, and lets us lodge free, else I don't know what we should do."

Martin sighed. "Haven't you any warmer clothing?" he asked.

"How could I get warm clothing?" said she. "Why, I pawned my last shawl for sixpence yesterday."

Then the woman came and took the child, and Martin got up. He went and looked among some things that were hanging on the wall, and brought back an old cloak.

"Here," he said, "though it's a worn-out old thing, it will do to wrap him up in."

The woman looked at the cloak, then at the old man, and taking it, burst into tears. Martin turned away, and groping under the bed brought out a small trunk. He fumbled about in it, and again sat down opposite the woman. And the woman said:

"The Lord bless you, friend. Surely Christ must have sent me to your window, else the child would have frozen. It was mild when I started, but now see how cold it has turned. Surely it must have been Christ who made you look out of your window and take pity on me, poor wretch!"

Martin smiled and said, "It is quite true; it was He made me do it. It was no mere chance made me look out."

And he told the woman his dream, and how he had heard the Lord's voice promising to visit him that day.

"Who knows? All things are possible," said the woman. And she got up and threw the cloak over her shoulders, wrapping it round herself and round the baby. Then she bowed, and thanked Martin once more.

"Take this for Christ's sake," said Martin, and gave her sixpence to get her shawl out of pawn. The woman crossed herself, and Martin did the same, and then he saw her out.

After the woman had gone, Martin ate some cabbage soup, cleared the things away, and sat down to work again. He sat and worked, but did not forget the window, and every time a shadow fell on it he looked up at once to see who was passing. People he knew and strangers passed by, but no one remarkable.

After a while Martin saw an apple-woman stop just in front of his window. She had a large basket, but there did not seem to be many apples left in it, she had evidently sold most of her stock. On her back she had a sack full of chips, which she was taking home. No doubt she had gathered them at some place where building was going on. The sack evidently hurt her and she wanted to shift it from one shoulder to the other, so she put it down on the footpath and, placing her basket on a post, began to shake down the chips in the sack. While she was doing this a boy in a tattered cap ran up, snatched an apple out of the basket and tried to slip away; but the old woman noticed it, and turning, caught the boy by his sleeve. He began to struggle, trying to free himself, but the old woman held on with both hands, knocked his cap off his head, and seized hold of his hair. The boy screamed and the old woman scolded. Martin dropped his awl, not waiting to stick it in its place, and rushed out of the door Stumbling up the steps, and dropping his spectacles in his hurry, he ran out into the street. The old woman was pulling the boy's hair and scolding him, and threatening to take him to the police. The lad was struggling and protesting, saying, "I did not take it. What are you beating me for? Let me go!"

Martin separated them. He took the boy by the hand and said, "Let him go, Granny. Forgive him for Christ's sake."

"I'll pay him out, so that he won't forget it for a year! I'll take the rascal to the police!"

Martin began entreating the old woman.

"Let him go, Granny. He won't do it again. Let him go for Christ's sake!"

The old woman let go, and the boy wished to run away, but Martin stopped him.

"Ask the Granny's forgiveness!" said he. "And don't do it another time. I saw you take the apple."

The boy began to cry and to beg pardon.

"That's right. And now here's an apple for you," and Martin took an apple from the basket and gave it to the boy, saying, "I will pay you, Granny."

"You will spoil them that way, the young rascals," said the old woman. "He ought to be whipped so that he should remember it for a week."

"Oh, Granny, Granny," said Martin, "that's our way—but it's not God's way. If he should be whipped for stealing an apple, what should be done to us for our sins?"

The old woman was silent.

And Martin told her the parable of the lord who forgave his servant a large debt, and how the servant went out and seized his debtor by the throat. The old woman listened to it all, and the boy, too, stood by and listened.

"God bids us forgive," said Martin, "or else we shall not be forgiven. Forgive every one, and a thoughtless youngster most of all."

The old woman wagged her head and sighed.

"It's true enough," said she, "but they are getting terribly spoilt."

"Then we old ones must show them better ways," Martin replied.

"That's just what I say," said the old woman. "I have had seven of them myself, and only one daughter is left." And the old woman began to tell how and where she was living with her daughter, and how many grandchildren she had. "There now," she said, "I have but little strength left, yet I work hard for the sake of my grandchildren; and nice children they are, too. No one comes out to meet me but the children. Little Annie, now, won't leave me for anyone. It's grandmother, dear grandmother, darling grandmother!" And the old woman completely softened at the thought.

"Of course it was only his childishness, God help him," said she, referring to the boy.

As the old woman was about to hoist her sack on her back,

the lad sprang forward to her, saying, "Let me carry it for you, Granny. I'm going that way."

The old woman nodded her head, and put the sack on the boy's back, and they went down the street together, the old woman quite forgetting to ask Martin to pay for the apple. Martin stood and watched them as they went along talking to each other.

When they were out of sight Martin went back to the house. Having found his spectacles unbroken on the steps, he picked up his awl and sat down again to work. He worked a little, but could soon not see to pass the bristle through the holes in the leather; and presently he noticed the lamplighter passing on his way to light the street lamps.

"Seems it's time to light up," thought he. So he trimmed his lamp, hung it up, and sat down again to work. He finished off one boot, and turning it about, examined it. It was all right. Then he gathered his tools together, swept up the cuttings, put away the bristles and the thread and the awls, and, taking down the lamp, placed it on the table. Then he took the Gospels from the shelf. He meant to open them at the place he had marked the day before with a bit of morocco, but the book opened at another place. As Martin opened it, his yesterday's dream came back to his mind, and no sooner had he thought of it than he seemed to hear footsteps, as though someone were moving behind him. Martin turned round, and it seemed to him as if people were standing in the dark corner, but he could not make out who they were. And a voice whispered in his ear: "Martin, Martin, don't you know me?"

"Who is it?" muttered Martin.

"It is I," said the voice. And out of the dark corner stepped Stepánich, who smiled, and vanishing like a cloud, was seen no more.

"It is I," said the voice again. And out of the darkness stepped the woman with the baby in her arms, and the woman smiled and the baby laughed, and they too vanished.

And Martin's soul grew glad. He crossed himself, put on his spectacles, and began reading the Gospel just where it had opened: and at the top of the page he read:

"I was an hungered, and ye gave me meat: I was thirsty, and ye gave me drink: I was a stranger, and ye took me in."

And at the bottom of the page he read:

"Inasmuch as ye did it unto one of these my brethren, even these least, ye did it unto me" (Matt. xxv.).

And Martin understood that his dream had come true; and that the Saviour had really come to him that day, and he had welcomed him.

(III)

THE THREE HERMITS

An Old Legend Current in the Volga District

(Translated by Mr. and Mrs. Aylmer Maude)

"And in praying use not vain repetitions, as the Gentiles do: for they think that they shall be heard for their much speaking. Be not therefore like unto them: for your Father knoweth what things ye have need of, before ye ask Him."—Matt. vi. 7, 8.

A BISHOP was sailing from Archangel to the Solovétsk Monastery, and on the same vessel were a number of pilgrims on their way to visit the shrines at that place. The voyage was a smooth one; the wind favourable and the weather fair. The pilgrims lay on deck, eating, or sat in groups talking to one another. The Bishop, too, came on deck, and as he was pacing up and down he noticed a group of men standing near the prow and listening to a fisherman, who was pointing to the sea and telling them something. The Bishop stopped, and looked in the direction in which the man was pointing. He could see nothing, however, but the sea glistening in the sunshine. He drew nearer to listen, but when the man saw him, he took off his cap and was silent. The rest of the people also took off their caps and bowed.

"Do not let me disturb you, friends," said the Bishop. "I came to hear what this good man was saying."

"The fisherman was telling us about the hermits," replied one, a tradesman, rather bolder than the rest.

"What hermits?" asked the Bishop, going to the side of the vessel and seating himself on a box. "Tell me about them. I should like to hear. What were you pointing at?"

"Why, that little island you can just see over there," answered the man, pointing to a spot ahead and a little to the right. "That is the island where the hermits live for the salvation of their souls."

"Where is the island?" asked the Bishop. "I see nothing."

"There, in the distance, if you will please look along my hand. Do you see that little cloud? Below it, and a bit to the left, there is just a faint streak. That is the island."

The Bishop looked carefully, but his unaccustomed eyes could make out nothing but the water shimmering in the sun.

"I cannot see it," he said. "But who are the hermits that live there?"

"They are holy men," answered the fisherman. "I had long ago heard tell of them, but never chanced to see them myself till the year before last."

And the fisherman related how once, when he was out fishing, he had been stranded at night upon that island, not knowing where he was. In the morning, as he wandered about the island, he came across an earth hut, and met an old man standing near it. Presently two others came out, and after having fed him and dried his things they helped him mend his boat.

"And what are they like?" asked the Bishop.

"One is a small man and his back is bent. He wears a priest's cassock and is very old; he must be more than a hundred, I should say. He is so old that the white of his beard is taking a greenish tinge, but he is always smiling, and his face is as bright as an angel's from heaven. The second is taller, but he also is very old. He wears a tattered peasant coat. His beard is broad, and of a yellowish-grey colour. He is a strong man. Before I had time to help him, he turned my boat over as if it were only a pail. He too is kindly and cheerful. The third is tall, and has a beard as white as snow and reaching to his knees. He is stern, with overhanging eyebrows; and he wears nothing but a piece of matting tied round his waist."

"And did they speak to you?" asked the Bishop.

"For the most part they did everything in silence, and spoke but little even to one another. One of them would just give a glance, and the others would understand him. I asked the tallest whether they had lived there long. He frowned, and muttered something as if he were angry; but the oldest one took his hand and smiled, and then the tall one was quiet. The oldest one only said: 'Have mercy upon us,' and smiled."

While the fisherman was talking, the ship had drawn nearer to the island.

"There, now you can see it plainly, if your Lordship will please to look," said the tradesman, pointing with his hand.

The Bishop looked, and now he really saw a dark streak—which was the island. Having looked at it a while, he left the prow of the vessel, and going to the stern, asked the helmsman:

"What island is that?"

"That one," replied the man, "has no name. There are many such in this sea."

"Is it true that there are hermits who live there for the salvation of their souls?"

"So it is said, your Lordship, but I don't know if it's true. Fishermen say they have seen them; but of course they may only be spinning yarns."

"I should like to land on the island and see these men," said the Bishop. "How could I manage it?"

"The ship cannot get close to the island," replied the helmsman, "but you might be rowed there in a boat. You had better speak to the captain."

The captain was sent for and came.

"I should like to see these hermits," said the Bishop. "Could I not be rowed ashore?"

The captain tried to dissuade him.

"Of course it could be done," said he, "but we should lose much time. And if I might venture to say so to your Lordship, the old men are not worth your pains. I have heard say that they are foolish old fellows, who understand nothing, and never speak a word, any more than the fish in the sea."

"I wish to see them," said the Bishop, "and I will pay you for your trouble and loss of time. Please let me have a boat."

There was no help for it; so the order was given. The sailors trimmed the sails, the steersman put up the helm, and the ship's course was set for the island. A chair was placed at the prow for the Bishop, and he sat there, looking ahead. The passengers all collected at the prow and gazed at the island. Those who had the sharpest eyes could presently make out the rocks on it, and then a mud hut was seen. At last one man saw the hermits themselves. The captain brought a telescope and, after looking through it, handed it to the Bishop.

"It's right enough. There are three men standing on the shore. There, a little to the right of that big rock."

The Bishop took the telescope, got it into position, and he saw the three men: a tall one, a shorter one, and one very small and bent, standing on the shore and holding each other by the hand.

The captain turned to the Bishop.

"The vessel can get no nearer in than this, your Lordship. If you wish to go ashore, we must ask you to go in the boat, while we anchor here."

The cable was quickly let out, the anchor cast, and the sails furled. There was a jerk, and the vessel shook. Then, a boat having been lowered, the oarsmen jumped in, and the Bishop descended the ladder and took his seat. The men pulled at their oars and the boat moved rapidly towards the island. When they came within a stone's throw, they saw three old men: a tall one with only a piece of matting tied round his waist; a shorter one in a tattered peasant coat, and a very old one bent with age and wearing an old cassock—all three standing hand in hand.

The oarsmen pulled in to the shore, and held on with the boathook while the Bishop got out.

The old men bowed to him, and he gave them his blessing, at which they bowed still lower. Then the Bishop began to speak to them.

"I have heard," he said, "that you, godly men, live here saving your own souls and praying to our Lord Christ for your fellow-men. I, an unworthy servant of Christ, am called, by God's mercy, to keep and teach His flock. I wished to see you, servants of God, and to do what I can to teach you also."

The old men looked at each other, smiling, but remained silent.

"Tell me," said the Bishop, "what you are doing to save your souls, and how you serve God on this island."

The second hermit sighed, and looked at the oldest, the very ancient one. The latter smiled, and said:

"We do not know how to serve God. We only serve and support ourselves, servant of God."

"But how do you pray to God?" asked the Bishop.

"We pray in this way," replied the hermit. "Three are ye, three are we, have mercy upon us."

And when the old man said this, all three raised their eyes to heaven, and repeated:

"Three are ye, three are we, have mercy upon us!"

The Bishop smiled.

"You have evidently heard something about the Holy Trinity," said he. "But you do not pray aright. You have won my affection, godly men. I see you wish to please the

Lord, but you do not know how to serve Him. That is not the way to pray; but listen to me, and I will teach you. I will teach you, not a way of my own, but the way in which God in the Holy Scriptures has commanded all men to pray to Him."

And the Bishop began explaining to the hermits how God had revealed Himself to men; telling them of God the Father, and God the Son, and God the Holy Ghost.

"God the Son came down on earth," said he, "to save men, and this is how He taught us all to pray. Listen, and repeat after me: 'Our Father.' "

And the first old man repeated after him, "Our Father," and the second, said "Our Father," and the third said, "Our Father."

"Which art in heaven," continued the Bishop.

The first hermit repeated, "Which art in heaven," but the second blundered over the words, and the tall hermit could not say them properly. His hair had grown over his mouth so that he could not speak plainly. The very old hermit, having no teeth, also mumbled indistinctly.

The Bishop repeated the words again, and the old men repeated them after him. The Bishop sat down on a stone, and the old men stood before him, watching his mouth, and repeating the words as he uttered them. And all day long the Bishop laboured, saying a word twenty, thirty, a hundred times over, and the old men repeated it after him. They blundered, and he corrected them, and made them begin again.

The Bishop did not leave off till he had taught them the whole of the Lord's Prayer so that they could not only repeat it after him, but could say it by themselves. The middle one was the first to know it, and to repeat the whole of it alone. The Bishop made him say it again and again, and at last the others could say it too.

It was getting dark and the moon was appearing over the water before the Bishop rose to return to the vessel. When he took leave of the old men they all bowed down to the ground before him. He raised them, and kissed each of them, telling them to pray as he had taught them. Then he got into the boat and returned to the ship.

And as he sat in the boat and was rowed to the ship he could hear the three voices of the hermits loudly repeating the Lord's Prayer. As the boat drew near the vessel their voices could no longer be heard, but they could still be seen in the moonlight, standing as he had left them on the shore, the shortest in the middle, the tallest on the right, the middle one on the left. As soon as the Bishop had reached the vessel and got on board, the anchor was weighed and the sails unfurled. The wind filled them and the ship sailed away, and the Bishop took a seat in the stern and watched the island they had left. For a time he could still see the hermits, but presently they disappeared from sight, though the island was still visible. At last it too vanished, and only the sea was to be seen, rippling in the moonlight.

The pilgrims lay down to sleep, and all was quiet on deck. The Bishop did not wish to sleep, but sat alone at the stern, gazing at the sea where the island was no longer visible, and thinking of the good old men. He thought how pleased they had been to learn the Lord's Prayer; and he thanked God for having sent him to teach and help such godly men.

So the Bishop sat, thinking, and gazing at the sea where the island had disappeared. And the moonlight flickered before his eyes, sparkling, now here, now there, upon the waves. Suddenly he saw something white and shining, on the bright path which the moon cast across the sea. Was it a seagull, or the little gleaming sail of some small boat? The Bishop fixed his eyes upon it, wondering.

"It must be a boat sailing after us," thought he, "but it is overtaking us very rapidly. It was far, far away a minute ago, but now it is much nearer. It cannot be a boat, for I can see no sail; but whatever it may be, it is following us and catching us up."

And he could not make out what it was. Not a boat, nor a bird, nor a fish! It was too large for a man, and, besides, a man could not be out there in the midst of the sea. The Bishop rose, and said to the helmsman:

"Look there, what is that, my friend? What is it?" the Bishop repeated, though he could now see plainly what it was —the three hermits running upon the water, all gleaming white, their grey beards shining, and approaching the ship as quickly as though it were not moving.

The steersman looked, and let go the helm in terror.

"O Lord! The hermits are running after us on the water as though it were dry land!"

The passengers, hearing him, jumped up and crowded to the stern. They saw the hermits coming along hand in hand, and the two outer ones beckoning the ship to stop. All three were gliding along upon the water without moving their feet. Before the ship could be stopped, the hermits had reached it, and raising their heads, all three as with one voice began to say:

"We have forgotten your teaching, servant of God. As long as we kept repeating it we remembered, but when we stopped saying it for a time, a word dropped out, and now it has all gone to pieces. We can remember nothing of it. Teach us again."

The Bishop crossed himself, and leaning over the ship's side, said:

"Your own prayer will reach the Lord, men of God. It is not for me to teach you. Pray for us sinners."

And the Bishop bowed low before the old men; and they turned and went back across the sea. And a light shone until daybreak on the spot where they were lost to sight.

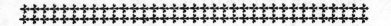

NICHOLAS LESKOV

(1831–1896)

✢✢

THE SENTRY

(Translated by Roman Sagovsky)

I

T H E event, a narration of which is hereby brought to the reader's notice, is touching and terrible with regard to the chief dramatic personage of the piece, while the *dénouement* of the entire business is so original that it would seem improbable and grotesque in any other country but Russia.

It is partly a court, partly an historical anecdote, and happily portrays the manners and tendency of an interesting yet poorly recorded period in the 'thirties of this our closing century.

There is not a shred of fiction in the following tale.

II

In the winter of 1839, about Epiphany, Petersburg was visited by a sudden thaw. So slushy was the weather that it seemed like the advent of spring: the snows melted, water dripped from the roofs in the daytime and the ice in the rivers swelled with moisture. On the Neva, directly before the Winter Palace itself, stretched deep pools of free water. A warm westerly wind was blowing, steadily increasing in strength: the flood tide of the river was threatening the city and the signal guns boomed.

In the Palace the guard was provided by a company of the Ismailovski Regiment under the command of Nicolai Ivanovitch Miller, a young officer of brilliant scholarly attainments and excellently placed in the social world (Miller eventually became a full general and the director of the Lycée). He was a man with what was then termed "humane" propensities, a trait that was noticed at the outset of his career and deemed by the superior command a shortcoming that tended to mar his prospects.

Nevertheless, Miller was an efficient and reliable officer, and mounting guard at the Palace presented in those days no element of danger. They were days of profound peace and tranquillity. Nothing more was required of the Palace guard than a scrupulous discharge of their duties by the sentries, and yet, as luck would have it, it was precisely during Captain Miller's turn as C.O. of the guards in the palace that the most extraordinary and alarming event occurred, doubtless hardly remembered now by those few contemporaries who are ending their days in our midst.

III

At first all went well with the guard: the duties were allotted, the men posted and everything was in perfect order. The Emperor Nicholas Pavlovitch was in good health, had gone for a drive in the evening, returned home and retired to bed. The Palace too had sunk into slumber. The calmest of nights descended. Stillness reigned in the guard-room. Captain Miller, with the aid of two pins, carefully tacked his white handkerchief to the high and traditionally greasy leather back of the officers' armchair and settled down to while away the hours with a book.

Captain Miller had always been a passionate lover of reading, and consequently was not bored and never noticed the progress of the night; but suddenly, just before 3 a.m., he was aroused by a fearful disturbance: before him stood the sergeant of the guard, pale as death, quaking with terror, and jabbering volubly.

"A mishap, your Honour, a mishap!"

"What's the matter?"

"A terrible misfortune has occurred!"

Captain Miller leapt up in extreme alarm, and with difficulty obtained a coherent account of the "mishap" and
"terrible misfortune."

IV

This is what had happened: a sentry, a private of the
Ismailovski Regiment named Postnikov, posted outside the
Jordan entrance, had suddenly become aware that a man was
in difficulties in a hole in the Neva ice and was shrieking for
help.

Private Postnikov, a household serf to a country family, was
a very highly strung, sensitive man. He listened for some
time to the distant yells and groans and they were reducing
him to a state of numbness. Sick with horror, he kept on
glancing to right and left, scanning the entire visible stretch
of the embankment, but unfortunately neither here nor on
the Neva was there a living soul in sight.

There's no one to render aid to the drowning man and he's
sure to go under. . . .

And meanwhile the victim struggles, oh, so long, so
desperately. . . .

It would almost have seemed easier for the unfortunate man
to be calm and drown than to struggle in that way. But he
would not submit to fate. His howls and entreaties kept breaking out anew and getting nearer and nearer to the Palace
Quay. Evidently the man had not yet lost his bearing and
was heading straight for the lights, only he hadn't got the
ghost of a chance, because precisely there in front of him lay
the Jordan water-hole. There he was bound to shoot under
the ice and be done for. . . . Again all was silence, and a
minute later, again the splashing in the water and the cry—
"Help! help!" Then now he was so near that the splashing
could almost be seen. . . .

Private Postnikov began to conjecture that the rescue of the man was a simple matter. If he were to run down on to the ice, the man was sure to be just there. Merely to pass him the end of a line, or a pole, or extend his gun to him would save him. He was so near that he could grasp help with his hands and jump out. But Postnikov remembered the service regulations and his oath: he knew he was a sentry, and a sentry dares never, under any excuse, leave the sentry-box.

On the other hand, Postnikov's heart was ungovernable: it ached for the man, it fluttered with anxiety. Oh, to pluck it out, that unregimental heart of his, and throw it away. The tension was unbearable. It was horrible, of course, to hear another man agonising and deny him a helping hand, when, honestly speaking, there was every opportunity for doing so; for the sentry-box won't run away and no other irreparable harm could result. "Or, perhaps, I'll just risk it, what? . . . No one will know. . . . Oh, God, to get it over! There he goes again. . . ."

In the course of the half-hour that all this was going on Private Postnikov worried his heart out and began to experience "doubts of the mind." Yet he was an intelligent and efficient soldier with a head on his shoulders, and clearly aware that the quitting of his post by a sentry constituted so great a crime as to entail immediate court-martial, public flogging, banishment, perhaps even death. But from the river, nearer and nearer rose the soul-tormenting cries, and he distinctly heard the gurgles and desperate floundering of the death-struggle. . . .

"I-am-d-rr-owning! . . . Help, drowning!"

Now he's reached the ice-hole. . . . God have mercy on him!

Postnikov again cast a helpless glance to right and left, all round. . . . Not a soul about anywhere—just the lanterns swaying and flickering in the wind, and with the wind is borne that halting, faltering cry . . . the last cry, perhaps. . . .

Another splash, another monotonous wail, and a rasping gurgle in the water. . . .

The sentry could stand it no longer. He deserted his post.

V

Postnikov raced up to the wooden planks, rapidly descended with thumping heart on to the ice, then plunged into the icy waters of the pool, and quickly locating the struggling, gasping body, stretched his musket towards it.

The drowning man clutched at the butt end, while Postnikov tugged at the bayonet and drew him to the shore.

Both rescuer and rescued were wringing wet, and since the latter was quite exhausted and trembled and could not keep to his legs, the rescuer, Private Postnikov, had not the heart to leave him on the ice, but hauled him on to the embankment and proceeded to look about for someone to take charge of him. In the meantime, while all this was taking place, a sleigh had made its appearance on the Quay, and in it was seated an officer of the then extant Household Company of Invalids (subsequently disbanded).

This most untimely (for Postnikov) new arrival was—it must be presumed—a most irresponsible gentleman, rather a scatterbrained fellow, and an impudent liar to boot. He skipped from his sleigh and broke into a torrent of questions:

"What's all this? . . . What's this man? . . . What are all these people?" . . .

"Drowning, going under . . ." began Postnikov.

"What do you mean, drowning? Who was drowning—*you*? Why at this spot?"

But the man merely spluttered and gasped. Postnikov himself had vanished: he had quietly shouldered his musket and returned to the sentry-box.

Whether the officer guessed what had occurred, or out of some other consideration, he cut short his interrogation abruptly and bundled the rescued man into his sleigh. Then he sped off to the Morskaya, where the Admiralty Divisional Police Station was situated.

Here the officer made a statement to the sergeant on duty that the dripping man he had brought with him was drowning in an ice-pool in the river in front of the Palace and was rescued by him—Mr. Officer—at great personal risk.

The man who had been thus gallantly rescued was still very wet, chilled and exhausted. As a result of the shock and immense expenditure of energy, he had swooned and was quite indifferent to the identity of his rescuer.

At his side pottered a sleepy police surgeon, while in the office the sergeant was drawing up a report based on the verbal statement of the Invalid officer, and with inherent police suspicion marvelled how he had succeeded in remaining dry as a pin himself. And the officer, who was moved by a desire to win the established medal "For the delivery of those in mortal danger," explained it all by a happy concurrence of circumstances, but explained it awkwardly and improbably. They went to wake the inspector and sent round for inquiries.

Meanwhile, in the Palace this occurrence was the cause of a rapid series of events, of a different nature.

VI

In the Palace guard-room, the above-mentioned developments, following the departure of the officer with the rescued man in his sleigh, were unknown. There the officer and soldiers of the Ismailovski Regiment merely knew that one of their privates, Postnikov, having deserted his post, went to save a man, and since this is a great breach of military duty, the said Private Postnikov would now inevitably be court-martialled and flogged, while all his superiors, beginning with the C.O., were apprehensive of the trouble which this must inevitably cause them.

The wet and trembling Postnikov was, of course, immediately relieved on his post. He was brought to the guard-room, and there made a clean breast of the matter to the captain, telling him all that we have already learnt, with every detail, including the circumstance that the Invalid officer had picked up the rescued man and told his driver to hurry to the Admiralty Police Division.

This complication caused the whole matter to be much more dangerous. The officer of the Invalids would naturally describe the whole episode to the police-sergeant, and the sergeant would instantly bring it to the notice of the Prefect of the Police, Kokoshkine, who would report it in the morning to the Emperor, and "panic" would be let loose.

There was no time to be lost in speculation, the opinion of the superior officer must be obtained.

Nicolai Ivanovitch Miller at once despatched a worried note to his battalion commander, Lieut.-Col. Svinin, asking him to come as quickly as he could, and assist him by every possible means in his awful predicament.

This was about 3 a.m. Kokoshkine presented himself to the Emperor very early in the morning, so there was little time left for reflection and action.

VII

Lieut.-Col. Svinin was not possessed of that feeling of clemency and kindness that had always distinguished Nicolai Ivanovitch Miller: Svinin was by no means a heartless man, but he was primarily and above everything a "service man" (a type which is again recalled to-day with some regret). Svinin had a reputation for severity, and even enjoyed parading his strictness in matters of discipline. He had no taste for evil and never sought to cause unnecessary suffering; but if a man transgressed any of the rules of service he was inexorable. He deemed it inexpedient to enter into a discussion regarding the motives that in those instances guided the

guilty party, but held to the rule that on service every fault
is a fault. Hence everyone in the company on guard knew
that whatever it was Postnikov was to suffer, suffer he would,
and Svinin would shed no tears about it.

Thus did this staff officer appear to his superiors and comrades, amongst whom were men who did not altogether
share his point of view. For the spirit of "humaneness" and
other delusions were not entirely absent at that period.
Svinin was quite indifferent as to whether the "humanitarians" applauded or censured him. To beg or entreat of
Svinin or even attempt to influence him was a hopeless task.
Against all this he was hardened. He had the temper of the
career-makers of his day, but, like Achilles, he too possessed a
weak spot.

Svinin's career had begun well, and he was naturally careful to do nothing that might give him a set-back. He saw to it
that there was never a speck of dust on his career, any more
than upon his uniform. But this unfortunate escapade of a
man of the battalion entrusted to his charge was bound to cast
a shadow on the discipline of the entire unit. Whether any
blame or not attached to the battalion commander for a deed
committed under the impulse of noble compassion—that
would not enter the minds of those on whom depended the
well-launched and meticulously well-maintained career of
Svinin; there were many who would gladly roll a log across
his path to make it better for some relative of theirs, or help
some influential protégé. This would, of course, be easy if the
Tsar, as was quite likely, proved to be annoyed by the affair
and called the attention of the Colonel-in-Chief to the slack-
ness of discipline. Svinin would be held to blame. And the
rumour would go round that "Svinin is slack," and so, perhaps, a blot would for ever remain upon his reputation.
There would be no chance then of becoming anything remarkable amid his contemporaries, no chance of leaving his
portrait in the gallery of historical personages of the Empire
of Russia.

Although the study of history was at a discount at the time, yet nevertheless everyone believed in history, and with eager willingness aspired to lend a hand in its manufacture.

VIII

The moment Svinin received, about three in the morning, the alarming note from Captain Miller, he leapt out of bed, donned his uniform, and fearfully and angrily descended upon the guard-room of the Winter Palace. Here he at once proceeded to examine Private Postnikov, and satisfied himself that the incredible incident had indeed occurred. Private Postnikov again frankly repeated to his battalion commander all the events of his watch, as he had previously narrated them to his officer, Captain Miller. The soldier stated that he was "guilty before God and the Tsar, and expected no mercy." He told how he was on his post, heard the groans of the man sinking in the pool, how he had suffered agonies of sympathy, and waged a stubborn battle against pity, but in the end pity won—he left his box, leapt on to the ice and brought the drowning man to shore. And he recounted how, by a stroke of ill-luck, he had been sighted by an officer of the Palace Company of Invalids.

Lieut.-Col Svinin was in despair. He permitted himself the only possible satisfaction; he at once placed Postnikov under arrest. And he reproached Miller bitterly with his "humanitarianism," which was of no earthly use in military service. But all this failed to mend matters. To invent even an excuse, to say nothing of a defence to such a crime as the desertion of his post by a sentry, was quite impossible, and there remained but one means of escape—that was, to conceal the entire business from the Emperor.

But was it possible to suppress an occurrence of this nature?

To all appearance it seemed impossible, because the facts of the rescue were known not only to all the guards, but also to

that hateful Invalid officer, who by now had doubtlessly
succeeded in bringing the whole matter to the knowledge
of General Kokoshkine.

Where was he to rush to now? To whose mercy would it be
best to appeal? Where was he to seek aid and protection?

Svinin was on the point of galloping off to the Grand Duke
Michael Pavlovitch and disclosing everything to him. This
was an habitual move of officers in trouble. Let the quick-
tempered Grand Duke fly into a rage about it. That would
not matter, because the more insulting he was to begin with,
the sooner he relented and himself acted as intercessor.
These *volte-faces* were quite common in the Grand Duke,
sometimes deliberately staged. Svinin was most anxious to
do what he could in that way. But how could he gain admission to the Palace at night and disturb the Grand Duke? To
wait till the morning, till after Kokoshkine's report to the
Tsar, was useless. And while Svinin was frantic with perplexity amid all these difficulties, he suddenly relaxed and his
brain began to see another way out, a way which till that
moment had remained hidden in the general fog.

IX

Among the existing rules of military tactics, there is one to
the effect that at a moment of supreme danger threatening
from the walls of a besieged fortress, the troops should not be
retired, but driven close in under the walls. Svinin decided
to do nothing as originally conceived, but go straight to
Kokoshkine.

Many horrible and absurd stories were then current in
Petersburg concerning the Prefect of Police, Kokoshkine, but
it was also asserted that he possessed wonderful resource and
tact, and that with the aid of this tact he could not only
"make an elephant out of a fly, but with equal ease turned
elephants into flies."

Kokoshkine was indeed very harsh and stern and inspired

everyone with a fear of his person, but he sometimes blinked at the pranks and escapades of the gay young dogs of the capital, and there were in those days many rips in the army who found in him a powerful and warm champion. Generally speaking he was able, and managed to do a lot if he only wished it. Both Svinin and Miller knew that much about him. Miller also strengthened his chief in his resolve to venture on immediately interviewing Kokoshkine and entrusting his fate to his magnanimity and tact. Kokoshkine would no doubt tell him just exactly how he would be able to extricate himself from this mess without angering the Tsar, which, to give the devil his due, Kokoshkine always avoided doing by every artifice at his disposal.

Svinin got into his greatcoat, fixed his eyes heavenwards, and exclaiming "God! God!" several times, departed to see Kokoshkine.

That would be a little after four in the morning.

X

The Prefect of Police, Kokoshkine, was roused from his sleep and informed of the arrival of Svinin on a business of the utmost importance and urgency.

The General rose in no time and appeared before Svinin clad in a dressing-gown, rubbing his forehead, yawning and shivering. All that Svinin related, Kokoshkine heard with the greatest attention, but quite unmoved. Throughout these explanations and pleas for indulgence he interrupted but once:

"A soldier left his sentry-box and rescued a man?"

"Precisely," answered Svinin.

"And the sentry-box?"

"Remained vacant in the meanwhile."

"Umph . . . I know it remained vacant. I am relieved to hear it has not been stolen."

This remark strengthened Svinin's conviction that he was

already aware of everything, and had no doubt already made up his mind how he was going to present the case in his morning report to the Emperor, and nothing would alter the decision. Otherwise such an incident as the desertion of his post by a sentry in the Palace guard would doubtlessly have perturbed the energetic Prefect of Police much more.

But Kokoshkine knew nothing. The inspector to whom the Invalid officer had presented himself with the rescued man did not think the matter very important. In his judgment it was not at all a business with which to worry the harassed Prefect of Police in the middle of the night, and besides, the occurrence itself appeared most suspicious to the inspector, because the clothes of the Invalid officer were quite dry, which would have been impossible had he saved the man at the risk of his own life. The Inspector thought the officer merely an ambitious liar, who was fishing for another medal to adorn his bosom, and therefore, while his junior was preparing the official statement, the inspector detained the officer with pleasant conversation and endeavoured to worm the truth out of him by a series of questions about small details.

Also the inspector was annoyed that the incident had taken place in his division and that the victim was brought to the shore, not by a policeman, but by a Palace officer. The equanimity of Kokoshkine was simply explained, firstly, by the extreme fatigue which he experienced after a day full of bustle and a night attendance at two fires, and secondly by the fact that the breach of discipline committed by the sentry Postnikov did not directly concern him as Prefect of Police.

Nevertheless, Kokoshkine gave certain instructions.

He sent for the chief of the Admiralty Division and ordered him to appear forthwith together with the Invalid officer and the rescued man, while Svinin was asked to wait in a little waiting-room adjoining his private work-room. Then

Kokoshkine went into his private office and, without closing the door, sat at his desk to sign some letters. A moment later he bowed his head into his hands and fell fast asleep over the desk as he sat there in his upholstered chair.

XI

There were then no city telegraphs and telephones, and for the prompt conveyance of administrative orders galloped the "forty thousand couriers" of whom Gogol wrote in his immortal "Revizor."

They were not so speedy as the telegraph or telephone, but, on the other hand, they lent to the city an atmosphere of considerable animation and testified to the unremitting vigilance of the authorities.

By the time the breathless inspector, the doughty Invalid officer and the rescued man were rushed up from the Admiralty Police Station, the nervous and energetic General Kokoshkine had had a quiet nap and felt refreshed. This was noticeable from the expression on his face and the new decision in his manner.

He summoned the new arrivals to his room and invited Svinin to come in also.

"The report?" inquired Kokoshkine curtly in refreshed tones.

The inspector without a word handed him a folded sheet of paper and whispered something in his ear.

"I have to beg permission to report to your Excellency a few things in private," said he.

"All right."

Kokoshkine stepped into the recess of a window and was joined by the inspector there.

"What is it?"

Followed the inaudible buzz of the inspector and the grunts of the General.

"Umph. . . . Yes. . . . Well, what about it? . . . That's

possible. . . . They always get a ducking without getting wet. . . . Nothing else?"

"Nothing."

The General emerged from the embrasure, dropped back into his chair and began to read. He read the paper to himself, betraying neither fear nor doubt, and immediately afterwards turned to the rescued man with a loud and firm query:

"How is it, man, you found yourself in that water in front of the Palace?"

"Sorry," replied the victim.

"That's just it! Drunk?"

"Sorry; I wasn't drunk, just shaky."

"How did you get into all that water?"

"I wanted to take a short cut across the ice, lost my bearings and slipped in a hole."

"So you couldn't see where you were going?"

"It was pitch dark all round, your Excellency!"

"And you never saw who pulled you out?"

"Sorry, I saw nothing. They did it, I believe." He pointed to the officer and added: "I couldn't be certain of anything. I was scared to death."

"That's it; prowling round when honest folk are all asleep! Take a good look now, and remember always who your benefactor was. A noble man risked his life for you!"

"I'll remember as long as I live."

"Your name, Mr. Officer,"

The officer gave his Christian name.

"Do you hear that?"

"I heard it, your Excellency!"

"Are you Orthodox?"

"An Orthodox, your Excellency."

"Enter that name for prayer in church."

"I'll put it down, your Excellency."

"Pray the Lord for him and clear out: I don't want you any more."

The man bowed to the ground and bounced out, highly delighted with having been allowed to go.

Svìnin stood dumb with amazement at the unexpected turn everything was taking, by the grace of God!

XII

Kokoshkine turned to the Invalid officer:

"You saved this man at the risk of your life?"

"That is so, your Excellency."

"There were no witnesses of the incident, and I presume, owing to the late hour, there could not be any?"

"No, your Excellency. It was dark and the Embankment was deserted save for the sentries."

"There is no need to mention the sentries: a sentry guards his post and must not be disturbed by any extraneous happening. I believe this report. It was written from your statement, was it not?"

This sentence Kokoshkine uttered with particular stress as though threatening or upbraiding.

But the officer stood his ground and with eyes bulging and chest well forward, replied:

"From my own words and perfectly correct, your Excellency."

"Your action deserves recognition."

The officer began to bow and scrape gratefully.

"There's nothing to thank me for," continued Kokoshkine. "I'll report your gallant deed to the Emperor, and your breast, maybe this very day, will be adorned by a medal. And now you can go home, have something hot to drink and don't leave your house, because, perhaps, I may require you."

The Invalid officer, shining and smiling, bowed and left.

Kokoshine gazed after him and remarked:

"It's quite possible the Emperor himself may desire to see him."

"Yes, sir," replied the inspector knowingly.

"I don't need you any more."

The inspector went out, and on closing the door after him, immediately crossed himself, as was his pious habit.

The Invalid officer awaited the inspector below and they departed together on infinitely warmer terms than when they had entered.

In the Prefect's room there remained only Svinin, whom Kokoshkine first scrutinised with a long fixed stare and then asked:

"You have not been to see the Grand Duke?"

In those days, when the words "the Grand Duke" were mentioned, everyone knew that they referred to the Grand Duke Michael Pavlovitch.

"I came straight to you," answered Svinin.

"Who is the officer in charge of the guard?"

"Captain Miller."

Kokoshkine again surveyed Svinin with an earnest gaze and then said:

"I believe you told me something different before."

Svinin had no idea what he alluded to and said nothing, while Kokoshkine added: "Oh, never mind: sleep well."

The audience closed.

XIII

The same afternoon, at one o'clock, the Invalid officer was indeed again summoned to Kokoshkine, who very graciously informed him that the Emperor was extremely pleased that the *Corps des Invalides* at his Palace included officers of such vigilance and gallantry and had bestowed upon him the medal "For the delivery of those in mortal danger." With these words Kokoshkine himself handed the decoration to the hero, and the latter went off to display it. The business might therefore have been considered at an end, but Lieut.-Col. Svinin felt some incompleteness about it and thought himself called upon to give some finishing touches. The whole incident so upset him that he was ill for three days, and on the fourth he rose from his bed, visited Peter the Great's hut, held a Thanksgiving Mass before the image of the Saviour, returning home in a calmed spirit, and sent to ask Captain Miller to come and see him.

"Well, thank the Lord, Nicolai Ivanovitch," said he to Miller. "Now the storm that has been brooding over our heads is completely dispersed and our unfortunate business with the sentry is liquidated. I believe we can now breathe freely again. All this we doubtlessly owe, first of all to the grace of God, and secondly to General Kokoshkine. People may say what they please about his being unkind and heartless, but I am filled with gratitude for his magnanimity and with profound respect for his presence of mind and tact. It was marvellous the way he took advantage of the boast of that Invalid rascal, who, as a matter of fact, deserved a damned good thrashing in the stable for his impertinence, but it could not be helped: he had to be made use of to save many, and Kokoshkine handled the business so cleverly that there were no unpleasant consequences for anybody concerned—on the contrary, everybody is very happy and pleased. Between you and me and the doorpost, I have been informed from reliable sources that Kokoshkine himself is very *pleased* with me. It flattered his vanity that I had gone nowhere else, but had come straight to him and did not argue with the whipper-snapper who got the medal. In other words, no one got into trouble and everything was done with such tact that there is nothing to fear for in the future, but there is a little short-coming on our part. We also must tactfully follow Kokoshkine's example and close the matter on our part in a manner calculated to protect us in case of future emergencies. There is one person whose position remains unformulated. I am speaking of Postnikov. He is still under arrest in the cells, and is, no doubt, full of apprehension as to his fate. It is time we put his mind at rest."

"Yes, high time," said Miller with relief.

"Well, naturally, and you are the person best suited to do it: will you please go immediately to the barracks, muster your company, take out Postnikov and see that he receives, in the presence of all ranks, two hundred lashes."

XIV

Miller, flabbergasted, tried to persuade Svinin to the view, that with the general relief and jubilation, complete clemency and a free pardon might be extended to Private Postnikov, who had already endured so much mental torture while awaiting the decision of his fate in the regimental lock-up; but Svinin flared up and even prevented Miller from continuing.

"No, no," he interrupted. "You stop that: I have only just spoken to you of tact and you immediately begin a piece of tactlessness! Stop it!"

Svinin changed his tone to a drier and more official one and added firmly:

"And since in this matter you too carry a share of the blame and are even much to blame, because you possess a certain mildness quite intolerable in a military man, and this fault in your character is reflected in the discipline of your subordinates, I command you to be personally present at the punishment and to insist that the lashing is carried out seriously, as thoroughly as possible. To that end, kindly give orders that the thrashing be done by young soldiers from among the new arrivals from the army, because our old-timers are in this respect all steeped in Guardsmen's liberalism: they don't thrash a comrade, they only worry the fleas on his back. I will call later in person and see for myself how well he has been flayed."

Any evasion of official orders by a superior officer was, of course, out of the question, and the tender-hearted Captain Miller was obliged to carry out the instructions.

The company was paraded in the yard of the Ismailovski

barracks, the rods were brought up in sufficient quantities from the stores, and Private Postnikov, who was marched up from the lock-up, was "done" with the zealous aid of young comrades, recently arrived from the army. These men, untainted with Guardsmen's liberalism, printed perfectly upon his back the necessary "finishing touches" required by his battalion commander. Then Postnikov, having received his punishment, was lifted up in the same greatcoat on which he had been thrashed and taken to the regimental hospital.

XV

Battalion-Commander Svinin, upon receiving the report of the execution of the punishment, at once paid a personal fatherly visit to Postnikov in the hospital, and at a glance obtained gratifying evidence that his orders had been carried out to the letter. The compassionate and highly strung Postnikov had been "done to a turn." Svinin was satisfied, and instructed that the chastised Postnikov be issued on his, Svinin's, behalf a pound of sugar and a quarter-pound of tea, so that he could find some solace during the period of convalescence. Postnikov, lying in his bunk, overheard the instructions regarding tea, and exclaimed:

"I am infinitely pleased, your Honour, and thank you for your fatherly kindness."

And "pleased" he was indeed, because while sitting in the lock-up he had steeled himself for incomparably worse results. Two hundred lashes in those harsh days meant little compared with the punishments people suffered under sentence of a court-martial; and such punishment would doubtless have befallen Postnikov had it not been for certain other bold moves and tactful interventions as before related.

But the number of persons pleased by the incident did not end there.

XVI

By various devious ways the story of Postnikov's exploit spread among the different social circles of the capital, which in those days of journalistic suspension existed in an atmosphere of endless rumour. Gossip forgot the name of the actual hero, Private Postnikov, but, on the other hand, the story gained in detail and soon assumed a very interesting and romantic character. It was whispered that some extraordinary swimmer was swimming across the river from the fortress of Peter and Paul to the Palace, and that one of the sentries on guard in the Palace shot at him and wounded him, while an Invalid officer jumped into the water and saved him; for which was meted out, to the one due recompense and to the other the punishment which he had deserved. This absurd rumour also reached the Abbey where lived at the time a most discreet dignitary of the Church, not entirely indifferent to "the affairs of the world," one who was benevolently attached to the devout Moscow family of the Svinins.

It seemed to this shrewd ecclesiastic that the legend was lacking in clarity. Who, after all, was this swimmer of the night? If he was an escaped prisoner, why was the sentry punished when he performed his duty by firing at the fugitive as he was swimming from the fortress across the Neva? If, again, he was not a prisoner but some other mysterious personage who needed rescuing, why should the sentry know it? He also averred that gossip must be wrong. The laity are prone to accept a lot of gossip as truth, but those who dwell in monasteries and abbeys regard things more seriously and are more in touch with truth.

XVII

One day when Svinin happened on a visit to his Eminence to receive his blessing, his host took the opportunity of sounding him "about that shot." Svinin then related the whole truth, which, as we know, had little in common with what was mooted around.

His Eminence heard the authentic account in silence, softly fingering his little white rosary, his eyes fixed on the speaker. But when Svinin concluded his recital, his Eminence murmured in soft warbling accents:

"Hence it should be deduced that in this matter not all has been set forth in strict accordance with the truth?"

Svinin shifted uneasily and made an evasive reply to the effect that it was not he, but General Kokoshkine, who made the report.

His Eminence silently let the beads trickle several times through his waxen fingers and then remarked:

"One must distinguish between what constitutes a lie and what is incomplete truth."

Again the beads, again silence, and finally the gentle flow of speech:

"Incomplete truth is not a lie. But the less said about it the better."

"That is indeed so," broke out Svinin, encouraged by the remark. "What of course worries me most is, that I was compelled to punish this soldier, who, although he had transgressed the regulations . . ."

The beads and a soft, warbling interruption:

"The regulations of service should never be transgressed."

"Yes, but this was done by him from sheer generosity, from compassion, and then after such a fearful struggle and at so great a risk: he understood that in saving the life of another man he was ruining himself. It was a noble, a holy feeling!"

"Holiness is only known by God; a punishment, on the other hand, upon the body of a common man is not ruinous and is not incompatible with the custom of human beings or the spirit of the Scriptures. The rod is more easily endured by a coarse body than a delicate suffering of the soul. In this respect justice was not in the least impaired by your action."

"But he has also been deprived of his reward for the rescue."

"Rescue is not an act of excellence deserving reward, but primarily a duty. He who could save and failed to do so is liable to punishment by law, but he who saves, discharges only his duty."

A pause, the beads and a warbling murmur:

"For a soldier to receive disgrace and wounds for his bravery is sometimes incomparably preferable to decoration. But what is of paramount importance in this matter, is that the secret be guarded carefully, and that never, under any circumstances, should what anyone has said be mentioned to anybody."

To all appearance his Eminence also was pleased.

XVIII

Did I possess the boldness of the Blessed Elect of Heaven, who through their boundless faith are suffered to penetrate the mysteries of God's guidance, I would perhaps have presumed to permit myself the supposition that the Lord Himself was pleased by the conduct of the humble soul of Postnikov that He had created. But my faith fails me; it does not provide my intellect with sufficient impetus to rise to such heights. I keep to the earthly, the material. I think of those mortals who love virtue simply for its own sake and expect no reward for it whatever the circumstances. These true and faithful people, it seems to me, will also be quite pleased by the blessed impulse of love and the not less holy endurance of the humble hero of my true and artless narrative.

ALEXIS APUKHTINE

(1841–1891)

THE ARCHIVE OF COUNTESS D——

1. From Alexander Vassilievitch Mozhaisky.
   (*Received at Petersburg, 25th March, 18—.*)

RESPECTED Countess Catherine Alexandrovna,—As I promised, I hasten to write to you immediately upon my arrival in this old long-since-abandoned nest of mine. I know that my letters can have no interest for you and that your insisting upon my writing was merely politeness on your part; but I wish to tell you that your merest whim is law for me although you might only have been jesting.

First of all I will answer the question with which we began our last conversation at Marya Ivanovna's; why, and with what object, did I go away from Petersburg. I answered you evasively at the time, but now I will tell you the whole truth. I went away because I was ruined; I went away in order to save what remained of my once large estate. Petersburg holds one's feet like a bog, and whilst one lives in it, it is quite impossible to put anything right. That is why I decided upon this radical measure which, truth to say, did not cause me much effort, because Petersburg life had become rather tedious to me.

But as by some incomprehensible irony of fate, my last day in Petersburg forced me to repent bitterly of my decision. In the morning I went to the English shop to buy a portmanteau, and there I met Marya Ivanovna, who invited me to come to her in the evening. That evening you were most charming to me. You showed me so much friendship and gave me such sympathy that you almost caused me to waver in my decision. And I remembered an occasion two years previously at the house of that same Marya Ivanovna. You were conversing as warmly with Kudryashin, and how intensely I envied him. I reflected at the time that Dmitri Kudryashin, my companion, was just as little of an aristocrat as I am . . . why therefore should he enjoy such exclusive attention on the part of the princess of Petersburg beauties? Will my hour never strike? Alas! my hour, when it did strike, was too late, but nevertheless I do from my soul thank the one who in one hour rewarded me for the years I spent in Petersburg cold and tedium.

I do not dare to hope, respected Countess, that you will answer this letter, but in any case I give you my address, which is Slobodsk. My estate is some twenty versts from Slobodsk, and I receive letters daily.

With deep respect, I have the honour to remain, sincerely devoted to you,

A. MOZHAISKY.

2. From the same.
(*Received 3rd April.*)

How can I thank you, respected Countess, for your warm and friendly lines? Being ignorant of your handwriting, I had opened the envelope with indifference, but when I looked at the signature I just leapt with joy. You are surprised that, living so long in the same city, I should only now have noticed you . . . oh, how cruelly you are mistaken. Each meeting which I have had with you left a deep impression in my heart, some sort of mingling of ecstasy and sadness. . . . Yes, and how could anyone fail to observe that severe classical beauty, that royal bearing, that reflective glance which seemed to pierce to one's very soul; such a glance that even when you turned your eyes away from the man you were talking to it seemed that you still looked at him through closed eyelids . . . but what can I do to express my delight? You have seemed so inaccessible to me, and you have paid me so little attention . . . the time when I overcame my timidity and called upon you, of course I did not find you at home, and three days later, I noticed that the Count had left his card at my house. There our progress in acquaintance stopped short.

You ask why I mentioned Kudryashin, and wish to know my opinion concerning him. I have known Kudryashin since childhood, and we were educated together at the same school. He was a very handsome boy, a charming creature, and a jolly drinking companion; he remained the same when he entered the Hussars, and is the same now, in retirement. There is nothing at all exalted about him, he is too much *terre-à-terre;* that is why I was surprised at your attention to him and why I spoke of him. I had no other object in view in writing about this.

Now all my efforts are directed to the reconstruction or to the destruction of my affairs here, so that I can return to Petersburg in the winter. At the same time as your letter came, I received another letter from a well-known rich man of Odessa, Sapunopoulo. He called upon me lately, he thoroughly inspected my estate, and now invites me to Odessa, proposing some sort of very tricky deal. I am leaving to-morrow, hoping in ten days to return, and—who knows?—perhaps I shall find on my writing-desk a small envelope with your coronet upon it. I can assure you that I shall not be particularly indifferent when I unseal the next envelope of yours.

But what do you mean by the enigmatical phrase: "Perhaps we shall meet sooner than you expect"? I recall that you once spoke of a very infirm old lady, living in the province of Slobodsk, an aunt, I think. Are you not proposing to visit her? Now, that would be pleasant! How sorry I am I did not ask you her name; I would certainly have looked her up and have covered her old hands with kisses, just because

she is your aunt, because she is so old and sick, and because
I feel myself young once more and capable of life and joy.

And since I have not these old hands of an aunt of yours to
kiss, permit me at least in thought to press my lips respectfully to that snow-white little hand which will be holding this
letter.

Endlessly devoted to you,

A. MOZHAISKY.

3. From the same.
  (*Received* 15*th April*.)

Hurrah, dear, precious Countess, I just cannot call you
merely respected,—hurrah! I guessed it: you *are* going to
visit your aunt. You could not have thought of anything
better. Had I known that your aunt's name was Anna
Ivanovna Kretchetova, I might long since have been able to
give you the most accurate news concerning her. Truth to
say, I have never met her, but from earliest childhood I heard
much concerning her, because she had some sort of lawsuit
with my father. She lives in that same village in which you
spent part of your childhood; I mean, in Krasny Khryashtchy
(what a dreadful name!). This village is thirty versts from
Slobodsk, but it is on the other side of my estate. However, if you avoided the town and kept to the villages, I
should say that the distance between us would be no more
than thirty-two or thirty-three versts.

Of course, when I received your letter yesterday I galloped
off at once to the town, to do what you asked me. It proved
very easy for me to find the friend of your childhood, because
I am well acquainted with Nadezhda Vassilievna; her husband is director of the local Government Estates Office.
Nadezhda Vassilievna was much touched by your remembering her, and to-day, I took her to Khryashtchy, to find out
how things were with your aunt. I have the honour to report
most humbly the results of that visit.

Your aunt, hearing that you were thinking of visiting her, was obviously overjoyed. She said that you were her nearest living relative, that she loved you as a daughter, that the quarrel she has had with you had been the greatest sorrow of her life, and that now if you had decided to forget the past, she would receive you with open arms. She will herself write to you about this, if she finds she has the strength. She is certainly very old and sick. There are two cousins staying with her, the Princesses Peeshetsky, who, as Nadezhda Vassilievna remarked, did not seem particularly pleased with the news of your coming visit. I suspect these princesses are afraid that they may lose your aunt's inheritance,—much use that would be to you! There is also someone else who has been living for a long while with your aunt. Perhaps you saw her when you were a child, I think she is called Vasilisa Ivanovna Mediashkina. She is just a parasite, but she has obtained such power over your aunt that everything is in her hands.

There were two other questions which I have to answer. My trip to Odessa did not prove fruitless. The plan is this: Sapunopoulo engages to discharge all my debts out of hand, and in return he will hold a mortgage on my estate and enter into possession for an indefinite number of years. We are fighting about details, but I suppose we shall come to ultimate agreement. The liquidation of this business has been complicated by the fact that he has a daughter, Sonitchka, who flirts with me considerably. It seems to me that it is not simply my person that is attractive to her, but my position at Court. She is rather younger than I am, naughty as sin, and possesses all sorts of accomplishments: speaks five languages, plays both on the piano and on the harp; and more than that, sings, and even writes verses. Of course, I do not intend to get caught in such an encyclopædical conspiracy.

Then you were very eager to know from whom I had heard of your friendship with Kudryashin. I swear I have heard absolutely nothing, and I only spoke of Kudryashin because I did once genuinely envy him, seeing that you were on such friendly terms with him. And in any case, what could I have heard? You are not only a Tsaritsa by virtue of your beauty —you stand so high in every way that no evil gossip could ever reach your person.

And now, permit me to forget Kudryashin and Sapunopoulo and his daughter, and everything else, that I may give myself up to one occupation: the counting of the days and the hours to that happy moment when your arrival will drive out of his mind one who is already bereft of his senses, but sincerely devoted to you.

A. MOZHAISKY.

4. From Vasilisa Ivanovna Mediashkina.
   (*Received 17th April.*)

Your Excellency,—Your aunt and my benefactress, Anna Ivanovna, has ordered me to write to you that she will await you with impatience and joy. She is unable to write because of her great weakness. And I also will be glad to see you! You will, of course, have forgotten me, but I well remember you as a child, how you ran about and smacked me upon the face with your innocent little hands, saying, "Take that, Silisia!" And Anna Ivanovna asks if you will bring some French prunes in blue boxes; we cannot buy these prunes here for any money; auntie is very fond of them and they are good for her digestion.

I kiss your Excellency's little hand, and remain your most humbly devoted Vasilisa Mediashkina.

Come quickly, my friend Katia.

Thy ANNA KRETCHETOVA.

5. Telegram from A. V. Mozhaisky.
   (*Received in Moscow 22nd April.*)

Implore do not telegraph aunt date arrival; will meet you at the station with closed carriage and horses which will take you anywhere you wish.—MOZHAISKY.

6. From the same.
   (*Received at Krasny Khryashtchy, 29th April.*)

Need I tell you, dear precious Countess, that the memory of
the day spent with you will never be effaced from my memory
and that the heavy dishes prepared for us by Nadezhda
Vassilievna will seem to me to have been the most light
repast, and that those three hours which I spent with you
waiting for the horses were the most happy hours of my life?
At parting you asked me why I had not invited you to spend
that day at my house. My God! why . . . why . . . well,
of course, because I did not dare! Surely you don't think
that I did not desire it. Surely you can see that my whole
life belongs irrevocably to you? I ask nothing of you, nor do
I hope,—my happiness lies in feeling myself your slave, and
in knowing that I have some aim in life.

Of course, you have not forgotten, dear Countess, your
promise to dine with me and Nadezhda Vassilievna to-
morrow. Now imagine what has happened; this dinner has
to be postponed because your friend declares that she cannot
visit me without her husband (what provincial propriety!),
and her husband is meeting some official or other who happens to be passing through Slobodsk at six o'clock. Nadezhda
Vassilievna asks that the dinner may be put off until the
day after to-morrow, and I hope that you have nothing
against that, though there appear to be the following complications. You agreed to travel in Nadezhda Vassilievna's
carriage, but your aunt's equipage will be in the town, and as
Nadezhda Vassilievna will be with her husband in a two-seat
phæton, there would not be place for you. Won't you agree
to come here cross-country without going into the town?
Your *march route* would be as follows: you ride to the ferry
by the familiar road, after the crossing you turn on the left
toward Selikhovo and Ogarkovo, then you turn into the
main road and, seven versts further on, you will see the old
house, Gnezdilovsky, on the right. The house itself will

blossom when you step over its threshold, as my old but not yet worn-out heart has blossomed. Come as early as you can, say about nine. We will have breakfast in the summer-house, in the depth of the garden, the one I described to you, and we will patiently wait for our kind but tedious Nadezhda Vassilievna and that husband of hers who proves to be so indispensable.

I have decided to send this letter by personal messenger. I am waiting a favourable reply upon my knees.

A. MOZHAISKY.

7. From the same.
   (*Received 4th May.*)

My dear Kitty,—For God's sake let me come to Khryashtchy and meet your aunt; it is terrible to live so near you and at the same time feel so far away. Be calm; I will conduct myself with discretion, and neither betray yourself nor me.

Thy A. M.

8. From Count D——.
   (*Received 6th May.*)

At last, then, dear Kitty, I receive intelligence of your safe arrival at your aunt's in Khryashtchy. I absolutely do not understand what you find to do that keeps you so long in Moscow. However, Moscow, as my friend said, is different from Petersburg, in the fact that we live in Petersburg and our relatives live in Moscow. It is difficult to get away from the dinners of Moscow kinsfolk. How strange that your aunt did not receive your telegram from Moscow, and how lucky it was that this Mozhaisky met you at the station with his carriage. What sort of person is this Mozhaisky? A chamberlain? A Lyceum man? I have met him in the Palace and somewhere or other in society, but for the life of me I do not remember his ever calling upon us, or that I visited him.

However, whether I remember him or whether it was some-body else I met, in either case, many thanks to him!

I rejoice that your first impressions have been pleasant, and that your aunt liked the prunes. I have asked Smurof to send her two boxes regularly every week. As Henry the Fourth said: *"Paris vaut bien une messe,"* and in the same way I may say that Khryashtchy is worth several boxes of prunes. That is not to say that you and I have not enough; but of course forty thousand or so a year in addition would never be in our way. I should say her income did not amount to less.

Within an hour of your departure Marya Ivanovna or, as you call her, Mary, hurried in to me in a state of great agita-tion, and began to rummage in your chests for some very important note. I could not convince her that you kept your archive in such order that one could only wish that the State archives were kept as well. I told her that it was seven times locked, that even I could not open it—nevertheless, she went on turning things over and at last went off much afflicted, having found nothing. I can imagine what sort of a valuable note this is!

There is nothing particularly new here. On Tuesday, when I returned from the club, I was astonished to see a whole mountain of visiting cards; I had completely forgotten that it was your reception day. The house-porter answered every one quite simply according to your directions. "To-day there will be no reception." I do not quite understand why you thought it necessary to surround your departure with such mystery. One could hide the fact if you had gone away for five days, but how could one hide it if you were invisible for two or three weeks? Yes, and already some people know. Yesterday the Baroness Wizen, the messenger of Europe, as I call her, inquired of me whether you had not gone to receive a large inheritance. We are invited to dinner at the Austrian Embassy to-morrow. I wrote that you were unwell, and I suppose I shall have to go myself, however tedious it may be. There is once more a great deal of talk about the affairs of the Society for saving Fallen Women. They want to make Princess Krivobokaya president, but she hesitates to accept, because she does not yet feel sure how this society is looked upon *en haut lieu*. I have success at cards at the club; I met Sophia Alexandrovna on Morskaya yesterday, and she invited me to come to-morrow and play vint informally, frockcoat.

Good-bye, dear Kitty. Come back quickly, unless you see that it may be profitable to remain a little longer at your aunt's, in which case, of course, do not hesitate to do so. However, it's not for me to teach you anything, seeing how wise and tactful you are. Having such a wife as you, I can sleep peacefully, whatever happens. The children are well and send kisses.

Your husband and friend,
D——.

If you see Mozhaisky, please thank him in my name for all he did for you.

9. From Marya Ivanovna Boyarova.
   (*Received 7th May.*)

I expressed such pleasure, dear Kitty, at receiving your letter, that it resulted in a family drama. We were sitting at luncheon when your letter came. Recognising the handwriting, I exclaimed and blushed. Hippolyte Nikolaitch at once "conceived some suspicion," as he expresses it, and when the children went out he began to insist that I should show him the letter. I got angry, and I teased him for a whole hour about it, he preaching at me and making satirical stabs. At last, when he had compared me with Cleopatra, with the wife of Pentephrius, and with someone else, I showed him your signature. He was quite confused, *et à mon tour, je lui ai dit les choses pénibles*. I said that such a stupid suspicious man, with such an acid expression, would never be made a

Cabinet Minister, and would remain an Under-Secretary all his life. That is his most vulnerable spot.

On the day of your departure there was a terrible rumpus over that note of Kostia Neverof's which I brought to show you in the morning. I imagined that I must have left that note at your house, and I came and searched all your drawers. The Count assured me that your archive was shut away behind seven locks, but that did not disturb me in the least: you could not have put a letter addressed to me in your archive! *Je ne suis pas te cacher, qu'a cette occasion ton mari m'a fait un brin de cour.* I was in despair at the thought that Kostia's note might get into someone else's hands, *car ce billet compromettait tout autant son maître d'orthographe que moi*, and just imagine, I found it next morning on the floor in my bedroom.

But what is it you are doing at your aunt's? I can imagine how you have hidden your *airs de reine*, and step with downcast eyes like a Madonna, and how your aunt and all her hangers-on were captivated and entranced by you. What of Mozhaisky? How is it you tell me nothing? Who is the better, he or Kudryashin? If I had to choose between them, I should choose Kudryashin. Mozhaisky *n'est qu'un poseur*, and is acting all the time, but Kudryashin's whole soul is open to gaze. However, you must know more about that than I; as for me, I need no one except my Kostia. You know I never thought that I should love him so much. He spends whole days here, and Hippolyte Nikolaitch *avec la perspicacité qui le caractérise n'en est nullement jaloux*. The new tutor, Vassily Stepanitch, I believe you saw him, begins to fall in love with me a little, and there are most amusing passages between him and Kostia every day. Vassily Stepanitch is a strong Liberal, and Kostia a dreadful Conservative, and they both utter such stupidities that one's ears ache. I am ashamed to confess, but you know I hide nothing from you, I have never loved Kostia more than when I hear him utter his characteristic stupidities. His face burns, his eyes glitter, he stares at his opponent so boldly and threateningly that the words do not seem to matter. But I am not blind about Kostia. I know that he is not particularly intelligent, *son éducation laisse à désirer;* I know that it is foolish to get so attached to him, but what is one to do? *c'est plus fort que moi.* Yesterday he brought his brother Misha to see me; in two months he will receive his commission. This Misha is also very handsome, but neither by his face nor by his manners does he in any way remind one of his brother; *il est très doux, très blond et très distingué.* I would bet that they are of different fathers. *On dit que la vieille madame Neverof ne se refusait rien dans le temps,* and only at the approach of old age decided to become a saint.

Nothing new has been happening; the same old round. There is much talk about Nina Karskaya, who is still living abroad and doing God knows what. That Parisian scandal, which you said you could not believe, turns out to be absolutely true; Baroness Wizen now has the whole story, with all details . . . only I can't imagine from whom she heard it all. What if Nina herself wrote to her!

Well, good-bye, dear Kitty; I must finish this letter or I might go on gossiping till this time to-morrow. Write me more often, and continue to combine the useful and the pleasant. I have always reckoned you to be an uncommon woman, but what you're doing now is the *comble* of smartness. Indulge your caprice of the moment and, for your pains, receive forty thousand a year—*c'est un trait de génie, ou je ne m'y connais pas.*

Your MARY.

10. From Count D——.
   (*Received* 15*th May.*)

Well, it seems you've got quite stuck down there, at aunty's, my dear runaway. I dare not murmur about it, because if you remain there it means that it is necessary, but all the same, it is rather difficult to bear the separation from such a beautiful and dear wife. Yes, and I imagine you also have been yearning for me. . . . Who can be tender to you, my poor dear, down there?

All that you write me about aunty inspires the hope that our separation will in any case bear some fruit. Those very significant words, "All that is yours is mine," seemed to me as if they ought to have been said the other way round. May I not give you some advice concerning the presents' you make when you leave? Whatever you give to the Princesses Peeshetsky, our rivals, you will not buy them out, and therefore I think that one need not give them any presents at all. Vasilisa is different; she can and must be bought, though it's not wise to give such people much at a time. You need only indicate a perspective of future benefits. I should give her some clothes now, and promise to send a shawl at the next holiday-time, and if possible just slip her a little money.

I think I wrote you that Sophia Alexandrovna asked me to an informal party to play vint. It appears that she told everybody she met about this, for three days afterward. I came in about eleven o'clock and found about fifty people crushed in her little apartment; in a word, it was an evening *en forme*. Fortunately I had been dining at the Austrian Embassy, and so had not dressed informally, and I arrived in full dress. I saw your friend Mary there, and we had a very pleasant conversation—pleasant, because in a way she reminded me of you. Only why does she have that immense locust Neverof always standing by her? Mary is too intelligent a woman to take pleasure in his company.

The day before yesterday I was much upset because we could not get the pug to eat, and he whimpered all day. I at once sent for the veterinary surgeon; he rubbed the dog with some stuff and dosed it; thank God, it seems quite well to-day. The children are well and send kisses.

Your husband and friend,

D.——

11. From M. I. Boyarova.
   (*Received* 16th *May.*)

Thank you, dear Kitty, for your long and friendly letter. Even such an unfathomable woman as yourself feels the necessity of a confidant, someone with whom she can speak *a cœur ouvert*. And whom would you choose but me, who have adored you since childhood? *Mais pourquoi me recommandes-tu la discrétion?* I am ready to chatter endlessly about myself if you wish it, but in anything concerning you I am capable of silence. I have no archive. All your letters I read when I receive them, and then at once tear up. I have much to tell you that is amusing, and much that is sad. First of all, we have had another family drama. Hippolyte Nikolaitch, when he was looking through Mitya's exercise books, must have taken a peep into the tutor's box, where he discovered an epistle in verse in which Vassily Stepanitch declared his passion for me. I don't think he would ever have dared to bring me these verses; he merely wrote them for his own personal pleasure, *mais il a eu la sottise de placer mes initiales à la tête*. Of course, Hippolyte Nikolaitch at once conceived suspicion, paid the tutor off, ordered him to leave the house within an hour and then came to me to make a scene. I was still in bed, and waked up in fright, thinking that he had found out something about Kostia, but when he began to read out this criminal poetry I could not refrain from giggling. What these verses were like you may be able to judge from the last lines:

> Throw down the velvet, blondes,
> Listen, listen to my love.
> And before the majesty of Nature
> Bow thy little head!

No matter how much I tried to reconcile Hippolyte Nikolaitch with the tutor, he remained inexorable, declaring that poetry has a dreadful influence on the weak heart of woman. I should think that there never was an example in the history of the world of a woman betraying her husband because of verses, certainly not because of verses that rhyme as these did, making "blondes" rhyme with "Nature." And why did he need to say blondes? He wrote of blond lace, but I've never worn blond lace in all my life. I am afraid that as part of his "principles of prudent economics", Hippolyte Nikolaitch had cheated the tutor out of some of his money, so I sent Mitya to him with a packet of notes, but he at once returned it, and wrote to me that he would preserve the brightest recollection of me all his life. I am sorry for Vassily Stepanitch: he said sometimes many stupid things, and wrote bad verses, but he was a fine fellow. Kostia also is sorry for him, because now he has no one to attack and annihilate after dinner. But Kostia is such a Conservative that he even considers my husband to be a Liberal and hinted to me that he would have no scruple about hanging rams' horns on his head. The expression rams' horns so pleased him that he must have repeated it quite five times. I was quite opposed to this; coarse sallies of this kind on the part of Kostia have humiliated me several times. I had been silent, but at last I lost patience and we had a serious quarrel. I ought to tell you that at Sophia Alexandrovna's evening I met your husband. He came on from some dinner or other *très élégant et très rajeuni;* he is combing his hair back, and that suits him very well, because it hides his greyness. He sat down beside me and began at once to court me in the most direct way. It amused me, but Kostia suddenly took offence and began to look at us with the eyes of a wild beast, and as I was afraid some scandal might ensue I hastened to go home. Next day, I joked Kostia about it, but he accused me quite seriously of flirting, and went on to say that I was the sort of woman who was ready to see any man hanged for her sake. I lost patience and blurted out all that I had been boiling to say for some time. He took offence, and went out without saying good-bye, and I lay awake all night, thinking what miserable creatures we women are. And indeed, why should we sacrifice ourselves as we do?

Towards morning, I found myself firmly resolved to break with Kostia, and if he had arrived at the house that day at his customary hour, I swear that all would have been over between us. But something kept him; he neither came to luncheon nor to dinner. Then I imagined that he had thrown me over and would never come again. The thought was so humiliating that I wrote to him immediately after dinner, asking him to come for a final explanation. But my messenger could find him nowhere, and the note was returned to me at nine o'clock. I had to go to Princess Krivobokaya, but I could not summon up the strength to dress myself, and I sat in the small drawing-room the whole evening in a kind of stupor. All my injuries, all my decisive plans, disappeared like smoke. I had only one wish, and that was to see him, be it for one second, that I might be sure that we had not quarrelled finally. At last, at midnight, there was a noisy ring at the door. It might be either he or Hippolyte Niko-laitch, who sometimes works surprises on me and comes home from the club two hours earlier than usual. I was all trembling when I heard the ring, but what was I like when I heard Kostia's steps in the hall and saw his dear face smiling a sort of guilty smile! . . . You will understand, Kitty, that after such a time it was possible to suffer much and forgive all! Do not scold, but pity

Your poor MARY.

P.S.—Petersburg is emptying, almost every one has gone away. On the day after to-morrow we are leaving for Peter-hof. I had been hoping that Hippolyte Nikolaitch would be sufficient of a spendthrift to take the large villa near yours; but, alas! while he was considering the matter and weighing up the advantages and disadvantages, someone else took it. Now I shall have to live at quite a distance from you, in Old Peterhof, and we shall be paying three hundred roubles more for it. That's what it means to follow the principles of prudent economy.

12. From Count D——.
    (*Received on the* 18*th May.*)

Dear Kitty,—Princess Krivobokaya has just informed me that she has agreed to be the President of the Society for Fallen Women, and she proposes that you become Vice-president. I have answered that I will write you about it and that in all probability you would not refuse. At the same time, I gave her your address, and she will write to you to-morrow after the election. In my opinion, you cannot refuse. If the Princess has agreed to be President, that means that the Society is in good odour. Although the Princess is rather feather-brained, you may rest assured she is not making a mistake here. I suppose that it may mean some expense, but we ought to get it back with interest. As the first floor of our large house is likely to remain empty all the winter, I hinted to the Princess that she might do worse than take it as premises for the Society. She said: "And why not, especially if your wife consents to be my helper?"

I hope, dear Kitty, that this will be my last letter to Krasny Khryashtchy. You've spent enough time with those folk, better go there again another time. The children are well and send kisses.

Your husband and friend,
D——.

13. From Princess Krivobokaya.
    (*Received* 19*th May.*)

Dear Countess,—I beg to inform you that at to-day's meeting of the Society for Fallen Women I proposed you as Vice-president, and you were voted with acclamation, and without ballot. I should like to think that after such a flattering reception of my nomination you will not refuse. For I cannot manage all this business alone; even my domestic worries make my head go round.

How fortunate you are, dear Countess, in having but two children, and both of them sons, whereas God has thought fit to reward me with five daughters, whom I shall have to fuss over all my life. There's an old fairy-tale about five sillies, and I think it must have been written about me. You will say it is sin for me to complain, because I have placed four of the girls with nice people, but, believe me, I have more trouble over Nadenka than over all the others. Of course, she's already twenty-four . . . you'd think there was no reason why she shouldn't find a husband. A wealthy bride, and personally not at all bad-looking, but she just does not get off, and that's all there is about it! I think it's because she has been brought up too well, and the young people nowadays do not like that. You know, Countess Anna Mikhailovna grasped that. Last year but one, she arranged living pictures at her house, and had her Katya pose as the Maid of Orleans. The curtain rises, and I see Katya almost entirely without clothes. I say to myself: "How can this be the Maid of Orleans? On the contrary, this is beauteous Helen", but Anna Mikhailovna explained the matter to me. "Katya's costume," says she, "is quite historical; don't you see the helmet and mail laying on the ground? only Katya chose to represent the Maid of Orleans at the moment when she wanted to lie down and rest." I do not think it at all surprising that Katya did not remain Maid of Orleans for long after this incident, and that very same evening, after supper, that little stupid, Fedya Varaxin, who had been courting Nadenka, made a proposal to Katya. There you see the sense in making a successful choice of moment.

Au revoir, dear Countess. In a week I am going to the country, but I should like to see you personally before then, as there is much to talk over with you. Come quickly, and meanwhile force the telegraph wires to play, and send me your consent.

Yours truly

E. KRIVOBOKAYA.

14. Telegram from Dmitri Dmitrievitch Kudryashin.
    (*Received 21st May.*)

Shall expect you in Moscow; do not know where staying;
obtain address from gipsies at Strielnia.—KUDRYASHIN.

15. From M. I. Boyarova.
    (*Received at Petersburg 1st June.*)

I have just heard from your husband that you are coming
back to-morrow. At last! I hope that you will drive over to
Peterhof to-morrow,—for there is nothing to do in town
just now. Get the people to cart your things over and come
yourself with your husband and children and have dinner
with us. How happy I am that you are coming,—how much
there is that I must tell you.

Your MARY.

16. From Princess Krivobokaya.
    (*Received 1st June.*)

Dear Countess,—I am sorry, but I cannot possibly wait
for your arrival, as I am going to the country. A certain Ivan
Ivanitch Optin, who used to be my steward, will come and
see you at Peterhof; I have made him secretary of our
Society. You do not need to stand on ceremony with him at
all. I have given him the post, but no authority. He will
hand over to you all the correspondence and give you what
details are necessary. You will be President until my return,
though I do not think there will be anything special to
trouble about. We are not going to have general meetings in
the summer, though there will be one at the end of August,
as I am returning then, because Olya is going to have a child.
You can judge from that, dear Countess, what a cross my
daughters are to me. To have to leave the country, at the
very best time,—and for what? Childbed does not seem to

me to be a very intricate affair, and a child can be born without my being present. But I shouldn't worry about all that, if only Nadenka would hurry and get a husband. She has certainly had a splendid upbringing, but she has a most intolerable character. Well, I must do my packing, my head's going round, and that girl's always buzzing round me. Write me at Znamenskoe, dear Countess; there is no one with whom I like to talk more than with you. At least, one can relieve one's heart.

Yours truly,

E. Krivobokaya.

P.S.—Yesterday I received the very happy news that my old confessor and friend, the Most Reverend Nicodemus, has been appointed to the Synod, and will spend the winter in Petersburg. He is a man of such intelligence and saintly life that you must certainly make his acquaintance. Our Society will go well under his guidance, and I shall undertake nothing without his blessing.

17. From A. V. Mozhaisky.
    (*Received in Peterhof, 6th June.*)

I have only this moment received your telegram, dear Kitty, telling me of your safe arrival in Petersburg. For the life of me, I cannot understand what there was to keep you so long in Moscow. I hope you were not ill there? Still less can I understand why you so firmly forbade my seeing you to Moscow. How I should have looked after you, if you had been ill, and how gay we should have been, if you had been well! But why worry! The time will not return, nor will those wonderful days of May, which passed like a dream, come back; and I might well repeat Zhukovsky's lines in thinking of them:

> Do not complain that they are not,
> But be thankful that they were!

After I had seen you off, I returned to Gniezdilovka and have remained there since. I have walked to our summer-house each day. The lilac which grew about it on all sides and pushed in at the windows, filling it with fragrance, has now faded. Yes, and everything around seems to have faded now for me. A beam of bright sunshine fell unexpectedly on my dreary, lonely life, but the moment has passed,—and that sun is somewhere afar, lighting and warming others.

This is the prose of life, which does not pass and does not let one rest. Yesterday I received an ultimatum from Sapunopoulo: either I must agree to all of his conditions, which means to become his slave, or he will renounce the contract, and then my whole fortune will go up in smoke. I shall have to go to Odessa and surrender. I will make but one condition, and that is that it shall be possible for me to go at once to Petersburg and exist there, be it one last year, and after that, let come what may!

Au revoir, may it be soon, my goddess, my sun, my dear, incomparable Kitty.

Yours to the last breath,

A. M.

18. From V. I. Mediashkina.
    (*Received 15th June.*)

Your Excellency, dear mother Countess, Catherine Alexandrovna,—Your aunt and my benefactress just received your little letter, in which you thank us for the hospitality shown you. Anna Ivanovna has asked me to answer that it is not for you to be grateful to us, but we to you, for having spent almost an entire month with us, and one can say, that you have sweetened her last days. And furthermore, your aunt has asked me to write that you will not repent the good work.

But what melancholy settled down upon us at your departure,—you cannot imagine it! If by chance I glance into the room which you occupied, my tears begin to flow in spite of myself. If I look at the clothes with which you presented me, I cry again, and I do not know when I shall wear these charming things. Perhaps on Easter Day. And you generously promised to send me a shawl for the New Year. That's not necessary, I swear I don't need it! Perhaps I shall not live until the New Year, but if you were to send me now something which you had yourself worn, that would be a real gift for me.

The whole house is grieving because you have gone. Even our young princesses, commonly so difficult and spiteful, express themselves in raptures about you. Recently I overheard the elder princess talking to her sister about you. "That's the sort of *bon ton* which you do not always come across abroad," said she. "Everything depends upon *bon ton*." And that is true, dear mother Countess, really true!

Falling at the feet of your Excellency, I kiss your little hands, and remain, till the grave shall take me,

Your devoted

VASILISA MEDIASHKINA.

19. From M. I. Boyarova.
    (*Received* 20*th June.*)

Dear Kitty,—For God's sake invite Hippolyte Nikolaitch to come to tea with you after the music, and arrange a party of vint for him.

Your MARY.

20. From Princess Krivobokaya.
    (*Received* 29*th June.*)

I sincerely thank you, dear Countess, for your dear letter. You write that Optin appears to be a doubtful character. That in no way surprises me, and only shows your great knowledge of people and things. I ought to acknowledge that

I dismissed him from my estate for swindling, but he has seven children, and I made him secretary of the Society out of pity, just until he finds employment. But we will not keep him long, as I hope to recommend him to Countess Anna Mikhailovna, who, they say, is in need of a steward.

Things are very lively here at Znamenskoe: for all the daughters, except Olya, have come here with their husbands and children. I am very glad to have my daughters and the grandchildren, but, of course, I'd just as soon have the husbands stay at home. Even Peter Ivanitch, who has been sulking for two years and has not put a foot on my doorstep, has thought fit to arrive, and continues to sulk and hardly says a word to me. I do not pay him the least attention, and twice a day when he kisses my hand very lingeringly, I turn away and try to kiss air instead of his brow, because he has such a smell of boot-polish. Imagine it, they have now invented a new perfume, *cuir de Russie*, and Peter Ivanitch deliberately sprinkles quantities of it on himself in order to make it unpleasant for me. I am a very great patriot, otherwise I should not write and speak Russian so well, and I am ready to love even the smoke of the fatherland, but I will not tolerate the smell.

Will you explain to me, dear Countess, why it is a mother-in-law is considered such a reprobate character that everyone must hate her? Still, I do think that in other families a mother-in-law is at least considered a human being, while I, for my pains, am considered not even a human being, but just a turkey stuffed with money, you know, as turkeys are with truffles. And really it sometimes seems to me that they're all standing round me with forks and turning me over from every side to try and find a bigger truffle. Yet aren't they all decent people?—I'm sure if they were strangers all would go splendidly, and I should receive them with pleasure, if only Peter Ivanitch did not carry a leather factory in his pocket. God only grant that I shall soon find Nadenka a husband,—then I'll share out all I've got, and leave myself a mere thirty thousand a year, just so as not to starve, and go to live in Florence or Rome. And by the way, what do you think of the way things are going at the Vatican? Poor Pope! I should like to embroider him a pair of slippers and send them to him (from an unknown lady in Russia). Good-bye, dear Countess. Write me more often.

Yours, sincerely devoted,

E. KRIVOBOKAYA.

P.S.—To-day after dinner Peter Ivanitch, to annoy me, called the Pope an idiot, for his unpracticality. I replied that it is not for all to be such practical people as State Councillor Bubnovsky. And you should know that Bubnovsky is a money-lender, to whom Peter Ivanitch owes a lot of money. He punished me for this by going off to sleep without further greeting, and I seized the opportunity to write you a letter, while my hands did not smell of boots.

21. From M. I. Boyarova.
    (*Received* 10*th July.*)

Dear Kitty,—As I just had to go to town, I left Hippolyte Nikolaitch a note saying that you had asked me to come along on business connected with the Society. *Si tu le vois, invente quelque chose.*

MARY.

22. From A. V. Mozhaisky.
    (*Received* 16*th July.*)

Dear Kitty,—Perhaps I seem much to blame in your eyes. I think it quite likely that there is a letter from you waiting for me in the country, and I have not yet been able to get away from Odessa. My business is nearly finished; I have agreed to everything: there was no other course. I hope to show up at your Peterhof dinner in about three weeks, and meanwhile they are entertaining me at Sapunopoulo's magnificent villa on the coast, and are trying to convince me by every means that I shall have to marry the Greek girl. Her aunt, the most disgusting creature, I have nicknamed the Virgin Fury. She has actually advised me to pop the question, assuring me that I would probably not be refused. Refused! However, I am holding back for the time being, and am saying neither yes nor no, but when everything has been sealed and signed at the notary's, I shall hasten to remind them of their famous countryman, swift-footed Achilles, and with such pleasure!

Hoping to meet you soon, my dear Kitty; write to me in Odessa.

Your A. M.

23. From M. I. Boyarova.
     (*Received* 19*th July.*)

Dear Kitty,—For God's sake, keep Hippolyte Nikolaitch at your house till the last train. If he is not playing cards, suggest a drive to *Mon Plaisir*. At midnight I shall go there and am prepared to wait till sunrise.

Your MARY.

24. From Princess Krivobokaya.
     (*Received* 15*th August.*)

Dear Countess,—I have just got in to Petersburg and feel worn off my feet. I found Olya in good condition, but she is dreadfully afraid of childbed, and for that reason I simply can't get away for a few hours to visit you at Peterhof. Do be so kind as you always are, and come and have dinner with me to-morrow. You can hand over the papers and we will have a good talk.

I wonder, dear Countess, if you could take Nadenka off my hands for a week or two, so that she might stay with you at

Peterhof until after Olya's childbed. I should be much obliged if you would; do not be afraid of her character, she is only intolerable with me, but with you she will be as gentle as anything. She can be an absolute angel when she wants to.

Sincerely devoted,

E. KRIVOBOKAYA.

P.S.—If you should hear that one of your Peterhof acquaintances is about to elope with Nadenka with a view to marriage, pray be deaf. Let her go and get married. I forgive her and bless her in advance.

25. From M. I. Boyarova.
    (*Received 29th August.*)

Dear Kitty,—We returned to town in such a hurry that I had not time to drop in and say good-bye. Kostia unexpectedly informed me that in a week he must leave for the country and that he will be away two months. His brother Misha has joined the same regiment, and old mother Neverof insists that they come to her for the sharing out of the estate. You can understand that, having to separate from Kostia for so long, I must want to see him as often as possible during these last days. And Hippolyte Nikolaitch has become so tired of travelling every morning from Peterhof to the Ministry that he was quite delighted when I suggested returning to town. Yes, and I think, seeing the sort of weather we are having, it's about time for you to pack up too.

Surely that intolerable Nadenka is not with you still? Last time we had dinner together she flirted so with Kostia that one felt ashamed. Kostia has been saying ever since that he likes her very much. Of course, he says it merely to annoy me . . . is there anything good in her?

Your MARY.

26. From M. I. Boyarova.
   (*Received 2nd September.*)

Dear Kitty,—Princess Krivobokaya has just told me that
you are bringing Nadenka back to her to-morrow, and so I
insist upon your coming to have dinner with me. By the way,
you will meet Misha Neverof. I think he's quite a nice little
officer, but I should be interested to know your opinion.
Can you guess who called on me yesterday? Nina Karskaya!
I had thought that after her Parisian scandals she would not
dare show her face in society. Of course, I did not receive
her; I hope you won't either. She has come thus early to
Petersburg to decorate her house entirely afresh. She is
thinking of holding large receptions in the winter, but who
will go to her? One must draw a line somewhere and make a
distinction between immoral women and . . . others.

Your MARY.

27. From A. V. Mozhaisky.
   (*Received 4th September.*)

Dear Kitty,—The Greeks have diddled me. It is not for
nothing that we read in the chronicle of Nestor, "The Greeks
remain seductive even to this day." I am still trying, without
success, to remind them of swift-footed Achilles, but Sapunopoulo already reminds me of the wily Odysseus. He has so
entangled me in deals and combinations that I seem to be
entirely in his power.

I awaited your letter with feverish impatience, hoping to
find in it some moral support, and now what do I find? *You*
advise me to get married! It is quite true that we seldom
have love-marriages in our world and that in each marriage
there is some sort of calculation . . . but then, you do not
know, Kitty, what sort of a girl this Sophia Sapunopoulo is.
I would not mind if she were sympathetic; I could overlook
her being ill-looking and yellow if only she were calm. But
she never leaves me a second's peace. She is not a woman,

but some sort of walking yellow fever. Let me tell you how we've been spending our time for the last three days. On Wednesday we had amateur theatricals at the villa, and the whole Odessa grand-monde (and it has its own grand-monde —it cannot get on without that) visited us. We presented something of her own composition; a proverb: "What a woman wishes, her husband will wish." Of course, I had to play the part of the husband, and I must kiss her hand ten times, and this intolerable rubbish had a colossal success. The day before yesterday it was decided to close the house to visitors, and the evening was consecrated to a reading Æschylus in the original. Can you understand the whole horror of these words: Æschylus in the original! For five whole hours she read on to me pathetically a tragedy in a language unknown to me, translating it phrase by phrase into French; and I must believe that it is a correct translation, though I am convinced that she does not know ancient Greek much better than I do; but when it seemed to be going very well, she must put out her hand to me and I must press it, whereupon Aunt Fury closes her eyes and nods her head with approbation. Yesterday we had another swarm of guests, and we put on fancy costumes and went for a sail. I was made up to represent a Turkish Pasha, with a turban on my head and a hubble-bubble in my hand. I have been bearing up patiently because Sapunopoulo gave me "his Greek word of honour" that on the fifteenth of September the whole business would be finished and he would release me to go to Petersburg with five thousand in hand. . . . But if he is fooling me again, will he not name another date and still fool me? Is it possible that I really have got to marry her?

No, Kitty, no! That's impossible, and cannot happen! I will never sell myself so ingloriously, never graft this Greek nut tree on to the old trunk of the Mozhaiskys. Better be a beggar and ask alms, or put a bullet through my head, than to fulfil the pitiful rôle marked out for me in that disgusting proverb.

Good-bye, my dear Kitty. Either you will see me in a fortnight, happily oblivious in your presence of this Hellas of Odessa, or you will never see me again, because I shall be no longer in this world. In such an eventuality, pray think nothing evil of one who loves you warmly.

A. M.

28. From Princess Krivobokaya.
    (*Received 26th September.*)

What can you be doing all this time in Peterhof, dear Countess! I have been yearning for your company, and our meetings go very poorly without you. These ladies come to no decision, and they are beginning to quarrel. Countess Anna Mikhailovna upsets everybody. Her son-in-law, Varaxin, was not made kamer-junker on the thirtieth of August, and she is just as malicious as she can be. That idiot Optin, in one of the declarations of the Society, called her Anna Fedorovna by mistake, and she was so offended that I had to go to her personally and apologise. But the worst trouble we have had has been through Nina Karskaya. I was assured that one ought not to receive her now, but she began by making a donation of five hundred roubles to our Society, and on the day after she paid us a visit. Well, how could one not receive her? Of course, she wished to become a member of the Society, but when at our first meeting I made a tentative proposal, Anna Mikhailovna attacked me so violently that I was forced to be silent. What ought I to have done? I did not wish to send back the money. Optin presents me with the accounts regularly, as if he were bringing them from the Countess, and I see that our treasury is always empty. But to take the money and not make her a member is also awkward. So I have descended to a piece of cunning. I called a meeting for eight o'clock yesterday evening, knowing in advance that Anna Mikhailovna would not be able to be present. As soon as Baroness Wizen and Vera Bielevskaya had arrived, I declared that the session had commenced and proposed Nina straight away. These two agreed: Vera out of kindness, and the Baroness in order to enrage Anna Mikhailovna, so I ordered Optin to record it in the minutes at once. Anna Mikhailovna came at nine o'clock, and when she heard of it, she went green with rage. It will be interesting to see how she will behave when she meets Nina at the next session, which will be held the day after to-morrow; do come, dear Countess.

Your
E. KRIVOBOKAYA.

P.S.—Baroness Wizen told me as a secret that Peter Ivanitch calls us "the Society for saving others for a few hours, from their mothers-in-law." You'd think from that, that I bored him often by my visits!

29. Telegram from D. D. Kudryashin.
    (*Received in Petersburg 10th October.*)

Arriving to-morrow for one day; stopping—usual place, shall expect news at nine o'clock evening.—KUDRYASHIN.

30. From A. V. Mozhaisky.
    (*Received 16th October.*)

Respected Countess Catherine Alexandrovna,—I have the honour to announce that I was legally married yesterday to Sophia Sokratovna Sapunopoulo. I make this announcement at the insistent desire of my wife.

Unalterably devoted to you,
A. MOZHAISKY.

Madame la Comtesse,

L'admiration tout-à-fait exceptionelle que professe pour Vous mon mari et l'amitié, dont Vous l'honorez, me donnent le courage de me recommander à Vos bontés. Comme nous avons le projet de passer une partie de l'hiver à S.-Petersbourg, permettez moi d'espérer que Vous voudrez bien guider mes premiers pas dans le monde qui, dit-on, est si sévère et si froid pour les nouveaux-arrivés. Une rose alpestre supporte difficilement le souffle glacial du Nord.

En attendant veuillez agréer, Madame la Comtesse, l'assurance de ma haute considération. Sophie de Mojaisky, née de Sapunopoula.

I unseal the envelope in order to make a correction in the wording of my announcement. It should read thus. "Alexander Vassilievitch Mozhaisky announces, with profound regret, the decease of all his precious and sacred ideals. It occurred on the tenth of October, in the city of Odessa, after a severe and prolonged struggle.

A. M.

31. From M. I. Boyarova.
    (*Received 3rd November.*)

Dear Kitty,—I have just received an invitation for Nina Karskaya's evening reception, although up till now I have not visited her. She asks for an answer, and I do not know what to do. Write me whether you are going or not; I will do as you do. *Après tout*, I do not know why we shouldn't go. They say that Princess Krivobokaya, her daughters, and all her coterie, will be there. The chief thing that moves me is that I have a most charming dress from Worth's, and I want to wear it as soon as possible. When may one expect the grand receptions?

Your MARY.

P.S.—Kostia is coming the day after to-morrow; he writes that his brother Misha is still off his head about you. But he only saw you once. *En voilà une charmeuse!* What a good thing it is that Kostia does not attract you, or you would long since have taken him away from me.

32. Telegram from V. I. Mediashkina.
   (*Received* 10*th November.*)

Anna Ivanovna died at ten o'clock last night; funeral
Friday.—MEDIASHKINA.

33. From M. I. Boyarova.
   (*Received* 10*th November.*)

How desperate I feel, dear Kitty, learning that you are
leaving us and that our *partie de plaisir* will fall through. As
there was snow last night, Kostia and I decided to ask you to
make a four, not to go to the theatre but to go in a troika to
the island and have supper somewhere. That would have
been delightful. Kostia declares that his brother has been
looking forward to it with as much impatience as when he
was about to receive his commission. And suddenly, it all
falls through, just because of some trifle! I cannot understand why you should want to go so far to a funeral. Your
aunt is now dead, and nothing can change that. What's more,
Nina Karskaya is going to have a big dinner next week, and
five Italians are going to sing. Her first evening party was,
as Baroness Wizen declares, *une colombe d'essai;* she wanted to
know upon whom she could count. Now she only invites the
most select people to the concert, and she is giving a great
ball in January. One must admit that she has arranged
things very cleverly. Who would have thought that she
would be in the swim again? Nicodemus has helped her
most of all, as he, with good reason, has an immense influence. And of course, Nina made quite substantial donations
to his hospital! It's the same everywhere: if you have
money, you can do anything you like. It is sad, but it is
true!

The Baroness says that you are in the list of guests to be
invited, are you really going away before such an interesting
evening? Why not send your husband to the funeral? It

would do him good to get a little air. He's been sitting in Petersburg for a hundred years. Send me an answer.

Your MARY.

34. From M. I. Boyarova.
(*Received 10th November.*)

Since your husband is going, would it not be better to return to your house after the troika party? Order supper at home; that would be much more pleasant than at a restaurant.

MARY.

35. From Count D——.
(*Received 18th November.*)

Dear Kitty,—I am writing you days later than I promised because yesterday evening when I got to my room I literally collapsed from fatigue and slept like the dead. I got here quite safely. I travelled from Moscow with Bublik-Bielevsky, and we played picquet all the way. I got to Slobodsk at eleven at night; horses were awaiting me at the station, but it was impossible to go on because of the great snow-storm. I had to stay the night, and only at nine o'clock in the morning got to Krasny Khryashtchy. The funeral was timed for ten o'clock, but was also delayed because the bishop had been held up by the snow-storm. Everything was done in fine style. There were a great number of neighbours and Slobodsk officials; one could see that the deceased was much respected. The very fatiguing funeral-dinner began at three o'clock in the afternoon. My neighbour was Mrs. Mozhais-kaya, who stuck to me like a leech and never let me get free from her for a moment. An astonishing person! If her complexion were not so yellow one would call her an absolute blue-stocking. She pelted me with names of books and authors which I heard for the first time in my life, and she bothered me terribly; she wants to know if there is some

Egyptologist in Petersburg, as she is now particularly interested in Egyptian antiquities. She is going to Petersburg in a month, and counts very much on you, I think, to help her climb into society, but probably she is mistaken in her hopes. *Ce n'est pas une femme à orner le salon, comme le tien.* Her husband also made a strange impression on me: he has a lost air, and when I thanked him for his kindness in looking after you in the Spring, he merely murmured some disconnected words. However, I have managed to extract some profit from these Mozhaiskys: they have leased the first floor of our large house, which remains empty for the second winter in succession, and since they are giving a very good price (a thousand roubles a month), will you please call the agent in and have him clean the place up; new decorations, etc.? As far as I can remember, the furniture in the second room is too old-fashioned; will you have it removed and put the blue satin-wood from the villa in instead? Everything ought to be ready by the New Year; they are arriving at the beginning of January. Just imagine it, the dinner lasted till nearly six o'clock; after the roast, the bishop and priests stood with goblets of champagne in their hands and sang "Give rest, O Lord." I was alarmed, thinking that they had got drunk, but it appears that this is an old Russian custom, still kept up in these parts. My neighbour assured me that they used to do something of the kind in Egypt. The guests remained a long while after dinner, and it was ten o'clock before I was conducted to that same bedroom which you occupied in the Spring.

I had hoped that the will would be read to-day, but that will happen either to-morrow or the day after. I could not very well ask about it, but it seems they are waiting for some sort of executor. Innumerable relatives of the deceased have arrived; they're all simple people, but quite pleasant. *Tout le monde est charmant pour moi, on m'entoure de petits soins.* One can quite see that they already look upon me as owner of the place. The Princesses Peeshetshky seem to me very attractive, especially the younger one. If your aunt has left them nothing, we ought to do something for them; find them some place in Petersburg. *La fameuse Vasilisa est d'un ridicule achevé, mais bonne femme au fond, elle a une véritable adoration pour toi.*

This morning I made a round of visits on the estate. The stables, the wings, the coach-house,—all these are much decayed, and should somehow be removed to a distance from the main building. I am sorry, but I have not been able to form any idea of the grounds. I wanted to see the orangery, but so much snow fell yesterday that the way was blocked up. There's a good deal of excellent old furniture in the house. One mahogany whatnot pleases me so much that I think of bringing it back with me and putting it in your boudoir.

I observe that I am disposing mentally of Krasny Khryashtchy as if it belonged to me, while perhaps it may be bequeathed to someone else. Still, to whom could it be? But in any case, whether your aunt has left us everything or even nothing, it must have been her will, and I am glad from my heart that I did not neglect to come to the funeral of this saintly worthy woman,—and I am certainly staying here till the ninth day. Certainly Anna Ivanovna was like a mother to you at one time; and in that quarrel, if we admit the truth, we were more to blame than she was. Of course, the old lady had her strangenesses and eccentricities, but we ought to have behaved towards her differently. How fortunate that in the last year of her life we undid this wrong, and I am so grateful to you for having thought of going to visit her this Spring. Whether we shall gain anything as a result of your trip is still uncertain, but that which we have gained, calm of conscience, is much more valuable than any inheritance, and we ourselves have got to die some time or other; of course, that is a stale truth, but how often we forget it! The ninth day will be the eighteenth of November. Having paid the last debt to the departed, I propose to leave on that same day in the evening, and spend next day with my brother near Moscow. In any case, I shall be home again for your name-day. Good-bye, dear Kitty. The children are well and send kisses.

Your husband and friend,
D——.

P.S.—You are arranging a party for the evening of St. Catherine's Day. But will that be quite fitting? Granted that no one in Petersburg knew your aunt, everyone is bound to know about her when we receive a large inheritance. In my opinion, it would do no harm if you wore mourning for a month or two; the more so, as the interesting balls only begin in January.

Reading over my letter, I see that I absent-mindedly sent you greetings from the children. That shows how constantly I think of them. Kiss them from me.

36. From Count D——.
(*Received 20th November.*)

The will was read this morning at nine o'clock. The elder princess is to have Krasny Khryashtchy; the younger gets the Pedza estate. As regards money, Vasilisa received thirty thousand, and there is about eighty thousand for various relatives, servants, and funeral expenses. All the rest, over three hundred thousand, is bequeathed to monasteries and charities. You are to receive her diamonds and other jewellery. That might not have been so bad, because Anna Ivanovna had all the Kretchetovsky diamonds, and all her life was buying valuable things, but just imagine it, the whole lot has disappeared. When the seals were removed, all that was found was one cheap brooch and a vast quantity of seed pearls, beads, and like rubbish. I am absolutely convinced that Vasilisa stole the rest, for the old lady was completely in her hands. I am not the inheritor, so it does not strictly concern me, and I made no claim; but you might write to Vasilisa and scare her with the threat of bringing her to court; you never know; she might surrender something out of the plunder. I tried *faire bonne mine à mauvais jeu*, and showed myself light-hearted and pleasant with everyone. At first, I succeeded in this, but when, after breakfast, the post arrived, just imagine what was the first thing I saw—the Smurof boxes of prunes! The sight of these made me so furious that I was obliged to go to my room, to hide my discomfiture, and write you this letter. Please send at once to Smurof's, and ask them to stop sending the prunes; I have not the least desire to improve the digestion of that underhand Vasilisa!

Of course, I shall not stay here till the ninth day. *J'ai assez de tout ce monde interlope!* And, truth to say, it was stupid to have come to the funeral. You and I are much too idealistic and inclined to judge other people by ourselves. God forbid that I should pass judgment on the dead, but one needs to express the truth: she was an eccentric all her life, and she died an eccentric. I note that all these old maids are the same. They have always got some Vasilisa hanging round them; someone who has power over them and can do what she likes because she knows of the affairs they had when they were young. And you know well enough that auntie had quite a few adventures in her early years. Of course, I will not go over them, and in a Christian spirit I desire from the depths of my soul that the Lord will forgive her everything, and among other things her ingratitude toward us.

I am leaving to-night. I shall spend three days with my brother, and will be in Petersburg on the eve of your name-day. In my last letter I gave you some advice about wearing mourning, but that now seems to me entirely superfluous. Send out invitations by the twenty-fourth, if you wish to give the party.

Your husband and friend,

D——.

37. From Princess Krivobokaya.
     (*Received 3rd December.*)

Dear Countess,—If you are going to the English ball to-night, I wish you would take Nadenka under your protection. As you know, I am not at all eager to let her go out even in the company of her married sisters. You're the only woman in whom I have sufficient confidence to trust my treasure. I am not going myself, first, because Peter Ivanitch visited me this morning and upset me for the rest of the day, and second, out of patriotism, because the English are putting spokes in our wheel wherever they can. In general, I do not like the political situation in Europe. Though I have no special news, I am convinced that Bismarck is again inventing something. What exactly, I do not yet know, but it disturbs me.

Sincerely devoted to you,

E. Krivobokaya.

38. From M. I. Boyarova.
     (*Received 7th December.*)

Dear Kitty,—Do please try and find out from Misha Neverof where Kostia was yesterday from eight to twelve. He assured me that he was going to the Opera with his brother, but Baroness Wizen was there and did not see either of them. You will agree that it is difficult to miss seeing Kostia, if he is in a theatre. You would not believe how these deceits enrage me . . . but why not tell you the truth? Since returning from the country, he has several times deceived me.

Your Mary.

39. From V. I. Mediashkina.
     (*Received 15th December.*)

Your Excellency,—The death of my unforgotten benefactress was such a heavy blow to me that I thought I could never again in my life experience any other grief, but your letter proved that there are no limits to one's trials if the Lord thinks fit to send them. You ask me what was done with the diamonds. Why does your excellency think that I know? The key of the case with the diamonds was always in your aunt's possession, and she could have given them to anyone she thought fit, and she had many relatives and friends and acquaintances. It is possible that someone stole the diamonds, only not, of course, I. I served Anna Ivanovna more than forty years in faith and truth, and never stole anything. But unfortunately, someone has slandered me in your eyes, and I see that in one place you hint at bringing me to court. But, gracious me, I am not afraid of the court. I could bring witnesses to my innocence from the whole province, beginning with your friend, Alexander Vassilievitch Mozhaisky, whom I have lately got to know you visited several times at his estate. Of course, I shall say nothing about that, because I am convinced you are incapable of anything wrong, though if brought to court I could not be silent, because one is obliged to tell the whole truth. But perhaps I was mistaken, and there were no threats in your letter, and I have only been imagining things when I thought you were hinting at bringing me to court. If so, I ask you to be so generous as to forgive me,—when one is in grief it is not surprising if one sees things in a crazy light!

I quite understand that it was unpleasant for your Excellency to be deprived of the inheritance on which you so counted, but I had nothing to do with it! Still, I think you may obtain great comfort in the thought that the Lord blessed your aunt with such a beautiful and truly Christian death. Anna Ivanovna several times mentioned your name and blessed you. It was difficult to make out what she was saying, but I knew the deceased too well to be mistaken. The very last word that she said was "prune." The elder princess at once went to the window and brought a new unopened box. Anna Ivanovna took a little prune, but was unable to eat it, squeezed it up in her little hand and dropped it on the floor. She probably wished to show in that way that she was thanking you for the prunes which you sent her so regularly. But I ought to say that Doctor Vetrof, whom we sent for from Moscow, declared in confidence that the prunes had been doing her a lot of harm. With true respect, I have the honour to remain, your Excellency, at your service,

V. Mediashkina.

40. From M. I. Boyarova.
   (*Received* 20*th December*.)

Dear Kitty,—Kostia was absent the whole day yesterday, and tells me that he was on duty. But I happen to have read the regimental orders for the day, and find that Sirotkin 2nd was on duty. Do ask Misha what it means, and who actually was on duty. See to what depths I have to go: I had to bribe Kostia's batman to bring me the orders; but what is one to do, when he constantly deceives me? . . . I do not wish to stand in his way in anything, but I do wish, I *ought* to know what he is doing.

Your Mary.

41. From Princess Krivobokaya.
   (*Received* 21*st December*.)

Dear Countess,—Imagine what a surprise I have received for the New Year! Optin announces that there is not only nothing in the treasury but that I am four thousand in debt. How this could come about, I absolutely cannot understand. I did sign some papers or other, which he handed to me, but I had not the remotest idea of paying anything on them. How right you were, in warning me against Optin, and how dare he bear the name of Optin, when that is the name of a monastery for which I have such reverence, and in which my uncle Vassily is buried. Of course, I am very much to blame in all this, but Countess Anna Mikhailovna served me out: had she taken Optin as her steward, nothing of all this would have happened.

Do come and see me, dear Countess, and help me to find out what these papers mean. My head's in a whirl; Nadenka is buzzing round me as usual, and I absolutely cannot understand anything. Awaiting you with the greatest impatience,

E. KRIVOBOKAYA.

P.S.—A fine Society—you can't deny it! It has not saved one fallen woman, and has placed me four thousand in debt.

42. From A. V. Mozhaisky.
   (*Received 4th January.*)

Dear Countess,—We arrived in Petersburg to-day, and the house-porter, at your orders, met us with bread and salt. I do not know how to thank you for this attention. I think the apartment to be excellent in every way, but my wife wishes to add some decorations, and we have been out together to make some purchases. We were gadding around the shops until six o'clock, and I could not find a minute in which to break away and see you. Now she has dressed for dinner, and asks me to inquire of you when you would be able to receive us, and to fix a day and hour. Kill her with magnanimity, and call on us simply one evening; I know that you attach no weight to stupid formalities. According to the original programme, we intended to spend our first Petersburg evening at the theatre, but fortunately we have been unable to find seats. If you only knew how madly I thirst to hear one accent of your voice and to see your smile, were it for one second!

A. M.

43. From M. I. Boyarova.
  (*Received 5th January.*)

Dear Kitty,—I have been unwell these last days, and so was unable to come to the meeting. Baroness Wizen came to me direct from it and gave me all the news, and I hear that Princess Krivobokaya has resigned from the Presidency and that you have been unanimously elected in her place. If I could have foreseen these happenings, I would, of course, have made an effort and come, if only to be a witness of your triumph. I congratulate you on this new success with all my heart.

I forgot to ask the Baroness if you were present at Nina Karskaya's ball last night. *La baronne m'dit, qu'en general c'était très brillant.* I was thinking of going, but suddenly felt myself worse, and truth to say, I feel too low-spirited to drag about at balls. Kostia will scarcely speak with me in the open nowadays, declaring that he does not wish to compromise me. How strange, that formerly he never used to think of that at all, and now when it's all the same to me what people say about me, and when I am ready to give everything for just one caressing word of his, he is beginning to bother about my reputation. And what is more, he visits me less and less frequently. You said to me that I had myself to blame, because I was boring him by my questions, my spying and jealousy, and that if I wished to keep him I must be always calm and gay. . . . But where am I to find calm or pretend to be gay, when cats are clawing at my heart? You say I am jealous, but I am absolutely jealous of no one. He does not seem to be paying court to anyone, and merely dances with such young ladies as Nadenka Krivobokaya, so that to be jealous would be just absurd. If I knew that he was in love with another woman, I would the sooner become reconciled to the fact, but it is dreadful to be thrown over without any reason.

The Baroness told me a very interesting thing about Anna

Mikhailovna. You know how she cut Nina Karskaya at the Society meeting, did not acknowledge her bow, and stalked majestically out of the hall. Two months later, they met again, and neither bowed to the other, but afterwards, *quand Nina a repris sa place dans le monde avec plus d'éclat que jamais,*— Anna Mikhailovna began to make up to her again, paid her a visit at New Year and began to try through various people to make sure of receiving an invitation to the ball. Nina acted very cleverly; she did not return her visit, but she sent her an invitation, *et pour l'humilier davantage* sent it on the day before the ball. And just think of it, she went to the ball, with her two daughters, and was the last to leave. *Voilà ce qui s'appelle avoir du toupet!*

Your MARY.

44. From Princess Krivobokaya.
    (*Received 17th January.*)

Dear Countess,—I have just received the statement of the changes you think of making in the Society. And I value it highly that you should think it necessary to consult such a silly old woman as I am. Everything you suggest is fine, and I am only sorry that I did not think of these things for myself. However, it did occur to me that our secretary ought to serve without wages and be one of our circle; unfortunately, that Optin turned up with his seven children, and out of pity I assigned him fifteen hundred a year. That's what pity does for one!

I am certain that my bosom friend, Countess Anna Mikhailovna, will go out of her mind by the end of the winter. Every day one hears something new. Yesterday Baroness Wizen was visiting her, and as she was going up the staircase she heard moaning somewhere. She rushed in as usual, without being announced, and saw Anna Mikhailovna rolling in hysterics on the carpet. Varya, also all in tears, came in and explained. "What do you think, we have not been invited to the little ball. It has so upset mother that she has gone like this, though it is the first time in her life she has been like it." Best of all is, that these tears were quite unnecessary. There was merely a mistake; the invitation was handed in just before dinner, and a few hours later all these sisters of affliction drove to the ball with swollen eyes. Knowing Countess Anna Mikhailovna as I do, I quite believe this story, but also I do think that this Baroness is marvellously fortunate! She always drops in on some scene which she can talk about for a whole week. Why is it this never happens to me?

Your E. KRIVOBOKAYA.

45. From A. V. Mozhaisky.
   (*Received 20th January.*)

Dear Countess,—When we returned from the theatre we found the official notification of the election of my wife as a member of your Society, and the proposal that I should be honorary secretary. My wife is absolutely delighted, and we are coming to you to-morrow to thank you; meanwhile, I cannot but express my rapture at this stroke of genius on your part. Up till this time I have literally been unable to escape from home, but now, willy-nilly, I shall have to bear all sorts of reports and estimates to the President. I promise to serve well, though without material recompense. It is also good that you have hired premises for the Society on Vassili-evsky Island, at a little distance from unwanted observation. Let us hope that even the all-seeing eye of Baroness Wizen will not be able to penetrate to the private meetings there.

Yesterday you asked my wife whence she had that pearl necklace which made such a sensation at the ball, and she told you she received it from her grandmother. That's not true. She bought it at Slobodsk, for almost nothing (for three thousand five hundred roubles) from Mediashkina, your.

deceased aunt's dependent. Mediashkina declared that only need forced her to part with this gift of her benefactress, and made my wife swear that she would tell no one about the purchase. But I did not swear, and so am able to tell you the truth.

Your submissive secretary kisses warmly the hand of his new chief.

A. M.

P.S.—If I could only find some Egyptologist or other who would agree to decipher hieroglyphics with my wife, I should think that my family life was on good foundations.

46. From M. I. Boyarova.
(*Received 2nd February.*)

It is now nearly two weeks since I have seen you, my dear Kitty. Of course, I do not reproach you, as I know how occupied you are with the affairs of the Society, which, under your direction, seems to be at last bearing fruit. But if you happen to have a free moment, do come and visit a sick woman, and you will really be doing good. I still feel very weak.

I scarcely ever see Kostia. I tried to follow your advice, and last time he was here, avoided asking him any questions, and did not reproach him once, trying to appear gay. But what came of it? He went away, and a week has passed since then, and I have not heard a word about him. His name has never been mentioned once in regimental orders.

No, Kitty, I am not to blame in this at all. At first I was jealous, quarrelled with him, cried, and all the same he would come back next day. Something has happened since then, something I do not know, and it is that which has gradually been bearing my happiness away. I felt it long ago, during the first days after his return from the country. You will laugh at my poetical comparison, and again call me a Russian

Madame Girardin. But I see happiness as a large and very beautiful bird, which once flew high over the earth, but who now is having its feathers plucked from its wings every day. It flies lower and lower, and soon will cease flying altogether.

It is Carnival in two days, and I have a heap of invitations, but I shan't go out anywhere, and will save my strength instead for *folle-journée*. I hope I shall be invited as in previous years. I don't know why, but I dreadfully want to be at the *folle-journée*. Perhaps because it is the last ball of the season, and I am not destined to live till the following season. I will look for the last time on these vanities, which once I loved so much, and afterwards. . . . What will be afterwards? Something dreadful to think of. I am not expecting immediate death,—for of course, I have no serious disease,—but, all the same, I have the feeling that something in me is just about to break, and then it will all be over. Perhaps my life is also somewhat like that bird of which I spoke; it seems to me its feathers also are getting fewer.

This morning I wakened up feeling as healthy and light-hearted as I did a year ago. My first thought, as always, was of Kostia, and I looked at the clock: it was ten—that meant that in two hours and fifteen minutes I might expect his arrival. That condition of mind lasted for a minute or so, until I remembered just how things were, and it seemed so intolerable that I fell back on the pillows, and lay for a long while with closed eyes. I would have liked to have remained so the whole day and have seen no one, but the doctor came and I had to get up, because I was expecting a few uninteresting guests. Baroness Wizen came in before dinner, and brought a quantity of all kinds of gossip. She was very amusing in her description of the way our ladies besiege the Most Reverend Nicodemus, who does not know where to go to get away from them. Anna Mikhailovna goes to him for advice regarding the toilettes of her daughters; Katya Varaxina calls him the pre-sanctified Host, because Princess Krivobokaya asked him was there not a special prayer to hasten the marriage of her daughter, and Nina Karskaya invited him to a dinner at which he was forced to fast, because all the courses were meat dishes, etc., and more things like that. I was a little diverted by these foolishnesses; we had dinner afterwards, and Hippolyte Nikolaitch several times cast severe and questioning glances at me. He does not know what is the matter, but all the same, looks sternly at me. We had a long and tiresome evening. For some reason or other I had a faint hope that Kostia would come to-day, but no one came. The children went off to sleep at last, Hippolyte Nikolaitch went to the Club, and I remained alone. So I am seeking some consolation chattering to you. I would write much more, but my head is beginning to ache again. Do come and see me to-morrow, if you can. I don't dare to ask you to dinner, but how glad that would make me! *Ne m'abandonne pas, ma chère, ma bien bonne Kitty! Si tu savais a quel point je suis seule et misérable!*

A toi comme toujours, MARY.

47. From Princess Krivobokaya.
    (*Received 12th February.*)

Dear Countess,—My great joy prevents my sleeping; I have just got up from bed, lit the candles, and wish to share my joy with you. Immediately upon returning from the *folle-journée*, Nadenka announced that she was engaged to Kostia Neverof. To-morrow, at one, he is coming formally to ask her hand, and I cannot sleep, so impatient I feel. To-day when I called your attention as they were dancing a mazurka, you shrugged your shoulders and said: "Nothing will come of it." But you see, dear Countess, that though you are much more wise than I am, there are occasions when the heart, especially the heart of a mother, aching from long expectation, becomes more penetrative than the mind.

Of course, if one looks on the whole matter dispassionately, one cannot possibly say that it is a very brilliant match for Nadenka. Though he bears the name of an ancient house his people are quite unknown, and he has no connections whatever. I knew his mother when she was a young girl, and at the time when she began to go loose; but when she threw her nightcap over the mill I stopped seeing her. She is now an honourable and respected woman; the Reverend Nico-demus knows her well. She has a very large fortune, but it is uncertain whether she will bequeath it to her sons. She invited the sons to come to her in the Autumn in order to share out the estate between them, and then she changed her mind and put it off. Truth to tell, I see two good points in my son-in-law: he has the physique of a hero, and is a perfect dancer. As regards other things, it is better to say nothing, though in the carriage coming home Nadenka buzzed in my ears: "He is very, very clever; only he hides that from every-one on purpose, but he let me know." Well, thank God that he let her know! If Neverof had been an older man, and had begun by courting one of my elder daughters, I would have closed my doors to him. But he's all right for Nadenka; you know she—now one can tell the truth—she's not twenty-four, but twenty-six and a bittock. And then, it is true, that every marriage is a lottery. I thought those bridegrooms, four sons-in-law, very much worth having, and yet I cannot get on with them. Who knows, perhaps I will get on with one who does not seem so good.

Although it is now late, I have not got the strength of character to postpone the announcement of such good news, and I therefore invite both you and the Count to come to me on Tuesday at seven o'clock, for a Lenten dinner, and drink the health of bridegroom and bride. It's no sin to drink champagne in Lent. At dinner you will see how kind and enchanting Peter Ivanitch will be, and you will probably be astonished at the riddle of his countenance, but the answer to the riddle is that I promised to pay all his debts (for the third time), as soon as Nadenka became engaged.

And so good-bye till we meet, my dear Countess.

Sincerely devoted to you,

E. KRIVOBOKAYA.

P.S.—I dare say your friend, Marya Ivanovna, will not be pleased with this wedding, but what can one do! You can't please everyone.

48. From Hippolyte Nikolaevitch Boyarof.
(*Received* 12*th February.*)

Respected Countess Catherine Alexandrovna,—Excuse me for troubling you at such an early hour. My wife, who has not been out of doors for nearly a month, thought of going yesterday to the *folle-journée*, but when she was dressed I found her to be in such a fever that almost by force I kept her at home. She was delirious most of the night, but about five in the morning she calmed down and fell asleep. At ten this morning, that intolerable Baroness Wizen arrived, broke into my wife's bedroom, wakened her, and, I suppose, said something which greatly upset her, because after the Baroness's departure, Mary got into such a dreadful nervous state that I was beside myself. She absolutely refuses to see a doctor, and keeps asking for you. For God's sake, come at once. You alone can soothe her. To save time, I send you the carriage, which was in readiness for myself. Profoundly devoted to you,

H. BOYAROF.

49. From Baroness Wizen.
(*Received* 12*th February.*)

Dear Countess,—It is now only one o'clock, and you have already gone out! I called to give you the very interesting news that the elder Neverof is marrying Nadenka Krivo-bokaya; they became engaged yesterday, at the *folle-journée*. He had to marry someone this year, or else his mother would not give him her Kursk estate. It seems that that old fox, Nicodemus, *a aussi manigancé* in this affair; it was not for nothing that Princess Krivobokaya went to see him every Sunday. *Excusez mon griffonage;* I am writing you at the porter's lodge, on a scrap of paper, and am in a great hurry, *j'ai encore une masse de courses a faire.*

Bien a Vous, CATHERINE WIZEN.

P.S.—Nina Karskaya, after her winter triumph, is going abroad to-morrow, but is hiding the fact from everyone, in order to avoid questions, such as: "Where?" "Why?" etc. Anna Mikhailovna has had another funny adventure. She wrote Prince Boris Ivanitch lately, asking him to be sure that her son-in-law, Varaxin, was made Kamer-junker by Easter, but she was so agitated at the time that she made a mistake and wrote Kamer-page instead of Kamer-junker. The prince, who finds her a terrible bore, answered her, saying that her request ought to have been addressed to the school of pages. . . . *Vous voyez d'ici sa fureur!*

50. From H. N. Boyarof.
     (*Received 25th February.*)

Most kind and respected Countess Catherine Alexandrovna, —As I promised, I hasten to let you know how our poor patient is going on. Her spiritual condition gives me the most serious anxiety. She is obstinately silent, and if she has to answer to some question addressed to her, she gives way helplessly to hysterical weeping. Our departure was so sudden that I had no time to make the necessary arrange-ments at our country-house, where we have not been for five years. The steward got my telegram only a few hours before our arrival, and was obliged to give us his own quarters, because living in the damp house was unthinkable. So we stayed the first three days, all of us, the children, the governess and the tutor, in four tiny cages, and suffered a great deal. Things are gradually getting into order now; fortunately our old friend, Doctor Flesher, lives in a provincial town only ten versts from us. Mary has known him since childhood, and agreed to be attended by him. The chief medicine which he prescribes is movement in fresh air, and Mary takes that willingly. We are having magnificent weather, two or three degrees of frost, and no wind. To-day we have been here just a week, and my wife has visibly improved. Her appetite has reappeared, she sleeps longer, and is willing to converse on various subjects, though her judgments are tinged with extreme pessimism. That, however, can easily be explained by long nervous tension. It's remarkable, that from the moment we left Petersburg she has not had one attack of fever.

I can find no words to thank you, most dear Countess, for the trouble you have taken for Mary's sake, and your warm sympathy; for it was you who convinced her that she must leave Petersburg at once. Flesher says that that saved her, and that with every hour she spent in Petersburg the danger of complications increased. My wife acknowledges the whole value of your help and has several times tried to write to you. Yesterday she even started a letter, but after two or three sentences she could not restrain her tears, so I persuaded her to postpone it till a later day, and took upon myself the responsibility for her silence, a silence which under other circumstances would have been inexcusable.

Flesher's opinion, which I share, is that Mary's illness was due to her weak physique; the absurd fashion of life of society, combined with sleepless nights, was too much for her. We must hope that my wife will learn from bitter experience and lead a different sort of life next winter.

If her health makes as sure progress as it has been doing, I propose to come to Petersburg in ten days, to attend to my official duties, but at the end of April I will take leave of absence and come here for the whole summer. It goes without saying that directly I arrive I will come to you and give you all the latest news personally.

Infinitely devoted to you,

H. BOYAROF.

51. From Count D——.
(*Received 10th March.*)

Dear Kitty,—I send you the key of my writing-desk. Please take out two thousand and send them to me at the Club. I have been losing heavily, and do not wish to remain in debt. As Gregory is unwell, and the others are unreliable, will you ask Misha Neverof, who is probably with you as always, to take the packet to the Club and ask for me to come out to the door. You will find the money on the left, under a large blue envelope.

52. Telegram from D. D. Kudryashin.
(*Received 11th March.*)

Stiosha, Manya, Pisha, Pasha, the whole choir and the whole gang, including myself and Mitka, drink the health of our adored Countess, and remind her of her promise to visit white-stoned mother Moscow once again.—KUDRYASHIN.

53. From the Most Reverend Nicodemus.
(*Received 11th March.*)

Most kind sister in Christ, and Excellent Countess,—I have received your generous gift in aid of my diocesan fund for the suffering, and send you my heart-felt thanks, though it is not unknown to me that your modesty evades gratitude when it can. . . . But what do I say? It not only evades gratitude, but strives always to minimise what you have done and to deny it.

But though it may be justifiable to allow your almsgiving to remain hidden behind a mist, nevertheless, your life dedicated to the service and well-being of mankind must not be allowed to remain like a light under a bushel. A true and virtuous wife, a loving and tender mother, an obedient and zealous daughter of the one true Church, you are like a lamp set on a high place, open to the gaze of everyone. And people passing by doubt at which to marvel more, the beauty of the priceless vessel or of its interior unquenchable fire.

The donation of this sum by your Excellency will be reported by me to-morrow to a certain exalted personage.

I send you my pastoral blessing and remain your humble servant and intercessor,

                                            NICODEMUS.

54. From M. I. Boyarova.
    (*Received* 25*th March.*)

I have been going to write to you for more than a month, my dear, dear friend, Kitty, but every time I have tried my pen has fallen out of my hands. I have gone over so much in my mind and changed my point of view so often that I really do not know where to begin. But to-day I have made a great effort, and will begin by telling you how deeply thankful I am to you. You were positively my salvation, when you persuaded my husband to take me as soon as possible to the country. That showed how well you knew me, and how well you understand the fashionable world in which we live. For what could I have done, had I remained in Petersburg? It would have been impossible to refuse to see everybody, and I should have had to see ladies whose real object was not concerned with my health but the interest of seeing my sufferings and torments, and I should have had to listen to their false sympathy and poisonous insinuations. . . .

Three days of that would be sufficient to drive me out of my mind! I am not going to write to you about our journey, nor about myself, nor my life here. Hippolyte Nikolaitch went to see you and probably told you everything in detail. I must give Hippolyte Nikolaitch his due: he has been very tactful and kind the whole time; *il me soignait comme une véritable sœur de charité*—and although he probably guessed everything he never made the slightest hint about it. Only on the day of his departure, he said, laconically: "Won't you write a few words to Princess Krivobokaya? you ought to congratulate her on her daughter's engagement, and I could take the letter to her myself." So I sat down submissively at the writing-table and wrote congratulations to that witch; I wrote: "*Je fais des vœux bien sincères pour le bonheur de Nadine. . . .*"

Can one live in society and not tell lies? I just cannot imagine what a true and honourable life would mean in the midst of all the hypocrisies and lies. I thought of this once or twice before, but it was impossible to hear the voice of conscience in the constant hubbub of fashionable society. Now, however, I see everything clearly. Please do not think that I am attacking society in order to justify myself. I am not seeking any justification for my actions, for even before, when my life was swallowed up in a sort of mist, I did not think I was doing right. On St. Catherine's day, after your great dinner, I went to spend the evening at another Catherine party—at Baroness Wizen's. I was much struck by the sort of people gathered together. There were seven or eight women, each of whom had some liaison in society, and each knew something that the others did not know. The men present at the party, of course, knew also; unless perhaps some foreigner in the diplomatic service did not know, and that's hardly likely. The diplomats who visit the Baroness know everything. But what was there to be proud of in that? And then, how majestically we bowed to one another, and walked from place to place, how superior was the tone of our conversation, how severely we condemned the behaviour of ·certain people in our circle, and with what ineffable contempt we viewed the rest of humanity! I remember we were talking about a certain unfortunate little girl . . . you know she was governess at Anna Mikhailovna's, fell in love with her son, and broke her heart . . . my God! what thunders of indignation we let loose upon that unfortunate girl! And strangely enough, the one who was most indignant and loudest in condemnation was that Nina Karskaya, whom three months previously no one in Petersburg wished to receive. I also joined with the rest and expressed condemnation, though I immediately felt that I had not the right to say what I did. My words at that party troubled my conscience for a long while afterwards, and I always blushed when I thought of them. When lately I communicated some of these thoughts to Hippolyte Nikolaitch, he answered: "You should not consider falsehood and hypocrisy as the exclusive characteristics of our society; these sins exist in all societies and all peoples." That is very possible, but I do not know any other society; I speak of ours, which I know very well. But even if it is indeed so, have we the right to despise other people because they are as bad as we are?

But society is not only lying and hypocritical; it is also cruel and pitiless. Our former tutor, Vassily Stepanitch, once explained to me the theory of a well-known scholar, that everything in Nature must struggle in order to exist. We fashionable people carry on just such a cruel struggle, but there is this difference, that it is in no way necessary to our existence. Every success, every little personal gleam of fortune, prevents other people living; but while you have it, everybody is on your side. But let one but falter in one's steps, and fortune change,—then you need expect no mercy! And what is the object, what is the *raison d'être* of all our dresses and ornaments, on which we spend such mad money? It is said that everything is done to attract the men; but that is not true. The majority of men do not even notice what we are wearing. Of course, they like it when we are dressed to suit our faces, but, of course, we could dress to suit our faces on next to nothing. No, our dresses and jewels are our weapons for struggling one with another. They are our guns and cannon. Our victory consists in Mme. A. blushing with chagrin, or our friend B. paling with rage. . . . You see, Kitty, when I reflect that I have spent all my life in this darkest hell and must again go back to it, I feel cold shivers down my spine. I told Hippolyte Nikolaitch that I wanted to stay in the country for ever, but he replied that that was the fantasy of a convalescent woman, and that I owed it to his official career and the training of the children to spend the winter in Petersburg. But only imagine; how shall I face society? imagine how I shall feel when I meet Kostia again. . . . I will not write any more, I will finish this letter to-morrow.

The day before yesterday, when I began this letter, we had dreadful weather: wet snow, and such a piercing wind that it was impossible to go out on the verandah. But yesterday there was a burst of hot bright sunshine, and Spring began down here. If you could only know what happiness this is— the beginning of Spring in the country: I experienced this special sort of feeling in childhood, but afterwards forgot about it. Only usually Spring comes very gradually; yesterday something moved suddenly, and Spring was everywhere. *Le printemps est entré sans s'annoncer, comme la baronne Wizen.* The day before yesterday the mountain was quite white, but to-day there is a blackness on the summit, and some little blue flowers have appeared among the trees. We spent the whole of yesterday in the open air. In the evening, when the others had gone to bed, I thought of finishing this letter, but something drew me irresistibly out of doors once more. I wrapped myself up in a big plaid and sat for several hours on the steps of the verandah. It is a long while since I have felt so light-hearted. It was very pleasant, to breathe in the fresh and powerful and somehow caressing atmosphere; the bright stars looked at me so enigmatically; the unceasing murmur of innumerable streams was so clear in the deep silence of the night! On the right and on the left of the verandah streams purred softly downward and fell with a splash somewhere in the depths of the garden. And they all seemed to be saying to me: "Listen how we run, as if we were doing something and hastening somewhere, but to-morrow not a trace of us will remain. Thus everything that now agitates you and torments you will flow away and vanish. Yes; and life itself will also go away and leave no trace. Is it worth while remembering and speculating, is it worth while complaining and getting tired? Do not regret the past, do not fear what will be. . . . Be calm, forgive, forget!"

Do not laugh at me, dear Kitty, and think that I am trying to write in a high-flown style; truly, I write you all that I feel. This is not like Petersburg; where sometimes one expresses oneself ecstatically about Nature while thinking of something quite different. There is another feeling about which I used to speak much previously, a feeling that I only experience in its fullness now, and that is, love of my children. Of course, I loved my children in the old days, but there was simply no time to think of them. My Mitya is only ten, and I have only just understood how intelligent and dear he is. Every day he either astonishes me with some apt remark or puts such questions to me as quite bewilder me, and I have to delve in books to find an answer for him. One thing surprises and vexes me: in going over the names of our acquaintances in Petersburg, he never once mentions Kostia's name. Is it possible he understands something? Several times I have thought of disembarrassing myself and saying something about him, but some irresistible force held me back. What if I blushed at mentioning his name? What if Mitya blushes? The questioning glance of these ten-year-old eyes has more power to confuse me than the frowning brow and important bearing of Hippolyte Nikolaitch.

But I have said enough about myself: let me write something about you. I have always considered you to be in all ways an uncommon woman. All the successes and honours which others struggle for all their lives come to you of themselves. You are able to materialise every whim that comes into your mind, and you will go without hesitation beyond the limit where another woman would stop short in fear. You have some sort of conviction that it is impossible for anyone to suspect you. Up till now, this has not failed you, but you know as well as I do, dear Kitty, *les jours se suivent, mais ne se ressemblent pas.* Do you remember how you answered me, that night at Mon Plaisir, when I asked you what possessed you to keep all those compromising letters? You then said: My husband has such faith in me that even if he saw me in someone's embrace he would not believe his own eyes. Of course, that was a great exaggeration, Kitty, *au fond, cè n'est qu'une phrase.* Some negligence on your part, some merest trifle, may be your undoing, and then the whole building will tumble down, and your husband will hate you even more than he now believes in you, and society will attack you bitterly in order to be revenged for the admiration with which it has so long surrounded you. Society does not love those whom it has involuntarily to respect. Take my advice, my dear kind friend Kitty, burn that famous archive of yours, and with it all that makes that archive interesting for you; in a word, be actually what others reckon you to be. That will not cost much effort on your part. I know well enough that you have never had a serious affair. I am sure you would not experience a hundredth part of the suffering I have gone through as a result of my first and last affair if you resolved to have done with your caprice. My affair lasted about two years, but I expended so much strength and feeling in that time that it seems like a whole lifetime, and from the beginning I never understood how it could possibly end. Now I do not understand how it could possibly have begun, and, of course, I would give half of the

rest of my life if thereby it could be understood never to
have begun.

Be not angry, my dear Kitty, that your hare-brained, crazy
Mary gives you advice, but believe that that advice comes
out of the depth of my heart, which is overflowing with love
and gratitude towards you. You will show that you are not
angry by writing me just such a long letter as this to you.
Write and let me know what everybody is doing. When
Hippolyte Nikolaitch gets enraged with his chief, he keeps
saying all day long, "I will go into private life." And see, I
have gone into private life. But all the same, fashionable
gossip interests me as an actor is interested after he has left
the stage in all that his companions are acting. Tell me, are
people saying very much about me? *On me déchaire à belles
dents, n'est ce pas?* I can imagine how Baroness Wizen tries!
Of course, you will go to Kostia's wedding, so describe it all
to me, down to the very smallest details. I am not angry
with him in the very least. God be with him,—perhaps it's
all for the best, but I am deeply sorry for him: he will not
be happy. How can that stupid Nadenka love as once I
loved! I have written: *once* . . . but was that long ago? I
kiss you warmly.

                                        Your MARY.

P.S.—Remember me to Misha Neverof. He is a fine charming boy. Surely, society life will not spoil him. I shall never
forget the expression on his face when he came to say good-
bye to me at the railway station and made excuses for his
brother. He said: "My brother is on duty to-day," and
blushed up to his ears. He has not even yet learned how to
tell a lie without blushing! And I knew very well that it was a
lie, because I had read in the orders the day before that
Sirotkin 1st was on duty that day. I got dreadfully interested
in these Sirotkin brothers, because they seem to be on duty
the whole Winter—one one day, the other the next. Shall I
see the Sirotkins some day, and will they be on duty all the

coming year in the same way? Yes, and how will it be with me next winter? Shall I have to play some comedy rôle in our world, or shall I remain an indifferent looker-on at this aimless vanity, this eternal struggle of all possible ambitions and interests? Who knows? *Qui vivra verra.*

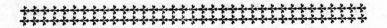

VLADIMIR SOLOVYOF

(1853–1900)

❖❖

THE TWO HERMITS

I n the desert in Egypt two hermits were saving their souls. Their caves were quite near one another, but they never entered into conversation unless it were to sing psalms at one another or call one another by name now and then. In this way of life they passed many years, and the fame of their sanctity spread beyond Egypt and into many lands. But in course of time the devil, mortified by their holiness, succeeded in tempting them. He snared them both at the same time, and, not saying a word to one another, they gathered the baskets and pallets which in their long spare time they had plaited from grasses and palm leaves, and they set off together for Alexandria. There they sold their work, and on the money they got for it they spent three gay days and nights with drunkards and sinners, and on the fourth morning, having spent everything, they returned to their cells in the desert.

One of them wept bitterly and howled aloud; the other walked at his side with bright morning face and sang psalms joyfully to himself. The first cried:

"Accursed that I am, now am I lost for ever. I shall never out-pray my hideous sin, never, never. All my fasts and hymns and prayers have been in vain. I might as well have sinned all the time; all lost in one foul moment! Alas! alas!"

But the other hermit went on singing, quietly, joyfully.

"What!" cried the first hermit. "Have you gone out of your mind?"

"Why?" asked the joyful one.

446

"Why don't you repent?"

"What is there for me to repent of?" asked the joyful one.

"And Alexandria, have you forgotten it?" asked his companion.

"What of Alexandria? Glory be to the Almighty who preserves that famous and honourable town!"

"But what did we do in Alexandria?"

"What did we do? Why, we sold our baskets, of course; prayed before the ikon of holy St. Mark, visited several churches, walked a little in the town hall, conversed with the virtuous and Christly Leonila . . ."

The repentant hermit stared at the other in pale stupefaction.

"And the house of ill-fame in which we spent the night.. . ." said he.

"God preserve us!" said the other. "The evening and night we spent in the guest-house of the Patriarch."

"Holy martyrs! God has already blasted his reason," cried the repentant hermit. "And with whom did we get drunk on Tuesday night? Tell me that."

"We partook of wine and viands in the refectory of the patriarchate, Tuesday being the festival of the Presentation of the most Blessed Mother of God."

"Poor fellow! And whom did we kiss, eh?"

"We were honoured at parting with a holy kiss from that father of fathers, the most blessed Archbishop of the great city of Alexandria and of all Egypt, yes, and of Libya, and of Pentapolis, and of Kur-Timothee with its spiritual court, and with all the fathers and brothers of his divinely appointed clergy."

"Ah, why do you make a mock of me? Does it mean that after yesterday's abominations the devil has entered into possession of you? You embraced sinners, you accursed one."

"I can't say in whom the devil has found a home, in me or in you," said the other; "in me when I rejoice in God's gifts and His holy will, when I praise the Creator and all His works, or in you who rave and call the house of our most blessed father and pastor a house of ill-fame, and defame the God-loving clergy, calling them sinners as it were."

"Ah, you heretic!" screamed the repentant hermit. "Arian monster! Thrice accursed lips of the abominable Apollonion!"

And the repentant hermit threw himself upon his companion and tried to killhim. But failing to do that, he grew tired of his efforts, and the two resumed their journey to their caves. The repentant one beat his head on the rock all night and tore his hair and made the desert echo with his howls and shrieks. The other calmly and joyfully went on singing psalms.

In the morning the repentant hermit made the following reflections:

"Just think of it. I had earned from Heaven especial blessings and holy power by my fasts and *podvigs*.[1] This has already become evident by the miracles and wonders I have lately been enabled to perform, but after this that has happened, all is lost. By giving myself up to fleshly abomination I have sinned against the Holy Ghost, and that sin, according to the word of God, will be forgiven me neither in this life nor in the life to come. I have thrown the pearl of heavenly purity to be trampled under foot by swine, by devils. The devils have taken my pearl, and, no doubt, having stamped it into the mire, they will come after me and tear me. Well, well, if I am irrecoverably lost, whatever is there for me to do out here in the desert?" And he returned to Alexandria and gave himself up to a life of debauch. Eventually, on one occasion when he was hard up, he conspired with other vagabonds, fell upon a rich merchant, killed him and robbed him. He was tracked down, caught and tried in the courts. The judge condemned him to death and he died without repentance.

[1]*Podvig* is a Russian word for holy exploits and victories, especially in those consisting in a denial of the world.

But his old companion continued his holy life, his *podvizhnit-chestvo*[1] attained a high degree of sanctity and became famous through the many miracles wrought at his cave-mouth. At a word from his holy lips a woman past the age of child-bearing yet conceived and brought forth a male child. When at last the good man died, his shrivelled and worn-out body suddenly, as it were, blossomed in beauty and youth, becoming translucent and filling the air with a heavenly perfume. Over his holy relics a monastery was built, and his name went forth from the church of Alexandria to Byzantium and thence to the shrines of Kief and Moscow.

The lesson of this story is, according to Varsonophy, who told it, that there are no sins of any importance except despondency. Did not both these hermits sin alike, and yet but one of them was lost, namely, he who desponded?

---

[1] *Podvizhnitchestvo*, i.e. the life of going on doing *podvigs*, the continuance denial of the world.

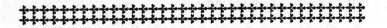

VLADIMIR KOROLENKO

(1853–1919)

MAKAR'S DREAM

T H I S is the tale of the dream which poor Makar dreamt on Christmas Eve—the very Makar who is mentioned by the Russian proverb as the step-child of Fate. He lived in the little out-of-the-way village of Chalgan, in Siberia, which is inhabited by a medley of Russians and Yakouts. That is to say, many years ago some Russian emigrants settled in the *taiga* (virgin forest), cleared a small piece of ground, and built a couple of *yourtas* (huts) on it. By and by they married Yakout women, and gradually, almost without knowing it themselves, adopted the customs and the language of their wives. And Makar was an offspring of that curious mixed race which had settled down in a little village lost in the wide *taiga* to a life of misery and starvation.

It was Christmas Eve, and Makar remembered that to-morrow was a great holiday. He was tormented by an intense craving for vodka, which was not to be satisfied, for he had no money wherewith to buy liquor. The corn was nearly all sold, and he was already in debt with the shopkeepers and the Tartars who lived in the place. And to-morrow was the great holiday . . . on which he could not work. . . . What was he to do if he could not get drunk? He felt utterly wretched at this prospect, and bemoaned his miserable life. Not to be able to drink a single bottle of spirits on the greatest feast-day in the whole winter!

Suddenly a happy thought struck him. He rose and began to draw on his ragged fur-coat. His wife, who was a tall, wiry,

450

exceedingly strong and equally ugly woman, who knew all his tricks, guessed at once what he was about.

"What are you about, you devil? Are you going to drink all the vodka by yourself?"

"Hold your tongue! I am going to buy one bottle, and we will drink it together to-morrow."

He gave her a slap on the shoulder which nearly threw her on the floor, and winked cunningly with one eye. Such is the heart of woman! She knew that Makar was deceiving her, and yet she felt flattered by her husband's caress!

He left his hut, caught his old horse, and was soon seated in his sleigh and driving towards the outskirts of the village.

A small *yourta* stood at the very end of the hamlet. A column of smoke, rising slowly from the chimney, hid the cold, glittering stars and the bright moon behind a thick, undulating veil. One could see the fire-light within shining through the blocks of ice which are used in those regions instead of panes of glass in the window. Everything was quiet without. Two strangers from afar[1] dwelt in this wilderness. Makar did not know what had brought them to this distant spot, nor did he care in the least. He liked to do a little job for them now and then because they were not exacting and did not haggle about the pay, nor did they trouble him about his small debts.

Makar entered the *yourta*, walked straight up to the fireplace, and stretched out his hands, which were benumbed with the frost.

"Tcha!" ejaculated he, to inform them that he was cold.

The strangers were at home. A candle burned on the table. One of them was lying on his bed smoking and gazing thoughtfully at the rings of blue smoke as they rose in the air —perhaps he was following some train of thought. The other was seated by the fireplace watching the flames dancing round the logs of wood and licking them.

"Be ye well?" asked Makar, who wished to break the silence, which was making him feel uncomfortable.

[1]Political exiles.

How could he know the load of sorrow which lay heavily on the hearts of the strangers, or guess what memories haunted their brains on that very night, and what pictures they saw in the firelight and the smoke? And besides, he himself was in great trouble.

The young man who was sitting by the fire raised his head and stared at Makar as if he did not recognise him at once. Then, giving himself a shake as if to rouse himself, he jumped up from his chair.

"Oh, it is you, Makar! How are you? I'm glad you came. You'll take a glass of tea with us?"

Makar was pleased with this proposal.

"Tea?" repeated he inquiringly. "That's good. . . . Yes, mate; that is capital."

He began at once to take off his things. As soon as he had laid aside his cap and coat he felt at home, and the sight of the samovar with the coals glowing inside warmed him into a burst of feeling. "I love you! It is the truth. I love you so well, oh, so well! I can't sleep at night thinking of you!"

The stranger turned round with a bitter smile on his face.

"Indeed," said he. "You love us. What is it you want?"

Makar was taken aback by this sudden question.

"I have something on my mind," replied he. "But how could you know it? Well, I will tell you all about it when I have had my tea." Seeing that his hosts had offered him the tea, Makar thought that he might go further. "Have you a piece of roast meat? I love roast meat," said he.

"No."

"Never mind," said Makar, soothingly; "I will have some another day. . . . Sure," added he in an inquiring tone, "you will let me have some another day?"

"Of course we will."

Now Makar regarded the strangers as his debtors for a piece of roast meat; and he never forgot debts of that kind. An hour later he was sitting in his sleigh, having earned a whole rouble by selling five cartloads of fuel on comparatively easy conditions. He had promised them solemnly not to spend the money on drink on that same day, having all the time fully made up his mind that he would do so. He was so absorbed in the prospect of this treat that he quite forgot the beating which his wife most certainly would give him.

"Where are you going to, Makar?" called out the young man, laughing, when he saw that Makar's horse turned to the left instead of going straight on.

"Tprou-ou, Tprou-ou! Did you ever see such a wretched horse? . . . Where are you going to?" shouted Makar, tugging hard at the left rein and giving the animal an innocent-looking slap with the right. The clever little horse whisked its tail reproachfully and trotted quietly in the required direction till the sledge stopped at the door of the tavern.

Several horses with high Yakout saddles on their backs were standing at the gate waiting for their masters.

The little hut was crammed full of men. The acrid fumes of bad tobacco floated in a dense cloud over the heads of the guests, and were slowly absorbed by the fire. Yakouts were sitting on benches behind the tables, on which stood cups and glasses of vodka; some men were playing at cards. The faces of the customers were red and streaming with perspiration. The eyes of the players followed eagerly the cards. Money was rapidly changing owners. A drunken Yakout was sitting on a bundle of straw in one corner of the room rocking himself to and fro and singing an endless song, in which he repeated in different tunes the plain fact that to-morrow was a great holiday and that he was drunk to-day.

Makar put down his money and had a bottle handed him, which he put into his bosom and crept unperceived into the dark corner with the Yakout. Here he poured out one glassful after another, which he swallowed greedily. The vodka was very bitter! it had been mixed three-quarters with water on occasion of the holiday, but tobacco had been put in freely.[1] After each glassful Makar gasped for breath and saw red rings dancing before his eyes.

He was soon drunk, and sinking down on the straw, he embraced his knees with his arms and laid his heavy head on them. In this position he began to utter strange uncouth sounds which meant a song. He sang that to-morrow was a great holiday and that he had spent on drink the money he had earned by selling five loads of fuel.

Meanwhile the crowd increased. New customers kept coming; they had come to the place to attend the service in the church and drink vodka. The landlord, foreseeing that in a short time there would be no room for any new-comers, looked round to see whom he might expel! his eyes fell on Makar in his corner beside the Yakout, and, without wasting words, he dragged up the latter by the collar of his coat and flung him out of the hut. Then came Makar's turn. Being an inhabitant of the place, he was entitled to a more courteous treatment. The Tartar opened the door wide and gave him such a hearty kick that Makar flew out of the hut and fell on his nose upon a mound of snow. It is difficult to tell whether he felt morally hurt on finding himself thus summarily disposed of. The cold, hard snow stuck to his face and filled his gloves. He gathered himself together, and, rising from his mound, he limped towards his sledge.

The moon had risen in the sky. The tail of the Great Bear pointed downwards. It was freezing hard. The aurora borealis was shining in the north, half hidden by a round black cloud, round which its flames were leaping up like fiery darts. The horse evidently understood its master's condition and slowly wended its way home. He had crawled somehow upon the sledge and was huddled up in it, rocking to and fro and singing his endless song about the five loads of firewood and the beating which was in store for him. As he drove he saw the

[1]In Siberia bad tobacco is often put into vodka and allowed to stand for a certain time, till the latter has acquired a certain strength. This mixture is extremely unwholesome, as may easily be imagined.

taiga in the distance, and the snow-capped hills which glittered in the moonlight reminded him of the traps he had set for birds and animals. This incident filled his heart with joy, and he sang that a fox had been caught in his trap; he would sell the skin to-morrow, and thus escape the beating. The church bells were ringing when Makar entered his hut and told his wife that a fox was caught in his trap. He had forgotten that his wife had not shared his bottle of brandy, and was rather taken aback when in answer to the joyful tidings she struck him a heavy blow. And before he had time to throw himself on his bed she struck him a second blow on the back.

Meanwhile the bells were ringing for the midnight mass, and their merry sound floated far away in the air over the village of Chalgan and the boundless snowbound *taiga*. . . .

He was lying on his bed. His head was burning hot, and a fire seemed to be raging in his inside. The mixture of spirits and tobacco was flowing in his arteries like liquid fire. The snow on his face and clothes was melting and running down his forehead and back in ice-cold streamlets. The old woman thought he was asleep, but he was not.

He could not forget the fox; he was sure it had been trapped, he even knew in which trap. He could see it distinctly— crushed by the heavy board—tearing the soil with its claws and trying to escape. The rays of the moon were shining through the thick underwood and playing on its yellow fur, while its eyes were glowing like live coals—he could see them glowing.

He could bear it no longer, and, rising from his bed, he directed his steps towards his faithful horse to drive to the *taiga*.

What was that? Did his wife take him by the collar of his coat and pull him back?

No; he has left the village behind him. The runners of the sledge glide along the hardened snow with that peculiar creaking sound one knows so well in winter. He has left Chalgan far behind. The bells are still ringing solemnly, and he can see lines of black figures standing out sharply against the sky. They are Yakouts on horseback riding to church.

Meanwhile the moon has sunk lower in the sky. A whitish cloud has appeared in the zenith, which shines with a phosphorescent light; it grows and expands: suddenly it bursts asunder—many-coloured flames shoot forth, leaping across the semicircular dark cloud, which looks blacker from the contrast.

The path winds between low shrubs; right and left rises a row of hills. The trees grow taller as he drives on, and the underwood becomes more thick and tangled. A mystery seems to hover over the boundless *taiga*. The bare branches of the trees are covered with silvery hoar-frost. Makar stops his horse, for he has reached the spot where all the traps are laid. He sees distinctly the top of the hill and the first trap: it consists of three heavy beams, which rest on a pointed piece of wood that slants a little. The whole thing is kept together by a clever combination of hooks and cord made of hair.

Now, this happened to be another man's trap, but foxes will sometimes go into other people's traps. Makar got down quickly from his sledge, left the horse standing on the road, and listened attentively. All was still. Only the bells still rang in the distant village.

He was safe. The owner of these traps, Alioshka Chalganov, who was Makar's neighbour and worst enemy, was probably in church. Makar walked up and down in front of the traps. They were wide open, waiting with gaping mouths for their prey.

Hist! . . . There was a slight rustling. . . . A reddish fur gleamed in the moonlight so close to Makar that he could see the ears of the fox and its bushy tail sweeping the ground. It disappeared between the trees in the direction of Makar's traps, and a dull thud soon informed him that the board had

fallen. His heart beat faster as he burst through the underwood, running towards his capture. The cold twigs struck
him in the eyes and covered his face with snow; he stumbled
and gasped for breath. He had reached a clearing which he
had made himself . . . he was close to the spot . . . when,
behold, a figure appeared between the trees: he recognised
Alioshka Chalganov—that was his square, short figure, his
stooping shoulders and clumsy, shuffling gait like a bear's.
Makar thought that his enemy's face looked blacker and his
teeth gleamed whiter than usual. He felt deeply hurt and
angry with him for sneaking about other people's traps. "The
scoundrel! He is after my traps." To be sure, Makar had
done exactly the same thing with regard to Alioshka's traps,
but then that was different—he was afraid of being caught in
the act of prowling about other people's traps, whereas he felt
angry with them for trespassing on *his* ground.

He ran quickly towards the trap in which the fox had been
captured. Alioshka shuffled in the same direction. Who was
to be first?

The fox was tearing the soil with its claws, exactly as he had
seen it do in his vision, and glared at him with burning, eager
eyes. "Tytyma!" (Don't touch it). . . . "It's mine," shouted
Makar.

"Tytyma!" replied Alioshka, like an echo, "It's mine."

They both ran towards the trap, and hurriedly lifted the top
board, thereby setting the fox free. It rose, took a little jump,
stopped, looked at both men with a somewhat sarcastic expression, licked the spot which had been bruised by the board,
and ran away, waving its tail merrily in the moonlight.

Alioshka was going to rush off after it, but Makar caught
hold of him by the tails of his coat. "Tytyma!" he shouted.
"It's mine." And he rushed after the fox.

"Tytyma!" repeated Alioshka, like an echo, and Makar felt
that someone was holding by his coat-tails. He grew very
angry, and, forgetting all about the fox, he ran after Alioshka,
who was trying to escape.

Faster and faster they ran. The branches of the trees tore Alioshka's cap from his head, but he had no time to stop and pick it up, for Makar was close behind him shrieking angrily. However, Alioshka had more cunning than poor Makar. He stopped suddenly, turned round and stooped, putting out his head, against which Makar came full rush, and tumbled down. While he fell the wily Alioshka twisted his cap off his head and disappeared in the *taiga*.

Makar rose slowly, feeling miserable and vanquished. Streams of cold water trickled down his body where the snow had penetrated between the skin and his clothes. He had lost his warm gloves, and he knew only too well that it is no joke to be out on such a night in the *taiga* without one's cap and gloves. He turned to go home, but the way seemed endless. According to his calculations he ought to get out of the *taiga* and see the church steeple by this time. He could still hear the bells ringing, and though he thought he was drawing nearer the sound, it became fainter. And then his heart sank, and he began to despair.

He was thoroughly tired out: his legs failed him, he gasped for breath, and felt his hands and feet grow as cold as ice. The thought that he was lost now became uppermost in his mind. The *taiga* was as still as death. A white hare ran across the road, sat down on her hind legs, moved her long ears, and began to wash her face, winking at Makar and making mouths at him. She evidently wished to let him know that she knew quite well that he had been her foe, setting traps to catch her, and that now he was being caught himself.

His heart grew heavy. The branches struck him in the face, and the trees stretched out long twigs to catch him by the hair, and hit him in the eyes and face. The *taiga* suddenly became alive; the partridges came out of their holes and stared at him with their round eyes, and the ptarmigan rushed about with outspread wings, chattering angrily, and telling their wives about him and his tricks. Thousands of foxes peeped out of the thicket, sniffing the air, moving their ears, and looking scornfully at Makar. The hares sat on their hind legs and giggled as they told each other his adventures.

"I am lost!" thought Makar, as he lay down on the snow.

The frost increased. The last flames of the aurora played on the sky, peeping at Makar from above between the branches of the trees. A few faint sounds came floating through the air from distant Chalgan. The aurora vanished. The sounds ceased.

Makar had died.

He did not know how he died. He only knew that something ought to go out from him, and expected it, but nothing did go out. Meanwhile, he knew that he was dead, and remained lying motionless till he grew tired of it. It was quite dark when Makar felt something touching his feet. He turned his head in that direction and opened his eyes.

The trees were as still as death; they looked ashamed of the pranks they had been playing on him. The moss-grown fir trees stretched out their huge snow-covered arms as they waved slowly to and fro. Little flakes of snow were softly floating through the air. The bright, kind-looking, tiny stars peeped out of the blue sky between the branches and seemed to say, "Oh dear, oh dear, the poor man is dead!"

The old priest Ivan was standing by Makar's side and gently kicking him. There was snow on his long robe and on his fur cap, on his shoulders and on his long beard. But what struck him most was, that this apparition was evidently the identical priest Ivan who died four years ago!

He had been good-natured and kind-hearted during his lifetime, never troubling his parishioners about the tithes and his fees. Now, Makar had always settled the money matters himself, and he remembered with a pang of shame that he had been rather close and stingy when the fees for christenings and masses had to be paid—once or twice he had even forgotten to pay them.

But the priest Ivan was never angry, he was even perfectly happy, provided he got his bottle of spirits. If Makar had no money to buy some, priest Ivan would send for it, and share its contents with his parishioner. At such times the priest had generally to be carried home dead drunk, and delivered to the tender care of his *matouchka*. Sometimes these proceedings would be enlivened by a little fight, but this seldom happened.

Yes, he had been a kindly "little father," and he had met with a terrible death. One day, as he was lying dead drunk on his bed, alone in his cottage (the others having gone out for a few hours), he wanted to smoke, and, getting up from his couch in order to light his pipe, he reeled to the fireplace, overbalanced himself, and fell into the fire. When his family returned there was nothing left of Father Ivan except his legs. His parishioners mourned for him, but as no doctor in the world could cure him of his disease, they buried his legs; and another priest came in his place.

And at this moment Father Ivan was standing before Makar and poking him with his foot, saying, "Get up, Makaroushko. Get up, and come along with me!"

"Where to?" asked Makar, sulkily. He had expected to lie still after his death, and to be no longer obliged to wander aimlessly about the *taiga*. If not, what would have been the good of dying?

"Let us go to the *Great Taion*" (Great Chief).

"And why should I go to him?" retorted Makar.

"To be judged," said the priest, somewhat sadly, and in a deprecating tone of voice.

Then Makar remembered that he was expected to appear at a judgment after his death. He had heard it in church. There was no help for it; the priest was right, and he got up accordingly, grumbling that there was no rest for a body even after death. The little father went on and Makar followed him. The trees moved aside as they passed them going eastwards. Makar noticed wonderingly that the priest left no footprints behind him as he glided over the snow. Looking round he saw that the snow was perfectly smooth and even, and bore no trace whatever of his footsteps either. He was just thinking how convenient it would be for him to visit other people's traps, because nobody would know anything about it, when the priest, who evidently had read his hidden thoughts, turned round, saying, "Stop that! You do not know what each thought may cost you."

"Oh, indeed!" growled Makar. "Can't a body think what he likes? What's the matter with you? You used not to be so dreadfully strict in old times. Hold your tongue!"

The priest shook his head deprecatingly and walked on.

"Have we far to go?" asked Makar.

"Very far!" replied the other in the same mournful manner.

"But what shall we eat?" asked Makar anxiously.

"Have you forgotten that you are dead, and that henceforth you need neither food nor drink?" retorted the other, turning round.

Makar did not like this at all. He would not have minded so much if he had been left in peace on the snow.

"But you cannot expect a man to walk far without eating," he grumbled again.

"Do not grumble!" said the priest.

"Very well!" retorted he, sulkily. But he went on grumbling in his heart and finding fault with everybody and everything. "Whoever heard of such a thing? They make you walk for ever without eating. That is too bad!"

He stalked on behind the priest in high dudgeon. They had walked very far; it seemed to Makar as if they had been on the road for a whole week or more. They had passed high-peaked mountains without end, and skirted numberless precipices, and gone by many woods and glades, rivers and lakes. Whenever Makar looked round it seemed to him as if the dark *taiga* vanished behind them, and the high snow-mountains disappeared in the darkness and hid themselves behind the horizon. They seemed to be going uphill. The stars shone brighter, then the setting moon peeped from behind the ridge of the hill which they were ascending. She seemed to be running away from them, but Makar and the priest ran after her till she rose again above the horizon. They were walking on the top of a broad, even ridge, when it grew lighter than it had been during the first part of the night. The stars were as big as apples and shone brightly, while the moon was of the size of the bottom of a golden cask, and shone like the sun, illuminating the whole plain. Each snowflake was visible in the dazzling light. Several roads ran across the plain, and they all went towards the east. Many people, dressed in all kinds of garbs, were walking and riding on those roads.

Makar had for some time been looking attentively at a man on horseback, when he suddenly left the road and ran after him.

"Stop! stop!" shouted the priest; but Makar did not heed him. He had recognised in the rider a Tartar who had stolen his horse six years ago, and had been dead for five years. And there he was riding on that very same horse, which galloped wildly across the plain, raising a cloud of snow at each leap. Makar was astonished to see how easily and quickly he had reached the Tartar, who was flying like the wind. The other stopped his horse at once when he saw his pursuer come up with him. Makar was exceedingly angry. "Come with me to the *starosta*!" he shouted. "The horse is mine! I know it by its right ear, which has been slit open! . . . You scoundrel! You ride another man's horse while its owner walks like a beggar!"

"Stop!" said the Tartar. "There is no need to go to the *starosta*. Take your confounded brute back. This is the fifth year I ride it, and I have not moved one inch. . . . The people who are on foot leave me behind. It is a shame for an honest Tartar not to get on any quicker!"

He had raised his leg and was going to jump down, when the priest came running up breathless, and dragged Makar away, shouting:

"You wretch! What are you doing? Do you not see that the Tartar is going to cheat you?"

"That's what he has been doing!" vociferated Makar, gesticulating furiously. "The horse was a capital horse, a horse fit for a nobleman. . . . They offered me forty roubles for it some time ago. . . . No, my fellow, you shall not escape scot free. If you have spoiled the horse I shall kill it and eat the flesh, and you shall fork out the money and pay the damages. Do you think you will be let off because you are a Tartar?"

He had been shouting and working himself into a passion on purpose, because he hoped to attract a crowd, as he was afraid of the Tartars. But the priest said calmly:

"Be quiet, Makar. Have you forgotten that you are dead? . . . What do you want the horse for now? And do you not see that you are getting on far more quickly on foot than the Tartar on horseback? How would you like to have to ride for a thousand years?"

And Makar understood now why the Tartar had been so eager to return the horse. "What a cunning people they are!" thought he; then, turning to the other, he added, "Ride on, my fellow, till you hear from me. I intend to go to law about this affair."

The Tartar angrily pulled his cap over his eyes, and struck the horse. The animal rose on its hind legs; a shower of snow fell on them, but it did not advance one step.

He spat out angrily, and said, turning to Makar: "Listen, dʒgor (friend), have you a little tobacco to spare? I am dying to have a smoke, but my tobacco was finished four years ago."

"A dog is your friend, not I!" retorted Makar, angrily. "There is a fine fellow for you! He steals your horse, and then asks you for tobacco. I don't care if you go to perdition!"

And he walked away.

"You were wrong not to give him a poor little leaf of

tobacco. If you had done it the Taion would have forgiven you no less than a hundred sins on the day of judgment."

"Why did you not tell me that before?" snarled Makar.

"It is too late to teach you now. Your priests ought to have told you so when you were alive."

Makar was very angry. What was the use of having priests? You pay them your tithes and dimes, and they cannot even teach you when you ought to let a Tartar have a leaf of tobacco in order to obtain forgiveness for your sins. It is no joke . . . one hundred sins . . . and all that for one leaf! To be sure, that is worth something!

"Stop!" exclaimed he. "One leaf will do for us, and I will give the rest to the Tartar. That will make four hundred sins!"

"Look round!" said the priest.

Makar obeyed. Behind them stretched the boundless plain covered with snow, and on that white sheet the Tartar seemed a mere black spot, which disappeared presently.

"Oh, well," said Makar, "he will get on all right even without my tobacco. He has spoilt my horse—the scoundrel!"

"No," said the priest, "he has not spoilt your horse, but he stole it. Do you not remember the saying, that you do not ride far on a stolen horse?"

Yes, Makar remembered having heard this saying from the old man, but as he had frequently seen during his life that the Tartars rode to town on their stolen horses, he had forgotten it. He began to think now that old men sometimes spoke the truth.

He passed many people on horseback, who all rode as fast as the first and yet remained far behind. Some of the riders were Tartars, others came from Chalgan. These were riding on oxen, which they had probably stolen, and urged them on with long goads. Makar glared at the Tartars, and each time he met one he remarked that he deserved a still greater punishment. He stopped to chat with the people from Chalgan, because, after all, they came from the same place; he even went so far as to help them to drive the animals with a cudgel he had picked up, but the men who were riding always remained behind, and soon dwindled away into mere specks. The plain seemed boundless; notwithstanding the number of people they were constantly meeting it appeared almost deserted. Hundreds—nay, thousands—of versts seemed to lie between two travellers.

Among others, Makar met an old man whom he had never seen before. He was dressed in a ragged coat, old leather breeches, a mangy fur cap, and worn-out shoes, made of calf-skin. He seemed very old, and what was stranger still, he carried on his back an old woman, whose feet dragged on the ground. The poor wretch gasped for breath as he dragged himself painfully along, leaning heavily on his staff. Makar felt sorry for him. He stood still, the old man did the same.

"Kapsé" (speak), said Makar, speaking kindly for once in his life.

"No," replied the old man.

"What news have you heard?"

"Nothing."

"What did you see?"

"Nothing."

A short silence ensued, which Makar broke by asking the old man who he was, and where he was going.

The old man told him that many years ago, when he lived on earth, he had left the village of Chalgan and gone to live on the mountain to save his soul. He left off working, lived on berries and roots, neither ploughed nor sowed, nor ground the corn, nor did he pay any taxes. When he died and appeared before the Great Taion the latter asked him who he was, and what he had been doing. He replied that he had lived on the mountains to save his soul. "Very well," said the Taion, "but where is your old woman? Go and fetch her." He had gone accordingly, and met her on the way. She had lived in great poverty, having neither house, nor cows, nor bread, and had grown so weak that she had lost the use of her limbs, and so he was obliged to carry her on his back to the Taion. He cried while he told his story, but the old woman struck him a blow with her heel as if he had been a beast of burden, and said, in a feeble, cross voice, "Go on!"

Makar pitied the old man, and felt very glad that he had never gone to the hills for his soul's sake. His wife was a very tall, large old woman, and he could not have carried her. And if she had taken it into her head to strike him as if he were an ox or a cow, he must have died again.

He tried to help his friend, and raised the old woman's legs in order to carry them a little, but he was obliged to let go after two or three steps for fear of tearing her feet off. So quickly did the old man move with his burden that they had disappeared in one minute.

Many more people they passed on their way: there were thieves loaded with stolen goods like beasts of burden, and creeping slowly along; fat Yakout *taions* seated on their high saddles, while by their side ran poor light-footed workmen. A gloomy murderer slunk past them casting wild glances around him. He was bespattered with blood, and from time to time he threw himself on the ground, trying to wash off the criminal stains. In vain. The snow turned dark red, and the marks on the unhappy wretch seemed to become more visible, while he crept on, the picture of abject misery, trying to escape from the terrified glances of his fellow-travellers.

The souls of little children fluttered·in the air like little birds.

They were very numerous, and no wonder: the coarse food, the dirt, the open fireplaces, and the icy draughts of the *yourtas* killed the poor little things by hundreds. As they flew past the murderer his aspect frightened them; they fluttered away horror-stricken, and long afterwards the rustling of their little wings could be heard in the air.

Makar noticed that they, he and the priest moved with considerable quickness, and he ascribed this fact to his goodness. He drew near the priest and asked him: "Listen, my father, I have been, perhaps, a little too fond of the brandy-bottle in my time, but after all I was a good man. . . . What do you say? Do you not think that God loves me?" He watched the priest's face closely as he spoke, for he wanted to find out certain things from him.

But the priest only said, "Do not be proud. We are near our goal. You will soon know yourself."

Then Makar noticed that the plain seemed less dark. Rays of light darted forth from the east, extinguishing the bright stars. A golden mist rose over the snow-bound steppe, the sun was veiled for a second—then he burst forth in all his glory, flooding the plain with his golden light. Suddenly Makar thought that he heard a beautiful but strange song. It was the same hymn with which the earth greets the rising sun every day. Only Makar had never heeded it hitherto, and this was the first time in all his life that he understood how beautiful the song was. He stood still to listen, and refused to go any further . . . he wanted to stand there, listening, for ever. . . .

But Father Ivan touched his arm, saying, "Let us go in. We have arrived."

And then only did Makar behold a big door which had been hid by the fogs. He would have preferred to remain without, but he obeyed the summons notwithstanding.

They entered a handsome, roomy *izba* (peasant house), in the centre of which stood a beautifully carved fireplace. It was made of pure silver, and in it burned a few golden logs, which diffused a pleasant warmth. Then only did Makar notice how cold it had been out of doors. The flame in this wonderful fireplace did not hurt the eyes, nor did it scorch the skin; it gave such an agreeable sensation of warmth that Makar would have liked to stand there warming himself for ever. Father Ivan walked up to the fireplace and stretched out his hands, which were benumbed with cold.

There were four doors in the *izba*: the door through which they had entered, and three others, which evidently led to other rooms. Several young men, dressed in long, white shirts, were constantly coming and going. Makar thought they were servants of the Taion. He vaguely remembered having seen them somewhere, but he could not exactly remember where. He was much struck by the fact that each lad had two large white wings folded on his back, and he said to himself that the Taion must have other servants besides these, because it was impossible to cut wood in the thicket with such a pair of wings. One of the serving-men walked up to the stove, and turning his back to the fire, he began the following conversation with Father Ivan:

"Speak out!"

"I have nothing to say," replied the priest.

"What did you hear in the world?"

"Nothing!"

"What did you see?"

"Nothing!"

Both were silent for a short time, then the priest observed, "I have brought someone with me."

"Is it a man from Chalgan?" asked the servant.

"Yes, he comes from Chalgan."

"In that case I must get the big scales." And he left the room.

In answer to Makar's question why he had gone to fetch the scales, and what was going to be weighed, the priest informed him, with an embarrassed air, that all his actions, both good and bad, which he had committed during his life were going to be weighed in those scales. As a rule, the number of good and bad actions was much the same, so that the scales were even with most people, but the inhabitants of Chalgan were such a wicked set that the Taion had a gigantic balance made on purpose to weigh all their sins.

Makar was not a little frightened on hearing these words. His heart quailed and his courage left him.

The servants came in carrying a huge balance. One scale was made of gold and was very small, the other was made of wood and was very large. As they arranged it on the floor the latter suddenly opened, and a large, black hole yawned beneath it. Makar immediately went up to see that the scales were in order. He did not understand them at all, and would have preferred another system with which he was well acquainted. He had used all his life the *bezmen*,[1] and knew sundry little tricks which turned the balance in his favour.

"The Taion comes!" said Father Ivan, smoothing down his robe.

The middle door opened, and the Taion entered the room. He was a very old man, with a beautiful silvery beard which reached to his waist. He was dressed in robes made of rich furs, and materials such as Makar had never seen, and wore warm boots, trimmed with plush, on his feet. Makar remembered having seen an old painter of ikons wearing similar boots. He saw at once that the Taion was the old man whose picture he had seen in the church. He was without his Son, who was, perhaps, away on some business of his own. A dove flew into the room, and, after fluttering for some time over the old man's head, settled down on his knee.

He sat down on a chair which had been prepared for him, stroking the bird tenderly. He had a kind face, and whenever Makar felt his heart grow too heavy, one glance at that face gave him new comfort.

His heart had grown heavy because he suddenly remembered his whole life down to the slightest incidents; he remembered each step, each stroke of his axe, each tree which he had cut down, and each time he had cheated another person, and each glass of brandy which he had drunk. And he felt frightened and ashamed, but one glance at the face of the old Taion comforted him, and as soon as he felt comforted he hoped to be able to hide some of his evil deeds. The old Taion looked at him for some time, and then asked him who he was, and where he came from, and how old he was. When

[1] A balance consisting of an arm with a hook on which the object which is going to be weighed is hung.

he had answered all those questions the old Taion asked him:

"What have you been doing during your life?"

"You know that as well as I do," retorted Makar. "I daresay you have got it all somewhere in your books." He only said so on purpose, because he wanted to find out if it was true that everything was written down.

"Tell me yourself," replied the old man.

And Makar began forthwith to enumerate all his works, and although he remembered perfectly well each tree he had cut down, and each furrow he had made with his plough, he added thousands of faggots, and hundreds of cartloads of wood, and hundreds of *pouds*[1] of corn for sowing.

When he had done the old Taion told the priest Ivan to fetch the book. Makar understood that the priest was secretary to the Taion. This made him very angry, because he might have dropped him a hint.

Father Ivan brought an immense book, opened it, and began to read.

"How many faggots did you say?" asked the old Taion.

The priest looked at the book and said, sadly, "He has added three thousand faggots."

"He lies!" shouted Makar angrily. "He must be mistaken, because he is a drunkard and died an ugly death."

"Hold your tongue!" said the old Taion. "Did he ever make you pay too much for your wedding, or your christenings? or did he force you to pay the tithes?"

"N-no," replied Makar.

"There, you see!" said the old Taion, growing angry. "I know myself that he was fond of the wine-glass. . . . Let me hear all his sins as they are put down in the book, because I no longer trust him, he is a cheat!"

Meanwhile the servants had weighed the faggots and the wood, and the ploughing and sowing—in short, all his works. There was such a heap of them that the golden scale went

[1] A *poud* is about thirty-six English pounds.

down, while the wooden flew so high that the young serving-men were obliged to fly up and tie a rope to it so that it could be pulled down again.

And Father Ivan went on reading his sins. He had cheated 21,933 times, and drunk four hundred bottles of vodka. And as he read, Makar saw the wooden scale going down till it reached the hole. He was afraid lest it might disappear altogether, and drawing near he tried secretly to keep it up with his foot. But one of the serving-men caught him in the act, and they made a great noise.

"What is the matter?" asked the old Taion. And when he had been told he turned angrily towards Makar, saying, "I see that you are a cheat, a lazy fellow, and a drunkard! You have not paid all your debts, you have left the tithe unpaid, and you cause the *ispravnik*[1] to sin by making him swear at you!" Then he asked of the priest what man in Chalgan was cruellest to his horses, and laid too heavy loads on them.

Ivan the priest answered: "The Elder of the Church. He keeps the post-horses and drives the *ispravnik*."

"Let this lazy wretch become one of his horses," said the Taion. "He shall draw the *ispravnik's* carriage till he can work no more. . . . After that we will see. . . ."

He had hardly finished speaking when the door opened, and his Son came into the room and sat down at his right hand. He said: "I heard your sentence. . . . I have lived long in the world, and I know it well: it will be very hard on that poor wretch to draw the *ispravnik's* carriage. . . . Well . . . be it so. . . . Yet, he has perhaps something to say for himself! Speak, my poor man!"

And then something wonderful happened. Makar, who in all his life had never been able to say ten words, had suddenly become eloquent. He was no longer afraid, and the old Taion, who had been angry at first, listened to him wonder-ingly. The priest tried to keep him quiet, and pulled him by his coat-tails, but Makar shook him off impatiently, **and**

[1]Head police officer and chief of the district.

the priest listened with a pleased smile to his parishioner's speech, and he saw that the old Taion liked it too. And the serving-men in their white robes and wings came running to the door from the inner department, and listened wonderingly to Makar's bold speech, nudging each other whenever anything struck them.

He began by saying that he did not want to become a horse and belong to the Elder of the Church: not because he feared the work, but because the sentence was unjust. And he was not going to obey it—not if he were given up to the devils. He was not afraid of being a horse; for if the Elder overworked his horses he fed them with oats. Now, he had been overworked all his life, but had never had the oats afterwards.

"Who overworked you?" asked the old Taion.

Who? Why, everybody did so all his life through. The *ispravniki* and justices and *starostas* were always clamouring for their taxes, and the priests for their tithes. Hunger and misery had driven him hither and thither; he had suffered from the drought in summer and the cold in the bitter winter time; the *taiga* and the frozen soil that brought forth nothing. He had lived like the cattle who are always being driven on and do not know where they are going. . . . Did he know what the priest was saying in church, and why he wanted the tithes? Did he know what had become of his eldest son, who had been taken as a soldier? He did not know where he died, nor in what corner his poor bones were mouldering! They reproached him with drinking four hundred bottles of vodka. Did they know what kind of vodka it was? Three-quarters of it were water, and one quarter was vodka in which tobacco had been distilled to make it stronger. Therefore they might boldly strike off three hundred bottles.

"Is this true?" asked the Taion of the priest.

"It is the truth," replied the latter, hurriedly.

And Makar went on:—He had added three thousand faggots. Perhaps so. He had made only sixteen thousand. Was that not enough? He had made two thousand faggots when

his first wife was lying ill . . . his heart was heavy, he longed
to sit by his sick wife, but he was obliged to go to work in the
taiga. . . . And there he had wept bitterly, and his tears
had frozen to his eyelashes, and his very heart was freezing
within his body. And he had gone on working. His wife
died. She must be buried, but he had no money. And he
hired himself out to a merchant as a woodcutter to be able to
pay for his wife's last house. . . . The merchant knew that he
was poor, and gave him only two kopecks for each load.
. . . And meanwhile his dead wife was lying alone in the
cold *izba* while he was cutting wood and weeping bitterly.
Surely these loads of wood were worth five times their value!

There were tears in the eyes of the old Taion, and Makar
saw that the scales moved: the wooden one rose, while the
golden one sank.

And Makar went on speaking. Everything was put down
in their books, they said. Would they just look if he had ever
been caressed and petted by anyone, or had a pleasure in all
his life? Where were his children? If they died young he
mourned for them, but when they grew up they left him to
struggle through life alone. He had grown old alone with
his second wife, and had felt old age creeping on slowly,
his strength leave him, and looked hideous poverty in the
face. They were alone, alone like two lonely fir trees in the
prairie that are scourged by the cruel snow-storms.

And again the Taion asked: "Is this true?" And the priest
answered: "It is perfectly true!"

The scales trembled again . . . but the old Taion was lost
in thought.

"How is this?" said he. "There are good people still
living on the earth. Their eyes are bright, and their faces
shine, and their robes are spotless . . . their hearts are as
tender as good soil; they receive the good seed, and bring
forth beautiful fruit, and the perfume is sweet in my nostrils.
Look at yourself. . . ."

All eyes were turned towards Makar, who felt ashamed of

his appearance. He knew that his eyes were not bright, and his face was begrimed, his hair and beard matted and tangled, and his clothes torn. True, he had been thinking of buying a pair of boots before his death, in order to appear at the judgment-seat as behoves an honest peasant. But he had always spent the money on drink, and now he stood before the Taion in ragged shoes, like the last of the Yakouts. . . . He would gladly have sunk under the ground.

"Thy face is dark," went on the Taion; "thy eyes are not bright, and thy clothes are torn. And thy heart is overgrown with weeds and thorns. That is the reason why I love mine own that are pure and good and holy, and turn my face away from such as you are. . . ."

Makar's heart was ready to break. He felt ashamed of his existence. He hung his head, but suddenly lifted it and began to speak again.

Who were those just and good men the Taion was speaking about? If he meant those who were living in fine palaces on the earth at the same time as Makar did, he knew them well enough. . . . Their eyes were bright because they had not shed as many tears as he had, and their faces shone because they were bathed in perfume, and their clean garments had been wrought by other people's hands. Did he not see that he too had been born like the others with bright open eyes, in which heaven and earth were reflected as in a mirror, and with a pure heart which was ready to take in all that was beautiful in the world? And if he longed now to hide his wretched self under the ground, it was no fault of his . . . he did not know whose it was . . . all he knew was that all the patience had died in his heart.

If Makar had seen the effect which his speech had produced on the old Taion, and that every word he said fell on the golden scale like a weight of lead, his rebellious heart would have been soothed. But he saw nothing, because his heart was full of blind despair.

He thought of his past life which had been so hard. How had he been able to bear it so long? He had borne it because the star of hope had shone through the darkness. And now the star had vanished, and the hope was dead. . . . Darkness fell on his soul, and a storm rose in it like the storm-wind which flies across the steppe in the dead of night. He forgot where he was, before whom he stood—forgot everything except his anger.

But the old Taion said to him: "Wait, poor man! You are no longer on earth. There is justice for you here."

Makar trembled. He felt that they pitied him, and his heart was softened, and as he thought of his wretched life he burst into tears, weeping over himself. The old Taion wept too . . . and so did the old Father Ivan, and tears flowed from the eyes of the young serving-men, and they wiped them with their wide sleeves.

And the scales trembled, and the wooden scale rose higher and higher!

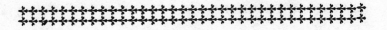

VSEVOLOD GARSHIN
(1855–1888)

✥

(I)

FOUR DAYS

(Translated by HELEN MATHESON)

I REMEMBER how we ran through the wood, how the bullets whistled, how the broken branches fell, how we pushed through the hawthorn bushes. On the edge of the wood something red appeared, darting hither and thither. Sidorov, of the first company ("How does he come to be in our detachment?" flashed through my mind), suddenly squatted on the ground and looked at me with big, frightened eyes. A stream of blood poured from his mouth. Yes, I remember it all perfectly. And I remember that on the edge, among the bushes, I saw—*him*. He was a big, fat Turk, but I ran straight at him though I was thin and puny. Something crashed, something enormous, as it seemed to me, whizzed past me, there was a ringing in my ears. "He is shooting at me," I thought. But, with a cry of terror, he tried to press back into the bush. He might have gone round it, but he was so frightened that he forgot everything and thrust himself into the thorny branches. With one blow, I knocked the rifle from his hand, and then I plunged my bayonet into him. I heard something like a roar or a groan. Then I dashed on. Our men were crying "Hurrah," they were firing, falling. I remember firing several shots when I emerged from the wood into the open. Suddenly the hurrahs grew much louder, and we all pressed forward. At least, not "we," but our men, for I remained. This seemed very

476

strange, but stranger still was the fact that everything was unexpectedly blotted out; the firing, the shouting, were silenced. I heard nothing. I saw only something blue— probably the sky. Then that, too, disappeared.

I have never been in such a strange position. I seem to be lying on my stomach, and can see nothing but a tiny patch of earth. A few blades of grass, an ant crawling upside down along one of them, wisps of dried leaves from last year—that constitutes my whole world. And I can only see it with one eye, because something hard is pressing on the other, probably the branch on which my head is resting. I am frightfully uncomfortable and I want to move, and cannot understand why I am unable to do so. Time passes. I hear the chirruping of grasshoppers, the buzz of bees, and nothing more. At last, making an effort, I free my right arm from beneath my body, and, leaning on the earth with both hands, I try to raise myself to a kneeling posture.

Something sharp, and as rapid as lightning, penetrates my whole body from my knees to my chest, to my head. I fall back again, and again all is darkness, oblivion.

I awaken. Why do I see stars shining brightly in the blue-black Bulgarian sky? Am I not in my tent? Why did I leave it? I move and feel an agonising pain in my legs.

Yes, I have been wounded in battle. Dangerously or not? I touch the place that hurts. Both legs are covered with congealed blood. When I touch them the pain increases. The pain is like toothache, constant, soul-destroying. My ears buzz, my head is heavy. I realise dimly that I am wounded in both legs. But what has happened? Why have I not been picked up? Is it possible that the Turks have beaten us? I try to recall all that has happened to me, at first hazily, then more and more clearly, and I reach the conclusion that we cannot have been beaten. Because I fell on the open space at the top of the hill. (I did not actually remember this; but I remembered how they all rushed forward while I could not run and could see nothing but a patch of blue.) It had been pointed out to us earlier by our short company commander. "Boys, we shall be there," he had cried in his ringing voice, and we were there, so we were not beaten. Then why had I not been picked up? It is an open space. Everything on it is visible. And I cannot be the only one here, the firing was so fierce. I must turn my head and look around. It is easier to do this now, because, on coming to, when I saw the grass and the ant crawling upside down, I had tried to get up and had fallen again, but not as before face downwards, but on my back. That is why I can see the stars.

I raise myself and sit up. It is very difficult to do this when both legs are wounded. Despair overwhelms me more than once, but eventually I achieve it, though my eyes are full of tears from the acute pain. Above me a speck of blue-black sky in which one bright star and several small ones are shining. All around me something tall, dark—bushes! I am in the bushes; they have not noticed me!

I feel my hair stand on end.

But however did I get into the bushes when they shot me in the open? I must have crawled here wounded, stunned by pain. How strange that I should have been able to do that, whereas now I cannot move. Perhaps I had only one wound then, and the second got me when I was already in the bushes.

Pale flashes of pink appear, the bright star fades, some of the small ones disappear—the moon is rising. How lovely it must be at home!

Strange sounds reach me. It is as though someone were groaning. Is there someone near me, forgotten like me, with broken legs or a bullet in his stomach? No, the groans are quite close, but there is no one. Great heavens! It is I, I myself. Low, pitiful moans; does it really hurt as much as that? I suppose it does, but I cannot grasp it because my head is confused and as heavy as lead.

I had better lie down again and go to sleep, sleep, sleep. . . . Shall I ever wake up? What does it matter?

Just at the moment when I am getting ready to lie down, a broad, pale moonbeam lights up the place, and I notice something dark and big lying within a few yards of me. Small, bright specks are lit by the moon—that must be buttons or ammunition. It is either a corpse or a wounded man. I don't care, I shall lie down . . .

No, it is impossible. Our men have not gone. They are here. They beat the Turks and retained the position. Why do I not hear voices, the crackle of camp fires? Surely because I am too weak to hear. They must be here.

"Help! Help——!"

Wild, mad hoarse cries tear themselves from my chest, but there is no answer. They resound loudly in the night air. All the rest is silence except for the crickets that chirrup as incessantly as before. The round-faced moon looks down at me pityingly.

If *he* were wounded, such cries would awaken him. He is a corpse. Ours or the Turks'? Good God, what does it matter? Sleep once again closes my burning eyes.

I lie with my eyes closed, though I have been awake for some time. I do not want to open them, because, through my closed lids I can feel the sunlight, and if I open them it will hurt them. Besides, it is better not to move. . . . Yesterday (I think it was yesterday) I was wounded. A day has passed, others will pass, and I shall die. It doesn't matter. Better not to move, let the body stay still. How good it would be to stop the brain from working; but nothing will stop that. My head is full of thoughts and memories. However, it cannot last long, the end will soon come. Nothing will remain except a few lines in a newspaper to the effect that our losses were light: so many wounded, and one volunteer, Private Ivanov, killed. No, they won't put in the name, they will simply say: "one killed." One soldier, just as one might say—one dog. A whole picture rises vividly before my mind's eye. It is of something a long time ago, but all, all my life, all *that* life, before lying here with broken legs, was a long time ago. . . . I am walking along a street, and am stopped by a crowd. It stands silently staring at something white, covered with blood and howling piteously. It is a pretty little dog that has been run over by a tram. It is dying, just as I am dying now. A hall-porter pushes through the crowd, lifts the dog by the scruff of its neck and carries it away. The crowd disperses.

Will anyone carry me away? No, lie here and die. And how lovely life is! That day, the day the accident happened to the dog, I was happy. I walked as though I were intoxicated, and with good reason. Oh, memories, leave me, do not torment me! The happiness of the past, the horror of the present! . . . Better simply suffer the pain, better avoid the torment of memories which evoke comparisons. Oh, anguish, anguish, you are worse than wounds!

It is becoming hot, the sun is burning. I open my eyes and see the same bushes, the same sky, but by daylight, and—there is my neighbour. Yes, it is a Turk, a corpse. How enormous he is. I recognise him, it is he——

Before me lies a man that I have killed. Why did I kill him? He lies there dead, bloody. Why did Fate drive him here? Who is he? Perhaps, like me, he has an old mother? For a long time she will sit at the door of her poor mud hut, gazing northward, waiting: is her darling, her support, her breadwinner, coming? And I? I also—I would change places with him. He is happy, he hears nothing, he feels no pain from his wounds, no deadly anguish, no thirst. My bayonet pierced his heart. There is a big, black hole in his chest, and all around it is blood. *I did that.*

I did not want to. When I went to fight I had no wish to hurt anyone. The thought that I should have to kill escaped me. In my imaginings I only saw myself offering my own chest to the bullets. I went and I offered it.

And then what? Fool, fool! But this wretched fellaheen (he wore an Egyptian uniform) is even less to blame than I am. He had never even heard of Russia or Bulgaria until, with others, he was packed on the boat like a herring in a barrel, and carried off to Constantinople. He was ordered to go, and he went. Had he refused to go, he would have been beaten with sticks or shot by a bullet from some pasha's revolver. He had made long, difficult marches from Stamboul to Rustchuk. We attacked, they defended themselves. But seeing that we, horrible people, were unafraid of his patent English Peabody and Martini gun, seeing that we continued to advance, he became terrified. When he wanted to run away, a small man, whom he could have killed with one blow of his black fist, sprang towards him and plunged a bayonet into his heart. How was he to blame?

And how was I to blame, although I had killed him? How was I to blame? Why am I tortured by thirst? Thirst! Who knows what that word means? Even when we were going through Roumania, doing fifty-verst marches with the thermometer at 105 degrees, even then I never experienced anything like this. Oh, if only someone would come! Good God! There must be water in that great canteen of his. Only, I have got to get to him, and what will that cost? But I will get to him for all that.

I crawl, my legs dragging, my arms barely able to move, my body inert. The corpse is about a dozen yards away, but for me that is further, or rather it is worse, than a dozen miles. Still, I must crawl. My throat is burning, parched as if by fire. One dies more quickly without water. Still, perhaps—and I crawl. My feet catch in the ground, and every movement causes excruciating pain. I moan. I scream, but I still crawl on. At last I reach him. There is the canteen, there is water in it, a lot of water! It is more than half full. Ah, the water will last me a long time, to my death!

You have saved me, my victim! Leaning on one elbow, I begin to unfasten the canteen, when suddenly I lose my balance and fall, face downward, on my saviour's chest. The body already has a strong, cadaverous smell.

I drink. The water is warm but untainted, and, above all, there is a lot of it. I shall live several days more. I remember reading in *The Physiology of Everyday Life* that a man can live for over a week so long as he has water. And in the same book there was an account of a man who committed suicide by starvation. He lived a long time because he drank.

Well, what about it? If I live five, six days more, what does it matter? Our men have gone. The Bulgarians have run away. There is no road anywhere near. I shall die all the same. Only, instead of three days' agony I am making it a week. Would it not be better to make an end of it? My neighbour's gun lies by his side, an excellent English gun. I need only stretch out my hand, then—a moment, and all is over. A heap of cartridges lie spilled on the ground, those that he had not had time to use.

Well, shall I end it all? Or shall I wait? What for? Rescue? Death? Wait till the Turks come and begin to skin my wounded legs? Better do it myself. No, I must not lose heart, I will struggle to the end, to my last breath. Once they find me, I am saved.

Perhaps my bones are whole; they may make me well. I shall see my country again, my mother, Masha—— Lord, don't let them ever learn all the truth. Let them think that I was slain outright. What would happen to them if they learnt that I suffered for two, three, four days!

My head swims. The journey to my neighbour has utterly exhausted me. And now there is this fearful stench. He is all black. What will he be like to-morrow or next day? I am lying here only because I have not strength enough to drag myself away. I will rest a little, and then crawl back to my old place. Luckily the wind is coming from that direction and will carry the smell from me. I lie there completely worn out. The sun burns my face and my hands. There is nothing to cover myself with. I long for the night—it will be the second one, I think.

My thoughts become confused, and I doze off.

I must have been asleep for a long time, because when I wake it is night. Everything is just as it was: my wounds hurt, my neighbour lies there, huge, motionless. I cannot help thinking about him. Is it possible that I left all that is near and dear to me, that I travelled a thousand versts to join this campaign, that I hungered, froze, burned in the heat, and, finally, is it possible that I lie here now, suffering this agony, in order that that poor fellow might cease to live? But, apart from this murder, what have I done to further our military aims?

Murder? Murderer? Who? I!

When I made up my mind to join up, mother and Masha did not dissuade me, though they wept over me. I was blinded by my idea, and did not notice their tears. I did not understand (but I understand now) what I was doing to those nearest to me. But why recall all this? The past cannot be undone. How strangely some of my acquaintances acted to my enlistment. "What a crank, taking on a job he knows nothing about." How could they say that? How could they reconcile such words with their own notions of heroism and patriotism? In *their* eyes I was possessed of all those virtues, and yet I was a "crank."

I am off to Kishinev; I am laden with a haversack and various military implements. I wait, together with thousands, among whom only a few are going, like myself, of their own free will. The rest would have stayed at home if they had been allowed. Nevertheless, they go, just as we go, "conscientiously" marching thousands of miles and fighting, as well as, or better than, we do. They do their duty although they would chuck it all and go home if that were permitted.

A strong morning breeze springs up. The bushes rustle, a sleepy bird flies out. The stars fade. The dark sky pales and is covered with soft fleecy clouds. A grey mist rises from the ground. It is the beginning of my third day of—what shall I call it? Life? Or agony?

The third—— How many more will there be? In any case, not many. I am very weak, and unable to move further from the corpse. We shall soon be alike, and cease to be unpleasant to one another.

I must drink. I am going to drink three times a day, morning, noon and evening.

The sun has risen. Its enormous disc, streaked and veined by the black hawthorn branches, is as red as blood. It looks as though the day would be hot. Neighbour mine, what will happen to you? Even now the smell is terrible.

Yes, he is appalling. His hair is coming out, his skin, naturally dark, has become pallid and so tightly stretched over the swollen yellowish face that it has cracked behind the ears. He is crawling with maggots. His calves, encased in tight gaiters, are swollen, and there are enormous blisters in the spaces between the buttons. He is so inflated that he looks mountainous. What will the sun do to him to-day?

It is insufferable to lie so close to him. I must crawl further from him at any cost. But can I do it? I can still raise my hand, open the canteen and drink; but move my heavy, inert body? Still, I will move, however little at a time, if only half a yard an hour.

The whole morning is occupied in making this change of place. The pain is bad, but what does that matter now? I can no longer remember, I cannot even imagine, what it is like to feel well. I seem inured to pain. I actually manage that morning to crawl about half a dozen yards; and find myself back at my old place. But I do not enjoy the fresh air for long, if the air can be called fresh at a distance of six yards from a decaying corpse. The wind changes, and once more blows the dreadful smell towards me, and it is so strong that I feel sick. My empty stomach contracts in painful spasms, everything inside me seems to be turned. The stink-infected air blows in my face. Giving way to despair, I weep.

Broken, stunned, I lie there unconscious. Suddenly—— Is it the delusion of a disordered brain? I seem to hear—— No,—yes—I hear voices, human voices and the tramping of horses' hoofs. I nearly scream, but I restrain myself. What if they are Turks? What would happen if they were? To all my other sufferings, other, more terrible, torture would be added, the mere thought of which makes my hair stand on end. They would tear off the skin and roast my wounded legs—— And it would be well if that were all, they are so ingenious. Would it really be better to meet death at their hands than to die here?

But what if they were ours? Oh, cursed bushes, why do you surround me so thickly? I can see nothing through them, except at one place where there is a gap in the boughs and I get a glimpse of a distant dell. I seem to remember a stream in that dell at which we drank before the battle. Yes, and there is the enormous slab of sandstone thrown across the stream to make a bridge. They are certain to ride over that stone. The voices die down. I cannot distinguish the language, my hearing is failing too. God! If they are ours—— I will shout, and even from the stream they will hear me. Better that than risk falling into the hands of the Bashibazouks.

Why are they so long in coming? I am sick with impatience. I no longer notice the stench of the corpse, though it has not diminished.

And suddenly Cossacks appear at the crossing over the stream. Blue uniforms, red braiding, lances. There is half a squadron of them. In front of them is a black-bearded officer astride a magnificent horse. No sooner have the men crossed the stream than the officer turns right round in his saddle and shouts:

"Tro-o-o-t! Ma-a-arch!"

"Stop, stop, for God's sake. Help, brothers, help!" I cry.

But the tramping of the horses, the rattle of swords, the noisy chatter of the Cossacks, drown my hoarse voice. They do not hear me. Oh, damnation! Utterly exhausted, I bury my face in the ground and sob. The water trickles from the canteen which I have upset, the water which is my life, my salvation, my only respite from death. But I do not notice it until there is only about half a glassful left; the rest has soaked into the greedy, parched earth.

How can I describe the torpor which overwhelmed me after this frightful incident? I lie motionless, with half-closed eyes. The wind is for ever changing, now bringing a breath of pure freshness, then enveloping me in stench. My neighbour that day was horrible beyond description. Once when I opened my eyes and glanced at him, I was filled with revulsion. There was no face, the flesh had gone from the bone, leaving a terrible, perpetual grin which horrified and disgusted me, although I had often held skulls in my hands and had dissected heads. That skeleton in a uniform with shining buttons made me shudder. "This is war," I thought, "and that is its emblem."

The sun is as scorching hot as ever. My hands and face had long ago been grilled. I drank the remaining water to the last drop. I was so tortured by thirst that, having decided to take a sip, I swallowed it all at one gulp. Oh, why had I not shouted to the Cossacks when they were near? Even if they had been Turks, it would have been better than this. They would have tortured me for an hour or two, but, as it is, I do not know how long I may have to lie here and suffer.

Mother mine! Darling mother! You will tear your grey

hair, you will beat your head against the wall, you will curse the day you gave birth to me, you will curse the world which invented war to torture mankind.

But you and Masha will probably never hear of my sufferings. Good-bye, mother; good-bye, my bride, my love. Oh, how hard, how bitter, it all is. My heart fails me——

Again that little white dog! The hall-porter had no mercy, he dashed its head against a wall and threw it into the sewer into which the slops and garbage are thrown. But it was alive. And it suffered a whole day. Miserable wretch that I am, I have already suffered for three days. To-morrow will be the fourth, then the fifth, the sixth—— Death, where are you? Come to me, take me, take me!

But death does not come, does not take me. And I lie under this terrible sun, and I have not a single mouthful of water to moisten my burning throat, and the corpse infects me. It is a mass of putrefaction. Myriads of maggots drop from it. How they swarm! And only the mere form is left. When he is completely devoured, and nothing remains but bones and a uniform—it will be my turn. I shall become like that.

The day passes, and the night. Everything is just as it was. Dawn breaks, and still it is the same. The day drags on——

The bushes stir and rustle as though whispering, "You will die, you will die, you will die."

And the bushes opposite seem to answer, "You won't see, you won't see, you won't see."

"Why, you won't be able to see them here," says a loud voice close to me.

I regain consciousness with a start.

Takovlev, our lance-corporal, is looking down at me through the bush with his kind blue eyes.

"Spades," he cries; "there are two more here; one of ours and one of theirs."

I want to cry out, "You must not bring spades, you must not bury me, I am alive." But only a low moan escapes from my dry lips.

"Good Lord, is it possible that he is alive? It is Ivanov. Here, boys, quick. Our young gentleman is alive. Fetch the doctor."

A moment later, water, vodka and something else is being poured down my throat. Then all is darkness.

The stretcher sways rhythmically, and the rhythm soothes me. I wake for a moment, and lose consciousness again. My dressed wounds do not pain me. An inexpressible feeling of joy fills my whole being.

"Sto-o-p! Lo-o-wer! Bearers of the Fourth Squad, march! Take the stretcher, lift it, go!" The orders are given by Peter Ivanovitch, our Red Cross officer, a tall, thin, kindly man, so tall that if I turn my eyes towards him I can see his head and shoulders although the stretcher is being carried on the shoulders of four big men.

"Peter Ivanovitch," I whisper.

"What is it, sweetheart?" Peter Ivanovitch bends over me.

"Peter Ivanovitch, what did the doctor tell you? Shall I soon die?"

"Nonsense, Ivanov. You're not going to die. All your bones are whole. Lucky fellow, no bones and no arteries. But how on earth did you live those three and a half days? What did you eat?"

"Nothing."

"And drink?"

"I took the Turk's water-bottle. I can't talk now, Peter Ivanovitch; later——"

"All right, God be with you, sweetheart, go to sleep again."

Again sleep and unconsciousness.

I wake up in the Divisional Hospital. Doctors and nurses surround me, and among them I distinguish the face of a celebrated Petersburg surgeon, who is bending over my feet.

There is blood on his hands. He busies himself with my legs
for a moment and then looks at me:

"Well, you may thank God for your luck. You will live.
We've had to take one foot away, but that's nothing. Can
you talk?"

I can, and I tell them all that I have written here.

(II)

THE CRIMSON FLOWER

(IN MEMORY OF IVAN SERGEEVITCH TURGENIEV)

(Translated by ROSA GRAHAM)

I

"IN the name of his Imperial Majesty, the Sovereign Emperor Peter the First, I give notice that this lunatic asylum
is to be inspected."

These words were spoken in a loud, harsh, ringing tone.
The secretary of the hospital, who was seated at an ink-
spattered table, writing down particulars about the sick person in a large tattered register, could not refrain from smiling.
But the two young people who accompanied the invalid did
not laugh: they could hardly stand on their feet after two
whole days' sleepless journeying, alone with the madman
whom they had just brought here by train. At the last
stopping-place but one their companion's madness had got
worse; they had procured a strait-jacket from somewhere or
other, and with the help of conductors and a gendarme had
put it on him. In this way they had brought him to the
town, and arrived at the hospital.

He looked awful. Over his grey suit, which had been torn
to rags in his mad fits, was a short jacket of coarse sail-cloth

of a very large size. This was wrapped round his body, and its long sleeves kept his crossed arms close to his breast and were tied in a knot behind his back. His bloodshot, staring eyes (he had not slept for ten days) shone with a steady burning brilliance, his lower lip was trembling nervously, his tangled curly hair fell mane-like on his forehead; he walked with a quick heavy step from corner to corner of the office, looking inquisitively at the old cupboards and books and oilcloth-covered chairs, rarely turning his glance upon his fellow-travellers.

"Take him into the annexe. On the right."

"I know, I know. I was here with you last year. We inspected the hospital. I know all about it, and it will be difficult to deceive me," said the sick man.

He turned towards the doors. The warder opened them for him, and with the same quick, heavy, decided step, holding his mad head high, he went out of the office and almost at a run turned to the right towards the section for the mentally-afflicted patients. His companions could hardly keep up with him.

"Ring the bell. I cannot. You have tied up my arms."

A porter opened the door, and the travellers went into the hospital.

It was a large stone building of an old government-office type. Two large rooms—one the dining-room, the other a common room for the quieter patients—a broad corridor with glass doors leading into the flower-garden; and twenty-two separate rooms for the sick people, occupied the lower story. There were also two darkened rooms, one with plank walls, the other padded, where they put the obstreperous patients, and an immense room, arched and gloomy—the bathroom.

The upper story was occupied by women. A noise of disorder, mingled with howlings and wailing, came thence. The hospital had been built to accommodate eighty patients, but because it was the only one for several neighbouring provinces, they took up to three hundred. Each small room had four or five beds in it, and in the winter-time, when the patients were not allowed to go into the garden and all the windows behind their iron bars were tightly closed, the air of the place was intolerably smelly and close.

The new patient was taken into the bathroom. This room would have made a gloomy impression upon a healthy person, but to anyone whose mind was disturbed and excited it must have appeared much worse. It was a large vaulted room with a slippery stone floor, lighted by only one window in a corner; the walls and arches were painted a dark red colour. The floor was black with dirt, and two stone baths on a level with it looked like two oval pits filled with water. A large copper stove with a cylindrical boiler for heating the water and a whole system of copper pipes and taps occupied the corner opposite the window. To a disordered mind the whole place would appear as extraordinarily gloomy and fantastic, and the man in charge, a Little Russian, thick-set and taciturn, had a look which intensified this impression of gloom.

When the patient was brought into this terrible room to be bathed, and, in accordance with the doctor's method, to have a large blister applied to the nape of his neck, he was terrified and enraged. His head was dizzy with absurdities, each more monstrous than the other. What's this? The Inquisition? A place of secret execution, where his enemies had decided to make an end of him? Perhaps it was hell? He concluded that it must be a place of torture. They undressed him in spite of his desperate struggles. With the double strength of madness he easily tore himself away from several warders and threw them down. It took four men to overcome him finally, and, gripping him by his arms and legs they dropped him into a warm bath. He thought it was boiling water, and through his crazy brain rushed disconnected thoughts of ordeal by red-hot iron and scalding water.

Choking and spluttering, he struggled convulsively to free his limbs from the grasp of the warders. Gasping, and babbling senselessly, he gabbled and shouted, and no one could understand a word of it. There were prayers and there were curses. He shouted till he had no strength left, and then at last, quietly, with warm tears in his eyes, he uttered a sentence which was entirely unconnected with his previous railings.

"O holy and mighty martyr Saint George! Into thy hands I give up my body. But my soul—no, oh no . . .!"

The warders were still holding him though he had ceased to struggle. The warm bath and the ice-bag on his head were having effect. Yet when at last he was taken out of the water almost unconscious, a remnant of strength and insanity showed itself, and he burst forth again.

"For what reason? For what reason?" he shouted. "I've never wished evil to anyone. Why do you want to kill me? Oh-o-o! O God! Oh, all you who have been martyred before me! I beseech you, deliver me. . . ."

The burning touch of the blister on his neck caused him to struggle desperately. The attendants could not cope with him and did not know what to do.

"We can't go on with it," said the soldier who had applied the blister; "we'll have to take it off."

These simple words made the patient shudder. "Take it off! Take what off? Take whom off? Me?" he whispered, and in mortal terror closed his eyes. The soldier took a rough towel by both ends and rubbed it violently and rapidly across the back of the patient's neck, wrenching away the blister and a layer of skin with it—leaving a raw red wound. The pain of this operation would have been intolerable for anyone who was self-possessed and healthy, but to the madman it seemed like the end of everything. His whole body lurched in desperate physical fright, and he tore himself from the warders' hands. He ran naked across the stone floor. He thought they had just cut off his head, and that he wished to cry but could not. He was taken to his bed in an unconscious condition and there fell into a prolonged and death-like stupor.

II

He woke up in the night. Everything was quiet; he could hear the breathing of the people sleeping in the adjoining room. From a distance came the sound of a patient talking to himself in a terrible monotone—shut up for the night in one of the dark rooms. Upstairs a woman was singing a wild song in a hoarse contralto. The sick man listened attentively to these noises. He felt strangely weak and exhausted. His neck ached terribly.

"Where am I? What's the matter with me?" he thought. And suddenly with extraordinary clearness he remembered his life of the past month—and understood that he was ill and what was the matter with him. He remembered a host of absurd thoughts, words and deeds, and his whole being shuddered at the recollection.

"But it's come to an end, glory be to God; it's come to an end," he muttered, and fell asleep again.

The open window with an iron grating looked on to a little lane between high buildings and stone walls. No one ever came into this lane, and it was all overgrown with wild bushes and lilacs, in full flower at this time of the year. . . . Behind the bushes, exactly opposite the window, was the high wall of a garden, above which could be seen the tops of tall trees bathed in the light of the moon. To the right rose the white walls of the hospital with its iron-barred windows lighted up from the inside; to the left the dull walls of the mortuary gleamed white in the moonlight. The moonlight fell also across the iron grating of the window and into the room, illuminating the floor and part of the bed and the tortured pale face of the sick man, who lay with his eyes closed. Now he was not insane at all. He was sleeping the heavy dreamless sleep of a worn-out man, lying perfectly still and almost without breathing. For a few moments he woke to full consciousness, as if he were quite sane, only to get up in the morning as mad as before.

III

"How are you to-day?" the doctor asked him next morning. The sick man, only just awake, was still lying under the bed-clothes.

"Splendid!" said he, jumping out of bed and putting on his dressing-gown and slippers. "There's only one thing—look!"

He pointed to the back of his neck.

"I can't turn my head without pain. But it doesn't matter. Everything's all right, if one understands it, and I do understand."

"You know where you are?"

"Of course I do, doctor. I'm in the lunatic asylum. But you see, if one understands, it's absolutely all the same. It's absolutely all the same."

The doctor looked fixedly into his eyes. His handsome well-fed face, his excellently-combed golden beard, his calm blue eyes behind gold-rimmed spectacles—his whole countenance was immobile and inscrutable. He was observing.

"Why do you look at me so earnestly? You cannot read what is in my soul," continued the sick man. "But I can read yours quite clearly. Why do you do evil? Why have you gathered together this crowd of unfortunates and shut them up here? It doesn't matter to me. I understand it all, and I don't worry; but what about them? Why must they suffer? To a man who has a great idea in his mind—a universal idea—it's all the same where he lives and what he feels—or even whether he lives or doesn't live. . . . Isn't it so?"

"Yes, perhaps," answered the doctor, sitting down on a chair in a corner so as to watch the invalid, who was now walking rapidly from corner to corner of his room, shuffling along in his immense horse-leather slippers and letting his striped and flowered cotton dressing-gown wave from side to side as he walked.

The doctor's assistant and an inspector who had come with him stood erect in the doorway.

"And I have this idea," exclaimed the patient. "When I came upon it, I felt as if I were born again. My senses became keener, and my brain worked better than ever before. What formerly I only reached after a great deal of logical reasoning and guess-work, I now understand intuitively. I have attained that which is the conclusion of philosophy. I am experiencing in myself this great idea— that space and time are fictions. I am living in all ages. I am living outside space—everywhere or nowhere, just as I like. And so it makes no difference to me whether you keep me here or whether you let me go; whether I am bound or free. I have noticed that there are several others here like me. But for the rest of the crowd such a position is terrible. Why don't you set them free? Who wants . . .?"

"You said," interrupted the doctor, "that you were living outside space and time. But you must agree, nevertheless, that you and I are in this room and that it is now" (the doctor looked at his watch) "half-past ten o'clock on the sixth of May, in the year eighteen hundred and something. What do you make of that?"

"That doesn't matter. It's just the same to me where I may be or when I live. If it's all the same to *me*, doesn't that mean that I am everywhere and always?"

The doctor laughed.

"That's unusual logic," said he, getting up. "Perhaps you're right. Good-bye. Wouldn't you like a cigar?"

"Thank you." The patient stood still, took the cigar, and nervously bit off the end of it. "It helps one to think," said he. "This world is the microcosm. On the one hand— alkalies; on the other—acids. Such is the equilibrium in the world, that opposing elements neutralise each other. Good-bye, doctor."

The doctor went on to visit other patients. The majority of these were awaiting him, standing by their beds. No official receives such respect from his subordinates as a doctor-psychiatrist gets from his madmen.

The sick man, now left by himself, strode nervously from corner to corner of his room. Tea was brought to him, and, without sitting down, he drank off in two gulps the contents of a large mug, and almost in an instant ate the large slice of white bread that accompanied it. Then he left his room and for some hours ceaselessly tramped with his quick, heavy step from one end of the building to the other.

The weather was wet and the patients were not allowed to go into the garden. When the doctor's assistant came in search of the new patient he was pointed out at the end of the corridor. He was standing there with his face pressed against the glass doors leading into the garden, staring at the flowers. His attention was attracted to an unusually bright crimson flower—a kind of poppy.

"Please come and be weighed," said the assistant, tapping him on the shoulder. But when the patient turned his face round to him he nearly stepped back in horror—such un-restrained malice and hate burned in his mad eyes. Seeing the assistant, however, he at once changed the expression of his face and obediently followed him without saying a word, as if he were oppressed by some profound thought. They went to the doctor's private room; the patient himself climbed up on to the platform of the scales. The assistant weighed him and noted down in a book opposite his name, 109 pounds.

Upon being weighed next day it was 107—and the day after 106.

"If this goes on," said the doctor, "he won't live." And he gave orders for him to receive extra nourishing food.

But in spite of this and of the patient's good appetite, he

got thinner every day, and every day the assistant wrote in the book a lower number of pounds. The patient hardly slept at all, and spent whole days in unceasing movement.

He realised that he was in a mad-house; he even realised that he was ill. Sometimes, as on his first night there, he awoke in the stillness of that time after a whole day of continuous movement, feeling as if his bones were broken and having a terribly heavy head, but in full consciousness. Perhaps it was due to the absence of impressions in the silence and peace of the night, perhaps to the weak working of the brain of a man who was only half awake, but in such moments he clearly understood his position and was, as it were, quite sane. But with the dawn, the sounds of awakening life in the hospital and the bright light of day overwhelmed his brain with a new flood of impressions. He was not strong enough to cope with them, and he became mad once more.

His mind was a strange mixture of reasonableness and nonsense. He grasped that all those around him were sick people, but at the same time he thought he recognised in each of them someone he had either known previously or heard about or read about, and he thought they were all endeavouring to hide themselves in this place. It seemed to him that the hospital was crowded with people of all nationalities and all ages in history. There were living people there and there were dead people; famous men, potentates, and soldiers killed in the late war now risen from the dead. He seemed to be in a kind of magic circle, and in an ecstasy of egotism he imagined himself to be the actual human centre of that circle. All these people in the hospital had their mission, and he dimly understood this as a stupendous enterprise having as its object the destruction of all evil upon earth. He did not exactly know how this would be achieved, but he felt that he had in himself sufficient strength for the purpose. He was able to penetrate the thoughts of others. He could see into things and read their whole anterior history, as, for instance, the tall elms in the hospital garden sang him complete legends of the experience of man. The hospital building itself, which certainly was old-fashioned, he considered to be a construction of Peter the Great. He felt sure that the Tsar Peter had lived there at the time of the battle of Poltava. He obtained this knowledge from the walls and the decaying stucco and from the fragments of brick and tile which he found in the garden. The whole history of the place was written on them. He peopled the small mortuary building with tens and hundreds of the long-ago dead, and he stared continually at its little cellar-window in a corner of the garden, seeing in the uneven, rainbow-like reflections of its dirty panes faces familiar to him in real life or in portraits.

The weather was now becoming clear and lovely. He spent the whole of the long days walking in the fresh air. The part of the garden allotted to the patients had many trees in it, and wherever it was possible flowers had been planted. The superintendent made everyone who could do so take some share of the gardening—and all day the patients were occupied in sweeping and scattering sand upon the paths, in weeding and watering the flower-beds, and the cucumber and melon beds which they themselves had made. Great cherry trees grew in one corner, and there was a long avenue of elms down one side, but in the middle, on a small artificial mound, had been planted the most beautiful beds. Bright flowers grew at the edge of the topmost bed, and in the middle of it blossomed a large rare dahlia—yellow with crimson edges. This formed the centre and the highest point of the whole garden, and it was noticeable that many of the patients looked upon it as having some sort of mysterious significance. The new-comer also regarded it as something out of the ordinary—as a kind of crown of the whole place.

Along all the paths grew flowers planted by the patients. There were all the flowers one could possibly meet in a Little Russian garden—tall roses, bright petunias, high bushes of tobacco-plants with their small pink blossoms, verbenas, cockscombs, nasturtiums and poppies. There also, not far from the porch, grew three clumps of a special kind of poppy—they were much smaller than ordinary poppies and were distinguished by the unusual brilliance of their bright crimson hue. It was this flower which had so attracted the new patient when he had looked out at the glass doors on his first day at the hospital.

When he came into the garden for the first time, he stood on the steps and looked intently at these bright flowers. There were only two of them—they had grown accidentally apart from the others in a waste corner, so that they were surrounded by coarse grass and reeds.

The patients filed out at the door where a warder was standing, and he gave to each of them a thick white knitted cotton cap, having a red cross on the front. They had been used in a military hospital in war-time and bought up at an auction. But the sick man, occupied with his own thoughts, gave a special meaning of mystery to the red·cross. He took off his cap, and looked first at the cross and then at the poppy-flower. The flower was of a brighter colour.

"That's victorious now," said he, "but we shall see."

And he went down the steps into the garden. Taking no notice of the warder behind him, he stepped over a flower-border and stretched out his hand towards the flower, but he could not make up his mind to pluck it. He began to feel a heat and a prickly sensation in his outstretched arm, extending to his whole body; it was as if some kind of strong current of an unknown power exuded from the crimson petals and penetrated all his frame. He moved closer and put out his hand towards the blossom, but it seemed to him that the flower protected itself by breathing out a terrible poisonous and deathly odour. His head grew dizzy—he made a last and desperate effort and just succeeded in getting hold of the stalk when suddenly a heavy hand fell on his shoulder. It was the warder.

"You mustn't pick the flowers," said the old man, "nor step over the borders. We have many lunatics here, and if each of them picked a flower there wouldn't be any left in the garden," he went on conclusively, still keeping a hand on the man's shoulder.

The sick man looked in the warder's face, silently released himself from his grasp, and agitatedly went back to the path. "O unhappy people!" thought he. "You do not see, you are so blind that you protect it. But no matter how much it costs me, I will destroy it. Not to-day, but to-morrow, we will measure our strength. And if I perish, it won't make any difference. . . ."

He walked in the garden all day long, making the acquaintance of other patients and holding strange conversations with them, they for their part hearing only answers to their own absurd ideas, expressed in nonsensically mysterious language. The sick man walked now with one companion, now with another, and as the day wore away he became more than ever convinced that "all was ready," as he said to himself. Soon, very soon, the iron gratings would fall away, and all the miserable people would go hence and disappear to the ends of the earth. The whole world would tremble and shake off its ancient garments and appear anew in marvellous beauty. He almost forgot about the flower, but, leaving the garden, as he was going up the steps, he once more descried the two crimson heads in the midst of the thick and now dewy grass. So he stepped out from the rest of the crowd and, standing behind the warder, waited for a convenient moment. Nobody saw how he jumped over the flower-border, grabbed the poppy, and hurriedly hid it under his blouse against his bosom. When the fresh dewy petals touched his body he went pale as death, and his eyes dilated with horror. Cold sweat trickled down his brow.

The lamps were lighted in the hospital. Most of the patients lay on their beds waiting for supper-time, but a few unquiet ones paced restlessly along the corridor and through the rooms. The sick man was one of these. He walked about, clenching his hands convulsively and crossing them on his breast as if he wanted to crush and press the life out of the flower he was hiding. When the others came near him he carefully avoided them—afraid of their touching even the edge of his clothes. "Don't come near me; don't come near me!" he cried. But in the hospital they paid little attention to such exclamations. He walked quicker and quicker, with longer and longer strides—walked for two whole hours with the same intensity.

"I will wear you out. I'll suffocate you," said he, darkly and maliciously.

And every now and then he gnashed his teeth.

Supper was served in the dining-room. On the long bare tables were placed several painted and gilded wooden basins of thin porridge; the patients sat on benches, and to each was given a hunk of black bread. Eight of them shared a basin of porridge and ate it with wooden spoons. Some of them, who were allowed better food, were served separately. Our sick man hastily swallowed the portion brought to his room by a warder and, not satisfied with it, went into the general dining-room.

"Allow me to eat here," said he to the superintendent.

"Haven't you had your supper yet?" asked the superintendent, serving him out an extra portion in a basin.

"I'm very hungry. And I need to keep up my strength. Everything depends on my food; you know that I don't get any sleep at all."

"Eat, my dear man, and get strong. Tarass, give him a spoon and some bread!"

He sat down in front of one of the basins and ate another large helping of porridge.

"Well, that's enough, that's enough," said the superintendent at last, when all the rest had finished their supper and our sick man still sat by his basin, scooping up the remaining porridge with one hand and pressing the other firmly on his breast. "You will over-eat yourself."

"Oh, if you only knew how much strength I need—how very much! Good-bye, Nikolai Nikolaich," said the sick man, getting up from the table and warmly shaking hands with the superintendent. "Good-bye."

"Where are you going?" asked the superintendent, with a smile.

"I? Nowhere. I'm staying here. But perhaps to-morrow we shan't see one another. Thank you for your kindness to me." And he once more shook hands. His voice trembled and tears came into his eyes.

"Calm yourself, my dear man, calm yourself," answered the superintendent. "What's the good of such gloomy thoughts? Go along, get to bed and have a good sleep. You need to sleep more; if you slept better you'd soon get well."

The sick man groaned. The superintendent turned away to see that the warder took away the supper-things more quickly.

In half an hour everyone in the hospital was sleeping, except one man who lay still dressed on his bed in the corner room. He shook as in a fever, and clutched convulsively at his chest, which, it seemed to him, must now be saturated with an unheard-of deadly poison.

He did not sleep all night. He had plucked this flower because he saw in that action a great exploit which he was obliged to accomplish. When he had first seen it through the glass door its crimson petals had attracted his attention, and it seemed to him at that moment that upon him alone in the whole world was this task imposed. All existent evil was concentrated in this bright red flower. He knew that opium was made from poppies—and perhaps it was this thought, increasing in his mind and reaching gigantic proportions, which caused him to create for himself this dreadful and phantasmal idea. In his eyes the flower had realised in itself all existent evil, and he sampled in it all the innocently-shed blood which had made it so red, all the tears, all the malice of humanity.

It was a mysterious and dreadful being, standing in opposition to God, Arimanes, taking on a modest and innocent appearance. It must be plucked and destroyed. But that was only part of the work—it must be prevented from breathing out its evil into the world. That was why he had hidden it in his breast. He hoped that by the morning the flower would lose all its evil power. That evil would pass into his body and into his soul, and there either be overcome or overcome him. Then he himself would perish and die, but die as an honourable warrior, the warrior of humanity, because until then no one had had the daring to struggle alone against all the evil of the world.

"They didn't see it. But I did. Could I have let it go on living? Better dead."

And he lay there, helpless in a phantasmal and unreal struggle, but helpless all the same.

In the morning the assistant found him scarcely breathing. But in spite of this, after a little while, excitement got the upper hand of him, and he jumped out of bed and strode about the hospital talking with the other patients in a louder and more incoherent fashion than ever. He was not allowed to go into the garden—and when the doctor saw that his weight was decreasing and that he had no sleep and was continually on the move, he ordered a strong injection of morphia.

The patient did not resist—fortunately, his mad thoughts just then were in accord with this operation. He soon fell asleep, his furious movement ceased, and he no longer heard that loud singing in his ears which had been constant until then and had given its rhythm to his agitated steps. He lost consciousness and forgot everything, even the other flower which he thought he had to pluck.

He did gather it though, three days later, under the very eyes of the old man, who did not succeed in preventing him.

The warder chased him, but with a loud yell of triumph the sick man ran into the hospital and, dashing into his own room, hid the flower in his bosom.

"Why are you picking the flowers?" asked the warder, running after him.

But the sick man had already lain down in his usual fashion on the bed, with his arms crossed on his breast, talking such nonsense that the warder only removed his white cotton cap with the red cross on it, which he had forgotten to take off in his hasty flight, and went out.

The spectral struggle began anew. The sick man felt that from the flower long currents of evil came forth, crawling like snakes, encircling him, pressing down and crushing his limbs, and pouring into his whole body their horrible poison. He wept and prayed to God in the intervals between the curses which he hurled at his enemy. By the evening the flower had faded—and the sick man trampled underfoot its blackened remains and then gathered up the pieces and carried them to the bathroom. Throwing the wilted plant on to the red-hot coals of the stove, he watched for a long while how his enemy sizzled and shrivelled and finally changed into a delicate snow-white heap of ash. He blew on it and it entirely disappeared.

Next day he was much worse. Dreadfully pale, with hollow cheeks and deeply sunken, burning eyes, he continued his mad wandering about, though his steps were uncertain and his body was covered with perspiration—and he talked and talked unceasingly.

"I do not wish to resort to force," said the old doctor to his assistant.

"And yet one must stop this continual movement. He only weighs ninety-three pounds to-day. If this goes on he will die in a couple of days."

The old doctor reflected. "Morphia—or chloral," said he, half-questioningly.

"Yesterday the morphia had no effect."

"Tell them to tie him up. I doubt, however, if he can be cured."

So the sick man was tied up. He lay on his bed in a strait-jacket, firmly held down by strips of linen to the iron bars of his bed. But his insane movements did not decrease, they grew. For many hours he stubbornly strove to free himself from his bandages. At last, by a vigorous jerk he broke out of his bands and freed his legs; then he wriggled from under the other fastenings, and with his arms still tied up, walked about his room, shouting wild and incomprehensible sounds.

"Oh, what *is* the matter with you?" cried the warder, coming in to him. "The devil must have helped you to get free. Grishka, Ivan, come here! The madman has untied himself!"

Both assistants came to the sick man, and a long struggle began—very tiring for the attendants and agonising for the patient, who was exhausting the last remnant of his strength. At length they got him on to the bed again and bound him up more firmly than before.

"You don't understand what you are doing," cried the patient, out of breath. "You will perish. I saw a third flower, hardly open. Now it will be quite ready. Let me finish my work. I must kill it, kill it, kill it. Then all will be finished, and everyone will be saved. I could send you, but it is only I myself who can do this. You would die if you only touched it."

"Be quiet, sir, be quiet," said the old warder who had been left in charge of him and stood by his bed.

The sick man suddenly became quiet. He made up his mind to trick the warder. He was kept bound all that day and left in the same position for the night. After giving him some supper the warder spread a mattress on the floor and lay down upon it. In an instant he was fast asleep, and the sick man set himself to work.

He wriggled his whole body until he could reach the iron bar of the bed and feel it with his wrists through the long sleeves of the strait-jacket. Then he began to rub the sleeve rapidly and forcibly against the iron. After a little while the thick sail-cloth material was worn through, and he was able to free his index finger. Then the matter was easier. With a suppleness and agility quite impossible for a sane person, he undid the knot which tied the sleeves behind his back, unlaced the jacket, and after that, listened for a long time to the snores of the warder. But the warder slept soundly. Then the sick man got out of the jacket and released himself from the bed. He was free.

He went to the door. It was locked on the inside, and the key, no doubt, was in the warder's pocket. Fearful of awakening him, he dared not feel in his pocket, and he resolved to get out through the window.

It was a calm, warm, dark night. The window was open; the stars glittered in the dark heaven. He looked at them, recognising the familiar constellations and rejoicing because he thought they understood and sympathised with him. Blinking his eyes, he saw the endless rays of light which they were sending down to him, and his insane resolve grew stronger. He must bend the thick bars of the iron grating, squeeze himself through the narrow opening into the little lane overgrown with bushes, and climb the high stone wall. Then would come the final struggle—and after that—what mattered death?

He tried to bend the thick iron bar with his bare hands, but the iron did not give. Then he twisted the strong sleeves of the strait-jacket to make a rope, and fastening it to a spike of the grating, swung himself upon it. After desperate efforts, which almost exhausted his remaining strength, the spike bent—a narrow passage was opened. He pushed himself through it, rubbing the skin from his shoulders and elbows and bare knees; got through the bushes, and stood in front of the wall.

All was quiet. Night-lights from within feebly illumined the windows of the great building; no one was to be seen at them. He was unobserved. The old man lying by his bed was probably sound asleep. The stars twinkled kindly at him; their rays of light went right to his heart.

"I am coming to you," he whispered, looking up at the sky.

Bleeding after his initial efforts, his finger-nails were torn, his hands and knees smeared with blood. He began to seek some way to scale the wall. Some bricks had fallen out at the place where the wall of the mortuary and the garden-wall met. The sick man felt for the gaps and made use of them. He got to the top of the wall and, grasping the branches of an elm growing there, gently let himself down by the tree on to the ground.

He ran to the familiar spot by the steps. The flower hung its shadowy head; its petals were curled back and it stood out clearly in the dewy grass.

"This is the last one," whispered the sick man—"the very last. To-day it is victory or death. But whichever it is, it's all the same to me now. Wait a little," said he, looking up at the sky. "I shall soon be with you."

He pulled up the plant, tore it to bits, crushed it, and holding it in his hand went back by the way he had come to his own room. The old man still slept. The sick man had hardly touched his bed when he fell unconscious upon it.

Next morning he was found dead. His face was calm and radiant—his emaciated features with their thin lips and deeply-sunken closed eyes expressed triumphant joy. When they laid him on the bier they tried to open his fingers and take away the crimson flower. But his hand was stiff, and he carried his trophy to the grave.

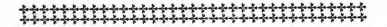

ALEXANDER ERTEL

(1855–1908)

✢✢

(I)

A SPECIALIST

(Translated by NATALIE DUDDINGTON)

ON November the 12th Yegor Petrovitch Kapliuzhny came home late from his work.

The fact was he had been summoned by his chief. And not by his direct "immediate" chief, but by the one at the head of affairs who had power to plunge Yegor Petrovitch into nothingness by merely blowing upon him or to fill him with joyful tremors by a playful poke in the ribs. It was that high and mighty chief who had graciously patted Yegor Petrovitch on the shoulder that day and, dismissing him kindly, deigned to say:

"Another such case, Kapliuzhny, and you will be a real specialist." In the entry Yegor Petrovitch threw back his arms and patiently waited for the zealous man-servant, an old soldier, to pull off his overcoat.

"Is that you, Yurok?" a woman's voice asked languidly, and Yegor Petrovitch's wife, a plump and handsome blonde with an ample bust, appeared in the doorway of the dimly lighted entry.

"Daddy, daddy has come!" cried a shrill childish voice to the accompaniment of the quick and uncertain patter of soft little shoes. "Mammy, let me go! Let me go to daddy!"

Yegor Petrovitch smiled blissfully. He saw his two-year-old daughter put her fat, rosy little arms round her mother's knees, trying to push by her. The doorway was too narrow.

508

"I'll teach you to shout and run about, you little imp!"
Yegor Petrovitch said with feigned severity, and turning to
the modestly smiling soldier he added, "Zaharov, take Galka
to the police station!"

The child gave a playful scream, let go her mother and ran
back with her arms thrust forward, hardly able to balance
herself on her fat little legs and in danger of stumbling at the
first obstacle in her way. One heard her babbling breathless with joyous laughter:

"G'anny, g'anny, daddy told him to take me to the police
station!"

"Mind you brush the overcoat and give a rub to the braiding," Yegor Petrovitch said to the servant with unfeigned
sternness this time.

The old soldier understood the change instantly, and instead of the modest smile assumed an expression of concentrated attention.

"Yes, sir," he answered deferentially, and hanging the coat
on a peg, calmly withdrew to the kitchen. "One might be at
it for ever!" he muttered.

Meanwhile Yegor Petrovitch, giving his wife a luscious kiss
on her rosy half-open lips, followed her through an unlighted
parlour into a neat little dining-room where a brightly
polished samovar was boiling noisily, a damask tablecloth
gleamed white under the crockery and an elegant alabaster
lamp glowed with a soft even light.

"Well, give me my dressing-gown, Polina Mihailovna.
Dressing-gown and slippers. I am tired out," said Yegor
Petrovitch, clinking his spurs as he came up to the table. (He
always brought his heels together smartly when he came to a
standstill.)

"Why are you so late to-day?" Polina Mihailovna asked,
following her husband slowly and gracefully.

Yegor Petrovitch eagerly picked up a sandwich, and as he
demolished it, answered that he had been to see his Excellency, and that his Excellency had been most kind and had

actually patted him on the shoulder. Polina Mihailovna smiled and looked at her husband with joyful eyes.

"Well done, Yurok!" she said gaily. "At that rate you'll soon be made a superintendent!" and all at once, abandoning her languor, she threw her arms round Yegor Petrovitch's neck, made him sit down, and jumping on to his lap pressed herself against the buttons of his uniform.

"Buy me a cloak, Yurok," she whispered between ardent kisses. "A velvet one, like Madame Tchurkin's. . . . Do get it me, poppet, please!"

Yegor Petrovitch laughed, hastily finishing his sandwich; with his free hand he hurriedly straightened his moustache, freeing it from crumbs of bread and cheese. A quick patter of feet and childish laughter accompanied by an old woman's chidings interrupted them. Madame Kapliuzhny jumped up, and tidying her hair disappeared in the bedroom. Yegor Petrovitch assumed a sedate expression.

But the grandmother and Galka did not come into the dining-room till later, when Yegor Petrovitch had had time to put on his dressing-gown and slippers and, sipping hot tea, was dreamily smoking a cigarette.

The grandmother was a wrinkled old lady wearing a dress of some dark material, with quick movements and a gentle, rather frightened-looking face. She at once busied herself round the samovar, quickly and noiselessly moving the crockery, pouring out tea and cutting sandwiches; with extraordinary rapidity and as though by stealth she drank a cup of tea, nibbling at a bit of sugar instead of putting it in the cup, softly trying to keep the mischievous child quiet and evidently doing her utmost not to attract attention. She addressed Yegor Petrovitch with formal politeness, and each time that she handed him a glass of tea she got up from her seat and seemed to curtsy.

Yegor Petrovitch was happy. He stretched himself with sighs of content and addressed playful remarks to Galka.

"Galka! So you don't want to go to the police station?" he

said. "Wait a bit, as soon as you are naughty I'll take you there. At Christmas I'll catch a lot of pickpockets and lock you up with them."

But Galka was evidently used to Yegor Petrovitch's jokes. She climbed on to his knees, pulled his moustache, jumped down again and laughed delightedly without taking the slightest notice of the grandmother's gentle chiding. Yegor Petrovitch was infected by Galka's gaiety. At first he tickled her and gave her little slaps, obviously condescending to her age, fully conscious that he was a father and a serious-minded man; but gradually all condescension disappeared from his jokes. He began mooing like a cow, bleating like a sheep, grunting like a pig, and ended by seeming as much a child as Galka. Even the old lady brightened up and smiled without any timidity: she felt like a grown-up with these two naughty children.

But when Polina Mihailovna appeared, Yegor Petrovitch reverted to his normal condition. Setting Galka aside, he told his wife some news derived as usual from the latest police reports. A student unable to subsist by giving lessons and typewriting had hanged himself; but the student was only a Jew. A working man had cut his throat with a bit of bottle glass—he had been drinking for a fortnight on end. A boy of twelve had been caught in a cogwheel and killed. A girl had poisoned herself with sulphur matches—a wench of working class and doubtful character.

Madame Kapliuzhny uttered slight exclamations as she munched a sugared biscuit; sometimes she made suitable remarks, such as "Served him right!" "He shouldn't drink!" "He had no business to be there! (The idea of his getting into the wheel!)." But one could see that she made them merely from politeness. Yegor Petrovitch supplied her with such news almost every evening and she could not be expected to lavish her feelings on them every time.

She grew much more lively when Yegor Petrovitch told her of "daring robberies," burglaries, murders, escaped convicts.

"It would be just the thing for you, Yurok!" she cried then. "I wish you could catch him! I wish you would track him out!" and her eyes would sparkle with delight.

Yegor Petrovitch, however, never answered these remarks. He was one of those men who distrust a woman's tongue. He did tell Polina Mihailovna the results of his exploits and discoveries, repeated to her the praises he had had from his superiors, and gave her the money he received as a bonus, but he kept a modest and resolute silence with regard to his plans.

"Fetyuk has murdered the innkeeper at Vesyoly Gai," Yegor Petrovitch said, drinking his fourth glass of tea, and for the hundredth time tousling Galka's hair as she climbed on to his knees. "Armed burglary and murder."

"Hasn't he been caught?" Polina Mihailovna cried with interest.

Yegor Petrovitch did not answer at once. Galka was laughing so shrilly as she scrambled on to his knees that he was obviously growing tired of her. He tried to quieten her, but the child would take no notice of the change in his mood. Then Yegor Petrovitch looked at the old lady with a fixed stare in his grey eyes and said significantly:

"Mamma!"

The old lady, startled and flurried, rushed to the child and, whispering something in her ear, instantly carried her out of the room. Tea was finished.

Then Yegor Petrovitch brushed off the crumbs and answered lazily:

"He is in hiding, of course. There's no catching a man like that! He's escaped from Siberia twice. A notorious brigand!" and before Madame Kapliuzhny had had time to utter her usual "It would be just the thing for you, Yurok!" he went on: "Stasyonok has promised to send you your boots to-morrow."

The conversation naturally turned to domestic matters. Rolling a cigarette for her husband, Polina Mihailovna told him her news and revealed her plans for the future. She wanted Galka to have a winter outfit like the Pobochnys' child: blue silk edged with swansdown. It was most charming! The gaiters were also blue, to match; and the muff was white. Then "mamma's" coat had to be mended—that shabby old garment, with worn bits of fur hanging down: it would have to be patched if only with a sheepskin, and re-covered with some old piece of stuff.

"I feel so ashamed of her!" Madame Kapliuzhny said indignantly. "She looks like a costermonger. No sense of what's fitting!"

"You can't expect sense at her age!" Yegor Petrovitch remarked kindly. But he had evidently touched Polina Mihailovna's sore spot: her face flushed and her eyes looked hard.

"I have always been ashamed of her," she said, speaking quickly and irritably. "Always going about begging for favours and fawning on people. And kissing hands like a servant. I hate it! Papa was a captain and he never demeaned himself . . . but she seems to like doing it!"

But it was not in Madame Kapliuzhny's character to be angry and she soon calmed down. And once more the panorama of household plans was unrolled before Yegor Petrovitch. It was necessary to buy a new mattress, to repair the washing-stand, to re-upholster the furniture, to have the saucepans tinned.

Yegor Petrovitch purred contentedly and let out fanciful spirals of smoke. He agreed to everything: he had the necessary money and, besides, he had hopes; but of that he said nothing.

When the household matters had been discussed the conversation seemed to flag, and Yegor Petrovitch yawned once or twice, stretching himself spasmodically and luxuriously; but Madame Kapliuzhny gave their talk a new and lively turn and he was thoroughly roused again. She was now speaking of their friends and acquaintances, their families, their private affairs, big and small quarrels and what went on behind the scenes.

It was always like that with the Kapliuzhnys: the husband's news, the domestic and so to speak intimate conversation was inevitably followed by gossip about their friends. It was a rest for the Kapliuzhnys' heart and mind—a recreation which held the place of literature and the fine arts for them, sharpening their powers of observation and developing their intellects, increasing their sense of their own dignity and making them feel superior to other people.

One must do justice to Madame Kapliuzhny: she was a master-hand at gossip. Her tongue did not hiss with malice and there was no venom on her rosy lips (as is sometimes the case with gossips). Her chatter was frankly malicious, innocently derisive, candidly disparaging.

Spreading over her plump knees a piece of embroidery for a summer dress, she quickly plied her needle and talked of the police superintendent Petiushkin. There was a game of *vint* at his house. Doctor Beznadiozhny had Pechtel the grocer for partner, and had just declared four hearts when the grocer called out "Doctor!" and blew his nose violently; the doctor put down his cards and said "Pass." Petiushkin could not stand this and said to Pechtel, "How dare you blow your nose, you German?" Then there was a regular flare-up. Pechtel was offended, the doctor was offended; Pechtel flung down his cards and began taunting Petiushkin about some caviare.

"Oh, that was the caviare served on his name-day. It was bad," Yegor Petrovitch remarked indifferently.

"They had a fearful row. You haven't heard, but it appears Pechtel went to lodge a complaint against Petiushkin, only he couldn't make himself clear. He kept repeating that the superintendent doesn't allow him to blow his nose, but couldn't explain why. But what is the doctor to do now? He is an old friend of Pechtel's, but he can't have his groceries from him any more: Petiushkin is keeping an eye on them and wants to convict the doctor of taking bribes. He asks: How does the doctor's account with Pechtel stand? and says it's all bribery and corruption!"

"He is a sharp one, that man!" Yegor Petrovitch cried delightedly.

Polina Mihailovna quite agreed and told several more stories about the cleverness of Petiushkin and his subordinates in private life. Then she passed to her husband's friends and colleagues—well-groomed, amiable and business-like men, burdened for the most part with smart wives who had to be kept in style. All this provided much material for the Kapliuzhnys' intimate talk. Cards, flirtations, drink— these predominant peculiarities of the police officers' social life—gave rise to plenty of incidents, of which one could not help talking and disapproving.

"I can't imagine why that Tchurkin woman is so stuck up!" Madame Kapliuzhny prattled, tracing neatly the pattern of a cock in red cotton. "Would you believe it, she has ordered a hat from Moscow, and now there's simply no going near her! She does fancy herself! And what is her Vassily Vassilyitch, after all? He is a superintendent, it is true, but he is an officer like everybody else—and yet other women don't address their husbands in French! Why must it be in French? *Basile, Basile!* He is nothing out of the way. And before other people too! It always makes me laugh."

"Swank!" Yegor Petrovitch commented briefly.

"'When Christmas comes,' she says, 'I'll spend all the holidays in Moscow.' Whom does she expect to impress by that? Certainly no one will be impressed except her *Basile.* Horrid woman! And I wonder at the way her husband spoils her. Would you believe it, she goes ransacking the shops before every holiday! She is either buying a hat, or a *sorti de bal,* or gloves in dozens. Every blessed holiday! Ah, Yurok, if you had only seen her cloak! She is as flat as a board, you know, but the velvet gives her a lovely figure!"

"We'll see about it!" Yegor Petrovitch muttered kindly, but being a man of character said no more.

And so they talked on, enjoying themselves. Zaharov cleared away the samovar. The grandmother brought in Galka for her to say "Good-night, daddy" and "*Bonne nuit, maman.*" (That *nuit* had cost a lot of trouble to Madame Kapliuzhny: she had to press the child's lips with her fingers to achieve the right pronunciation of the *u*, but she did achieve it. Yegor Petrovitch, being a patriot at heart, did not want a French greeting.) Galka was rubbing her sleepy eyes with her fists and was obviously glad to go to bed.

"See if she doesn't ask in the night for papa to take her!" said Madame Kapliuzhny with a smile and a tender look at her husband.

"I say, make her that blue coat you spoke of," Yegor Petrovitch said, trying to conceal the emotion ready to betray itself in his voice. And to conceal it more successfully he added, laughing, "We'll send her to the high school presently and make a lady of her."

"And you know, Yurok," Madame Kapliuzhny chimed in, "we must see to it that she marries a barrister. The fortunes those barristers make!"

"Well, that's as it happens," Yegor Petrovitch remarked doubtfully. "Some of them haven't a decent pair of trousers. My work, now, is really worth something."

"Oh, don't say that, Yurok!" Polina Mihailovna retorted, in the heat of the argument, putting aside her embroidery. "It's all very well for you because you have a special gift for it, and of course they prize you because of your talent. But take Minkin, Ohlebyshev, Pobochny. If it weren't for his wife, what would Pobochny do? A repulsive red-faced man—that's all he is. But of course you have a talent for it, that's why you talk like that."

Yegor Petrovitch was flattered. He patted his wife on her bare arm and said:

"Of course there's a difference." He paused, and with sudden playfulness pinched his wife under the chin. "I say, Polka, and what if I am made a chief of police?" he cried. "We'd show them what's what! We'd teach them what living in style means!"

Madame Kapliuzhny answered him with a long moist look. She felt once more a longing to sit on her husband's knee, to press herself against his breast and cling to his lips, so admirably bordered with an elegant, truly military moustache. But "mamma's" voice called her: she had to see to something.

Yegor Petrovitch was left alone. He settled more comfortably in the armchair and stretched out his legs still further. Pleasant dreams clouded his mind, a sweet languor overpowered him. He did not look around him, but his inner vision showed him clearly and conclusively that life was good, since it was all arranged in a gay and harmonious pattern. The lamp, the furniture, the coloured prints on the walls, the narrow strips of carpet on the shining floor, the flowers on the windows, the clean warm rooms—all was comfort and orderliness; his wife was a perfect little mamma with her plumpness and prettiness; his daughter was fat and rosy; in the bank a necessary sum was accumulating for buying state lottery tickets; his superiors liked him and often praised him in official reports; his poor relations sat quietly in the wilds of Kostroma, and, so far from disturbing him with their existence, sent presents of mushrooms and whortleberries for every big holiday.

Yegor Petrovitch was not thinking of all this distinctly, but he felt light-hearted because of it all; life seemed so easy and the prospects on all sides clear and unclouded. Yegor Petrovitch knew from the Scriptures that life was a burden and heaved deep sighs about it when he went to church in Lent, or had to comfort a colleague who had lost a chance of receiving an order of merit. But conscientiously analysing his own life, Yegor Petrovitch could not call it a burden; it was rather like resilient waves on which he rose triumphantly, almost chortling at times with sheer delight.

He remained in this mood all the evening. Madame Kapliuzhny had long been asleep with her back to him; the soft light of the sanctuary lamp fell on Galka's bed gently and peacefully; "mamma," curled up on a box outside the bedroom door, snored diffidently. But Yegor Petrovitch could not go to sleep, and lay in a kind of torpor, with half-shut eyes. His soul was melting in sweet languor.

Later on he put it down to a presentiment: promotion was mysteriously descending upon him from higher spheres, bringing disturbing dreams; vistas of the future were opening before his inner eye. It does happen sometimes.

Suddenly there was a gentle pull at the bell and a whispering of two voices. Yegor Petrovitch pricked up his ears. His face seemed to stiffen and assumed a business-like expression as befitted a police officer; a dry, penetrating look came into his eyes. He quickly put his feet down and fumbled for his slippers. Zaharov appeared at the bedroom door.

"Moseika has turned up, sir," he whispered.

Yegor Petrovitch flung his dressing-gown over his shoulders and went to the kitchen. A dirty, ragged Jew stood there hugging himself and trembling with fear as in a shivering fit. Yegor Petrovitch took him to the dining-room and they whispered together for a few minutes. One could hear Moseika's cracked voice breaking as though in terror and Yegor Petrovitch saying sternly: "Mind, you dirty Jew, it's either twenty-five roubles reward or the lock-up. I mean what I say." Then Yegor Petrovitch dressed hastily, buckled on his sword, took a revolver, put an old civilian overcoat over his uniform and went out with Moseika. As he left the house he gave strict orders to Zaharov to bolt the door and not go out. The sleepy servant stood to attention and answered, "Yes, sir! Don't you worry, sir"; but the moment Yegor Petrovitch went out he stretched himself on the floor where his felt mattress lay and snored beyond all belief.

The night was dark and damp. Slippery mud squelched underfoot. Bare trees that grew in places along the road shook in the wind, making a dismal noise. Pious towns-people's sanctuary lamps glimmered in the windows. All was asleep. Somewhere in the distance a dog howled pitifully.

Yegor Petrovitch walked behind Moseika.

"Oie, he'll give us the slip! Oie, we must be quick, your honour," squeaked the Jew hurriedly, sliding through the mud in his torn boots, shuddering and bending down every minute.

The poor feeble creature was filled with terror; suspicious shapes seemed to him to lurk in the darkness, and waves of sharp, prickly cold reached him from every corner. Fear, agonising fear, tortured him.

They reached the policeman's box. The man had gone to sleep, but Yegor Petrovitch roused him rudely, whispered some order, and the policeman disappeared quickly and quietly. Then Moseika turned into a gloomy and deserted part of the town. An endless succession of dilapidated fences stretched alongside the street; the few street lamps flickered dimly, throwing uncertain reflections on the dark and as it were tear-stained windows; evil-smelling mud covered the narrow pavements.

Yegor Petrovitch's mind was assailed by doubts: Moseika was a notorious rascal, and it was solely owing to a few private services that he had not yet been despatched to Siberia.

"What if . . ." Yegor Petrovitch whispered fearfully—"What if the dirty rogue is deceiving me?" But he immediately grew angry with himself for his doubt and cried in vexation, "Oh, damn!"

The Jew was overwhelmed.

"Oie, my God, my God!" he whispered. "Is it possible to make such a noise!" and moving stealthily like a cat he slowly and hesitatingly walked by a broken-down fence.

Yegor Petrovitch seized him from behind.

"Go on, go on!" he said insistently, holding on to the rags in which Moseika was clothed.

Moseika shrank and muttered piteously, "Let me go, your honour," trying to disengage himself from Yegor Petrovitch's hands; but suddenly he subsided and submitted to his fate. And so they walked on, possessed by fear, suspecting each other and looking searchingly and mistrustfully around them.

All at once a brightly lighted window caught their eyes. A tumbledown cottage backing on to a deep ravine, its thatched roof dishevelled by the wind, was all astir with the jarring sound of a barrel organ, hoarse voices of drunken men whistling and stamping.

> "I want to tell the tale, tell the tale,
> Of three beauties going for a stroll, for a stroll.
> They walked down the vale, forest vale,
> And they met an archer young and bold . . ."

The words of the song reached Yegor Petrovitch clear and loud. He stole up to the window and stood stock-still, his eyes rivetted on what he saw. Yes, there was no doubt of it: it was Fetyuk "on the spree." Deadly pale and with red blotches on his excited face he sat dressed in a new red shirt, aimlessly waving his arms, and shouting in a hoarse and angry voice, "Go it! Make merry, you wretched tipplers, frisk away!" He was in that state of drunkenness when the movements are still unimpeded, but the nerves are painfully strained and irritated. Crumpled paper money lay on the wine-stained table beside him. A haggard drunken woman with a black eye turned the barrel-organ handle as she sang, screeching at the top of her voice. A sturdy red-haired peasant seconded her, out of tune, stamping about with his huge boots and whistling with a deafening noise; suddenly he stopped and tried to kiss the woman. They wrangled; the barrel organ wheezed and gasped with a kind of choking sound. "Sing away, Agneshka!" Fetyuk shouted furiously, and the barrel organ began again playing the *Archer* with startled haste, and the red-haired peasant stamped with his huge boots once more. Agneshka screeched more shrilly than ever. A young man with a greenish, puffy face and a stupid, set smile moved his fingers in a pool of vodka on the table, saying thickly, as though trying to convince someone, "We have plenty—we have plenty to live on—plenty!" And getting up suddenly he grinned delightedly and shouted with all his might: "Haven't we, Fedot Semyonitch?" But Fetyuk pushed him violently in the chest and the lad fell with a thud on the floor. The sounds of stamping, whistling, the barrel organ and the singing drowned his voice. "I'll smash you!" Fetyuk shouted in a fury, rolling up the sleeves over his sinewy arms. "I'll smash it all!" he repeated, and dealt a tremendous blow on the window-pane. The tinkle of broken glass strangely disturbed the night stillness of the quiet, stuffy street. The drunken voices and the sounds of the barrel organ suddenly grew extremely loud and clear. Somewhere in a backyard a dog barked in alarm. "Help!" the young man shouted, running up to the window.

Yegor Petrovitch had barely time to jump back when the glass was smashed. He caught a glimpse of the young man's blood-stained face, of a small revolver glistening in Fetyuk's hands, and of arms in red and bright yellow sleeves waving and then clasping one another.

Yegor Petrovitch ran back a few steps and put his whistle to his lips. A long piercing sound cut through the air. Instantly something dreadful happened in the cottage. Fetyuk wrenched out the window-pane, jumped out and rushed away. From the opposite side the policemen were coming at a fast run.

Then there began a desperate pursuit. Yegor Petrovitch shouted to the policemen to arrest those in the hut, and dashed after Fetyuk, throwing off his overcoat and unbuckling his sword as he ran.

It seemed as though Heaven had decided to take the side of

justice: the clouds broke up and the thick darkness lifted slightly. Yegor Petrovitch saw before him the outline of Fetyuk's figure and could even make out the sleeves of his shirt blowing out like sails in the wind, and he ran headlong after him. He ran clenching his teeth, holding the revolver ready, prepared to pounce upon his prey at any moment. His whole soul was in the intent gaze he fixed upon Fetyuk, and all his strength seemed to be centred in his legs that moved with incredible rapidity over the slippery ground.

Fetyuk jumped on to the fence, flung out his arms and disappeared. Yegor Petrovitch screamed as though with unendurable pain, and for a moment he was himself surprised at this piercing scream; then he gave a whistle and jumped over the fence too. He could hear the policemen's heavy tread, the clank of their swords and the squelching of mud some thirty paces behind him.

Fetyuk rushed behind some bushes, jumped another low fence and coming level with the street made for the river. Yegor Petrovitch knew that if Fetyuk reached the bank, all would be lost: the whole bank was covered with timber and planks ready to be rafted; there were boats in the shallows. His heart fell. With a desperate effort he gained a few steps on Fetyuk, gasping hoarsely, "No, you shan't escape me." He actually touched Fetyuk's back with his finger-tips and was distinctly aware of the warm smell of Fetyuk's hot perspiring body. This sensation seemed to inspire Yegor Petrovitch with fresh energy. Suddenly Fetyuk jumped to one side and something glittered in his hand. Yegor Petrovitch swung back. At the same moment there was a flash, a report, and a strong smell of powder took Yegor Petrovitch's breath away. Then, without thinking, Yegor Petrovitch rushed at Fetyuk with a savage, furious roar. He had forgotten that it was essential to catch an important criminal alive, that the success of the judicial investigation depended upon it; he merely saw five steps before him Fetyuk's broad back and was overcome with a tearing rage which seemed to choke him, and suddenly, not knowing what he was doing, he fired at that back. Fetyuk fell down with a short moan. Yegor Petrovitch pounced upon him, seized him by the hair and with all his might struck him on the jaw with his fist. Fetyuk quivered all over like a bird that had been shot, made a convulsive movement with his shoulders and tried to rise, but Yegor Petrovitch was firmly sitting on him.

He came to himself as soon as he had struck Fetyuk. "Thank Heaven, he is alive," he thought, and once more put the whistle to his lips. A dozen whistles, vibrating and chirping like crickets, answered him.

When the policemen had taken Fetyuk (he was wounded in the neck), Yegor Petrovitch stood up and straightened himself. Only now he remembered that perhaps he too had been wounded, and suddenly he felt desperately frightened. He anxiously stretched his arms and legs, drew a deep breath, and as he did so the air seemed to cut his parched throat like a knife. There was no pain anywhere. Only his chest ached a little and his arms and legs trembled slightly.

Yegor Petrovitch joyfully crossed himself.

At the cottage they had arrested the barrel-organ woman and the young man. The red-haired peasant had escaped. Moseika too could nowhere be found.

Yegor Petrovitch sat in a shabby leather armchair in the dusty and dirty police-station office, dispensing justice. The collar of his coat was torn, his boots were muddy, there was a narrow blue bruise on his cheek, but his whole being was full of calm self-confidence, and his gay, slightly protruding eyes were clear and steady.

The business, however, was only half done. The beast had been caught, its trace was still fresh and blood-stained, but its lair was not yet discovered. Fetyuk did nothing but swear and clamour for a doctor, the barrel-organ woman proved to have had nothing to do "with all these goings-on," the young man with the damaged face spoke stupidly and incoherently. They were all tightly bound and locked up in the "secret cells."

Yegor Petrovitch had written a report and was about to telephone to his immediate chief when he suddenly changed his mind and began slowly rolling a cigarette.

Before he had finished smoking, a tearful female voice was heard in the entry. The policemen were driving away some old woman who demanded to see the "head officer." Yegor Petrovitch started; he jumped up instantly and shouted for her to be admitted. A wrinkled, dishevelled old woman came in, wearing a brand-new overcoat and dirty woollen stockings slipping down on to her coarse, shabby shoes. She came in and fell at Yegor Petrovitch's feet. It took him some time to grasp what the old woman wanted: she grovelled on the floor, kissed his feet, seized the skirts of his coat, and sobbed that she was "her mother" and "would give anything." She begged Yegor Petrovitch "to have mercy," to spare "the children, the angels, the little cherubs." Yegor Petrovitch could make nothing of it. He vaguely guessed that a guiding thread was being put into his hands which would enable him at last to unravel the skein. And so he assumed a kind manner. Softening as far as possible the hard and keen expression of his eyes, he raised the old woman, trying as he did so to move slowly and repress his joyful impatience.

"Speak plainly, my dear; what is it you want? To have mercy on whom? Whose mother are you?" he asked almost tenderly.

It appeared that the old woman was the mother of Alyona, and Alyona had two children—Lyovushka, a one-year-old boy, and Marfutochka, a girl of four.

"What do you want of me?" Yegor Petrovitch asked in an insinuating whisper.

The old woman flopped at his feet again and wailed: "Have pity! Spare us! We'd give anything!"

Then Yegor Petrovitch winked to the policemen and they went out.

"Look here, granny," Yegor Petrovitch said resolutely, "let us talk sensibly."

The old woman got up at once and stopped crying. Yegor Petrovitch's business tone sobered her: she listened attentively and with a cunning air, noiselessly moving her lips.

"Talk sensibly," Yegor Petrovitch hurried on as though he were anxious. "I know what you have come for. Fedot is bound hand and foot. To-morrow he will be taken to prison, and you know yourself what will happen to him next. But I haven't reported to my chief yet: I was just going to, but evidently your God has brought you in time. I will speak straight: how much are you going to give?"

The old woman hurriedly unbuttoned her coat, with feverish haste produced a dirty rag, and undoing the knot with her teeth, unfolded it before Yegor Petrovitch. There were two fifty-rouble notes in the rag.

"Not enough," said Yegor Petrovitch with a sidelong glance at the money. "Two hundred!" and laughing, he added playfully, "Why, he was your breadwinner!"

The old woman began whimpering again, but Yegor Petrovitch's resolute tone brought her to her senses once more.

"A hundred and fifty," he said, "and not another word, or I'll be angry. It's not worth soiling my hands for less."

The old woman had no such sum by her. Yegor Petrovitch said carelessly:

"Run where you like, but the money must be here in an hour's time. If you don't bring it, I'll send in my report. Your Fedot will be done for then."

The old woman walked to the door and stopped irresolutely.

"What about the policemen, sir?" she asked suspiciously.

"You need not worry your head about them, granny. They don't know who it is they have arrested; I'll let him out and say it had been a mistake."

This finally reassured the old woman; she scurried out of the police station and ran along the dark street, lifting her new coat above her knees.

But she did not run alone: policemen, headed by Yegor Petrovitch, glided after her like shadows, hardly breathing and keeping their swords from clanking as they moved stealthily along the walls and fences.

The old woman brought them to a new cottage and disappeared in the doorway. A light was gleaming through the badly-closed shutters. Yegor Petrovitch peeped through the chink. A lamp was burning in a lofty, well-kept room; a handsome woman was anxiously walking to and fro softly singing to sleep the baby in her arms.

"A nice little bit of goods!" Yegor Petrovitch thought, and for some reason he recalled his Polina Mihailovna. But there was no time to waste: from the other side of the road a policeman was coming with the witnesses—sleepy and frightened neighbours who had been roused for the purpose. The whole crowd quickly entered the room.

The woman cried out faintly and sank helplessly on to the bed. The baby rolled out of her arms; a policeman picked it up. The old woman was discovered in the next room: she stood bending over an open box, shoving small crumpled notes into her stockings. A pretty child, alarmed by the noise, jumped out from under a quilt and rushed to her mother, screaming and waving her arms; she looked blue with fright. But by that time her mother was firmly held by the arms, and Yegor Petrovitch was carefully searching her with an air of modest triumph, taking not the slightest notice of the convulsive movements of her legs and body that tried to repulse him and ward off his rapidly gliding hands.

The old woman was led in. She was trembling all over and glancing wildly about her.

"Mother, what have you done? You have ruined us all!" her daughter whispered with a note of bitter reproach in her voice.

"May the curse of God be upon you!" the old woman suddenly howled in a piercing voice, rushing at Yegor Petrovitch.

She was bound.

The search yielded excellent results. They found the murdered innkeeper's things. In the baby's napkins there was a Government lottery ticket; in the cradle there were broken golden bracelets, rings, ear-rings; in the boxes and the cellar money, clothes and a number of small articles. A great many of the things had been stolen during the recent Jewish *pogrom*. Many articles had traces of blood on them.

Alyona kept shuddering and muttering senselessly:

"The children, don't abandon the children. Take care of Marfutochka, kind gentlemen."

When the women had been taken and locked in secret cells and the things in their possession had been numbered and heaped up on the office table with a seal attached to them, Yegor Petrovitch breathed freely. He felt like rubbing his hands in the gay excitement of his triumph, but instead, he went to the telephone and boldly rang up not his immediate chief, but his Excellency's office.

"I, Kapliuzhny, have tracked and caught an escaped convict, Fedot Semyonov, nicknamed Fetyuk," said Yegor Petrovitch, speaking distinctly and clearly. "In view of his armed resistance, I have shot at him and slightly wounded him. Then I have also captured his mistress, an artisan's widow, Alyona Nosenkov, and her mother, who have proved to have in their possession much property looted during the Jewish *pogrom* and stolen from the murdered innkeeper at the Vesyoly Gai. All are locked up in secret cells. What are your orders?"

The answer came immediately.

"Three hundred roubles bonus and promotion. Fetyuk to be moved to the prison hospital. Inform the police superintendent and the examining magistrate. To-morrow at two o'clock come to me."

It was five o'clock when Yegor Petrovitch had at last washed, put his clothes to rights as best he could and went home, accompanied by a policeman with a lantern. The sky was clouded again. The autumn night seemed bent on lingering on. A piercing wind was blowing and the wet branches of the trees creaked piteously. Yegor Petrovitch was rather cold and hurried along impatiently, conscious that he must control himself lest he should display unseemly playfulness in his movements. Truth to tell, it was not his warm bed and the sleepy peace of his cosy bedroom he wanted at the moment—he was longing to tell some experienced, understanding people of the night's adventures, making a witty, amusing tale of it, to shout all over the town that he had been promoted and raised by his Excellency, to cry out that he was very happy and would certainly soon become "a real specialist."

He found his door unbolted and Zaharov fast asleep; but it did not enter his head to wake Zaharov with a good kick as he sometimes did. Now he carefully bolted the door and went quietly into the bedroom, trying not to make a noise with his boots. There the sanctuary lamp burned peacefully, shedding its dim soft light over the room, the Dutch stove radiated warmth and Galka could be heard breathing evenly behind the curtains of her cot. Yegor Petrovitch undressed and sat down on the edge of the bed. He was still feeling excited. Polina Mihailovna was fast asleep, and at first he did not venture to wake her, but after a few minutes he could resist no longer and lightly touched her shoulder.

"Mamma . . . Polka!" he whispered caressingly.

"Sleep, Yurok, sleep," Madame Kapliuzhny answered without waking, and turning over on the other side snored agreeably.

"But I say . . . listen what has happened," Yegor Petrovitch said in an excited whisper. "You shall have a velvet cloak—fur-lined—the very thing you want."

But Polina Mihailovna merely muttered "Presently" and dropped hopelessly asleep.

"Sleepy head!" Yegor Petrovitch said with vexation, diving irritably under the blanket.

But Galka's incoherent muttering attracted his attention; he rose, and going up to her cot drew back the curtain. The child, flushed with sleep, lay in a charming attitude, with her arms thrown back, and her lips were saying, "Papa, a picture—a picture for Galka, papa." Yegor Petrovitch smiled blissfully, and touching Galka's forehead with his lips reverently made the sign of the cross over her and closed the curtains.

As he did so he felt a pain in his right hand, his fingers seemed to smart on the outside. He went up to the sanctuary lamp and raised his hand to the light: the knuckles were grazed. This was the trace of the blow he had dealt to Fetyuk with his fist after he had shot him down. Yegor Petrovitch carefully laid a piece of cobweb on the sore place.

His excitement gradually subsided. Feeling calm and at peace he lay down, pulling the blanket over him with the greatest precision. But as he dozed off he started suddenly and opened his eyes: he had dreamed of Fetyuk as he was when they brought him, bound, to the police station. His face, convulsed with pain and helpless anger, was blood-stained and spattered with mud, and he looked at Yegor Petrovitch with a strangely fixed, feverish and disturbing stare.

"Curse the gaol-bird!" Yegor Petrovitch muttered—"making me dream of him like that!"

A few minutes later all the Kapliuzhny family was plunged in profound sleep.

(II)

A GREEDY PEASANT

(Translated by NATALIE DUDDINGTON)

I

I n the province of Oryol there is a village called the Great Springs. Some thirty years ago, in the times of serfdom, three brothers lived in that village: Ivan, Onisim and Yermil. Their master lived in foreign parts and was not hard upon the peasants; they paid him a tax, sending ten roubles from every family towards the first of October. The eldest brother, Ivan, and the one next to him, Onisim, were both married and had children: Onisim had two and Ivan three. The youngest, Yermil, was still a boy. The brothers had enough to live on but no more. They did not drink and were capital workers; when they came out to mow, they did the work of three. But as they had many mouths to feed, and Yermil was too young to do a full man's work, they just made both ends meet, and that was all. They never had to buy bread and they had two ploughs; the women sent a cow, a heifer and four sheep to graze with the village herd; they were always in time with their tax. But there was nothing to spare.

Then there was a war in Russia. The French came, the English came with the Turks and the Italians; they besieged a Russian town, Sebastopol, and killed a lot of people. The Tsar was short of soldiers, so he ordered that more men should be taken for the army. When the Great Springs turn came Onisim had to go. He was taken ill on the way and died of fever before the end of the campaign. He died, and his widow with two small children remained on Ivan's hands, and Ivan had a very hard time of it. Yermil learned to handle a scythe and gradually became used to it; so Ivan thought, "We'll find the lad a wife, let him do a man's work, and we'll manage somehow." He wanted to find Yermil a wife, but it proved to be a bad year: late frosts spoiled the rye when it was in flower; in the summer some kind of lice attacked the peas and hot winds ruined the oats. The peasants had nothing but straw to harvest. The brothers had a worse time than ever.

Meanwhile their master had troubles of his own. A letter came from him requesting an extra tax of six roubles from each family. The bailiff came to Ivan almost every day; he would come knocking his stick against the ground and stand there nagging. Ivan grew worried: he was ashamed of his neighbours seeing he was so poor.

They sat down to dinner one day, and Ivan said to Yermil: "Go and hire yourself out to a merchant, Yermil. We'll take some of your salary in advance and manage somehow. And meanwhile I'll do what I can without·you: perhaps I'll go as carrier or pick up some daily work."

Yermil grunted, scratched his head, scratched his back and said to his brother:

"It's not a job one is used to. One doesn't know what it's like in town. Their ways are different from ours—I won't know which foot to put forward, where to stand or sit down. . . ."

II

However, on thinking it over, Yermil made ready to go. He took a permit from the bailiff and went to the town. As luck would have it, he found a merchant who hired him at once and gave him twelve roubles in advance. Ivan paid the bailiff all that was due.

Yermil had struck upon a good master. He did not scold, did not work him hard, gave him plenty to eat and on holy days treated him to a glass of vodka. Yermil liked his new life. He was a quick, clever lad, and little by little he began to take stock of things.

He saw first of all that his master liked cleanliness; he had a big yard paved with brick, and when peasants brought corn from the market and littered the place with grain and manure, Yermil took a broom and swept it all clean. When there was a snowstorm and drifts of snow heaped up in the yard, Yermil took a spade and shovelled the snow on one side. If the merchant happened to pass by he smiled, stroked his beard and said to Yermil:

"Work away, my lad, your labour will not be wasted upon me."

For another thing, Yermil saw that his master liked respect: he liked people to be polite to him, to bow low. If a man called him "your worship" and bowed to him, the corn-dealer was glad and showed every favour to that man. Yermil tried to please him too: he addressed him respectfully and took off his cap in his presence, and made a cheerful face as though it were a joy to him to see his master. And the merchant was well satisfied with Yermil.

Yermil noticed yet another thing: the merchant bought corn from the peasants, and those of his men who bullied the peasants most and took heavier measure of corn from them were the merchant's favourites and he sometimes made them presents of money. Those men wore coats of fine cloth, good top-boots and had a gay time and plenty of money. So, being no fool, Yermil said to his master:

"Let me have a try at it, your worship. I have watched it done."

The merchant agreed and was well pleased with the way Yermil handled the work. He fought tooth and nail with the peasants: if grain was sold by the measure he pounded it with his fist in the bushel, knocked at the sides with a ladle and cunningly shifted it away from the edge, while in the centre it stood up in a mound; if it was sold by weight, Yermil fidgeted between the scales, caught the arrow with his finger, did his best to trip up the board with the weights with his foot. The peasants merely wagged their heads.

"That man of yours is a regular dog," they said to the corn-dealer.

The merchant pretended it was none of his business, but he watched Yermil's work and was glad. He called him to his house one day and said:

"I see your knack, Yermil. Your labour shall not be wasted with me." He treated him to a glass of vodka and at the same time pulled a five-rouble note out of his pocket and said, "Here is something for you. Go on doing your best."

Yermil was delighted. He bought himself leather gloves and a coat of fine cloth, and tried to please his master more than ever.

III

The merchant began to take him instead of a coachman. If he drove out to the landowners to buy corn, Yermil went with him; if he drove to the markets, Yermil went with him. His master could not praise him enough. He had a way of filling sacks, hiring horses, rattling the corn measure as though he had done it all his life; he did not look like a peasant any longer.

They were driving along one day. The sky was white, the fields were white, sign-posts were stuck in the snow to mark the road, the sledge runners creaked in the frost. The merchant felt dull and began talking to Yermil.

"Now, Yermil," he said, "we have bought two thousand sacks of oats. We have bought it cheap and will sell it dear. Look here"—and he showed him on his fingers—"it cost us ninety silver kopecks per sack; the storage will cost five kopecks per sack; the cost of sacks is three kopecks for each *pud* of grain: that's nine kopecks; carriage to Moscow is twenty-five kopecks per *pud*, or a rouble and a half per *pud*. What does it amount it, you reckon?"

Yermil counted it up and said:

"I make it nine roubles less ten kopecks, your worship."

"Why, you stupid! no one reckons in paper money nowadays. Count in silver."

Yermil thought it over and made it two silver roubles fifty-four kopecks per sack. He said so, but at once added, just to flatter the man:

"We are ignorant people; your worship knows best, of course, your mind sees more clearly."

His master was quite melted by these words. He stroked his beard, wrapped his coat round him and felt that he liked Yermil more than ever. And he showed him a letter.

"Look here, Yermil," he said; "you are a smart lad, but your one trouble is you can't read and write. But I have had some schooling. Because, you see, you are a peasant and your fathers may have worshipped stocks and stones, but my father was a merchant, my grandfather was a merchant, and I am one too. And so I have to be able to read and write. In this letter now they write me from Moscow that the price of oats is high—three silver roubles per sack, or more if it has been kiln-dried. Do you understand?"

"Yes," Yermil answered, and he kept wondering how much profit his master would make. And he reckoned it out that he would gain forty-six kopecks per sack because it was mostly peasants' oats, not dried. He said:

"You'll have forty-six kopecks left over for each sack, your worship."

"Left over! It is called profit, my boy. Reckon out now how much I'll gain on two thousand sacks."

Yermil could not do it, he was muddled. The merchant laughed and said: "Nine hundred and twenty roubles, you little stupid!" And he wanted to boast to Yermil. He pulled out his pocket-book, opened it and said:

"Look, there are seven hundred-rouble notes here. So if you add to that heap two notes of a hundred roubles each, that will be my profit on the oats. Understand?"

Yermil looked out of the corner of his eye and saw that the

merchant's pocket-book was swollen out with money and looked like a pillow.

"I understand," he said, and his heart glowed with greed within him.

"That's just it. It has been said that learning is light and ignorance darkness, and that is so. Now, my lad, whip up the piebald, the beast is moving at a snail's pace."

Yermil sighed and urged the horses on. From that time Yermil's heart was heavy. Whether he took up a broom, or shovelled the snow, or groomed his master's stallion his heart was not in his work.

After supper he would settle down for the night on the stove, and though he had enough to eat and felt warm, there was no peace in his thoughts. He kept seeing how he and his master drove along in the white fields with signposts stuck in the snow and a white sky above them, how the merchant wrapped his coat round him and his pocket-book stuck out from under the coat. Everyone round Yermil would be snoring, the cocks would crow, the cathedral bells would ring for matins, but Yermil still tossed from side to side. At first he had grown fat on the good food he had at his master's: his cheeks stood out, his neck was like a boar's and the coat he had brought with him from home hardly met round the waist: when he tried to fasten it the buttonholes gave way. But now his thoughts made him grow thin; he looked sallow and his eyes were sunken. He could not master his greed. And the more he looked at the merchant's life, the more he was stung with envy. The merchant would get up in the morning, put on a smart fox fur-coat and go to mass. When he came home there was a samovar on the table, white bread, rich rolls. His wife, wearing a fine dress and a cashmere shawl round her shoulders, sat drinking tea; her cheeks were red, she was plump and fat and soft like a rasp-berry. When the merchant had had his fill of food and drink he went for a walk in the arcade. Other merchants came too: they made merry, and calling in some crazy fellow

would tell him to sing and dance, while they rocked with
laughter; or they went to a tavern to drink tea and talk
business. When the merchant came home an ample dinner
was ready for him. He had roast goose every day, soup with
meat in it, porridge with butter in it, vodka and kvass to
drink. After dinner the merchant and his wife lay down on
their feather beds and slept till evening. When he woke up
he went to sit outside the gate, cracking nuts. Whoever
passed by bowed to him.

In the meantime business went on as usual. The peasants
brought corn; the merchant's men received it, wrangled
with the peasants and filled the sacks. Yermil's hands were
quite rough with using the needle and coarse thread. It had
all to be done in a hurry. Almost every day cartloads of the
merchant's corn were despatched to Moscow.

IV

Yermil understood that the chief thing for business was to
be able to read and write, to have money and employ other
people. And so he thought: "I must learn too, surely I am
no worse than anyone else." He heard that there was a man
just outside the town who taught reading and arithmetic.
One holiday Yermil asked his master's leave to go to the
cobbler's to fetch his boots, but in truth he went to find
that man. It took him some time. The man lived in a
peasant's back yard; there were snowdrifts round his hut;
the windows were tiny and one had to bend double to come
in at the door. Yermil went into the entry, knocked the snow
off his boots, took hold of the door ring and all at once felt
ashamed: a big lad like him wanting to learn to read—the
man would laugh at him!

However, he mastered himself, smoothed down his hair and
went in. He saw an elderly man, wrinkled and bony, dressed
in a clean shirt, reading a book.

"Good-day," said Yermil, and his throat was parched with

fear. The man left off reading, looked at Yermil, and Yermil saw from his eyes that he was a gentle, kind man who would not laugh at him, and all at once felt at ease. He told him of his trouble. When he said he wanted to learn to read, the man's eyes lit up with joy and he could not make enough of Yermil, but when Yermil told him what he wanted it for, he understood that Yermil was consumed by greed and was grieved.

"Do me the favour, teach me, good man," Yermil said. "I'll do anything for you, I'll be grateful to you all my life." The man said nothing and did not raise his eyes.

"Have no fear," Yermil said. "Your labour will not be wasted. I'll repay you one way or another."

The man raised his eyes and spoke, and Yermil saw quite a different man before him; his voice was stern, his face sorrowful.

"Your wish to learn is not from God, but from the devil," he said. "God has given you reason and understanding. But if you want to learn for the sake of gain, if you are envious of the merchants' easy life and want to do like them, that's not from God but from the devil. Learning is given us in order to save the soul, not to lose it."

"Why, my dear man, it's much easier to save your soul if you have money," Yermil answered jokingly, while he was really angry with the man. "Look, my master goes to Mass every morning, puts up candles worth a quarter of a rouble each, and has bought a bell for the cathedral."

The man shook his head, frowned, opened his book and read to Yermil:

"'Jesus looked up, and saw the rich men casting their gifts into the treasury. And He saw also a certain poor widow casting in thither two mites. And He said, 'Of a truth I say unto you, This poor widow hath cast in more than they all: for all these have of their abundance cast in unto the offerings of God, but she of her penury hath cast in all the living that she had'" (St. Luke xxi. 1-4).

Yermil took it in with one ear and let it out with the other; he was very much vexed with the old man and said:

"Look here, I have no time to waste talking to you: I haven't watered my master's stallion yet. Will you take a silver rouble for teaching me?"

"I don't want your money," the man said. "If you think it over and renounce your greed I'll teach you for nothing." And again he said, "Learning has been given us to save the soul, not to lose it."

"But, you queer fellow, what's the good of learning to read and write if I don't go in for business? If I remain a peasant I don't need any schooling to hold the flail properly. I want to find my line, my luck."

"Luck may be one's undoing," said the man.

Yermil grew angry, and without listening put his cap on, swore as he banged the door and went home.

V

As luck would have it, a shop assistant he knew agreed to teach him. Yermil ran to the market on the sly, bought himself an A B C and sharpened a bit of wood for a pointer; the shop assistant and he had a service sung to St. Nahum, then they went to a tavern and had a drink and Yermil set to work. He studied on the quiet so that people should not laugh at him and say, "Look, a big fellow like that wearing himself out over the A B C!" When everybody went to bed he sat over his book; when everyone went to sit by the gate he would hide himself in the stables and repeat his lesson. And he was so clever at it that before Lent was over he could make out printed words and began to understand the meaning of figures; and he could trace words with a pen.

Meanwhile his work went on as usual: he was either shovelling snow, filling sacks, or sewing them up; his master did not forget him and gave him sometimes one rouble, sometimes two. Yermil bought himself a whole new outfit and never troubled to think of his brother Ivan. He only sent him what he had promised of his salary. Sometimes he sent him fifty kopecks, sometimes twenty-five. The village was a long way off, some twenty-five miles, and the peasants came to the town seldom, only when there was some real need for it. It was by them Yermil sent money to his brother Ivan.

In the Easter week Ivan came to the town. He had grown thin during the winter; his coat was patched, his leg-wrappings were tied with string. He looked and saw Yermil was wearing a coat of fine cloth, a red shirt, velveteen trousers and top-boots. And Ivan was grieved to see it.

"You should give it a thought, Yermil," he said. "We've sold the heifer to buy flour, and the heifer wasn't enough, we had to pawn our clothes. I couldn't get any work as carrier. The cattle have all grown thin. Now I have to buy some oats for sowing and here you are showing off."

"What if I am?" Yermil replied. "I have been sending you what I received as salary, and there's five roubles or more still owing me. But the master chose to give me more than was my due—that's because I have pleased him. If you don't like my clothes, it's again my master's doing." And Yermil told a lie, saying that his master had given him presents of clothes, not of money.

Ivan had nothing to say to it. He was glad Yermil's master was pleased with the lad, but he felt sad when he looked at him. "Well," he thought, "when he takes up the plough he'll forget his fine ways. He'll come round."

They went to the tavern and had some tea with a roll and a drink of vodka. Then Ivan said to Yermil:

"Go to your master, Yermil, get your discharge and pack up your things, and I'll run to the market meanwhile. My women have asked me to sell the wool for them."

He took up his bag and went to the market.

What was Yermil to do? He was loth to leave the merchant, he had lost the habit of peasant work. He went to his master's house, stood in the entry for a few minutes and then decided not to go in. He went out at the gate and sat there eating sunflower seeds.

Ivan had another drink of vodka at the market. He was coming back feeling merry, with a new ploughshare under his arm, and some bread rings and two whistles for the children in his bag. He had sold the wool well.

When Yermil saw him he turned into the yard and went to the stables. "Yermil must have been ready and waiting for me by the gate," Ivan thought. He sat down and waited, but Yermil did not come. "What's the meaning of this?" he wondered. He went and found Yermil.

"Are you ready?" he asked. "Give me the bag, I will put the ploughshare in it. It's better for it to lie with something soft. Have you taken the money? How much was it?"

Yermil said nothing and merely snuffled. Ivan saw that the lad wanted to have his own way and grew angry. The spirit he had drunk went to his head, he lost his temper and shouted at his brother. Then he went to the merchant himself. After a while Yermil was sent for too.

"Look here, Yermil," his master said to him; "there is nothing much to do here in the summer, and your brother wants you at home and is angry about it. I don't like any nonsense of this sort. Come back again in the autumn, I'll engage you again: you are a sharp fellow. And now go home and God bless you."

He paid Yermil all he owed him and dismissed them. There was nothing for it; Yermil gathered up his belongings, slung them behind his shoulders and unwillingly followed his brother.

VI

In the week after Easter the brothers began ploughing. Yermil put on bark shoes and a hempen shirt and walked after the plough. At first he was breathless and his back ached, but then he got used to it and ploughing seemed to him easy.

But he had no liking for peasant work. He did not shirk it, but he kept thinking of his life in town.

When they sat down to dinner on a Sunday, Ivan would cut some bread and his wife pour out the cabbage soup. The bread was bitter, with notch-weed in it, the soup had just a little milk in it but no meat. Yermil would be eating it and thinking:

"Ah, in town they are having soup with meat in it and butter with their porridge."

The fallow land was ploughed; the rye was in flower; the oats began to form stems. Rain came just when it was needed, the weather was lovely and warm. Ivan went to have a look at his field, and his heart rejoiced within him.

"God has given us grace," he said to Yermil; "it will be a good harvest."

Yermil said nothing to this and went on fixing the blade to a scythe. Ivan was angry with him.

"You are like a stranger, Yermil. You should give it a thought. All good Christians are glad, but you don't seem to care."

"What is there to be glad about? We shall have enough to eat in the winter and then be short of food again. There isn't much profit in that."

"And what would you have? Not much profit—that's a nice thing to say! Too soft a life isn't good for one, my boy. You mustn't look at other people, but live as good men do."

Yermil said nothing to this. He turned away and went to the shed to sharpen the scythe.

Ivan saw that something had gone wrong with his brother. He worked as he should, did the ploughing and the mowing, but he took no pleasure in his work. He was not rude, he did not disobey Ivan, but they were not one in heart as in the old days. Yermil seemed like a stranger in the house; it was as though he had returned from the town another man.

"We must marry him," Ivan thought.

But Yermil had his own thoughts. He watched the peasants, and it was clear to him that a man with money could make much profit out of them. He saw that when a peasant was in need he was ready to put his head in the noose for money. Peasants sold cheaply and bought dearly. Yermil saw that the tavern-keepers, *kulaks* and merchants made a fortune out of them.

"Oh, if only I had money," Yermil thought, "I'd do something worth doing!"

On holy-days other young men liked to join the girls and sing with them, but Yermil had another thing in mind. He would stand near the old men and listen to their talk. What the price of flour or of salt was, how much a peasant had sold his pig for—he wanted to know it all. He took note of it and pondered it in his mind. He had grown thoughtful and sullen and shunned looking people in the face, afraid of their reading his thoughts. And he said to himself:

"Oh, if I only had a hundred roubles or so, I'd do something worth while."

The Assumption fast came. The harvest was gathered, the new rye threshed, the peasants enjoyed the good bread. Girls began to have work parties in the evenings. Songs were heard all over the village. The innkeeper was saving forty gallons of vodka for the feast of Our Lady's Intercession.

VII

"We must marry the lad," Ivan said to his wife, and she agreed. Her sister-in-law had been ill ever since Onisim died—she was melting away like a candle; the children were small and it was hard for Ivan's wife to run the house by herself. They bought a little pig and began wondering how they could find the money for the wedding. Ivan took to the market four cartloads of rye and seventeen bushels of oats, paid his tax, bought some salt, a pair of sheepskin gloves and two kerchiefs for the women and had five roubles left. That was not enough for the wedding. He talked things over with his wife and decided to get Yermil married, while Ivan would mortgage himself to a landowner close by and work for him through the winter. They broached the subject with Yermil. Ivan's wife began sighing and complaining about her life.

"All my bones ache with work," she said. "There's the cow to be milked, the pig's food to be mixed, the men's clothes to be made, the children to be fed. When I go to the fields to bind corn how can I keep pace with two scythes? My sister-in-law is sick and can't work. When the herd is driven home, there's no one to go and meet our beasts. In St. Peter's fast we very nearly lost the short-tailed sheep—we had to run over the whole village to find the wretched creature."

Yermil said nothing, as though it did not concern him.

Ivan would listen and then give a hint too.

"It's hard for my wife to manage alone," he would say; "it's very awkward."

But Yermil had only one thing in mind: "The merchant will be buying grain now and make no end of money. It's been a fine year, the holiday is coming, the tax has to be paid—the peasants will simply flood the markets. Ah, if only I had money!"

Seeing that Yermil's ears were closed, Ivan said to him straight:

"You should give it a thought, Yermil. My wife can't do more than she can. It's been a good year and we ought to make a marriage for you. Have you anyone in mind? What about Doonka Pavlikova—she is a fine worker."

Yermil said nothing and looked at the ground.

"What's the good of hanging about?" Ivan went on; "you are just the right age: you will be twenty-two on St. George's Day. You are a good-sized young colt. I will hire myself out for the winter and you get married. Any girl will marry you. We are not nobodies. We have two horses and a cow and a young pig, and plenty of flour to last us till next harvest."

Yermil shook his mop of hair, looked sideways and said, "I'll go to the corn-dealer."

"Whatever for?"

"To live."

Ivan was angry and did not know what to say. He cursed, and picking up his cap went to sit outside the cottage, looking into the street.

In the meantime Yermil made ready, packed his belongings, put on his top-boots, cut himself a stick and said to Ivan:

"I am going. If you want money, send me word by the peasants. Or will you come yourself?"

Ivan was very angry. He turned away and did not say a word to Yermil.

Ivan's wife was spreading out her homespuns in the threshing yard. Yermil found her and said:

"Good-bye, sister-in-law!"

Seeing him with a bag and a stick, she stared at him open-eyed and ran to her husband.

"Have you two quarrelled?" she cried. "Where is Yermil off to? Have you gone crazy, you devils, plague take you! We have always lived in peace and quiet, and all of a sudden you do a thing like that!"

"Let him!" Ivan said. "Peasant bread is bitter to him. Let him try the sweet. He'd better go."

However, the woman brought Yermil to reason, and he stayed over the feast of Intercession. And after the holy day Ivan opposed him no longer, but harnessed the gelding and took Yermil to the town.

VIII

Everything went on as before. Yermil haggled with the peasants, sewed up sacks and did his utmost to please his master. He felt as much at home in this life as a fish in water.

The merchant noticed that as Yermil was receiving the rye he marked the weight in figures.

"Why, have you learnt?" he asked.

Yermil grinned and said:

"Yes, your worship. I can write words too."

The merchant thought it over and added two roubles to his monthly salary.

"Do your best," he said; "your labours will not be wasted upon me."

Yermil lived at the merchant's the winter and the summer, and in the autumn it was a full year since he had been with him. He was to stay the following winter too Ivan gave up all hopes of Yermil and hired a man to help in the summer.

And the longer Yermil lived at the merchant's, the more eager he felt. His one dream was to grow rich. He kept puzzling his head about it. "If I could only begin," he thought, "if I could only save up a hundred or so; that would set me up, I could do a lot with a hundred." He noticed that some of the assistants pilfered their masters and so procured money for their pleasures; sometimes they put down the expenses wrongly or sold the grain out of the storehouse. They tried to tempt Yermil to do the same, but on thinking it over he refused. "If I join them, I'll have to go shares with them, but they want money for pleasure, and I—to set up in business. I had better try by myself." . . . He was very keen, so he found a man to whom he took oats from his master's horses. He transferred a whole bag to him, and then, choosing a good moment, went for the money.

"What money do you want?" the man asked.

"Why, don't you know? For the oats."

"Did you sow those oats?"

"I didn't, but give me the money!"

18

"And how would you like to go to prison?"

Yermil was frightened and decided never to steal again.

The winter came, and his master began taking him as coachman once more. They drove to markets and to the landowners, staying in various places two or three days at a time. Cartloads of the merchant's corn were being driven to the town night and day. Yermil was working hard. He got up at daybreak, watered the horses and gave them oats, unlocked the store-house, polished the bushel measures on the inside with brick, fixed the scales. The merchant drank his tea and walked along the market; when he bought corn from a peasant he wrote the price on the sack in chalk and told the man to take it to the store-house. Yermil was there to receive it, and he knew his business. All would have been well, but something seemed to be gnawing at Yermil's heart—he wanted to grow rich. He had thought at first that his master would let him do the paying, and he decided, "I'll take the money, hide it away somewhere and then say I've dropped it." But the corn-dealer was afraid that Yermil might make a mistake in reckoning and did not trust him with the money.

Yermil had thought too of coming to terms with the peasants, but he was afraid that when the sacks came to be filled, the wrong weight would be discovered and his master would have him put in prison. Besides, he did not know the peasants, so he could not trust them. And so for a time none of Yermil's plans succeeded.

IX

They were driving along one day. The sky was as white as the fields, signposts were stuck along the road, the runners creaked on the snow. The merchant felt dull. He wrapped his coat round him, put his head on the pillow and dropped asleep. Yermil looked round. A ground wind was whirling the snow, fluffy clouds hung low in the sky, it was snowing slightly. The merchant lay on his back, snoring. Yermil was thinking and felt afraid of his own thoughts. He jumped off the box, let the horses go slowly and walked behind the sledge.

He was thinking: "My master has a lot of money on him. If I took three or four hundred he would not notice it. And if he missed it later he would think he had made a mistake in reckoning."

The corn-dealer was fast asleep.

Yermil felt cold. He let the horses go at a trot—the road was smooth and even—and ran after the sledge. His heart was beating wildly; greed was blinding him, evil thoughts gave him no peace. "I shall never have another such chance," he thought; "he is fast asleep and will never notice my taking the money." And Yermil's face looked sullen and hard. He stopped the horses, jumped into the sledge and put his hand into the breast of the corn-dealer's coat.

The man woke up and looked at Yermil in consternation. "What are you up to, you dog?" he said.

Yermil lost his head. His hands shook, there was a darkness before his eyes; he seized the cushion and threw it over the corn-dealer's face. The man kicked convulsively and shook all over—he was choking. Yermil was frightened. He took away the cushion and saw that his master's eyes were bloodshot, the veins stood out on his face, his cheeks were blue and his mouth open. He was dead.

What was Yermil to do? He looked about him and there was nothing but the bare plain all round. The horses walked on, the harness creaked, the runners crunched in the snow, a few flakes of snow were falling. All was still. Yermil put his hand into his master's breast pocket, took out the money, and picking out the thickest bundle of notes hid it in the sledge lining. He put the rest of the money back into the dead man's coat and drove to town.

X

There was a great to-do in the town. Yermil was called up and severely cross-examined.

But apparently the corn-dealer had died of a stroke, and a great deal of money—several thousand—was found upon him. They tried to discover if any of it was missing, but the dead man had kept no proper accounts and he had a big turnover; it seemed he had a bigger sum with him than they reckoned, so they went no further and set Yermil free.

In the spring the corn-dealer's widow collected her debts, sold the corn and dismissed the assistants, as she wound up the business. Yermil came for his discharge.

"You'd better stay with me as coachman," she said. "I'll buy some good horses and you will drive me in a fine carriage."

"I can't possibly. My brother is angry and bids me go home. It's ploughing and sowing time with us."

"Why, give up the ploughing! I am well satisfied with you. You are a smart lad, and you used to drive out with my husband. Stay!"

But Yermil refused.

"I can't possibly," he said. "We are peasants and have land."

"Well, just as you like."

She gave him a rouble.

"Pray for your master's soul," she said.

And she thought: "Another man would have got away with the money, but this one has a conscience, he has brought it all back." Then she reckoned out how much was owing to him, paid him and let him go.

Yermil waited for the night, and climbing up to the hay-loft pulled out the bundle of notes from a hiding-place. He put them inside his boot, and slinging his bag behind his back went home.

He managed it all very cleverly. He hid the money and

worked as he had done before, keeping pace with his brother. He was wondering how he could declare his ill-gotten wealth and make use of it by putting it into business. He saw that the innkeeper had a grown-up daughter—a plain, ill-tempered girl and a slut. She spent her days sitting in the porch cracking nuts; when she went indoors she nagged at the servant and gave her no peace.

Yermil had his own plans. He did not care about her looks or temper. He took to walking by the inn, dropping a word to her now and then. The girl did not so much as look at him. She knew he came of a peasant family, so that nothing was to be gained by taking up with him. She dreamed of more genteel wooers—priests' sons or clerks.

Seeing that his advances were of no avail, Yermil found a suitable moment and walked into the inn. The innkeeper was a quick, clever man, thoroughly trained in his business. He was surprised to see Yermil, for Yermil had never come into the place before, but he showed no sign of it.

"What is it?" he asked.

Yermil looked round and saw that the room was empty.

"I have come on important business to you, Petrovitch!" he said.

"What sort of business?"

"I want to marry your Anfissa."

The innkeeper stared at him and said:

"Are you in your right mind, my boy? You'd better go and sleep it off."

Yermil was not discouraged.

"You can go to the town and find out about me—I can do anything in the commercial line, I know how to deal in grain or buy anything. I can read and write too, and add up figures."

The innkeeper sat drumming his fingers on the table and smiling broadly as he looked at Yermil.

"Talk away," he said. "I don't remember when I have heard anything more funny."

Yermil looked round, bent down to the man and said:

"And what if I have money? What if I can buy you up altogether, if it comes to that?"

The innkeeper started.

"How so? How did you come by it?"

But when he recalled that Yermil's master had died on the high-road and had a great deal of cash with him, he grasped at once where Yermil's money had come from. He thought it over and decided the offer would suit him. He glanced at the lad and liked the look of him.

He thought again.

"How much money have you?"

"Sixteen hundred."

"True?"

"I can show it you if you don't believe me."

"Bring it along."

"Not likely! I know those tricks. If you like to come to the kitchen gardens at dawn, I'll show it you."

"He is a smart lad, one has to look sharp with him," the innkeeper thought. "He'll get on," and he liked Yermil still better.

XI

At dawn the innkeeper stole into the kitchen gardens and hid in a ditch. As he lay there he saw Yermil walking towards him, looking round like a wolf and holding his hand in the breast of his coat. The innkeeper peeped out and waved to him, asking in a hoarse voice:

"Have you brought it?"

Yermil was still looking round. He glanced into the ditch and walked across the kitchen gardens. Seeing there was no one about, he said:

"Lie still, I'll bring it."

"But why do you hold your hand in the breast of your coat?"

"Oh, just to try you. I thought perhaps you had brought someone with you."

"Well, he is a sharp one," the innkeeper thought. "The very kind of man to make money!"

Yermil brought the money, and, true enough, it was sixteen hundred.

The innkeeper was very keen.

"Make an offer to my daughter," he said.

But this was not enough for Yermil, he thought of still another trick. He went to the town and called on his former mistress. He told her his story and said:

"Seeing that I can read and write and have grown used to trade while I lived at your house, our innkeeper wants me to marry his daughter and to live at his house. He is a rich man, but the girl is very plain."

And he asked the widow's advice whether he should accept the man's offer.

"You are our masters and we look to you for good counsel. We country people are an ignorant lot. You know more about these matters."

These words were like honey to the widow. She knit her brows and pondered.

"So the girl's father is rich, you say?" she asked.

"He is well off. I expect he has several thousand in his pocket."

"And you say he has only one child?"

"Only one."

"And the girl is plain?"

Yermil merely wagged his head. The widow considered the matter and gave her judgment:

"Well, Yermil, looks aren't everything and you shouldn't run away from your good fortune. I advise you to marry her."

She took an old shawl out of a box and gave him:

"Give it to your betrothed," she said.

Yermil bowed down to the ground before her, and after doing his shopping went back to the village.

As he drove home he thought:

"I have covered up my tracks now."

And so he had. The innkeeper died before the year was out.

XII

Meanwhile the serfs were set free.

Yermil went in for trade, hired his former owner's mill and did business on a big scale.

His life was one continual round of buying and selling. He bought cheaply, he sold dearly. And the only thing he had in mind was to make money. He had a chaise built, bought a fast horse and dashed from village to village.

"You give yourself no rest, Yermil Ivanitch," people said to him.

"A wolf has to be on the run," he answered.

And Yermil was indeed like a wolf. A wolf can smell a carcase a long way off, and Yermil seemed to have a keen nose for trouble. Wherever there was trouble he was sure to be. If peasants' cattle were being sold for arrears, Yermil was the first to come to the auction, and bought everything at half-price. If a village was burned down, Yermil turned up at once, lending money to the peasants for building and paying the taxes; but when the time of reckoning came, Yermil laid the village waste like the fire. If there was a cattle plague and the peasants lost their beasts, Yermil appeared immediately and gave a cow to that man, a heifer to this one; but when it was time to pay, he proved worse than the plague.

His heart seemed to have turned to stone. No sight of sorrow could melt him. There was no pity in him. If he had a chance to pocket a rouble he did so; if it was an orphan's last penny he did not scorn that either. He spread his web throughout the neighbourhood.

The peasants struggled in this web like flies. Poor men complained of Yermil bitterly and abused him behind his back, but when they needed money they took off their caps to him and spoke to him respectfully.

It was not only people's poverty that profited Yermil. He grew fat on their wrongs, weakness and ignorance. If a barn was broken in and stolen grain brought to his mill at night, he did not inquire where it came from so long as he made money on it. By that time the vodka monopoly was abolished and peasants began to drink a great deal. Yermil opened a dozen pot-houses. In drawing up contracts he inserted forfeit clauses, taking advantage of the peasants' illiteracy and going to law with them.

In this way he soon grew so rich that he would have lost count of his money had he not been able to read and write. He bought the mill he had rented and built many storehouses.

As he drove along the road he said to himself sometimes: "You are a clever man, Yermil Ivanitch! You have great luck. You will move to the town presently and keep company with the merchants. People will hold you in great respect."

In their simplicity the peasants forgave Yermil a great deal for his piety. He never missed a church service, he lighted thick candles before the ikons and put twenty-five kopecks or even half a rouble on the collection plate.

XIII

Yermil saw he was doing business on a large scale and had a big turnover. He could no longer go away from home. Every day cartloads of grain came to the mill; the pestle was pounding millet, and one had to add some dye to the mortars to make it look better; the millstones were grinding rye, and one had to see that each customer received the right kind: the peasants liked it coarse, and for Moscow fine flour was required; pigs were grunting in the pigsties, bulls were tied to the blocks in the stalls, geese were cackling and ducks quacking in the fenced pond. All this had to be fed, fattened, killed, plucked, singed, stored away. A master's eye was needed to keep watch over everything.

Yermil had long arms and keen eyes; he settled on the mill himself and let his assistants do business for him in the neighbourhood. And while in the old days he could not have managed it all by himself, now everything was caught in the same web. The peasants struggled like fish in Yermil's net.

All would have been well except that Yermil had no children. Anfissa had grown so stout with the easy life that she looked like a tree stump.

Her house was in disorder; there was dirt and dust everywhere, the servants did not stay with her. At first Yermil did not care because he had no thoughts to spare for it. He would sometimes shout at his wife or give her a blow and then go off on business again. But when he settled at home he saw that Anfissa was no good at all. He felt angry with her and took to beating her. The woman went about black and blue.

Anfissa was in a sad case. She was dull of wit; she had never heard a good word from anybody. Her father's one thought was to grab as much money as he could. All her mother had cared for while she lived was good food and sweet drink. Anfissa's idea of life was the same.

"The man must provide the money," she thought, "and I will sleep with him, bear children, have good food and sweet drink and wear fine clothes."

When Yermil began beating her, she wondered what she was to do and took to drinking vodka on the quiet. She would get drunk and limp in the body and lie flat on her feather bed, and Yermil might kill her for aught she cared. When she was drunk, the sea was knee-deep to her. Yermil would swear and turn black with anger, but he could do nothing.

However, five years after their marriage they had a son, and a year later another one. Yermil's spirits rose. He had been greedy before, but now that he had children he grew worse than ever. It was nothing to him that other people had children too. All he thought of was to snatch what he

could from others so that his children could live like the
gentry.

"I'll set them up in life and make gentlemen of them," he
thought. "Let everyone see what Yermil's sons are like!"

XIV

Meanwhile a bad time had come. One lean year followed
another; the peasants had grown poor, the cattle were getting scarce, the gentry had lost their wealth and the merchants began buying up their lands. And every merchant
who settled in the country tried to catch the peasants in
his net. Yermil felt cramped and thought that as things
were he could not make much money. Twice indeed the
merchants had tripped him up and he suffered severe loss.

"No, this won't do," he thought; "I must seek safer
ground."

Luckily for him he found a purchaser for his mill and sold
it; he sent the grain to Moscow, received the money for it
and moved to the town. It appeared he had fifty thousand
roubles.

Just before he moved, his brother Ivan came to see him.
His coat was torn and tied up with a piece of tow, his bark
shoes had holes in them, his face was thin and his hair grey.

"You should give it a thought, brother Yermil," he said.
"The Lord has visited me with trouble. My cow died, my
eldest son had to go for a soldier, and the village elders out
of spite against you took away your land. We have nothing
to live on, to say nothing of paying the tax. I've kept away
from you for many years, but I have come now. Help me,
for Christ's sake, save me from distress."

Yermil was sitting on a cloth-upholstered bench; his cheeks
were fat and ruddy, a gold chain was round his neck, his
waistcoat was of velvet and his boots polished like a mirror.

"I have children of my own," he said; "I have to bring
them up. You should have worked harder and then you

wouldn't have to go a-begging. This is what comes ot shirking your work."

Ivan turned round, and wiping his eyes walked home with a heavy heart.

"May God be your judge, Yermil Ivanitch!" he said.

Yermil had thought of calling his brother back, but felt too proud to get up from his seat.

"He is a nice one!" he said. "One might think he came for what was his own. It wouldn't have hurt him to bow down to my feet, I should have thought."

Yermil moved to the town. He bought a house and had thought to deal in corn, but he saw that trade was bad. He wondered what he had better do with his money. He looked about him and asked some of the merchants' advice. He saw that some of the chief among them were collecting money from all sides and lending it out to tradespeople for business. And those who gave money to those people could sit with their hands folded: profit would flow to them without any trouble on their part. That profit was called *interest*, and the men who managed the whole thing were called *bankers*. Merchants had opened many such banks throughout Russia.

Yermil wondered into which bank he had better put his money. He grasped that it was best to go to a bank that gave most profit; he did not do it at once, however, but made more inquiries.

"What more do you want?" other merchants said to him. "The director is a man of great repute and much respected."

So Yermil put his money into the bank they spoke of.

And at last his wish came true. He lived exactly as the corn-dealer whom he wanted to imitate had done. Yermil copied all his ways with regard to food and sleep and going out. Getting up in the morning, he washed, put on a fox fur coat and went to mass. When he came home from the service the samovar was on the table, white bread, rich rolls. After Yermil had had his fill of food and drink he went for a walk in the arcade. The merchants gathered there and made merry, calling in some simpleton and telling him to sing and dance while they rocked with laughter. Or they went to a tavern to drink tea, listen to the barrel organ and talk business. When Yermil returned home, dinner was waiting for him. He had roast goose every day, porridge with butter, vodka and kvass. After dinner Yermil lay down on his feather bed and slept till vespers. When he woke up he had a drink of kvass and went to sit by the gate, cracking nuts. And everyone who passed by bowed to him.

Yermil grew fat living like that. He had a big belly, his flesh was soft and flabby, his cheeks were puffy and he had the eyes of a dead codfish. Walking to church made him as hot as though he had been to the bath-house.

He lived in this way for a couple of years and he began to feel very dull. He slept so much that when he woke and sat up in bed his eyes were still dim with sleep. He would tell the servant to bring him some kvass, but when he had drunk the kvass there was again nothing to do. He would sit swinging his legs, yawn a dozen times, walk about the room and look round—he did not know what to do with himself.

Then he roused himself and walked to the arcade. He looked about—everything in the arcade was exactly the same as the day before. It was sickening. He came home, had the stallion harnessed and took Anfissa for a drive. Anfissa sat in the carriage like a log, dressed in fine clothes and with gold earrings in her ears, but her face looked drunken and she never spoke a word of sense. Yermil pondered and looked askance at her and felt more dull than ever.

"You've grown soft and weak, Yermil Ivanitch," he said to himself. And he thought he would recall his young days: he went to his garden, borrowed the gardener's scythe and tried mowing. It made him breathless and he gave it up before he had finished a row. "No," he said, "it isn't a merchant's work," and he peeped through a crack in the fence to see if anyone was watching him.

XV

Yermil ate and slept; after a meal he would go to sleep, and when he woke up he did not know what to do with himself. He was dull and his one thought was to amuse himself.

And he took to bad ways. He forgot God's law, he forgot that his children were not babies any longer; he beat Anfissa and carried on with other men's wives. He took to drinking too.

Meanwhile it happened that a poor widow's son had died of sore throat, and being very poor she went to sell his clothes. The widow had been fond of her boy and spent her last farthing on dressing him up; just before he died she had a velveteen jacket and breeches made for him. Yermil saw the widow and coveted the clothes. "I'll dress up my Vaska in this," he thought. He called the woman, fingered the stuff and saw it was quite a good velveteen and perfectly new. But he showed no sign of liking the clothes.

"What do you want for this rubbish?" he asked.

"It isn't rubbish, Yermil Ivanitch, it's a perfectly new suit. I had just had it made when my darling died. The velveteen alone cost me four roubles. If I weren't in such straits I wouldn't dream of selling it. But I am in dire need."

"Fiddlesticks! People in dire need don't go in for such clothes. Your boy could have worn a hempen shirt just as well. Paupers like yourself throw away money and then go a-begging. But it's no use talking; if you like taking fifty kopecks, here it is; if not—go along. I have no time to waste on you."

The widow hesitated; she had been trying to sell the clothes since the morning, and when she came home there would be no food in the house. She wiped her tears and gave Yermil the clothes. Yermil chucked fifty kopecks to her, called Vaska and told him to put on the jacket.

Before the week was out Vaska died of sore throat.

XVI

Yermil had now only one son left, Vanka. He sent him to school, but it did the boy no good. His mother drank, his father lived a bad life; the boy watched them and thought, "Why should I put myself out? My father has plenty of money and I can do without any schooling. My father can barely read and write and yet he has made a fortune, and I am provided for, so there is no need for me to worry. There's enough to last me a lifetime." As the boy grew up he picked up some friends, and noticing where his father kept money, helped himself to a little at a time to spend on his pleasures. Yermil saw that the lad was indulging himself, visiting taverns and being rowdy, so he gave him a beating. Vanka was angry and behaved worse than ever.

One day as Yermil sat in the tavern the merchants began reading a newspaper, and read that the bank in which Yermil had kept his money had gone bankrupt: the director had mismanaged the business and squandered the depositors' money. Yermil could not believe the news when he heard it; he looked at the paper himself and turned green with fright. He took the train to the town where the bank was. He made inquiries, called on this man and on that, and found that the director was in prison, his assistants had run away and the money was gone. Yermil gnashed his teeth, and when he returned to the inn he cried aloud, clutched at his hair and flung himself on the ground. On his way home he walked unsteadily as though he were drunk.

At home a spoiled son and a wife half-crazy with vodka were waiting for him—there was no one with whom he could share his grief. He dragged himself to the arcade and saw that rich merchants kept away from him, while others had no thought to spare for anyone: they too had lost money in the bank. Yermil felt very bitter.

"I think I'll go to Skliadnev," he said to himself; "when I was rich he was my best friend."

As he walked up he saw Skliadnev sitting by his gate warming himself in the sun. Seeing Yermil, Skliadnev wanted to hide indoors, but there was not time. Yermil walked up to him and took off his cap.

"I am in great trouble, Falalei Ivanitch," he said; "I have come to ask your advice."

Skliadnev scratched himself and yawned.

"I am too busy to talk to you just now," he answered, and thought to himself, "I hope he isn't going to ask for a loan."

Yermil was offended by his words, but there was nothing for it, he had to bear it.

"What am I to do?" he asked.

"Do what fools do. There is no written law for fools. If you hadn't hankered after a big interest on your money you wouldn't have lost it. You are much too greedy."

"You wouldn't refuse a chance of gain either, Falalei Ivanitch. You are greedy enough too."

"You are a fool and no mistake. Whatever I am, I am rich and you are a pauper. What extra money I had, I put into the state bank: the interest is less, but it's safer. And you were after profit—so now you have to repent of your foolishness."

"But do tell me what I am to do, advise me."

"Think for yourself. You have a head on your shoulders like everyone else."

Yermil sat still for a few minutes and then said, getting up:

"Well, good-bye then, Falalei Ivanitch. I didn't think you would speak to me like that."

"I am sorry, that's the best I can do for you."

Yermil bowed his head and walked home. Skliadnev's dogs ran out and barked at him, and their owner did not trouble to call them away.

XVII

Yermil paced up and down his rooms, and thought and thought. When he went to bed he could not sleep. The nights were long, his pillow felt hot, he could find no peace. Anfissa lay beside him snoring, with no care in the world. Vanka climbed over the fence as soon as it was dark and disappeared till morning. The house was deserted. A sanctuary lamp burned before the ikons and the Saviour's face looked down from the wall.

And Yermil fancied that the Saviour was looking into his soul. He would turn to the wall, pull the blanket over his face and lie quietly, but no sleep came to him. "Ah," he thought, "there is no one with whom I can share my misery." And he recalled his peasant life. If anyone had trouble, the other peasants did not avoid him like the plague; they did something to help him or at least spoke a kind word, and that made one feel better. It is not for nothing the proverb says that in company death itself has no terrors. "Townspeople are a bad sort," Yermil thought; "while you are rich they can't make enough of you, but if you are poor you might not exist. It truly says in that song they sing here, 'All your friends forsake you when days of sorrow come.' There is no mercy in town." And when he recalled his life and the way he had wronged the peasants and grieved his brother Ivan, he felt more sad than ever. He threw off the blanket and looked about him; the rooms were deserted, a sanctuary lamp was burning before the ikon, and Christ was looking at him sternly and sorrowfully. Yermil sat up in bed, clutched at his head and wept bitterly.

Trouble never comes alone. While Yermil was grieving over his loss, wondering how he could mend his affairs and thinking about his life, Anfissa had a stroke. Yermil was sitting in the garden when they ran to tell him. He rushed to the house, and when he saw Anfissa he trembled all over. It was not that he felt sorry for her, but her death recalled to him how he had strangled his master. Anfissa looked exactly like the dead man. Her head was thrown back, her eyes were bloodshot, the veins stood out on her face, her cheeks were blue and her mouth twisted. Yermil was completely overcome; he sat down in a corner and could not get up—his legs gave way under him.

Anfissa was buried and Yermil remained alone with his son Vanka.

He sold his house and moved into lodgings. He tried to begin trade again and bought a truck-load of rye from the peasants. But it was hard for him: he had lost the habit of work and was no longer strong. And as he looked at Vanka he saw that he would be a poor helper to him. His thoughts too gave him no rest. He sold the rye and locked up in a chest the money he received for it. "I have many sins on my conscience," he thought. "I will now live quietly on what I have and try to save my soul." Yermil went to mass and to matins and to vespers, and his knees ached with kneeling. He took to fasting and ate only one plain roll a day—tea and a roll was all he had.

He lay in bed one night and anguish was gnawing at his heart; he was alone in the room, a sanctuary lamp was burning before the ikons. He fancied he and his master were driving along the high-road, white fields around them and a white sky overhead; signposts were stuck on either side and the runners creaked in the snow. Yermil could not lie still and sat up in bed—his heart was breaking within him. And he prayed to God: "Remember my devotions, O Lord, the money I have given to the churches, the candles I have put up, the masses I have heard. Forgive me my sins! Give me peaceful sleep!" He stood before the ikon and began bowing down to the ground. When he was tired out he lay down and dozed.

Through his sleep he heard something rustle close to his head. He tried to open his eyes but dozed off again. He heard once more a clank and a bang and then all was quiet. He wanted to see what it was, but sleep overcame him. And suddenly he felt a hand moving stealthily. Yermil started and saw Vanka standing before him in his stockinged feet with his hand under his father's pillow. Yermil shuddered.

"What are you up to, you dog?" he asked.

Vanka rushed out of the room and disappeared.

Yermil jumped out of bed and looked under the pillow—the keys of his chest were there. Lighting a candle he unlocked the chest and gasped. There was no money in it, only a wrapper.

Yermil tried to run, but his legs would not obey him; he tried to shout, but his voice failed him. And so he sat barefoot on the chest till dawn.

In the morning people saw that Yermil's hair, that had been black as a beetle, had turned grey and one could hardly recognise him. It happened in a single night.

Vanka ran away from the town, and some time afterwards a rumour reached Yermil that he had been caught in some wrongdoing and sent to Siberia.

Then Yermil prayed. "Let me die, O Lord!" But God did not send him death.

XVIII

Ivan heard that Yermil was in trouble. He put on his coat, took a stick, thrust a slice of bread into the breast of his coat and walked to the town to find his brother. He saw a wrinkled bent old man sitting on a bench. Tears came into Ivan's eyes.

"Good-day, brother Yermil!" he said. "How are you?"

Yermil started and cried out, his face lit up, and his arms and legs trembled with joy. They sat down and began to talk. Ivan saw that his brother was in a bad way. His voice was breaking, tears trickled down his beard. He seemed quite shattered.

"You should give it a thought, Yermil," he said. "Despair is a sin."

Yermil looked down and wept.

Ivan felt so sorry for him that there was a mist before his own eyes. He turned away, and wiping his eyes with the skirt of his coat, cleared his throat and said:

"It's no use talking, make ready to go with me. Your land in the village is safe enough, they haven't eaten it. Come along!"

Yermil did as his brother told him. He sold his things and got a hundred roubles for them; half of that money he gave to the church and half to his brother Ivan; then he slung a bag behind his back and walked to the village with his brother.

Ivan's affairs were better. He had found husbands for all his daughters and a wife for his nephew and sent him to live in her family; his son was married and grandchildren were born to him; he built another cottage and the place was swarming with people; they could live fairly well, but they had not enough land. The children were born after the census and no land was allotted to them. Ivan set to work: he treated the village elders to ten roubles' worth of vodka and, consulting the registers, they found that Yermil had never ceased to belong to the commune and returned him his land. Yermil tried ploughing, but his back ached so badly that he could hardly walk home.

He settled in the outer room. He helped the women in their work, mixed the pigs' food or emptied the slops or fetched water. He never came out into the street. He had done so at first, but the children gave him no peace. As soon as they saw him they began to shout:

"Merchant! Merchant! Buy some spittle from us!" or a woman would go past him and, recalling his wrongs, could not resist giving him a piece of her mind.

"So you've choked at last, you greedy soul?" she would say. "They've stopped your mouth after all!"

And Yermil kept out of people's way.

When he first returned to the village he felt easier in his mind. "I'll live with my own people," he thought, "and rest from my thoughts." When he came out into the fields he rejoiced at every blade of grass. He looked at the meadow and thought, "That's where we used to take the horses for the night." He was glad he recognised the place. When he saw the willow at the cross-roads he remembered it too.

XIX

But after a time Yermil's troubles began again. Autumn came and the nights were long and dark. Yermil would go to bed, but he could not sleep. He listened—all was quiet. A cow stirred in the shed. The pig in its sty scratched itself sleepily against the post. A dog barked in the village and then started howling. The cocks crew. Yermil turned over, but still he could not sleep.

His past rose before him. He had ruined one man, cheated another, deceived a third, went to law with a fourth.

Yermil felt wretched. He banished one set of thoughts and another one would come instead.

He saw a coffin covered with blue brocade and his son Vaska in it. His little nose stood out sharply on his bluish face, and he was dressed in the velveteen jacket and breeches. The sexton stood reading the Psalms over him. Yermil shut his eyes and buried his face in the pillow. He did not know what to do with himself in his misery, and jumping off the bed, knelt down in prayer. When he was tired out he lay down again and dozed off.

But just as his thoughts grew vague he suddenly heard through his sleep that a hand was creeping to his pillow. He started and sat up. All was still. The room was dark and cool. The church bell was tolling the hour, and the sound of it was like a human voice.

Yermil dropped off to sleep. And he dreamed he was in the open road. The horses walked slowly, the harness creaked, the runners crunched in the snow, a few snowflakes were falling. The dead man lay on his back, his mouth was open, the veins stood out on his face and his eyes were blood-shot. And as Yermil looked on he suddenly saw in his dream that the corpse quivered and sat up, saying, "What are you up to, you dog?" Yermil gasped, and crying aloud, ran out of his room, shaking with terror. Sometimes he woke others with his shouts.

Rumours spread about the village that a demon attacked Yermil at nights. Ivan saw that his brother was in a bad way; he was grieved and wondered how he could comfort Yermil.

One day Ivan was summoned to the village meeting. Ivan found Yermil and said to him:

"Put on your coat and come along to the meeting with me. It's no use your talking. You are one of us too."

XX

Yermil did as his brother told him, and putting on his coat took a stick and went. When they had come to the meeting, Yermil took off his cap and bowed to the peasants; then he hid behind other men's backs and stood hanging his head.

The peasants discussed their affairs, and Yermil heard them talking about the land. Their own was not enough and the land all round was leased by merchants at fancy prices. It appeared that a merchant rented an estate close to the village; there was plenty of arable land there, ponds, meadows and forest, and the merchant's lease had only another six months to run. It would be fine if the villagers could rent that estate, but it was difficult. For one thing they did not know where the gentleman lived; for another, the merchant had paid him the rent in advance and the peasants had no such money. And besides, it was all a subtle, intricate business, and the peasants in their ignorance did not know how to tackle it. There's many a slip between the cup and the lip. Yermil listened to them and recalled that he had once bought some millet from the gentleman and paid him in instalments, sending the money to him in Petersburg. He wanted to tell this to the peasants, but his courage failed him and he stood in silence throughout the meeting. When they came home Yermil took an old notebook out of his bag and found in it the name of the street and house where the gentleman lived—he had it all written down. He told Ivan, and when the other peasants heard of it, they called a meeting. Yermil went to it too, told them the gentleman's address and hid behind people's backs. And the elders said, "Let us send Yermil to do the business for us. He can read and write and he is a clever man, he will do his best for us." There was a great uproar. Some said that Yermil had cheated them, some that he had extracted twice their due from them, and others shouted that if they let Yermil act for them he wouldn't scruple to sell the village. Yermil looked down and never said a word, but after listening for a time he turned round and hobbled home like one in disgrace. And he said to himself:

"There, Yermil Ivanitch, your sins have found you out!"

When the peasants saw that Yermil had left the meeting they calmed down. Ivan stood up for his brother.

"You should give it a thought, good people," he said. "God has punished Yermil, and it is not for us to finish him off. He has done much wrong, there's no denying it, but then God alone is without sin."

The peasants talked it over and decided to send Yermil on behalf of the village; word was passed that they were to keep it quiet, lest, heaven forbid, the merchant should hear and snatch the bargain from them. They collected twenty-five roubles and let Yermil go to Petersburg.

XXI

Yermil was glad to be of service to the peasants. He travelled to Petersburg partly on foot, partly by train, and found the gentleman. A man who can read and write can easily find his way about.

The gentleman had a good memory. He recalled how he sold the millet and recognised Yermil.

"Well, what is it, Yermil Ivanitch?" he asked.

But when he looked at him he noticed how the man had changed: his face was lined, his hair grey, and he wore peasant's clothes. The gentleman was surprised.

"What has happened to you?" he asked.

Yermil told him of his troubles—of how his family perished, of how he lost his money, and said:

"God has punished me for my sins. I had no mercy, I paid no heed to people's tears and wronged many."

And he told the gentleman that the peasants had sent him to hire the land for them. And since Yermil had seen the peasants' need and the merchants' way of living, he put the case before the gentleman very clearly. And when he told how poor the peasants were, how little land they had, how the merchants oppressed them, the gentleman was moved to pity. He liked Yermil's words. He let the peasants have the land cheaper than the merchant had it, and arranged for the money to be paid in instalments. He had a deed drawn up, gave it to Yermil and dismissed him.

Yermil's heart rejoiced within him. He put up at an inn and went to bed, and God sent him sweet, peaceful sleep.

When he returned to the village the peasants called a meeting; Yermil accounted for his expenses, and read the deed the gentleman had drawn up about the land. The peasants were beside themselves with joy. They forgot all the wrong Yermil had ever done them.

When Yermil came out into the village street, people were kind and friendly to him. If the children started teasing him, the women ran out at once to stop them and bowed to Yermil.

And Yermil's mind found peace. When night came and he lay down on his sacking, the old thoughts would stir within him and die down again. And God gave him sweet and peaceful sleep.

XXII

Meanwhile his bankers had been tried, stock was taken of the money they had left and it was settled that the depositors were to receive three thousand roubles each. A notice came to Yermil from the town.

He was perturbed and felt ill at ease. He could not sleep and his old thoughts returned to him. He pondered for a while and went to the town to receive the money. Sixteen hundred of it he sent to his master's widow, not saying from whom it was; then he went to find the man who lived in a peasant's back yard, earning his living by teaching children to read and write and count. Yermil was surprised when he saw him: the man had not changed at all; dressed in a clean shirt, he sat on a bench reading a book; he was thin as before, but his hair had turned grey. He glanced at Yermil and asked what he wanted; he did not recognise him.

Yermil reminded him how he had come to him for lessons and been refused, and how the man had warned Yermil against greed but he had not listened. And Yermil told him his whole life from first to last.

And the man's heart melted within him and his face seemed to light up. Yermil wept for his sins and the man wept with him; and he looked at Yermil gently and kindly.

Yermil told him what he had decided to do, and the man approved of it.

XXIII

And Yermil went to the town, to the market-place and the bazaars, and gave money to beggars. And he went to the prison and the hospitals and the inns and the almshouses and among the destitute outside the town, and everyone who was in need took money from Yermil in Christ's name. And Yermil had no money left, not even to buy a pound of bread. Then he thought to himself:

"The time has come!"

He went to church just as mass was over, and when he saw that the people were about to leave he went up the church steps, took off his cap and stopped the people.

"Listen, Orthodox Christians!" he said. "I am a great sinner. I was tempted by gain. I killed a man; I strangled a corn-dealer in the open road." He confessed it all.

The people gasped and shuddered. Some were scared and hurried home for fear of being involved as witnesses; others blamed Yermil and thought, "The man is a fool not to keep it quiet," but many pitied him. The police heard what he said and led him away to prison.

Yermil fell ill in prison; he felt stifled, shut up in the bad air and the stench; it was too much for an old man.

Meanwhile the news came to Ivan. He ran to the town, bailed his brother out and brought him home.

And death came to Yermil.

He was lying in the outer room, and one day he felt very bad. He beckoned to his brother Ivan and begged him to carry him out of doors.

It was a warm spring day. They laid him on some sacking and carried him out. And Yermil saw that the people crowded round him, grieved for him and pitied him. And Yermil understood that God had forgiven him and he was happy. His face looked bright and joyful . . . and he died.

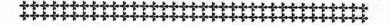

ANTON CHEKHOV

(1860–1904)

**

(I)

DUSHECHKA

(Translated by ROSA GRAHAM)

OLENKA PLEMYNIKOVA, daughter of a retired college assessor, was sitting on the steps in the yard, dreaming. It was hot; the flies would not let one alone, and it was pleasant to think that evening was coming. Dark rainy clouds were moving over from the east, and every now and then a little rain fell.

In the middle of the yard stood Kukin—lessee and manager of the "Tivoli" pleasure-garden, who had his lodging in the little cottage in the yard. He was looking up at the sky.

"Again!" said he, in despair. "It's raining again! It rains every day; every day it rains, as if on purpose. You can't get away from it. It's ruin. Heavy losses every day!"

He wrung his hands and went on, turning to Olenka:

"There you are, Olga Semenovna, that's our life. I could cry! You work, and strive, and worry! you can't sleep thinking how things could be improved; and then what? On the one hand, the public, uncultured and illiterate. I give them the very best operetta, fairies, splendid artists; but do they really want it? Do they understand anything about it? They'd like a rowdy show. They want rubbish! On the other hand, just look at the weather! Almost every evening it rains. From the tenth of May, when we opened, right on through the whole of May and June—it's just dreadful. The public doesn't come, so how can I pay the rent? And the artists?"

Next day, as evening was coming on, the sky was again overcast, and Kukin said with a hysterical guffaw:

"Well, what if it does rain! Let it! Let it wash all the garden away and me with it! There's no happiness for me in this world or the next. Let the artists bring me to court! What does it matter? Let them send me to Siberia!—or the scaffold! Ha, ha, ha!"

And the next day, just the same.

Olenka listened to Kukin in silence. She took him seriously, and sometimes the tears came into her eyes. In the end the misfortunes of Kukin moved her to pity, and she fell in love with him.

He was of squat stature, short and sallow; his hair was combed back from his temples; he had a thin tenor voice and twisted his mouth as he spoke; despair was always written on his face, but all the same he aroused in her a deep and genuine emotion. She had always been in love with somebody or other, and could not exist otherwise. Formerly she had loved her father, who was now an invalid and sat all the time in an armchair in a darkened room, breathing with difficulty; then she had loved her aunt, who sometimes, perhaps once in two years, came to visit them from Briansk; and before that, when she was still a young schoolgirl, she had been in love with the French master. She was a gentle, good-natured, sympathetic girl, with a sweet engaging manner, and healthy-looking. She had plump rosy cheeks, a soft white neck with a little dark mole upon it, and her smile, whenever she heard anything pleasant, was naïve and friendly. When men observed her they commonly said to themselves, "Yes, not at all bad . . ." and they would smile also. As for other women, they went into raptures over her and, unable to restrain themselves, would snatch up her hand in theirs and exclaim in a burst of pleasure:

"Dushechka!"[1]

The house in which she had lived ever since she was born, and which she had now inherited, was on the outskirts of the town, in the Gipsy Suburb, not far from the "Tivoli" pleasure-garden. In the evenings and at night she could hear the orchestra playing and the bursting of the rockets as they fell. It seemed to her that this Kukin was at war with his destiny and was rushing to the final assault of his chief enemy —an indifferent public; her heart was sweetly anxious for him; she liked to lie awake all night so that towards morning when he returned home she could tap lightly on her bedroom window-pane, and, pulling aside the curtains, show him just her face and one shoulder and smile tenderly at him. . . .

He proposed to her, and they were married. And when he saw the curves of her neck and of her full healthy shoulders he clasped his hands as in prayer and exclaimed:

"Dushechka!"

He was happy, but as the wedding day and the whole evening after it had been rainy, a despairing expression had become fixed on his face and did not wear off.

They lived happily together after their marriage. She kept the accounts, saw that everything was in order in the garden; she tabulated the expenses, and paid the wages, and her rosy cheeks and gentle naïve smile looked like a sunbeam gleaming from the little office-window, in the wings of the open theatre, or in the restaurant. And very soon she began to say to her acquaintances that the most remarkable, the most necessary and important thing on earth was the theatre, and that one could only get real pleasure and become cultured and human by means of the theatre.

"But do you think the public understands that?" she would say. "No; they want a show. Yesterday we had 'Faust Reversed,' and the stalls were almost empty; but if Vanitchka

---

[1] Dushechka means *dear-little-soul*, and is an expression of endearment. In Chekhov's story the word obtains a further significance, as Olenka had no life of her own, but had to be the soul of someone else. [Ed.]

and I were to put on any kind of rubbish, would you believe it, the theatre would be crowded out. We're giving 'Orpheus in Hell' to-morrow—come and see it."

And she would repeat everything Kukin said about the theatre and about the actors. Like him, she despised the public for its indifference toward Art and for its lack of culture; she interfered in the rehearsals, corrected the actors, looked after the behaviour of the musicians, and when the local newspaper commented unfavourably on their productions she would weep and afterwards go to the editor to obtain an explanation.

The actors loved her and called her "Vanitchka and I" and "Dushechka." She was sorry for their poverty and made them little loans now and then, and when, as sometimes happened, the actors told her a false story or did not pay her back, she would have a little cry on the quiet but made no complaint to her husband about it.

They had a good winter—they leased the town theatre for the whole season and sub-let it for short periods to Ukrainian singers, a conjuror, the local amateurs, and others. Olenka put on flesh and just radiated happiness, but Kukin grew thinner and more yellow, complaining of dreadful losses, though as a matter of fact business remained pretty good all the time. He coughed at nights, and she gave him lime-tea and raspberry syrup, rubbed him with eau-de-Cologne, and wrapped her own soft shawls about him.

"What a splendid man I've got!" said she, smoothing his hair with her hand, and she was absolutely sincere. "What a fine man I've got!"

He went to Moscow in Lent, to get together a new company, and while he was away she could not sleep, but sat at the window at night and looked at the stars. She compared herself with the hens who, when they are shut up in their coop without a cock, cannot sleep at all at nights and remain in a state of constant flutter. Kukin was held up in Moscow, but wrote that he would return in Holy Week. In his letters he gave various orders regarding the "Tivoli." But on the Monday before Easter, late in the evening, there was a sinister knocking at the outside gate. Someone was beating upon it as upon a barrel—boom, boom, boom. The sleepy cook jumped out of bed and splashed through the puddles of the yard in her bare feet to find out who it was.

"For goodness' sake, open!" cried someone in a deep bass voice. "There's a telegram."

Olenka had received telegrams from her husband at various times, but she took this one with trembling hands, and for some reason or other went white as chalk. She unsealed it, and read the following words:

"Ivan Petrovitch died suddenly this morning. Sutchala. Awaiting instructions for funeral Tuesday."

The word funeral was mis-spelt, and the telegram contained the incomprehensible word *sutchala;* it was signed by the stage-manager.

"My darling!" sobbed Olenka. "My darling Vanitchka, my loved one! Why did we ever meet? Why did I know you and love you? For whom have you abandoned your poor, poor, unhappy Olenka?"

Kukin was buried on the Tuesday, in Moscow, in the Vagankof cemetery; Olenka came home again on the Wednesday, and as soon as she got indoors she threw herself on the bed and sobbed so loudly that all the people in the street and in the neighbouring houses could hear her.

"Dushechka!" said the neighbours, crossing themselves. "Dushechka! Olga Semenovna 'll die of grief!"

Three months later, Olenka was coming home from church one day, grief-stricken and in deep mourning. One of her neighbours, also returning from church, walked along with her—Vassily Andreitch Pustovalof, managing director of the merchant Babakaief's timber warehouse. He wore a straw hat and a white waistcoat with a gold chain, and he looked more like a landowner than a trader.

"There's a certain fitness in things, Olga Semenovna," said

he, sombrely, with sympathy in his voice. "If one of our near ones dies, it means that it is God's will, and in that case we ought to recognise it and bear it with humility."

He accompanied Olenka to her little gate, said good-bye, and went on. And during the whole day she could hear his sombre voice, and directly she closed her eyes at night in fancy she saw again his dark beard. She was much attracted to him. And evidently she also made an impression on him, for soon after, a slight acquaintance of hers, a middle-aged woman, came to drink coffee with her, and Olenka had no sooner sat herself down at the table than she began to talk of Pustovalof, saying what a good reliable man he was and how any woman would be pleased to marry him. Three days later Pustovalof himself visited her; he only stayed about ten minutes and said little, but Olenka was in love with him, so much in love that all that night she could not sleep and was burning as if with fever. Next morning she sent a message to the middle-aged lady. An engagement soon followed, and then the wedding.

Pustovalof and Olenka lived happily together after their marriage. He generally sat in the timber warehouse up till dinner-time; then he went out on business and Olenka took his place, sitting in the office till evening, writing up accounts and sending out the goods.

"Nowadays timber gets twenty per cent. dearer every year," she would say to her customers and friends. "We used to get wood from the forests near by, but now Vassitchka has to go every year to the forests in Mogilyovsky Government. And the cost of freight!" said she, covering her face with her hands in horror. "The cost of freight!"

It seemed to her that she had traded in timber for long long years, that timber was the most important and necessary thing in life, and that there was something familiar and touching in the sound of words like beam, joist, planks, props, deal, laths, beadings, matchboard.

She used to dream at night of wood, and saw mountains of

planks and boards, endless fences, stretching like forests far
beyond the town. Once she dreamed that a whole regiment
of twelve-yard poles was advancing to assault the timber-
yard; there was a terrific collision and collapse, boards and
beams rolling down with the dull sonorous sound of dry
wood. The yard-timber fell and then stood up again and
ranged itself in piles. Olenka cried out in her sleep, waking
Pustovalof, who said tenderly:

"What's the matter, Olenka dear? Cross yourself!"

Whatever were her husband's thoughts, hers were the same.
If he felt that it was hot in the room, so did she, and if he
remarked that business was becoming rather quiet, the same
thing had occurred to her. Her husband took little pleasure
in outside amusements; he just sat indoors on holidays, and
so did she.

"You're always either at home or in the office," said her
acquaintances. "If I were you, Dushechka, I'd go to the
theatre or the circus sometimes!"

"Vassitchka and I never go to theatres," said she, unmoved.
"We are working people. We haven't time for nonsense.
What is there in all these theatres?"

The pair went to church on Saturday evenings regularly, and
to early mass on Sundays and Saints' days, and they returned
from church side by side. There was a sweet expression on
their faces, and a sort of pleasant odour about them; her silk
dress rustled agreeably as she walked along. When they got
home they would have tea, sweet rolls, and saucer-fulls of
various jams, and later, munched hot meat-pies together.
Their beetroot soup smelt good each day at noon; you could
smell it in the street and in the yard; yes, and there was roast
mutton there, or duck, though it would be fish on fast-days;
no one passed their door without suddenly feeling hungry. A
samovar was always in the office, always on the boil, and they
could offer tea and buttered bubliks to the customers. Once a
week this happy couple went to the public bath, and might be
seen returning thence together, both their faces red with steam.

"Yes, it's all right. We live well, glory be to God," said Olenka to her friends. "God grant everyone such a life as He has given to Vassitchka and me."

When Pustovalof went off to Mogilyof to buy timber, Olenka was terribly miserable; she wept, she could not sleep at night. Sometimes she would receive visits from the regimental veterinary surgeon, Smirnin, a young fellow who was lodging in the wing of the house. He told her stories, or played cards with her, and that distracted her a little. She was much interested in the stories he told of his private family life; he was a married man and had a son, but had separated from his wife because she had been unfaithful to him, and now he hated her. He sent her forty roubles a month for the upkeep of the child. And when Olenka heard this sad story she sighed and shook her head and was sorry for him.

"Well, God bless you!" she would say, as she showed him down the stairs, candle in hand. "Thank you for coming to cheer me; God keep you, and may the Queen of Heaven . . ."

She spoke slowly and thoughtfully, imitating her husband. The surgeon had got to the outside door, and she called to him once more:

"Vladimir Platonitch, d'you know, I think it would be better if you made it up with your wife. I would forgive her, if it were only for the child's sake! You may be sure the little lad understands everything."

And when Pustovalof returned, she told him in a half-whisper about the veterinary surgeon and his unhappy married life, and they both sighed and shook their heads and spoke of the little boy, who no doubt fretted for his father. And afterwards, by some strange association of ideas, they both stood before the ikons and, bowing down to the ground, prayed that God would send them children.

And so the Pustovalofs spent the first six years of their married life, quietly and humbly, in love and complete har-

mony. But one winter day, Vassily Andreitch, after drinking
tea in the office and getting heated, went off without his hat
to despatch some timber. He took cold and was laid up.
They had the best doctors for him, but the illness took a fatal
course; after six months' illness, he died. And Olenka once
more was a widow.

"For whom have you abandoned me, my darling?" sobbed
she, at her husband's funeral.. "How can I live now without
you, in grief and bitterness? Good people, pity me, the
complete orphan!"

She wore black; she wore a widow's veil, and renounced
hats and gloves for ever. She rarely left the house, only going
out to church or to her husband's grave, and lived the life
of a nun. Only after six months did she put her veil aside,
and open the shutters of her windows. Sometimes she could
be seen in the mornings, going to the bazaar with her cook
to buy provisions, but no one knew how she was living at that
time, or what was happening in her home; they could only
guess. For instance, people guessed something because upon
occasion they had seen her in her garden drinking tea with
the veterinary surgeon while he read a newspaper aloud to
her; and one day, meeting a lady whom she knew at the
post-office, Olenka had said to her:

"There's no proper veterinary supervision in our town—
that's why there's so much illness. One hears often that
people get ill from drinking milk, and they get infection from
horses and cows. Really we ought to look after the health of
our domestic animals as much as after our own."

She repeated the ideas of the veterinary surgeon, and came
to have just the same opinions as he had. It was clear that
she could not live one year without becoming attached to
somebody, and that she had found her new happiness in the
wing of her own house. Another person might have been
censured for this, but no one could think badly of Olenka,
and her life was quite clear to everybody. Neither she nor
the veterinary surgeon told anyone of the change in their

relationship, and they tried to hide it, but they were not successful because Olenka could never keep a secret. When he received guests, Olenka, while pouring out tea or serving supper, would begin talking about foot-and-mouth disease, the so-called pearly disease, and of the municipal slaughter-houses. On these occasions Smirnin would get dreadfully embarrassed, and after the guests had gone he would seize her hand and hiss out angrily:

"Didn't I ask you to keep quiet about things you don't understand? When we veterinary surgeons talk among ourselves, please don't interfere. It really becomes annoying!"

And she would look at him in wonder and alarm, and ask: "But, Voloditchka, what was there for me to talk about?"

And she would tearfully embrace him, and beg him not to be angry, and both would be happy again.

But this happiness, however, did not last long. The veterinary surgeon went off with his regiment—went off for ever, it seemed, for the regiment had been transferred to some place very distant, almost to Siberia. And Olenka was left alone.

And now she really was quite alone. Her father had died long ago, and his armchair, with one leg missing, reposed in the dust in the attic. Olenka grew thinner and less good-looking, and when her acquaintances met her in the street they no longer looked on her as they used to do, with a smile; it was evident that her best years had passed, and that now a kind of new life was beginning for her, an unfamiliar life concerning which it were best not to think. In the evenings Olenka sat on the steps, and she could hear the orchestra of the "Tivoli" and the bursting of the rockets there, but they did not arouse in her mind any thought at all.

She gazed with indifference on her empty yard—she thought of nothing and wished for nothing—and when, later, night came on, she went to sleep and saw in her dreams the same empty yard. She ate and drank as if against her will.

And, worst of all, she had no opinions of any kind. She saw

the things around her and she understood all that was going
on, but she couldn't form an opinion about anything, and
she didn't know what to talk about. And how dreadful it is
not to have any opinions! You see, for instance, that a bottle
is standing there, or that it rains, or that a peasant is going
by in his cart, but what the bottle is there for, or the rain,
or the peasant, and what they all mean, you can't say, and
if anyone were to give you a thousand roubles, you couldn't
say. In Kukin's time, or Pustovalof's, and later, with the
veterinary surgeon, Olga could explain everything and give
her opinion on anything you like; but now, in her thought
and in her heart, there was just the same emptiness as in her
yard. And it was as dreary and as bitter as the taste of
wormwood in the mouth.

The town was spreading itself by degrees in all directions.
The Gipsy Suburb was now called a street, and where the
"Tivoli" and the timber warehouse had been, houses had been
built, and there was a row of little streets. How quickly time
flies! Olenka's house grew shabby in appearance, the roof
rusted, the shed caved in, and the whole yard was overgrown
with burdock and nettle. Olenka herself had become older
and plainer. In summer she sat, as of old, on the steps of her
house, and her soul was empty and dreary. In winter she sat
at the window and looked out at the snow. When a gleam
of spring sunshine came in at the window, or when she heard
the chiming of the cathedral bells on the wind, she would
have a sudden stab of recollection; her heart would ache
sweetly, and her eyes would fill with abundant tears; but
then that would be only for a moment, and once more,
emptiness and the unanswerable question, "What is life for?"
Breeska, her black cat, would rub itself against her and purr
gently, but cat's caresses could not touch Olenka. She didn't
want them. She wanted such a love as would satisfy her
whole being, her whole soul and mind, would give her ideas,
direction in life, and would warm up her ageing heart. She
would push the cat off her skirt and say sadly:

"Run along . . . I've nothing for you."

And so day after day, year after year, and no joy, and no opinions whatsoever. Whatever the cook Mavra said was all right for her.

But one hot July day, towards evening, when the cows were all being driven home down the street, and the whole yard was in dust, someone suddenly knocked. Olenka herself went to open the door, and when she saw who it was she nearly fainted. There on the threshold stood Smirnin, now a grey-headed man in civilian clothes. Suddenly the past flooded back to her consciousness, and she could not restrain herself; she rested her head on his breast and wept. She did not say one word, and was so agitated that she did not even observe how they went inside the house and sat down to take tea.

"Darling!" murmured she, trembling with joy. "Vladimir Platonitch! Where on earth have you come from?"

"I want to come and live here for always," he told her. "I've retired from the army, and I want to try and get a little happiness in freedom, and live a settled life. What's more, it's time for my boy to go to the high school. He's growing up! And, you know, I've made it up with my wife."

"And where is she?" asked Olenka.

"She's living in a hotel with the boy, and I'm just looking for lodgings."

"Good Lord! Dear man, come and take my house. Isn't that better than lodgings? And, Lord knows, I shouldn't want any rent," said Olenka, in excitement, and she began to weep again. "You live here, and I will take the lodging in the wing. O Lord, what a pleasure it is!"

And the very next day the roof was painted and the walls whitewashed, and Olenka walked about the yard with her hands on her hips, and gave her orders. Her old radiant smile had come back, and she was as fresh and vivacious as if she had just awakened from a long sleep. The veterinary surgeon's wife arrived. She was lean and ugly, wore her hair short, and her face wore a petted, difficult expression. With her came the boy. Sasha was small for his years—he was not yet ten—but he was chubby; he had bright blue eyes and dimpled cheeks. Directly he came into the yard he ran after the cat, and at once you could hear his gay, joyful laughter.

"Auntie, is this your cat?" asked he of Olenka. "When she has kittens, please give us one. Mother's dreadfully afraid of mice."

Olenka talked to him and gave him tea, and her heart felt suddenly warm and sweetly happy, as if this little boy were her own child. And when in the evening he sat at the table and went over his lessons, she looked at him with tenderness and sympathy, whispering:

"My darling, my handsome one, my little child; what a clever boy you are, and what a nice white skin you have."

"An island . . ." he was reading, "is a piece of land, entirely surrounded by water."

"An island is a piece of land . . ." she repeated after him, and this was the first opinion which she had expressed with conviction after so many years of silence and emptiness of mind.

And now she had her own opinions, and after supper she told the parents how difficult it is for children nowadays in the high school, but that a high school education is better than the ordinary school, because from the high school the way stands clear if you want to be a doctor, or if you want to be an engineer.

Sasha started going to school. His mother went off to Kharkov to visit her sister, and did not come back; his father went out every day to inspect cattle, and sometimes he was away for three days at a time, and it seemed to Olenka as if Sasha were quite forsaken—he was all alone in the house, and she thought he might die of hunger, so she brought him over to her own wing and put a little room in order for him.

Six months passed, and Sasha was still living with Olenka in the wing. Every morning she would go into his room; he slept soundly, with his hand under his cheek, breathing gently. She felt sorry to awaken him.

"Sashenka," she would say, sorrowfully. "Get up, dearie! Time to go to school!"

He would get up and dress and say his prayers, and then sit down to drink tea—he would drink up three glasses of tea and eat two large bubliks and half a French roll and butter. Generally he was but half awake, and not in a very good humour.

"Sashenka, you didn't learn your fable very well," Olenka would say, and look at him as if he were setting out on a long journey. "What a trouble I have with you! You're getting older, darling, and you must learn. Do what your teacher tells you!"

"Oh, stop it, please!" Sasha would say.

Then he would go along the street to the school—such a little boy, but wearing a big cap and a satchel on his back. Olenka would tip-toe after him.

"Sashenka-a!" she would cry.

He would look round, and she would slip into his hand a date or a caramel. When he turned into the side street where the school stood, he would become self-conscious because of this tall stout woman behind him, and he would look round and say:

"Now, Auntie, you go home. I can go along by myself now."

She would stand still and watch him, unmoving, until he was hidden in the school entrance. Oh, how she loved him! None of her previous attachments had been so deep as this; never had her soul submitted so absolutely, so disinterestedly, and with such joyful abandon, as at this time when her maternal feeling developed in her. She would have been ready to give her whole life and all her happiness for the sake of this other person's child, with the dimpled cheeks and the cap, yes, with joyful tears. Why would she have done that? And who knows—just why?

When she had seen Sasha off to school she would return home with soft steps, most happy, contented and loving. Her face had grown younger in these six months; it smiled, it radiated. People who met her took pleasure from her appearance.

"Good-day, Dushechka Olga Semenovna," they would say. "How are you getting on, Dushechka?"

When she went out to shop, she would gossip with the stall-keepers. "It's getting quite difficult for a boy in the high school now," she would say. "It's no joke to have to learn a fable by heart—and that's what they set for home-work in the first class yesterday, and a Latin translation, and a problem . . . that's a lot for a little boy, isn't it?"

She began to discuss the teachers, the lessons, the school-books, and said about them just what Sasha said.

Olenka and Sasha had dinner together at three in the afternoon, and in the evenings they worked together on the home-work, and grieved over the difficulties. When at last she tucked him into bed, she would make the sign of the cross over him many times and whisper her prayers. Then she would lie down to sleep herself, and dream of that distant and misty future when Sasha, having passed through the University, would become a doctor or an engineer, would have his own large house, his horse and carriage, would marry and have children. . . . With gentle tears trickling down her cheeks from her shut eyes, she would slumber on, still thinking of the same thing, while the black cat lying curled up against her side purred steadily:

"Mur . . . mur . . . mur."

One night Olenka was awakened by a sudden knocking at the outside door and could hardly breathe for terror, her heart beat so powerfully. Half a minute passed, and the knocking was repeated.

"It's a telegram from Kharkov," she thought, beginning to tremble all over. "The mother wants Sasha to be sent to her at Kharkov . . . Lord help me!"

She was in despair, and went cold all over, feeling that she was the most unfortunate being in the whole world. But another minute passed, and she heard voices: it was only the veterinary surgeon returning from the club.

"Well, glory be to God!"

The burden was gradually lifted from her heart. Once more she was at ease. She stretched herself on her bed and thought of Sasha, who was fast asleep in the adjoining room but kept calling out in a dream:

"I'll—I'll give it you! You go away! Don't tug!"

(II)

ON THE WAY

(Translated by MARIAN FELL)

"A golden cloud lay for a night
On the breast of a giant crag."
                              LERMONTOFF.

I N the room which the Cossack innkeeper, Simon Tchisto-plui, himself calls the "visitors' room," meaning that it is set aside exclusively for travellers, a tall, broad-shouldered man of forty sat at a large, unpainted table. His elbows were resting upon it, his head was propped in his hands, and he was asleep. The stump of a tallow candle, which was stuck in an empty pomade jar, lit his red beard, his broad, thick nose, his sunburned cheeks, and the heavy eyebrows which over-hung his closed eyes. Nose, cheeks and brows—each feature in itself was heavy and coarse, like the furniture and the stove in the "visitors' room"; but, taken altogether, they made up a harmonious and even a beautiful whole. And this is, generally speaking, the structure of the Russian physi-ognomy; the larger and more prominent the features, the gentler and kinder the face appears to be. The man was dressed in a gentleman's short coat, worn but bound with new braid, a plush waistcoat, and wide black trousers tucked into high boots.

On one of the benches which formed a continuous row along the wall, on the fur of a fox-skin coat, slept a little girl of eight wearing a brown dress and long black stockings. Her face was pale, her hair was curly and fair, and her shoulders were narrow; her whole body was lithe and thin, but her nose stood out, a thick ugly knob, like the man's. She was sleeping soundly and did not feel that the round little comb which she wore in her hair had slipped down and was pressing into her cheek.

The "visitors' room" wore a holiday look. The air smelled of its freshly scrubbed floor, the usual array of cloths was missing from the line which was stretched diagonally across the whole room, and a little shrine lamp was burning in a corner over the table, casting a red spot of light on the ikon of Gregory the Bringer of Victory. Two rows of bad wood-cuts started at the corner where hung the ikon and stretched along either wall, observing in their choice of subjects a rigid and careful gradation from the religious to the worldly. By the dim light of the candle and of the little red lamp they looked an unbroken band covered with dark blotches, but when the stove drew in its breath with a howl, as if longing to sing in tune with the wind, and the logs took heart and broke out into bright flames, muttering angrily, then ruddy splashes of light would flicker over the timbered walls and the monk Seraphim or the Shah Nasr-ed-Din would start out over the head of the sleeping man, or a fat brown child would grow out of the darkness, staring and whispering something into the ear of an uncommonly dull and indifferent Virgin.

Outside a storm was roaring. Something fiendish and evil but profoundly unhappy was prowling about the inn with the fury of a wild beast, trying to force its way into the house. Banging the doors, knocking on the windows and on the roof, tearing at the walls, it would first threaten, then implore, then

grow silent awhile, and at last rush down the flue into the
stove with a joyous, treacherous shriek. But here the logs
would flare up and the flames leap furiously to meet the
enemy like watch-dogs on the chain; a battle would ensue,
followed by a sob, a whine, and an angry roar. Through it
all could be heard the rancorous anguish, the ungratified
hatred, and the bitter impotence of one who has once been a
victor.

It seemed as if the "visitors' room" must lie for ever spell-
bound by this wild, inhuman music; but at last the door
creaked and the tavern boy came into the room wearing a new
calico shirt. Limping and blinking his sleepy eyes, he snuffed
the candle with his fingers, piled more wood on the fire, and
went out. The bells of the church, which at Rogatch lies only
a hundred steps from the inn, rang out for midnight. The
wind sported with the sound as it did with the snowflakes;
it pursued the notes and whirled them over a mighty space
so that some were broken off short, some were drawn out into
long, quavering tones, and some were lost entirely in the
general uproar. One peal rang out as clearly in the room as
if it had been struck under the very window. The little girl
that lay asleep on the fox skins started and raised her head.
For a moment she stared blankly at the dark window and at
Nasr-ed-Din, on whom the red light from the stove was
playing, and then turned her eyes towards the sleeping man.

"Papa!" she said.

But the man did not move. The child frowned crossly and
lay down again, drawing up her legs. Someone yawned long
and loud in the tap-room on the other side of the door. Soon
after this came a faint sound of voices and the squeaking of a
door pulley. Someone entered the house, shook off the snow,
and stamped his felt boots with a muffled sound.

"Who is it?" asked a lazy female voice.

"The young lady Ilovaiskaya has come," a bass voice
answered.

Again the pulley squeaked. The wind rushed noisily in.

Someone, the lame boy most likely, ran to the door of the "visitors' room," coughed respectfully, and touched the latch.

"Come this way, dear young lady; come in," said a woman's singsong voice. "Everything is clean in here, my pretty——"

The door flew open and a bearded peasant appeared on the threshold wearing the long coat of a coachman and bearing a large trunk on his shoulder. He was plastered with snow from his head to his feet. Behind him entered a little female form of scarcely half his height, showing neither face nor arms, muffled and wrapped about like a bundle and also covered with snow.

A dampness as from a cellar blew from the coachman and the bundle towards the little girl and the candle flame wavered.

" How stupid!" cried the bundle crossly. "We could go on perfectly well! We have only twelve more miles to go, through woods almost all the way, and we shouldn't get lost."

"Lost or not lost, miss, the horses won't go any farther," answered the coachman. "Lord! Lord! One would think I had done it on purpose!"

"Heaven knows where you've brought me to. But hush! There seems to be someone asleep here. Go away."

The coachman set down the trunk, at which the layers of snow were shaken from his shoulders, emitted a sobbing sound from his nose, and went out. Then the child saw two little hands creep out of the middle of the bundle, rise upward, and begin angrily to unwind a tangle of shawls and kerchiefs and scarfs. First a large shawl fell to the floor and then a hood; this was followed by a white knitted scarf. Having freed her head, the new-comer threw off her cloak and at once appeared half her former width. She now wore a long, grey coat with big buttons and bulging pockets. From one of these she drew a paper parcel and from the other a bunch of large, heavy keys. These she laid down so carelessly that the sleeping man started and opened his eyes. For a minute he looked dully round him as if not realising where he was, then he threw up his head and walked across to a corner where he sat down. The new-comer took off her coat, which again narrowed her by half, pulled off her plush overshoes, and also sat down.

She now no longer resembled a bundle but appeared as a slender brunette of twenty, slim as a little serpent, with a pale, oval face and curly hair. Her nose was long and pointed, her chin, too, was long and pointed, and the corners of her mouth were pointed; in consequence of all this sharpness the expression of her face, too, was piquant. Squeezed into a tight black dress with a quantity of lace at the throat and sleeves, she recalled some portrait of an English lady of the Middle Ages. The grave, concentrated expression of her face enhanced this resemblance.

The little brunette looked round the room, glanced at the man and at the child, shrugged her shoulders, and sat down by the window. The dark panes shook in the raw west wind; large snowflakes, gleaming whitely, fell against the glass and at once vanished, swept away by the blast. The wild music grew ever louder and louder.

After a long period of silence the child suddenly turned over and, crossly rapping out each word, said:

"Lord! Lord! How unhappy I am! Unhappier than anyone else in the world!"

The man got up and tiptoed across to her with apologetic steps that ill suited his great size and his large beard.

"Can't you sleep, darling?" he asked guiltily. "What do you want?"

"I don't want anything. My shoulder hurts. You are a horrid man, papa, and God will punish you. See if he doesn't!"

"My baby, I know your shoulder hurts, but what can I do, darling?" said the man in the voice of a husband who has been drinking and is excusing himself to his stern spouse. "Your shoulder aches from travelling, Sasha. To-morrow we will reach our journey's end, and then you can rest and the pain will all go away."

"To-morrow, to-morrow! Every day you say to-morrow. We're going to travel for twenty days more!"

"But, my child, I promise you we will get there to-morrow. I never tell a story, and it is not my fault that this snow-storm has delayed us."

"I can't stand it any more! I can't! I can't!"

Sasha rapped her foot sharply and rent the air with shrill, unpleasant wails Her father made a helpless gesture and glanced in confusion at the little brunette. The girl shrugged her shoulders and went irresolutely toward Sasha.

"Listen, darling," she said. "Why do you cry? I know it is horrid to have an aching shoulder, but what can we do?"

"You see, madam," said the man hastily, "we have not slept for two nights and have been travelling in a terrible carriage, so of course it is natural that she should feel ill and distressed. And then, too, we have struck a drunken driver, and our trunk has been stolen, and all the time we have had this snow-storm. But what's the use of crying? The fact is, this sleeping in a sitting position has tired me. I feel as if I were drunk. For Heaven's sake, Sasha, it's sickening enough in this place as it is, and here you are crying!"

The man shook his head, waved his hand in despair, and sat down.

"Of course, one ought not to cry," said the little brunette. "Only little babies cry. If you are ill, darling, you had best get undressed and go to sleep. Come, let's get undressed!"

When the child had been undressed and quieted, silence once more reigned. The dark girl sat by the window and looked about the room, at the ikon, and at the stove in per-plexity. It was obvious that the place, the child with its thick nose and boy's shirt, and the child's father all appeared strange to her. This odd man sat in his corner as if he were drunk, looked off to one side, and rubbed his face with the palm of his hand. He sat silent and blinked, and anyone seeing his apologetic appearance would hardly have expected him to begin talking in a few minutes. But he was the first to break silence. He stroked his knees, coughed, and began:

"What a comedy this is, I declare! I look about me and can hardly believe my eyes. Why, in the name of mischief, should Fate have driven us into this infernal inn? What was meant by it? Life sometimes makes such a *salto mortale* that one is fairly staggered with perplexity. Have you far to go, madam?"

"No, not far," answered the girl. "I am on my way from our estate, which is twenty miles from here, to our farm where my father and brother are. My name is Ilovaiskaya and our farm is called Ilovaiski, too. It is twelve miles from here. What terrible weather!"

"It couldn't be worse."

The lame boy entered the room and stuck a fresh candle-end into the pomade jar.

"Here, you might bring us a samovar as quick as you can!" the man said to him.

"Who wants to drink tea now?" the lame boy laughed. "It's a sin to drink before the morning service."

"Never mind, be quick. We shall burn in hell for it, not you."

Over their tea the new acquaintances fell into conversation. Ilovaiskaya discovered that her companion was called Gregory Likarieff; that he was a brother of the Likarieff who was marshal of the nobility in one of the neighbouring counties; that he himself had once been a landowner, but had been ruined. Likarieff learned that Ilovaiskaya's name was Maria, that her father's estate was a very large one, and that she had the entire charge of it herself, as her father and brother were too easy-going and were far too much addicted to coursing.

"My father and brother are all, all alone on the farm," said Ilovaiskaya, twiddling her fingers. (She had a habit of mov-

ing her fingers before her piquant face when she was speaking,
and of moistening her lips with her pointed little tongue at
the end of each sentence.) "Men are careless creatures and
never will raise a finger to help themselves. I wonder who
will give my father and brother their breakfast after this fast.
We have no mother, and the servants we have won't even
lay the table-cloth straight without me. You can imagine the
position my father and brother are in. They will find themselves without food to break their fast with while I have to sit
here all night. How strange it all is !"

Ilovaiskaya shrugged her shoulders, sipped her tea, and
continued :

"There are some holidays that have a scent of their own.
At Easter and Christmas and on Trinity Sunday the air
always smells of something unusual. Even unbelievers love
these holidays. My brother, for instance, says that there is no
God, yet on Easter Sunday he is always the first to run to the
vigil service."

Likarieff raised his eyes to Ilovaiskaya's face and laughed.

"They say there is no God," the girl continued and laughed
too. "But tell me, why do all great writers and students and
all wise people in general believe in God at the end of their
lives ?"

"If a man has not been able to believe in his youth, my lady,
he will not believe in his old age, were he never so many times
a great writer."

Judging from the sound of his cough, Likarieff possessed a
bass voice, but, whether from fear of talking loud or whether
from excessive timidity, he now spoke in a high one. After
a short silence he sighed and said :

"My idea is this, that faith is a gift of the soul. It is like any
other talent : one must be born with it to possess it. Judging
from my own case, from the people I have known in my life,
and from all I have seen going on about me, I believe this
talent to be inherent in Russians in the highest degree.
Russian life is made up of a constant succession of beliefs and

enthusiasms, and Russians have not yet scented unbelief and negation. If a Russian doesn't believe in God, then he believes in something else."

Likarieff accepted a cup of tea from Ilovaiskaya, swallowed half of it at a gulp, and went on:

"I will tell you how it is with me. Nature has placed in my soul an unusual faculty for believing. Between you and me, half of my life has been spent in the ranks of the atheists and nihilists, and yet there has never been an hour when I have not believed. All talents, as a rule, make their appearance in early childhood, and my gift showed itself when I could still walk upright under the table. My mother used to like to have her children eat a great deal, and when she was feeding me she used to say:

" 'Eat! Soup is the most important thing in life!' I believed it. I ate soup ten times a day. I ate like a wolf till I swooned with loathing. When my nurse told me fairy stories I believed in hobgoblins and demons and every kind of deviltry. I used to steal corrosive sublimate from my father and sprinkle it on little cakes and spread them out in the attic to poison the house sprites. But when I learned how to read and could understand the meaning of what I read I kept the whole province in an uproar. I started to run away to America; I turned highwayman; I tried to enter a monastery; I hired little boys to crucify me as if I were Christ. You will notice that my beliefs were all active and never lifeless. If I started for America I did not go alone, but seduced some fool like myself, and I was glad when I froze outside the walls of the town and got a thrashing. If I turned highwayman I invariably came home with a face all beaten up. I had an extremely agitated childhood, I can assure you! And then, when I was sent to school and had such truths instilled into me as that, for instance, the earth revolves round the sun, or that white light is not white but is made up of seven different colours, then how my little brain did hum! Everything was in a whirl in my head now: Joshua arresting the sun in its course, my mother denying the existence of lightning-rods on the authority of the prophet Elijah, my father indifferent to the truths I had discovered. My own insight stifled me. Like one insane, I roved through the house and stables preaching my truths, overcome with horror at the sight of ignorance and burning with indignation towards all those who in white light saw only white—but all that is childish nonsense. My serious enthusiasms began when I was at the university. Have you ever taken a course of learning anywhere, madam? "

"Yes, in Novotcherkass, at the Donski Institute."

"But you have never followed a course of lectures? Then you probably don't know what a science is. Every science in the world must possess one and the same passport, without which it is senseless; it must aspire to the truth. Every one of them, down to pharmaceutics even, has its object, and this object is not to bring usefulness or comfort into life but to seek the truth. It is wonderful! When you set to work to learn a science it is the beginning which first astounds you. Believe me, there is nothing more splendid, more captivating, nothing that so stuns and grips the human soul as the beginnings of a science. After the first five or six lectures the highest hopes beckon you on. You already fancy yourself the master of truth. And I gave myself up to science, heart and soul, as passionately as I would give myself to a beloved woman. I was its slave, and there was no sun for me but science. Night and day I pored and howled over my books without raising my head, weeping when I saw people exploiting science for their own personal ends. The joke is that every science, like a recurring decimal, has a beginning and no end. Zoology has discovered thirty-five thousand five hundred different species of insects; chemistry can count sixty-five elements; if you were to add ten zeros to the right of each of these figures, zoology and chemistry would be no nearer the end of their labours than they are now; all contemporary scientific work consists in exactly this augmentation of numbers. I saw through that hocus-pocus when I discovered the three thousand five hundred and first species and still did not attain contentment. However, I had no time for disillusionment, for I soon fell a prey to a new passion. I plunged into nihilism with its manifestos, its secret trans-formations, and all its tricks of the trade. I went among the people; I worked in factories, as a painter, as a boatman on the river Volga. Then, as I roamed across Russia and the scent of Russian life came to my nostrils, I changed into its ardent worshipper. My heart ached with love for the Russian people. I believed in their God, in their language, in their creative power, and so on and so on. I have been a Slavophil and have wearied Aksakoff with letters; I have been an Ukrainophil, and an archæologist, and a collector of examples of native genius—I have fallen in love with ideas, with people, with events, with places, time upon time without end. Five years ago I was the slave of the denial of the right of ownership. Non-opposition of evil was my latest belief."

Sasha stirred and heaved a shuddering sigh. Likarieff rose and went to her.

"Do you want some tea, my little one?" he asked tenderly.

"Drink it yourself!" the child answered roughly. Likarieff was embarrassed and returned guiltily to the table.

"So you have had an amusing life," said Ilovaiskaya. "You have much to remember."

"Well, yes, it all seems amusing when one is sitting over one's tea gossiping with a sweet companion, but figure to yourself what that amusement has cost me! What has it led to? You see, I did not believe 'zierlich-manierlich' like a German doctor of philosophy; I did not live in a desert; every passion of mine bowed me under its yoke and tore my body limb from limb. Judge for yourself. I used to be as rich as my brothers, and now I am a beggar. On the offspring of my enthusiasms I have squandered my own fortune, that of my wife, and a great deal of the money of others. I am now forty-two, old age is upon me, and I am as homeless as a dog that has strayed at night from a train of wagons. I have never in my life known what peace is. My soul has always been weary and has suffered even from hoping. I have wasted away under this heavy, disorderly labour; I have endured privations; I have been five times to prison; I have trailed all over the provinces of Archangel and Tobolsk. I ache to remember it. I have lived, and in the fumes that enveloped me I have missed life itself. Can you believe it? I cannot recall one single spring; I did not notice that my wife loved me; I did not notice when my children were born. What else can I tell you? To all who have loved me I have brought misfortune. My mother has already worn mourning for me for fifteen years; my proud brothers, for my sake, have endured agonies of soul and blushed for me and hung their heads, and have wasted their money on me till at last they have come to hate me like poison."

Likarieff rose and then sat down again.

"If I alone were unhappy I would give thanks to God," he continued without looking at Ilovaiskaya. "My own personal happiness vanishes into the background when I remember how often in my passions I have been absurd, unjust, cruel, dangerous, far from the truth! How often I have hated and despised with my whole soul those whom I should have loved, and—on the contrary! I have changed a thousand times. To-day I believe and prostrate myself, to-morrow I run like a coward from my gods and my friends of to-day, silently swallowing the charge of dastard that is flung after me. God only knows how often I have wept and gnawed my pillow for shame at my enthusiasms! I have never in my life wittingly told a lie or done an evil deed, but my conscience is not clear; no, I cannot even boast of not having a death on my mind, for my wife died under my very eyes, exhausted by my restlessness. Listen! There now exist in society two ways of regarding women. Some men measure the female skull and prove in that way that woman is the inferior of man; they seek out her defects in order to deride her, in order to appear original in her eyes, in order to justify their own bestiality. Others try with all their might to raise woman to their own level; they oblige her to con the three thousand five hundred species and to speak and write the same folly that they speak and write themselves."

Likarieff's face darkened.

"But I tell you that woman always has been and always will be the slave of man," he said in a deep voice, banging on the table with his fist. "She is a soft and tender wax out of which man has always been able to fashion whatever he had a mind to. Good God! For a man's penny passion she will cut off her hair, desert her family, and die in exile. There is not one feminine principle among all those for which she has sacrificed herself. She is a defenceless, devoted slave. I have measured no skulls, but I say this from grievous, bitter experience. The proudest, the most independent of women, if I can but succeed in communicating my passion to her, will follow me unreasoningly, unquestioningly, doing all I desire. Out of a nun I once made a nihilist who, I heard later, shot a policeman. In all my wanderings my wife never left me for an instant, and, like a weathercock, changed her faith with each of my changing passions."

Likarieff leaped up and walked about the room.

"It is a noble, an exalted bondage!" he cried, clasping his hands. "In that bondage lies the loftiest significance of woman's existence. Of all the terrible absurdities that filled my brain during my intercourse with women, my memory has retained, like a filter, not theories nor wise words nor philosophy, but that extraordinary submission, that wonderful compassion, that universal forgiveness——"

Likarieff clenched his hands, fixed his eyes on one spot, and with a sort of passionate tension, as if he were sucking at each word, muttered between set teeth:

"This—this magnanimous toleration, this faithfulness unto death, this poetry of heart—— The meaning of life lies in this uncomplaining martyrdom, in this all-pardoning love that brings light and warmth into the chaos of life——"

Ilovaiskaya rose slowly, took a step in the direction of Likarieff, and fixed her eyes on his face. By the tears which shone on his lashes, by his trembling, passionate utterance, she saw clearly that women were not a mere casual topic of conversation; they were the object of a new passion or, as he called it himself, a new belief. For the first time in her life Ilovaiskaya saw before her a man inspired by passionate faith. Gesticulating, with shining eyes, he appeared to her insane, delirious, but in the fire of his glance, in his speech, in the movements of his whole great frame she felt such beauty that, without being conscious of it herself, she stood paralysed before him and looked into his face with rapture.

"Take my mother!" he cried, holding out his arms to her with a face of supplication. "I have poisoned her existence; I have dishonoured her name; I have harmed her as much as her bitterest enemy could have done—and what is her answer? My brothers give her pennies for holy wafers and Te Deums, and she strangles her religious sentiments and sends them in secret to her worthless Gregory. Those little coins are far stronger to teach and ennoble the soul than all the theories and wise sayings and three thousand five hundred species. I could cite to you a thousand examples. Take, for instance, yourself! Here you are, on your way to your father and brother at midnight, in a blizzard, because you want to cheer their holiday by your tenderness, and all the time, perhaps, they are not thinking of you and have forgotten your existence! Wait until you love a man! Then you will go to the North Pole for him. You would, wouldn't you?"

"Yes, if—I loved him."

"There, you see!" rejoiced Likarieff, and he even stamped his foot. "Good Lord! How glad I am to have known you! It is my good fortune to keep meeting the most magnificent people. There is not a day that I do not meet someone for whom I would sell my soul. There are far more good people in this world than bad ones. See how freely and openheartedly you and I have been talking together, as if we had been friends for a century! Sometimes, I tell you, a man will have the courage to hold his tongue for ten years with his wife and friends, and then will suddenly meet a cadet in a railway carriage and blurt out his whole soul to him. This is the first time I have had the pleasure of seeing you, and yet I have confessed to you things I have never confessed to anyone before. Why is that?"

Rubbing his hands and smiling happily, Likarieff walked about the room and once more began to talk of women. The church-bell rang for the vigil service.

"Oh! oh!" wept Sasha. "He talks so much he won't let me sleep!"

"Yes, that is true," said Likarieff, recollecting himself. "I'm sorry, my little one. Go to sleep; go to sleep——"

"I have two little boys besides her," he whispered. "They live with their uncle, but this one couldn't survive for a day without her father. She complains and grumbles, but she clings to me like a fly to honey. But I have been chattering too much, my dear young lady, and have kept you from sleeping. Will you let me prepare a couch for you?"

Without waiting for her permission, he shook out her wet cloak and laid it along the bench with the fur side up, picked up her scattered scarfs and shawls, folded her coat into a roll, and placed it at the head of the couch. He did all this in silence, with an expression of humble reverence on his face, as if he were busied not with feminine rags but with the fragments of some holy vessel.

His whole frame had a guilty and embarrassed look as if he were ashamed of being so large and strong in the presence of a weak being.

When Ilovaiskaya had lain down he blew out the candle and took a seat on a stool beside the stove.

"And so, my little lady," he whispered, puffing at a thick cigarette and blowing the smoke into the stove, "nature has given the Russian an extraordinary facility for belief, an investigating mind, and the gift of speculation; but all this is scattered like chaff before his laziness, his indifference, and his dreamy frivolity. Yes——"

Ilovaiskaya stared wonderingly into the shadows and saw only the red spot on the ikon and the flickering firelight on the face of Likarieff. The darkness, the ringing of the church-bells, the roar of the storm, the lame boy, the grumbling Sasha, the unhappy Likarieff and his sayings—all these flowed together in the girl's mind and grew into one gigantic impression. The world seemed fantastic to her, full of marvels and forces of magic. All that she had just heard rang in her ears, and the life of man seemed to her to be a lovely and poetical fairy tale without an ending.

The mighty impression grew and grew, engulfed her consciousness, and changed into a sweet dream. Ilovaiskaya slept, but she still saw the little shrine lamp and the large nose on which the ruddy firelight was playing.

She heard weeping.

"Dear papa!" a tender child's voice besought. "Do let us go back to uncle! There they have a Christmas tree, and Stephen and Nicolas are there!"

"My darling, what can I do?" entreated the deep, low voice of a man. "Understand me, do understand!"

And a man's weeping was joined to that of the child. This voice of human woe in the midst of the howling storm seemed to the girl's ears such sweet, human music that she could not endure the delight of it, and also wept. Then she heard a large, dark shadow quietly approach her, pick up her shawl, which had slipped to the floor, and wrap it about her feet.

Ilovaiskaya was awakened by a strange sound of bawling. She jumped up and looked about her in astonishment. The blue light of dawn was already peeping in at the windows, which were almost drifted over with snow. A grey half-light lay in the room, and in it the stove, the sleeping child, and Nasr-ed-Din were distinctly visible. The stove and the shrine lamp had gone out. Through the wide-open door could be seen the large tap-room with its counter and tables. A man with a dull, gipsy face and wondering eyes was standing in the middle of the floor in a pool of melted snow and was holding a large red star on a stick. A throng of little boys surrounded him, motionless as statues, all plastered over with snow. The light of the star shone through the red paper and shed a crimson glow on their wet faces. The little crowd was bawling in a disorderly fashion, and all that Ilovaiskaya could distinguish was the single couplet:

> "Ho, youngster, you tiny one,
> Take a knife, a shiny one.
> We'll kill, we'll kill the Jew,
> The weary son of rue——"

Likarieff was standing near the counter gazing with emotion at the singers and beating time with his foot. At sight of Ilovaiskaya a smile spread over his whole face and he went up to her. She, too, smiled.

"Merry Christmas!" he cried. "I saw that you were sleeping well."

Ilovaiskaya looked at him, said nothing, and continued to smile.

After their talk of last night he no longer appeared tall and broad-shouldered to her, but small, as the largest ship appears small when we are told that it has crossed the ocean.

"Well, it is time for me to go," she said. "I must put on my things. Tell me, where are you going now?"

"To the station of Klinushka; from there I shall go to Sergyevo, and from Sergyevo I shall drive forty miles to some coal-mines belonging to an old fool of a general named Shashkofski. My brothers have found me a place there as manager. I am going to mine coal."

"Why, I know those coal-mines! Shashkofski is my uncle. But—why are you going there?" asked Ilovaiskaya, staring at Likarieff in astonishment.

"To be manager. I am going to manage the coal-mines."

"I don't understand," said Ilovaiskaya, shrugging her shoulders. "You are going to the mines. But don't you know that they lie in a barren, uninhabited waste? It's so lonely there you won't be able to stand it a day. The coal is horrible; no one will buy it; and my uncle is a maniac, a despot, a bankrupt—you won't even get a salary!"

"Never mind," said Likarieff indifferently. "I'm thankful even for the mine."

Ilovaiskaya shrugged her shoulders and walked excitedly up and down.

"I don't understand; I don't understand!" she cried, waving her fingers in front of her face. "It's impossible and—and senseless! Oh, understand that it's—it's worse than exile; it's a living tomb! Oh, Heavens!" she cried hotly, going up to Likarieff and waving her fingers before his smiling face. Her upper lip trembled and her piquant face paled. "Oh, imagine that barren plain, that solitude! There is not a soul there with whom to speak a word, and you—have an enthusiasm for women! A coal-mine and women!"

Ilovaiskaya suddenly grew ashamed of her ardour and, turning away from Likarieff, walked across to the window.

"No, no, you mustn't go there!" she cried, rapidly fingering the panes.

She felt not only in her soul but even in her back that behind her stood a man who was immeasurably unhappy and neglected and lost, but he stood looking at her, smiling kindly, as if he did not realise his unhappiness, as if he had not wept the night before. It would be better were he still crying! She walked back and forth across the room several times in agitation and then stopped thoughtfully in a corner. Likarieff was saying something but she did not hear him. She turned her back to him and drew a little bill from her purse. This she crushed in her hands for a long time; then she glanced round at Likarieff, blushed, and thrust it into her pocket.

The voice of the coachman was now heard outside the door.

Ilovaiskaya began to put on her things with a stern, concentrated expression on her face. Likarieff chatted merrily as he wrapped her up, but each word of his fell like a weight on her heart. It is not gay to hear an unhappy or dying man jest.

When the transformation of a living being into a bundle had been effected, Ilovaiskaya gave one last look at the "visitors' room," stood silent for a moment, and went slowly out. Likarieff followed her to see her off.

Out-of-doors, Heaven knows for what purpose, the winter wind was still raging.

Whole clouds of soft, heavy snow were whirling restlessly along the ground, unable to find peace. Horses, sleighs, trees, and a bull tied to a post—all were white and looked fluffy and soft.

"Well, God bless you," muttered Likarieff, seating Ilovaiskaya in her sleigh. "Don't think ill of me——"

Ilovaiskaya was silent. As the sleigh moved away and made the tour of a huge snow-drift she looked round at Likarieff as if wishing to say something. He ran toward her, but she said not a word and only glanced at him between her long lashes, on which hung the snowflakes.

Either his sensitive soul had really been able to read the meaning of this glance or else his fancy deceived him, but it suddenly seemed to him that, had he but added two or three more good, strong strokes to the picture, this girl would have forgiven him his failure, his age, and his misfortune, and would have followed him unquestioningly and unreasoningly. He stood there for a long time as if in a trance, staring at the track left by the runners of her sleigh. The snowflakes settled eagerly on his hair, on his beard, on his shoulders— the track of the sleigh soon vanished and he himself was covered with snow; he began to resemble a white crag, but his eyes still continued to search for something among the white snow-clouds.

(III)

ROTHSCHILD'S FIDDLE

(Translated by MARIAN FELL)

I T was a tiny town, worse than a village, inhabited chiefly by old people who so seldom died that it was really vexatious. Very few coffins were needed for the hospital and the jail; in a word, business was bad. If Jacob Ivanoff had been a maker of coffins in the county town, he would probably have owned a house of his own by now, and would have been called Mr. Ivanoff, but here in this little place he was simply called Jacob, and for some reason his nickname was Bronze. He lived as poorly as any common peasant in a little old hut of one room, in which he and Martha, and the stove, and a double bed, and the coffins, and his joiner's bench, and all the necessities of housekeeping were stowed away.

The coffins made by Jacob were serviceable and strong. For the peasants and townsfolk he made them to fit himself, and never went wrong, for, although he was seventy years old, there was no man, not even in the prison, any taller or stouter than he was. For the gentry and for women he made them to measure, using an iron yardstick for the purpose. He was always very reluctant to take orders for children's coffins, and made them contemptuously without taking any measurements at all, always saying when he was paid for them:

"The fact is, I don't like to be bothered with trifles."

Beside what he received for his work as a joiner, he added a little to his income by playing the violin. There was a Jewish orchestra in the town that played for weddings, led by the tinsmith Moses Shakess, who took more than half of its earnings for himself. As Jacob played the fiddle extremely well, especially Russian songs, Shakess used sometimes to invite him to play in his orchestra for the sum of fifty kopecks a day, not including the presents he might receive from the guests. Whenever Bronze took his seat in the orchestra, the first thing that happened to him was that his face grew red, and the perspiration streamed from it, for the air was always hot, and reeking of garlic to the point of suffocation. Then his fiddle would begin to moan, and a double bass would croak hoarsely into his right ear, and a flute would weep into his left. This flute was played by a gaunt, red-bearded Jew with a network of red and blue veins on his face, who bore the name of a famous rich man, Rothschild. This confounded Jew always contrived to play even the merriest tunes sadly. For no obvious reason Jacob little by little began to conceive a feeling of hatred and contempt for all Jews, and especially for Rothschild. He quarrelled with him and abused him in ugly language, and once even tried to beat him, but Rothschild took offence at this, and cried with a fierce look:

"If I had not always respected you for your music, I should have thrown you out of the window long ago!"

Then he burst into tears. So after that Bronze was not often invited to play in the orchestra, and was only called upon in cases of dire necessity, when one of the Jews was missing.

Jacob was never in a good humour, because he always had to endure the most terrible losses. For instance, it was a sin to work on a Sunday or a holiday, and Monday was always a bad day, so in that way there were about two hundred days a year on which he was compelled to sit with his hands folded in his lap. That was a great loss to him. If anyone in the town had a wedding without music, or if Shakess did not ask him to play, there was another loss. The police inspector had lain ill with consumption for two years while Jacob impatiently waited for him to die, and then had gone to take a cure in the city and had died there, which, of course, had meant another loss of at least ten roubles, as the coffin would have been an expensive one lined with brocade.

The thought of his losses worried Jacob at night more than at any other time, so he used to lay his fiddle at his side on the bed, and when those worries came trooping into his brain he would touch the strings, and the fiddle would give out a sound in the darkness, and Jacob's heart would feel lighter.

Last year on the sixth of May, Martha suddenly fell ill. The old woman breathed with difficulty, staggered in her walk, and felt terribly thirsty. Nevertheless, she got up that morning, lit the stove, and even went for the water. When evening came she went to bed. Jacob played his fiddle all day. When it grew quite dark, because he had nothing better to do, he took the book in which he kept an account of his losses, and began adding up the total for the year. They amounted to more than a thousand roubles. He was so shaken by this discovery that he threw the counting board on the floor and trampled it underfoot. Then he picked it up again and rattled it once more for a long time, heaving as he did so sighs both deep and long. His face grew purple, and perspiration dripped from his brow. He was thinking that if those thousand roubles he had lost had been in the bank then, he would have had at least forty roubles interest by the end of the year. So those forty roubles were still another loss! In a word, wherever he turned he found losses and nothing but losses.

"Jacob!" cried Martha unexpectedly, "I am going to die!"

He looked round at his wife. Her face was flushed with fever and looked unusually joyful and bright. Bronze was troubled, for he had been accustomed to seeing her pale and timid and unhappy. It seemed to him that she was actually dead, and glad to have left this hut, and the coffins, and Jacob at last. She was staring at the ceiling, with her lips moving as if she saw her deliverer Death approaching and were whispering with him.

The dawn was just breaking and the eastern sky was glowing with a faint radiance. As he stared at the old woman it somehow seemed to Jacob that he had never once spoken a tender word to her or pitied her; that he had never thought of buying her a kerchief or of bringing her back some sweetmeats from a wedding. On the contrary, he had shouted at her and abused her for his losses, and had shaken his fist at her. It was true he had never beaten her, but he had frightened her no less, and she had been paralysed with fear every time he had scolded her. Yes, and he had not allowed her to drink tea because his losses were heavy enough as it was, so she had had to be content with hot water. Now he understood why her face looked so strangely happy, and horror overwhelmed him.

As soon as it was light he borrowed a horse from a neighbour and took Martha to the hospital. As there were not many patients, he had not to wait very long—only about three hours. To his great satisfaction it was not the doctor who was receiving the sick that day, but his assistant, Maksim Nicolaitch, an old man of whom it was said that although he quarrelled and drank, he knew more than the doctor did.

"Good-morning, your Honour," said Jacob, leading his old woman into the office. "Excuse us for intruding upon you with our trifling affairs. As you see, this subject has fallen ill. My life's friend, if you will allow me to use the expression——"

Knitting his grey eyebrows and stroking his whiskers, the doctor's assistant fixed his eyes on the old woman. She was sitting all in a heap on a low stool, and with her thin, long-nosed face and her open mouth she looked like a thirsty bird.

"Well, well—yes——" said the doctor slowly, heaving a sigh. "This is a case of influenza and possibly fever; there is typhoid in town. What's to be done? The old woman has lived her span of years, thank God. How old is she?"

"She lacks one year of being seventy, your Honour."

"Well, well, she has lived long. There must come an end to everything."

"You are certainly right, your Honour," said Jacob, smiling out of politeness. "And we thank you sincerely for your kindness, but allow me to suggest to you that even an insect dislikes to die!"

"Never mind if it does!" answered the doctor, as if the life or death of the old woman lay in his hands. "I'll tell you what you must do, my good man. Put a cold bandage around her head, and give her two of these powders a day. Now then, good-bye! Bon jour!"

Jacob saw by the expression on the doctor's face that it was too late now for powders. He realised clearly that Martha must die very soon; if not to-day, then to-morrow. He touched the doctor's elbow gently, blinked, and whispered:

"She ought to be cupped, doctor!"

"I haven't time, I haven't time, my good man. Take your old woman, and go in God's name. Good-bye."

"Please, please, cup her, doctor!" begged Jacob. "You know yourself that if she had a pain in her stomach, powders and drops would do her good, but she has a cold! The first thing to do when one catches cold is to let some blood, doctor!"

But the doctor had already sent for the next patient, and a woman leading a little boy came into the room.

"Go along, go along!" he cried to Jacob, frowning. "It's no use making a fuss!"

"Then at least put some leeches on her! Let me pray to God for you for the rest of my life!"

The doctor's temper flared up and he shouted:

"Don't say another word to me, blockhead!"

Jacob lost his temper too, and flushed hotly, but he said nothing and, silently taking Martha's arm, led her out of the office. Only when they were once more seated in their wagon did he look fiercely and mockingly at the hospital and say:

"They're a pretty lot in there, they are! That doctor would have cupped a rich man, but he even begrudged a poor one a leech. The pig!"

When they returned to the hut, Martha stood for nearly ten minutes supporting herself by the stove. She felt that if she lay down Jacob would begin to talk to her about his losses, and would scold her for lying down and not wanting to work.

20

Jacob contemplated her sadly, thinking that to-morrow was St. John the Baptist's day, and day after to-morrow was St. Nicholas the Wonder-worker's day, and that the following day would be Sunday, and the day after that would be Monday, a bad day for work. So he would not be able to work for four days, and as Martha would probably die on one of those days, the coffin would have to be made at once. He took his iron yardstick in hand, went up to the old woman, and measured her. Then she lay down, and he crossed himself and went to work on the coffin.

When the task was completed Bronze put on his spectacles and wrote in his book:

"To 1 coffin for Martha Ivanoff—2 roubles, 40 kopecks."

He sighed. All day the old woman lay silent with closed eyes, but towards evening, when the daylight began to fade, she suddenly called the old man to her side.

"Do you remember, Jacob?" she asked. "Do you remember how fifty years ago God gave us a little baby with curly golden hair? Do you remember how you and I used to sit on the bank of the river and sing songs under the willow tree?" Then with a bitter smile she added: "The baby died."

Jacob racked his brains, but for the life of him he could not recall the child or the willow tree.

"You are dreaming," he said.

The priest came and administered the Sacrament and Extreme Unction. Then Martha began muttering unintelligibly, and towards morning she died.

The neighbouring old women washed her and dressed her, and laid her in her coffin. To avoid paying the deacon, Jacob read the psalms over her himself, and her grave cost him nothing, as the watchman of the cemetery was his cousin. Four peasants carried the coffin to the grave, not for money but for love. The old women, the beggars, and two village idiots followed the body, and the people whom they passed on the way crossed themselves devoutly. Jacob was very glad that everything had passed off so nicely and decently and cheaply, without giving offence to anyone. As he said farewell to Martha for the last time he touched the coffin with his hand and thought:

"That's a fine job!"

But walking homeward from the cemetery he was seized with great distress. He felt ill, his breath was burning hot, his legs grew weak, and he longed for a drink. Beside this, a thousand thoughts came crowding into his head. He remembered again that he had never once pitied Martha or said a tender word to her. The fifty years of their life together lay stretched far, far behind him, and somehow, during all that time, he had never once thought about her at all or noticed her more than if she had been a dog or a cat. And yet she had lit the stove every day, and had cooked and baked and fetched water and chopped wood, and when he had come home drunk from a wedding she had hung his fiddle reverently on a nail each time, and had silently put him to bed with a timid, anxious look on her face.

But here came Rothschild towards him, bowing and scraping and smiling.

"I have been looking for you, uncle!" he said. "Moses Shakess presents his compliments and wants you to go to him at once."

Jacob did not feel in a mood to do anything. He wanted to cry.

"Leave me alone!" he exclaimed, and walked on.

"Oh, how can you say that?" cried Rothschild, running beside him in alarm. "Moses will be very angry. He wants you to come at once!"

Jacob was disgusted by the panting of the Jew, by his blinking eyes, and by the quantities of reddish freckles on his face. He looked with aversion at his long green coat and at the whole of his frail, delicate figure.

"What do you mean by pestering me, garlic?" he shouted. "Get away!"

The Jew grew angry and shouted back:

"Don't yell at me like that or I'll send you flying over that fence!"

"Get out of my sight!" bellowed Jacob, shaking his fist at him. "There's no living in the same town with swine like you!"

Rothschild was petrified with terror. He sank to the ground and waved his hands over his head as if to protect himself from falling blows; then he jumped up and ran away as fast as his legs could carry him. As he ran he leaped and waved his arms, and his long, gaunt back could be seen quivering. The little boys were delighted at what had happened, and ran after him screaming: "Sheeny! Sheeny!" The dogs also joined barking in the chase. Somebody laughed and then whistled, at which the dogs barked louder and more vigorously than ever.

Then one of them must have bitten Rothschild, for a piteous, despairing scream rent the air.

Jacob walked across the common to the edge of the town without knowing where he was going, and the little boys shouted after him. "There goes old man Bronze! There goes old man Bronze!" He found himself by the river, where the snipe were darting about with shrill cries, and the ducks were quacking and swimming to and fro. The sun was shining fiercely and the water was sparkling so brightly that it was painful to look at. Jacob struck into a path that led along the river bank. He came to a stout, red-cheeked woman just leaving a bath-house. "Aha, you otter, you!" he thought. Not far from the bath-house some little boys were fishing for crabs with pieces of meat. When they saw Jacob they shouted mischievously: "Old man Bronze! Old man Bronze!" But there before him stood an ancient, spreading willow tree with a massive trunk, and a crow's nest among its branches. Suddenly there flashed across Jacob's memory with all the vividness of life a little child with golden curls, and the willow of which Martha had spoken. Yes, this was the same tree, so green and peaceful and sad. How old it had grown, poor thing!

He sat down at its foot and thought of the past. On the opposite shore, where that meadow now was, there had stood in those days a wood of tall birch trees, and that bare hill on the horizon yonder had been covered with the blue bloom of an ancient pine forest. And sail-boats had plied the river then, but now all lay smooth and still, and only one little birch tree was left on the opposite bank, a graceful young thing, like a girl, while on the river there swam only ducks and geese. It was hard to believe that boats had once sailed there. It even seemed to him that there were fewer geese now than there had been. Jacob shut his eyes, and one by one white geese came flying towards him, an endless flock.

He was puzzled to know why he had never once been down to the river during the last forty or fifty years of his life, or, if he had been there, why he had never paid any attention to it. The stream was fine and large; he might have fished in it and sold the fish to the merchants and the government officials and the restaurant keeper at the station, and put the money in the bank. He might have rowed in a boat from farm to farm and played on his fiddle. People of every rank would have paid him money to hear him. He might have tried to run a boat on the river, that would have been better than making coffins. Finally, he might have raised geese, and killed them, and sent them to Moscow in the winter. Why, the down alone would have brought him ten roubles a year! But he had missed all these chances and had done nothing. What losses were here! Ah, what terrible losses! And, oh, if he had only done all these things at the same time! If he had only fished, and played the fiddle, and sailed a boat, and raised geese, what capital he would have had by now! But he had not even dreamed of doing all this; his life had gone by without profit or pleasure. It had been lost for a song. Nothing was left ahead; behind lay only losses, and such terrible losses that he shuddered to think of them. But why shouldn't men live so as to avoid all this waste and these losses? Why, oh, why should those birch and pine forests have been felled? Why should those meadows be lying so deserted? Why did people always do exactly what they ought not to do? Why had Jacob scolded and growled and clenched his fists and hurt his wife's feelings all his life? Why, oh, why had he frightened and insulted that Jew just now? Why did people in general always interfere with one another? What losses resulted from this! What terrible losses! If it were not for envy and anger they would get great profit from one another.

All that evening and night Jacob dreamed of the child, of the willow tree, of the fish and the geese, of Martha with her profile like a thirsty bird, and of Rothschild's pale, piteous mien. Queer faces seemed to be moving towards him from all sides, muttering to him about his losses. He tossed from side to side, and got up five times during the night to play his fiddle.

He rose with difficulty next morning, and walked to the hospital. The same doctor's assistant ordered him to put cold bandages on his head, and gave him little powders to take; by his expression and the tone of his voice Jacob knew that the state of affairs was bad, and that no powders could save him now. As he walked home he reflected that one good thing would result from his death: he would no longer have to eat and drink and pay taxes, neither would he offend people any more, and, as a man lies in his grave for hundreds of thousands of years, the sum of his profits would be immense. So, life to a man was a loss—death, a gain. Of course this reasoning was correct, but it was also distressingly sad. Why should the world be so strangely arranged that a man's life which was only given to him once must pass without profit?

He was not sorry then that he was going to die, but when he reached home, and saw his fiddle, his heart ached, and he regretted it deeply. He would not be able to take his fiddle with him into the grave, and now it would be left an orphan, and its fate would be that of the birch grove and the pine forest. Everything in the world had been lost, and would always be lost for ever. Jacob went out and sat on the threshold of his hut, clasping his fiddle to his breast. And as he thought of his life so full of waste and losses he began playing without knowing how piteous and touching his music was, and the tears streamed down his cheeks. And the more he thought the more sorrowfully sang his violin.

The latch clicked and Rothschild came in through the garden-gate, and walked boldly half-way across the garden. Then he suddenly stopped, crouched down, and, probably from fear, began making signs with his hands as if he were trying to show on his fingers what time it was.

"Come on, don't be afraid!" said Jacob gently, beckoning him to advance. "Come on!"

With many mistrustful and fearful glances Rothschild went slowly up to Jacob, and stopped about two yards away.

"Please don't beat me!" he said with a ducking bow. "Moses Shakess has sent me to you again. 'Don't be afraid,' he said, 'go to Jacob,' says he, 'and say that we can't possibly manage without him.' There is a wedding next Thursday. Ye-es, sir. Mr. Shapovaloff is marrying his daughter to a very fine man. It will be an expensive wedding, ai, ai!" added the Jew with a wink.

"I can't go," said Jacob, breathing hard. "I'm ill, brother."

And he began to play again, and the tears gushed out of his eyes over the fiddle. Rothschild listened intently with his head turned away and his arms folded on his breast. The startled, irresolute look on his face gradually gave way to one of suffering and grief. He cast up his eyes as if in an ecstasy of agony and murmured: "Ou—ouch!" And the tears began to trickle slowly down his cheeks, and to drip over his green coat.

All day Jacob lay and suffered. When the priest came in

the evening to administer the Sacrament he asked him if he could not think of any particular sin.

Struggling with his fading memories, Jacob recalled once more Martha's sad face, and the despairing cry of the Jew when the dog had bitten him. He murmured almost inaudibly:

"Give my fiddle to Rothschild."

"It shall be done," answered the priest.

So it happened that everyone in the little town began asking:

"Where did Rothschild get that good fiddle? Did he buy it or steal it or get it out of a pawnshop?"

Rothschild has long since abandoned his flute, and now only plays on the violin. The same mournful notes flow from under his bow that used to come from his flute, and when he tries to repeat what Jacob played as he sat on the threshold of his hut, the result is an air so plaintive and sad that everyone who hears him weeps, and he himself at last raises his eyes and murmurs: "Ou—ouch!" And this new song has so delighted the town that the merchants and Government officials vie with each other in getting Rothschild to come to their houses, and sometimes make him play it ten times in succession.

FEDOR SOLOGUB
(1863—1927)

❖❖

(I)

TURANDINA

(Translated by ROSA GRAHAM)

I

P E T E R   A N T Ò N O V I T C H   B U L A N I N was spending the
summer in the country with the family of his cousin, a teacher
of philology. Bulanin himself was a young advocate of thirty
years of age, having finished his course at the University
only two years before.

The past year had been a comparatively fortunate one. He
had successfully defended two criminal cases on the nomination of the Court, as well as a civil case undertaken at the
instigation of his own heart. All three cases had been won
by his brilliant pleading. The jury had acquitted the young
man who had killed his father out of pity because the old
man fasted too assiduously and suffered in consequence ; they
had acquitted the poor seamstress who had thrown vitriol at
the girl her lover wished to marry ; and in the civil court the
judge had awarded the plaintiff a hundred and fifty roubles,
saying that his rights were indisputable, though the defendant
asserted that the sum had previously been paid. For all this
good work Peter Antònovitch himself had received only
fifteen roubles, this money having been paid to him by the
man who had received the hundred and fifty.

But, as will be understood, one cannot live a whole year on
fifteen roubles, and Peter Antònovitch had to fall back on his

own resources, that is, on the money his father sent him from home. As far as the law was concerned there was as yet nothing for him but fame.

But his fame was not at present great, and as his receipts from his father were but moderate, Peter Antònovitch often fell into a despondent and elegiac mood. He looked on life rather pessimistically, and captivated young ladies by the eloquent pallor of his face and by the sarcastic utterances which he gave forth on every possible occasion.

One evening, after a sharp thunder-storm had cleared and refreshed the air, Peter Antònovitch went out for a walk alone. He wandered along the narrow field paths until he found himself far from home.

A picture of entrancing beauty stretched itself out before him, canopied by the bright blue dome of heaven besprinkled with scattered cloudlets and illumined by the soft and tender rays of the departing sun. The narrow path by which he had come led along the high bank of a stream rippling along in the winding curves of its narrow bed—the shallow water of the stream was transparent and gave a pleasant sense of cool freshness. It looked as if one need only step into it to be at once filled with the joy of simple happiness, to feel as full of life and easy grace of movement as the rosy-bodied boys bathing there.

Not far away were the shades of the quiet forest; beyond the river lay an immense semicircular plain, dotted here and there with woods and villages, a dusty ribbon of a road curving snake-like across it. On the distant horizon gleamed golden stars, the crosses of far-away churches and belfries shining in the sunlight.

Everything looked fresh and sweet and simple, yet Peter Antònovitch was sad. And it seemed to him that his sadness was but intensified by the beauty around; as if some evil tempter were seeking to allure him to evil by some entrancing vision.

For to Peter Antònovitch all this earthly beauty, all this

enchantment of the eyes, all this delicate sweetness pouring itself into his young and vigorous body, was only as a veil of golden tissue spread out by the devil to hide from the simple gaze of man the impurity, the imperfection, and the evil of Nature.

This life, adorning itself in beauty and breathing forth perfumes, was in reality, thought Peter Antònovitch, only the dull prosaic iron chain of cause and effect—the burdensome slavery from which mankind could never get free.

Tortured by such thoughts, Peter Antònovitch had often felt himself as unhappy as if in him there had awakened the soul of some ancient monster who had howled piteously outside the village at night. And now he thought:

"If only a fairy tale could come into one's life and for a time upset the ordered arrangement of predetermined Fate! Oh, fairy tale, fashioned by the wayward desires of men who are in captivity to life and who cannot be reconciled to their captivity—sweet fairy tale, where art thou?"

He remembered an article he had read the day before in a magazine, written by the Minister of Education; some words in it had specially haunted his memory. The article spoke of the old fairy-tale tradition of the forest enchantress, Turandina. She had loved a shepherd and had left for him her enchanted home, and with him had lived some happy years on earth until she had been recalled by the mysterious voices of the forest. She had gone away, but the happy years had remained as a grateful memory to mankind.

Peter Antònovitch gave himself up to the fancy—oh, for the fairy tale, for a few enchanted years, a few days! . . . And he cried aloud and said:

"Turandina, where art thou?"

II

The sun was low down in the sky. The calm of even had fallen on the spreading fields. The neighbouring forest was hushed. No sound was heard, the air was still, and the grass still sparkling with raindrops was motionless.

It was a moment when the desires of a man fulfil themselves, the one moment which perhaps comes once in his life to every man. It seemed that all around was waiting in a tension of expectation.

Looking before him into the shining misty vapour, Peter Antònovitch cried again.

"Turandina, where art thou?"

And under the spell of the silence that encompassed him, his own separate individual will became one with the great universal Will, and with great power and authority he spoke as only once in his life a man has power to speak:

"Turandina, come!"

And in a sweet and gentle voice he heard the answer:

"I am here."

Peter Antònovitch trembled and looked about. Everything seemed again quite ordinary and his soul was as usual the soul of a poor human being, separate from the universal Soul—he was again an ordinary man, just like you and me, who dwell in days and hours of time. Yet before him stood she whom he had called.

She was a beautiful maiden, wearing a narrow circlet of gold upon her head, and dressed in a short white garment. Her long plaits of hair came below her waist and seemed to have taken to themselves the golden rays of the sunlight. Her eyes, as she gazed intently at the young man, were as blue as if in them a heaven revealed itself, more clear and pure than the skies of earth. Her features were so regular and her hands and feet so well-formed, so perfect were the lines of the figure revealed by the folds of her dress, that she seemed an embodiment of perfect maiden loveliness. She would have seemed like an angel from heaven had not her heavy black eyebrows met and so disclosed her witchery; if her skin had not been dark as if tanned by the rays of a burning sun.

Peter Antònovitch could not speak for wonder at her, and she spoke first:

"Thou didst call me and so I came to thee. Thou calledst to me just when I was in need of an earthly shelter in the world of men. Thou wilt take me to thy home. I have nothing of my own except this crown upon my brow, this dress, and this wallet in my hand."

She spoke quietly, so quietly that the tones of her voice could not have been heard above earthly sounds. But so clear was her speech and so tender its tone that even the most indifferent man would have been touched by the least sound of her voice.

When she spoke about going home with him and of her three possessions, Peter Antònovitch saw that she held in her hand a little bag of red leather drawn together by a golden cord—a very simple and beautiful little bag; something like those in which ladies carry their opera-glasses to the theatre.

Then he asked:

"And who art thou?"

"I am Turandina, the daughter of King Turandon. My father loved me greatly, but I did that which was not for me to do—out of simple curiosity I disclosed the future of mankind. For this my father was displeased with me and drove me from his kingdom. Some day I shall be forgiven and recalled to my father's home. But now for a time I must dwell among men, and to me have been given these three things: a golden crown, the sign of my birth; a white garment, my poor covering; and this wallet, which contains all that I shall need. It is good that I have met with thee. Thou art a man who defendeth the unhappy, and who devoteth his life to the triumph of Truth among men. Take me with thee to thy home; thou wilt never regret thy deed."

Peter Antònovitch did not know what to do or what to think. One thing was clear: this maiden, dressed so lightly, speaking so strangely, must be sheltered by him; he could not leave her alone in the forest, far from any human dwelling.

He thought she might be a runaway, hiding her real name and inventing some unlikely story. Perhaps she had escaped from an asylum, or from her own home.

There was nothing in her face or in her appearance, however, except her scanty clothing and her words, to indicate anything strange in her mind. She was perfectly quiet and calm. If she called herself Turandina it was doubtless because she had heard someone mention the name, or she might even have read the fairy story of Turandina.

III

With such thoughts in his mind Peter Antònovitch said to the beautiful unknown:

"Very well, dear young lady, I will take you home with me. But I ought to warn you that I do not live alone, and therefore I advise you to tell me your real name. I'm afraid that my relatives will not believe that you are the daughter of King Turandon. As far as I know there is no such king at the present time."

Turandina smiled as she said:

"I have told thee the truth, whether thy people believe it or not. It is sufficient for me that thou shouldst believe. And if thou believest me, thou wilt defend me from all evil and from all unhappiness, for thou art a man who hast chosen for thyself the calling in which thou canst uphold the truth and defend the weak."

Peter Antònovitch shrugged his shoulders.

"If you persist in this story," answered he, "I must wash my hands of the matter, and I cannot be answerable for any possible consequences. Of course I will take you home with me until you can find a more suitable place, and I will do all I can to help you. But as a lawyer I very strongly advise you not to hide your real name."

Turandina listened to him with a smile, and when he stopped speaking she said:

"Do not be at all anxious; everything will be well. Thou wilt see that I shall bring happiness to thee if thou canst show me kindness and love. And do not speak to me so much about my real name. I have spoken the truth to thee, and more I may not say, it is forbidden me to tell thee all. Take me home with thee. Night is coming on; I have journeyed far and am in need of rest."

Peter Antònovitch was quick to apologise.

"Ah pardon me, please. I am sorry that this is such an out-of-the-way place; it's quite impossible to get a carriage."

He began to walk in the direction of his home, and Turandina went with him. She did not walk as though she were tired; her feet seemed hardly to touch the ground, though they had to walk over stiff clay and sharp stones, and the moist grass and rain-soaked pathway did not seem to soil her little feet.

When they reached the high bank of the river and could see the first houses of the village, Peter Antònovitch glanced uneasily at his companion and said somewhat awkwardly:

"Pardon me, dear young lady . . ."

Turandina looked at him, and with a little frown interrupted him, saying reproachfully:

"Hast thou forgotten whom I am and what is my name? I am Turandina, and not 'dear young lady.' I am the daughter of King Turandon."

"Your pardon, please, Mademoiselle Turandina—it is a very beautiful name, though it is never used now—I wanted to ask you a question."

"Why dost thou speak so to me?" asked Turandina, interrupting him once more. "Speak not to me as to one of the young ladies of thy acquaintance. Say 'thou' to me, and address me as a true knight would speak to his fair lady."

She spoke with such insistence and authority that Peter

Antònovitch felt compelled to obey. And when he turned to Turandina and for the first time spoke to her intimately and called her by her name, he at once felt more at ease.

"Turandina, hast thou not a dress to wear? My people would expect thee to wear an ordinary dress."

Turandina smiled once more and said:

"I don't know. Isn't my one garment enough? I was told that in this wallet I should find everything that I should need in the world of men. Take it and look within; perhaps thou wilt find there what thou desirest."

With these words she held out to him her little bag. And as he pulled apart the cord and opened it, Peter Antònovitch thought to himself: "It will be good if someone has put in some kind of frock for her."

He put his hand into the wallet, and feeling something soft he drew out a small parcel, so small that Turandina could have closed her hand over it. And when he unwrapped the parcel, there was just what he wanted, a dress such as most young girls were wearing at that time.

He helped Turandina to put it on, and he fastened it for her, for, of course, it buttoned at the back.

"Is that all right now?" asked Turandina.

Peter Antònovitch looked regretfully at the little bag. It looked much too small to hold a pair of shoes. But he put in his hand again and thought: "A pair of sandals would do nicely."

His fingers touched a little strap, and he drew forth a tiny pair of golden sandals. And then he dried her feet and put on the sandals and fastened the straps for her.

"Now is everything all right?" asked Turandina again.

There was such a humility in her voice and gesture as she spoke that Peter Antònovitch felt quite happy. It would be quite easy to manage her now, he thought. So he said: "Oh yes; we can get a hat later on."

IV

And so there came a fairy story into the life of a man. Of course, it seemed sometimes as if the young lawyer's life were quite unsuited for such a thing. His relatives were utterly unable to believe the account their young guest gave of herself, and even Peter Antònovitch himself lacked faith. Many times he begged Turandina to tell him her real name, and he played various tricks on her to trap her into confessing that her story was not really true. But Turandina was never angry at his persistence. She smiled sweetly and simply, and with great patience said over and over again:

"I have told you the truth."

"But where is the land over which King Turandon reigns?" Peter Antònovitch would ask.

"It is far away," Turandina would answer, "and yet if you wish it, it is near also. But none of you can go thither. Only we who have been born in the enchanted kingdom of King Turandon can ever get to that wonderful country."

"But can you not show me how to go there?" asked Peter Antònovitch.

"No, I cannot," answered Turandina.

"And can you return yourself?" said he.

"Now I cannot," said she; "but when my father calls me, I shall return."

There was no sadness in her voice and expression, nor any joy, as she spoke of her expulsion from the enchanted land and of her return. Her voice was always calm and gentle. She looked on all she saw with inquiring eyes, as if seeing everything for the first time, but with a quiet calmness, as if knowing that she would soon become accustomed to all new and strange things, and would easily recognise them again. When she once knew a thing she never made a mistake nor confused it with anything else. All ordinary rules of conduct that people told her, or that she herself noticed, were lightly and easily followed, as if she had been accus-

GREAT RUSSIAN SHORT STORIES

tomed to them from her childhood. She remembered names and faces of people after having once seen them.

Turandina never quarrelled with anyone, and she never said anything untrue. When she was advised to use the ordinary Society evasions she shook her head and said:

"One must never say what is untrue. The earth hears everything."

At home and in the company of others Turandina behaved with such dignity and graciousness that all who could believe in a fairy tale were obliged to believe that they were in the presence of a beautiful princess, the daughter of a great and wise king.

But the fairy tale was somewhat difficult to reconcile with the ordinary life of the young lawyer and his people. There was a perpetual struggle between the two, and many difficulties arose in consequence.

V

When Turandina had been living with the family for a few days, an official came to the house and said to the servant:

"They say there's a young lady visitor here. She must send in her passport and have it signed."

The servant told her mistress, who spoke to her husband about the matter. He asked Peter Antònovitch about the passport, and the latter went to find Turandina and ask her. Turandina was sitting on the verandah and reading a book with much enjoyment.

"Turandina," said Peter Antònovitch, going out to her, "the police have sent to ask for your passport. It must be sent to be signed."

Turandina listened very attentively to what Peter Antònovitch had to say, and then she asked:

"What is a passport?"

"Oh, a passport," said he, "don't you know, is—a passport.

A paper on which is written your name and your father's name, your age, your rank. You can't possibly live anywhere without a passport."

"If it's necessary," said Turandina calmly, "then, of course, it ought to be in my little bag. Look, there's the bag, take it and see if the passport is inside."

And in the wonderful little bag there was found a passport— a small book in a brown cover, which had been obtained in the province of Astrakhan, in which was inscribed the name of the Princess Tamara Timofeevna Turandon, seventeen years of age, and unmarried. Everything was in order: the seal, the official signature, the signature of the princess herself, and so on, just as in all passport books.

Peter Antònovitch looked at Turandina and smiled.

"So that's who you are," said he, "you are a princess, and your name is Tamara."

But Turandina shook her head.

"No," said she, "I've never been called Tamara. That passport doesn't tell the truth; it's only for the police and for those people who do not know and cannot know the truth. I am Turandina, the daughter of King Turandon. Since I have lived in this world I have learnt that people here don't want to know the truth. I don't know anything about the passport. Whoever put it in my little bag must have known that I should need it. But for thee, my word should be enough."

After the passport had been signed, Turandina was known as the princess, or Tamara Timofeevna, but her own people continued to call her Turandina.

VI

Her own people—for they came to be her own people. The fairy tale came into a man's life, and, as often happens in a fairy tale, so it now occurred in life. Peter Antònovitch fell in love with Turandina and Turandina loved him also. He made up his mind to marry her, and this led to slight difficulties in the family.

The teacher-cousin and his wife said:

"In spite of her mysterious origin and her obstinate silence about her family, your Turandina is a very dear girl, beautiful, intelligent, very good and capable, and well brought up. In short, she is everything that one could wish. But you ought to remember that you have no money, and neither has she.

"It will be difficult for two people to live in Petersburg on the money your father allows you.

"Especially with a princess.

"You must remember that in spite of her sweet ways she's probably accustomed to live in good style.

"She has very small soft hands. True, she has been very modest here, and you say she was barefoot when you met her first and had very little clothing. But we don't know what kind of garments she will want to wear in a town."

Peter Antònovitch himself was rather pessimistic at first. But by and by he remembered how he had found a dress for Turandina in the little bag. A bold thought came into his mind, and he smiled and said:

"I found a house-frock for Turandina in her little bag. Perhaps if I were to rummage in it again I might find a ball-dress for her."

But the teacher's wife, a kind young woman with a genius for housekeeping, said:

"Much better if you could find some money. If only she had five hundred roubles we could manage to get her a good trousseau."

"We ought to find five hundred thousand—for a princess's dowry," said Peter Antònovitch, laughing.

"Oh, a hundred thousand would be quite enough for you," laughed his cousin in reply.

Just then Turandina came quietly up the steps leading

from the garden, and Peter Antònovitch called to her and said:

"Turandina, show me your little bag, dear. Perhaps you have a hundred thousand roubles there."

Turandina held out her little bag to him and said:

"If it's necessary, you will find it in the bag."

And Peter Antònovitch again put his hand into the little bag and drew forth a large packet of notes. He began to count them, but without counting he could see they represented a large quantity of money.

VII

So this great fairy tale came into the young man's life. And though it didn't seem well suited to the taking-in of a fairy tale, yet room was found for it somewhere. The fairy tale bought a place in his life—with its own charm and the treasures of the enchanted bag.

Turandina and the young lawyer were married. And Turandina had first a little son and then a daughter. The boy was like his mother, and grew up to be a gentle dreamy child. The girl was like her father, gay and intelligent.

And so the years went by. Every summer, when the days were at their longest, a strange melancholy overshadowed Turandina. She used to go out in the mornings to the edge of the forest and stand there listening to the forest voices. And after some time she would walk home slowly and sadly.

And once, standing there at midday, she heard a loud voice calling to her:

"Turandina, come. Your father has forgiven you."

And so she went away and never returned. Her little son was then seven years old and her daughter three.

Thus the fairy tale departed from this life and never came back. But Turandina's little son never forgot his mother.

Sometimes he would wander away by himself so as to be quite alone. And when he came home again there was such an expression upon his face that the teacher's wife said to her husband in a whisper:

"He has been with Turandina."

(II)

THE HERALD OF THE BEAST

I

I t was quiet and peaceful, neither gladness nor sadness was in the room. The electric light was on. The walls seemed solid, firm as adamant, indestructible. The window was hidden behind heavy dark green curtains, and the big door opposite the window was locked and bolted, as was also the little one in the wall at the side. But on the other side of the doors all was dark and empty, in the wide corridor and in the melancholy hall where beautiful palms yearned for their southern homes.

Gurof was lying on the green divan. In his hands was a book. He read it, but often stopped short in his reading. He thought, mused, dreamed—and always about the same thing, always about *them*.

They were near him. He had long since noticed that. They had hid themselves. *They* were inescapably near. They rustled round about, almost inaudibly, but for a long time did not show themselves to his eyes. Gurof saw the first one a few days ago; he wakened tired, miserable, pallid, and as he lazily turned on the electric light so as to expel the wild gloom of the winter morning he suddenly saw one of them.

A wee grey one, agile and furtive, pattered over his pillow, lisped something, and hid himself.

And afterwards, morning and evening, they ran about Gurof, grey, agile, furtive.

And to-day he had expected them.

Now and then his head ached slightly. Now and then he was seized by cold fits and by waves of heat. Then from a corner ran out Fever, long and slender, with ugly yellow face and dry bony hands, lay down beside him, embraced him, kissed his face and smiled. And the rapid kisses of the caressing and subtle Fever and the soft aching movements in his head were pleasant to him.

Weakness poured itself into all his limbs, and tiredness spread over them. But it was pleasant. The people he knew in the world became remote, uninteresting, entirely superfluous. He felt he would like to remain here with *them*.

Gurof had been indoors for several days. He had locked himself up in the house. He permitted no one to see him. Sat by himself. Thought of them. Waited them.

II

Strangely and unexpectedly the languor of sweet waiting was broken. There was a loud knocking at an outer door and then the sound of even unhurrying footsteps in the hall.

As Gurof turned his face to the door a blast of cold air swept in, and he saw, as he shivered, a boy of a wild and strange appearance. He was in a linen cloak, but showed half his body naked, and his arms were bare. His body was brown, all sunburnt. His curly hair was black and bright; black also were his eyes and sparkling. A wonderfully correct and beautiful face. But of a beauty terrible to look upon. Not a kind face, not an evil one.

Gurof was not astonished at the boy's coming. Some dominant idea had possession of his mind. And he heard how *they* crept out of sight and hid themselves.

And the boy said:

"Aristomakh! Have you forgotten your promise? Do noble

people act thus? You fled from me when I was in mortal danger. You promised me something, which it seems you did not wish to fulfil. Such a long time I've been looking for you! And behold, I find you living in festivity, drowning in luxury."

Gurof looked distrustfully at the half-naked beautiful boy and a confused remembrance awakened in his soul. Something long since gratefully buried in oblivion rose up with indistinct feature, and asking for remembrance tired his memory. The enigma could not be guessed though it seemed near and familiar.

And where were the unwavering walls? Something was happening round about him, some change was taking place, but Gurof was so obsessed by the struggle with his ancient memory that he failed to take stock of those changes. He said to the wonderful boy:

"Dear boy, tell me clearly and simply without unnecessary reproaches what it was I promised you and when it was I left you in mortal danger. I swear to you by all that is holy that my honour would never have allowed me to commit the ignoble act with which for some reason you charge me."

The boy nodded, and then in a loud and melodious voice gave answer:

"Aristomakh! You always were clever at verbal exercises, and indeed as clever in actions demanding daring and caution. If I said that you had left me in a moment of mortal danger it is not a reproach. And I don't understand why you speak of your honour. The thing purposed by us was difficult and dangerous, but why do you quibble about it? Who is here that you think you can deceive by pretending ignorance of what happened this morning before sunrise and of the promise you had given me?"

The electric light became dim. The ceiling seemed dark and high. There was the scent of a herb in the room—but what herb? Its forgotten name had one time sounded sweetly

on his ear. On the wings of the scent a cool air seemed
wafted into the toom. Gurof stood up and cried out:

"What thing did we purpose? I deny nothing, dear boy,
but I simply don't know of what you are speaking. I don't
remember."

It seemed to Gurof that the child was at one and the same
time looking at him and not looking at him. Though the
boy's eyes were directed towards him they seemed to be
staring at some other unearthly person whose body coincided
with his but who was not he.

It grew dark around him and the air became fresher and
cooler. A gladness leapt in his soul and a lightness as of
elementary existence. The room disappeared from his remembrance. Above he saw the stars glittering in the black
sky. Once more the boy addressed him:

"We ought to have killed the Beast. I shall remind you of
that when under the myriad eyes of the all-seeing sky you are
again confused with fear. And how not have fear! The thing
that we purposed was great and dreadful, and it would have
given a glory to our names in far posterity."

In the night quietude he heard the murmuring and gentle
tinkling of a brook. He could not see the brook, but he felt
that it was deliciously and tantalisingly near. They were
standing in the shadow of spreading trees, and the conversation went on. Gurof asked:

"Why do you say that I left you in a moment of mortal
danger? Am I the sort of man to take fright and run away?"

The boy laughed, and like music was his laughter. Then in
sweet melodious accents he replied:

"Aristomakh, how cleverly you pretend to have forgotten
all! But I don't understand why you take the trouble to
exercise such cunning, or why you contrive reproaches
against yourself which I for my part should not have thought
of alone. You left me in the moment of mortal danger because it was clearly necessary, and you couldn't help me
otherwise than by abandoning me there. Surely you won't

remain obstinate in your denial after I remind you of the
words of the oracle."

Gurof suddenly remembered. It was as if a bright light had
flooded into the dark abyss of the forgotten. And he cried
out loudly and excitedly:

"He alone will kill the Beast!"

The boy laughed. Aristomakh turned to him with the
question:

"Have you killed the Beast, Timaride?"

"With what? Even were my hands strong enough I am not
he who has the power to kill the Beast with a blow of the fist.
We were incautious, Aristomakh, and without weapons. We
were playing on the sands and the Beast fell upon us suddenly and struck me with his heavy paw. My fate was to give
my life as a sweet sacrifice to glory and in high exploit, but
to you it remained to finish the work. And whilst the Beast
tore my helpless body you might have run, swift-footed Aristomakh, might have gained your spear, and you might have
struck the Beast whilst he was drunk with my blood. But the
Beast did not accept my sacrifice; I lay before him motionless
and looked up at his blood-weltering eyes, and he kept me
pinned to the ground by the heavy paw on my shoulder.
He breathed hotly and unevenly and he growled softly, but
he did not kill me. He simply licked over my face with his
broad warm tongue and went away."

"Where is he now?" asked Aristomakh.

The night air felt moist and calm, and through it came the
musical answer of Timaride:

"I rose when he had left me, but he was attracted by the
scent of my blood and followed after me. I don't know why
he has set upon me again. Still, I am glad that he follows,
for so I bring him to you. Get the weapon that you so
cleverly hid, and kill the Beast, and I in my turn will run
away and leave you in the moment of mortal danger, face to
face with the enraged Beast. Good luck, Aristomakh!"

And saying that, Timaride ran away, his white cloak gleaming but a minute in the darkness. And just as he disappeared there broke out the horrible roaring of the Beast and the thud of his heavy paws on the ground. Thrusting to right and left the foliage of the bushes there appeared in the darkness the immense monstrous head of the Beast, and his large eyes gleamed like luminous velvet. The Beast ceased to roar, and with his eyes fixed on Aristomakh approached him stealthily and silently.

Terror filled the heart of Aristomakh.

"Where is the spear?" he whispered, and immediately he turned to flee. But with a heavy bound the Beast started after him, roaring and bellowing, and pulled him down. And when the Beast held him, a great yell broke through the stillness of the night. Then Aristomakh moaned out the ancient and horrible words of the curse of the walls.

And up rose the walls about him. . . .

III

The walls of the room stood firm, unwavering, and the barely reflected electric light seemed to die upon them. All the rest of the room was customary and usual.

Once more Fever came and kissed him with dry yellow lips and caressed him with wizened bony hands. The same tedious little book with little white pages lay on the table, and in the green divan lay Gurof, and Fever embraced him, scattering rapid kisses with hurrying lips. And once more the grey ones rustled and chattered.

Gurof raised his head a little as if with great effort and said hollowly:

"The curse of the walls."

What was he talking about? What curse? What was the curse? What were the words of it? Were there any?

The little ones, grey and agile, danced about the book and turned with their tails the pallid pages, and with little squeaks and whimpers answered him:

"Our walls are strong. We live in the walls. No fear troubles us inside the walls."

Among them was a singular-looking one, not at all like the rest. He was quite black and wore dress of mingled smoke and flame. From his eyes came little lightnings. Suddenly he detached himself from the others and stood before Gurof, who cried out:

"Who are you? What do you want?"

The black guest replied:

"I . . . am the Herald of the Beast. On the shore of the forest stream you left long since the mangled body of Tima-ride. The Beast has sated himself with the fine blood of your friend—he has devoured the flesh which should have tasted earthly happiness; the wonderful human form has been destroyed, and that in it which was more than human has perished, all to give a moment's satisfaction to the ever-insatiable Beast. The blood, the marvellous blood, godly wine of joy, the wine of more than human blessing—where is it now? Alas! the eternally thirsting Beast has been made drunk for a moment by it. You have left the mangled body of Timaride by the side of the forest stream, have forgotten the promise given to your splendid friend, and the word of the ancient oracle has not driven fear from your heart. Think you, then, that saving yourself you can escape the Beast and that he will not find you?"

The voice and the words were stern. The grey ones had stopped in their dancing to listen. Gurof said:

"What is the Beast to me? I have fixed my walls about me for ever, and the Beast will not find a way to me in my fortress."

At that the grey ones rejoiced and scampered round the room anew, but the Herald of the Beast cried out once more, and sharp and stern were his accents:

"Do you not see that I am here? I am here because I have found you. I am here because the curse of the walls has lost power. I am here because Timaride is waiting and tirelessly questioning. Do you not hear the gentle laughter of the brave and trusting child? Do you not hear the roaring of the Beast?"

From beyond the wall broke out the terrible roaring of the Beast.

"But the walls are firm for ever by the spell I cast, my fortress cannot be destroyed," cried Gurof.

And the Black One answered, imperiously:

"I tell thee, man, the curse of the walls is dead. But if you don't believe, but still think you can save yourself, pronounce the curse again."

Gurof shuddered. He indeed believed that the curse was dead, and all that was around him whispered to him the terrible news. The Herald of the Beast had pronounced the fearful truth. Gurof's head ached, and he felt weary of the hot kisses that clinging, caressing Fever still gave him. The words of the sentence seemed to strain his consciousness, and the Herald of the Beast as he stood before him was magnified until he obscured the light and stood like a great shadow over him, and his eyes glowed like fires.

Suddenly the black cloak fell from the shoulders of the visitor and Gurof recognised him—it was the child Timaride.

"Are you going to kill the Beast?" asked Timaride in a high-sounding voice. "I have brought him to you. The malicious gift of godhead will avail you no longer, for the curse is dead. It availed you once, making as nothing my sacrifice and hiding from your eyes the glory of your exploit. But to-day the tune is changed; dead is the curse, get your sword quickly and kill the Beast. I was only a child; now I have become the Herald of the Beast. I have fed the Beast with my blood, but he thirsts anew. To you I have brought him, and do you fulfil your promise and kill him—or die."

He vanished.

The walls shuddered at the dreadful roaring. The room filled with airs that were cold and damp.

The wall directly opposite the place where Gurof lay collapsed, and there entered the ferocious, immense and monstrous Beast. With fearful bellowing he crept up to Gurof and struck him on the chest with his paw. The merciless claws went right into his heart. An awful pain shattered his body. And looking at him with gleaming bloody eyes, the Beast crouched over Gurof, grinding his bones in his teeth and devouring his yet-beating heart.

(III)

ADVENTURES OF A COBBLE-STONE

THERE was in the town a cobbled roadway. A wheel of a passing cart loosened one of the stones. The stone said to himself: "Why should I lie here close packed with others of my kind? I will live separately."

A boy came along and picked up the cobble-stone.

Thought the stone to himself: "I wanted to travel and I travel. I only had to wish sufficiently strongly."

The boy threw the stone at a house. Thought the stone: "I wish to fly and I fly. It's quite simple—I just willed it."

Bang went the stone against the window-glass. The glass broke, and in doing so cried out:

"Oh, the scoundrel! What are you doing?"

But the stone replied:

"You'd have done better to get out of the way. I don't like people getting in my way. Everything arranged for my benefit—that's my motto."

The stone fell on a soft bed and thought: "I've flown a bit, and now I'll lie down for a while and rest."

A servant came and took the stone off the bed and threw it out at the window again so that it fell back on the cobbled roadway.

Then the stone cried out to his fellow-cobbles: "Brothers, good health, I've just been paying a call at one of the mansions, but I did not at all care for the aristocracy, my heart yearned for the common people, so I returned."

(IV)

EQUALITY

A B I G fish overtook a little one and wanted to swallow him.

The little fish squeaked out: "It is unjust. I also want to live. All fishes are equal before the law."

The big fish answered: "What's the matter? I won't discuss whether we are equal, but if you don't want me to eat you, then do you please swallow me if you can—swallow me, don't be afraid, I shan't set on you."

The little fish opened his mouth and poked about trying to get the big fish in, sighed at last and said: "You have it. Swallow me."

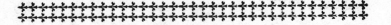

EUGENE CHIRIKOF

(*b.* 1864)

✳✳

(I)

BOUND OVER

(Translated by Leonide Zarine)

I

O L D Marya Timofeevna went each evening to the railway station to meet the passenger train. The train would glide alongside the wooden platform and seemed always to startle her, as though it somehow were unexpected. Her head was full of thoughts of what had happened to her son Nicholas, and what was going to happen now . . . the clanging of the signal bell and the whistle of the steam would arouse her from these thoughts and she would rush from one carriage to another searching for her son. She would stare eagerly among the crowd on the platform and peep into the windows of the carriages, and her heart would jump whenever she saw gold buttons or the peaked cap with blue band.

The same thing happened for several days; the train would glide along into the station, small groups of unimportant people would alight, the shrieking whistle would answer, as if in haste, the station bell, and the train would depart, leaving in its wake torn ribbons of grey smoke. On one occasion the local chief of police arrived, his wife and a lot of children were there to meet him; another time the lady doctor and Father Porfery of the monastery came, but there was no Nicholas. . . . "What does it mean? . . . Ah, these children, these children!" Marya Timofeevna would hastily wipe the tears from her eyes and would continue to scan the platform. Unable to believe her own eyes, she would ask one of the railway men:

"Where does this train go now?"

"To Moscow, grannie, to bright Moscow, grannie," would answer the man as he continued sweeping the platform.

"And has it come from Kief?"

"Yes, from Kief, from Kief," the man would answer, becoming annoyed.

Marya Timofeevna would gaze in the direction where, according to her reckoning, Kief must be, and a strange smile would steal over the face of the old woman, a smile sad and tender, for there, far, far away in the mist of the approaching darkness of the spring evening, the dear image of a dark young fellow in student uniform would appear before her.

"Just a minute, grannie, step to one side a little," the railwayman would say, brushing against the feet of Marya Timofeevna with his broom.

She would tear herself away from Kief, the image of the dark young man would disappear and, sighing, full of anxiety and sorrow, helpless and bewildered, Marya Timofeevna would depart, looking like one of those very old women whom everyone feels must be called "grannie." First she would walk slowly, then begin to hurry; there always came the hope that perhaps she had missed Nicholas and would find him at home when she arrived. . . . Her sight was failing . . . it was so easy to miss anyone in that bustle. . . . She really ought to get some spectacles. . . . The nearer Marya Timofeevna approached the house, the more real seemed the hope that she would find Nicholas there, and with a throbbing heart she would enter the gate of the small creeper-covered house, a house as old as Marya Timofeevna herself. Certainly Nicholas would be there and his father would be scolding him. . . . What was there to scold him for? You cannot undo what has been done. The main thing was that he would be in good health. It was not everyone who finished his term and remained alive. . . . Marya Timofeevna would anxiously take hold of the latch of the gate, anxiously raise it, and anxiously she would ascend the steps of the porch and with a tremor would open the door. . . .

No! he had not arrived!

Her husband, old Stepan Nikiforovitch, would be moving about the room in his very worn slippers, coughing nervously, trying to hide his excitement, and when Marya Timofeevna appeared in the doorway, always without Nicholas, he would turn away and growl:

"And there was no need to go and meet him!" . . .

Then he would turn to the old woman and with arms outstretched would add:

"Isn't it quite clear!"

A long silence usually would follow. Their hearts were heavy, their thoughts were of the same thing. Both would be on the verge of tears, but in trying to be firm would be obstinate, silent . . . and in the silence the room would fill with a feeling of sadness and a stifling atmosphere. The large clock on the wall ticked in slow, deliberate measure, and seemed to be repeating the words of the old man . . .

"And there is no need to wait! . . . and there is no need to wait! . . ."

And the old people began to imagine all kinds of terrible things.

The local accountant, an old friend of Stepan Nikiforovitch, sometimes visited them. He would tell them that people convicted for political offences are imprisoned in a fortress cell with small windows in the roof and apertures in the walls through which water could be let on to drown the prisoner.

"I have read about it and have even seen the picture," he would say—"a young girl standing on a bed and water pouring through the aperture."

"My God! My God!" would whisper Marya Timofeevna, and tears would tremble in her eyes.

"They often hang people also," the accountant would continue dreamily. "Of course some are liberated, but that seldom happens," he would add in an attempt to console the old people. "If you have sinned you must atone. . . . I was reading a paper about these . . . what are they called? . . . December revolutionaries." . . .

And the accountant would relate what he had read, adding at the same time a great deal that he imagined, muddling up the old paper with all sorts of historical novels, and filling the old people with such terror that all through the night they tossed about and sighed, and were unable to sleep. . . .

And for this reason Stepan Nikiforovitch would say to his wife on her return alone from the station:

"How could you expect to see him!"

He would say this quite gruffly, but would then go out into the garden. They had there an old grass-covered bathing hut with a small square window. The old man would go stealthily into the hut and lock himself in, and there in the freedom of solitude would cry like a child and would mutter in despair:

"My God! If only he is alive . . . if only that . . . nothing else matters." . . .

One morning when Stepan Nikiforovitch was at his place of employment and Marya Timofeevna was busying herself in the kitchen, an old-fashioned cab with rattling rusty mudguards drove up to the house. Marya Timofeevna looked through the window and the duster fell from her hand. Near the cab was standing a thin, lanky student waiting for the cabman to lift down an old trunk. A student stood with his back to the window, but the sight of the old trunk was enough to send Marya Timofeevna rushing to the porch.

"Kolia! . . . dear Kolia! . . ." she exclaimed, and laughing through her tears she threw herself on the young man and began to kiss him. She could hardly believe that her Kolia had come back, she gazed into his face and kept on asking:

"Are you in good health? are you in good health?" . . .

"Not bad." . . .

"And we have been worried to death, thinking I don't know what about you! Have they pardoned you? . . . My God, and you are really alive!" . . .

The young man, dark, with a thin sensitive face, answered somehow confusedly with a sad smile, as though he felt uncomfortable before this old woman, who was choking with happiness, and her overwhelming tenderness to which he had been so long unaccustomed.

"Give me the parcel! . . . I myself! . . . Just when one had given up expecting you! . . . and I have been going every day to meet you. . . . We simply couldn't make up our minds what had happened." . . .

"Nothing out of the ordinary. . . . I was imprisoned for a time." . . .

"In a fortress? . . . And God has helped you out? I have prayed so, Kolia dear. Have they granted you . . . full pardon?" . . .

"No, not full pardon, but . . . they have sent me to you bound over . . ." said the student, smiling confusedly.

"And then what will they do with you?" . . .

"Nothing in particular. . . . I shall enter the university again in two years." . . .

"I saw a student one day passing through the station. . . . I asked him, but he knew nothing about you." . . .

"How could we all know each other? There are so many of us, mother."

"You really must want something to eat! . . . How thin you are! . . . I won't be a moment!" . . .

II

At last he is home!

Everything just as it was in the old days. The small rooms so cleanly arranged . . . curtains on the windows . . .

drooping flowers . . . geraniums . . . ivy . . . the well-remembered clock on the wall and the horseshoe to keep it balanced, the round table before the elaborate couch covered with homespun linen whose design reminded one of something long past. . . . It seemed as though he had seen these designs from the very day of his birth, and also that inkstain on the table! On the wall between the windows was a nail on which was hanging a neat file of the newspaper *Light*. Through the windows one could see a wide expanse of green grass, and the street . . . quiet and deserted. . . . Just in the old way the dove sanctuary projected from the corner of the house, and over the gate was the miniature windmill. . . . Geese wandered about the green with their fluffy yellow goslings, and in the nettles under the fence a sleeping pig flicked its ears.

Nicholas smiled . . . it seemed only yesterday since he had seen those geese, that pig!

The blue cloudless sky spread over the town, so gentle, so kind and so lazy. Swallows circled high up in the sky . . . a jackdaw rested with open beak and lowered wings on the long fence. A dog, dejected and indifferent, with tongue hanging out, stepped over pools of water. And there also walked a man! Nor did he hurry; raising the dust as he walked, eyes cast downwards and spitting out the shells of the sunflower seeds as he chewed. A small chubby boy careered along the street riding on a stick and whipping himself with a small whip, while another standing against the gate began to cry. Probably the chubby one had stolen his horse! . . . Sparrows chirped in the lilac bushes and hedges, fussing, fighting, scrambling and screaming like women at a bazaar. . . . One sparrow jumped on to a branch quite near the window and with measured curiosity peeped in at Nicholas, then immediately flew chirping away, and two more sparrows flew over to the same branch. . . . On the window-sill was a plate covered with brown paper bearing the design of one large fly surrounded by innumerable small ones. On the paper, feet upwards, lay one dead fly. . . . Father began his fight with the flies in the early spring. He enjoyed the occupation. . . . There really must be a fly-paper somewhere. Of course . . . there it is hanging on the wall above the small table, just in the place where it was hanging so long ago!

Nicholas seated himself near the window and began to look into the street, and the joy which had risen in the heart of the young man as the cab had rattled towards his home behind the hedge suddenly deadened, became uncertain, and departed. Nicholas began to feel dispirited. With the view of this street, with the dove sanctuary, the geese on the green and the pig under the fence, he began to feel lonely in these clean cosy little rooms with the file of *Light* on the wall, the knitted table-cloth and the fly-paper. . . . . Nobody here thinks that there is anything important or even interesting happening somewhere far away in the large towns, where life seethes like the water in the small kettle over the fire, and where all that had happened during the past months was so pregnant with significance for every human soul. . . . Nicholas began to feel that he had two entirely separate and distinct lives, neither having anything in common with the other : two lives everlastingly at variance; the one there where he had come from and the other here. And the life there now seemed like a fairy tale which he must have read, while this life in the village was the real life, unalterable and unvaried like a law of nature.

"You like fish, Kolia dear?"

Nicholas looked round. His mother, fussing, full of happiness, was standing, with sleeves rolled up, in the doorway.

"Fish. . . . All right. . . . I don't mind." . . .

"Then I will cook you some fish . . . some carp in sour cream! . . .

"And now come and have a bite! You used to like this very much," said mother, putting on the table a steaming dish. "You rebels! What do you rebel for! What do you want?"

Marya Timofeevna did not wait for her son's answer and apparently had no interest in "what they want"; she went immediately into the kitchen, where butter was sizzling in the pan on the fire. . . . Then she brought a whole pile of bread on a plate and advised:

"Do not quarrel with your father: he will be angry, but that will pass. Agree with him, he is old, has lived long and you are only learning to walk. To have lived a lifetime is not merely like walking through a meadow." . . .

"And when does father come home?"

"Just as usual, at three."

"Where does he work now?"

"Just at the same place, assessor to the guardians . . . and his salary is just the same . . . he never had a rise! All the same we must thank God, as he is old now and can scarcely write, his hand trembles so." . . .

"Trembles?" asked Nicholas anxiously.

"Yes, trembles, Kolia dear. I wrote to you about it, some sort of paralysis has taken hold of him. We always hoped that . . . but what about it! . . . You can't bring that back . . . eat while the food is hot!" . . .

Nicholas was eating slowly, glancing from time to time at his mother and thinking how very old she had become during those past two years whilst he had been in Kief; more grey hairs and the corners of her mouth drooped still lower, her hands seemed more bony and her back still more bent.

Marya Timofeevna glanced anxiously at the clock; she was awaiting the return of Stepan Nikiforovitch from the office of the guardians, and was agitated with feelings of joy, fear and impatience. She wished that he would come the sooner to enjoy the arrival of his son, but she was afraid lest the father in heat should offend his son, and hoped that the son would not say something too much for his father, and she trembled with joy and fear for what might happen.

"Father has still two hours at the office . . . they have such a lot of flies there, they irritate father and cause him always

to come home in a bad temper," forewarned Marya Timofeevna.

Nicholas also was agitated. He wished to meet his father
more quickly and feared lest the reunion should be spoiled
by recriminations. The fact was he would never understand,
however one might try to explain, that one could not have
acted otherwise. And to talk about this was unavoidable.
Nicholas felt that he was in the right, but still was anxious;
a disagreeable shyness was disturbing his heart. He glanced
at the clock, the hand of which was slowly creeping to three.

"Here comes father!"

Stepping slowly and decorously over pools of water, Stepan
Nikiforovitch approached the house. Nicholas recognised
him in the distance by his pompous walk. It seemed that
Stepan Nikiforovitch felt himself to be of no small importance
in his native town. He was wearing a glossy steel-grey cape,
a peaked cap with a badge, in his hand a massive umbrella
and under his arm a portfolio.

"What is father carrying?"

"It is a portfolio!" said mother gently. "He always carries
it with him; sometimes it is empty, but he still carries it.
And the umbrella too, even when it doesn't rain, just in
case . . ."

When Stepan Nikiforovitch neared the geese and the mother
goose with outstretched neck rushed at him with the intention of pinching his leg, he came to a halt, raised his head
high and wagged an admonishing finger. The mother goose
immediately lowered her neck, took it in and with jerking
tail returned to her goslings, and Stepan Nikiforovitch decorously and importantly proceeded, the wings of his wide cape
waving at his sides.

Nicholas went out to the gate.

Stepan Nikiforovitch did not hurry. He already knew that
Nicholas had arrived, he had been told about it in the office.

"Ah, ahah! You have arrived!" said he, smiled slightly,
but did not hasten, continuing on his way with the same

pomposity. It seemed to Stepan Nikiforovitch that it would be wrong to show before the young offender the joy which overflowed his father's heart at the sight of his Kolia, the same Kolia whom only the previous night he had seen in a dream in some terrible plight; it was as if he had been condemned to be shot and had run home to say good-bye, pale and dishevelled, with parched lips and for some reason barefooted

"Good-day, father!"

"Good-day, my boy!"

The old man embraced Nicholas somewhat coldly, coughed sharply and asked:

"Have you been here long?"

"I came this morning."

"I am very pleased, very pleased!" said Stepan Nikiforovitch in the tone in which he would greet a visitor.

Marya Timofeevna rushed to the porch. As usual she had missed the important moment. She had not seen the manner of the reunion of father and son. Seeing that they were walking in silence, not even looking at each other, she tried to ease the situation:

"Thank God, father, our Kolia has returned. And you frightened me unnecessarily yesterday by your dream. He is alive and in good health, which is the chief thing. . . . Come and have dinner! And did the flies worry you much, father?"

Stepan Nikiforovitch did not answer the question about the flies; he grasped that they were mentioned for quite a different reason. They sat at the table. The father ate seriously as though performing some kind of ceremony, breaking the bread and dipping his spoon into the stew almost with reverence. Now and again he put short questions to his son:

"So they let you out?"

"Yes."

"So you were a jail-bird?"

"Yes."

"It means that you return to your parents bound over?"

"Yes."

Not until the stew was finished did the old man begin to talk at greater length.

"And what do you intend to do now, my boy?"

"I will take up my studies again later on."

"It means starting afresh. And if they kick you out again? Then once more you start from the beginning?"

"Come now, father, always the start and the beginning. . . . God will allow an end to come some time," smoothed over Marya Timofeevna.

"Everything has an end, that is the law of nature, Marya Timofeevna," answered Stepan gruffly, wiping his mouth with his serviette. "The end will come for both of us one day . . . we live . . . it will be time to die. . . . For what reason did they kick you out, my boy?"

"For taking part in disorders."

"Oh, excellent! . . . and why did they lock you up?"

"Well, really, I don't know myself."

"So . . . 'm . . . 'm. . . . Things don't happen for nothing, my boy. What we have but do not keep, when we lose, we cry for! I must say I never expected such a performance from you, my boy."

"Performance! What a strange idea!" murmured Nicholas to himself, and he began to run his fingers through his hair impatiently.

"And so . . . for eight years we had to pay preparatory school, we paid a tutor, bought satchels, books, stationery, jackets, trousers. . . . I counted that some day all this would come back to me, but it seems that will be in another world, my boy, with burning coals."

"But, father, there is no reason for you to count," interposed Marya Timofeevna, seeing that the conversation was taking a wrong turn. "Everyone has children and has to spend money on them. It cannot be otherwise. The boy cannot be blamed because he needed a jacket and trousers. . . . And it doesn't seem somehow right to count! It is a sin!"

"I just happened to say that . . . the word came . . . what sort of count!" retorted the old man, coughing confusedly. "You and I need nothing. We haven't long to live, and in any case there is nothing for us to gain by this. I just mentioned it . . . but it is regrettable, a pity and vexing! We wanted to put him on his feet more quickly, to make a man of him, though we might have only one eye left, to see that he had succeeded, then to lie at rest. . . . But why talk about it? . . . One can see that everyone is the maker of his own happiness." . . .

"There is happiness and happiness," said Nicholas quietly, with a break in his voice; "everyone understands happiness in his own way, and there lies the cause of all the unhappiness. . . . For some, honour is dearer than any happiness. . . ."

"It is great honour to have nothing to eat!" answered the old man, raising his voice in anger, and he began to give thanks after dinner.

"How can we understand?" he said, having finished his prayer, "we worn-out old people, why do we exist? To be thrown quickly into the grave like dust, that is all!"

Marya Timofeevna blinked with her old eyes at Stepan Nikiforovitch and made a gesture of vexation.

"You didn't eat anything, Kolia, with all your talking," said she.

"That's all right, thanks," said Nicholas.

"There is nothing to thank for," answered his father with a sigh.

Nicholas put on his peaked cap.

"Where are you going, Kolia dear?" asked his mother anxiously.

"I will just go for a walk."

When Nicholas had gone out into the porch, one could hear through the open window the angry whisper of the old people; Marya Timofeevna was saying that one really couldn't attack the boy so soon; whatever might be said, he was their only son! One must pity the child! He himself was not proud of what had happened, and Stepan Nikiforovitch was repeating in lowered tones:

"But what in particular did I say, what in particular, mother?"

III

Nicholas went along, leaving the town behind; whistling sadly he stepped slowly down the road, and as he passed he tore the young sticky leaves from the branches which grew near the road, crumbling them in his hand. He was in deep thought. From time to time he paused and took in the view of the endless sea of green wheat, the blue stretch of the unending plain, and again his heart was possessed by a sort of hopeless desperation. Everything around was still. A lark trilled somewhere in the sky; white clouds hovered in the unattainable heavens above . . . a cuckoo called morosely from the bushes in the ravine. Everything lived its own life, and everything for which he had lived in the large town, everything he had considered great and important, seemed to be transient and negligible here. In the country the chief thing seemed to be health, and if the health was all right, then the whole problem of life was solved. It was only necessary to gaze on this peaceful picture of green plains, to give your heart to the contemplation of these unending fields and these kindly skies and to take rest; to expect nothing, as these fields, this passionless sky, these immovable white clouds expected nothing. Everything would be as it always had been; winter would come and then the summer; the fields would be green and then covered with a white cover of snow; the larks would sing and the crows utter their discordant noises in the dry pines; the peasant carts would screech on the winding paths; the markets would be held each Monday on the town square, with the shrieks and screeches of unoiled wheels; drunken peasants and blind beggars. . . . And nothing else would happen.

The sun began to set. . . . He heard the cuckoo in the forest . . . how much sorrow there was in her cry! She seemed to complain that everything was going on just as it did a hundred years ago and that nothing new would ever happen in the world. . . .

"I will go to the river, in the forest, in the meadows . . . I will hunt," thought Nicholas, turning back towards the town.

The setting sun was playing on the windows of the houses. The children with their chattering voices were occupied with their games. Peasant women, chewing sunflower seeds, were sitting on benches behind their gates, with their babies feeding at their breasts. The mill-owner passed importantly along the road, raising the dust with his heavy boots. Nicholas studied the appearance of the streets, recognising houses, side streets, small pastures and dirty ponds as though it was only yesterday that he had last seen them. . . .

"Good-day to you!"

Nicholas looked at the young peasant who raised his hat and remembered him.

"Gavrilo?"

"Yes. You remember me?"

"How could I not remember?"

"Of course, we played together, we fought together. . . ."

"How are you getting on, Gavrilo?"

"I am very happy. I am serving in the 'Madrid' bar, eight roubles and all found. And how about you, Nicholas, how have you got on? Have you finished your studies, or are you still wearing yourself out?"

"I had a break . . . for two years."

"But why?" asked Gavrilo in astonishment.

Nicholas wanted to tell the story of how there had come such a break, but glancing at the stupid, self-satisfied face of the fellow, he decided to say nothing.

"Good-bye, Gavrilo!"

"Good-bye, Nicholas! Perhaps you will look in some time at our place? There is always a bottle of beer to drink, or a game of billiards. Do come, we have quite a decent crowd of people!"

Gavrilo raised his cap, smiled broadly and bowed familiarly to a gentleman walking on the other side of the street.

"That is our controller . . . Ivan Petrovitch. . . . Quite a good fellow!" remarked Gavrilo, and he called across the street:

"There is a small debt outstanding from you, Ivan Petrovitch!"

Nicholas looked at this gentleman and asked Gavrilo:

"Isn't that Kaliagin?"

"Yes, Kaliagin," confirmed Gavrilo gaily.

Kaliagin was moving along the pavement as though he had long ago become too tired to walk, as though he only moved his feet now in order that he should not fall. . . . Nicholas remembered Kaliagin at the time when he himself was a pupil at the public school and Kaliagin was a student, the object of general attention and the envy of all the younger ones. Kaliagin had then appeared to Nicholas as the most happy of men, the most clever and interesting in the whole town. He had given Nicholas books and pamphlets to read, and had confided that he thought he would devote himself to some holy cause. And now here was Kaliagin with a beard, dressed in an official cap, an alpaca jacket and checked trousers, gone stout and looking just like an ordinary workman. His eyes were kindly, his shoulders had become more broad and the whole of his appearance had the finish of a well-nourished man who need never hurry, who had come to a full-stop, who liked to eat, to have a good sleep after dinner, and during the evening to read the paper and talk about national affairs.

"Ivan Petrovitch!"

Kaliagin looked across and smiled affably at Nicholas, but

he remained where he was, waiting for the younger man to go over to him.

"Ah, so you have arrived!" said Kaliagin, giving Nicholas his soft hand.

"Yes, I have arrived."

"You are studying science?"

"Oh, science? . . . That's not in keeping with my character!"

"How so?"

"Science goes with a quiet character, while I am . . ."

"Quarrelsome, like my wife!" finished Kaliagin with a good-humoured laugh at his own joke.

Nicholas explained how it was he had given up science, but got no response from Kaliagin.

"It is no good, my friend. . . . Nothing will come of all this . . . it is a pity for our young people. . . . What do you wish to do with our aristocracy? . . . You can't alter it! . . . They are all idiots and imbeciles! They only want to stuff themselves, to drink and to sleep!"

Kaliagin was indignant about the aristocracy and had found that it was not worth while to sacrifice a worn official shoe, let alone a career, on account of "such pigs."

"I, my friend, also sacrificed something, but now I am sorry; my colleagues are now collegiate counsellors and I am still a Government clerk! It is hot to-day!"

Kaliagin took off his cap and wiped his head. Then he informed Nicholas that he was serving in the Excise Department, that it was good to serve in the Excise Department, which had quite a big future. On parting he said:

"Here is the Red House! . . . It looks like a University! This is our Excise Department," and he pointed with his finger down the street. "We shall soon all be there," and laughing again at his own joke they parted.

The flocks returned from the pastures; the little town seemed to become more filled with sound, cows lowed in varying tones, sheep bleated, calves shrieked in contralto and bulls bellowed deeply. Intermingling with these animal sounds were the cries of women calling the hens by name to their coops; at times the long whips of the shepherds coiled in the air and cracked like the shot of a revolver, and an angry voice shouted, "Oh, you cursed ones, where are you going? Are you blind?" A golden dust hung around the houses. This was the liveliest time of the day in the country town.

IV

Days followed days. A week passed. Stepan Nikiforovitch was called to the police and they took from him some sort of statement. They requested Nicholas would call at the police station: "It is necessary that he too should sign something." Stepan Nikiforovitch also visited the police captain. The latter was a stout, good-humoured old man who was proud that people found in him a likeness to General Dragomiroff. The police captain was godfather of Nicholas. What he said to Stepan Nikiforovitch remained a secret, but from the time of the visit the father was a little kinder to the boy and only urged from time to time:

"The chief thing is—behave yourself more discreetly. Why don't you call on your godfather? It isn't polite." . . .

"I will call some time . . ." Nicholas would say, but he went neither to his godfather nor to the police, though he had already been invited several times. Nicholas liked to be alone, and would wander occasionally the whole day with a gun on his shoulder along the river bank, in the meadows and the forest.

One evening he returned from such an excursion. The old people were seated in the hedgerow near the samovar. His father was sipping his tea and reading *Light;* mother was darning his father's socks. His father had a frowning and ill-humoured expression, and his mother looked frightened. Probably they had been discussing Nicholas again and had quarrelled. His mother poured out a glass of tea and handed it to Nicholas, asking sympathetically:

"Where have you been?"

"Strolling around," answered Nicholas, and throwing his peaked cap on to the lilac bush seated himself at the table.

"A very good occupation!" grunted Stepan Nikiforovitch without raising his eyes from *Light*. Nicholas blushed but kept his temper this time as he had to keep it so often. They sat at the table in silence, and only Marya Timofeevna broke the heavy silence with such abrupt phrases as "I hope there won't be any rain," or "I will make some hash for supper."

After a long silence his father put aside the paper and said:

"A notice has come from the police! I have told you time after time! You must go there, you must go! You have delayed long enough. What sort of position do you want to put me into?"

Nicholas began to say that this was nothing important, a notice from the police was quite an ordinary matter, but the old man lost his temper and cut him short:

"Don't try to teach me! I can think for myself! It is enough for me that everyone points at me and you continue your tricks! Why don't you go to see your godfather? It is an affront to me, to me, your father!"

"Good appetite!" an old voice shrieked from behind the fence and a head stuck out. This was the accountant, a bosom friend of Stepan Nikiforovitch.

"Having tea?" he asked in a small honeyed voice.

"Come in, come in!" called Marya Timofeevna kindly, pleased to have the newcomer, who in her opinion was just in time.

The gate squeaked and a short old man wearing a straw hat, resembling in both voice and manner nothing so much as a stage uncle, entered. They exchanged greetings. Father presented Nicholas.

"Ah, the socialist! I am very pleased, very pleased to meet you!" said the visitor. "I have already had the pleasure of seeing you in the distance, but this is the first time close at hand."

They set the samovar boiling again and began to drink tea. The usual cross-examination of Nicholas, which took place every time the old people had a guest, began.

"You say you were taking the medical course?"

"Yes."

"For two years, you say?"

"Yes."

"A pity! You are probably sorry now?"

And to this question Nicholas's father usually answered:

"Of course! But, as they say, the elbow is near and still you cannot bite it!"

"It is a great pity. What didn't you like?"

Nicholas found it difficult to answer these questions which the visitors asked in all sincerity.

"Well, perhaps . . . the whole thing in general . . ."

"They don't know themselves!" said Stepan Nikiforovitch, and added angrily:

"A good thrashing would do them good, a thorough one!"

Then the old people would talk about disorders. The accountant expressed his political views. He was greatly opposed to England and was ready to see in every move "vile trickery." Though he didn't say straight out, he inferred that even in the students' disorders there was "foreign influence." This appeared paradoxical even to Stepan Nikiforovitch, who always had the greatest respect for the cashier as a well-read man.

"But . . . I don't quite see how . . ." said Stepan Nikiforovitch.

"Oh, through the Jews . . . it is through the Jews that this vile England is acting!" exclaimed the accountant in a voice full of ill-feeling.

"Ah . . . ah . . ." drawled Stepan Nikiforovitch.

"Yes, most certainly, through the Jews!"

"Of course that is quite a different thing, quite possible, quite possible," agreed Stepan Nikiforovitch.

Then the old men began to discuss how the matter could be remedied. The accountant had a very simple solution:

"And the police captain? . . . Is he godfather or not? . . . If he only wished to . . . he, a relation of General Drago-miroff!"

"No, he only resembles him, he is not a relation!"

"But I tell you—a relation! I know it perfectly well. . . . Let him go to the police captain and plead earnestly . . . and you yourself, Stepan Nikiforovitch, ought to go and talk to him."

"I have been, and I have told him a hundred times to go! I have said: Go to see your godfather! But what is the use? Will he go to ask for anything? . . . he has more pride than a general!"

Then began one of the usual tirades which Nicholas and Marya Timofeevna feared so much, because they made both so uncomfortable and gave such a feeling that at any moment there would be break and a family catastrophe.

"I am an old man . . . my hand trembles! Please look . . . look, you hero!" shrieked Stepan Nikiforovitch, and he stretched out a hand which trembled as though he had the ague. But the hero was not there; he had slipped out unnoticed and was wandering away beyond the hedgerow. He wandered about until late at night and had no wish to return to his home. Seeing through a crack in the wall a light in the "Madrid," he knocked with his stick at the window. The door was partially opened and the sleepy face of Gavrilo peered out.

"Let me in, Gavrilo."

"With pleasure."

"Give me some beer."

"Here you are, thanks."

Nicholas sat alone in the "Madrid" for a long time, a bottle of beer before him, his head resting on his hand. . . . He thought about what he must do now, and his thoughts filled him with sadness; in the loneliness and quietness he muttered: "Alas, comrades, anguish has cut deeply into my heart."

"Gavrilo, give me another bottle!"

He drank again and the sad thoughts gave place to pleasant memories, and as these memories multiplied the pain in his heart ceased to gnaw. He forgot his home town, heard no longer the clicking of the billiard balls in an adjoining room, ceased to see the dirty floor and walls of the bar. Before Nicholas appeared Kief, glistening with electric lights, full of people, full of light, noise, laughter, music, songs and pealing bells.

The face of Nicholas brightened and on his lips hovered a smile, he asked the drowsy Gavrilo, standing behind the bar:

"Were you ever in Kief?"

"No!" answered Gavrilo sleepily, then after some thinking he added with animation:

"But, I say, there must be a lot of bars like this there?"

Nicholas laughed loudly, and waving his hand took his peaked cap.

"Thanks for the beer!"

It was night, moonlight, quiet, thoughtful. The moon lit up the whole town; the hour was striking from the bell-tower, and the sound of the bells, melancholy and ponderous, fell from the tower and slowly dispersed in the silent rays of the moonlight. Nicholas returned to his home leisurely, and his steps sounded loudly on the wooden pavement and echoed down the street. He went on and on and then stopped. Looking up into the starry sky he suddenly began to sing the "Marseillaise." Behind one of the gates a dog began to bark, and Nicholas stopped his song abruptly. The dog ceased barking and everything was quiet again. Only his steps in the empty street broke the silence of the thoughtful starry night.

V

For a long time that night Nicholas was unable to sleep. He lay on the couch in the hall and thought of all that had happened to him in Kief. One memory stood out very clearly in his mind and gave him both pain and pleasure. . . . Once, while Nicholas was in the prison and each day seemed to him to be a year, when all that he had seen for a long time were the grey walls of the cell in which he was kept in solitary confinement, when he felt himself to be forgotten by everyone, lonely, buried alive in a stone coffin, the door of the cell had suddenly opened and the prison superintendent announced:

"Someone to see you!"

He said this and went away. A warder armed with sword and revolver remained behind.

"Come along!" said the warder.

Nicholas threw his greatcoat over his shoulders, put on his peaked cap and followed the warder. They went along a gloomy corridor, passing the doors of cells at regular intervals, and Nicholas thought to himself how like a Zoo this was: each door numbered, and behind each door the door of a cage with a beast inside. . . . Who could have come to see Nicholas? Was it possible that his mother had arrived? No, that could not be! She had not yet heard that he was in prison. Perhaps one of his colleagues? No, all his colleagues were either in prison or exiled . . . besides, they would not admit a colleague . . . there was nobody who could come!

"Who has come?" asked Nicholas of the warder.

The warder let Nicholas pass and followed behind him, but did not answer the question. Nicholas repeated it.

"We are not permitted to talk to you!"

"Perhaps it is . . . a mistake? Not for me?"

The warder looked round and quietly said:

"Your fiancée?" . . .

"Fiancée?" . . . Nicholas paused for a moment and took a deep breath. His heart jumped and he wanted to laugh loudly through the whole prison.

"Go on, go on." . . .

Nicholas knew that only very near relatives were allowed to visit, and that the only outsider likely to be admitted would be a fiancée; one had the right to visit her sweetheart. That meant that he was betrothed. . . . Betrothed! What a funny, strange word! Nicholas went on, smiling; his eyes sparkled with happiness and excitement and his heart beat more quickly. "Who can she be, my fiancée?" he thought to himself, and went along quickly in front of the warder, who led him into a small room; in this room was a small square window which looked into another dull yellow room; in this window there was no glass, instead there was a grating of brass bars. And through this grating Nicholas saw a young girl in a spring dress and a straw hat trimmed with corn-flowers.

"Good-day!" said the girl, smiling kindly and nodding her head.

Near the girl stood a moustached warrant officer whose spurs clinked as he moved from one foot to the other.

"Good-day!" answered Nicholas, and they began to stare at each other.

"Are you grieving?"

"No, not really."

Nicholas looked into the face of the girl and tried to think whether he had ever met her before. Her face was covered with a light bluish veil and the bars of the grating cast a shadow on it. Perhaps this was the reason he could not recognise her. . . .

"Take off your veil," he asked shyly.

"Very well."

The warrant officer became more attentive, and each time the girl moved her hands he clinked his spurs and coughed, thus giving to understand that he could see and hear everything. The girl raised her veil and Nicholas was spell-bound by two bright brown eyes. . . . What a nice face! Nicholas blushed and again lowered his eyes. . . . No, he had never seen her before. . . .

"You have certainly forgotten your Galia already!"

"No," vaguely answered Nicholas, and smiled.

The girl laughed like a bell, her teeth glistened through the bars, and her eyes became so large and so strange. . . . The warrant officer clinked his spurs and said:

"May I ask you to be more quiet!"

"Now there you are! Is it possible that I am not allowed to laugh!" asked the girl flightily.

"You are not permitted to laugh loudly here."

"And cry? . . . Do you ever laugh here?" she asked Nicholas.

"One neither wants to laugh nor to cry here." . . .

They remained silent, then Nicholas asked:

"It is probably very nice outside now?"

Galia began to tell hurriedly how spring had come, how the Dnieper was swollen, very swollen; the storks were there, spring flowers were blooming and their scents filled the air; the stars were large and glistened so brightly as if they had come nearer the earth. . . .

"Next time I come I will bring you some flowers. Do you like violets?"

"I will put them in my cell and they will remind me of . . . you!" said Nicholas with a trembling voice, and he gazed steadily into the eyes of the girl and blushed. What a nice face! . . .

"Do not be sad, I will come to see you each Saturday."

They looked at each other, then lowered their eyes. Then the clock struck two and the meeting ended.

"Please!" said the warder, opening the door.

"Good-bye! Do not be so sad! Wherever you are, remember that you have friends!" called Galia brightly, and smiling kindly she again began to nod her head quickly. . . .

Nicholas smiled sadly, nodded his head and followed the warder. On his eyelashes trembled a tear, and his heart was so full that he wanted to cry from delight and happiness. And when he entered his cell and the iron bolt shot behind his back he began to sing loudly an old Russian song: "I will walk out with you, I will love you." . . .

"Singing and dancing are not permitted here," pronounced a severe voice. The voice entered the cell through the small aperture in the door, and it seemed as though the door itself had spoken with a human voice. Nicholas stopped singing and asked:

"And to love! Is that permitted here?"

There was no reply.

"And have feeling, may I?"

There was no reply. All that day Nicholas was very gay, and he seemed as though he wanted to forget that he was in prison. Either he murmured a song, or with upraised head he walked about his cell like a beast in a cage, shaking his fist at someone, or like a schoolboy he jumped up and down on one spot, even tried to dance.

"Just look at him, as though it is his birthday," thought the man on duty in the corridor, peeping stealthily through the aperture.

Evening came. It was Saturday.

In the distance the church bells began to ring. Their chimes, clashing one against the other, filled the heart with a sad, quiet thoughtfulness and aroused memories of childhood. Nicholas composed himself. His gaiety vanished and into his heart flowed a sweet quietness; he opened the window and listened to the sound of the bells, looked at the blue sky. The ruddy reflection of the setting sun was playing on the prison walls, and passing pigeons appeared and disappeared across the stretch of blue sky; this setting sun awakened the sorrow in his heart and the passing birds reminded him of liberty.

The night was warm, quite springlike. In the visible piece

of sky a star shone brilliantly and it seemed to look directly on the window of the cell. From somewhere, probably the residence of the prison superintendent, snatches of music floated on the breeze, and at times, quite near the prison walls, a nightingale burst into song. . . . The sorrow and loneliness in the heart of Nicholas became more acute, he felt that he must talk to somebody about that loneliness.

"Who is she, this charming Galia?"

He wanted to express his feelings in verse. He took a match stick and began to scribble on the grey wall:

> Brightly shine the stars in the blueness of the sky,
> Through the window flows the aroma of the spring;
> O'er the earth that sleeps, they foregather in a swarm,
> Fairies of visions and dreams, floating on wing.

The nightingale began to sing. He could hear someone's provoking laugh, the scent of the spring flowers was wafted in the room. Nicholas hastily wiped the writing from the wall with his sleeve, and throwing himself on the bed began to cry quietly:

"Who is she, this nice Galia?"

All the week Nicholas waited for Saturday, and it seemed that the day would never come. He lived for it, thought of nothing else. . . . During the night he slept badly, waking up every moment and thinking of Saturday, counting how many more days before it arrived. At last the Saturday came. It was a gloomy day, the sky overcast, a fine rain was drizzling outside, but Nicholas did not notice this. He was on the alert, listening to every sound, every rustle outside the door of his cell. His dinner was brought in.

"Any visitor?"

He received no answer. The dinner remained untouched . . . he waited, waited. . . . Then he rang for the warder:

"Any visitor?"

Again no answer. The prisoners in the choir began to sing the supper prayer . . . it meant that she would not come. . . . After supper the prison superintendent making the round of the prison peeped into the cell of Nicholas and gave him a fading bunch of violets. Nicholas blushed, trembled, nearly tore the flowers from the hand of the superintendent, and asked with a note of despair in his voice:

"And my visitor?"

The superintendent smiled and went out, and when the door of his cell closed Nicholas heard a voice outside the door:

"All the lot of you here are engaged!"

Nicholas looked at the flowers and thought that not long ago they were in Galia's hand, and that seemed to him to make them special, extraordinary violets. . . . He buried his face in the petals and inhaled the aroma, their perfume of spring and liberty. . . . Like a child he nursed these flowers, trying to keep the life in them, but they soon darkened and shrivelled. Death approached them quickly and they had no strength to withstand it. The flowers perished. Just one violet remained, and this Nicholas put in a book. On opening this book Nicholas would stare at the faded flower and think: "Who is she, this charming Galia?" . . .

VI

Nicholas was awakened by some sort of strange whisper. It seemed that this whisper filled the entire house and disagreeably disturbed the quiet spring air. What was it? Nicholas listened and remembered, it was his father offering prayers to God. The whisper was first low, then became louder and almost angry, at times he could hear the old bones creak when his father kneeled at his devotions. Stepan Nikiforovitch was praying for the well-being and health of innumerable relations. . . .

"Also my erring son, your servant Nicholas," with a sigh whispered the old man, and raising himself from his knees he dusted his trousers.

"Get up! You must go to-day to the police!" said he as he passed Nicholas.

"Very well!"

"Not 'well'! But it is time to get up and wash, to say your prayers and go to the police!"

The old man moved the curtain and opened the window. The gentle morning breeze freshened the room, the twittering of birds could be heard and the sunshine entered the room. Nicholas could hear his mother in the hedgerow frightening away the hens which surrounded her as she rattled the glasses. Nicholas did not move. He lay with closed eyes and tried to remember what he had been dreaming about. Something good and bright like the early morning, which seemed to linger agreeably in the heart. Ah, yes, Galia had appeared in the dream, in a white dress and a straw hat trimmed with cornflowers, and bending over him she had whispered something in his ear. . . . What she had whispered he could not remember.

"Get up! You must go to the police!" said Marya Timofeevna kindly through the open window. Nicholas trembled and his thoughts of Galia took flight, flying away like the birds which had been frightened by the old woman as she crept through the lilac bushes to the window.

"Do you hear? You must go to the police!"

"I hear!" answered Nicholas irritably.

For some time past the word "police" had filled Nicholas with a nervous excitement, as did the word "godfather"; somehow they linked themselves together in his mind. Nicholas dressed, splashed the water in annoyance, combed his hair with such fury that he tore the tangles from his head without mercy, then he went out into the hedgerow. They took tea in silence. His mother placed before him the cream, scones, put sugar into his glass, and in general devoted a lot of attention to him. The old woman attached great importance to the fact that he would now go to the police: to her it seemed an important and difficult affair, it frightened and at the same time pleased her, awakening in her heart some sort of vague hope. "May God help you!" she was saying to herself as she passed the scones to Nicholas, and she gazed at him with such love and pity as though she was seeing him off on some dangerous mission. . . . Stepan Nikiforovitch did not look at his son at all but just frowned and grunted; breaking the sugar, he collected from the cloth the scattered crumbs and scooped them into his glass. All this made Nicholas feel uncomfortable, he could not eat or drink because he felt that he was being blamed for not earning his keep.

"It would be as well to trim your hair—you will have to speak with the assistant police captain! And please be more polite when you get there and do not spoil my relations with decent people!" said the old man severely as he left for his work.

When the old man had gone, Marya Timofeevna spoke more naturally and Nicholas regained his appetite.

"Where did you disappear yesterday?" asked his mother. "We waited and waited, we did not know what to think. We nearly went to inquire of the police!"

Nicholas blushed and stopped eating.

"Police, police! . . . at every turn I get 'police'; you don't let me drink my tea without 'police'!"

"But, Kolia, we were anxious, you are bound over to us. There mustn't be any trouble for your father."

"Very well! Very well!"

"You cannot be absent for a long time . . . they took an undertaking from your father."

"I will not go away, there is nowhere I can go."

"Of course! And during the evening Kaliagin sent for you . . . there is some correspondence . . . some sort of reports."

Nicholas was silent, and his mother began to talk in great detail about the Kaliagins.

"He finished his studies, got a good position, found a girl, married. . . . everything as it should be," she said with a sigh, and looked sorrowfully at her son.

"I also found a girl for myself," said Nicholas with an ironical smile.

"Who is she?" asked his mother incredibly.

"I do not know." . . .

"There you are! Was she of noble birth or of a business family?"

"I do not know."

"What is her family name?"

"I do not know."

Marya Timofeevna began to laugh.

"There are such a lot of girls, and they are all eligible . . . but nobody will have you now, Kolia dear."

"Oh yes, she will have me!"

"Perhaps she is desperate? Ah, you, would that you had finished you studies, found work and taken a decent girl. You have lost your chance of happiness, Kolia."

"I wish you would cease lamenting, you are making me quite ill!" said Nicholas, flicking away the flies.

"Do not be angry. I am only speaking the truth. I am so sorry for you!" said his mother tearfully.

"Do not be sorry . . . I have my own faith." . . .

When Nicholas left to go to the police his mother stood by the gate and made the sign of the cross behind his back. "May God help you!" she whispered.

Facing the cathedral square stood an old yellow house with an ugly tower raised over the roof. In the wide entrance porch of this house there were always peasant men and women, and their attitude was one of infinite patience. When Nicholas saw this gloomy house he remembered his "godfather," remembered all the monologues of his father and all the sighs and sorrowful looks of his mother, and once again he endured all the pangs of loneliness. It seemed to be one of the fatal houses of which he had read in some terrifying fairy tale in childhood. . . . When he entered the porch the peasants rose with respect for his glistening student's buttons, the men took off their hats and the women bowed their heads.

Someone whispered, "Oh, merciful God," and in this whisper was a whole avalanche of anguish and humility. . . . The wide half-dark entrance smelled of dampness and mice; here again peasant women were seated on the floor, and near by a messenger went about, twirling his moustache and joking with the younger women. . . . Nicholas inquired why all these people waited, and several voices answered in reply:

"We are witnesses, friend, witnesses."

And in these hurried answers there sounded clearly a hope: perhaps this gentleman with shining buttons would do something for the tired witnesses. . . . Nicholas went upstairs. In the anteroom stood an attendant who asked: "What do you want?" He had to wait in the private waiting-room. As he sat there he heard the various noises of the house—the scratching of pens, the steps of someone tiptoeing on the stairs, the rustling of paper—and all this produced a heaviness, a desire to yawn and to go to sleep. . . . It seemed to Nicholas that little by little life was leaving his body, his thoughts becoming dull and the capacity for speech departing, so that in the end he would become some kind of inanimate article.

"Come along!"

Nicholas opened his eyes. The attendant was pulling his sleeve and waving his hand towards the door to which Nicholas had to go. Nicholas got up, but did not move immediately, there was a buzzing in his head and one leg was asleep and refused to function.

"Is your leg asleep?" said the attendant, pointing again to the door.

Nicholas entered a large grey room where several people were sitting at tables, writing. One table was better than the others, and at it sat a man who evidently sensed his superiority over all the others. Probably this was the secretary.

"You are . . . the secretary?"

"I am," answered this man proudly. "Please. . . . I beg

you be seated. . . . You are the son of Stepan Nikiforovitch?"

"Yes, the son."

"I am very pleased to see you. You are, I believe, bound
over to your parents? . . . Stepan Nikiforovitch and I are
good friends. Would you like a cigarette? . . . This transfer
certificate will be retained by us; will you please be good
enough to read these regulations and sign? . . . this is just a
formality," smiled the secretary apologetically.

Nicholas read the regulations.

"You are not allowed to leave the town, not allowed to give
lessons, not allowed to join various societies, not allowed to
take part in theatricals, not allowed. . . ." There were many
paragraphs, and each began with "You are not allowed."

"All this is really only terrible on paper, there are much
worse things happen in life to us," said the secretary, as if
with apology and a desire to set Nicholas at ease, and he
obligingly passed a pen which he had already dipped in the
ink. Nicholas signed and the secretary immediately blotted
the signature and said with relief:

"That is all."

Nicholas heard whispering behind him, and when he turned
round he saw that all the other people in the room were
gazing at him with curious and astonished eyes.

"If I am not mistaken, our police captain is your godfather?"

"Godfather, yes, my godfather!"

"You haven't been to see him?"

"No."

"You should ask your godfather to stop the inspector visiting
your home. It would be better if you came here once a week.
We can sit together and have a chat and a smoke. . . . All
this is only a matter of form." . . .

Nicholas felt as though the grime from the grey walls was
settling on his soul. He felt stuffy and wanted to get out as
quickly as he could into the fresh air, but some other man in

uniform came along and said that the assistant police captain ordered Nicholas to see him in his study. Nicholas blushed as though the word "ordered" displeased him.

"What does he want?"

"He ordered. . . . I do not know!"

"You will have to go in," whispered the secretary, "it is the regulation."

Nicholas lighted a cigarette and went with an angry step behind the man. . . . They went along a corridor where there was again the smell of mice, and the man said:

"We have a lot of mice . . . last year the mice ate up a very important document . . . the hands become greasy. . . . It was after Shrove Tuesday . . . the pancakes certainly . . . the papers smelled of grease . . . they ate the whole file, leaving only the cover and the binding." . . .

"You have probably very tasty documents," said Nicholas ironically.

They entered a large room, in the middle of which stood a long table covered with a red cloth hemmed with gold braid.

"Here we are!" said the man; "you ought to throw your cigarette away!"

"I will finish smoking immediately."

Nicholas took a vigorous puff and blew the smoke out from his nose, and the man said:

"It is not allowed here, it is not proper!" and he dispersed the smoke with his handkerchief.

Nicholas threw the end of the cigarette on the floor. The man took it up quickly, and not knowing how to dispose of it at last put it in his waistcoat pocket. Then he approached the door on tiptoe, opened it timidly and then said in a low voice: "He has arrived, he is here."

"Ask him in!" said a bass voice from the other side of the door.

"Please!" said the man, and opening the door a little wider he allowed Nicholas to pass.

Nicholas entered. The assistant police captain was seated at a writing-desk, poring over some documents. He silently beckoned Nicholas to a chair and continued to read, accompanying the reading with a low muttering. Nicholas looked at him in anger and tried to refrain from screaming, "What do you want of me?" At last the muttering ended, the assistant police captain put aside the documents, stroked his sidewhiskers and asked:

"You are the son of Stepan Nikiforovitch?"

"Yes."

"Ah, ah!" The assistant police captain shook his head reproachfully. "What have you been up to?" asked he. Then he rose, shut the door and sat down again. Nicholas was looking aside and was silent.

"What do you want, eh? Equality? But that, young man, can never be! . . . See here, you are bony and thin and I am stout. One likes melon, the other grisly pork. One man is naturally capable, another just stupid. Nature herself, young man, doesn't want it . . . and you . . ."

"I want nothing!"

"I must tell you that you ought not to have listened to the agitators who talk about this equality . . . no, there is no equality and never will be, young man. . . . I like your father very much, and I am telling you all this, not as assistant police captain, but as one who is well disposed towards you, one who has lived, a man of experience. Do you think I have never dreamed of equality? My God! . . . All of us as young men dream and make mistakes . . . but the time comes when sense is uppermost . . . everything can be repaired . . . everything smoothed over. . . . Now you are here with us bound over, and, certainly . . ."

"Forgive me, I have no time!"

Nicholas got up and went out. His face was pale, drawn and tired, his hands were trembling, and in his eyes glistened the cold light of hatred.

VII

White and pink lilac was blooming in the hedgerows, pigeons were cooing in the early morning and nightingales were singing in the lime trees in the garden. The little house was absolutely covered with verdure, tufts of grass even peeped out between the half-rotted beams of the roof. The days were warm and the water attracted one to go and swim. When at home there was nothing but a continual grumbling and complaint about the hardness of fate and the scarcity of money, of trembling hands and that Nicholas had not fulfilled parental expectations; then he would usually take up his gun and wander towards the river. In the meadows beyond the river there were lakes, such quiet meditative lakes, framed in laburnums and reeds, they resembled large mirrors reflecting the blue sky and the fleecy clouds; and how pleasant it was to sit there and hear the reeds whispering their tales, to hear them made the heart more restful, more contented, all the hurts of life seemed quietened, the peaceful gladness of life and the happiness of youth began to be reflected in the heart like the blue sky in the lakes. . . . Sometimes these quiet thoughts and dreams were interrupted by a water-fowl descending on a lake; it would sail elegantly and proudly on the water, circling round the reeds and calling quietly to its mate. It could have been killed very easily, but Nicholas would not take up his gun, he held his breath and continued in rapt contemplation, and he felt that he was sharing some of the most intimate secrets of nature. . . . He would forget his home and himself and would be relieved of the reproaches, the complaints and the advice which everyone he met in the street offered to him. These reproaches, complaints and advice were becoming more pointed and more frequent. His mother only sighed the more, but his father could not be near him without making some vexatious remark. If the son was reading a book in the garden, then father would say, "What is the use of reading?"; if lounging on the grass and doing nothing, father would say, "It is pleasant, comfortable, plenty to eat, which is the main thing, and nothing to do!"; if Nicholas was absent for some time from the house, then the old man would talk about pitying the soles of the boots as well as the parents . . . and Stepan Nikiforovitch would say all this, not with the intention of offending or reproaching his son, but because he hoped to improve "poor Kolia," hoped to influence his "turn of mind"; that was how Stepan Nikiforovitch expressed himself after the assistant police captain had told him how Nicholas had behaved in his office. . . . The old man would find a wrong motive in the least little thing. Taking up a cigarette end thrown on the floor by Nicholas he would grumble: "Throw your ash wherever you like, we don't mind anything!" Noticing his dirty boots the old man would sigh and say:

"Why clean them? Thinking as we do we can walk about the town in anything." . . .

One day Stepan Nikiforovitch met the police captain in the street and was quite confused. He was now afraid to meet anyone of importance in the town. It seemed that in some way he was at a disadvantage before them, that he had done something very ugly which none of these people would expect from a person of good birth and such an esteemed official who had a medal for thirty years' unblemished service.

"Why don't you look in?" asked the police captain.

"We intend to . . . but somehow it never comes about," answered Stepan Nikiforovitch, lowering his eyes, and inferred that Marya Timofeevna had not been in good health of late.

"Now my godson is a fine one! Doesn't show his nose!" . . .

Stepan Nikiforovitch felt definitely out of place and thought to himself, "This is certainly the limit of rudeness on the part of Nicholas, to whom I have talked a thousand times, pointing out, insisting. Now he has done it."

"He is embarrassed . . . he did some stupid things there,

and now he hides . . . is ashamed to show his face,"
Stepan Nikiforovitch replied, shaking his head and sighing
deeply.

"Oh, that is nothing, nothing . . . one cannot reproach
the fellow for past mistakes," said the police captain.

"But he is embarrassed . . . he thinks that you are very
displeased and perhaps do not want . . . because really, you
know . . . although on the one hand his godfather . . . on
the other, say what you may . . . police captain."

The police captain began to laugh good-humouredly

"That is nothing. It is all over. No one is blameless. . . .
Let him come to see me. I will scold him, but as a godfather,
not as police captain. . . . What troublesome youths they
are nowadays . . . no sooner do the hairs of their moustaches grow than they begin to demand a republic!"

The stout figure of the police captain shook with his mirth.
Stepan Nikiforovitch was terribly confused by all this kindness and condescension, small tears even began to form on
the eyelids of the old man and his shaking hand began to
tremble with pleasure, he must make the most of this
occasion.

"We were all young, we old stupid things. . . . He is really
a good boy, kind, quiet, respectful . . . and what has suddenly happened to him I cannot understand."

The police captain nodded his head in sympathy, and the
old man took courage and began to ask, "Could he not by
some means repair the blunder of youth . . . go back to his
studies?"

"We will wait a little longer and then we will see. Perhaps
we can arrange something," said the police captain, then he
shook the old man's trembling hand and went on his way.
Stepan Nikiforovitch looked round twice towards the slowly
departing police captain and said to himself:

"W-o-n-d-e-r-f-u-l man!"

The old man returned home light-heartedly, swinging his
umbrella and lisping from his toothless mouth:

> "Lanterns, little masters,
> Burn and burn. . . .
> What they see, what they hear,
> Of this they do not talk."

During dinner he looked kindly at his son, joked with Marya Timofeevna and quite forgot his trembling hands. There were milk scones for the third dish, and as he handed the soft sugar to Nicholas he joked:

"Do salt your pancake, Mr. Socialist!"

And after dinner, having prayed to God with special fervour, the old man put his two hands behind his back and walked about the room singing:

> "Lanterns, little masters
> Burn and burn." . . .

"What makes you sing to-day?" asked Marya Timofeevna with astonishment; but the old man instead of answering stood still, and conducting with his trembling hand under the nose of Marya Timofeevna continued to sing:

> "What they see, what they hear,
> Of this they do not talk."

Marya Timofeevna also became more gay, she prepared tea under the hedgerow on a clean cloth, brought out newly-made jam and fussed about with the well-polished samovar under the bushes. They sat down to take tea, and Stepan Nikiforovitch at last showed his hand:

"Socialist, please come here! There is some really good news! Come here! I will not bite you!"

Nicholas trembled and turned pale. A strange fright took hold of the young man by reason of his father's joy, and as he seated himself on the bench he almost seemed to shrivel from a premonition that something was about to happen. He listened and composed himself, expecting the worst. . . . .

"I have told you a hundred times that you must go to see your godfather."

"So that's it . . . Godfather again!"

The old man told of his meeting with the police captain, related the whole conversation, changing at the same time, without really intending to do so, the words of the police captain so that it appeared that he had definitely promised to arrange for Nicholas to return to his studies if he came to his senses and put out of his head this "socialistic rot."

"W-o-n-d-e-r-f-u-l man!" repeated Stepan Nikiforovitch several times, and ended his talk with the instruction:

"Go to church on Sunday and from there to your godfather. Do the proper thing and everything will be all right."

Nicholas was seated, gazing in silence at the design on the tablecloth: his father was saying that it was time to leave these foolish things alone and understand that even Nature herself does not permit this stupid equality . . . and so on.

"Your head will not fall off because once in your life you bend it too low!"

"But it happens that it falls off!"

The old man went red with anger. He looked at the pale Nicholas, and banging down a teaspoon, shouted:

"It means then that you are a fool . . . do you understand?"

"I understand."

"You must go . . . I gave my word . . . do you hear?"

"I will not go," said Nicholas dully, and he got up.

"What?"

Mother did not know how to stop this scene. She looked imploringly at Stepan Nikiforovitch, touched his sleeve and whispered imploringly:

"In the name of God!"

Nicholas seized his cap and went out quickly from the garden. He went towards the river. He sat for a long time on the bank, motionless, silent, gazing into the distance. His lips trembled and compressed themselves into a smile and his eyes became misty with tears. . . . The summer day slowly departed and the approaching evening dimmed the outlines on the horizon; the setting sun looked with a sad smile on the darkening nature. Shadows began to creep and to take definite shape on the dark green water. The stream, the meadows, the forest, all became thoughtful: the last red rays of sunset played on the bend of the river. The dampness, the smell of rotting grass and clay came more strongly from the bank. The skies becoming more dark and the clouds more heavy, took definite shape and assumed the fantastic forms of strange monsters. Sometimes in the twilight Nicholas heard the passing shrieks of a water-fowl; or a wild duck, startled by something, would fly out from the lakes behind the river, clapping the air excitedly with its strong wings. . . . A warm breeze crept furtively through the birches under which Nicholas was sitting, and the mysterious whisper of the young leaves mingled with the murmuring of the stream running against the clay bank.

Nicholas watched the slowly fading summer evening and his thoughts flew far beyond the river, beyond the meadows in the direction of the darkening forest . . . where, he did not know. Somewhere towards the Dnieper, in a quiet corner of an old house with balconies, storks on the roof, a sombre park, a bathing establishment near the green bank . . . there in the quiet evening could be heard the sweet voice of a girl with brown eyes, in the thick cluster of the trees in the old park twinkled the agile form in a white dress and a straw hat trimmed with cornflowers.

He sat thinking of Galia and was content that there was no one to interrupt his thoughts; the quiet sleeping river and the bluish mist in the distance seemed to tell a story of that dear land where lived the girl with hazel eyes . . . and as he thought of her Nicholas sang quietly, with a sweet, oppressive plaintiveness, gazing beyond the river: "The wind roars between the mountains and in the forest there is a great noise." . . . All around was quietness and solitude, and the song sounded sadly on the slopes as though bearing a complaint to someone; the wind carried it along the river and dispersed it like a cloud in the darkness. . . . Perhaps even now Galia was sitting somewhere on the banks of the Dnieper thinking of him. Nicholas stared with sad eyes in the distant blue mists beyond the river, and still more sadly sounded his song:

> "Oh, Galia, my little girl, my dear one,
> How sad I am. . . . You are alone!"

The new moon sailed forth, the river began to glisten and a silvery shadow rippled on the water. Peasants lit bonfires on the meadows. . . .

"You are singing in solitude!"

Nicholas broke off his song and became confused as though he had been caught in some unlawful act. He looked round and saw in the half-light a form wearing a straw hat and carrying an umbrella.

"You don't recognise me? I am the accountant at the local bank—a friend of your father."

"Ah!" . . .

"A wonderful evening, wonderful evening! . . . Splendid weather! . . . Do sing! . . . I will listen. . . . I love singing . . . I used to conduct the cathedral choir, but I cannot do it now." . . .

The accountant descended the bank, and with the grunting of an old man sat down on the grass near Nicholas.

"Have you been to see your godfather?"

Nicholas jumped to his feet, pulled on his peaked cap and went away.

"You can all go to the devil!" he said in a tearful voice without turning round, and disappeared behind the bushes.

"Oh . . . go . . . go . . ." said the stupefied accountant, and for a long time he stared in the bushes where this rude young man had disappeared.

VIII

Nicholas wandered for a long time along the bank of the river and then on the outskirts of the town. It was moonlight. The frogs croaked in the marshes behind the road, someone was singing a mournful song in a tremulous tenor. Here and there small lights twinkled in the windows of the cottages. All was quiet, wonderfully quiet, it seemed that even the moon paused to wonder at the silence. . . . A dog barked somewhere at the other end of the town, and its bark resounded in the silvery light of the night, so passionless and so clear. From time to time the chimes would ring out from the bell-tower, and their ringing would waver in the air for a long time, each sound joining with the other as though it did not wish to be silenced. . . . Behind the hedges long branches of trees looked out mysteriously, and it seemed that they inquired what manner of man was this who wandered at night along lonely pathways, and what could he want. The town crier, on nearing the dejected figure of Nicholas, sounded his rattle more loudly, and its clatter resounded from the hedges with an echo which troubled the air with discordant noises.

"Who is that?" he asked severely when he reached Nicholas, but immediately began to smile and said quietly:

"I did not recognise you, sir . . . unable to sleep?"

"That's right."

"It is such a fine night . . . and you young people . . . when alone you are not sleepy! . . . ah ah, ah ah!"

And the old man went on, rolling from one leg to the other. In the field, in the silvery night the mournful song continued, the frogs croaked in the marshes, again the chimes from the bell-tower sounded the hour. Nicholas counted, and when the last ring died in the quietness, turned homewards. On the way he peeped through the lighted window of the cosy room of a small house: at the table was seated a man in his waistcoat, eating with relish some porridge from a deep plate; he was opening his mouth to admit the spoon, and his hair, cropped like a brush, moved as he chewed the porridge. Opposite stood a sturdy young woman, and with chin resting on her hand she watched with pleasure as her man enjoyed his food.

"God has given us food, and nobody has seen," said the man, laying down his spoon and getting up and stretching himself.

"And if anyone has seen, he has done us no harm!" said the woman, removing the plate.

The man in the waistcoat grunted, stretched himself and gave the woman a pat. Nicholas smiled and went on his way. "They want nothing there, and nothing in the world interests them." . . . The nearer Nicholas came to his home, the slower became his steps; there, in that cosy little house behind the hedgerow where he had passed his care-free childhood, and where he was so long and dearly loved, he felt now so burdened and so stifled that he had no wish to return, as though behind that green enclosure something terrible awaited him.

Stepan Nikiforovitch was sitting on the bench behind the gate. Nicholas did not immediately see his father because the shadow of a lilac tree screened his motionless figure. He had already taken hold of the latch of the gate when the old man coughed and asked in a hoarse voice:

"Is that you, Nicholas?"

Nicholas trembled at the unexpectedness of this, became confused and said:

"You are sitting outside?"

"And you are always roaming about. Just a moment, my dear friend!"

"Well!"

"Not well! I visited the police captain to-day . . . a won-der-ful man! . . . although you are so stupid, you are still his godson . . . do you understand?"

"I understand."

"He orders that you write a petition stating that all you did was a mistake . . . that you were led into it . . . you understand?"

"I understand."

"That you are sorry about everything and beg to be pardoned for all your foolishness . . . that you will never again be mixed up in such things . . . you hear?"

"I hear."

"And I, on my part, will write a petition. . . . I am an old man with a trembling hand . . . I have worked hard for thirty-five years, conscientiously and honestly . . . you hear?"

"I hear."

"And everything will be arranged. The police captain on his side will write . . ."

Nicholas stood by the gate like one condemned to death, he looked dazedly at the earth, his hands hanging at his sides, and he repeated silently: "I understand" and "I hear." A mosquito buzzed as though with pity in his ear; its buzzing, long, dull and persistent, resounded in his brain like a long and endless pitying groan. A dog barked somewhere. Brilliant stars shone coldly and passionlessly in the heavens. All round was intense quiet, as if the night was holding its breath to hear what was happening in the soul of Nicholas.

"You must go to-morrow and thank him."

Nicholas was silent.

"And everything will be all right . . . you will return to your studies again."

"I will go nowhere and write nothing!" said Nicholas in a choking whisper and he moved away.

"Why?" screamed the old man, getting up from the bench and following his son.

"I can't."

"But you can fill your stomach!"

"Leave me alone!" shouted Nicholas wildly, and quickening his steps he went beyond the porch towards the kitchen garden, to the bathing hut which he had made his quarters a few days ago.

"Ah, you scoundrel !" whispered the old man, and when the gate leading to the kitchen garden creaked he shouted loudly : "Scoundrel !"

And this shriek awoke the silent night. It trembled and with a vibrating echo repeated " Scoundrel." . . .

Nicholas entered the bathing hut and lighted a candle-end. Shadows flickered across the floor, along the black smoke-covered logs of the walls and lost themselves in the corners. The red flame wavered in the darkness of this black hut, and the crickets on the hearth stopped their noise. The place was damp and had a sooty smell. On an overturned tub lay books and writing materials; one chair stood near a wide bench and a student's jacket hung over its back. Nicholas opened the small window and then paced about the hut like a caged animal, then he suddenly felt a terrible weariness in all his limbs, blew out the candle and threw himself face upwards on the bench, covering his eyes with the palm of his hand. When he was quiet the summer night filtered through the small window, in the nettles behind the wall a grass-hopper rustled; the tinkling of small bells could be heard, rather loudly at first, then dying away in the distance. . . . Someone was going away somewhere, the lucky fellow. . . . One must go away somewhere . . . must certainly go away . . . go away very quickly. . . . My God, how tired he was, how unbearably tired ! The cricket began its noise again and some other kind of rustling sound could be heard, creeping outside the bathing hut and up to the window. . . . A cock began to crow and beat his strong wings somewhere. What was it? Nicholas raised himself on his elbow and in fright asked:

"Who is there?" and he seized his gun.

"It is I, Kolia dear, just I, dear," whispered an old tearful voice at the window, and in the bright background of the night his mother's head took shape.

"It is you?"

"You do not sleep? . . . You grieve?" with infinite tenderness and pity whispered the old woman; then she became silent and one could hear how she was crying softly, leaning against the small window. Nicholas went over to his mother.

"Don't, for God's sake!" he whispered imploringly, trying to choke back the sobs in his own throat.

"Oh, my dear, my heart aches so for you that I cannot keep back my tears."

Nicholas rushed away from the window, and thrusting his face in one of the dark corners began to weep tears of bitter anguish and despair. . . . His mother, feeling her way gradually, entered the bathing hut, put her head on the back of her son and also began to cry. And they stood thus for a long time, crying in the dark corner. Then they both ceased and seated themselves in silence on the bench. Mother took the hand of Nicholas and held it firmly in her own, and he felt how the old bones were trying more strongly to clasp his hand. . . .

"I . . . I cannot stay here with you," sobbed Nicholas at last in a tremulous whisper. . . . "I must go away somewhere."

"Your father hurt you? . . . Hurt you very much? . . . What did he say to hurt you?" The old woman leaned over to her son and began to stroke his hair. Nicholas lowered his head submissively under this caress, and it seemed to him that he was becoming small, quite small, that he was again a young schoolboy, and that just as before he loved his mother, loved her unceasingly and was ready even to give his life for her.

"What must I do? . . . I do not know. . . . I can bear it no longer. . . . You understand? . . . I can go on no more," he whispered, pressing his parched lips on her hand. "I ought to have gone away somewhere . . . run away." . . .

"And are you not sorry for your father? He is crying now. . . . Do you think it is easy for him? . . . Have thought

for his old age. Do what he asks. . . . Do not be so proud.
. . . Ah, you . . ."

Mother spoke quietly and tenderly about life, old age, death,
and of the heart of the parents. The sense of her words did
not reach the consciousness of Nicholas, but he was soothed
by the quiet, kind chatter in which there was so much love
and tenderness.

"Do write what he asks you to do."

Nicholas remembered and shook his head.

"I can't. . . . You understand? . . . I can't. . . . If you
love me, do not ask me to do it. . . . I will go away somewhere." . . .

"Where can you go, Kolia dear? You can go nowhere. . . .
Father has to answer for you." . . .

"No, I can't," gently agreed Nicholas, lapsing into silence.

And they sat for a long time, thinking in silence of all sorts
of things.

The warm night looked on through the small window and
seemed as though listening to what happened in the hearts
of these people, hidden in the darkness.

And in a room of the small house behind the hedgerow
radiated a reddish little flame; there before the burning lamp
of the holy image was Stepan Nikiforovitch, prostrate in
humility, praying fervently to his Maker that He would
restrain and guide the erring youth.

IX

The sky was cloudless and the midday summer sun shone so
brilliantly that it was impossible to look upon it. Sparrows
bathed in the dust on the road and crows sat with outstretched wings on the roof. The little town was overcome
with heat. Everything was silent, sleepy and gently quiet.
The inhabitants hid themselves in their rooms, and it seemed
that no one had anything to do, had no interest whatever in
the little house behind the hedgerow. A horse harnessed to a

dogcart was standing by the gate flicking away the troublesome flies with its tail; the driver was sitting on the fence,
leisurely prodding the dirt from his boots with his whip.
From an open window of the house could be heard prolonged
groans, some voices talking in whispers in the porch and
someone's heels tapping hasty noisy steps on the staircase.
. . . For a moment everything became silent as though
everyone in the little house had fallen asleep, then again the
groan was heard, as though someone was gasping in pain;
then again the voices, the steps and the rustling. . . .

"Who has come?" asked the accountant in a breathless
whisper.

"The doctor."

The accountant took his breath, folded his umbrella and
began to peep fearfully through the fence into the hedgerow.
. . . He beckoned somebody with his finger and stepped a
few paces outside, wiping the perspiration from his face with
his handkerchief. The gate was partially opened and a
peasant woman, Anisia, peeped out. Her face was terrible,
she had a confused expression, and as soon as she saw the
accountant her eyes began to blink and tears to flow.

"What is happening now in the house?"

The peasant woman waved her arm and covered her face
in her apron. She said sobbingly that they were bringing
him round, the poor old master . . . he was broken up . . .
quite broken up . . . could move neither his hands nor his
feet . . . and he could not speak . . . only stare so pitifully.
. . . She sobbed all this as she sniffed in her apron.

"But do come in!"

"What is the use? . . . one cannot help," whispered the
accountant with a sigh, and he seated himself on the bench.
The driver got up, considering it impolite to sit near a
gentleman.

"And the young one . . . you haven't seen him?" asked
Anisia.

"No . . . where is he?"

"He is laid so prettily in the bathing hut, as though alive . . . just as though he is sleeping, poor dear!" said Anisia with tearful tenderness, and with her face covered in the apron she disappeared behind the gate. . . . Across the meadow came another old man with blue spectacles and a peaked cap. He approached the accountant, and in a low voice asked him something and then began to peer through the fence.

"Should we go in? . . . it will seem rather bad if we don't!"

The accountant shook his head and the two old men went thoughtfully across the green meadow away from the little house behind the hedgerow. Both opened their umbrellas, which made them look like two large retreating mushrooms. . . .

Near the old bathing hut had gathered a small crowd of peasant women and children. They stood near the small window and were peeping through with large fearful eyes. . . . The door of the hut was locked and a sentry was standing before it. . . . Through the window one could see the legs of a man stretched on the bench. These legs, clad in newly-knitted socks and somehow strangely long, were attracting and frightening the inquisitive women and children. They were pulling each other back, frightening themselves and whispering to each other:

"Are they his legs?"

"Yes, his."

"Make room! . . . You have seen enough!"

"Will they hold an inquest?"

"Certainly. . . . Oh, Jesus Christ!"

It was Nicholas who lay on the bench, so quiet, as though he slumbered the sweet sleep of a tired man, no longer interested in what the living world was saying, or doing, or thinking. . . . On the floor, near the bench, lay a note-book and a faded violet.

X

They buried Nicholas on the Tuesday.

The whole of the small town followed him to the cemetery, and there was the cathedral choir. The day was fine, bright, glorious, and the chimes of the bells were heard sadly and solemnly in the silent morning air. The choir were singing, and when they were silent the birds sang in the garden behind the fence. The coffin cloth waved over the crowd and the sun glistened on the bright coffin lid. Marya Timofeevna stumbled along with difficulty behind the coffin; on one side she was supported by the police captain, on the other by his assistant. She did not cry. With her dull eyes fixed on the departing coffin she was muttering and shaking her head. The accountant was with the choir, and he uttered in a high broken tenor his "Oh, God Almighty!". He conducted, by habit, with his hand; his face was preoccupied and business-like, and it seemed that for him the important thing was not that they were burying Nicholas, but how the choir sang. From time to time he looked round angrily and made some sort of sign to the choristers, but they kept their eyes on their own conductor and paid no attention to these signs. Then the accountant would shrug his shoulders and stop singing. . . .

All the important people of the town tried to keep as near as possible to the police captain, and gazed with sad eyes on Marya Timofeevna and the coffin. Everyone was sorry for Nicholas and for this old woman.

At the cemetery Kaliagin came forward, and lowering his close-cropped head began to say his farewell to Nicholas. This farewell began with the words, "Do not cry so bitterly over him, it is good to die young." No sooner had Kaliagin said that it was good to die than Marya Timofeevna began to sob and to tear herself away from the arms of the godfather and his assistant. The godfather tried to quieten the old woman, with tears in his eyes he leaned over her and gently and sorrowfully said:

"What can you do? . . . You must be resigned. . . . It is a sin to cry. Everything is in God's hands."

And on her other side the assistant leaned over and whispered:

"We all have to die, all of us."

But Marya Timofeevna did not listen, she continued sobbing, louder and louder, so that no one could hear what Kaliagin was saying as he sadly moved his head in time with his speech.

"Kolia, what have you done?" sobbed the mother as the coffin swung over the grave and began to disappear below.

The police captain took out his handkerchief and began to blow his nose violently. Tears glistened in the eyes of those who stood around the grave. . . . Birds sang in the leafy sprays of the birch trees, whose branches peeped over into the grave, lumps of clay thudded dully on the coffin lid. . . . When the earth covered Nicholas, everyone, quietly and thoughtfully, went away from the cemetery and the place was soon deserted. Only the birds and Marya Timofeevna remained. The birds were singing and the old woman was seated on the clay bank covered with bunches of white and pink lilac, staring with dull eyes on the ground and reproachfully whispering:

"Ah, you young ones . . . ah, you young ones!"

(II)

THE MAGICIAN

(Translated by LEONIDE ZARINE)

THE town was in a nervous, frightened state: the strike was spreading. It started in the factories and workshops, then like a fire fanned by the wind spread from one end of the town to the other, and detachments of mounted

police were careering through the streets like firemen,
always in haste and always too late. Occasionally soldiers
with gloomy, morose faces marched quickly by to the
accompaniment of the beat of drums, stepping out as one
man, their bayonets glistening. Sometimes a Cossack in
fluffy bearskin galloped along like a madman and the
passers-by dashed quickly in various directions to avoid
being trampled down.

The noisy turbulent life of the town went on as before,
shop-windows in the main street glistened brightly and
colourfully, crowds of people swarmed along the pavements and there were the usual straggling rows of cabs,
but there was something unusually hurried and fearful in
it all. The least important occurrence would create a
scurry and bustle; the blowing of a near-by policeman's
whistle, a hatless man running down the street, a drunken
brawl, all these produced panic and curiosity. Some people
rushed to see what was happening, others hid for safety
in the shop doorways . . . safety from what? No one knew.
Everybody expected something unusually terrible and exciting, but what it would be they could not tell.

Sometimes large crowds of sullen, gloomy workmen appeared in the streets. They moved quietly along the pavements, talked in hushed whispers with the comrades they
met and glared with animosity at the well-dressed public
who took no interest at all in these ill-clad people with their
pale, sickly faces and dirty hands. Such people only spoiled
the streets, generally so clean, so beautiful and refined, full
of natural charm on such a fine autumn day, the leaves of
the boulevard trees shining golden as though receiving a
parting kiss from the waning sun, with the glistening enamel
of carriages and cabs, the new tramcars with their clattering
bells, the hooting motor-cars and the passing cyclists.

These strange people, like unwanted and unnecessary pilgrims from another world, wandered among the elegant
passers-by, who avoided them with aversion as though they

feared to soil themselves with something unclean, then suddenly, like a pack of wandering dogs, they would scatter in different directions when the galloping Cossacks appeared, and would impart their fear to the crowd.

"Mother, are these workmen?"

"Yes, yes. . . . Go on, don't look round!"

"But why do they run?"

"From the police. . . . Go on, don't chatter."

"But why? . . . Can't they walk in the street?"

"It is not allowed!"

"Why isn't it allowed?"

"Oh, please don't worry me! . . . Give me your hand and come along . . . otherwise, perhaps . . . the whip." . . .

Serge clasped his mother's hand and dragged along behind her. The disturbance caused by the dispersal of the crowd of workmen filled his mother with terror, and this was communicating itself to Serge, but all the time curiosity was uppermost, he wanted to gaze round on what was happening.

"Are they wicked, mother?"

"Who, who?"

"The workmen."

"I don't know . . . there are good and bad . . . they won't work."

"Are they lazy, mother?"

"Yes, yes! . . . But come along . . . you also, if you are lazy . . ."

"Are they nasty, mother?"

But just then some Cossacks galloped by. One whistled shrilly and lashed out with his whip. The whip cracked like a revolver and Serge's mother screamed, and without stopping to bargain with the driver pushed Serge into the first passing cab and jumped in herself, and digging the cabman in the back shouted in a voice choking with excitement:

"Quick!"

"But where, madam?"

"There! Straight on! Ah! how disgusting. . . . Turn quickly!"

"Don't be afraid, lady, they won't touch us."

When they had turned the corner Serge's mother felt more safe, regained her breath and became more normal and talkative.

"Don't forget. . . . I shall not pay more than twenty kopecks."

"That's not enough, lady."

"Then we will get out. Stop, we will take a tramcar."

"Very well then, lady, stay where you are. . . . The tramcars will soon stop running."

"Who says so?"

"They will be out on strike. I heard yesterday that they will stop on Sunday."

Again a crowd of workmen was passing along the street. Serge's mother gave the cabman a push in the back. Serge was gazing fearfully at these people and nestling close to his mother.

"I don't see why they should fuss about with them. If they don't want to work, then let them walk about, they will feel hungry and return."

"You are quite right there, lady, hunger is no good," said the cabman, and he turned round and began to mumble in his beard. "You can train a beast as you like by starving it, and you can do that with a man too . . . but it seems a sin to wrong a poor man." . . .

After a few moments' silence the cabman suddenly turned round and said:

"Now you, lady, have a rich cloak, and I have only a peasant coat, and who dresses us?"

"Don't worry yourself, man, if you have money you can always be shod and clothed . . . if our people won't work the things can be obtained abroad." . . .

"But what if the railways stop? . . . You won't be able to have things brought for you."

"Nonsense, of course they won't stop. . . . It won't be allowed!"

"Who knows? They say that they will stop soon."

Serge listened attentively to his mother's conversation with the cabman. He found it impossible to understand this sort of people who clothed and fed them and at the same time ran away from policemen.

His mother had just bought for him a new winter overcoat; it lay in a paper wrapper on his knees, and the boy was very glad that it was already bought and that no one could deprive him of it.

"And did they make my new overcoat, mother?"

"Everything, young sir! Everything. You haven't a stitch on you which they didn't make," answered the cabman, and the mother, pulling Serge by his sleeve, said in an angry whisper:

"Shut up! You mustn't talk to him."

And the cabman continued to philosophise in the same strain until Serge's mother said:

"You yourself, my man, ought to be in jail!"

Then the cabman whipped up his horse vigorously, swore, and ceased talking.

So Serge returned home with his doubts concerning these people called workmen still unsolved.

"Sonia, we have seen some workmen," he informed his sister mysteriously. "Really, we did."

"What are they like?"

"They are . . . well, they just look like peasants."

Each day in the house and in the yard where Serge played after his meals there was more talk about these people who stopped the factories and workshops and who did not want work; but from all the talk one could not gather whether they were good or bad. In the house it seemed they were bad; in the yard, good. Once Serge questioned Ignatius, the under-porter.

"But can they stop a factory?"

"Very easily, Master Serge."

"But how do they do it?"

"They let out the steam and finish, or else they merely clear out."

"And without them the factory must stop?"

"But how can it be otherwise? They can't go on without them."

"Oh, so it is like that. And without them my new overcoat would never have been made?"

"It would not."

"And my little jacket?"

"And the little jacket, and the trousers, and the shirt. . . . You would have to walk about as you were born."

"Naked! . . . oh, you silly man! But mother would get them from abroad."

"You would have to wait for them, and then they have to be made. And what if there was a strike there too, or on the railway?"

"Will the railway stop?"

"There is a rumour that all the trains will stop."

"And what about father? How will he come home?"

"Oh, perhaps he will ride on a stick!"

"H'm! . . . you talk nonsense. I will tell that to mother and she will scold you for talking about father in such a way."

Serge became silent and looked thoughtful. Then he stroked the sleeve of his new overcoat and said:

"And you will say that the workmen also had to sew this?"

"Yes, they did that too! Your mother merely gave birth to you, and all the rest . . ."

In two days' time the clattering tramcars ceased running, newspapers were not published, the public baths closed and the streets, usually lit by gas, were in darkness. Two days later the regular train service was discontinued and there was panic at the railway stations . . . a complete cessation of communications was expected hourly.

Serge's father should have come but did not arrive. The mother was uneasy and angry with everybody. Everybody in the house blamed the workmen. Serge was not allowed to go into the yard, and he sat for hours at the window tortured by a devouring curiosity to know what was now happening in the streets.

"And will father come home at once, mother?"

"He cannot come."

And his mother began to rate against the strike, and the workmen, and father.

"Is it possible, mother, that they can?"

"They can what?"

"Prevent travelling on the railway?"

"It seems they can. . . . Don't worry me!"

Tears appeared in his mother's eyes, and she became so angry that Serge was silent, and turning towards the window again began to gaze with curiosity and fear on the street.

"If I only could . . . I . . . I would kill them all!"

Each day matters became worse in the town. The streets were deserted from early evening, the shops closed, doors and windows were protected with strong shutters, and all through the night Cossacks and policemen were stationed round flaring bonfires. Sometimes in the middle of the night Serge would jump from his bed and run barefooted to the window, looking out into the street to see what might be happening there.

The bonfires flared, enormous shadows of people in furry bearskins, like savages, stirred and moved about in the red glare of the flames. . . . Something terrifying and mysterious must be happening during the night in the streets. . . . A cold shiver would run down Serge's spine, he would shudder and shrink back . . . just like cannibals they would catch him and roast him on the bonfire, and eat him. . . . "Oh, mother, mother! I am frightened and cold!" Then Serge would run back to his bed where it was warm and soft, and his mother, awakening, would ask:

"Why are you not asleep? Why are you out of bed?"

"The fire is always burning, mother, and those people stand opposite our window."

"Go to sleep. It is nothing, do not be afraid. If only your father would come!"

"Mother!" . . .

"What, darling?"

"I want to come to you, I am afraid."

"Of what, darling?"

"The magician."

"What magician?"

"Different . . ."

"Then come along."

Serge jumped from his bed with delight and ran over to his mother's bed. Hiding beneath the cover he took hold of his mother's hand and said in a whisper:

"They can do everything." . . .

His mother quickly went to sleep again, and Serge, thrusting his head from beneath the cover, looked at the wall where he could see the red reflections of the street bonfire and thought about good and bad magicians, and of the people called workmen. What were they? Good or bad?

Once, when he went down for his breakfast, Serge found that there were no warm scones on the table as was usual. Instead there was only hard, cold, unappetising bread.

"Give me some scones. Where are the scones? Why have you given me this nasty stuff?" protested Serge, pushing away the basket containing the bread.

"But you must thank God, Master Serge, that we have some bread."

"What? Give me some scones! . . . Mother, why can't I have some scones?"

"But where can we get them from, Serge dear? all the bakeries are closed."

"Why?"

"Because all the workmen are on strike."

Again workmen. Serge scratched behind his ear and asked:

"And what shall we do without scones?"

"We shall manage somehow."

"But can't the governor make them bake scones?"

"Not very well, Serge dear. They are not afraid."

"Of the governor?"

"They are afraid of nobody."

"So they are . . . important?"

"Nothing can be done with them. Eat this dry bread. There will soon be none of that."

"But I cannot eat black bread!"

"Yes, and you will be glad of black bread!"

"But why?"

Serge became more puzzled, wondering what sort of people were these who were not even afraid of the governor, not afraid of anybody, and yet ran away from Cossacks and policemen. How was it? They could stop a factory, tramways, railways, newspapers, deprive you of scones and even black bread, and you could do nothing with them. . . . And he began to remember and think again about magicians and wizards of whom he had read in various fairy tales. They had magic caps which made them invisible, you could not catch them. The governor would say: "Now, work!" and they would put on their magic caps and disappear.

And the unrest from the streets invisibly but insistently crept into the stone houses, to people who were unaccustomed to trouble. Each day, every hour, chaos spread in these houses, upsetting all established rules of procedure, forcing the inhabitants to change their customs and habits. Gaiety disappeared, there was no more laughing and joking, the joy of living departed. Fright crept in instead, and some unknown fear such as had never before been experienced grew each day . . . this fear especially took hold of such large and splendid houses as that in which Serge lived. There the gates were locked from early morning, the heavy locks and chains had to be unfastened to let in the late-comers, armed porters stood in front of the porches, exchanging conversation with the sentries and patrols and blowing piercing blasts on their whistles.

One evening in Serge's home the electric lamps would not burn.

"There is something wrong with the electricity, mother."

"Light the lamp in the drawing-room!"

"And that one, too, mother . . . and here also. . . ."

"Can it be possible . . . a strike there too?"

"It won't burn anywhere, mistress. They say there is a strike."

"Candles, candles. Have we any candles?"

"We have, but not many."

The house darkened. Instead of bright lights in the windows the small yellow flames of candles flickered, the imposing vestibule and staircase were hidden in gloom.

The whole family gathered in the dining-room round a dimly flickering candle and looked fearfully at the dark ballroom where the armchairs, settees and piano in their covers looked like corpses in shrouds standing in deep meditation. Alarming news was brought from the kitchen by the servants who had been gossiping in the servants' hall:

"They say there will soon be no water."

"We have just heard that the holding of funerals has been stopped."

"There will be no meat to-morrow—if it lasts another week there will be a famine in the town."

Serge heard this alarming news with wide-opened eyes; the workman had already appeared as the chief actor, and in the child's mind grew the thought that the workman was a magician, an all-powerful magician who could be summoned with an Aladdin's lamp.

He could do everything; all depended on the magician— if he willed it the railways could start again and father would arrive, if he willed it the electricity would come on and the rooms would once again be as bright as day, at his behest there would be warm scones; but if he did not wish it the water would not run from the taps, there could be no bath and no tea. And he was afraid of nobody, absolutely nobody, this magician.

Serge was quite certain of this when a fortnight later many miracles happened during the course of one day—the trams started again, the electric lamps could be lighted, the streets were flooded with the bright light of the standards, and the shop-windows, newspapers and letters were delivered, warm scones were served with the tea—and father arrived! . . . So many good things at once. . . . Then they drove with his father round the streets and saw the magicians thronging in merry crowds down the streets, carrying floating banners and singing cheerful choruses, and no one dared disperse them—they were afraid of nobody. . . . Serge longed to get out into the street alone, but his mother wouldn't allow him.

"Mother dear, the magicians are going down the street again, do let me go out."

"You can't go."

"They are not bad but good now, mother, aren't they?"

Several months passed. Everything was running in the old smooth way in the house. Gaiety and laughter had returned and fear was banished. Everyone in the house had forgotten the alarming time which had just passed. One day Serge's mother and father went to the theatre, the governess disappeared somewhere, his grandmother who had fallen ill during the strike was still confined to her bed, his sister was playing with her dolls in the nursery. Serge felt dull—there was nothing that he could do. As he moved idly from room to room he could find nothing to occupy his time.

"Grandma, what can I do?"

"Rub my leg, it aches again." . . .

"I don't want to do that, it isn't interesting."

He wandered from his grandmother's room into the nursery and broke the arm of his sister's doll. The nurse sent him away. He wanted to go to the kitchen to see the new cook, but the maid would not allow him.

"Your mother says you are not to go into the kitchen, young master. You have no business there."

"But what if I am lonely?"

"There is nothing there to amuse you."

"But who is talking there?"

"The cook's husband has called."

"Now that is interesting."

"Why interesting? He is just an ordinary man, a workman."

"The cook's husband a workman?"

"Yes."

"A magician! I must go in."

"You must not. I will complain to the governess, and when your mother comes in I will tell her."

"So you are a tell-tale—a tell-tale! I will say that you drank the cream!" . . .

"It is not true. I took a fly out!"

Serge quarrelled with the maid but dared not go into the kitchen; he had once before been scolded for it by his mother. However, his curiosity was overpowering and he edged down the corridor towards the kitchen door. He was anxious to have a close look at the magician. When one of the servants went through into the kitchen, Serge hastened to peep within but didn't manage it; he could hear a voice but could not see the magician himself, the door was not opened widely enough. His curiosity became more acute and he could not withstand it.

"Thank goodness," whispered Serge when he saw the maid move away. As soon as she had gone he began to open the door little by little with the handle of a broom. At last it was wide open. . . . Serge dare not look in at once and stood for a moment or two with lowered eyes, holding his breath.

At last he plucked up courage and looked in: a shabby man sat at the table eating food from a steaming plate. He looked round fearfully as he was eating, as though afraid that someone might take away the food which was before him— he even held the plate with his other hand.

But where was the magician? Serge peered forward and looked all round the kitchen. There was no one there except the cook and this man. Could he possibly be the magician?

Serge, unable to restrain himself any longer, went into the kitchen. The magician jumped from his chair and dropped his spoon, which fell from the table to the floor.

"It is all right; get on with your eating," said the cook, "the little master won't say anything."

"What about?" asked Serge.

"Don't tell your mother and father that a man was eating soup, it was left over."

"Very well."

"The man is hungry, you must pity him, young master."

"Who?"

"Why, this man, my husband."

"Your husband?"

Serge looked askance at the fidgeting, short, ill-fed man near the table. "Surely he has transformed himself," he thought, and said:

"So you, you are a magician. . . . I know."

"Who?"

"You, you!"

"I am a workman, young sir, but out of work."

"But you are a magician . . . I know. . . . You can do everything. It was you who did all this mischief . . . but just see that you don't do it again. It is very dark with candles, and I like hot scones with my tea."

"I have done nothing, young sir, I will go away at once."

"And you are not at all frightful. . . . I thought that you

would be big, like a house, and angry also. . . . But you . . .
have you transformed yourself?"

"You are making fun because I have had nothing to eat.
. . . It is a sin to laugh."

"And I thought that you were important . . . and you are
. . . funny. Your hands tremble when you eat your soup.
. . . I am not a bit afraid of you!"

However, Serge dived quickly out of the kitchen and
stood in the doorway so that he could run away if the
magician decided to chase him. But nothing happened. He
did not run. He turned away to the wall. What was he
doing there? Who was crying? But it was he! HE! Standing and sobbing quietly and wiping away the tears with his
sleeve.

"A magician, and you cry! Oh, you, it serves you right!
. . . Why didn't you let father come back? . . . Why did you
put out the electricity? . . . You didn't let us have any hot
scones. . . . Now God has punished you! . . . Hurrah! hurrah!" suddenly shrieked Serge so loudly that he could be
heard all through the house, and with a triumphant laugh
he informed the approaching governess:

"I am not afraid of him now. My word; not a bit afraid!"

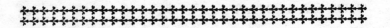

VLASY DOROSHEVITCH
(1864—1922)

❖❖

HOW HASSAN LOST HIS TROUSERS

(Translated by Rosa Graham)

Y e s, yes—that's how it's called—
"How Hassan's trousers came off."
And this is how it happened.
Once upon a time, in the great and famous city of Bagdad,
there lived a rich and popular merchant.
"What was his name?"
When he played at his mother's knee . . .
"Oh, where's heaven? On his mother's knee?"
His mother called him Hassan-Hakki, Happy Hassan.
Hassan was young, handsome, wise and rich.
Enormously rich.
There was nothing he hadn't got.
Hassan made up his mind to one thing.
He would get married.
No sooner said than done.
His bride was the most beautiful young girl in the whole
town.
She was . . . she was . . . no, there are no words to describe
her.
Only music could tell you how beautiful she was.
In a word, she was as beautiful as the girl you're in love
with, sir.
And as yours.
And as yours, my good man.
(In this way, I hope I shall please all tastes.)
All Bagdad was invited to Hassan's wedding-feast.

The Bagdad cooks were ordered to show themselves to be in very truth the best cooks in the whole world.

And among the sheep-flocks went the rumour:

The end of the world has come. Hassan has made up his mind to kill all the young lambs and have them stuffed with pistachio nuts and roasted.

When they saw this gay, rich and luxurious wedding, the women all wept sweet tears of envy, while they ate sherbets and rosy Turkish delight and honeyed jam made from the petals of peach and almond and apricot flowers.

The young ladies only ate the crystallised leaves of lilac and violet blossoms and vowed they couldn't eat anything more, even if it were their own wedding.

The musicians played so long that everybody felt dizzy.

The young folk's legs gave way with so much dancing.

The Koran forbade elderly and corpulent people to drink wine which had the power to grasp them by their legs like slaves and throw them on to the floor.

Midnight sounded—the wished-for hour arrived.

The women took the bride and led her away to the chamber prepared for her.

With laughs and jests they undressed her and laid her on the bridal bed, all hung with lace.

The busybodies went for Hassan: those who had arranged the match.

Accompanied by his friends, the bridegroom bore himself as a young and wise man should.

He walked eagerly and gaily—but he did not hurry.

For no wise man is ever in a hurry, either for punishment or for his wedding.

And nothing is gained by hurrying to live.

Hassan sat leisurely down on the couch opposite the lace-hung bed, leisurely listened to the congratulations and good wishes of his friends, leisurely arose, and said:

"I salute you, dear friends of my youth, as I bid farewell to my bachelor life."

He stepped leisurely towards the bed.

But . . . at that moment, suddenly . . . his trousers came down.

Loud bursts of laughter resounded on all sides, like thunder. The old women squealed as if they were having their throats cut.

The young women giggled together like church-bells ringing. His men friends rolled on the floor.

Ringing laughter resounded from the young bride, who could see everything through the lace canopy of the bed, and in order to deaden the sound of her wild mirth, she began to jingle all her bracelets and bangles.

Everybody just died of laughter.

And Hassan stood helplessly there with his bare legs and his trousers down.

Even his legs blushed a little.

In his confusion he grabbed up his trousers and ran right out of the house.

He ran out into the yard, jumped on the first saddle-horse he came to, one that happened to belong to one of the guests, spurred it with all his might, and galloped into the street.

And from the house came shrieks of derision.

On such trifles does human happiness so often depend.

Hassan galloped like a madman along the road as far as he could see.

Nearly out of his senses, he galloped faster and faster.

And in the early morning he was rapidly approaching the city of Damascus.

They say that the bread of exiles is bitter.

How untrue!

The bread of exiles is neither bitter nor sweet.

The land of exile makes no bread at all for exiles.

There's not a taste of bread for them. . . .

In the streets of a strange town, Hassan looked like a beggar without a coin in his purse.

In a strange town, behind every gate is a dog ready to spring at you as at a robber.

Every door in a strange town is only waiting for you to knock at it, and it will slam itself in your face.

On the cobbled roadway of a strange town every stone is ready to fly at your head.

And in a strange town it is only the trees which meet you with welcome, stretching out to you their blossoming branches.

To hang yourself on!

In the strange town Hassan gazed about him with horror.

He went into the bazaar.

He sold the worn-out horse on which he had come, and with the money he bought some roasted almonds.

He threw a sack of these over his shoulder and walked through the town, stopping in front of the wooden-barred windows of the harems.

"Behold a man, come from afar! I'm looking for the teeth of ladies which will vie in whiteness with my almonds. Hey! Which ladies here have the whitest teeth?"

"Oh, we can't break our teeth on your almonds," they called out from behind the bars.

"Don't trouble yourselves," answered Hassan, with a bow. "My almonds would burst with envy if they fell into your mouths. Seeing your white teeth, they would burst with envy. You wouldn't even have to crack them!"

And by midday he had sold all his almonds.

He reckoned up his profit, and bought some blood oranges.

"Where are to be found the red lips which can compare with my oranges?"

"And are your oranges juicy?" they asked from behind the wooden bars.

"Oh, ladies, my oranges would burst into tears with envy if they found themselves in your mouths."

And long before sunset he had sold all his oranges.

In the same way he sold off a basket of Turkish delight

and all sorts of sweetmeats. His face became familiar in the bazaars; the merchants gave him credit, and after selling confectionery he went in for jewellery.

On Mondays, when according to the Eastern custom only women go to the bazaars, Hassan would spread out his wares and, smiling craftily behind his curly black beard, he would say:

"Oh, beautiful ladies! beautiful ladies! Would you like to be sure that you will never more shed tears? Then buy these earrings. Look, what brilliants! Tears! Real tears! A woman should use tears for ornaments. That's their destiny. Kismet! Buy these earrings, and tears will never glisten in your eyes. Give a hostage to Fate. Why should tears gleam in your eyes when you have them sparkling in yours ears?

"Beautiful ladies! peerless ladies! Don't buy anything from me, but only look! Only look! Your glance will make these turquoises look like bits of the sky. Tell your lover to buy you a turquoise brooch! Then he will see a little bit of the sky on the bosom of his loved one!

"Here are sapphires, dark and blue, like the sea. And rubies, like drops of blood. They shine even in the dark. Ladies! beautiful ladies! Ask your sweethearts to give you either the sea or some drops of blood. I should advise you to take some drops of blood. In a drop of blood there is more emotion than in the bottomless sea.

"Beauteous ladies, here are pearls, here are pearls!"

"I'm afraid. Pearls mean tears!"

"Only the little ones ladies—only the little ones. Only small pearls bring tears. Never yet did large pearls cause a woman to weep!"

So, laughing and joking, and with gay chatter, Hassan sold his wares and grew rich, and soon he was known everywhere in Damascus.

His fame reached even the ears of the Sultan himself.

Allah is the only Sultan.

There are no Sultans, except the Sultan of Sultans, Allah himself.

Allah-Akbar!

The Sultan wished to see the general favourite, and the wisdom and judgment of Hassan pleased him. In conversation with him he said:

"The most difficult matter for a Sultan is to nominate for himself a Vizier.

"You know best, mighty Sovereign," answered Hassan bowing very low. "But it seems to me that it should not be so difficult. The way we commonly do it is this: We take any man, make him Vizier, and say, 'Here is a wise man for you; you must obey him—and if you don't, off with your head!' What else can you do? You can't all at once make human beings into wise men and Viziers. But what if you took the wisest man you have and made him Vizier?"

The Sultan only shook his head.

"That's very simple. But such an idea never came into my mind. Take the wisest man and make him Vizier. Hassan, *you* are the wisest man, and I will make you my Vizier."

"Sovereign Lord, to hear you means to obey."

So Hassan became the Grand Vizier.

He was good and wise and just.

Good people loved him; evil ones feared him.

The laws that he made pleased everybody, and everyone in Damascus marvelled and said:

"What a Vizier we have—neither eminent nor glorious nor famous, but just simply a wise man."

And so it went on for ten years.

Then the Sultan of Damascus called his favourite Vizier to him and said:

"Hassan, may that day be blest when the wind blew you out of your home tree and brought you to us. Praise be to the great and holy Koran which commands us to be hospitable to strangers! It's already ten years, Hassan, since I took your advice and fulfilled your will for the blessing of my city. Now I want you to listen to *my* words and fulfil my will. Listen to me, Hassan! I shan't be here much longer to follow your good counsel. I've such a little way to go to the grave that I have hardly time to look around. And I see that my own city of Damascus is happy under your wise government, and I should like to preserve this happiness for her as long as you live.

"Listen, Hassan! I have no heir. I will give you my favourite daughter to wife and make you Sultan of Damascus. Listen and obey!"

Hassan kissed the earth at the feet of the Sultan, and said:

"To hear you is to obey. But, Sultan! Allah alone is Sultan. There is no Sultan but the Sultan of Sultans, and this is what the Sultan of Sultans has commanded me:

" 'Hassan,' said he, 'Damascus is beautiful, but your home is Bagdad.

" 'There are many beautiful women in this world, but there's no face of any beauty which is as lovely as the wrinkled face of a mother.

" 'Anyone who thinks it better to be Sultan of a foreign land than to be a simple citizen of his own country is not worthy to be either such a simple citizen or Sultan of a foreign city.'

"So spake to me the Sultan of Sultans, and when the Sultan of Sultans speaks, all other Sultans must hold their peace."

The sultan was enraged.

"And is that the way, slave, that you fulfil the will of your Sovereign? I wanted to make you happy. And I *will* make you happy. I will do that which I have resolved."

That's a little weakness of Sultans.

They think that they can make people not only famous and rich and powerful, but also happy.

And in order to make Hassan happy the Sultan ordered that he should be shut up in prison.

But Hassan escaped.

He saddled a horse, filled his purse with gold, and at midnight set off at a gallop for Bagdad.

Just as ten years before, he gave his horse no rest, and when dawn flooded over the mountain-tops, Hassan found himself at the gates of the city of Bagdad.

It seemed to him that nowhere in the world were the trees so fragrant and full of blossom as around Bagdad. And that nowhere else in the world did the minarets rise so straight and so high into the heavens.

He leapt from his horse, fell on his knees, and kissed the earth.

And just at that moment an old woman was sitting at the gates of the city, combing out the hair of her little grandchild.

"Look, granny, look what that man is doing!" said the little girl; "is he eating the earth?"

"No, he's not eating it, he's kissing it. Be quiet, silly, be quiet!" answered the old dame. "What business is it of yours? Perhaps it's a man who loves his country very much, or, it may be, a drunkard. We don't want to get mixed up with either one or the other. You ought to be ashamed. You're not a little girl any longer."

"But how old am I, granny?" asked the girl, making a face.

"You—you're more than ten. You were born in the very year when the merchant Hassan's trousers came down at his wedding."

It was as if his native land had spat in Hassan's face.

He jumped to his feet.

"Allah Akbar! O Allah! Great, Merciful and All-gracious! They now number the years from the day when I had that mishap with my trousers! And some disgusting little girl who does not know how old she is, does know that ten years ago Hassan's trousers came down. I have lived two lives, and, beginning life afresh, from a beggar once more became a rich man. I reached the height of power, governed a state, proclaimed wise laws, made a whole country happy, and could have become Sultan, and now some unkempt, dirty beggar, with a disgusting child at her knee, still cannot forget that ten years ago my trousers came down!"

And leaping on his horse again, Hassan turned him about and galloped away at random over the desert.

That is what Hassan learned about people.

But, of course, Allah alone knows everything about them.

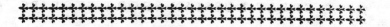

MAXIM GORKY (PESHKOV)
(1868—1936)

❖❖

(I)

TWENTY-SIX AND ONE

(Translated by NISBET BAIN)

THERE were twenty-six of us—twenty-six living machines shut up in a damp cellar, where from morning to evening we kneaded dough to make cakes and biscuits. The windows of our cellar looked upon a ditch yawning open before them and crammed full of bricks, green with damp; the window-frames were partly covered from the outside by an iron grating, and the light of the sun could not reach us through the window-panes covered with flour dust. Our master had closed up the windows with iron in order that we might not give away a morsel of his bread to the poor, or to those of our comrades who were living without work, and therefore starving; our master called us galley-slaves, and gave us rotten entrails for dinner instead of butcher's meat.

It was a narrow, stuffy life we lived in that stone cage beneath the low and heavy rafters covered with soot and cobwebs. It was a grievous evil life we lived within those thick walls, plastered over with patches of dirt and mould. . . . We rose at five o'clock in the morning, without having had our sleep out, and—stupid and indifferent—at six o'clock we were sitting behind the table to make biscuits from dough already prepared for us by our comrades while we were still sleeping. And the whole day, from early morning to ten o'clock at night, some of us sat at the table kneading the

yeasty dough and rocking to and fro so as not to get benumbed, while the others mixed the flour with water.
And all day long, dreamily and wearily, the boiling water
hummed in the cauldron where the biscuits were steamed,
and the shovel of the baker rasped swiftly and evilly upon
our ears from beneath the oven as often as it flung down
baked bits of dough on the burning bricks. From morning
to evening, in one corner of the stove, they burned wood,
and the red reflection of the flames flickered on the wall of
the workshop as if silently laughing at us. The huge stove
was like the misshapen head of some fairy-tale monster—
it seemed to stick out from under the ground, opening its
wide throat full of bright fire, breathing hotly upon us, and
regarding our endless labour with its two black vent-holes
just over its forehead. Those two deep cavities were like
eyes—the passionless and pitiless eyes of a monster; they
always regarded us with one and the same sort of dark
look, as if they were weary of looking at their slaves and,
not expecting anything human from us, despised us with
the cold contempt of worldly wisdom.

From day to day in tormenting dust, in dirt brought in by
our feet from the yard, in a dense malodorous steaming
vapour, we kneaded dough and made biscuits, moistening
them with our sweat, and we hated our work with a bitter
hatred; we never ate of that which came forth from our
hands, preferring black bread to the biscuits. Sitting behind
the long table face to face with each other, nine over against
nine, we mechanically used our arms and fingers during the
long hours, and were so accustomed to our work that we no
longer noticed our own movements. And we had examined
one another so thoroughly that everyone of us knew all the
wrinkles in the faces of his comrades. We had nothing to
talk about, so we got accustomed to talking about nothing,
and were silent the whole time unless we quarrelled—there
is always a way to make a man quarrel, especially if he be
a comrade. But it was rarely that we even quarrelled—how

can a man be up to much if he is half dead, if he is like a figure-head, if his feelings are blunted by grievous labour? But silence is only a terror and a torture to those who have said everything and can have nothing more to say; but for people who have not begun to find their voices, silence is simple and easy. . . . Sometimes, however, we sang; it came about in this way. One of us in the midst of his work would suddenly whinny like a tired horse and begin to croon very softly one of those protracted ditties, the sadly caressing *motif* of which always lightens the heaviness of the singer's soul. One of us would begin singing, I say, and the rest would, at first, merely listen to his lonely song, and beneath the heavy roof of the cellar his song would flicker and die out like a tiny camp-fire in the steppe on a grey autumn night when the grey sky hangs over the earth like a leaden roof. Presently the first singer would be joined by another, and then two voices, softly and sadly, would float upwards from the stifling heat of our narrow ditch. And then, suddenly, several voices together would lay hold of the song, and the song would swell forth like a wave, and become stronger and more sonorous, and seem to amplify the heavy grey walls of our stony prison.

And so it came about that the whole six-and-twenty of us would find ourselves singing—our sustained, soncrous concert would fill the work-room, and the song would seem not to have room enough therein. It would beat against the stone wall, wail, weep, stir within the benumbed heart the sensation of a gentle tickling ache, reopen old wounds in it, and awake it to anguish. The singers would sigh deeply and heavily; one of them would unexpectedly break off his own song and listen to the singing of his comrades, and then his voice would blend once more with the common billow of sound. Another of us, perhaps, would utter an anguished "Ah!" and then continue singing with fast-closed eyes. No doubt the broad, dense wave of sound presented itself to his mind as a road stretching far, far away—a broad road lit up by the bright sun, with he himself walking along that road. . . .

And all the time the flame of the furnace was flickering and the baker's shovel was harshly scraping the brick floor, and the boiling water was humming in the cauldron, and the reflection of the fire was quivering on the wall and laughing at us noiselessly. . . . And we were wailing forth in the words of others our dull misery, the heavy anguish of living beings deprived of the sun, the anguish of slaves. Thus we lived, twenty-six of us, in the cellar of a large stone house, and life was as grievous to us as if all the three upper stories of this house had been built right upon our very shoulders.

But, besides the singing, we had one other good thing—a thing we set great store by and which, possibly, stood to us in the place of sunshine. In the second story of our house was a gold-embroidery factory, and amongst the numerous factory girls employed there was a damsel sixteen years old, Tanya by name. Every morning she would come to the little window pierced through the door in the wall of our workshop, and pressing against it her tiny rosy face, with its merry blue eyes, would cry to us with a musical, friendly voice: "Poor little prisoners! give me some little biscuits!"

All of us would instantly turn round at the familiar sound of that bright voice, and gaze good-naturedly and joyously at the pure virginal little face smiling upon us so gloriously. It became a usual and very pleasant thing for us to see the little nose pressed against the window-pane, to see the tiny white teeth gleaming from under the rosy lips parted by a smile. There would then be a general rush to open the door, each one trampling upon his fellows in his haste, and then in she would come, always so bright and pleasant, and stand before us, her head perched a little on one side, holding up her apron and smiling all the time. The long thick locks of her chestnut hair, falling across her shoulders, lay upon her breast. We dirty, grimy, misshapen wretches stood there looking up at her—the threshold of the door was four steps above the level of the floor—we had to raise our heads to look at her, we would wish her good-morning, and would address her in especial language—the words seemed to come to us expressly for her and for her alone. When we conversed with her our voices were gentler than usual, and our jests were less rough. We had quite peculiar and different manners—and all for her. The baker would take out of the oven a shovelful of the ruddiest, best-toasted biscuits, and skilfully fling them into Tanya's apron.

"Take care you don't fall into the clutches of the master!" we would always caution her. And she, roguishly laughing, would call to us: "Good-bye, little prisoners," and vanish as quickly as a little mouse.

Only—long after her departure, we would talk pleasantly about her among ourselves; we always said the same thing, and we said it late and early, because she and we and everything around us was always the same early and late. It is a heavy torment for a man to live where everything around him is unchanging, and if this does not kill the soul within him, the longer he lives the more tormenting will the immobility of his environment become. We always spoke of women in such a way that sometimes it went against the grain with us to listen to our own coarse, shameful speeches, and it will be understood that the sort of women we knew were unworthy to be alluded to in any other way. But we never spoke ill of Tanya. None of us ever permitted himself to lay so much as a finger upon her; nay, more, she never heard a loose jest from any of us. Possibly this was because she never remained very long with us: she twinkled before our eyes like a star falling from heaven and vanished; but, possibly also, it was because she was so tiny and so very pretty, and everything beautiful awakens respect for it even in coarse people. And there was something else. Although our prison-like labour had made dull brutes of us, for all that we were still human beings, and, like all human beings, we could not live without worshipping something or other. We had nothing better than she, and nobody but she took any notice of us who lived in that vault; nobody, though scores of people lived in that house. And finally—and that, after all, was the chief thing—we all of us accounted her as in some sort our own, as, in some sort, only existing thanks to our biscuits; we looked upon it as our duty to give her biscuits piping hot, and this became to us a daily sacrifice to our idol; it became almost a sacred office, and every day bound us to her more and more. Besides the biscuits we gave to Tanya a good deal of advice—she was to put on warmer clothes, not run rapidly upstairs, not to carry heavy loads of wood. She listened to our advice with a smile, responded to it with laughter, and never followed it at all; but we were not offended with her on that account, we only wanted to show her that we were taking care of her.

Sometimes she asked us to do different things for her; such, for instance, as to open the heavy cellar door, to chop up wood and so on, and we joyfully, nay, with a sort of pride, did for her all that she asked us to do.

But once, when one of us asked her to mend his only shirt, she sniffed contemptuously and said: "What next! do you think I've nothing better to do?"

We laughed heartily at the silly fellow—and never asked her to do anything more. We loved her—and when that is said all is said. A man always wants to lay his love upon someone, although sometime he may crush her beneath the weight of it, and sometimes he may soil her; he may poison the life of his neighbour with his love, because in loving he does not revere the beloved. We were obliged to love Tanya because we had none else to love.

At times one or other of us would begin to reason about it like this: "Why are we spoiling the wench like this? What is there in her after all? Eh? We are making a great deal of fuss about her!"

The fellow who ventured to use such language was pretty roughly snubbed, I can tell you. We wanted something to love, we had found what we wanted, and we loved it; and what we six-and-twenty loved was bound to be inviolate, because it was our holy shrine, and everyone who ran contrary to us in this matter was our enemy. No doubt people often love what is not really good—but here we were, all twenty-six of us, in the same boat, and therefore what we considered dear we would have others regard as sacred.

Besides the biscuit factory our master had a fancy-bakery; it was located in the same house, and only separated from our hole by a wall; but the fancy-bakers—there were four of them—kept us at arm's-length, considering their work as cleaner than ours, and for that reason considering themselves as better than we. So they did not come into our workshop, and laughed contemptuously at us when they met us in the yard. We, too, did not go to them; our master had forbidden us to do so for fear we should steal the milk scones. We did not like the fancy-bakers because we envied them. Their work was lighter than ours; they got more than we did and were better fed; they had a spacious, well-lighted workshop, and they were all so clean and healthy— quite the opposite to us. We indeed, the whole lot of us, looked greyish or yellowish; three of us were suffering from disease, others from consumption, one of us was absolutely crippled by rheumatism. They, on feast-days and in their spare time, put on pea-jackets and boots that creaked; two of them had concertinas, and all of them went strolling in the Park—we went about in little better than dirty rags, with down-at-heel slippers or bast shoes on our feet, and the police would not admit us into the Park—how could we possibly love the fancy-bakers?

Presently we heard that their overseer had taken to drink, that the master had dismissed him and hired another, and that this other was a soldier who went about in a rich satin waistcoat, and on great occasions wore a gold chain. We were curious to see such a toff, and, in the hope of seeing him, took it in turns to run out into the yard one after the other.

But he himself appeared in our workshop. He kicked at the door, it flew open, and, keeping it open, he stood on the threshold, smiled, and said to us: "God be with you! I greet you, my children!"

The frosty air, rushing through the door in thick smoky clouds, whirled round his feet, and there he stood on the threshold looking down upon us from his eminence, and from beneath his blond, skilfully twisted moustaches gleamed his strong yellow teeth. His vest really was something quite out of the common—it was blue, embroidered with flowers, and had a sort of sparkle all over it, and its buttons were made of pretty little pearls. And the gold chain *was* there. . . .

He was handsome, that soldier was, quite tall, robust, with ruddy cheeks, and his large bright eyes looked good and friendly and clear. On his head was a white stiffly starched cap, and from beneath his clean spotless spats appeared the bright tops of his modish, brilliantly polished boots.

Our baker asked him, respectfully, to shut the door. He did so, quite deliberately, and began asking us questions about our master. We outdid each other in telling him that our master was a blood-sucker, a slave-driver, a malefactor, and a tormentor; everything in short that we could and felt bound to say about our master, but it is impossible to write it down here. The soldier listened, twirled his moustache, and regarded us with a gentle, radiant look.

"And I suppose now you've a lot of little wenches about here?" he suddenly said.

Some of us laughed respectfully, others made languishing grimaces; one of us made it quite clear to the soldier that there *were* wenches here—a round dozen of them.

"Do you amuse yourselves?" asked the soldier, blinking his eyes.

Again we laughed, not very loudly, and with some confusion of face. . . . Many of us would have liked to show the soldier that they were as dashing fellows as himself, but none dared to do so; no, not one. One of us indeed hinted as much by murmuring: "Situated as we are . . ."

"Yes, of course, it would be hard for you!" observed the soldier confidentially, continuing to stare at us. "You ought to be—well, not what you are. You're down on your luck—there's a way of holding one's self—there's the look of the thing—you know what I mean! And women, you know, like a man with style about him. He must be a fine figure of a man—everything neat and natty, you know. And then, too, a woman respects strength. Now what do you think of that for an arm, eh?"

The soldier drew his right arm from his pocket, with the shirt-sleeve stripped back, bare to the elbow, and showed it to us. It was a strong, white arm, bristling with shiny, gold-like hair.

"Legs and breast the same—plenty of grit there, eh? And then, too, a man must be stylishly dressed, and must have nice things. Now look at me—all the women love me! I neither call to them nor wink at them—they come falling on my neck by the dozen."

He sat down on a flour-basket and discoursed to us for a long time about how the women loved him, and how valiantly he comported himself with them. After he had gone, and when the creaking door had closed behind him, we were silent for a long time, thinking of him and of his yarns. And after a bit we suddenly all fell a-talking at once, and agreed unanimously that he was a very pleasant fellow. He was so straightforward and jolly—he came and sat down and talked to us just as if he were one of us. No one had ever come and talked to us in such a friendly way before. And we talked of him and of his future successes with the factory girls at the gold-embroiderer's, who, whenever they met us in the yard, either curled their lips contemptuously, or gave us a wide berth, or walked straight up to us as if we were not in their path at all. And as for us, we only feasted our eyes upon them when we met them in the yard, or when they passed by our window, dressed in winter in peculiar little fur caps and fur pelisses, and in summer in hats covered with flowers, and with sunshades of various colours in their hands. But, on the other hand, among ourselves, we talked of these girls in such a way that, had they heard it, they would have gone mad with rage and shame. . . .

"But how about little Tanya—I hope he won't spoil her!" said our chief baker suddenly with a gloomy voice.

We were all silent, so greatly had these words impressed us. We had almost forgotten about Tanya: the soldier had shut her out from us, as it were, with his fine burly figure. Presently a noisy dispute began. Some said that Tanya would not demean herself by any such thing; others maintained that she would be unable to stand against the soldier; finally, a third party proposed that if the soldier showed any inclination to attach himself to Tanya, we should break his ribs. And, at last, we all resolved to keep a watch upon the soldier and Tanya, and warn the girl to beware of him. . . . And so the dispute came to an end.

A month passed by. The soldier baked his fancy-rolls, walked out with the factory girls, and frequently paid us a visit in our workshop, but of his victories over the wenches he said never a word, but only twirled his moustaches and noisily smacked his lips.

Tanya came to us every morning for her "little biscuits," and was always merry, gentle and friendly with us. We tried to talk to her about the soldier—she called him "the goggle-eyed bull-calf," and other ridiculous names, and that reassured us. We were proud of our little girl when we saw how the factory girls clung to the soldier. Tanya's dignified attitude towards him seemed to raise the whole lot of us, and we, as the directors of her conduct, even began to treat the soldier himself contemptuously. But her we loved more than ever, her we encountered each morning more and more joyfully and good-humouredly.

But one day the soldier came to us a little the worse for liquor, he sat him down, began laughing, and when we asked him what he was laughing about, he explained:

"Two of the wenches have been quarrelling about me, Liddy and Gerty," said he. "How they did blackguard each other! Ha, ha, ha! They caught each other by the hair, and were down on the floor in a twinkling, one on the top of the other; ha, ha, ha! And they tore and scratched like anything, and I was nearly bursting with laughter. Why can't women fight fair? Why do they always scratch, eh?"

He was sitting on the bench; there he sat so healthy, clean, and light-hearted, and roared with laughter. We were silent. Somehow, or other, he was disagreeable to us at that moment.

"No, I can't make it out. What luck I do have with women, it is ridiculous. I've but to wink, and—she is ready. The d-deuce is in it."

His white arms, covered with shining gold down, rose in the air and fell down again on his knees with a loud bang. And he regarded us with such a friendly look of amazement, just as if he himself were frankly puzzled by the felicity of his dealings with women. His plump, ruddy face regularly shone with happiness and self-complacency, and he kept on noisily smacking his lips.

Our chief baker scraped his shovel along the hearth violently and angrily, and suddenly remarked, with a sneer:

"It is no great feat of strength to fell little fir trees, but to fell a full-grown pine is a very different matter. . . ."

"Is that meant for me, now?" queried the soldier.

"It *is* meant for you."

"What do you mean?"

"Nothing. . . . Never mind."

"Nay, stop a bit! What's your little game? What pine tree do you mean?"

Our master-baker didn't answer, he was busily working with his shovel at the stove, shovelled out the well-baked biscuits, sifted those that were ready, and flung them boisterously on to the floor to the lads who were arranging them in rows on the bast wrappings. He seemed to have forgotten the soldier and his talk with him. But the soldier suddenly became uneasy. He rose to his feet and approached the stove, running the risk of a blow in the chest from the handle of the shovel which was whirling convulsively in the air.

"Come, speak—what *she* did you mean? You have insulted me. Not a single she shall ever get the better of me, n-no—I say. And then, too, you used such offensive words to me. . . ."

He really seemed to be seriously offended. No doubt he had but a poor opinion of himself except on this one point: his ability to win women. Possibly, except this one quality, there was nothing really vital in the man at all, and only this single quality allowed him to feel himself a living man.

There are people who look upon some disease, either of the body or of the soul, as the best and most precious thing in life. They nurse it all their lives, and only in it do they live at all. Though they suffer by it, yet they live upon it. They complain of it to other people, and by means of it attract to themselves the attention of their neighbours. They use it as a means of obtaining sympathy, and without it—they are nothing at all. Take away from them this disease, cure them, and they will be unhappy because they are deprived of the only means of living—there they stand empty. Sometimes the life of a man is poor to such a degree that he is involuntarily obliged to put a high value on some vice, and live thereby; indeed, we may say straight out that very often people become vicious from sheer ennui.

The soldier was offended, rushed upon our master-baker, and bellowed: "Come, I say—speak out! Who was it?"

"Speak out, eh?" and the master-baker suddenly turned round upon him.

"Yes! Well?"

"Do you know Tanya?"

"Well!"

"Well, there you are!—try her!"

"I?"

"You."

"Pooh! That's nothing."

"Let us see!"

"You shall see. Ha-ha-ha!"

"She look at you!"

"Give me a month!"

"What a braggart you are, soldier!"

"A fortnight! I'll show you. Who's she? Little Tanya! Pooh!"

"And now be off!—you're in the way."

"A fortnight, I say—and the thing's done. Poor you, I say!"

"Be off, I say."

Our baker suddenly grew savage, and flourished his shovel. The soldier backed away from him in astonishment, and observed us in silence. "Good!" he said at last with ominous calmness—and departed.

During the dispute we all remained silent, we were too deeply interested in it to speak. But when the soldier departed, there arose from among us a loud and lively babble of voices.

Someone shrieked at the baker: "A pretty business you've set a-going, Paul!"

"Go on working, d'ye hear?" replied the master-baker fiercely.

We felt that the soldier would make the assault, and that Tanya was in danger. We felt this, and yet at the same time we were all seized by a burning curiosity that was not unpleasant—what would happen? Would Tanya stand firm against the soldier? And almost all of us cried, full of confidence. :

"Little Tanya? She'll stand firm enough!"

We had all of us a frightful longing to put the fortitude of our little idol to the test. We excitedly proved to each other that our little idol was a strong little idol, and would emerge victorious from this encounter. It seemed to us, at last,. that we had not egged on our soldier enough, that he was forgetting the contest, and that we ought to spur his vanity just a little bit. From that day forth we began to live a peculiar life, at high nervous tension, such as we had never lived before. We quarrelled with each other for days together, just as if we had all grown wiser, and were able to talk more and better. It seemed to us as if we were playing a sort of game with the devil, and the stake on our part was —Tanya. And when we heard from the fancy-bread-bakers that the soldier had begun "to run after our little Tanya," it was painfully well with us, and so curious were we to live it out, that we did not even observe that our master, taking advantage of our excitement, had added 14 poods [1] of paste to our daily task. We practically never left off working at all. The name of Tanya never left our tongues all day. And every morning we awaited her with a peculiar sort of impatience.

Nevertheless we said not a word to her of the contest actually proceeding. We put no questions to her, and were kind and affectionate to her as before. Yet in our treatment of her there had already crept in something new and strangely different to our former feeling for Tanya—and this new thing was a keen curiosity, keen and cold as a steel knife.

[1] 560 lbs.

"My friends, the time's up to-day," said the master-baker one morning as he set about beginning his work.

We knew that well enough without any reminder from him, but we trembled all the same.

"Look at her well, she'll be here immediately," continued the baker.

Someone exclaimed compassionately:

"As if eyes could see anything!"

And again a lively, stormy debate arose among us. To-day we were to know at last how clean and inviolable was the vessel in which we had placed our best. That morning, all at once and as if for the first time, we began to feel that we were really playing a great game, and that this test of the purity of our divinity might annihilate it altogether so far as we were concerned. We had all heard during the last few days that the soldier was obstinately and persistently persecuting Tanya, yet how was it that none of us asked her what her relations with him were? And she used to come to us regularly, every morning, for her little biscuits, and was the same as ever.

And this day also we very soon heard her voice.

"Little prisoners, I have come. . . ."

We crowded forward to meet her, and when she came in, contrary to our usual custom, we met her in silence. Looking at her with all our eyes, we knew not what to say to her, what to ask her. We stood before her a gloomy, silent crowd. She was visibly surprised at this unusual reception —and all at once we saw her grow pale, uneasy, fidget in her place, and inquire in a subdued voice:

"What's the matter with you?"

"And how about yourself?" the master-baker sullenly said, never taking his eyes off her.

"Myself? What do you mean?"

"Oh, nothing, nothing."

"Come, give me the biscuits!—quick!"

Never before had she been so sharp with us.

"You're in a hurry," said the baker, not moving and never taking his eyes from her face.

Then she suddenly turned round and disappeared through the door.

The baker caught up his shovel and, turning towards the stove, remarked quietly:

"It means—she's all ready for him. Ah, that soldier . . . the scoundrel . . . the skunk!"

We, like a flock of sheep, rubbing shoulders with each other, went to our table, sat down in silence, and wearily began to work. Presently, someone said: "Yet is it possible . . .?"

"Well, well, what's the good of talking?" screeched the baker.

We all knew that he was a wise man, far wiser than we. And we understood his exclamation as a conviction of the victory of the soldier. . . . We felt miserable and uneasy.

At twelve o'clock—dinner-time—the soldier arrived. He was, as usual, spruce and genteel and—as he always did—looked us straight in the eyes. But we found it awkward to look at *him*.

"Well, my worthy gentlemen, if you like, I'll show you a bit of martial prowess," said he, laughing proudly. "Just you come out into the outhouse and look through the crevices—do you understand?"

Out we went, elbowing each other on the way, and glued our faces to the crevices in the boarded-up wall of the outhouse looking upon the courtyard. We had not long to wait. Very soon, at a rapid pace, and with a face full of anxiety, Tanya came tearing through the yard, springing over the puddles of stale snow and mud. Shortly afterwards, in not the least hurry and whistling as he went, appeared the soldier, making his way in the same direction as Tanya, evidently they had arranged a rendezvous. His arms were thrust deep down in his pockets, and his moustaches were moving up and down. . . . He also disappeared. . . . Then the rain came and we watched the raindrops falling into the puddles, and the puddles wrinkle beneath their impact. The day was damp and grey—a very wearying day. Snow still lay upon the roofs, and on the earth dark patches of mud were already appearing. And the snow on the roofs also got covered with dirty dark-brown smuts. The rain descended slowly with a melancholy sound. We found it cold and unpleasant to stand waiting there, but we were furious with Tanya for having deserted us, her worshippers, for the sake of a common soldier, and we waited for her with the grim delight of executioners.

After a while—we saw Tanya returning. Her eyes—yes, *her* eyes, actually sparkled with joy and happiness, and her lips—were smiling. And she was walking as if in a dream, rocking a little to and fro, with uncertain footsteps. . . .

We could not endure this calmly. The whole lot of us suddenly burst through the door, rushed into the yard, and hissed and yelled at her with evil, bestial violence.

On perceiving us she trembled—and stood as if rooted in the mud beneath her feet. We surrounded her and, maliciously, without any circumlocution, we reviled her to our hearts' content, and called her the most shameful things.

We did not raise our voices, we took our time about it. We saw that she had nowhere to go, that she was in the midst of us, and we might vent our rage upon her as much as we liked. I don't know why, but we did not beat her. She stood in the midst of us, and kept turning her head now hither, now thither, as she listened to our insults. And we —bespattered her, more and more violently, with the mud and the venom of our words.

The colour quitted her face, her blue eyes, a minute before so radiant with happiness, opened widely, her bosom heaved heavily, and her lips trembled.

And we, surrounding her, revenged ourselves upon her,

for she had robbed us. She had belonged to us, we had expended our best upon her, and although that best was but a beggar's crumb, yet we were six-and-twenty and she was but one, therefore we could not devise torments worthy of her fault. How we did abuse her! She was silent all along—all along she looked at us with the wild eyes of a hunted beast, she was all of a tremble.

We ridiculed, we reviled, we baited her. . . . Other people came running up to us. . . . One of us pulled Tanya by the sleeve.

Suddenly her eyes gleamed, she leisurely raised her hands to her head and, tidying her hair, looked straight into our faces, and ejaculated loudly but calmly:

"Ugh! you miserable gaol-birds!"

And she walked straight up to us, unhesitatingly as if we were not standing there in front of her at all, as if we were not obstructing her way. And for that very reason not one of us was actually standing in her way when she came up to us.

And as she passed by, without so much as turning her face towards us, she added as loudly and as haughtily:

"Oh you riff-raff! you . . . you filth!"

And—away she went, erect, beautiful, haughty.

We remained standing in the yard, in the midst of the mud, beneath the pouring rain and the grey, sunless sky.

Presently we returned in silence to our grey, stony dungeon. As before, the sun never looked through our window to us, and—Tanya did not come again.

(II)

CREATURES THAT ONCE WERE MEN

(Translated by Dora Montefiore and Emily Jakovlef)

I

T h e High Street consists of two rows of one-storied hovels, squeezed close one against another; old hovels with leaning walls and crooked windows, with dilapidated roofs, disfigured by time, patched with shingles, and overgrown with moss; here and there above them rise tall poles surmounted with starling houses, whilst the roofs are shaded by the dusty green of pollard willows and elder bushes, the sole miserable vegetation of suburbs where dwell the poorest classes.

The windows of these hovels, their glass stained green with age, seem to watch each other with the shifty, cowardly glance of thieves. Up the middle of the street crawls a winding channel passing between deep holes, washed out by the heavy rain; here and there lie heaps of old, broken bricks and stones overgrown with weeds, the remains of the various attempts made from time to time by the inhabitants to build dwellings; but these attempts have been rendered useless by the torrents of storm-water sweeping down from the town above. On the hill nestle, amongst the luxuriant green of gardens, magnificent stone-built houses; the steeples of churches rise proudly towards the blue heavens, their golden crosses glittering in the sun.

In wet weather the town pours into this outlying suburb all its surface water, and in the dry weather all its dust, and this miserable row of hovels has the appearance of having been swept down at one of these moments by some powerful hand.

Crushed into the ground, these half-rotten human shelters seem to cover all the hill, whilst, stained by the sun, by the dust, and by the rains, they take on them the dirty non-descript colour of old decaying wood.

At the end of this miserable street stood an old, long, two-storied house, which seemed to have been cast out in this way from the town, and which had been bought by the merchant Petunikoff. This was the last house in the row, standing just under the hill, and stretching beyond it were fields, ending at a distance of half a verst from the house in an abrupt fall towards the river. This large and very old house had a more sinister aspect than its neighbours; all its walls were crooked, and in its rows of windows there was not one that had preserved its regular form; whilst the remnants of the window-panes were of the dirty green colour of stagnant water.

The spaces between the windows were disfigured with discoloured patches of fallen plaster, as if time had written the history of the house in these hieroglyphics. Its roof, sagging forwards towards the street, increased its pathetic aspect; it seemed as if the house were bowing itself towards the ground, and were humbly waiting for the last stroke of fate to crumble it into dust, or into a deformed heap of half-rotten ruins.

The front gates were ajar. One side, torn from its hinges, lay on the ground, and from the cracks between the boards sprang grass, which also covered the great desolate yard. At the further end of this yard stood a low, smoke-blackened shed with an iron roof. The house itself was uninhabited, but the shed had been converted into a doss-house which was kept by a retired cavalry officer, Aristide Fomitch Kuvalda.

Inside, this doss-house appeared as a long, dark den, lighted by four square windows and a wide doorway. The brick unplastered walls were dark with smoke, which had also blackened the ceiling. In the middle stood a large stove, round which, and along the walls, were ranged wooden bunks containing bundles of rags which served the dossers for beds. The walls reeked with smoke, the earthen floor with damp, and the bunks with sweat and rotten rags.

The master's bunk was on the stove, and the beds in its immediate neighbourhood were looked upon as places of honour, and were granted to those inmates who rejoiced in his favour and friendship. The master spent the greater part of the day seated at the door of the shed in a solid chair, which he had himself constructed of bricks, or else in the beerhouse of Jegor Vaviloff, just across the way, where Aristide dined and drank vodka.

Before starting the lodging-house Aristide Kuvalda used to keep a servants' registry office in the town; and glancing further back into his life we should find he had had a printing establishment, and before the printing business, according to his own account, he had lived—and " lived, devil take it, well; lived as a connoisseur, I can assure you!"

He was a broad-shouldered man of about fifty, with a pock-marked face, bloated with drink, and a bushy, yellow beard. His eyes were grey, large, audaciously gay; he spoke with a bass voice, and almost always held between his teeth a German china pipe with a curved stem. When he was angry the nostrils of his red crooked nose would dilate wide, and his lips would quiver, showing two rows of large yellow teeth like those of a wolf. Long-armed and bow-legged, he dressed always in an old dirty military overcoat and a greasy cap with a red band, but without a peak; and in worn felt boots reaching to his knees. In the morning he was always in a state of drunken stupor, and in the evening he became lively. Drunk he never could be, for however much liquor he stowed away he never lost his gay humour.

In the evening he might be seen seated in his brick arm-chair, his pipe between his teeth, receiving his lodgers.

"Who are you?" he would ask, on the approach of some ragged, depressed-looking individual, who had been turned out of house and home for drunkenness or for some other reason. And after the man had answered he would say:

"Show me your papers, to prove that you are not lying!"

The papers were shown, if there were any forthcoming. The master would push them into his shirt, not caring to look at their contents.

"All right! For one night two kopecks; a week, ten kopecks; a month, twenty kopecks; go and take your place, but mind not to take anyone else's, or you will catch it. The people who live here are particular."

The new-comer would ask him, "Can one get tea and bread and grub? Don't you sell them?"

"I sell only walls and roof, for which I pay the rogue Judas Petunikoff, the owner of this hole, five roubles a month," Kuvalda would explain in a business-like tone. "People who come to me are not used to luxury, and if you are in the habit of guzzling every day, there's a beershop just opposite. But you'd better get out of that bad habit as soon as possible, you skulker; you are not a gentleman, so why do you want to eat? You had better eat yourself!"

For these and like speeches, uttered in a voice of pretended severity, but always with a laugh in his eyes, and for his attention to his lodgers, Kuvalda was very popular among the outcasts of the town.

It sometimes happened that a former client would come into the doss-house, no longer ragged and down-trodden, but in more or less decent clothes, and with a cheerful face.

"Good-day, your honour; how are you?"

"All right; quite well; what do you want?"

"Don't you recognise me?"

"No, I don't."

"Don't you remember last winter I spent a month with you, when you had a police raid and three were taken away?"

"Oh, my good fellow, the police often come under my hospitable roof!"

"And, good Lord! don't you remember how you cheeked the police officer?"

"Well, that will do with recollections; just say simply what you want."

"Let me stand you something. When I lived with you, you were so——"

"Gratitude should be always encouraged, my friend, for we seldom meet with it. You must be a really good fellow, though I can't remember you; but I'll accompany you to the vodka shop with pleasure, and drink to your success in life."

"Ah! you're always the same—always joking."

"Well, what else can one do when one lives among a miserable set like you?"

Then they would go off, and often the former lodger would return staggering to the doss-house. Next day the entertainment would begin anew; and one fine morning the lodger would come to his senses to find that he had drunk away all that he possessed.

"See, your honour! Once more I am one of your crew; what am I to do now?"

"Well, it's a position you can't boast about, but being in it, it's no use crying," argued the captain. "You must look at your position with equanimity, my friend, and not spoil life with philosophising and reasoning. Philosophy is always useless, and to philosophise before the drink is out of one is inexpressibly foolish. When you are getting over a bout of drinking you want vodka, and not remorse and grinding of teeth. You must take care of your teeth, otherwise there will be none to knock out. Here are twenty kopecks; go and bring some vodka and a piece of hot tripe or lights, a pound of bread and two cucumbers. When we get over our drink then we'll think over the state of affairs."

The state of affairs would become clear in two or three days, when the master had nothing more left of the four or five roubles which had found their way into his pocket on the day of the return of the grateful lodger.

"Here we are, at the end of our tether!" the captain would

say. "Now, you fool, that we have drunk all we had, let us try to walk in the paths of sobriety and of virtue. As it is, how true is the saying, 'If one hasn't sinned one can't repent; and if one hasn't repented one can't be saved!' The first commandment we have fulfilled; but repentance is of no use, so let's go straight for salvation. Be off to the river and start work. If you are not sure of yourself, tell the contractor to keep your money back, or else give it to me to keep. When we've saved a good sum I'll buy you some breeches and what is necessary to make you look like a decent, tidy, working man persecuted by fate. In good breeches you will still stand a good chance. Now be off with you!"

The lodger went off to work on the towpath, down by the river, smiling to himself at the long, wise speeches of Kuvalda. The pith of the wisdom he did not understand, but watching the merry eyes, and feeling the influence of the cheerful spirit, he knew that in the discursive captain he had a friend who would always help him in case of need.

And, indeed, after a month or two of hard work, the lodger, thanks to the strict supervision of the captain, found himself in a pecuniary position which enabled him to rise a step above that condition into which he had fallen, thanks also to the kind assistance of the same captain.

"Well, my friend," Kuvalda would say, critically inspecting his renovated acquaintance, "here you are now with breeches and a coat. These matters are very important, believe me. As long as I had decent breeches I lived as a decent man in the town; but damn it all! as soon as these fell to pieces, I fell also in the estimation of mankind, and I had to leave the town and come out here. People, you fool, judge by the outer appearance only; the inner meaning is inaccessible to them, because of their innate stupidity. Put that into your pipe and smoke it. Pay me half your debt if you like, and go in peace. Seek and you will find."

"How much, Aristide Fomitch, do I owe you?" the lodger would ask confusedly.

"One rouble and seventy. You may give me the rouble or the seventy kopecks, whichever you like now; and for the rest I'll wait for the time when you can steal or earn more than you have now."

"Many thanks for your kindness," replied the lodger, touched by such consideration. "You are—well, you are—such a good soul; it's a pity that life has been so hard on you. You must have been a proud sort of eagle when you were in your right place."

The captain could not get on without grandiloquent phrases. "What do you mean by being in my right place? Who knows what his right place should be? Everyone wants to put his neck into someone else's yoke. Judas Petunikoff's place should be in penal servitude, but he walks freely about the town, and is even going to build a new factory. Our schoolmaster's place should be by the side of a nice, fat, quiet wife, with half a dozen children round him, instead of lying about drunk in Vaviloff's vodka shop. Then there's yourself, who are going to look for a place as a waiter or porter, whereas I know you ought to be a soldier. You can endure much, you are not stupid, and you understand discipline. See how the matter stands! Life shuffles us up like cards, and it's only now and then we fall into our right places; but when that does happen, it's not for long; we are soon shuffled out again."

Sometimes such farewell speeches would serve only as a preface to a renewed friendship, which would start with a fresh drinking bout, and would end with the lodger being surprised to find that he had nothing left, when the captain would again stand treat, till both were in the same state of destitution.

These backslidings never spoilt the good understanding on either side. The afore-mentioned schoolmaster was amongst those friends who only got put on his feet in order to be knocked over again. Intellectually he was more on a level with the captain, and this was perhaps just the reason that,

24

once having fallen to the doss-house, he could never rise again.

He was the only one with whom Aristide Kuvalda could philosophise and be sure that he was understood. He appreciated the schoolmaster for this reason, and when his renovated friend was about to leave the doss-house, having again earned some money with the intention of taking a decent room in town, Aristide Kuvalda would begin such a string of melancholy tirades, that both would recommence drinking, and once more would lose all. In all probability Kuvalda was conscious of what he was doing, and the schoolmaster, much as he desired it, could never get away from the doss-house. Could Aristide Kuvalda, a gentleman by birth, and having received an education, the remnants of which still flashed through his conversation, along with a love of argument acquired during the vicissitudes of fortune —could he help desiring to keep by his side a kindred spirit? It is always ourselves we pity first. This schoolmaster once upon a time used to give lessons in a training school for teachers in a town on the Volga, but as the result of some trouble he was expelled; after that he became a clerk at a tanner's, and was forced, after a time, to leave that place as well; then he became a librarian in a private library, tried various other professions, and at length, having passed an attorney's examination, he began drinking, and came across the captain. He was a bald-headed man, with a stoop, and a sharp-pointed nose. In a thin, yellow face, with a pointed beard, glittered restless, sad, deep-sunk eyes, and the corners of his mouth were drawn down, giving him a depressed expression. His livelihood, or rather the means to get drunk, he earned by being a reporter on the local newspapers. Sometimes he would earn as much as fifteen roubles a week; these he would give to the captain, saying, "This is the last of it! Another week of hard work, and I shall get enough to be decently dressed, and then—*addio, mio caro!*"

"That's all right; you have my hearty approbation. I

won't give you another glass of vodka the whole week," the captain would reply severely.

"I shall be very grateful. You must not give me a single drop."

The captain heard in these words something approaching very near to a humble appeal, and would add still more severely, "You may shout for it, but I won't give you any more."

"Well, that's an end of it," the teacher would sigh, and go off to his work. But in a day or two, feeling exhausted, fatigued, and thirsty, he would look furtively at the captain, with sad, imploring eyes, hoping anxiously that his friend's heart would melt. The captain would keep a severe face, making speeches on the disgrace of a weak nature, on the bestiality of drunkenness, and the like. To give him his due, it is right to add that he was sincere in his rôle of mentor and of moralist, but the patrons of his doss-house were always inclined to be sceptical, and while listening to the scathing words of the captain, would say to each other with a wink, "He's a sly one; he knows how to get rid of all responsibility himself: 'I told you so; but you wouldn't listen to me; now blame yourself.'"

"The gentleman is an old soldier; he doesn't advance without preparing a retreat."

The schoolmaster would catch his friend in a dark corner, and holding him by his dirty cloak, trembling and moistening his parched lips with his tongue, would look into the captain's eyes with an expression so deeply tragic that no words could describe it.

"Can't you?" the captain would question sombrely.

The schoolmaster would nod silently, and then drop his head on his chest, trembling through all his long, thin body.

"Try one more day; perhaps you will conquer yourself," proposed Kouvalda.

The schoolmaster would sigh and shake his head in a hopeless negative. When the captain saw that his friend's lean body was shaken with thirst for the poison, he would take the money out of his pocket.

"It's generally useless to argue with fate," he would say, as if wishing to justify himself.

But if the schoolmaster held out the whole week, the farewell of the friends terminated in a touching scene, the end of which generally took place in Vaviloff's vodka shop.

The schoolmaster never drank all his money; at least half of it he spent on the children of the High Street; poor people are always rich in children, and in the dust and ditches in this street might be seen from morning till night groups of ragged, hungry, noisy youngsters. Children are the living flowers of the earth, but in the High Street they were like flowers faded before their time; probably because they grew on most unfertile soil.

Sometimes the schoolmaster would gather the children round him, buy a quantity of bread, eggs, apples, nuts, and go with them into the fields towards the river. There they would greedily eat up all he had to offer them, filling the air with merry noise and laughter. The lank, thin figure of the drunkard seemed to shrivel up and grow small like the little ones round him, who treated him with complete familiarity, as if he were one of their own age. They called him "Philippe," not adding even the title of "uncle." They jumped around him like eels, they pushed him, got on his back, slapped his bald head, and pulled his nose. He probably liked it, for he never protested against those liberties being taken. He spoke very little to them, and his words were humble and timid, as if he were afraid that his voice might soil or hurt them. He spent many hours with them, sometimes as plaything, and at other times as playmate. He used to look into their bright faces with sad eyes, and would then slowly and thoughtfully slink off into Vaviloff's vodka shop, where he would drink till he lost consciousness.

Almost every day when he returned from his reporting, the schoolmaster would bring back a paper from the town, and the outcasts would form a circle round him. As soon as they saw him coming, they would gather from the different corners of the yard, some drunk, some in a state of stupor, all in different stages of raggedness, but all equally miserable and dirty.

First would appear Alexei Maximovitch Simtzoff, round as a barrel; formerly a surveyor of forest lands, but now a pedlar of matches, ink, blacking and bad lemons. He was an old man of sixty, in a canvas coat and a broad-brimmed crushed hat, which covered his fat, red face with its thick, white beard, out of which peeped forth a small, red nose, and thick lips of the same colour, and weak, running, cynical eyes. They called him "Kubar," a top, and this nickname well portrayed his round, slowly-moving figure and his thick, humming speech.

Luka Antonovitch Martianoff, nicknamed Konetz, "The End," would come out of some corner, a morose, black, silent drunkard, formerly an inspector of a prison; a man who gained his livelihood at present by playing games of hazard, such as the three-card trick and thimble-rig, and by the display of other talents equally ingenious, but equally unappreciated by the police. He would drop his heavy, often ill-treated body on the grass beside the schoolmaster, his black eyes glistening, and stretching forth his hand to the bottle, would ask in a hoarse bass voice:

"May I?"

Then also would draw near the mechanic Pavel Sontseff, a consumptive of about thirty. The ribs on his left side had been broken in a street row; and his face, yellow and sharp, was constantly twisted into a cunning, wicked smile; his thin lips showed two rows of black, decayed teeth, and the rags on his thin shoulders seemed to be hanging on a peg. They used to call him "Scraps"; he earned his living by selling brooms of his own making, and brushes made of a certain kind of grass, which were very useful for brushing clothes.

Besides these, there was a tall, bony, one-eyed man with uncertain antecedents; he had a scared expression in his large, round, silent and timid eyes. He had been three times condemned for thefts, and had suffered imprisonment for them. His name was Kisselnikoff, but he was nicknamed "Tarass and a half" because he was just half the size again of his inseparable friend Tarass, a former Church deacon, but degraded now for drunkenness and dissipation. The deacon was a short, robust little man with a broad chest and a round, matted head of hair; he was famous for his dancing, but more so for his swearing; both he and "Tarass and a half" chose as their special work wood-sawing on the river-bank, and in their leisure hours the deacon would tell long stories "of his own composition," as he expressed it, to his friend or to anyone who cared to hear them. Whilst listening to these stories, the heroes of which were always saints, kings, clergy, and generals, even the habitués of the doss-house used to spit the taste of them out of their mouths, and opened wide eyes of astonishment at the wonderful imagination of the deacon, who would relate these shameless, obscene, fantastic adventures with great coolness, and with eyes closed in rapture. The imagination of this man was powerful and inexhaustible; he could invent and talk the whole day long, and never repeated himself. In him the world lost perhaps a great poet, and certainly a remarkable story-teller, who could put life and soul even into stones, by his foul but imaginatively powerful thought.

Besides these there was an absurd youth, who was called by Kuvalda "The Meteor." He once came to seek a night's lodging, and to the astonishment of all he never left the place again. At first no one noticed him, for during the day he would go out to earn a livelihood, as did the rest, but in the evening he stuck closely to the friendly doss-house society. One day the captain asked him:

"My lad! What do you do in this world?"

The boy answered shortly and boldly, "I? I'm a tramp."

The captain looked at him critically. The lad had long hair, a broad, foolish face with a snub nose; he wore a blue blouse without a belt, and on his head were the remains of a straw hat. His feet were bare.

"You are a fool!" said Aristide Kuvalda. "What are you doing here? You are of no use to us. Do you drink vodka? No! And can you steal? Not that either? Well, go and learn all that, and make a man of yourself, and then come back."

The lad smiled. "No, I shan't; I'll stay where I am!"

"Why?"

"Because——"

"Ah! you're a meteor!" said the captain.

"Let me knock some of his teeth out," proposed Martianoff.

"But why?" asked the lad.

"Because——"

"Well, then, I should take a stone and knock you on the head," solemnly replied the boy.

Martianoff would have thrashed him if Kuvalda had not interfered. "Leave him alone; he is distantly related to you, brother, as he is to all of us. You, without sufficient reason, want to knock his teeth out, and he, also without sufficient reason, wants to live with us. Well, damn it all! We all have to live without sufficient reason for doing so. We live, but ask us why; we can't say. Well, it's so with him, so let him be."

"But still, young man, you had better leave us," the schoolmaster intervened, surveying the lad with sad eyes.

The lad did not answer, but remained. At last they grew accustomed to him, and paid no attention to him, but he watched closely all that they said and did.

All the above-mentioned individuals formed the captain's body-guard, and with good-natured irony he used to call them his "Has-beens." Besides these, there were five or six regular tramps in the doss-house; these were country-folk who could not boast of such antecedents as the has-beens, though they had undergone no less vicissitudes of fate; but they were a degree less degraded, and not so completely broken down. It may be that a decent man from the educated classes is somewhat above a decent peasant; but always a vicious townsman is immeasurably more degraded and vile than a sinner from the country. This rule was strikingly illustrated by the ex-peasants and ex-intelligentsia of Kuvalda's shelter.

The most prominent peasant representative was a rag-picker of the name of Tiapa. Tall, and horribly thin, he constantly carried his head so that his chin fell on his breast, and from this position his shadow always assumed the shape of a hook.

One could never see his full face, but his profile showed an aquiline nose, projecting underlip, and bushy grey eye-brows. He was the captain's first lodger, and it was rumoured that he possessed large sums of money hidden somewhere about him. It was for this money that two years ago he had been stabbed in the throat, since when he had been forced to keep his head so strangely bent. He denied having any money and said that he had been struck with a knife for fun; and this accident had made it convenient for him to become a rag-and-bone picker, as his head was always necessarily bent for-ward towards the ground. When he walked about with his swaying, uncertain gait, and without his stick and bag, the badges of his profession, he seemed a being absorbed in his own thoughts, and Kuvalda, pointing at him with his finger would say, "Look out! There is the escaped conscience of Judas Petunikoff, seeking for a refuge! See how ragged and dirty this fugitive conscience looks!"

Tiapa spoke with such a hoarse voice that it was almost impossible to understand him, and that was perhaps why he spoke little, and always sought solitude. Each time when a new-comer, driven from the village, arrived at the doss-house, Tiapa at sight of him would fall into a state of angry irritation and restlessness. He would persecute the miserable being with sharp, mocking words, which issued from his throat in an angry hiss; and he would set on him one of the most savage amongst the tramps; and finally threaten to beat and rob him himself in the night; he nearly always succeeded in driving out the terrified and disconcerted peasant, who never returned.

When Tiapa was somewhat appeased, he would hide himself in a corner to mend his old clothes or to read in a Bible as old, as torn, as dirty as himself. Tiapa would come out of his corner when the schoolmaster brought the newspaper to read. Generally Tiapa listened silently to the news, sighed deeply, but never asked any questions. When the schoolmaster closed the newspaper, Tiapa would stretch out his bony hand and say:

"Give it here."

"What do you want it for?"

"Give it; perhaps there is something written concerning us."

"Concerning whom?"

"The village."

They laughed at him, and threw the paper at him. He would take it and read those parts which told of corn beaten down by the hail; of thirty holdings being destroyed by fire, and of a woman poisoning a whole family; in fact all those parts about village life which showed it as miserable, sordid and cruel. Tiapa read all these in a dull voice, and emitted sounds which might be interpreted as expressing either pity or pleasure. On Sunday he never went out rag-picking, but spent most of his day reading his Bible, during which process he moaned and sighed. His book he always held resting on his chest, and he was angry if anyone touched it or interrupted his reading.

"Hullo! You magician!" Kuvalda would say; "you don't understand anything of that; leave the book alone!"

"And you? What do you understand?"

"Well, old magician, I don't understand anything; but then I don't read books."

"But I do."

"More fool you!" answered the captain. "It's bad enough to have vermin in the head. But to get thoughts into the bargain. How will you ever be able to live, you old toad?"

"Well, I have not got much longer to live," said Tiapa quietly.

One day the schoolmaster inquired where he had learnt to read, and Tiapa answered shortly:

"In prison."

"Have you been there?"

"Yes, I have."

"For what?"

"Because—I made a mistake. It was there I got my Bible. A lady gave it me. It's good in prison, don't you know that, brother?"

"It can't be. What is there good in it?"

"They teach one there. You see how I was taught to read. They gave me a book, and all that free!"

When the schoolmaster came to the doss-house, Tiapa had been there already a long time. He watched the schoolmaster constantly; he would bend his body on one side in order to get a good look at him, and would listen attentively to his conversation.

Once he began, "Well, I see you are a scholar. Have you ever read the Bible?"

"Yes, I have."

"Well, do you remember it?"

"I do! What then?"

The old man bent his whole body on one side and looked at the schoolmaster with grey, morose, distrustful eyes.

"And do you remember anything about the Amalekites?"

"Well, what then?"

"Where are they now?"

"They have died out, Tiapa—disappeared."

The old man was silent, but soon he asked again:
"And the Philistines?"
"They've gone also."
"Have they all disappeared?"
"Yes, all."
"Does that mean that we shall also disappear as well?"
"Yes, when the time comes," the schoolmaster replied in an indifferent tone of voice.
"And to which tribe of Israel do we belong?"
The schoolmaster looked at him steadily, thought for a moment, and began telling him about the Cymri, the Scythians, the Huns and the Slavs.
The old man seemed to bend more than ever on one side, and watched the schoolmaster with scared eyes.
"You are telling lies!" he hissed out when the schoolmaster had finished.
"Why do you think I am lying?" asked the astonished schoolmaster.
"Those people you have spoken of, none of them are in the Bible!" He rose and went out, deeply offended, and cursing angrily.
"You are going mad, Tiapa!" cried the schoolmaster after him.
Then the old man turned round, and stretching out his hand shook with a threatening action his dirty, crooked forefinger.
"Adam came from the Lord. The Jews came from Adam. And all people come from the Jews—we amongst them."
"Well?"
"The Tartars came from Ishmael. And he came from a Jew!"
"Well, what then?"
"Nothing. Only why do you tell lies?"
And he went off, leaving his companion in a state of bewilderment. But in two or three days' time he approached him again.

"As you are a scholar, you ought at least to know who we are!"

"Slavs, Tiapa—Slavs!" replied the schoolmaster.

And he awaited with interest Tiapa's rejoinder, hoping to understand him.

"Speak according to the Bible! There are no names like that in the Bible. Who are we, Babylonians or Edomites?"

The teacher began criticising the Bible. The old man listened long and attentively, and finally interrupted him.

"Stop all that! Do you mean that among all the people known to God there were no Russians? We were unknown to God? Is that what you mean to say? Those people, written about in the Bible, God knew them all. He used to punish them with fire and sword; He destroyed their towns and villages, but still He sent them His prophets to teach them, which meant He loved them. He dispersed the Jews and Tartars, but He still preserved them. And what about us? Why have we no prophets?"

"Well, I don't know," said the schoolmaster, trying in vain to understand the old man.

The old peasant put his hand on the schoolmaster's shoulder, rocking him gently to and fro whilst he hissed and gurgled as if swallowing something, and muttered in a hoarse voice:

"You should have said so long ago. And you went on talking as if you knew everything. It makes me sick to hear you. It troubles my soul. You'd better hold your tongue. See, you don't even know why we have no prophets. You don't know where we were when Jesus was on earth. And such lies too. Can a whole people die out? The Russian nation can't disappear; it's all lies. They are mentioned somewhere in the Bible, only I don't know under what name. Don't you know what a nation means? It is immense. See how many villages there are! And in each village look at the number of people; and you say they will die out. A people cannot die out, but a person can. A people is necessary to God, for they till the soil. The Amalekites have not died out; they are the French or the Germans. And see what you have been telling me. You ought to know why we don't possess God's favour; He never sends us now either plagues or prophets. So how *can* we be taught now?"

Tiapa's speech had a dreadful force in it. It was penetrated with irony, reproach, and fervent faith. He spoke for a long time, and the schoolmaster, who was as usual half drunk, and in a peaceful frame of mind, got tired of listening. He felt as if his nerves were being sawn with a wooden saw. He was watching the distorted body of the old man, and feeling the strange oppressive strength in his words. Finally, he fell to pitying himself, and from that passed into a sad, wearied mood. He also wanted to say something forcible to old Tiapa, something positive, that might win the old man's favour, and change his reproachful morose tone into one that was soft and fatherly. The schoolmaster felt as if words were rising to his lips, but could not find any strong enough to express his thought.

"Ah! You are a lost man," said Tiapa. "Your soul is torn, and yet you speak all sorts of empty, fine words. You'd better be silent!"

"Ah! Tiapa!" sadly exclaimed the schoolmaster, "all that you say is true. And about the people also. The mass of the people is immense! But I am a stranger to it, and it is a stranger to me. There lies the tragedy of my life! But what's to be done? I must go on suffering. Indeed there are no prophets; no, not any. And it's true I talk too much and to no purpose. I had better hold my tongue. But you mustn't be so hard on me. Ah! old man, you don't know. You don't know. You can't understand."

Finally, the schoolmaster burst into tears; he cried so easily and freely, with such abundant tears, that afterwards he felt quite relieved.

"You should go into the country; you should get a place as schoolmaster or as clerk. You would be comfortable there, and have a change of air. What's the use of leading this miserable life here?" Tiapa hissed morosely.

But the schoolmaster continued to weep, enjoying his tears.

From that time forth they became friends, and the creatures who once had been, seeing them together, would say:

"The schoolmaster is making up to old Tiapa; he is trying to get at his money."

"It's Kuvalda who has put him up to trying to find out where the old man's hoard is."

It is very possible that their words were not in agreement with their thoughts; for these people had one strange trait in common; they liked to appear to each other worse than they really were.

The man who has nothing good in him likes sometimes to show off as one who is bad.

When all of them were gathered round the schoolmaster with his newspaper the reading would begin.

"Now," the captain would say, "what does the paper offer us to-day? Is there a serial story coming out in it?"

"No," the schoolmaster would reply.

"Your editor is mean. Is there a leading article?"

"Yes, there is one to-day. I think it is by Guliaeff."

"Give us a taste of it! The fellow writes well.   He's a cute one, he is!"

"The valuation of real estate," reads the schoolmaster, "which took place more than fifteen years ago, continues still to form a basis for present-day rating, to the great advantage of the town."

"The rogues!" interjects Captain Kuvalda. " ' Still continues to form!' It's indeed absurd! It's to the advantage of the merchants who manage the affairs of the town that it should continue to form the basis, and that's why it does continue!"

"Well, the article is written with that idea," says the schoolmaster.

"Ah! is it? How strange: It would be a good theme for the serial story, where it could be given a spicy flavour!"

A short dispute arises. The company still listens attentively, for they are at their first bottle of vodka. After the leading article they take the local news. After that they attack the police news and law cases. If in these a merchant is the sufferer, Aristide Kuvalda rejoices. If a merchant is robbed all is well; it is only a pity they did not take more. If his horses ran away with him and smashed him up, it was pleasant to listen to, and only a pity that the fellow escaped alive. If a shopkeeper lost a lawsuit, that was a good hearing; the sad point was that he was not made to pay the expenses twice over.

"That would have been illegal," remarks the schoolmaster.

"Illegal?" Kuvalda exclaims hotly. "But does a shopkeeper himself act always according to the law? What is a shopkeeper? Let us examine this vulgar, absurd creature. To begin with, every shopkeeper is a peasant. He comes from the country, and after a certain time he takes a shop and begins to trade. To keep a shop one must have money, and where can a peasant get money? As everyone knows, money is not earned by honest labour. It means that the peasant by some means or other has cheated. It means that a shopkeeper is a dishonest peasant!"

"That's clever!" The audience shows its approbation of the orator's reasoning.

Tiapa groans and rubs his chest; the sound is like that which he makes after swallowing his first glass of vodka.

The captain is buoyant. They now begin reading provincial correspondence. Here the captain is in his own sphere, as he expresses it. Here it is apparent how shamefully the shopkeeper lives, and how he destroys and disfigures life. Kuvalda's speech thunders round the shopkeeper, and annihilates him. He is listened to with pleasure, for he uses violent words.

"Oh! if I could only write in newspapers!" he exclaims, "I'd show the shopkeeper up in his right colours! I'd show he was only an animal who was temporarily performing the duties of man. I can see through him very well! I know him. He's a coarse fool with no taste for life, who has no notion of patriotism, and understands nothing beyond kopecks!"

A ragged fellow, knowing the weak side of the captain, and delighting in arousing anger, would interpose:

"Yes, since the gentry are dying out from hunger there is no one of any account left in the world."

"You are right, you son of a spider and of a frog! Since the gentry have gone under no one is left. There are nothing but shopkeepers, and I hate them!"

"That's easy to see; for have they not trodden you underfoot?"

"What's that to me? I came down in the world through my love of life, while the shopkeeper does not understand living. That's just why I hate him so, and not because I am a gentleman. But just take this as said, that I'm no longer a gentleman, but just simply a creature who once was a human being, the shadow only of my former self. I spit at all and everything, and life for me is like a mistress who has deserted me. That is why I despise it, and am perfectly indifferent towards it."

"All lies!"

"Am I a liar?" roars Aristide Kuvalda, red with anger.

"Why roar like that?" says Martianoff's bass voice, coolly and gloomily. "What's the use of arguing? Shopkeeper or gentleman, what does it matter to us?"

"That's just it, for we are neither fish, nor fowl, nor good red herring," interposes Deacon Tarass.

"Leave him in peace," says the schoolmaster pacifically. "What's the use of throwing oil on the fire?"

The schoolmaster did not like quarrels and noise. When passions grew hot around him his lips twitched painfully, and he unobtrusively tried to make peace; not succeeding in which, he would leave the company to themselves. The captain knew this well, and if he was not very drunk he restrained himself, not wishing to lose the best auditor of his brilliant speeches.

"I repeat," he continued now with more restraint—"I repeat, that I see that life is in the hands of foes, not only of foes of the nobility, but foes of all that is noble; of greedy, ignorant people, who won't do anything to improve the conditions of life."

"Still," argues the schoolmaster, "merchants created Genoa, Venice, Holland. It was the merchants, the merchants of England, who won India. It was the merchants Stroganoffs——"

"What have I to do with those merchants? I am speaking of Judas Petunikoff and his kind, with whom I have to do."

"And what have you to do with these?" asked the school-master softly.

"Well, I'm alive. I'm in the world. I can't help being indig-nant at the thought of these savages, who have got hold of life, and who are doing their best to spoil it!"

"And who are laughing at the noble indignation of a captain and a retired human being!"

"It's stupid, very stupid! I agree with you. As a has-been I must destroy all the feelings and thoughts that were once in me. That's perhaps true; but how shall we arm ourselves, you and I, if we throw these feelings on one side?"

"Now you are beginning to speak reasonably," says the schoolmaster encouragingly.

"We want something different. New ways of looking at life, new feelings, something fresh, for we ourselves are a new phase in life."

"Yes, indeed, that's what we want," says the schoolmaster.

"What's the use of discussing and thinking?" asks a tramp nicknamed—The End; "we haven't got long to live. I'm forty, you are fifty. There is no one under thirty among us. And even if one were twenty, one could not live very long in such surroundings as these."

"And then, again, what new phase are we? Tramps, it seems to me, have always existed in the world," says the ragged fellow satirically. His nickname was "Leavings."

"Tramps created Rome," says the schoolmaster.

"Yes; that was so!" said the captain jubilantly. "Romulus and Remus, were they not tramps? And we—when our time comes—we shall also create."

"A breach of social peace!" interjects "Leavings", and laughs, well pleased with himself.

His laugh is wicked, and jars on the nerves. He is echoed by Simtsoff, by the deacon, and by "Tarass and a half." The naïve eyes of the lad "Meteor" burn with a bright glow, and his cheeks flush red. "The End" mutters in tones that fall like a hammer on the heads of the audience.

"All that's trash and nonsense, and dreams!"

It was strange, to hear these people, outcasts from life, ragged, saturated with vodka, angry, ironical and filthy, discussing life in this way.

For the captain such discussions were a feast. He spoke more than the others, and that gave him a chance of feeling his superiority. For however low a person may fall, he can never refuse himself the delight of feeling stronger and better off than the rest. Aristide Kuvalda abused this sensation, and never seemed to have enough of it, much to the disgust of "The Top," and the other outcasts, little interested in similar questions. Politics was with them the favourite topic. A discussion on the necessity of conquering India, and of checking England, would continue endlessly. The question as to the best means of sweeping the Jews off the face of the earth was no less hotly debated. In this latter question the leader was always "Leavings",. who invented marvellously cruel projects; but the captain, who liked always to be first in a discussion, evaded this topic. Women

were always willingly and constantly discussed, but with unpleasant allusions; and the schoolmaster always appeared as
women's champion, and grew angry when the expressions
used by the others were of too strong a nature. They gave in
to him, for they looked upon him as a superior being, and on
Saturdays they would borrow money from him, which he had
earned during the week.

He enjoyed besides many privileges. For instance, he was
never knocked about on the frequent occasions when the discussions finished in a general row. He was allowed to bring
women into the doss-house; and no one else enjoyed this
right, for the captain always warned his clients:

"I'll have no women here! Women, shopkeepers and
philosophy have been the three causes of my ruin. I'll
knock down anyone I see with a woman, and I'll knock the
woman down as well. On principle I would twist the neck
of——"

He could have twisted anyone's neck, for in spite of his
years he possessed wonderful strength. Besides, whenever he
had a fighting job on he was always helped by Martianoff.
Gloomy and silent as the tomb in the usual way, yet on these
occasions, when there was a general row on, he would stand
back to back with Kuvalda, these two forming together a
destructive but indestructible engine. If Kuvalda was
engaged in a hand-to-hand fight, "The End" would creep
up and throw his opponent on the ground.

Once when Simtsoff was drunk, he, without any reason,
caught hold of the schoolmaster's hair and pulled a handful
out. Kuvalda, with one blow of his fist, dropped Simtsoff
unconscious, and he lay where he fell for half an hour.
When the fellow came to his senses he was made to swallow
the hair he had pulled out, which he did for fear of being
beaten to death.

Besides the reading of the newspaper, discussions and
laughter, the other amusement was card-playing. They
always left Martianoff out, for he could not play honestly.

After being several times caught cheating, he candidly confessed:

"I can't help cheating; it's a habit of mine."

"Such things do happen," corroborated Deacon Tarass. "I used to have the habit of beating my wife every Sunday after mass; and, would you believe it, after she died I had such a gnawing feeling come over me every Sunday I can scarcely describe it. I got over one Sunday, but things seemed to go all wrong. Another Sunday passed, and I felt very bad. The third Sunday I could not bear it any longer, and struck the servant girl. She kicked up a row, and threatened to take me before a magistrate. Just imagine my position! When the fourth Sunday came I knocked her about as I used to do my wife; I paid her ten roubles down, and arranged that I should beat her as a matter of course until I married again."

"Deacon, you are telling lies! How could you marry again?" broke in "Scraps."

"Well—I—she—we did without the ceremony. She kept house for me."

"Had you any children?" asked the schoolmaster.

"Yes, five of them. One got drowned—the eldest. He was a queer boy. Two died of diphtheria. One daughter married a student, and followed him to Siberia. The other wanted to study in Petersburg, and died there; I am told it was consumption. Yes, five of them. We clergy are very prolific."

And he began giving reasons for this, causing by his explanations Homeric laughter. When they were tired of laughing, Alexei Maximovitch Simtsoff remembered that he also had a daughter.

"She was called Lidka. Oh, how fat she was!"

Probably he remembered nothing more, for he looked round deprecatingly, smiled, and found nothing more to say.

These people spoke but little of their past. They seldom

recalled it, and if ever they did so, it was in general terms and in a more or less scoffing tone. Perhaps they were right in treating their past slightingly, for recollections with most people have a tendency to weaken present energy, and destroy hope in the future.

On rainy days, and during dark, cold, autumn weather, these creatures who once were men would gather in Vaviloff's vodka shop. They were habitués there, and were feared as a set of thieves and bullies; on the one hand they were despised as confirmed drunkards, and on the other hand they were respected and listened to as superior people. Vaviloff's vodka shop was the club of the neighbourhood, and the has-beens were the intellectuals of the club.

On Saturday evenings, and on Sundays from early morning till night the vodka shop was full of people, and the has-beens were welcome guests. They brought with them, amongst these inhabitants of the High Street, oppressed as they were by poverty and misery, a rollicking humour, in which there was something that seemed to brighten these lives, broken and worn out in the struggle for bread. The has-beens' art of talking jestingly on every subject, their fearlessness of opinion, their careless audacity of expression, their absence of fear of everything which the neighbourhood feared, their boldness, their daredevilry—all this did not fail to please. Besides, almost all of them knew something of law, could give advice on many matters, could write a petition, or could give a helping hand in a shady transaction without getting into trouble. They were paid in vodka, and in flattering encomiums on their various talents.

According to their sympathies, the street was divided into two nearly equal parties. One considered that the captain was very superior to the schoolmaster: "A real hero! His pluck and his intelligence are far greater!" The other considered that the schoolmaster outbalanced Kuvalda in every respect. The admirers of Kuvalda were those who were known in the street as confirmed drunkards, thieves and scapegraces, who feared neither poverty nor prison. The schoolmaster was admired by those who were more decent, who were always hoping for something, always expecting something, and yet whose bellies were always empty.

The respective merits of Kuvalda and the schoolmaster may be judged of by the following example. Once in the vodka shop they were discussing the town regulations under which the inhabitants of the neighbourhood were bound to fill up the ruts and holes in the streets; the dead bodies of animals and manure were not to be used for this purpose, but rubble and broken bricks from buildings."

"How the devil am I to get broken bricks? I, who all my life have been wanting to build a starling house, and yet have never been able to begin?" complained in a pitiful voice Mokei Anissimoff, a seller of rolls which were baked by his wife.

The captain considered that he ought to give an opinion on the question, and thumped the table energetically to attract the attention of the company.

"Don't you know where to get bricks and rubble? Let's go, all of us, my lads, into the town together and demolish the Town Hall. It's an old, good-for-nothing building, and your work will be crowned by a double success. You will improve the town by forcing them to build a new Town Hall, and you will make your own neighbourhood decent. You can use the Mayor's horses to draw the bricks, and you can take his three daughters as well; the girls would look well in harness! Or else you may pull down Judas Petunikoff's house, and mend the street with wood. By the by, Mokei, I know what your wife was using to-day to heat the oven for baking her rolls! It was the shutters from the third window, and the boards from two of the steps!"

When the audience had had its laugh out, and had finished joking at the captain's proposal, the serious-minded gardener Pavlugin asked:

"But, after all, captain, what's to be done? What do you advise us to do?"

"I—I advise you not to move hand or foot. If the rain destroys the street, let it. It isn't our fault."

"Some of the houses are tumbling down already."

"Leave them alone, let them fall! If they come down the town must pay damages, and if the authorities refuse, bring the matter before a magistrate. For just consider where the water comes from; doesn't it come down from the town? Well, that shows the town is to blame for the houses being destroyed."

"They will say it's rain water."

"But in the town the rain doesn't wash down the houses, does it? The town makes you pay rates and gives you no vote to help you claim your rights. The town destroys your life and your property, and yet holds you responsible for them. Pitch into the town on every side!"

And one half of the dwellers in the street, convinced by the radical Kuvalda, decided to wait till the storm-waters of the town had washed down their hovels.

The more serious half got the schoolmaster to write out an elaborate, convincing report for presentation to the town authorities. In this report, the refusal to carry out the town regulations was based on such solid reasons that the municipality was bound to take them into consideration. The dwellers in the street were granted permission to use the refuse left after the rebuilding of the barracks, and five horses from the fire brigade were lent to cart the rubbish. Besides this it was decided to lay a drain down the street.

This, added to other circumstances, made the schoolmaster very popular in the neighbourhood. He wrote petitions, got articles put into the papers. Once, for instance, the guests at Vaviloff's noticed that the herrings and other coarse food were not up to the mark, and two days later Vaviloff, standing at the counter with the newspaper in his hands, made a public recantation.

"It's quite just. I have nothing to say for myself. The herrings were indeed rotten when I bought them, and the cabbage—that's also true—had been lying about too long. Well, it's only natural every one wants to put more kopecks into his own pocket. And what comes of it? Just the opposite to what one hopes. I tried to get at other men's pockets, and a clever man has shown me up for my avarice. Now we're quits!"

This recantation produced an excellent effect on his audience, and gave Vaviloff the chance of using up all his bad herrings and stale cabbage, the public swallowing them down unheeding their ancient flavour, which was concealed with the spice of a favourable impression. This event was remarkable in two ways; it not only increased the prestige of the schoolmaster, but it taught the inhabitants the value of the Press.

Sometimes the schoolmaster would hold forth on practical morality.

"I saw," he would say, accosting the house painter Yashka Turine, "I saw, Yakoff, how you were beating your wife to-day."

Yashka had already raised his spirits with two glasses of vodka, and was in a jovial mood. The company looked at him, expecting some sally, and silence reigned in the vodka shop.

"Well, if you saw it I hope you liked it!" said Yashka.

The company laughed discreetly.

"No, I didn't like it," answered the schoolmaster; his tone of voice was suggestively serious, and silence fell on the listeners.

"I did what I could; in fact I tried to do my best," said Yashka, trying to brave it out, but feeling he was about to catch it from the schoolmaster. "My wife has had enough; she won't be able to get out of bed to-day."

The schoolmaster traced with his forefinger some figures on the table, and whilst examining them said:

"Look here, Yakoff, this is why I don't like it. Let us go thoroughly into the question of what you are doing, and of what may be the result of it. Your wife is with child, you beat her yesterday all over the body; you might, when you do that, kill the child, and when your wife is in labour she might die or be seriously ill. The trouble of having a sick wife is not pleasant; it may cost you also a good deal, for illness means medicine and medicine means money. If, even, you are fortunate enough not to have killed the child, you have certainly injured it, and it will very likely be born hunchbacked or crooked, and that means it wont be fit for work. It is of importance to you that the child should be able to earn its living. Even supposing it is only born delicate, that also will be an awkward business for you. It will be a burden to its mother, and it will require care and medicine. Do you see what you are laying up in store for yourself? Those who have to earn their living must be born healthy and bear healthy children. Am I not right?"

"Quite right," affirms the company.

"But let's hope this won't happen," says Yashka, rather taken aback by the picture drawn by the schoolmaster. "She's so strong one can't touch the child through her. Besides, what's to be done? she's such a devil. She nags and nags at me for the least trifle."

"I understand, Yakoff, that you can't resist beating your wife," continued the schoolmaster, in his quiet, thoughtful voice. "You may have many reasons for it, but it's not your wife's temper that causes you to beat her so unwisely. The cause is your unenlightened and miserable condition."

"That's just so," exclaimed Yakoff. "We do indeed live in darkness—in darkness as black as pitch!"

"The conditions of your life irritate you, and your wife has to suffer for it. She is the one nearest to you in the world, and she is the innocent sufferer just because you are the stronger of the two. She is always there ready to your hand; she can't get away from you. Don't you see how absurd it is of you?"

"That's all right, damn her! But what am I to do? Am I not a man?"

"Just so; you are a man. Well, don't you see what I want to explain to you? If you must beat her, do so; but beat her carefully. Remember that you can injure her health and that of the child. Remember, as a general rule, it is bad to beat a woman who is with child on the breasts, or the lower part of the body. Beat her on the back of the neck, or take a rope and strike her on the fleshy parts of the body."

As the orator finished his speech his sunken dark eyes glanced at the audience as if asking pardon or begging for something. The audience was in a lively, talkative mood. This morality of a has-been was to it perfectly intelligible—the morality of the vodka shop and of poverty.

"Well, brother Yashka, have you understood?"

"Damn it all! there's truth in what you say."

Yakoff understood one thing—that to beat his wife unwisely might be prejudicial to himself.

He kept silence, answering his friends' jokes with shame-faced smiles.

"And then again, look what a wife can be to one," philosophises Mokei Anissimoff. "One's wife is a friend, if you look at the matter in the right light. She is, as it were, chained to one for life, like a fellow-convict, and one must try and walk in step with her. If one gets out of step, the chain galls."

"Stop!" says Jakoff. "You beat your wife also, don't you?"

"I'm not saying I don't, because I do. How can I help it? I can't beat the wall with my fists when I feel I must beat something!"

"That's just how I feel," says Yakoff.

"What an existence is ours, brothers! So narrow and stifling, one can never have a real fling."

"One has even to beat one's wife with caution," humorously condoles someone.

Thus they would go on gossiping late into the night, or until a row would begin, provoked by their state of drunkenness, or by the impressions aroused by these conversations.

Outside the rain beats against the window and the icy wind howls wildly. Inside the air is close, heavy with smoke, but warm. In the street it is wet, cold, and dark; the gusts of wind seem to strike insolently against the window-panes as if inviting the company to go outside, and threatening to drive them like dust over the face of the earth. Now and then is heard in its howling a suppressed moan, followed at intervals by what sounds like a hoarse, chill laugh. These sounds suggest sad thoughts of coming winter; of the damp, short, sunless days, and of the long nights; of the necessity for providing warm clothes and much food. There is little sleep to be got during these long winter nights if one has an empty stomach! Winter is coming—is coming! How is one to live through it?

These sad thoughts encouraged thirst among the dwellers in the doss-house, and the sighs of the has-beens increased the number of wrinkles on their foreheads. Their voices sounded more hollow, and their dull, slow thought kept them, as it were, at a distance from each other. Suddenly amongst them there flashed forth anger like that of wild beasts or the desperation of those who are overdriven and crushed down by a cruel fate, or else they seemed to feel the proximity of that unrelenting foe who had twisted and contorted their lives into one long, cruel absurdity. But this foe was invulnerable because he was unknown.

Then they took to fighting, and they struck each other cruelly, wildly. After making it up again they would fall to drinking once more, and drink till they had pawned everything that the easy-going Vaviloff would accept as a pledge.

Thus, in dull anger, in trouble that crushed the heart, in the uncertainty of the issue of this miserable existence, they spent the autumn days awaiting the still harder days of winter. During hard times like these Kuvalda would come to their rescue with his philosophy.

"Pluck up courage, lads! All comes to an end!—that's what there is best about life! Winter will pass and summer will follow; good times when, as they say, 'even a sparrow has beer'!"

But his speeches were of little avail; a mouthful of pure water does not satisfy a hungry stomach.

Deacon Tarass would also try to amuse the company by singing songs and telling stories. He had more success. Sometimes his efforts would suddenly arouse desperate, wild gaiety in the vodka shop. They would sing, dance, shout with laughter, and for some hours would behave like maniacs. And then——

And then they would fall into a dull, indifferent state of despair as they sat round the ginshop table in the smoke of the lamps and the reek of tobacco; gloomy, ragged, letting words drop idly from their lips while they listened to the triumphant howl of the wind; one thought uppermost in their minds—how to get more vodka to drown their senses and to bring unconsciousness. And each of them hated the other with a deadly, senseless hatred, but hid that hatred deep down in his heart.

II

Everything in this world is relative, and there is no situation which cannot be matched with a worse one.

One fine day at the end of September Captain Kuvalda sat, as was his custom, in his armchair at the door of the doss-house looking at the big brick building erected by the merchant Petunikoff by the side of Vaviloff's vodka shop. Kuvalda was deep in thought.

This building, from which the scaffolding had not yet been removed, was destined to be a candle factory; and for some time it had been a thorn in the captain's side, with its row of dark, empty, hollow windows and its network of wood surrounding it from foundation to roof. Blood-red in colour, it resembled some cruel piece of machinery, not yet put into motion, but which had already opened its row of deep, greedy jaws ready to seize and gulp down everything that came in its way. The grey, wooden vodka shop of Vaviloff, with its crooked roof overgrown with moss, leaned up against one of the brick walls of the factory, giving the effect of a great parasite drawing its nourishment from it. The captain's mind was occupied by the thought that the old house would soon be replaced by a new one and the doss-house would be pulled down. He would have to seek another shelter, and it was doubtful if he would find one as cheap and as convenient. It was hard to be driven from a place one was used to, and harder still because some merchant wants to make candles and soap. And the captain felt that if he had the chance of spoiling the game of this enemy of his he would do it with the greatest pleasure.

Yesterday the merchant, Ivan Andreevitch Petunikoff was in the yard of the doss-house with his son and an architect. They made a survey of the yard and stuck in pegs all over the place, which, after Petunikoff had left, the captain ordered "The Meteor" to pull up and throw away.

The merchant was for ever before the captain's eyes— short, lean, shrivelled up, dressed in a long garment something between an overcoat and a jacket, with a velvet cap on his head, and wearing long, brightly polished boots. With prominent cheekbones and a grey, sharp-pointed beard; a high, wrinkled forehead, from under which peeped narrow, grey, half-closed, watchful eyes; a hooked, gristly nose and thin-lipped mouth—taken altogether the merchant gave the impression of being piously rapacious and venerably wicked.

"Damned offspring of a fox and a sow!" said the captain angrily to himself as he recalled some words of Petunikoff's.

The merchant had come with a member of the town

council to look at the house, and at the sight of the captain he had asked his companion in the abrupt dialect of Kostroma:

"Is that your tenant—that lunatic at large?"

And since that time, more than eighteen months ago, they had rivalled each other in the art of insult.

Yesterday again there had been a slight interchange of "holy words," as the captain called his conversations with the merchant. After having seen the architect off, Petunikoff approached the captain.

"What, still sitting—always sitting?" asked he, touching the peak of his cap in a way that left it uncertain whether he were fixing it on his head or bowing.

"And you—you are still on the prowl," echoed the captain, jerking out his lower jaw and making his beard wag in a way that might be taken for a bow by anyone not too exacting in these matters; it might also have been interpreted as the act of removing his pipe from one corner of his mouth to the other.

"I've plenty of money; that's why I'm always on the go. Money needs putting out, so I'm obliged to keep it moving," says the merchant in an aggravating voice to the other, screwing up his eyes slyly.

"Which means that you are the slave of money, and not money your slave," replies Kuvalda, resisting an intense desire to kick his enemy in the stomach.

"It's all the same either way where money is concerned. But if you have no money!"—and the merchant looked at the captain with bold but feigned compassion, while his trembling upper lip showed large, wolfish teeth.

"Anyone with a head on his shoulders and with a good conscience can do without it. Money generally comes when the conscience begins to grow a little out-at-elbows. The less honesty the more money!"

"That's true, but there are some people who have neither honesty nor money."

"That describes you when you were young, no doubt," said Kuvalda innocently.

Petunikoff wrinkles his nose, he sighs, closes his narrow eyes, and says, "Ah! when I was young what heavy burdens I had to bear!"

"Yes, I should think so!"

"I worked! Oh, how I worked!"

"Yes, you worked at outwitting others!"

"People like you and the nobility—what does it matter? Many of them have, thanks to me, learnt to extend the hand in Christ's name."

"Ah! then you did not assassinate, you only robbed?" interrupted the captain.

Petunikoff turns a sickly green and thinks it is time to change the conversation.

"You are not an over polite host; you remain sitting while your visitor stands."

"Well, he can sit down."

"There is nothing to sit on."

"There is the ground. The ground never rejects any filth!"

"You prove that rule, but I had better leave you, you blackguard!" says Petunikoff coolly, though his eyes dart cold venom at the captain.

He went off, leaving Kuvalda with the agreeable sensation that the merchant was afraid of him. If it were not so he would have turned him out of the doss-house long ago. It was not for the five roubles a month that he let him remain on!
... And the captain watches with pleasure the slowly retreating back of Petunikoff, as he walks slowly away. Kuvalda's eyes still follow the merchant as he climbs up and down the scaffolding of his new building. He feels an intense desire that the merchant should fall and break his back. How many times has he not conjured up results of this imaginary fall, as he has sat watching Petunikoff crawling about the scaffolding of his new factory, like a spider crawling

about its net. Yesterday he had even imagined that one of the boards had given way under the weight of the merchant; and Kuvalda had jumped out of his seat with excitement—but nothing had come of it.

And to day, as always, before the eyes of Aristide Kuvalda, stands the great red building, so four-square, so solid, so firmly fixed into the ground, as if already drawing from thence its nourishment. It seemed as if mocking the captain through the cold dark yawning openings in its walls. And the sun poured on it its autumn rays with the same prodigality as on the distorted tumble-down little houses of the neighbourhood.

"But what if?" exclaimed the captain to himself, measuring with his eye the factory wall. "What if?"

Aroused and excited by the thought which had come into his mind, Aristide Kuvalda jumped up and hastened over to Vaviloff's vodka shop, smiling, and muttering something to himself. Vaviloff met him at the counter with a friendly exclamation: "How is your Excellency this morning?"

Vaviloff was a man of medium height, with a bald head surrounded by a fringe of grey hair; with clean-shaved cheeks, and moustache bristly as a toothbrush. Upright and active, in a dirty braided jacket, every movement betrayed the old soldier, the former non-commissioned officer.

"Yegor! Have you the deeds and the plan of your house and property?" Kuvalda asked hastily.

"Yes, I have."

And Vaviloff closed his suspicious thievish eyes and scrutinised the captain's face, in which he observed something out of the common.

"Just show them to me!" exclaimed the captain, thumping on the counter with his fist, and dropping on to a stool.

"What for?" asked Vaviloff, who decided, in view of the captain's state of excitement, to be on his guard.

"You fool! Bring them at once!"

Vaviloff wrinkled his forehead, and looked up inquiringly at the ceiling.

"By the by, where the devil are those papers?"

Not finding any information on this question on the ceiling, the old soldier dropped his eyes towards the ground, and began thoughtfully drumming with his fingers on the counter.

"Stop those antics!" shouted Kuvalda, who had no love for the old soldier; as according to the captain it was better for a former non-commissioned officer to be a thief than a keeper of a vodka shop.

"Well now, Aristide Kuvalda, I think I remember! I believe those papers were left at the law-courts at the time when——"

"Yegorka! stop this fooling. It's to your own interest to do so. Show me the plans, the deed of sale, and all that you have got at once! Perhaps you will gain by this more than a hundred roubles! Do you understand now?"

Vaviloff understood nothing; but the captain spoke in such an authoritative and serious tone that the eyes of the old soldier sparkled with intense curiosity: and saying that he would go and see if the papers were not in his strong box, he disappeared behind the door of the counter. In a few moments he returned with the papers in his hand, and a look of great surprise on his coarse face.

"Just see! The damned things were after all in the house!"

"You circus clown! Who would think you had been a soldier!"

Kuvalda could not resist trying to shame him, whilst snatching from his hands the cotton case containing the blue legal paper. Then he spread the papers out before him, thus exciting more and more the curiosity of Vaviloff, and began reading and scrutinising them; uttering from time to time interjections in a meaning tone. Finally, he rose with an air of decision, went to the door leaving the papers on the counter, shouting out to Vaviloff:

"Wait a moment! Don't put them away yet!"

Vaviloff gathered up the papers, put them in his cash box, locked it, felt to see that it was securely fastened. Then rubbing his bald head, he went and stood in the doorway of his shop. There he saw the captain measuring with his stride the length of the front of the vodka shop, whilst he snapped his fingers from time to time, and once more began his measurements—anxious but satisfied.

Vaviloff's face wore at first a worried expression; then it grew long, and at last it suddenly beamed with joy.

"Aristide Fomitch! Is it possible?" he exclaimed, as the captain drew near.

"Of course it's possible! More than a yard has been taken off! That's only as far as the frontage is concerned; as to the depth, I will see about that now!"

"The depth is thirty-two yards!"

"Well, I see you've guessed what I'm after. You stupid fool!"

"Well, you're a wonder, Aristide Fomitch! You've an eye that sees two yards into the ground!" exclaimed the delighted Vaviloff. A few minutes later they were seated opposite each other in Vaviloff's room, and the captain was swallowing great gulps of beer, and saying to the landlord:

"You see therefore all the factory wall stands on your ground. Act without mercy. When the schoolmaster comes we will draw up a report for the law courts. We will reckon the damages at a moderate figure, so that the revenue stamps shan't cost us too much, but we will ask that the wall shall be pulled down. This sort of thing, you fool, is called a violation of boundaries, and it's a stroke of luck for you! To pull a great wall like that down and move it further back is not such an easy business, and costs no end of money. Now's your chance for squeezing Judas! We will make a calculation of what the pulling down will cost, taking into consideration the value of the broken bricks and the cost of digging out the new foundations. We will calculate everything, even the value of the time, and then, O just Judas, what do you say to two thousand roubles?"

"He won't give it!" exclaimed Vaviloff anxiously, blinking his eyes, which were sparkling with greedy fire.

"Let him try and get out of it! Just look, what can he do? There will be nothing for him but to pull it down. But look out, Yegor! Don't let yourself be worsted in the bargain. They will try and buy you off! Mind you don't let them off too easily! They will try and frighten you; don't you be afraid; rely on us to back you up!"

The captain's eyes burnt with wild delight, and his face, purple with excitement, twitched nervously. He had succeeded in arousing the greed of the ginshop keeper, and after having persuaded him to commence proceedings as soon as possible, went off triumphant, and implacably revengeful.

That evening all the outcasts learnt the discovery that the captain had made, and discussed eagerly the future proceedings of Petunikoff, representing to themselves vividly his astonishment and anger, the day when he should have the copy of the lawsuit presented to him. The captain was the hero of the day. He was happy, and all around were pleased. A heap of dark tattered figures lay about in the yard, talking noisily and eagerly, animated by the important event. All knew Petunikoff, who often passed near them, blinking his eyes disdainfully, and paying as little attention to them as he did to the rest of the rubbish lying about in the yard. He was a picture of self-satisfaction, and this irritated them; even his boots seemed to shine disdainfully at them But now the shopkeeper's pocket and his self-esteem were going to be hurt by one of themselves! Wasn't that an excellent joke?

Evil had a singular attraction for these people; it was the only weapon which came easily to their hands, and which was within their reach. For a long time now, each of them had cultivated within himself dim half-conscious feelings of keen hatred against all who, unlike themselves, were neither hungry nor ragged. This was why all the dossers felt such an intense interest in the war declared by Kuvalda against the shopkeeper Petunikoff. Two whole weeks the dwellers in the doss-house had been living on the expectation of new developments, and during all that time Petunikoff did not once come to visit the almost completed building. They assured each other that he was out of town, and that the summons had not therefore yet been served upon him. Kuvalda raged against the delays of civil procedure. It is doubtful if anyone ever awaited the arrival of the merchant so impatiently as did these tramps.

> "He comes not, he comes not!
> Alas! he loves me not!"

sang the Deacon Tarass, leaning his chin on his hand, and gazing with a comically sad expression up the hill.

But one fine day, towards evening, Petunikoff appeared. He arrived in a strong light cart, driven by his son, a young man with red cheeks and wearing a long checked overcoat, and smoked blue spectacles. They tied up the horse; the son drew from his pocket a tape measure, gave one end of it to his father, and both of them silently, and with anxious expressions, began measuring the ground.

"Ah!" exclaimed triumphantly the captain.

All who were about the doss-house went and stood outside the gate watching the proceedings and expressing aloud their opinions on what was going forward.

"See what it is to have the habit of stealing! A man steals unconsciously, not intending to steal, and thereby risks more than he can gain," said the captain with mock sympathy; thereby arousing laughter among his body-guard, and provoking a whole string of remarks in the same strain.

"Look out! you rogue," exclaimed Petunikoff at length, exasperated by these jibes. "If you don't mind I'll have you up before the magistrate."

"It's of no use without witnesses, and a son can't give evidence for a father," the captain reminded him.

"All right; we shall see! Though you seem such a bold leader you may find your match some day."

And Petunikoff shook his forefinger at him. The son, quiet and deeply interested in his calculations, paid no heed to this group of squalid figures, who were cruelly mocking his father. He never looked once towards them.

"The young spider is well trained!" remarked "Leavings," who was following the actions and the movements of the younger Petunikoff.

Having taken all the necessary measurements, Ivan Andreevitch frowned, climbed silently into his cart and drove off, whilst his son, with firm decided steps, entered Vaviloff's vodka shop, and disappeared.

"He's a precious young thief! that he is. We shall see what comes of it!" said Kuvalda.

"What will come of it? Why, Petunikoff junior will square Yegor Vaviloff!" remarked "Leavings" with great assurance, smacking his lips, and with a look of keen satisfaction on his cunning face.

"That would please you perhaps?" asked Kuvalda severely.

"It pleases me to see human calculations go wrong!" said "Leavings," blinking his eyes and rubbing his hands.

The captain spat angrily, and kept silence. The rest of them, standing at the gate of the tumble-down house, watched silently the door of the vodka shop. An hour and more passed in this silent expectation. At length the door opened, and young Petunikoff appeared, looking as calm as when he had entered. He paused for a moment, cleared his throat, raised his coat collar, glanced at those who were watching his movements, and turned up the street towards the town.

The captain watched him till he was out of sight, and, turning towards "Leavings," smiled ironically and said:

"It seems after all as if you might be right, you son of a scorpion and of a centipede! You smell out everything that's evil. One can see by the dirty mug of the young rogue that he has got his own way! I wonder how much Yegor has screwed out of him? He's got something, that's sure! They're birds of a feather. I'm damned if I haven't arranged it all for them. It's cursed hard to think what a fool I've been. You see, mates, life is dead against us. One can't even spit into one's neighbour's face—the spittle flies back into one's own eyes."

Consoling himself with this speech, the venerable captain glanced at his body-guard. All were disappointed, for all felt that what had taken place between Vaviloff and Petunikoff had turned out differently from what they had expected, and all felt annoyed. The consciousness of being unable to cause evil is more obnoxious to men than the consciousness of being unable to do good; it is so simple and so easy to do evil!"

"Well! what's the use of sticking here? We have nothing to wait for except for Yegorka to stand us treat," said the captain, glowering angrily at the vodka shop. "It's all up with our peaceful and happy life under Judas's roof. He'll send us packing now; so I give you all notice, my department of *sans-culottes!*"

"The End" laughed morosely.

"Now then, jailer, what's the matter with you?" asked Kuvalda.

"Where the devil am I to go?"

"That indeed is a serious question, my friend. But never fear, your fate will decide it for you," said the captain, turning towards the doss-house.

The has-beens followed him idly.

"We shall await the critical moment," said the captain, walking along with them. "When we get the sack there will be time enough to look out for another shelter. Meanwhile, what's the use of spoiling life with troubles like that? It is at critical moments that man rises to the occasion, and if life as a whole were to consist of nothing but critical moments, if one had to tremble every minute of one's life for the safety of one's carcase, I'll be hanged if life wouldn't be more lively, and people more interesting!"

"Which would mean that people would fly at each other's throats more savagely than they do now."

"Well, what of that?" struck in the captain, who did not care to have his ideas enlarged on.

"Nothing! nothing. It's all right—when one wants to get to one's destination quickly, one thrashes the horse, or one stokes up one's machine."

"Yes, that's it; let everything go full speed to the devil. I should be only too glad if the earth would suddenly take fire, burst up and go to pieces, only I should like to be the last man left, to see the others."

"You're a nice one!"

"What of that? I'm a has-been, am I not? I'm freed from all chains and fetters; therefore I can spit at everything. By the very nature of the life I lead now, I am bound to drop everything to do with the past—all fine manners and conventional ideas of people who are well fed, and well dressed, and who despise me because I am not equally well fed and dressed. So I have to cultivate in myself something fresh and new—don't you see—something you know which will make people like Judas Petunikoff, when they pass by me, feel a cold shudder run down their backs!"

"You have a bold tongue!"

"You miserable wretch!" said Kuvalda. "What do you understand, what do you know? You don't even know how to think! But I have thought much, I have read books of which you would not have understood a word."

"Oh! I know I'm not fit to black the boots of such a learned man! But though you have read and thought so much, and I have done neither the one nor the other, yet we are not after all so far apart."

"Go to the devil!" exclaimed Kuvalda.

His conversations with "Leavings" always finished in this way. When the schoolmaster was not about, the captain knew well that his speeches were only wasted, and were lost for want of understanding and appreciation. But for all that, he couldn't help talking, and now, having snubbed his interlocutor, he felt himself lonely amongst the others. His desire for conversation was not, however, satisfied, and he turned therefore to Simtsoff with a question.

"And you, Alexei Maximovitch, where will you lay your old head?" The old man smiled good-naturedly, rubbed his nose with his hand, and explained:

"Don't know! Shall see by and by. I'm not of much account. A glass of vodka, that's all I want."

"A very praiseworthy ambition, and very simple," said the captain.

After a short silence Simtsoff added that he would find shelter more easily than the rest, because the women liked him.

This was true, for the old man had always two or three mistresses among the prostitutes, who would keep him sometimes for two or three days at a time on their scanty earnings. They often beat him, but he took it stoically. For some reason or other they never hurt him much; perhaps they pitied him. He was a great admirer of women, but added that they were the cause of all his misfortunes in life. The close terms on which he lived with women, and the character of their relations towards him, were shown by the fact that his clothes were always neatly mended, and cleaner than the clothes of his companions. Seated now on the ground at the door of the doss-house amidst his mates, he boastfully related that he had for some time been asked by Riedka to go and live with her, but that he had till now refused, not wanting to give up the present company.

He was listened to with interest, mingled with envy. All knew Riedka; she lived not far down the hill, and only a few months ago she came out of prison after serving a second term for theft. She had formerly been a wet nurse; a tall, stout, strapping countrywoman, with a pock-marked face, and fine eyes, somewhat dulled by drink.

"The old rogue!" cursed "Leavings," watching Simtsoff, who smiled with self-satisfaction.

"And do you know why they all like me? Because I understand what their souls need."

"Indeed?" exclaimed Kuvalda interrogatively.

"I know how to make women pity me. And when a woman's pity is aroused, she can even kill out of pure pity! Weep before her, and implore her to kill; she will have pity on you, and will kill."

"It's I who would kill!" exclaimed Martianoff in a decided voice, with a dark scowl.

"Whom do you mean?" asked "Leavings," edging away from him.

"It's all the same to me! Petunikoff—Yegorka—you if you like!"

"Why?" asked Kuvalda, with aroused interest.

"I want to be sent to Siberia. I'm tired of this stupid life. There one will know what to do with one's life."

"Hm!" said the captain reflectively. "You will indeed know what to do with your life there!"

Nothing more was spoken about Petunikoff, nor of their impending expulsion from the doss-house. All were sure that this expulsion was imminent, was perhaps a matter of a few days only; and they therefore considered it useless to discuss the point further. Discussion wouldn't make it easier; besides, it was not cold yet, though the rainy season had begun. One could sleep on the ground anywhere outside the town.

Seated in a circle on the grass, they chatted idly and aimlessly, changing easily from one topic to another, and paying only just as much attention to the words of their companions as was absolutely necessary to prevent the conversation from dropping. It was a nuisance to have to be silent, but it was equally a nuisance to have to listen with attention. This society of creatures that once were men had one great virtue; no one ever made an effort to appear better than he was, nor forced others to try and appear better than they were.

The August sun was shedding its warmth impartially on the rags that covered their backs, and on their uncombed heads—a chaotic blending of animal, vegetable and mineral matter. In the corners of the yard, weeds grew luxuriantly —tall agrimony, all covered with prickles, and other useless plants, whose growth rejoiced the eyes of none but these equally useless people.

In Vaviloff's vodka shop the following scene had been going forward.

Petunikoff junior entered, leisurely looked around, made a disdainful grimace, and slowly removing his grey hat, asked the landlord, who met him with an amiable bow, and a respectful smile:

"Are you Yegor Terentievitch Vaviloff?"

"That's myself!" answered the old soldier, leaning on the counter with both hands, as if ready with one bound to jump over.

"I have some business to transact with you," said Petunikoff.

"Delighted! Won't you come into the back-room?"

They went into the back part of the house, and sat down before a round table; the visitor on a sofa covered with oil-cloth, and the host on a chair opposite to him.

In one corner of the room a lamp burnt before a shrine, around which on the walls hung ikons, the gold backgrounds of which were carefully burnished, and shone as if new. In the room, piled up with boxes and old furniture, there was a mingled smell of paraffin oil, of tobacco, and of sour cabbage. Petunikoff glanced around, and made another grimace. Vaviloff with a sigh glanced up at the images, and then they scrutinised each other attentively, and each produced on the other a favourable impression. Petunikoff was pleased with Vaviloff's frankly thievish eyes, and Vaviloff was satisfied with the cold, decided countenance of Petunikoff, with its broad jaw and strong white teeth.

"You know me, of course, and can guess my errand," began Petunikoff.

"About the summons, I guess," replied the old soldier respectfully.

"Just so! I'm glad to see that you are straightforward, and attack the matter like an open-hearted man," continued Petunikoff encouragingly.

"You see I'm a soldier," modestly suggested the other.

"I can see that. Let us tackle this business as quickly and as straightforwardly as possible, and get it over."

"By all means!"

"Your complaint is quite in order, and there is no doubt but that you have right on your side. I think it better to tell you that at once."

"Much obliged to you," said the soldier, blinking his eyes to conceal a smile.

"But I should like to know why you thought it best to begin an acquaintance with us, your future neighbours, so unpleasantly—with a lawsuit?"

Vaviloff shrugged his shoulders, and was silent.

"It would have been better for you to have come to us, and we could have arranged matters between us. Don't you think so?"

"That indeed would have been pleasanter. But, don't you see? there was a little hitch. I didn't act altogether on my own. I was set on by someone else; afterwards I understood what would have been best, but it was too late then."

"That's just it. I suppose it was some lawyer who put you up to it!"

"Something of that sort."

"Yes, yes. And now you are willing to settle things out of court?"

"That's my great wish!" exclaimed the soldier.

Petunikoff remained silent for a moment, then glanced at the landlord and said in an abrupt dry voice:

"And why do you wish it now, may I ask?"

Vaviloff did not expect this question, and was not prepared for an immediate answer. He considered it an idle question, and shrugging his shoulders with a look of superiority, smiled sneeringly at Petunikoff.

"Why? Well, it's easy to understand: because one must live with others in peace."

"Come!" interrupted Petunikoff, "it isn't altogether that! I see you don't clearly understand yourself why it is so necessary for you to live in peace with us. I will explain it to you."

The soldier was slightly surprised. This queer-looking young fellow in his check suit was holding forth to him just as Commander Rashkin used to do, who when he got angry would knock out three teeth at a time from the head of one of his troopers.

"It is necessary for you to live in peace with us because it will be profitable to you to have us as neighbours. And it will be profitable because we shall employ at least a hundred and fifty workmen at first, and more as time goes on. If a hundred of these on each weekly pay-day drink a glass of vodka, it means that during the month you will sell four hundred glasses more than you do at present. This is taking it at the lowest calculation; besides that, there's the catering for them. You don't seem a fool, and you've had some experience; don't you see now the advantage that our neighbourhood will be to you!"

"It's true!" said Vaviloff, nodding his head. "I knew it."

"Well then——"

The young merchant raised his voice.

"Oh! nothing. Let's arrange terms."

"I'm delighted you make up your mind so promptly. I have here a declaration prepared in readiness, declaring that you are willing to stop proceedings against my father. Read it and sign it.

Vaviloff glanced with round eyes at his interlocutor, with a presentiment that something exceedingly disagreeable was coming.

"Wait a moment. Sign what—what do you mean?"

"Simply write your name and your family name here," said Petunikoff, politely pointing out with his finger the place left for the signature.

"That's not what I mean—that is, I mean, what compensation will you give me for the land?"

"The land is of no use to you," said Petunikoff soothingly.

"Still it's mine!" exclaimed the soldier.

"To be sure. But how much would you claim?"

"Well, let's say the sum named in the summons. The amount is stated there," suggested Vaviloff hesitatingly.

"Six hundred?" Petunikoff laughed as if highly amused. "That's a good joke!"

"I have a right to it! I can even claim two thousand! I can insist on your pulling down the wall; and that is what I want. That's why the sum claimed is so small. I demand that you should pull it down!"

"Go on with it then! We shall perhaps have to pull it down, but not for two or three years—not till you have been involved in heavy law expenses. After that we shall open a vodka shop of our own, which will be better than yours, and you will go to the wall! You'll be ruined, my friend, we'll take care of that. We might be taking steps to start the vodka shop at once, but we are busy just now, have got our hands full; besides, we are sorry for you. Why should one take the bread out of a man's mouth without a reason?"

Yegor Terentievitch clenched his teeth, feeling that his visitor held his fate in his hands. Vaviloff felt pity for himself, brought face to face as he was with this cold, mercenary, implacable person in his ridiculous check suit.

"And living so near us, and being on friendly terms with us, you, my friend, might have turned a pretty penny. We might have helped you also; for instance, I should advise you at once to open a little shop—tobacco, matches, bread, cucumbers, and so on. You'd find plenty of customers."

Vaviloff listened, and not being a fool, understood that the best for him at present was to trust to the generosity of his enemy. In fact, he ought to have begun by that; and not being able any longer to conceal his anger and his humiliation, he burst out into loud imprecations against Kuvalda.

"Drunkard! Cursed swine—may the devil take him!"

"That's meant for the lawyer who worded your report?" asked Petunikoff quietly, and added with a sigh: "Indeed he might have served you a bad turn if we hadn't taken pity on you!"

"Ah!" sighed the distressed soldier, letting his hands fall in despair. "There were two of them—one started the business, and the other one did the writing, the cursed scribbler!"

"How, a newspaper scribbler?"

"Well, he writes for the newspapers. They are both of them tenants of yours. Nice sort of people they are! Get rid of them, send them off for God's sake! They are robbers; they set everyone in the street against each other, there is no peace with them, they have no respect for law or order. One has always to be on one's guard with them against robbery or arson."

"But this newspaper scribbler, who is he?" asked Petunikoff in an interested tone.

"He? He's a drunkard. He was a school-teacher, and got turned away. He has drunk all he had, and now he writes for the newspapers, and invents petitions. He's a real bad 'un!"

"Hm-m! And it was he, then, who wrote your petition? Just so! Evidently it was he who wrote about the construction of the scaffolding. He seemed to suggest that the scaffolding was not built according to the bye-laws."

"That's he! That's just like him, the dog! He read it here, and was boasting that he would run Petunikoff into expense!"

"Hm-m! Well, how about coming to terms?"

"To terms?" the soldier dropped his head and grew thoughtful. "Ah! what a miserable dark existence ours is!" he exclaimed sadly, scratching the back of his head.

"You must begin to improve it!" said Petunikoff, lighting a cigarette.

"Improve it? That's easy to say, sir! But we have no liberty! that's what is the matter. Just look at my life, sir. I'm always in terror, always on my guard, and have no freedom of action. And why is that? Fear! This wretch of a schoolmaster may write to the newspapers about me, he sets the sanitary authorities at me, and I have to pay fines. One has always to be on one's guard against these lodgers of yours, lest they burn, murder or rob one! How can I stop them? They don't fear the police! If they do get clapped into prison, they are only glad; because it means free rations!"

"Well, we'll get rid of them if we come to terms with you," Petunikoff promised.

"And what shall the terms be?" asked Vaviloff, anxiously and gloomily.

"State your own terms."

"Well, then, let it be the six hundred mentioned in the summons!"

"Wouldn't a hundred be enough?" said the trader, in a calm voice.

He watched the landlord narrowly, and smiling gently, added, "I won't give a rouble more!"

After saying this he removed his spectacles, and began slowly wiping the glasses with his handkerchief. Vaviloff, sick at heart, looked at him, experiencing every moment towards him a feeling of greater respect. In the quiet face of young

Petunikoff, in his large grey eyes and prominent cheek-bones, and in his whole coarse, robust figure, there was so much self-reliant force, sure of itself, and well disciplined by the mind. Besides, Vaviloff liked the way that Petunikoff spoke to him; his voice possessed simple friendly intonations, and there was no striving after effect, just as if he were speaking to an equal; though Vaviloff well understood that he, a soldier, was not the equal of this man.

Watching him almost with admiration, the soldier felt within himself a rush of eager curiosity, which for a moment checked all other feeling, so that he could not help asking Petunikoff in a respectful voice:

"Where did you study?"

"At the Technological Institution. But why do you ask?" replied the other, smiling.

"Oh! nothing; I beg your pardon."

The soldier dropped his head, and suddenly exclaimed in a voice that was almost inspired, so full was it of admiration and of envy, "Yes! that's what education can do! Knowledge is indeed enlightenment, and that means everything! And we others, we are like owls looking at the sun. Bad luck to us! Well, sir, let us settle up this affair."

And with a decided gesture he stretched out his hand to Petunikoff, and said in a half-choking voice:

"Let's say five hundred!"

"Not more than a hundred roubles, Yegor Terentievitch!"

Petunikoff shrugged his shoulders, as if regretting not being able to give more, and patted the soldier's hairy hand with his large white one.

They soon clinched the bargain now, for the soldier suddenly started with long strides to meet the terms of Petunikoff, who remained implacably firm. When Vaviloff had received the hundred roubles, and signed the paper, he dashed the pen on the table, exclaiming: "That's done! Now I'll have to settle up with that band of tramps. They'll bother the life out of me, the devils!"

"You can tell them that I paid you all that you demanded in the summons," suggested Petunikoff, puffing out thin rings of smoke, and watching them rise and vanish.

"They'll never believe that! they are clever rogues; as sharp as——"

Vaviloff stopped just in time, confused at the thought of the comparison which almost escaped from his lips, and glanced nervously at the merchant's son. But this latter went on smoking, and seemed wholly engrossed with that occupation. He left soon after, promising Vaviloff, as he bade him good-bye, to destroy ere long this nest of noxious beings. Vaviloff watched him, sighing, and feeling a keen desire to shout something malicious and offensive at the man who walked with firm steps up the steep road, striding over the ruts and heaps of rubbish.

That same evening the captain appeared at the vodka shop; his brows were knit severely, and his right hand was firmly clenched. Vaviloff glanced at him deprecatingly.

"Well, you worthy descendant of Cain and of Judas! tell us all about it!"

"It's all settled!" said Vaviloff, sighing and dropping his eyes.

"I don't doubt it. How many shekels did you get?"

"Four hundred roubles down!"

"A lie! as sure as I live! Well, so much the better for me. Without any more talking, Yegorka, hand me over ten per cent. for my discovery; twenty-five roubles for the schoolmaster for writing out the summons, and a gallon of vodka for the company, with grub to match. Hand the money over at once, and the vodka with the rest must be ready by eight o'clock!"

Vaviloff turned green, and stared at Kuvalda with wide-open eyes.

"Don't you wish you may get it! That's downright robbery! I'm not going to give it. Are you in your senses to suggest such a thing, Aristide Fomitch? You'll have to keep your appetite till the next holiday comes round; things have changed, and I'm in a position not to be afraid of you now, I am!"

Kuvalda glanced at the clock.

"I give you, Yegor, ten minutes for your fool's chatter! Then stop wagging your tongue and give me what I demand! If you don't—then look out for yourself! Do you remember reading in the paper about that robbery at Bassoff's? Well, 'The End' has been selling things to you—you understand? You shan't have time to hide anything; we'll see to that; and this very night, you understand?"

"Aristide Fomitch! Why are you so hard on me?" wailed the old soldier.

"No more cackle! Have you understood? Yes or no?"

Kuvalda, tall and grey-headed, frowning impressively, spoke in a low voice, whose hoarse bass resounded threateningly in the empty vodka shop. At the best of times Vaviloff was afraid of him as a man who had been once an officer, and as an individual who had now nothing to lose. But at this moment he beheld Kuvalda in a new light; unlike his usual manner the captain spoke little, but his words were those of one who expected obedience, and in his voice there was an implied threat. Vaviloff felt that the captain could, if he chose, destroy him with pleasure. He had to give way to force, but choking with rage, he tried once more to escape his punishment. He sighed deeply, and began humbly:

"It would seem the proverb is right which says, 'You reap what you sow.' Aristide Fomitch, I have lied to you! I wanted to make myself out cleverer than I really am. All I got was a hundred roubles."

"Well! what then?" asked Kuvalda, curtly.

"It wasn't four hundred, as I told you, and that means——"

"It means nothing! How am I to know whether you were lying then or now? I mean to have sixty-five roubles out of you. That's only reasonable, so now."

"Ah! my God! Aristide Fomitch, I have always paid you your due!"

"Come! no more words, Yegorka; you descendant of Judas!"

"I will give it to you then, but God will punish you for this:!"

"Silence! you scab!" roared the captain, rolling his eyes savagely. "I am sufficiently punished by God already. He has placed me in a position in which I am obliged to see you and talk to you. I'll crush you here on the spot like a fly."

And he shook his fist under Vaviloff's nose, and gnashed his teeth.

After he had left, Vaviloff smiled cunningly and blinked his eyes rapidly. Then two large tears rolled down his cheeks. They were hot and grimy, and as they disappeared into his beard, two others rolled down in their place. Then Vaviloff retired into the back room, and knelt in front of the ikons; he remained there for some time motionless, without wiping the tears from his wrinkled brown cheeks.

Deacon Tarass, who had always a fancy for the open air, proposed to the creatures that once were men that they should go out into the fields, and there in one of the hollows in the midst of nature's beauties, and under the open sky, should drink Vaviloff's vodka. But the captain and the others unanimously scouted the deacon's ideas of nature, and decided to have their carouse in their own yard.

"One, two, three," reckoned Aristide Fomitch, "we are thirteen in all; the schoolmaster is missing, but some other waifs and strays are sure to turn up, so let's say twenty. Two cucumbers and a half for each, a pound of bread and of meat—that's not a bad allowance! As to vodka, there will be about a bottle each. There's some sour cabbage, some apples and three melons. What the devil do we want more? What do you say, mates? Let us therefore prepare to devour Yegor Vaviloff; for all this is his body, and his blood!"

They spread some ragged garments on the ground, on which they laid out their food and drink, and they crouched round in a circle, restraining with difficulty the thirst for drink which lurked in the eyes of each one of them.

Evening was coming on, its shadows fell across the foul, untidy yard, and the last rays of the sun lit up the roof of the half-ruined house. The evening was cool and calm.

"Let us fall to, brethren!" commanded the captain. "How many mugs have we? Only six, and there are thirteen of us. Alexei Maximovitch, pour out the drink! Make ready! Present! Fire!"

"Ach—h!" They swallowed down great gulps, and then fell to eating.

"But the schoolmaster isn't here! I haven't seen him for three days. Has anyone else seen him?" said Kuvalda.

"No one."

"That's not like him! Well, never mind, let's have another drink! Let's drink to the health of Aristide Kuvalda, my only friend, who during all my lifetime has never once forsaken me; though, devil take it, if he had deprived me of his society sometimes I might have been the gainer."

"That's well said," cried "Leavings," clearing his throat.

The captain, conscious of his superiority, looked round at his cronies, but said nothing, for he was eating.

After drinking two glasses the company brightened up; for the measures were full ones. "Tarass and a half" humbly expressed a wish for a story, but the deacon was eagerly engaged discussing with "The Top" the superiority of thin women over fat ones, and took no notice of his friend's words, defending his point of view with the eagerness and fervour of a man deeply convinced of the truth of his opinion. The naïve face of "The Meteor," who was lying beside him on his stomach, expressed admiration and delight at the suggestive words of the disputants. Martianoff, hugging his knees with his huge, hairy hands, glanced gloomily and silently at the vodka bottle, while he constantly made attempts to catch his moustache with his tongue and gnaw it with his teeth. "Leavings" was teasing Tiapa.

"I know now where you hide your money, you old ogre!"

"All the better for you!" hissed Tiapa in a hoarse voice.

"I'll manage to get hold of it some day!"

"Do it if you can!"

Kuvalda felt bored amongst this set of people; there was not one worthy to hear his eloquence, or capable of understanding it.

"Where the devil can the schoolmaster be?" he said, expressing his thought aloud.

Martianoff looked at him, and said:

"He will return."

"I am certain he will come back on foot, and not in a carriage! Let us drink to your future, you born convict. If you murder a man who has got some money, go shares with me. Then, old chap, I shall start for America, make tracks for those lampas—pampas—what do you call them! I shall go there and rise at length to be President of the United States. Then I shall declare war against Europe, and won't I give it them hot? As to an army, I shall buy mercenaries in Europe itself. I shall invite the French, the Germans, and the Turks, and the whole lot of them, and I shall use them to beat their own relations. Just as Ilia de Murometz conquered the Tartars with the Tartars. With money one can become even an Ilia, and destroy Europe, and hire Judas Petunikoff as one's servant. He'd work if one gave him a hundred roubles a month, that he would, I'm sure. But he'd be a bad servant: he'd begin by stealing."

"And besides, a thin woman is better than a fat one because she costs less," eagerly continued the deacon. "My first deaconess used to buy twelve yards for a dress, and the second one only ten. It's the same with food."

"Tarass and a half" smiled deprecatingly, turned his face towards the deacon, fixed his one eye on him and shyly suggested in an embarrassed tone:

"I also had a wife once."

"That may happen to anybody," observed Kuvalda. "Go on with your lies!"

"She was thin, but she ate a great deal: it was even the cause of her death."

"You poisoned her, you one-eyed beggar!" said "Leavings" with conviction.

"No! on my word I didn't; she ate too much pickled herring."

"And I tell you, you did! you poisoned her," "Leavings" repeated with further assurance.

It was often his way, after having said some absurdity, to continue to repeat it, without bringing forward any grounds of confirmation; and beginning in a pettish childish tone, he would gradually work himself up into a rage.

The deacon took up the cudgels for his friend.

"He couldn't have poisoned her, he had no reason to do so."

"And I say he did poison her!"

'Shut up!" shouted the captain in a threatening voice.

His sense of boredom was gradually changing into suppressed anger. With savage eyes he glanced round at the company, and not finding anything in their already half-drunken faces that might serve as an excuse for his fury, he dropped his head on his breast, remained sitting thus for a few moments, and then stretched himself full length on the ground, with his face upwards. "The Meteor" was gnawing cucumbers; he would take one in his hand, without looking at it, thrust half of it into his mouth, and then suddenly bite it in two with his large yellow teeth, so that the salt juice oozed out on either side and wetted his cheeks. He was clearly not hungry, but this proceeding amused him. Martianoff remained motionless as a statue in the position he had taken, stretched on the ground and absorbed in gloomily watching the barrel of vodka, which was, by this time, more than half empty. Tiapa had his eyes fixed on the ground, whilst he masticated noisily the meat which would not yield to his old teeth. "Leavings" lay on his belly, coughing from time to time, whilst convulsive movements shook all his small body. The rest of the silent dark figures sat or lay about in various positions, and these ragged objects were scarcely distinguishable in the twilight from the heaps of rubbish half overgrown with weeds which were strewn about the yard. Their bent, crouching forms, and their tatters gave them the look of hideous animals, created by some coarse and freakish power, in mockery of man.

> "There lived in Suzdal
> A lady of small renown;
> She suffered from cramps and pains,
> And very disagreeable they were . . ."

sang the deacon in a low voice, embracing Alexei Maximovitch, who smiled back stupidly in his face. "Tarass and a half" leered lasciviously.

Night was coming on. Stars glittered in the sky; on the hill towards the town the lights began to show. The prolonged wail of the steamers' whistles was heard from the river; the door of Vaviloff's vodka shop opened with a creaking noise, and a sound of cracking glass. Two dark figures entered the yard and approached the group of men seated round the vodka barrel, one of them asking in a hoarse voice:

"You are drinking?"

Whilst the other figure exclaimed in a low tone, envy and delight in his voice:

"What a set of lucky devils!"

Then over the head of the deacon a hand was stretched out and seized the bottle; and the peculiar gurgling sound was heard of vodka being poured from the bottle into a glass. Then someone coughed loudly.

"How dull you all are!" exclaimed the deacon. "Come, you one-eyed beggar, let's recall old times and have a song! Let us sing *By the waters of Babylon*."

"Does he know it?" asked Simtsoff.

"He? Why, he was the soloist in the archbishop's choir. Come now, begin! *By—the—waters—of—Babylon.*"

The voice of the deacon was wild, hoarse, and broken, whilst his friend sang with a whining falsetto. The doss-house, shrouded in darkness, seemed either to have grown larger, or to have moved its half-rotten mass nearer towards these people, who with their wild howlings had aroused its dull echoes. A thick, heavy cloud slowly moved across the sky over the house. One of the outcasts was already snoring; the rest, not yet quite drunk, were either eating or drinking, or talking in low voices with long pauses. All felt a strange sense of oppression after this unusually abundant feast of vodka and of food. For some reason or another it took longer than usual to arouse to-day the wild gaiety of the company, which generally came so easily when the dossers were engaged round the bottle.

"Stop your howling for a minute, you dogs!" said the captain to the singers, raising his head from the ground, and listening. "Someone is coming, in a carriage!"

A carriage in those parts at this time of night could not fail to arouse general attention. Who would risk leaving the town to encounter the ruts and holes of such a street? Who? and for what purpose?

All raised their heads and listened. In the silence of the night could be heard the grating of the wheels against the splashboards.

The carriage drew nearer. A coarse voice was heard asking:

"Well; where is it then?"

Another voice answered:

"It must be the house over there."

"I'm not going any further!"

"They must be coming here!" exclaimed the captain.

An anxious murmur was heard: "The police!"

"In a carriage? You fools!" said Martianoff in a low voice.

Kuvalda rose and went towards the entrance gates.

"Leavings," stretching his neck in the direction the captain had taken, was listening attentively.

"Is this the doss-house?" asked someone in a cracked voice.

"Yes, it is the house of Aristide Kuvalda," replied the uninviting bass voice of the captain.

"That's it, that's it! It's here that the reporter Titoff lived, is it not?"

"Ah! You have brought him back?"

"Yes."

"Drunk?"

"Ill."

"That means he's very drunk. Now then, schoolmaster, out with you!"

"Wait a minute. I'll help you; he's very bad. He's been two nights at my house; take him under the arms. We've had the doctor, but he's very bad."

Tiapa rose and went slowly towards the gates. "Scraps" sneered, and drank another glass.

"Light up there!" ordered the captain.

"The Meteor" went into the doss-house and lit a lamp, from which a long stream of light fell across the yard, and the captain, with the assistance of the stranger, led the schoolmaster into the doss-house. His head hung loose on his breast, and his feet dragged along the ground; his arms hung in the air as if they were broken. With Tiapa's help they huddled him on to one of the bunks, where he stretched out his limbs, uttering suppressed groans, whilst shudders ran through his body.

"We worked together on the same newspaper; he's been very unlucky. I told him, 'Stay at my house if you like; you won't disturb me'; but he begged and implored me to take him home, got quite excited about it. I feared that worrying would do him more harm, so I have brought him —home, for this is where he meant, isn't it?"

"Perhaps you think he's got some other home?" asked

Kuvalda in a coarse voice, watching his friend closely all the time. "Go, Tiapa, and fetch some cold water."

"Well now," said the little man, fidgeting about shyly, "I suppose I can't be of any further use to him."

"Who? You?"

The captain scanned him contemptuously.

The little man was dressed in a well-worn coat, carefully buttoned to the chin. His trousers were frayed. His hat was discoloured with age, and was as crooked and wrinkled as was his thin starved face.

"No, you can't be of any further use. There are many like you here," said the captain, turning away from the little man.

"Well, good-bye then!"

The little man went towards the door, and standing there said softly:

"If anything happens let us know at the office; my name is Reezhoff. I would write a short obituary notice. After all, you see, he was a worker in the press."

"H—m—m! an obituary notice, do you say? Twenty lines, forty kopecks. I'll do something better, when he dies; I will cut off one of his legs, and send it to the office, addressed to you. That will be worth more to you than an obituary notice. It will last you at least three or four days; he has nice fat legs. I know all of you down there lived on him when he was alive, so you may as well live on him when he is dead."

The little man uttered a strange sound, and disappeared; the captain seated himself on the bunk, by the side of the schoolmaster, felt his forehead and his chest, and called him by name:

"Philippe!"

The sound echoed along the dirty walls of the doss-house, and died away.

"Come, old chap! this is absurd!" said the captain, smoothing with his hand the disordered hair of the motionless schoolmaster. Then the captain listened to the hot gasping breath, noted the death-like, haggard face, sighed, and wrinkling his brows severely, glanced around. The lamp gave a sickly light; its flame flickered, and on the walls of the doss-house dark shadows danced silently.

The captain sat watching them, and stroking his beard.

Tiapa came in with a bucket of water, placed it on the floor beside the schoolmaster's head, and taking hold of his arm held it in his hand, as if to feel its weight.

"The water is of no use!" said the captain in a hopeless voice.

"It's the priest he wants," said the old rag-picker.

"Nothing's of any use," replied the captain.

They remained a few moments silent, watching the schoolmaster.

"Come and have a drink, old boy!"

"And what about him?"

"Can you do anything for him?"

Tiapa turned his back on the schoolmaster, and both returned to the yard, and rejoined the company.

"Well, what's going on?" asked "Leavings," turning his shrewd face round to the captain.

"Nothing out of the common. The man's dying," the captain replied abruptly.

"Has he been knocked about?" asked "Leavings," with curiosity.

The captain did not answer, for at that moment he was drinking vodka.

"It's just as if he knew that we had something extra for his funeral feast," said "Leavings," lighting a cigarette.

One of them laughed, and another sighed heavily, but on the whole the conversation of "Leavings" and the captain did not make much impression on the company; at least there were no apparent signs of trouble, of interest or of thought. All had looked upon the schoolmaster as a man rather out of the common, but now most of them were drunk, and the rest remained calm and outwardly detached from what was going forward. Only the deacon evinced signs of violent agitation; his lips moved, he rubbed his forehead, and wildly howled:

"*Peace be to the dead!* . . ."

"Stop it!" hissed "Leavings." "What are you howling about?"

"Smash his jaw!" said the captain.

"You fool!" hissed Tiapa. "When a soul is passing, you should keep quiet, and not break the silence."

It was quiet enough; in the cloud-covered sky, which threatened rain, and on the earth, shrouded in the still silence of an autumn night. At intervals the silence was broken by the snoring of those who had fallen asleep; by the gurgle of vodka being poured from the bottle, or the noisy munching of food. The deacon was muttering something. The clouds hung so low that it almost seemed as if they would catch the roof of the old house· and overturn it on this group of men.

"Ah! how one suffers when a dear friend is passing away!" stammered the captain, dropping his head on his chest.

No one answered him.

"He was the best among you all—the cleverest, the most honest. I am sorry for him."

"*May—the—sa-i-nts—receive—him!* . . . Sing, you one-eyed devil!" muttered the deacon, nudging his friend, who lay by his side half asleep.

"Will you be quiet!" exclaimed "Leavings" in an angry whisper, jumping to his feet.

"I'll go and give him a knock over the head," proposed Martianoff.

"What! are you not asleep?" exclaimed Aristide Fomitch in an extraordinarily gentle voice. "Have you heard? Our schoolmaster is——"

Martianoff turned over heavily on his side, stood up, and glanced at the streams of light which issued from the door and windows of the doss-house, shrugged his shoulders, and without a word came and sat down by the side of the captain.

"Let's have a drink," suggested he.

They groped for the glasses, and drank.

"I shall go and see," said Tiapa. "He may want something."

"Nothing but a coffin!" hiccoughed the captain.

"Don't talk about it!" implored "Leavings" dully.

After Tiapa, "The Meteor" got up. The deacon wanted to rise as well; but he fell down again, cursing loudly.

When Tiapa had gone, the captain slapped Martianoff's shoulder, and began to talk in a low voice.

"That's how the matter stands, Martianoff; you ought to feel it more than the rest. You were, but it's better to drop it. Are you sorry for Philippe?"

"No!" answered the former jailer, after a short silence. "I don't feel anything of that sort. I have lost the habit of it; I am so disgusted with life. I'm quite in earnest when I say I shall kill someone."

"Yes?" replied the captain, indifferently. "Well, what then? . . . let's have another drink!"

"We are of no account; we can drink, that's all we can do," muttered Simtsoff, who had just woke in a happy frame of mind. "Who's there, mates? Pour out a glass for the old man!"

The vodka was poured out and handed to him.

After drinking it he dropped down again, falling with his head on someone's body.

A silence, as dark and as miserable as the autumn night, continued for a few moments longer. Then someone spoke in a whisper.

"What is it?" the others asked aloud.

"I say that after all he was a good sort of fellow; he had a clever head on his shoulders, and so quiet and gentle!"

"Yes; and when he got hold of money he never grudged spending it amongst his friends."

Once more silence fell on the company.

"He is going!"

Tiapa's cry rang out over the captain's head.

Aristide Fomitch rose, making an effort to walk firmly, and went towards the doss-house.

"What are you going for?" said Tiapa, stopping him. "Don't you know that you are drunk, and that it's not the right thing?"

The captain paused and reflected.

"And is anything right on this earth? Go to the devil!" And he pushed Tiapa aside.

On the walls of the doss-house the shadows were still flickering and dancing, as if struggling silently with one another.

On a bunk, stretched out at full length, lay the school-master, with the death-rattle in his throat. His eyes were wide open, his bare breast heaved painfully, and froth oozed from the corners of his mouth. His face wore a strained expression, as if he were trying to say something important and difficult; and the failure to say it caused him inexpressible suffering.

The captain placed himself opposite, with his hands behind his back, and watched the dying man for a moment in silence. At last he spoke, knitting his brows as if in pain.

"Philippe, speak to me! Throw a word of comfort to your friend. You know I love you; all the others are brute beasts. You are the only one I look upon as a man, although you are a drunkard. What a one you were to drink vodka, Philippe! That was what caused your ruin. You ought to have kept yourself in hand and listened to me. Was I not always telling you so?"

The mysterious all-destructive force, called Death, as if insulted by the presence of this drunken man, during its supreme and solemn struggle with life, decided to finish its impassive work, and the schoolmaster, after sighing deeply, groaned, shuddered, stretched himself out and died.

The captain swayed backwards and forwards, and continued his speech. "What's the matter with you? Do you want me to bring you some vodka? It's better not to drink, Philippe! restrain yourself. Well, drink if you like! To speak candidly, what is the use of restraining oneself? What's the use of it, Philippe?"

And he took the body by the leg and pulled it towards him.

"Ah! you are already asleep, Philippe! Well, sleep on. Good night. To-morrow I'll explain it all to you, and I hope I shall convince you that it's no use denying oneself anything. So now, go to sleep, if you are not dead."

He went out, leaving dead silence behind him; and approaching his mates exclaimed:

"He's asleep or dead, I don't know which. I'm a—little —drunk."

Tiapa stooped lower still, and crossed himself. Martianoff threw himself down on the ground without saying a word. "The Meteor" began sobbing in a soft, silly way, like a woman who has been ill-treated. "Leavings" wriggled about on the ground, saying in a low, angry, frightened voice:

"Devil take you all! A set of plagues! Dead? . . . what of that? Why should I be bothered with it? When my time comes I shall have to die too! just as he has done; I'm no worse than the rest!"

"That's right! that's it!" exclaimed the captain, dropping himself down heavily on the earth. "When the time comes, we shall all die, just like the rest! Ha! ha! It doesn't much matter how we live; but die we shall, like the rest. For that's the goal of life, trust my word for it! Man lives that he may die. And he dies, and this being so, isn't it all the same what he dies of, or how he dies, or how he lived? Am I not right, Martianoff? Let's have another drink, and yet another, and another, as long as there is life in us."

Rain began to fall. Thick, heavy darkness enshrouded the figures of the outcasts, as they lay on the ground in all the ugliness of sleep or of drunkenness. The streak of light issuing from the doss-house grew paler, flickered, and finally disappeared. Either the wind had blown the lamp out, or the oil was exhausted. The drops of rain falling on the iron roof of the doss-house pattered down softly and timidly. The solemn sound of a bell came at intervals from the town above, telling that the watchers in the church were on duty.

The metallic sound wafted from the steeple melted into the soft darkness, and slowly died away; but before the gloom had smothered the last trembling note, another stroke was heard, and yet another, whilst through the silence of the night spread and echoed the sad booming sigh of the bell.

The following morning Tiapa was the first to awake.

Turning over on his back, he looked at the sky; for this was the only position in which his distorted neck would allow him to look upwards.

It was a monotonously grey morning. A cold, damp gloom, hiding the sun, and concealing the blue depths of the sky, shed sadness over the earth.

Tiapa crossed himself, and leaning on his elbow looked round to see if there was no vodka left. The bottle was near, but it proved to be—empty. Crawling over his companions, Tiapa began inspecting the mugs. He found one nearly full, and swallowed the contents, wiping his mouth with his sleeve, and then shook the captain by the shoulder.

"Get up! Can't you hear?"

The captain lifted his head, and looked at Tiapa with dim, bloodshot eyes.

"We must give notice to the police! so get up."

"What's the matter?" asked the captain in an angry, drowsy voice.

"Why, he's dead."

"Who's dead?"

"Why, the scholar."

"Philippe? Ah! yes, so he is!"

"And you had already forgotten!" hissed Tiapa reproachfully.

The captain rose to his feet, yawned loudly, and stretched himself till his bones cracked.

"Well, go and give notice."

"No, I shan't go. I'm not fond of those gentry!" said Tiapa gloomily.

"Well, go and wake the deacon, and I'll go and see what can be done."

"Yes, that's better. Get up, deacon!"

The captain entered the doss-house, and stood at the foot of the bunk where lay the schoolmaster, stretched out at full length; his left hand lay on his breast, his right was thrown backwards, as if ready to strike. The idea crossed the captain's mind that if the schoolmaster were to get up now, he would be as tall as "Tarass and a half." Then he sat down on the bunk at the feet of his dead friend, and recalling to his mind the fact that they had lived together for three long years, he sighed.

Tiapa entered, holding his head like a goat ready to butt. He placed himself on the opposite side of the schoolmaster, watching for a time his sunk, serene, and calm face; then hissed out:

"Sure enough he is dead; it won't be long before I go also."

"It's time you did," said the captain, gloomily.

"That's so!" agreed Tiapa. "And you also—you ought to die, it would be better than living on as you are doing."

"It might be worse. What do you know about it?"

"It can't be any worse. When one dies, one has to deal with God; whilst here, one has to deal with men. And men, we know what they are."

"That's all right, only stop your grumbling!" said Kuvalda angrily.

And in the half-light of early dawn an impressive silence reigned once more throughout the doss-house.

They sat thus for a long time quietly, at the feet of their

dead companion, occasionally glancing at him, but plunged both of them in deep thought. At length Tiapa inquired:

"Are you going to bury him?"

"I? No, let the police bury him."

"Ah! now it's you who ought to do it! You took the share of the money due to him for writing the petition for Vaviloff. If you haven't enough I'll make it up."

"Yes, I have his money, but I am not going to bury him."

"That doesn't seem right. It's like robbing a dead man. I shall tell everyone that you mean to stick to his money!"

"You are an old fool!" said Kuvalda, disdainfully.

"I'm not such a fool as all that, but it doesn't seem right or friendly."

"Very well! just leave me alone."

"How much money was there?"

"A twenty-five rouble note," said Kuvalda, carelessly.

"Come now! you might give me five out of that."

"What a rogue you are, old man!" scowled the captain, looking blankly into Tiapa's face.

"Why so? Come now, shell out!"

"Go to the devil! I'll erect a monument to him with the money."

"What will be the use of that to him?"

"I'll buy a mill-stone and an anchor; I'll put the stone on the tomb, and I will fasten the anchor to the stone with a chain. That will make it heavy enough."

"What's that for? Why do you talk such nonsense?"

"That's no business of yours."

"Never mind! I shall tell of you," threatened Tiapa once more.

Aristide Fomitch looked vaguely at him and was silent. And once more there reigned in the doss-house that solemn and mysterious hush which always seems to accompany the presence of death.

"Hark! They are coming," said Tiapa.

And he rose and went out at the door.

Almost at the same moment there appeared the police officer, the doctor and the magistrate. All three in turn went up to the body, and after glancing at it moved away, looking meanwhile at Kuvalda askance and with suspicion.

He sat, taking no notice of them, until the police officer asked, nodding towards the schoolmaster's body:

"What did he die of?"

"Ask him yourself. I should say from being unaccustomed——"

"What do you mean?" asked the magistrate.

"I say that, according to my idea, he died from being unaccustomed to the complaint from which he was suffering."

"Hm! Yes. Had he been ill long?"

"It would be better to bring him over here; one can't see anything in there," suggested the doctor in a bored voice. "There may be some marks on him."

"Go and call someone to carry him out!" the police officer ordered Kuvalda.

"Call them in yourself. I don't mind his staying here," retorted the captain coolly.

"Be off with you," shouted the police officer savagely.

"Easy there!" threw back Kuvalda, not stirring from his place, speaking with cool insolence and showing his teeth.

"Damn you!" roared the police officer, his face suffused with blood from suppressed rage. "You shall remember this! I——"

"Good-day to you, honourable gentlemen!" said the oily, insinuating voice of Petunikoff, as he appeared in the doorway. Scrutinising rapidly the faces of the bystanders, he suddenly stopped, shuddered, drew back a step, and taking off his cap, crossed himself devoutly. Then a vicious smile of triumph spread over his countenance, and looking hard at the captain, he asked in a respectful tone, "What is the matter here? No one has been killed, I hope."

"It looks like it," answered the magistrate.

Petunikoff sighed deeply, crossed himself again, and in a grieved tone said:

"Merciful heavens! That's what I always feared! Whenever I came here, I used to look in, and then draw back with fear. Then when I was at home, such terrible things came into my mind. God preserve us all from such things! How often I used to wish to refuse shelter any longer to this gentleman here, the head of this band; but I was always afraid. You see; they were such a bad lot, that it seemed better to give in to them, lest something worse should happen." He made a deprecating movement with one hand, and gathering up his beard with the other, sighed once more.

"They are a dangerous set, and this gentleman here is a sort of chief of the gang—quite like a brigand chief."

"Well, we shall take him in hand!" said the police officer in a meaning tone, looking at the captain with a vindictive expression. "I also know him well."

"Yes, my fine fellow, we are old pals," agreed Kuvalda in a tone of familiarity. "How often have I bribed you and the like of you to hold your tongues?"

"Gentlemen!" said the police officer, "did you hear that? I beg you will remember those words. I won't forgive that. That's how it is then? Well, you shan't forget me! I'll give you something, my friend, to remember me by."

"Don't holloa till you are out of the wood, my dear friend," said Aristide Fomitch coolly.

The doctor, a young man in spectacles, looked at him inquiringly; the magistrate looked at him with an attention that boded no good; Petunikoff stole a look of triumph; whilst the police officer shouted and gesticulated threateningly.

At the door of the doss-house appeared the dark figure of Martianoff; he came up quietly and stood behind Petunikoff, so that his chin appeared just above the merchant's head. The old deacon peeped from behind Martianoff, opening wide his small swollen red eyes.

"Well, something must be done," suggested the doctor.

Martianoff made a frightful grimace, and suddenly sneezed straight on to the head of Petunikoff. The latter yelled, doubled up his body, and sprang on one side, nearly knocking the police officer off his feet, and falling into his arms.

"There, you see now!" said the merchant, trembling and pointing at Martianoff. "You see now what sort of people they are, don't you?"

Kuvalda was shaking with laughter, in which the doctor and the magistrate joined; whilst round the door of the doss-house clustered every moment more and more figures. Drowsy, dissipated faces, with red, inflamed eyes, and dishevelled hair, stood unceremoniously surveying the doctor, the magistrate, and the police officer.

"Where are you shoving to?" said a constable who had accompanied the police officer, pulling at their rags, and pushing them away from the door.

But he was one against many; and they, paying no heed to him, continued to press forward in threatening silence, their breath heavy with sour vodka. Kuvalda glanced first at them and then at the officials, who began to show signs of uneasiness in the midst of this overwhelmingly numerous society of undesirables, and sneeringly remarked to the officials:

"Perhaps, gentlemen, you would like me to introduce you formally to my lodgers and my friends. Say so if you wish it, for sooner or later, in the exercise of your duties, you will have to make their acquaintance."

The doctor laughed with an embarrassed air; the magistrate closed his lips firmly; and the police officer was the only one who showed himself equal to the emergency; he shouted into the yard:

"Sideroff, blow your whistle, and when they come, tell them to bring a cart."

"Well, I'm off," said Petunikoff, appearing from some remote corner. "You'll be kind enough, sirs, to clear out my little shed to-day. I want to have it pulled down. I beg you to make the necessary arrangements; if not I shall have to apply to the authorities."

In the yard the policeman's whistle was sounding shrilly; and round the doss-house door stood the compact crowd of its occupants, yawning and scratching themselves.

"So you don't want to make their acquaintance; that's not quite polite," said Aristide Kuvalda, laughing.

Petunikoff drew his purse from his pocket, fumbled with it for a few minutes, finally pulling out ten kopecks; he crossed himself and placed them at the feet of the dead man.

"God rest his soul! Let this go towards burying the sinful dust."

"How!" roared the captain. "You! you! giving towards the burial? Take it back; take it back I command you, you rogue! How dare you give your dishonest gains towards the burial of an honest man! I'll smash every bone in your body!"

"Sir!" exclaimed the alarmed merchant, seizing the police officer imploringly by the elbow.

The doctor and the magistrate hurried outside, while the police officer shouted again loudly: "Sideroff! Come inside here!"

The creatures who once were men formed a barrier round the door of the doss-house, watching and listening to the scene with an intense interest which lighted up their haggard faces.

Kuvalda, shaking his fist over Petunikoff's head, roared wildly, rolling his bloodshot eyes:

"Rogue and thief! take the coppers back! you vile creature; take them back, I tell you, or I'll smash them into your eyes. Take them back!"

Petunikoff stretched out one trembling hand towards his little offering, whilst shielding himself with the other against Kuvalda's threatening fist, and said:

"Bear witness, you, sir, the police officer, and you, my good people."

"We are not good people, you damned old shopkeeper!" was heard in the creaking tones of "Leavings."

The police officer, distending his face like a bladder, was whistling wildly, whilst defending Petunikoff, who was writhing and twisting about in front of him, as if wishing to get inside the officer for protection.

"You vile thing! I'll make you kiss the feet of this dead body if you don't mind! Come here with you!"

And seizing Petunikoff by the collar, Kuvalda flung him out of the door, as he would have done a kitten.

The outcasts moved on one side to make room for the merchant to fall; and he pitched forward, frightened and yelling at their feet.

"They are killing me! Murder! They have killed me!"

Martianoff slowly lifted his foot, and took aim at the head of the merchant; "Leavings," with an expression of extreme delight, spat full into the face of Petunikoff. The merchant raised himself on to his hands and knees, and half rolled, half dragged himself further out into the yard, followed by peals of laughter. At this moment two constables arrived in the yard, and the police officer, pointing to Kuvalda, exclaimed in a voice of triumph!

"Arrest him! Tie him up!"

"Bind him, comrades!" implored Petunikoff.

"I defy you to touch me! I'm not going to run away! I'll go wherever I have to go," said Kuvalda, defending himself against the constables, who approached him.

The tramps dropped off one by one. The cart rolled into the yard. One or two ragged strangers, who had been called in, were already dragging the schoolmaster's body out of the doss-house.

"You shall catch it! just wait a bit!" said the police officer threateningly to Kuvalda.

"Well, captain, how goes it now?" jeered Petunikoff,

maliciously pleased and happy at the sight of his foe's hands being tied. "Well! you are caught now; only wait, and you will get something warmer by and by!"

But Kuvalda was silent; he stood between the two constables, terrible and erect, and was watching the schoolmaster's body being hoisted into the cart. The man who was holding the corpse under the arms, being too short for the job, could not get the schoolmaster's head into the cart at the same moment as his legs were thrown in. Thus, for a second it appeared as if the schoolmaster were trying to throw himself head-foremost out of the cart, and hide himself in the ground, away from all these cruel and stupid people, who had never given him any rest.

"Take him away!" ordered the police officer, pointing to the captain.

Kuvalda, without a word of protest, walked silent and scowling from the yard, and, passing by the schoolmaster, bent his head towards the body, without looking at it. Martianoff followed him, his face set like a stone.

Petunikoff's yard emptied rapidly.

"Gee-up!" cried the driver, shaking the reins on the horse's back. The cart moved off, jolting along the uneven surface of the yard. The schoolmaster's body, covered with some scanty rags, and lying face upwards, shook and tumbled about with the jolting of the cart. He seemed to be quietly and peacefully smiling, as if pleased with the thought that he was leaving the doss-house, never to return—never any more. Petunikoff, following the cart with his eyes, crossed himself devoutly, and then began carefully dusting his clothes with his cap to get rid of the rubbish that had stuck to them. Gradually, as the dust disappeared from his coat, a serene expression of contentment and of self-reliance spread over his face. Looking up the hill, as he stood in the yard, he could see Captain Aristide Fomitch Kuvalda, with hands tied behind his back, tall and grey, wearing a cap with an old red band like a streak of blood round it, being led away towards the town. Petunikoff smiled with a smile of triumph, and turned towards the doss-house, but suddenly stopped, shuddering. In the doorway facing him stood a terrible old man, horrible to look at in the rags which covered his long body, with a stick in his hand, and a large sack on his back, stooping under the weight of his burden, and bending his head forward on his chest as if he were about to rush forward at the merchant.

"What do you want?" cried Petunikoff. "Who are you?"

"A man," hissed a muffled, hoarse voice.

This hoarse, hissing sound pleased Petunikoff, and reassured him.

"A man!" he exclaimed. "Was there ever a man who looked like you?"

And moving on one side, he made way for the old man, who walked straight towards him, muttering gloomily:

"Men are of various kinds—as God wills. Some are worse than I am, that's all—much worse than I am."

The threatening sky hung silently over the dirty yard, and over the trim little old man with the sharp grey beard, who walked about measuring and calculating with his cunning eyes. On the roof of the old house sat a crow triumphantly croaking, and swaying backwards and forwards with out-stretched neck.

The grey lowering clouds, with which the whole sky was covered, seemed fraught with suspense and inexorable design, as if ready to burst and pour forth torrents of water, to wash away all that soiled this sad, miserable, tortured earth.

ALEXANDER KUPRIN

(1870—1938)

(I)

PSYCHE

23rd November.—It would be quite a fair question for anyone to ask me, Why have I resumed writing the diary which I started and then abandoned five years ago? Certainly there is nothing funnier than the idea of writing a diary or an autobiography. In the first place, it's funny how all these documents have the same beginning: the writer thinks it his first duty to swear by all the gods that he is not writing for the public but for his own private pleasure. In order that a substantial and white-haired old man, surrounded by a swarm of children, may re-experience and feel again what he felt as a young man in his prime, so that the lonely tears of reminiscence . . . or how is it one writes on such occasions? And he shows off and cuts capers even on the road to venerable grey hairs. He will read his reminiscences perhaps thirty times, though they be of interest to no one but himself, and he will choose as his victim some modest, high-minded provincial maid, who will listen tremulously to his strange experiences and stifle big yawns in her handkerchief. God, isn't it disgusting that even clever people will gloat over their tiny personal intimate feelings and find some special relish or sense in them!

As for me, this diary is extremely important to myself and I certainly do not intend to read it to anyone.

The doctor warned me to-day that in view of the sort of life I have been leading during the last three years, with my

headaches and insomnia and intolerable, almost mule-like labours, I must expect my nervous system to be overstrained. And despite the drawl this fashionable doctor gave me for my last five roubles, did he not advise me to go to the Crimea and have a good time, and I, with not the price of a pair of goloshes in my pocket, I understood quite well that I am in danger of going mad. And that's likely enough, seeing that all my esteemed ancestors were booze-fiends or crazy. I intend to write my impressions in this book until I notice that I am getting obviously wrong-headed. And then . . . then the asylum, or, if I have strength of will remaining, a bullet in my brow.

26th November.—Why this injustice? I am certainly possessed of powerful and original gifts, so there's no reason why I should show off just to flatter myself. I am confirmed in that opinion not merely by the Academy Gold Medal which entitles me to some pretensions in art, nor by the estimate of newspaper critics. I am no longer a child, I have got to the point where I can estimate inner worth, for popular success is as unreasonable as a dream. I am aware of a mighty and intense creativeness within me. I can grasp at a glance the slightest details of any object, and I have never done violence to my imagination, the way some artists do in quest of themes. Gigantic thoughts, one more daring and more original than another, so overflow my brain that sometimes I become afraid. But a more important characteristic is this: in the moment when I am creating I am filled with a religious ecstasy and am aware of the sweet presence of the muse unseen. There is a flame in my brain, there are waves of coldness up and down my spine, the hair on my head stands up on end, my whole soul rejoices. But fate has ridiculously decreed, as it were deliberately, that to incarnate completely any one of my precious conceptions must remain for me a grievous impossibility. Working for one's daily bread is not compatible with free creativeness. In danger of.

death or lunacy one has to steer a course between glorious dreams and a prospective death by starvation. Hunger is the worst nourishment for inspiration. But surely possessing my irresistible flight of fancy and that inner ferment which torments me, I could get a job as a clerk or a cobbler!

27th November.—To-day I have just finished my twelfth Pushkin. I have become so expert in doing them that I could work with my eyes shut, and they are as like one another as twins. Pushkins sell readily just now because of some fiftieth anniversary, but the shopkeeper who takes my work is dissatisfied. "There's no diversity in your statuettes," says he. "We need something in the nature of a series. Public taste varies."

Sometimes I am sick almost to vomiting at the thought that I must sell myself for this daily drudgery. I see with horror that after a week's work on some tombstone bust I am beginning to introduce facial characteristics of the local customers, officials and merchants, into my antique studies. But if ten or twenty roubles earned from them enables me to be the master of my inspiration for a whole month, why should I worry?

28th November.—Why is it accepted by all that a man who is tipsy is near to the condition of insanity? What an astonishingly incorrect conclusion! I suppose I ought to confess that thanks to my landlady, who, for economy's sake and because I am not particular, neglects my stove, I have become an addict of the vodka bottle. At first I limited myself to two or three glasses just to keep warm, but after a while I found that that did not satisfy me. I am almost drunk now as I write. My mind is working very powerfully and with surprising accuracy: it notes the detail of my sensations with a subtlety that it could never achieve in sobriety.

But my tongue and my feet are out of discipline and my eyes work poorly; it's as if everything were covered with

sand; the clear outlines are gone. But that does not amount
to anything; many great artists have produced immortal
work in just such a condition. I wanted to work to-day, but
I spent my time lying on that dog's mat my landlady calls a
couch, dreaming of fame.

29th November.—I awakened early, about noon, with a frightful headache. I had a strange dream last night. I was standing somewhere in the outskirts of the city. I suppose it would
be autumn. The wind was humming in the telegraph wires
and there was an uncommonly close, cold drizzle and a sort
of grey mist over everything. Twilight came on, and my
heart sank in apprehension of some calamity. . . .
Suddenly I heard the clatter of a score of horses' hoofs
behind me. I turned and saw a strange sight. Ten or twenty
horsemen clad all in black were galloping by with incredible
speed. They rode in pairs; they went straight ahead and
looked neither to the right nor to the left. Each one carried
a lighted torch which burned with a red and sooty flare. I
grasped that it was a funeral, and sure enough a bier appeared
drawn by six black draped horses. They galloped as fast as
the others and were not left behind. The coffin was covered
with a mass of flame-coloured roses. I ran and overtook the
cavalcade at the cemetery. It proved to be an unusually
gloomy place. The bare trees rocked their branches, scattering rain; there was a smell of damp earth and rotting
withered leaves.
The horsemen took the coffin from the bier and began to
lower it into the pit, but the lid was not shut down and I saw
that it contained a marble statue of a girl of rare and heavenly
beauty. It was lying on a bed of bright green grass and was
covered with red roses and camellias. I do not myself know
how I came to the conclusion, but I recognised the figure at
once—it was the sleeping Psyche!
I rushed into the midst of the crowd, crying and shouting.
that she who lay there was alive. The horsemen laughed

loudly and roughly pushed me back. But they could not stop me. I got down into the grave and clasped the beautiful cold body in my arms and lay there beside her. Then they shovelled earth upon us, shovelled and shovelled. . . .

At last there was so much earth upon me that I could not breathe. I wished to cry out, but my voice was a mere whisper. I made a desperate movement, and awoke.

30th November.—Another day has gone to waste. Suddenly my "Wrestlers" have become distasteful to me. I cannot look on those coarse, healthy muscles! Why then, one may ask, have I used whole months in devotion to them? Why did I go to Morozof's factory and pay fourpence to make two working men wrestle in front of me? On the other hand, I have been thinking of that wonderful statue all day. Where is it I saw that calm and beautiful face before, that delicate girl's body with the young breasts barely showing, fragile and gracious, and at the same time so naïve in all its nakedness? Why should it certainly be Psyche for me, and not Daphne or Flora? I am much interested in the psychology of dreams and have read much on the subject. I know very well that you cannot see anything in a dream that you have not previously encountered in reality. I must have met my Psyche some time or other.

But where? I have been going over the whole of classical sculpture in my mind and I absolutely cannot place it. The face is strangely familiar, but I should find it absolutely impossible to describe; it is beautiful in the highest degree, but at the same time just incredibly simple. When I want to recall it the face will not appear, but directly I begin thinking of something else it floats up before my eyes.

2nd December.—I could hardly find the time to wash the clay off my hands and write a few lines in this foolish exercise book. For three days I have been working uninterruptedly on my Psyche. My nerves are restored, I work quickly and

lightly; and each evening, when I lie down to rest, I feel I
have such a perfect balance of mind and heart as can only
be called a condition of bliss. Some sculptors show Psyche
as a fully-developed woman: incomprehensible error!

Psyche is almost a child, she is small and should give the
impression of just drawing level to a charming maturity, with
a vague and shamefaced consciousness of the change from
girlhood to womanhood. But in addition to this I have made
a somewhat larger discovery; it is that no body that is not
virginal has the right to the sculptor's art, for this art is the
purest and most exalted and most chaste of all the arts.
Therefore a sculptor should work without model and without
even a stone figure in front of him; a living model is certain
to spoil everything. For if a heavy and dirty reality becomes
confounded with the marble dream, then the dream gives
way, and pornography takes its place. It is worth considering
that our ancient art is served by the simplest of instruments,
the hands and the movement of the fingers.

No one will read this diary except myself, and so I will
pursue this thought to the end: neither Phidias nor Canova
nor Thorwaldsen, despite their mighty genius, could escape
from the coarse everyday thoughts of their private life. A
sculptor, to be in a condition to do great work, must be
pure and chaste. I represent Psyche sleeping. They say
that recumbent figures are lost, but that does not deter
me.

4th December.—God, what suffering, what hellish labour, and
nothing, nothing! I simply cannot remember that Psyche I
saw in my dream. I work from morning till evening, till I'm
stupefied, till I'm exhausted, and nothing. What is in front
of me is not the sleeping Psyche but a piquant little sweetie
in a state of amorous fatigue.

No! I have been overworking; that's about it—one simply
cannot go on six days without once taking off one's overall.
I'll try and rest a little.

6th December.—Devil take it if this is resting. I have not got up for two days, but I have had a senseless nightmare the whole time. My mind is in a most puzzling confusion as regards dates, and I cannot be sure did a certain thing happen this morning, or yesterday, or a week back, or did I read of it in a book, or was it a dream.

I have noticed more than once that my memory has been failing, and specially since the time I chucked my friends and almost ceased talking. I have an old man's memory, clear as regards the happenings of childhood, but becoming more and more confused and vague the nearer I approach to the present time. I have been sleeping the greater part of the day and dreaming a thousand dreams. In these dreams I am always aware of myself as lying on that couch and always repeating one and the same stupid word to myself till I simply do not know what to do with myself for ennui. And these wretched dreams are so closely interwoven with wretched actuality that I have long periods of worrying as to where one ends and the other begins. Once or twice I sobered up, as it were, and desperately desired to escape from this devilish half-trance. The desire is to shake myself free, to get out of it if only for a moment, but in a short while the cycle of sleep gets me again.

Night is terrible! I do not sleep one wink till dawn, but watch with horror, sometimes with wonder, a most immense series of pictures, statues, animals, familiar and unfamiliar faces floating into my vision and floating out again without the slightest participation of will or desire. Some of the faces are just monstrous. They grimace, they make dreadful eyes and thrust out their tongues, and when one comes near enough to touch me it is hateful, as if a hangman touched me. To be rid of these hallucinations I take a few glasses of vodka and feel better. Ought I not to go to the doctor?

8th December.—I've just taken a chance glance at myself in the mirror. I had not seen myself for three weeks, and was simply scared when I saw that long-drawn, green and haggard face looking at me with its hollow eyes and sunken, corpse-like cheeks. I simply hate my exterior. They say that man is the crown of creation. They should take a look at the sort of crown my person is at the present moment.

10th December.—Am I able to express what happened last night? I have not yet been able to dissociate myself personally from the mass of impressions of my experience. And although I could not put a hundredth part into words, I will nevertheless endeavour to tell it all in order. I awakened in the middle of the night, thinking someone had called me by name. This occurs frequently enough, especially when there is a bright moon. My room was flooded with a stream of silvery-green light and seemed quite unfamiliar; the walls seemed to have grown higher and to have got further apart, and all the furniture had taken on an unwonted and illusory appearance. I seemed to grasp in an intuitive way that something of immense importance was about to happen. I looked at my Psyche. She was prostrate on the floor, wrapped around with damp rags, and her body in this stream of radiance seemed transparent. I took my sticks mechanically and went over to her, and, as if obeying some foreign influence, indicated certain new lines. . . . Suddenly I trembled and cried out with joy: in front of me lay that same Psyche which I had seen in my dream, the marvellous figure which I had striven in vain to remember! There is not in human language the means to express the raging happiness which was born in my soul. . . . Now I have understood why her face seemed to me so simple and familiar. It is because it is the prototype of divine harmony and beauty and exists in the soul of every man from the day of his birth, the thing to which humanity has given the hackneyed name of "ideal." We artists are given the means of attaining to it, but until this great night we have been sorrowfully and vainly chasing its shadow. And I, I, so pale, ugly and feeble, have achieved what has been thought to be impossible, and put it into firm, palpable form. Oh, of course, I understand well enough that this has little to do with my talent, and that chance led my hands. But just for that reason, no one but myself must see this Psyche. For if mankind ever attains to this degree of perfection in human art it will hardly be in less than ten centuries. Man must first of all discover and subdue all the forces of Nature which at present enslave him, and when at last he gets to the ultimate thing, when he gets to eternal truth and eternal beauty, he will cease to be a man. God alone knows what consequences the popular exhibition of Psyche might have now. She must rest underground for centuries, like the works of the ancient Greeks, and await the time when fate brings her forth like a light that must be set on a hill.

Date not given.—For some days I have not written; I have had an intolerable headache. At times it has seemed as if someone were breaking my skull in bits, and the slightest movement has caused me dreadful pain. However, I spent my last money to-day and sent out for plaster of Paris.

No date.—Directly it got dark I carefully pulled the curtains together, lit the lamp and stood gazing for a long, long time on the unearthly beauty which I have created. It is certainly remarkable that man can tire of all those things which from time immemorial he has sought: fame, sensibility, service of the fatherland, duty, honour, the delights of the world; but I shall never tire of the exaltation which I now experience. I ask myself the question: What would happen if this were a living woman? It seems to me that someone would have to kill her, in the same way as I, in a few days, must bury her in the ground. But until that moment she is mine alone, and her beauty belongs only to me.

Mine! Oh, if that word had not been defiled with thousands of human lusts! My destiny is surprisingly strange. I am only thirty-five, but I am entirely worn out by life. But even in my first manhood, women's caresses meant nothing to me. Perhaps it was due to my unusual physical weakness, but I never had need of women. When women, scared by my irregular life, avoided meeting me, I was not humiliated by it, but rather rejoiced in it. I have never known a woman, never known kisses, hand-pressings, love looks. And now, as if in satisfaction of a feeling of justice, fate has sent me the purest, the most extravagantly exalted happiness, which, of course, has nothing in common with the feelings of those who defile the love of women. But this is still not all; I know, I foresee that even greater delight awaits me in the unseen future! Ah! I have finished the plaster cast, and she lies in front of me in dazzling whiteness.

15th December.—I forgot to date my diary; no time, I suppose. The landlady came in with a sad face this morning and told me that to-day being the 15th December, I have now been three months here without paying my rent. The poor woman seems to pity me and is a little afraid. Still, this may not be a wise reflection: Don't the working class confound the word artist with a synonym for a madman or a rogue?

I keep writing here, but I am a good deal troubled by one circumstance; I keep forgetting certain letters of the alphabet and it costs me much trouble to remember them. Why is that? But it is not important. One very rich thought has come into my head. If the proverb permits every squire to have his whim, who can deny something similar once in a lifetime to a free artist? This is my bright idea. . . . I forget, did I write in this diary about that dream in which I saw "her" for the first time in the grave? I think I wrote about it! I want to stage my first impression in actual life, that is, put her in a fine pine coffin, covered with dark velvet and strewn with grass. But where shall I find the money?

16th December.—My colleague at the Academy, Slivinsky, came to see me to-day. He is a very strange being. At first glance you might think him mad; his hair is always tousled, his gaze wanders aimlessly, sometimes when he stops and stares at you fixedly he does not see you nor hear you, being too much occupied with his own ideas. Sometimes he will interrupt you suddenly in the middle of a sentence with some quite irrelevant question, the outcome of his own private reflection. He is terribly absent-minded, he is a passionate lover of the fair sex, and that is sometimes awkward for me, and he is always on the look-out for adventures. At the same time, in the practical affairs of life he is an absolute child, and if the conversation turns to domestic details he becomes silent and bites his nails. I like talking to him now and then because he sometimes provokes me to such startlingly new ideas that anyone but he would think me mad to utter them. But he understands what I mean before I say half of it, and sometimes knows in advance what I am going to say; an uncommon gift on his part. At those times when we see a good deal of one another we get very close to one another, exploring the most secret corners of the soul and digging up such rubbish that we become enraged with one another to a degree. I heard his voice as he was coming up the stairs and thought to send word that I was not at home, but I was too late: I had just time to snatch a sheet from the bed and cover Psyche up. Not a soul shall see her while I live!

"What's the matter with your face?" asked Slivinsky, even before he had said "how d'ye do?", scanning my physiognomy with complete effrontery.

"What d'ye mean? Have I got horns growing?" I asked with deliberate coarseness, trying to divert his attention from this embarrassing question.

"Not horns. That would make you look even worse, but your face is like a squeezed lemon, and there are circles under your eyes."

I was silent.

"D'ye know what, brother?" cried Slivinsky in some agitation. "Has it ever occurred to you that you won't live very
long?"

"Please stop that."

"You don't believe me? But I see in your face a sort of
special spiritual beauty. Do you know what I mean? I
noticed the expression when I was in hospital; nervous people
a few weeks before their death have it, you can see how the
soul is freeing itself, is breaking through the prison bars.
However, let's not talk of that. What are you doing nowadays? Are you working?"

Ha! I understood the moment had come to use my mother-
wit. All the same I had anticipated his question, and I
answered him with such poise that I astonished myself. The
most talented actor in the world could not have answered
more naturally.

"I spend my time mostly lying on the couch thinking
vaguely of immortality; in the evenings I sit and talk with
my landlady. On the whole I am pretty well occupied, and
not unprofitably."

Slivinsky stared at me in his solemn way.

"No, that's all rot, little brother," said he conclusively.
"You've got something fizzing up inside you. But it does not
matter, I won't press you. I really came to talk with you of
something else. Do you know, spiritualism is by no means
the humbug people say!"

And with characteristic heat and eloquence he began to
develop his theory of mediumism, very daringly and at
times rather wittily.

Taking advantage of a moment's pause, I asked him what
he had been doing since I saw him last, and complained that
he told me nothing about himself.

"I've touched nothing," said he, dropping his spirit-rapping
with surprising rapidity. "Do you know why? In the first
place, because sculpture is not my vocation at all, but women.

I suppose it must have been love of women's bodies that caused me to take up art. In the second place, and I am speaking very seriously, I consider that our art is a very poor one: it is as cold as the marble in which we work, and as pure. Perhaps I am mistaken, but it seems to me that a sculptor whose rôle is to produce something immortal should be an abnormal person like you, a hermit." . . .

An astonishing phenomenon: this man expresses the thought in my mind which I dare not put into words. I was right when I called him my conscience. But it is interesting the way we come by different roads to the same place.

"Do you know," Slivinsky began again, and I knew by his soft accents that he was going to enlarge once more on his favourite theme, "I feel I might have done something once, but since my moral downfall I have been dead to art. The severe pure line and lifeless plaster no longer satisfy me. I might still do something at painting perhaps, because it has colours and tones. It has more feeling. But I do not wish to belong to any profession. Life is given us only once, and it is certainly not intended that we should spend it as you have done, on art alone. And to mix trades is the dream of the amateurs; I do not belong to their number. I do not know what to do with myself unless it is to make a wise use of the blessings of life, among which, of course, in the most important place, stands woman, and woman alone."

"Don't you ever think that that 'trade' may at last become tedious?"

"Never! Don't you grasp, sweetheart, that I belong to the chosen few who have more pleasure in the fine shades, the accessories of love, so to speak, than in love itself in the coarse sense? And as those accessories are endlessly diverse, as diverse as human character itself, I shall always possess the delight of novelty. Eh, I forget that you are some sort of sport of Nature and cannot understand me. Of course you do not know all the delicate degrees of charm there are in the actual approach to a woman, the hint whereby the eyes say everything, the quarrels and flames of jealousy, the primitive madness. . . . No, you could not understand that."

"I understand it perfectly," I exclaimed in chagrin. "That's all gastronomical debauch."

Slivinsky looked at me with curiosity. He had not thought me capable of such a rejoinder.

"Perhaps you're right," he drawled reflectively. Then suddenly he fired up again. "Yes! But think of the struggle of will and mind in that same debauch. Listen! Have you ever considered the distance to which a man's will can go? Did you ever think of that?"

This time I observed that Slivinsky awaited my reply with considerable interest.

"I am not certain if I have wholly understood your question," I answered. "But if by will you mean what I mean—every desire for life—then you must be aware that I believe the greatest denial of that will is the best service of man."

"Oh, leave your old Schopenhauer in his dust," exclaimed Slivinsky sadly. "I am speaking of will in the domestic sense, I mean the power of our most prosaic wishes. In my opinion each man, even you and I, has a power of wishing of such gigantic proportions that nothing in the world is impossible for us."

Evidently Slivinsky thinks that the will can be developed by a sort of constant and persistent gymnastics which consists in doing every minute the things which are opposed to your wishes. Suppose I want to eat, I ought to put off eating till the last possible moment; when I want to lie down, I ought to walk about; if I like a feather bed, I ought to accustom myself to sleep on stones, and so on. And when a man has thus completely subjected himself he finds that everyone about him, and not only people but also the animals, begins to obey his will involuntarily. Then nothing is impossible for a man; his only hindrance is the matter of time and season.

"Do you grasp," continued Slivinsky eagerly, "that by

obstinately and untiringly pursuing one idea I could not merely become Pope of Rome or Emperor of China, but even a supreme genius or scholar? Did you ever hear of the negro who had developed his memory to such a degree that he could repeat by heart five hundred numbers that had been dictated to him, each of eight figures? I could tell you something more; I could cite better examples. How do you think Napoleon rose from being a lieutenant to be the greatest emperor on earth? You may say, just luck. Of course there was some luck in it; circumstances frequently favoured his rise, but the chief factor was the power of his desire. Where you and I let opportunity slip tens of thousands of times, you have a man of such resolution that he would have profited by each one of them, undeterred by danger or the sacredness of tradition or hundreds of victims. The strength of desire and faith in himself! That's all, that is the famous lever of Archimedes. It is written in the Bible that with faith amounting to a grain of mustard seed one could remove mountains. And the fakirs heal the sick and raise the dead!"

Slivinsky had become so exalted that it would have been difficult to recognise him. He seemed to grow as he spoke; his eyes were lighted by the fire of his enthusiasm, his voice had become severe and grand.

"In that case," said I, "how is it that, possessing this strange theory, you remain such an idler?"

"I? Oh, I do not wish to employ it. But I have tried the power of my will on women. That is really what I was leading up to. Bear in mind the following great statement of truth; it will be useful to you when you come to write about me in your memoirs,—there is no man who with the aid of a strong and flexible will cannot win a woman's love. This does not apply to neurasthenical women alone, to the so-called temperamental, but even to one as inaccessible as a goddess or as cold as a statue."

"Oh, you believe one could hypnotise an actual statue in that way, do you?"

I felt, as I posed that question, how pale my cheeks went. It was as if I had glanced over the edge of a frightful precipice. I felt gaily light-headed and apprehensive at one and the same time.

"One could," answered Slivinsky seriously. "Think of the myth of Galatea. Everyone knows there is no myth without some foundation in fact. As I said before, for a person with a strong will there are no impossibilities. If you have not actually brought a statue to life, you do nevertheless *understand, you do yourself believe that it could be done.*"

Slivinsky did not stay much longer.

"What's that you've got covered up in the sheet?" he asked as he was leaving. "Can I have a look at it?"

If I had thrown myself upon him and seized him by the throat as I wished to do, he would probably have overcome me and uncovered my secret. But I stood calmly where I was and offered him my hand.

"Oh, just some rubbish," said I, summoning all the spiritual force at my command. But I must say I could never have suspected that I had such reserve of cunning and self-possession. Directly he went out I took the sheets and curtained off *that* corner.

No date.—My head is in a whirl and my hands refuse to obey me. I do not know whether I am in a condition to tell what has happened.

When night came on I drew the curtain and lit my lamp. The room at once became austere and strange. I could not take my eyes off the white-screened corner; I seemed to sense some inaudible and invisible life behind it. Some irresistible power attracted me to that screen. I was trembling feverishly, but I endeavoured to postpone approaching it till the last possible moment.

At last, when my agitation had become intolerable, I made the decision.

Holding my breath, and with cautious soundless steps, I

went up to those sheets hanging from the ceiling and trem-blingly pulled them apart. In the tiny inner room before my eyes there reigned such a sweet and subtle calm as could only be found in a shrine. *She* lay there clothed from head to foot in a sheet, her marvellous form just suggested in contour. She lay on her back on a pallet of coarse linen, her left leg bending slightly. Her head, turned somewhat to one side, rested on her left arm; her right arm hung negligently to earth.

I will not say that I should have been frightened if at that moment she had stood up and addressed words to me. I should not have been afraid; in fact I even expected some-thing of the kind. But I was almost overcome; my whole body seemed to be under a weight as if overborne with sand, and my eyes were dazzled by a multitude of fast-whirling sparkling dots. . . .

And I declare that although I was keeping a strict guard on my senses, I clearly perceived that her bosom, under the sheet, was rising and falling in quiet, steady respiration. My heart beat in my breast like a drum, and I was for the whole space of time the victim of a sweet exhausting anguish. . . . At that point I lose the thread. I only remember that I slid down quietly on to my knees, bowed my head to the floor and gently lifted the edge of the sheet to kiss her foot. . . . But when I felt with my lips how cold her body was, the intolerably sweet anguish about my heart flared up suddenly like flame when spirit has been poured upon it. For a second the thought flickered in my brain that this was death. I must have fallen into a faint, for when I next opened my eyes, morning light was already gleaming through the curtains.

What does all this mean? Was Slivinsky right when he said I was going to die soon? Well, what of it? I am ready to greet the arrival of death as a beloved guest; for after what happened last night, after that moment of delight, what dis-tractions can be left for me in life? Oh, how I bless the fact that in childhood my comrades turned away from me in derision, though I hated it at the time! That alone saved me from decay, and, while depriving me of the chief.human pleasure, nevertheless preserved me for destiny's great reward.

No date.—To-day for the first time for two months I have been out of the house. My appearance doubtless affected passers-by strangely; everyone gazed at me from head to foot with the utmost astonishment. I was quite drunk with the frosty air, my eyes watered from the strong sunlight; I staggered about, my weak body having become unaccustomed to walking. One ought to add that the cotton-wool padding protruding so plentifully from the holes in my overcoat heightened the effect. I wandered about the whole day and did not pick up one kopeck. I shall have to put off my plan for a grave. O Lord, what is happening to me?

The same date.—How is it I cannot get Slivinsky's rant out of my head? I brood all day on what he said and come to frightening conclusions. Slivinsky said that for the will nothing was impossible. Therefore it would follow that all that is necessary is to harness that will and learn how to wish persistently, passionately and untiringly! I understand perfectly that an object made out of stone cannot awake of itself, stand up and walk towards you. But do not hypnotised persons wander over seas and forests which in reality do not exist? Does it not, therefore, seem that people can experience what is non-existent, what, in fact, cannot exist? However, in discussing that question the devil himself bruised his heel!

The same date.—Something suddenly awoke me in the middle of the night and I sat up at once in my bed. The moon was shining with uncommon brightness, and it seemed to me that the beams were making a monotonous buzzing sound as they came into the room.

Did I see something in my sleep, or was I earlier in the day thinking of something very important? Something very important seemed to have slipped out of my recollection, and I strove hard to recapture it. Suddenly, like a flash of lightning, I received this dreadful thought: "It is necessary to learn how to wish." With great difficulty I got up from the bed and stole across to the partition. Agitation, cold, weakness, caused my body to rock. I trembled; my jaws chattered unpleasantly. With the utmost precaution, so as not to wake Psyche from her light sleep, I slowly withdrew the sheet from her body. She did not move a muscle: only her bosom heaved ever so lightly.

Oh, what a wealth of almighty beauty lay in that calm face, in that delicate, half-transparent, naked body! I mobilised all my reserves of strength of will, I clenched my fists so tightly that my nails cut the flesh of my palms, I shut my teeth so firmly that it was painful, and I called out in an imperative, confident voice: "Awake!"

Suddenly in the murmurous stillness there was a deep sighing, a catching of the breath. The still face took life in a smile, the eyes opened and met mine tenderly. But that blissful and yet poignant sensation about my heart again burst out and flooded my whole being with a monstrous flame. I shouted out and fell heavily downward; but before I lost consciousness, I felt her cold naked arms enclosed about my neck. . . .

The same.—I do not understand the meaning of this gloomy room with the grating, beyond which some strange faces with moustaches keep looking at me! Can this be that very dungeon from which Slivinsky said my soul must escape?

The same.—My God! How difficult the victory is! I beat my head against the walls of the dungeon, I tear out my hair, I claw bits of flesh from my face.

When will all this end?

Date unfixed.—Victory! My hands obey me no more. I am taking less and less air at a breath. But at an unattainable height, through waves of radiant light, I see thy tender smile, my divinity! my Psyche!

(II)

TEMPTING PROVIDENCE

Y o u ' r e always saying "accident, accident. . . ." That's just the point. What I want to say is that on every merest accident it is possible to look more deeply.

Permit me to remark that I am already sixty years old. And this is just the age when, after all the noisy passions of his youth, a man must choose one of three ways of life: money-making, ambition, or philosophy. For my part I think there are only two paths. Ambition must, sooner or later, take the form of getting something for oneself—money or power—in acquiring and extending either or heavenly possibilities.

I don't dare to call myself a philosopher, that's too high-flown a title for me . . . it doesn't go with my character. I'm the sort of person who might any time be called upon to show his credentials. But all the same, my life has been extremely broad and very varied. I have seen riches and poverty and sickness, war and the loss of friends, prison, love, ruin, faith, unbelief. And I've even—believe it or not as you please—I've even seen *people*. Perhaps you think that a foolish remark? But it's not. For one man to see another and understand him, he must first of all forget his own personality, forget to consider what impression he himself is making on his neighbours and what a fine figure he cuts in the world. There are very few who can see other people, I assure you.

Well, here I am, a sinful man, and in my declining years I love to ponder upon life. I am old, and solitary as well, and you can't think how long the nights are to us old folk. My heart and my memory have preserved for me thousands of living recollections—of myself and of others. But it's one thing to chew the cud of recollection as a cow chews nettles, and quite another to consider things with wisdom and judgment. And that's what I call philosophy.

We've been talking of accident and fate. I quite agree with you that the happenings of life seem senseless, capricious, blind, aimless, simply foolish. But over them all, that is, over millions of happenings interwoven together, there reigns—I am perfectly certain of this—an inexorable law. Everything passes and returns again, is born again out of a little thing, out of nothing, burns and tortures itself, rejoices, reaches a height and falls, and then returns again and again, as if twining itself about the spiral curve of the flight of time. And this spiral having been accomplished, it in its turn winds back again for many years, returning and passing over its former place, and then making a new curve—a spiral of spirals . . . and so on without end.

Of course you'll say that if this law is really in existence, people would long ago have discovered it and would be able to define its course and make a kind of map of it. No, I don't think so. We are like weavers, sitting close up to an infinitely long and infinitely broad web. There are certain colours before our eyes, flowers, blues, purples, greens, all moving, moving and passing . . . but because we're so near to it we can't make out the pattern. Only those who are able to stand above life, higher than we do, gentle scholars, prophets, dreamers, saints and poets, these may have occasional glimpses through the confusion of life, and their keen inspired gaze may see the beginnings of a harmonious design, and may divine its end.

You think I express myself extravagantly? Don't you now? But wait a little; perhaps I can put it more clearly. You mustn't let me bore you, though. . . . Yet what can one do on a railway journey except talk?

I agree that there are laws of Nature governing alike in their wisdom the courses of the stars and the digestion of beetles. I believe in such laws and I revere them. But there is *Something* or *Somebody* stronger than Fate, greater than the world. If it is *Something*, I should call it the law of logical absurdity, or of absurd logicality, just as you please . . . I can't express myself very well. If it is *Somebody*, then it must be someone in comparison with whom our Biblical devil and our romantic Satan are but puny jesters and harmless rogues.

Imagine to yourself an almost godlike Power over this world, having a desperate childish love of playing tricks, knowing neither good nor evil, but always mercilessly hard, sagacious, and, devil take it all, somehow strangely just. You don't understand, perhaps? Then let me illustrate my meaning by examples.

Take Napoleon: a marvellous life, an almost impossible great personality, inexhaustible power, and look at his end— on a tiny island, suffering from disease of the bladder, complaining of the doctors, of his food, senile grumblings in solitude. . . . Of course, this pitiful end was simply a mocking laugh, a derisive smile on the face of my mysterious *Somebody*. But consider this tragic biography thoughtfully, putting aside all the explanations of learned people—they would explain it all simply in accordance with law—and I don't know how it will appear to you, but here I see clearly existing together this mixture of absurdity and logicality, and I cannot possibly explain it to myself.

Then General Skobelef. A great, a splendid figure. Desperate courage, and a kind of exaggerated belief in his own destiny. He always mocked at death, went into a murderous fire of the enemy with bravado, and courted endless risks in a kind of unappeasable thirst for danger. And see—he died on a common bed, in a hired room in the company of prostitutes. Again I say: absurd, cruel, yet somehow logical. It is as if each of these pitiful deaths, by their contrast with the life, rounded off, blended, completed, two splendid beings.

The ancients knew and feared this mysterious *Someone*—you remember the ring of Polycrates—but they mistook his jest for the envy of Fate.

I assure you—*i.e.* I don't assure *you*, but I am deeply assured of it myself—that, some time or other, perhaps after thirty thousand years, life on this earth will have become marvellously beautiful. There will be palaces, gardens, fountains. . . . The burdens now borne by mankind—slavery, private ownership of property, lies and oppression—will cease. There will be no more sickness, disorder, death; no more envy, no vice, no near or far, all will have become brothers. And then *He*—you notice that even in speaking I pronounce the name with a capital letter—He, passing one day through the universe, will look on us, frown evilly, smile, and then breathe upon the world—and the good old earth will cease to be. A sad end for this beautiful planet, eh? But just think to what a terrible bloody, orgiastic end universal virtue might lead, if once people succeeded in getting thoroughly surfeited with it!

However, what's the use of taking such great examples as our earth, Napoleon and the ancient Greeks? I myself have, from time to time, caught a glimpse of this strange and inscrutable law in the most ordinary occurrences. If you like, I'll tell you a simple incident when I myself clearly felt the mocking breath of this god.

I was travelling by train from Tomsk to Petersburg in an ordinary first-class compartment. One of my companions on the journey was a young Civil engineer, a very short, stout, good-natured young man; a simple Russian face, round, well-cared-for, white eyebrows and eyelashes, sparse hair brushed up from his forehead, showing the red skin beneath . . . a kind, good " Yorkshireman." His eyes were like the dull blue eyes of a sucking-pig.

He proved a very pleasant companion. I have rarely seen

anyone with such engaging manners. He at once gave me his lower sleeping-place, helped me to place my trunk on the rack, and was generally so kind that he even made me feel a little awkward. When we stopped at a station he bought wine and food, and had evidently great pleasure in persuading the company to share them with him.

I saw at once that he was bubbling over with some great inward happiness, and that he was desirous of seeing all around him as happy as he was.

And this proved to be the case. In ten minutes he had already begun to open his heart to me. Certainly I noticed that directly he spoke of himself the other people in the carriage seemed to wriggle in their seats and take an exaggerated interest in observing the passing landscape. Later on, I realised that each of them had heard the story at least a dozen times before. And now my turn had come.

The engineer had come from the Far East, where he had been living for five years, and consequently he had not seen his family in Petersburg for five years. He had thought to dispatch his business in a year at the most, but at first official duties had kept him, then certain profitable enterprises had turned up, and afterwards it had seemed impossible to leave a business which had become so very large and remunerative. Now everything had been wound up and he was returning home. Who could blame him for his talkativeness? To have lived for five years far from a beloved home, and come back young, healthy, successful, with a heart full of unspent love! What man could have imposed silence upon himself or overcome that fearful itch of impatience, increasing with every hour, with every passing hundred versts?

I soon learnt from him all about his family. His wife's name was Susannah or Sannochka, and his daughter bore the outlandish name of Yurochka. He had left her a little three-year-old girl, and "Just imagine!" cried he, "now she must be quite grown up, almost ready to be married."

He told me his wife's maiden name, and of the poverty they

had experienced together in their early married days, when he had been a student in his last year, and had not even a second pair of trousers to wear, and what a splendid companion, nurse, mother and sister in one his wife had been to him then.

He struck his breast with his clenched fist, his face reddened with pride, and his eyes flashed as he cried:

"If only you knew her! A be-eauty! If you're in Petersburg I must introduce you to her. You must certainly come and see us there; you must, indeed, without any ceremony or excuse; Kirochnaya 156. I'll introduce you to her, and you'll see my old woman for yourself. A queen! She was always the belle at our Civil engineers' balls. You must come and see us, I swear, or I shall be offended."

And he gave us each one of his visiting-cards on which he had pencilled out his Manchurian address and written in the Petersburg one, telling us at the same time that his sumptuous flat had been taken by his wife only a year ago—he had insisted on it when his business had reached its height.

Yes, his talk was like a waterfall. Four times a day, when we stopped at important stations, he would send home a reply-paid telegram to be delivered to him at the next big stopping-place or simply on the train, addressed to such and such a number, first-class passenger So-and-so. . . . And you ought to have seen him when the conductor came along shouting in a sing-song tone, "Telegram for first-class passenger So-and-so." I assure you there was a shining halo round his head like that of the holy saints. He tipped the conductors royally, and not the conductors only either. He had an insatiable desire to give to everybody, to make people happy, to caress them. He gave us all souvenirs, knick-knacks made out of Siberian and Ural stones, trinkets, studs, pins, Chinese rings, jade images, and other trifles. Among them were many things that were very valuable, some on account of their cost, others for their rare and artistic work, yet, do you know, it was impossible to refuse them, though one felt embarrassed and awkward in receiving such valuable gifts— he begged us to accept them with such earnestness and insistence, just as one cannot continue to refuse a child who continues to ask one to take a sweet.

He had with him in his boxes and in his hand luggage a whole store of things, all gifts for Sannochka and Yurochka. Wonderful things they were—priceless Chinese dresses, ivory, gold, miniatures in sardonyx, furs, painted fans, lacquered boxes, albums—and you ought to have seen and heard the tenderness and the rapture with which he spoke of his loved ones when he showed us these gifts. His love may have been somewhat blind, too noisy and egotistical, perhaps even a little hysterical, but I swear that through these formal and trivial veilings I could see a great and genuine love—love at a sharp and painful tension.

I remember, too, how at one of the stations when another wagon was being attached to the train, a pointsman had his foot cut off. There was great excitement, all the passengers went to look at the injured man—and people travelling by train are the most empty-headed, the wildest, the most cruel in the world. The engineer did not stay in the crowd, he went quietly up to the station-master, talked with him for a few moments, and then handed him a note for a sum of money—not a small amount, I expect, for the official cap was lifted in acknowledgment with the greatest respect. He did this very quickly; no one but myself saw his action, but I have eyes that notice such things. And I saw also that he took advantage of the longer stoppage of the train and succeeded in sending off a telegram.

I can see him now as he walked across the platform—his white engineer's cap pushed to the back of his head; his long blouse of fine tussore, with collar fastening at the side; over one shoulder the strap of his field-glasses, and crossing it, over the other shoulder, the strap of his dispatch-case— coming out of the telegraph-office and looking so fresh and plump and strong, with such a clear complexion, and the look of a well-fed, simple, country lad.

And at almost every big station he received a telegram. He quite spoilt the conductors—running himself to the office to inquire if there was a message for him. Poor boy! He could not keep his joy to himself, but read his telegrams aloud to us, as if we had nothing else to think about except his family happiness. "Hope you are well. We send kisses and await your arrival impatiently.—SANNOCHKA, YUROCHKA." Or, "With watch in hand we follow on the time-table the course of your train from station to station. Our spirits and thoughts are with you." All the telegrams were of this kind. There was even one like this: "Put your watch to Petersburg time, and exactly at eleven o'clock look at the star Alpha in the Great Bear. I will do the same."

There was one passenger on the train who was owner, or book-keeper, or manager of a gold mine, a Siberian, with a face like that of Moses the Moor,[1] dry and elongated, thick, black, stern brows, and a long, full, greyish beard—a man who looked as if he were exceptionally experienced in all the trials of life. He made a warning remark to the engineer:

"You know, young man, it's no use you abusing the telegraph service in such a way."

"What do you mean? How is it no use?"

"Well, it's impossible for a woman to keep herself all the time in such an exalted and wound-up state of mind. You ought to have mercy on other people's nerves."

But the engineer only laughed and clapped the wiseacre on the knee.

"Ah, little father, I know you, you people of the Old Testament. You're always stealing back home unexpectedly and on the quiet. 'Is everything as it should be on the domestic hearth?' Eh?"

[1]One of the hermits of the Egyptian desert, a saint in the Russian Calendar.

But the man with the ikon face only raised his eyebrows and smiled.

"Well, what of it? Sometimes there's no harm in that."

At Nizhni we had new fellow-travellers, and at Moscow new ones again. The agitation of my engineer was still increasing. What could be done with him? He made acquaintance with everybody; talked to married folks of the sacredness of home, reproached bachelors for the slovenliness and disorder of bachelor life, talked to young ladies about a single and eternal love, conversed with mothers about their children, and always led the conversation to talk about his Sannochka and Yurochka. Even now I remember that his daughter used to lisp: "I have thome yellow thlipperth," and the like. And once, when she was pulling the cat's tail, and the cat mewed, her mother said, "Don't do that, Yurochka, you're hurting the cat," and the child answered, "No, mother, it liketh it."

It was all very tender, very touching, but I'm bound to confess a little tiresome.

Next morning we were nearing Petersburg. It was a dull, wet, unpleasant day. There was not exactly a fog, but a kind of dirty cloudiness enveloped the rusty, thin-looking pines, and the wet hills looked like hairy warts extending on both sides of the line. I got up early and went along to the lavatory to wash; on the way I ran into the engineer, he was standing by the window and looking alternately at his watch and then out of the window.

"Good-morning," said I. "What are you doing?"

"Oh, good-morning," said he. "I'm just testing the speed of the train; it's going about sixty versts an hour."

"You test it by your watch."

"Yes, it's very simple. You see, there are twenty-five sazhens between the posts—a twentieth part of a verst. Therefore, if we travel these twenty-five sazhens in four seconds, it means we are going forty-five versts an hour; if in three seconds, we're going sixty versts an hour; if in two seconds, ninety. But you can reckon the speed without a watch if you know how to count the seconds—you must count as quickly as possible, but quite distinctly, one, two, three, four, five, six—one, two, three, four, five, six—that's a speciality of the Austrian General Staff."

He talked on, with fidgety movements and restless eyes, and I knew quite well, of course, that all this talk about the counting of the Austrian General Staff was all beside the point, just a simple diversion of his to cheat his impatience.

It became dreadful to watch him after we had passed the station of Luban. He looked to me paler and thinner, and, in a way, older. He even stopped talking. He pretended to read a newspaper, but it was evident that it was a tiresome and distasteful occupation for him; sometimes he even held the paper upside down. He would sit still for about five minutes, then go to the window, sit down for a while and seem as if he were trying to push the train forward, then go again to the window and test the speed of the train, again turning his head, first to the right and then to the left. I know—who doesn't know?—that days and weeks of expectation are as nothing in comparison with those last half-hours, with the last quarter of an hour.

But at last the signal-box, the endless network of crossing rails, and then the long wooden platform edged with a row of porters in white aprons. . . . The engineer put on his coat, took his bag in his hand, and went along the corridor to the door of the train. I was looking out of the window to hail a porter as soon as the train stopped. I could see the engineer very well, he had got outside the door on to the step. He noticed me, nodded, and smiled, but it struck me, even at that distance, how pale he was.

A tall lady in a sort of silvery bodice and a large velvet hat and blue veil went past our carriage. A little girl in a short frock, with long, white-gaitered legs, was with her. They were both looking for someone, and anxiously scanning every

window. But they passed him over. I heard the engineer cry
out in a strange, choking, trembling voice:

"Sannochka!"

I think they both turned round. And then, suddenly . . .
a sharp and dreadful wail . . . I shall never forget it. A
cry of perplexity, terror, pain, lamentation, like nothing else
I've ever heard.

The next second I saw the engineer's head, without a cap,
somewhere between the lower part of the train and the
platform. I couldn't see his face, only his bright upstanding
hair and the pinky flesh beneath, but only for a moment, it
flashed past me and was gone. . . .

Afterwards they questioned me as a witness. I remember
how I tried to calm the wife, but what could one say in such
a case? I saw him, too—a distorted red lump of flesh. He was
dead when they got him out from under the train. I heard
afterwards that his leg had been severed first, and as he was
trying instinctively to save himself, he fell under the train,
and his whole body was crushed under the wheels.

But now I'm coming to the most dreadful point of my story.
In those terrible, never-to-be-forgotten moments I had a
strange consciousness which would not leave me. "It's a
stupid death," I thought, "absurd, cruel, unjust;" but why,
from the very first moment that I heard his cry, why did it
seem clear to me that the thing must happen, and that it was
somehow natural and logical? Why was it? Can you explain
it? Was it not that I felt here the careless indifferent smile of
my devil?

His widow—I visited her afterwards, and she asked me
many questions about him—said that they both had tempted
Fate, by their impatient love, in their certainty of meeting,
in their sureness of the morrow. Perhaps so . . . I can't
say. . . . In the East, that tried well of ancient wisdom, a
man never says that he intends to do something either to-day
or to-morrow without adding "*Insh-Allah*," which means
"In the name of God," or "If God will."

And yet I don't think that there was here a tempting of Fate, it seemed to me just the absurd logic of a mysterious god. Greater joy than their mutual expectation, when, in spite of distance, their souls met together—greater joy, perhaps, these two would never have experienced! God knows what might have awaited them later! Disenchantment? Weariness? Boredom? Perhaps hate?

(III)

THE SONG AND THE DANCE

W e lived at that time in the Government of Riazan, some 120 versts from the nearest railway station and even 25 versts from the large trading village of Tuma. "Tuma is iron and its people are of stone," as the local inhabitants say of themselves. We lived on an old untenanted estate, where in 1812 an immense house of wood had been constructed to accommodate the French prisoners. The house had columns, and a park with lime trees had been made around it to remind the prisoners of Versailles.

Imagine our comical situation. There were twenty-three rooms at our disposal, but only one of them had a stove and was warmed, and even in that room it was so cold that water froze in it in the early morning and the door was frosted at the fastenings. The post came sometimes once a week, sometimes once in two months, and was brought by a chance peasant, generally an old man with the packet under his shaggy snow-strewn coat, the addresses wet and smudged, the backs unsealed and stuck again by inquisitive postmasters. Around us was an ancient pine wood where bears prowled, and whence even in broad daylight the hungry wolves sallied forth and snatched away yawning dogs from the street of the hamlet near by. The local population spoke in a dialect we did not understand, now in a sing-song drawl, now coughing and hooting, and they stared at us surlily and without restraint. They were firmly convinced that the forest belonged to God and the peasant alone, and the lazy German steward only knew how much wood they stole. There was at our service a splendid French library of the eighteenth century, though all the magnificent bindings were mouse-eaten. There was an old portrait gallery with the canvases ruined from damp, mould and smoke.

Picture to yourself the neighbouring hamlet all overblown with snow, and the inevitable village idiot, Serozha, who goes naked even in the coldest weather; the priest who does not play "preference" on a fast day, but writes denunciations to the starosta, a stupid, artful man, diplomat and beggar, speaking in a dreadful Petersburg accent. If you see all this you understand to what a degree of boredom we attained. We grew tired of encompassing bears, of hunting hares with hounds, of shooting with pistols at a target through three rooms at a distance of twenty-five paces, of writing humorous verses in the evening. Of course we quarrelled.

Yes, and if you had asked us individually why we had come to this place, I should think not one of us would have answered the question. I was painting at the time; Valerian Alexandrovitch wrote symbolical verses, and Vaska amused himself with Wagner and played Tristan on the old, ruined, yellow-keyed clavichord.

But about Christmas-time the village began to enliven, and in all the little clearings round about, in Tristenka, in Borodina, Breslina, Shustova, Nikiforskaya and Kosli, the peasants began to brew beer—such thick beer that it stained your hands and face at the touch, like lime-bark. There was so much drunkenness among the peasants, even before the festival, that in Dagileva a son broke his father's head, and in Kruglitsi an old man drank himself to death. But Christmas was a diversion for us. We started paying the customary visits and offering congratulations to all the local officials and peasants of our acquaintance. First we went to the priest, then to the psalm-singer of the church, then to the church-watchman, then to the two schoolmistresses. After the schoolmistresses we fared more pleasantly. We turned up at the doctor's at Tuma, then trooped off to the district clerk, where a real banquet awaited us, then to the policeman, then to the lame apothecary, then to the local peasant tyrant who had grown rich and held a score of other peasants in his own grasp, and possessed all the cord, linen, grain, wood, whips in the neighbourhood. And we went and went on!

It must be confessed, however, that we felt a little awkward now and then. We couldn't manage to get into the *tempo* of the life there. We were really out of it. This life had creamed and mantled for years without number. In spite of our pleasant manners and apparent ease we were, all the same, people from another planet. Then there was a disparity in our mutual estimation of one another: we looked at them through a microscope, they looked at us as through a telescope. Certainly we made attempts to accommodate ourselves, and when the psalm-singer's servant, a woman of forty, with warty hands all chocolate colour from the reins of the horse she put in the sledge when she went with a bucket to the well, sang of an evening, we did what we thought we ought to do. She would look ashamed, lower her eyes, fold her arms and sing:

> "Andray Nikolaevitch,
> We have come to you,
> We wish to trouble you.
> But we have come,
> And please to take
> The one of us you love."

Then we would boldly make to kiss her on the lips, which we did in spite of feigned resistance and screams.

And we would make a circle. One day there were a lot of us there; four students on holiday from an ecclesiastical college, the psalm-singer, a housekeeper from a neighbouring estate, the two schoolmistresses, the policeman in his uniform, the deacon, the local horse-doctor, and we three æsthetes. We went round and round in a dance, and sang, roared, swinging now this way, now that, and the lion of the company, a student named Vozdvizhensky, stood in the middle and ordered our movements, dancing himself the while and snapping his fingers over his head:

> "The queen was in the town, yes, the town,
> And the prince, the little prince, ran away.
> Found a bride, did the prince, found a bride.
> She was nice, yes, she was, she was nice,
> And a ring got the prince for her, a ring."

After a while the giddy whirl of the dance came to an end, and we stopped and began to sing to one another, in solemn tones:

> "The royal gates were opened,
> Bowed the king to the queen,
> And the queen to the king,
> But lower bowed the queen."

And then the horse-doctor and the psalm-singer had a competition as to who should bow lower to the other.

Our visiting continued, and at last we came to the schoolhouse at Tuma. That was inevitable, since there had been long rehearsals of an entertainment which the children were going to give entirely for our benefit—Petersburg guests. We went in. The Christmas tree was lit simultaneously by a torch-paper. As for the programme, I knew it by heart before we went in. There were several little tableaux, illustrative of songs of the countryside. It was all poorly done, but it must be confessed that one six-year-old mite, wearing a huge cap of dog-skin and his father's great leather gloves with only places for hand and thumb, was delightful, with his serious face and hoarse little bass voice—a born artist.

The remainder was very disgusting. All done in the false popular style.

I had long been familiar with the usual entertainment items: Little-Russian songs mispronounced to an impossible point; verses and silly embroidery patterns: "There's a Christmas tree, there's Petrushka, there's a horse, there's a steam-engine." The teacher, a little consumptive fellow, got up for the occasion in a long frock-coat and stiff shirt, played the fiddle in fits and starts, or beat time with his bow, or tapped a child on the head with it now and then.

The honorary guardian of the school, a notary from another town, chewed his gums all the time and stuck out his short parrot's tongue with sheer delight, feeling that the whole show had been got up in his honour.

At last the teacher got to the most important item on his programme. We had laughed up till then, our turn was coming to weep. A little girl of twelve or thirteen came out, the daughter of a watchman, her face, by the way, not at all like his horse-like profile. She was the top girl in the school and she began her little song:

> "The jumping little grasshopper sang the summer through,
>   Never once considering how the winter would blow in his eyes."

Then a shaggy boy of seven, in his father's felt boots, took up his part, addressing the watchman's daughter:

> "That's strange, neighbour. Didn't you work in the summer?"
>   What was there to work for? There was plenty of grass."

Where was our famous Russian hospitality?

To the question, "What did you do in the summer?" the grasshopper could only reply, "I sang all the time."

At this answer the teacher, Kapitonitch, waved his bow and his fiddle at one and the same time—oh, that was an effect rehearsed long before that evening!—and suddenly in a mysterious half-whisper the whole choir began to sing:

"You've sung your song, you call that doing,
You've sung all the summer, then dance all the winter;
You've sung your song, then dance all the winter,
Dance all the winter, dance all the winter;
You've sung the song, then dance the dance."

I confess that my hair stood on end as if each individual hair were made of glass, and it seemed to me as if the eyes of the children and of the peasants packing the schoolroom were all fixed on me as if repeating that d——d phrase:

"You've sung the song, you call that doing,
You've sung the song, then dance the dance."

I don't know how long this drone of evil boding and sinister recitation went on. But I remember clearly that during those minutes an appalling idea went through my brain. "Here we stand," thought I, "a little band of *intelligentsia*, face to face with an innumerable peasantry, the most enigmatical, the greatest and the most abased people in the world. What connects us with them? Nothing. Neither language, nor religion, nor labour, nor art. Our poetry would be ridiculous to their ears, absurd, incomprehensible. Our refined painting would be simply useless and senseless smudging in their eyes. Our quest for gods and making of gods would seem to them stupidity, our music merely a tedious noise. Our science would not satisfy them. Our complex work would seem laughable or pitiful to them, the austere and patient labourers of the fields. Yes. On the dreadful day of reckoning what answer shall we give to this child, wild beast, wise man and animal, to this many-million-headed giant?" We shall only be able to say sorrowfully, "We sang all the time. We sang our song."

And he will reply with an artful peasant smile, "Then go and dance the dance."

And I know that my companions felt as I did. We went out of the entertainment-room silent, not exchanging opinions.

Three days later we said good-bye, and since that time have

been rather cold towards one another. We had been suddenly chilled in our consciences and made ashamed, as if those innocent mouths of sleepy children had pronounced death sentence upon us. And when I returned from the post of Ivan Karaulof to Goreli, and from Goreli to Koslof, and from Koslof to Zintabrof, and then further by railroad, there followed me all the time that ironical, seemingly malicious phrase, "Then dance the dance."

God alone knows the destiny of the Russian people.

. . . Well, I suppose, if it should be necessary, we'll dance it!

I travelled the whole night to the railway station.

On the bare frosted branches of the birches sat the stars, as if the Lord Himself had with His own hands decorated the trees. And I thought, "Yes, it's beautiful." But I could not banish that ironical thought, "Then dance the dance."

(IV)

MECHANICAL JUSTICE

T H E large hall of the principal club of one of our provincial towns was packed with people. Every box, every seat in pit and stalls was taken, and in spite of the excitement the public was so attentive and quiet that, when the lecturer stopped to take a mouthful of water, everyone could hear a solitary belated fly buzzing at one of the windows.

Amongst the bright dresses of the ladies, white and pink and blue, amongst their bare shoulders and gentle faces shone smart uniforms, dress coats and golden epaulettes in plenty.

The lecturer, who was clad in the uniform of the Department of Education—a tall man whose yellow face seemed to be made up of a black beard only and glimmering black spectacles—stood at the front of the platform, resting his hand on a table.

But the attentive eyes of the audience were directed, not so much on him as on a strange, high, massive-looking contrivance which stood beside him, a grey pyramid covered with canvas, broad at its base, pointed at the top.

Having quenched his thirst, the lecturer went on:

"Let me briefly sum up. What do we see, ladies and gentlemen? We see that the encouraging system of marks, prizes, distinctions, leads to jealousy, pride and dissatisfaction. Pedagogic suggestion fails at last through repetition. Standing culprits in the corner, on the form, under the clock, making them kneel, is often quite ineffectual as an example, and the victim is sometimes the object of mirth. Shutting in a cell is positively harmful, quite apart from the fact that it uses up the pupil's time without profit. Forced work, on the other hand, robs the work of its true value. Punishment by hunger affects the brain injuriously. The stopping of holidays causes malice in the mind of pupils, and often evokes the dissatisfaction of parents. What remains? Expulsion of the dull or mischievous children from the school—as advised in Holy Writ—the cutting off of the offending member lest, through him, the whole body of the school be infected. Yes, alas! such a measure is, I admit, inevitable on certain occasions now, as inevitable as is capital punishment, I regret to say, even in the best of states. But before resorting to this last irreparable means, let us see what else there may be. . . ."

"And flogging!" cried a deep bass voice from the front row of the stalls. It was the governor of the town fortress, a deaf old man, under whose chair a pug-dog growled angrily and hoarsely. The governor was a familiar figure about town with his stick, ear trumpet and old panting pug-dog.

The lecturer bowed, showing his teeth pleasantly.

"I did not intend to express myself as shortly and precisely, but in essence his Excellency has guessed my thought. Yes, ladies and gentlemen, there is one good old Russian method of which we have not yet spoken—corporal punishment. Yes, corporal punishment is part and parcel of the very soul of the great Russian people, of its mighty national sense, its patriotism and deep faith in Providence. Even the apostle said: 'Whom the Lord loveth He chasteneth.' The unforgotten monument of mediæval culture—Domostroi—enjoins the same with paternal firmness. Let us call to mind our inspired Tsar-educator, Peter the Great, with his famous cudgel. Let us call to mind the speech of our immortal Pushkin:

> 'Our fathers, the further back you go,
> The more the cudgels they used up.'

Finally, let us call to mind our wonderful Gogol, who put into the mouth of a simple, unlearned serving-man the words: 'The peasant must be beaten, for the peasant is being spoiled.' Yes, ladies and gentlemen, I boldly affirm that punishment with rods upon the body goes like a red thread throughout the whole immense course of Russian history, and takes its rise from the very depths of primitive Russian life.

"Thus delving in thought into the past, ladies and gentlemen, I appear a conservative, yet I go forward with outstretched hands to meet the most liberal of humanitarians. I freely allow, loudly confess, that corporal punishment, in the way in which it has been practised until now, has much in it that is insulting for the person being chastised as well as humiliating for the person chastising. The personal confrontment of the two men inevitably awakens hate, fear, irritation, revengefulness, contempt and, what is more, a competitive stubbornness in the repetition of crime and punishment. So you no doubt imagine that I renounce corporal punishment. Yes, I do renounce it, though only to introduce it anew, replacing man by a machine. After the labours, thoughts and experiments of many years, I have at last worked out a scheme of mechanical justice, and have realised it in a machine. Whether I have been successful or not I shall in a minute leave this most respected audience to judge."

The lecturer nodded towards the wings of the stage. A fine-looking attendant came forward and took off the canvas cover from the strange object standing at the footlights. To the eyes of those present, the bright gleaming machine was rather like an automatic weighing-machine, though it was obviously more complex and was much larger. There was a murmur of astonishment among the audience in the hall.

The lecturer extended his hand and pointed to the apparatus.

"There is my offspring," said he in an agitated voice. "There is an apparatus which may fairly be called the instrument of mechanical justice. The construction is uncommonly simple, and in price it would be within the reach of even a modest village school. Pray consider its construction. In the first place you remark the horizontal platform on springs, and the wooden platform leading to it. On the platform is placed a narrow chair, the back of which has also a powerful spring and is covered with soft leather. Under the chair, as you see, is a system of crescent-shaped levers turning on a hinge. Proportionately with the pressure on the springs of the chair and platform these levers, departing from their equipoise, describe half-circles, and close in pairs at a height of from five to eighteen *vershoks*[1] above the level of the chair—varying with the force of pressure. Behind the chair rises a vertical cast-iron pillar, with a cross-bar. Within the pillar is contained a powerful mechanism resembling that of a watch, having a 160-lb. balance and a spiral spring. On the side of a column observe a little door; that is for cleaning or mending the mechanism. The door has only two keys, and I ask you to note, ladies and gentlemen, that these keys are kept, one by the chief district inspector of mechanical flogging machines, and the other by the head master of the school. So this apparatus, once brought into action, cannot be stopped until

[1]A *vershok* is $\frac{1}{16}$ of an arshin, *i.e.* $1\frac{3}{4}$ inches.

it has completed the punishment intended—except, of course, in the eventuality of its being forcibly broken, which is a hardly likely possibility, seeing the simplicity and solidity of every part of the machine.

"The watch mechanism, once set going, communicates with a little horizontally-placed axle. The axle has eight sockets in which may be mounted eight long supple bamboo or metal rods. When worn out these can be replaced by new ones. It must be explained also that, by a regulation of the axle, the force of the strokes may be varied.

"And so we see the axle in motion, and moving with it the eight rods. Each rod goes downward perfectly freely, but coming upward again it meets with an obstacle—the cross-beam—and meeting it, bends and is at tension from its point, bulges to a half-circle, and then, breaking free, deals the blow. Then, since the position of the cross-beam can be adjusted, raised or lowered, it will be evident that the tension of the bending rods can be increased or decreased, and the blow given with a greater or less degree of severity. In that way it has been possible to make a scale of severity of punishment from o degree to 24 degrees. No. o is when the cross-beam is at its highest point, and is only employed when the punishment bears a merely nominal, or, shall I say, symbolical character. By the time we come to No. 6 a certain amount of pain has become noticeable. We indicate a maximum for use in elementary schools, that would be up to No. 10; in secondary schools up to 15. For soldiers, village prisons and students the limit is set at 20 degrees, and finally, for houses of correction and workmen on strike, the maximum figure, namely, 24.

"There, ladies and gentlemen, is the substance of my invention. There remain the details. That handle at the side, like the handle of a barrel-organ, serves to wind up the spiral spring of the mechanism. The arrow here in this slot regulates the celerity of the strokes. At the height of the pillar, in a little glass case, is a mechanical meter or indicator. This enables one to check the accuracy of the working of the machine, and is also useful for statistical and revisionary purposes. In view of this latter purpose, the indicator is constructed to show a maximum total of 60,000 strokes. Finally, ladies and gentlemen, please to observe something in the nature of an urn at the foot of the pillar. Into this are thrown metal coupons with numbers on them, and this momentarily sets the whole machine in action. The coupons are of various weights and sizes. The smallest is about the size of a silver penny,[1] and effects the minimum punishment—five strokes. The largest is about the size of a hundred-kopeck-bit—a rouble—and effects a punishment of just one hundred strokes. By using various combinations of metal coupons you can effect a punishment of any number of strokes in a multiple of five, from five to three hundred and fifty. But"—and here the lecturer smiled modestly—"but we should not consider that we had completely solved our problem if it were necessary to stop at that limited figure.

"I will ask you, ladies and gentlemen, to note the figure at which the indicator at present stands, and that which it reaches after the punishment has been effected. What is more, the respected public will observe that, up to the moment when the coupons are thrown into the urn, there is no danger whatever in standing on the platform.

"And so . . . the indicator shows 2900. Consequently, having thrown in all the coupons, the pointer will show, at the end of the execution . . . 3250. . . . I fancy I make no mistake!

"And it will be quite sufficient to throw into the urn anything round, of whatever size, and the machine will go on to infinity, if you will, or, if not to infinity, to 780 or 800, at which point the spring would have run down and the machine need rewinding. What I had in view in using these small coupons was that they might commonly be replaced by coins, and each mechanical self-flogger has a comparative table of

[1]Five kopecks silver—the smallest silver coin in Russia.

the stroke-values of copper, silver and gold money. Observe the table here at the side of the main pillar.

"It seems I have finished. . . . There remain just a few particulars concerning the construction of the revolving platform, the swinging chair and the crescent-shaped levers. But as it is a trifle complicated, I will ask the respected public to watch the machine in action, and I shall now have the honour to give a demonstration.

"The whole procedure of punishment consists in the following. First of all, having thoroughly sifted and got to the bottom of the motives of the crime, we fix the extent of the punishment, that is, the number of strokes, the celerity with which they shall be given, and the force, and in some cases the material of the rods. Then we send a note to the man in charge of the machine, or communicate with him by telephone. He puts the machine in readiness and then goes away. Observe, the man goes, the machine remains alone, the impartial, unwavering, calm and just machine.

"In a minute I shall come to the experiment. Instead of a human offender, we have, on this occasion, a leather manni-kin. In order to show the machine at its best we will imagine that we have before us a criminal of the most stubborn type. 'Officer!'" cried the lecturer to someone behind the scenes. "'Prepare the machine, force 24, minimum celerity.'"

In a tense silence the audience watched the attendant wind the handle, push down the cross-beam, turn round the celerity arrow, and then disappear behind the scenes again.

"Now all is in order," the lecturer went on, "and the room in which the flogging machine stands is quite empty. There only remains to call up the man who is to be punished, explain to him the extent of his guilt and the degree of his punishment, and he himself—remark, ladies and gentlemen, himself—takes from the box the corresponding coupon. Of course, it might be arranged that he, there and then, drops the coupon through a slot in the table and lets it fall into the urn; that is a mere detail.

"From that moment the offender is entirely in the hands of the machine. He goes to the dressing-room, he opens the door, stands on the platform, throws the coupon or coupons into the urn, and . . . done! The door shuts mechanically after him, and cannot be reopened. He may stand a moment, hesitating, on the brink, but in the end he simply must throw the coupons in. For, ladies and gentlemen," explained the pedagogue with a triumphant laugh, "for the machine is so constructed that the longer he hesitates the greater becomes the punishment, the number of strokes increasing in a ratio of from five to thirty per minute according to the weight of the person hesitating. . . . However, once the offender is off, he is caught by the machine at three points, neck, waist and feet, and the chair holds him. All this is accomplished literally in one moment. The next moment sounds the first stroke, and nothing can stop the action of the machine, nor weaken the blows, nor increase or diminish the celerity, until that moment when justice has been accomplished. It would be physically impossible, not having the key.

"Officer! Bring in the mannikin!

"Will the esteemed audience kindly indicate the number of the strokes. . . . Just a number, please . . . three figures if you wish, but not more than 350. Please . . ."

"Five hundred," shouted the governor of the fortress.

"Reff," barked the dog under his chair.

"Five hundred is too many," gently objected the lecturer, "but to go as far as we can towards meeting his Excellency's wish let us say 350. We throw into the urn all the coupons."

Whilst he was speaking, the attendant brought in under his arm a monstrous-looking leathern mannikin, and stood it on the floor, holding it up from behind. There was something suggestive and ridiculous in the crooked legs, outstretched arms and forward-hanging head of this leathern dummy.

Standing on the platform of the machine, the lecturer continued:

"Ladies and gentlemen, one last word. I do not doubt that my mechanical self-flogger will be most widely used. Slowly but surely it will find its way into all schools, colleges and seminaries. It will be introduced in the army and navy, in the village, in military and civil prisons, in police-stations and for fire-brigades, and in all truly Russian families.

"The coupons are inevitably replaced by coins, and in that way not only is the cost of the machine redeemed, but a fund is commenced which can be used for charitable and educative ends. Our eternal financial troubles will pass, for, by the aid of this machine, the peasant will be forced to pay his taxes. Sin will disappear, crime, laziness, slovenliness, and in their stead will flourish industry, temperance, sobriety and thrift.

"It is difficult to probe further the possible future of this machine. Did Gutenberg foresee the contribution which book-printing was going to make to the history of human progress when he made his first naïve wooden printing-press? But I am, however, far from airing a foolish self-conceit in your eyes, ladies and gentlemen. The bare idea belongs to me. In the practical details of the invention I have received most practical help from Mr. N——, the teacher of physics in the Fourth Secondary School of this town, and from Mr. X——, the well-known engineer. I take the opportunity of acknowledging my indebtedness."

The hall thundered with applause. Two men in the front of the stalls stood up timidly and awkwardly, and bowed to the public.

"For me personally," continued the lecturer, "there has been the greatest satisfaction to consider the good I was doing my beloved fatherland. Here, ladies and gentlemen, is a token which I have lately received from the governor and nobility of Kursk, with the motto! *Similia similibus.*"

He detached from its chain and held aloft an immense

antique chronometer, about half a pound in weight. From the watch dangled also a massive gold medal.

"I have finished, ladies and gentlemen," added the lecturer in a low and solemn voice, bowing as he spoke.

But the applause had not died down before there happened something incredible, appalling. The chronometer suddenly slipped from the raised hand of the pedagogue and fell with a metallic clash right into the urn.

At once the machine began to hum and click. The platform inverted, and the lecturer was suddenly hoist with his own petard. His coat-tails waved in the air; there was a sudden thwack and a wild cry.

2901 indicated the mechanical reckoner.

It is difficult to describe rapidly and definitely what happened in the meeting. For a few seconds everyone was turned to stone. In the general silence sounded only the cries of the victim, the whistling of the rods, and the clicking of the counting-machine. Then suddenly everyone rushed up on to the stage.

"For the love of the Lord!" cried the unfortunate man, "for the love of the Lord!"

But it was impossible to help him. The valorous physics teacher put out a hand to catch one of the rods as they came, but drew it back at once, and the blood on his fingers was visible to all. No efforts could raise the cross-beam.

"The key! Quick, the key!" cried the pedagogue. "In my trouser pocket."

The devoted attendant dashed in to search his pockets, with difficulty avoiding blows from the machine. But the key was not to be found.

2950, 2951, 2952, 2953, clicked the counting-machine.

"Oh, your honour!" cried the attendant through his tears. "Let me take your trousers off. They are quite new, and they will be ruined. . . . Ladies can turn the other way."

"Go to blazes, idiot! Oey, o-o! . . . Gentlemen, for God's

sake! . . . Oey, oey! . . . I forgot. . . . The keys are in my overcoat. . . . Oey! Quickly!"

They ran to the ante-room for his overcoat. But neither was there any key there. Evidently the inventor had left it at home. Someone was sent to fetch it. A gentleman present offered his carriage.

And the sharp blows registered themselves every second with mathematical precision; the pedagogue shouted; the counting-machine went indifferently on . . . 3180, 3181, 3182. . . .

One of the garrison lieutenants drew his sword and began to hack at the apparatus, but after the fifth blow there remained only the hilt, and a jumping splinter hit the president of the Zemstvo. Most dreadful of all was the fact that it was impossible to guess to what point the flogging would go on. The chronometer was proving itself weighty. The man sent for the key still did not return, and the counter, having long since passed the figure previously indicated by the inventor, went on placidly:

3999, 4000, 4001.

The pedagogue jumped no longer. He just lay with gaping mouth and protruding eyes, and only twitched convulsively.

At last, the governor of the fortress, boiling with indignation, roared out to the accompaniment of the barking of his dog:

"Madness! Debauch! Unheard of! Order up the fire-brigade!"

This idea was the wisest. The governor of the town was an enthusiast for the fire-brigade, and had smartened the firemen to a rare pitch. In less than five minutes, and at that moment when the indicator showed stroke No. 4550, the brave young fellows of the fire-brigade broke on the scene with choppers and hooks.

The magnificent mechanical self-flogger was destroyed for ever and ever. With the machine perished also the idea. As regards the inventor, it should be said that, after a considerable time of feeling sore in a corporal way and of nervous weakness, he returned to his occupation. But the fatal occasion completely changed his character. He became for the rest of his life a calm, sweet, melancholy man, and though he taught Latin and Greek he was a favourite with the schoolboys.

He has never returned to his invention.

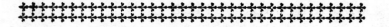

IVAN BUNIN
(1870—1957)

✢✢

(I)

NEVER-ENDING SPRING

(Translated by HELEN MATHESON)

. . . A n d then, my friend, something important happened to
me : in June I went into the country, to the provinces (to visit
one of my new acquaintances whom you do not know). Of
course, I remember the time when such things were not considered of any importance. I suppose that in Europe they
would not be counted important even now. But there are
still lots of things in Europe that we used to have. Two or
three hundred versts are no joke here. In Russia, which has
again become Muscovy, distances have again become enormous. And Muscovites do not travel much nowadays. Of
course, we are now so rich in rights that we could dispense
with some of them. But don't forget that all these rights,
which we had never hoped to see, are of very recent
date.

In a word, something very unusual happened, something I
had not experienced for years : one fine day, I took a cab and
drove to the railway station. You wrote to me once that the
Moscow of to-day looked "unutterable." Yes, it is very disgusting. I felt it acutely as I drove to the station, excited by
the novelty of being a traveller. The cab resembled one of
those old things that could only be found formerly in the
remotest depths of the country, and for which you paid, not
milliards as you do to-day, but about fourpence. What an
Asiatic crowd ; what a lot of street trading, on trays, in rag

markets, or "navels,"[1] to use the vulgar language which is becoming more and more fashionable here. How many dilapidated houses! What holes in the road! How the surviving trees have spread! There are "navels" in the square in front of the railway station, a constant buying and selling, a collection of the basest scum, jobbers, thieves, prostitutes, hawkers of every kind of rotten provisions. The stations still have refreshment-rooms and waiting-rooms of different classes, but they are nothing but barns, and hopelessly filthy. And always crowds of people—one can hardly push one's way through; the trains are infrequent; thanks to the general disorder and various restrictions, it is very difficult to obtain a ticket, while as to getting into the train, which is of course antediluvian, its wheels red with rust, that is a regular feat. Many people go to the station the evening before they want to start. I arrived two hours before the train was due to depart, and nearly paid for such rashness by being left ticketless. However, in some way (which, of course, means with a bribe) I did get a ticket. I got into the train, and even found a seat on a bench instead of having to sit on the floor. The train started, Moscow remained behind, and the woods, fields and villages, which I had not seen for so long, began to make their appearance. They, like Moscow, had returned to the drabbest of workadays after the dissipated debauchery in which Russia had indulged at such a fabulous price. Soon nearly all the people packed in the carriage began to shut their eyes, lean back, and snore with open mouths. A big, self-assured peasant was sitting opposite to me. At first he did nothing but smoke and spit on the floor, which he would then rub with the toe of his creaking boot. Later, he produced a bottle of milk from his pocket and began to drink in long gulps, removing his lips from the neck only to take breath. When he had emptied the bottle, he flung himself back, leaned against the partition, and proceeded to snore. The smell of the man nearly drove me mad, and, unable to

[1] Small trade centres.

bear it, I rose and went on to the platform between the cars. There I found an acquaintance whom I had not seen for about four years. He stood there swaying with the rocking of the train, the celebrated B——, formerly a professor and rich. I hardly recognised him, he looked an old man and something like a pilgrim to holy places. His shoes, his overcoat, his hat, were fearful, even worse than my own clothes. He had not shaved for ages; his long grey hair fell to his shoulders, and in his hand he held a bag of old sacking. Another sack lay on the floor at his feet. "I am returning home to the country," he told me. "I have been given an allotment on my former estate, where I live in the same way as the simple-lifer you are just going to stay with; that is, I get my food by doing manual labour. I devote my spare time to my historical *magnum opus*, which will be epoch-making."

The sun, a pale disc, was already low beyond the trunks of the forest trees. Half an hour later, the author of the epoch-making book got down at a halt, and trudged away in the cold evening twilight along a path through a green birch wood.

It was nearly dark when I reached my destination at about eleven o'clock. The train was late, and the peasant who had been sent to meet me had waited and waited and then gone home. I found myself in a ridiculous position. What was I to do? Spend my night at the railway station? But the station was locked up at night, and, even if it had not been, there was not a sofa or a bench in it—"nowadays, friend, there are no gentry"—but even a subject of the Soviets does not willingly spend a night on bare boards. Hire some other peasant from the village near the station? But in these times such a thing is practically impossible.

A peasant who was waiting for the night train to Moscow was sitting at the station entrance, sad and apathetic. I discussed it with him. He only shook his head. "Nobody would go. There are very few horses, and all the harness is broken.

You have to pay two milliards for a set of wheels—it is terrify-
ing to talk about such sums. How far do you want to go?"
So-and-so. "Well, that's about twenty versts, not more.
You'll do it."

"But," I said, "on foot through the forest?"

"What does the forest matter? You'll do it."

But he thereupon told me how in the spring two "chaps"
had hired a peasant in his village, and all three had disappeared. "They and he and the horse and the harness. And
nobody knows who killed which—they him or he them. No,
times aren't what they used to be."

Obviously, after such a tale, I lost all inclination to travel
by night. I decided to ask one of the station pubs to put me
up, and to wait till morning. "There are two here," the
peasant told me. But it turned out to be impossible to spend
the night in either—they refused to take me in. "You can
have some tea if you like," I was told in one, "we do serve
tea." I drank tea, or rather the sickening infusion of some
herb, for a long time in a dimly-lighted room. Then I said:
"At least let me sit on your porch till morning." "Oh, you
wouldn't be comfortable on the porch." "More comfortable
than on the road." "You aren't armed?" "Pray search me."
I turned out all my pockets, I unbuttoned my coat. "Well,
please yourself, I suppose you can stay on the porch, because
no one would let you into a cottage, and, for the matter of
that, everyone is asleep by now."

I went out and sat on the porch, and the lights in the inn
soon went out (the inn next door had been in darkness for
some time). It was night, still and slumberous. What a long
night! In the distant sky, beyond the black forest, the hazy
sickle of the moon was setting. When it disappeared, summer
lightning illuminated the place. I sat still, I paced up and
down in front of the porch, along the barely defined white
road. I sat down again, I smoked cheap tobacco on an empty
stomach. About two o'clock I heard the sound of wheels,
the patting of traces between the shafts. A little later some-

body drove up to the inn next door and tapped on the window in a manner suggestive of a thieves' code. A head peered from the door, then the landlord stealthily crept out, that same landlord who, earlier in the evening, had refused with such astonishing rudeness and ferocity to take me in. Then a mysterious process began: innumerable bundles of what looked like sheepskins were dragged from the house and packed into the visitor's cart, while the summer lightning lit up the road, the forest, the huts more and more vividly. A fresh wind had sprung up, and thunder muttered menacingly in the distance. I sat there, lost in admiration. Do you remember the thunderstorms in the nights at Vasileusk? Do you remember how the entire household was frightened by them? Just think, I have lost all that fear now. And, sitting on the porch of the inn that night, I was enraptured by the rainless storm which seemed to come to nothing. In the end, however, I felt dead tired from my wakeful hours. And I felt discouraged: how was I to walk twenty versts after a sleepless night?

But at dawn, when the clouds behind the forest paled and dispersed and everything took on a normal appearance, a bit of luck came my way. An open carriage drove quickly past the inn, taking to the Moscow train the Commissar who was administering the former estate of Prince D——, which was situated in the very district to which I was going. The landlady, who was leaning out of the window, gave me this information, so when the coachman was driving out of the station yard, I ran towards him and, with extraordinary readiness, he agreed to give me a lift.

He turned out to be charming; a childishly ingenuous giant who, all through the journey, told me the most awful things with an air of happy surprise. He kept on repeating, the whole way, "It was more than eyes could bear to see. It made you weep!"

Meanwhile, the sun was rising, and the crazy, broad-backed, grey-white stallion, deaf from old age, took the carriage along the forest road easily and quickly. The carriage was old but very good, and as comfortable as a cradle. It was a long time since I had ridden in a carriage, my friend!

The acquaintance with whom I spent my few days in the forest was in many respects a strange man. He was self-taught and only half educated. He had been living in Moscow, but had left there the year before to return to his native soil, where he had inherited a peasant farm. He passionately hated the Moscow of to-day, and had often insisted that I ought to get out of it and go to stay with him for a rest. He laid stress on the beauties of his country, and it was indeed wonderful. Imagine a well-to-do, peaceful, decorous village in which it seemed as though nothing had ever happened, not only all the recent events, but even the Napoleonic invasion and the liberation of the serfs. And surrounding it were the virgin forest, silence and peace indescribable. Dark, echoing pine forests predominated, and in its depths in the evening I was conscious not merely of the past, of antiquity, but of eternity itself. Light only came through in spots, it was only here and there that the glow of the slowly setting sun could be seen through the tree-tops. The warm aromatic scent of the pine needles, dried by the day's heat, mingled with the sharp freshness of the marshy banks of the deep, narrow river, from the hidden windings of which white mists rose in the evening. There was no sound of birds—a dead silence, except for the monotonous and everlasting note of the young fern-owls, so like the sound of a spindle. And, when it was quite dark and the stars shone above the forest, from all sides came the happy calls of the owls. There is something pre-creation, pre-time in their voices, in which the love-call, in awed anticipation of union, sounds like a sob and a laugh and a cry of dread on the verge of the abyss of destruction. So I spent my evenings wandering in the forest, full of the whirring of the fern-owls, and I dedicated my days to the enchantment of the one-time princely palace. It is indeed "one-time," for not a single member of the princely family is alive. The place is unexpectedly beautiful.

The days were hot and sunny. The way to the estate led me along a sandy path, now shaded, now in the sun, airless as it wound through the sweet scent of the pines, then along the overgrown banks of the river, where I scared a kingfisher and looked down, sometimes at open shallows, covered with water-lilies and dragon-flies, sometimes at shaded rapids where the water seemed black, though it was as transparent as a tear, in which tiny silver fish shimmered, and flat greenish heads showed their bulging eyes. Then I crossed the old stone bridge and went up to the manor.

It has, by good fortune, remained untouched, unlooted. It has all the usual characteristics of such manors. There is a church, built by a famous Italian; there are several wonderful ponds; there is a lake called the swan lake, in the centre of which is an island with a pavilion, where many a fête was given to Catherine when she visited the place; further on there is a gorge where the firs and pines are so tall that your hat falls off if you try to see their tops. Their branches are heavy with the nests of kites, herons and big black birds with funereal topknots of feathers on their heads.

The house, or rather the palace, was built by the same Italian who built the church. Passing through the enormous stone gateposts, on which reclined two superciliously drowsy lions, and where tall grass was already growing (the very grass of forgetfulness), I made my way straight to the palace. In the vestibule a one-armed Chinaman sat all day in an antique satin chair, a short rifle lying across his knees. For, you see, the palace is now a museum, "the property of the people," and has to be guarded.

No one, of course, but a Chinaman could have borne that idiotic sitting still in an empty house; indeed, there was something gruesome about it. But the one-armed, short-legged fool, with yellow, wooden face, sat calmly there smoking vile tobacco, crooning pathetically to himself like an old woman, and staring indifferently at me as I passed him.

"Don't you be afraid of him, sir," said the coachman, as one speaks of dogs. "I've told him about you, and he won't touch you." And indeed the Chinaman did not touch me. If he had been ordered to kill me, he would have done so without turning a hair. But, as there was no need to kill me, he merely glanced at me sleepily. I was free to spend hours in the palace as though it were my own. I wandered from one room to another in contemplation, thinking my own thoughts. The ceilings glittered with gilt mouldings, gilded coats of arms, Latin mottoes. (If you only knew how unaccustomed my eyes are not only to things of beauty, but even to cleanliness!) Priceless furniture was reflected in the polished floors. In one room there was a lofty bed of some dark wood under a canopy of red satin, and a Venetian chest which opened mysteriously to the sound of sweet music. In another, a whole wall was occupied by a clock with chimes, and in a third was a mediæval organ. And, on every side, busts, statues, portraits, gazed down at me. Heavens! What beautiful women! What handsome, blue-eyed men in their uniforms, their tunics, their wigs and their diamonds! And, more regal, more radiant than all the rest—Catherine! With what gay grace she adorned and dominated that brilliant circle!

In one of the studies, on a small writing-table, I found, to my astonishment, a brown log bearing a golden plate. The engraved inscription was to the effect that this was a relic of the flagship *St. Eustace*, which went down in the battle of Chesma "to the honour and glory of the Russian Empire." Yes—the honour and glory of the Russian Empire. It sounds strange now, doesn't it?

I often visited the ground floor. You know my passion for books, and the library was housed in those vaulted rooms. It was always cool there; the sun never penetrated to these vaults. The windows were barred by thick iron grilles, and

through them one could see the joyous green bushes, the
happy summer day, everything just as it used to be, just as
it was a century, two centuries ago. There were shelved
recesses in the walls, containing thousands of volumes with
dull-gold backs—nearly all the important literary works of
Russia and Europe for the last two hundred years. In one
hall was an enormous telescope, in another a gigantic planet-
arium; on the walls more portraits, priceless engravings.

I picked out an exquisite volume, dating from the beginning
of the last century, and read:

> "Tempestuous soul, find peace;
> Thy burning passions quell:
> Shepherd, thy piping cease;
> My soul at rest would dwell."

For a long while I stood enchanted. What rhythm, what
charm! With what graceful steps the transitions of feeling
were accomplished! Now, when nothing but "navels"
remain of "the honour and glory of the Russian Empire,"
they write differently: "The sun, like a pool of horse
urine. . . ."

On another day I happened to take up a volume of Baratinsky, and, as though predestined to do so, opened it at this
poem:

> "Though vanished the past, like a dream that has fled,
> Still lovely, Elysian, art thou,
> And thy magical charm, in spite of neglect,
> Fills my soul as I turn to thee now."

Just before leaving I went to the celebrated church. It is
in the forest, on the edge of a ravine, circular, primrose-
hued, its golden dome glittering under the blue sky. Inside
the church a circle of yellow marble columns support the
airy, luminous dome. In the circular aisle between the
columns and the wall hang pictures of saints who have
the conventionalised faces of the dead who are buried in the
church vaults. Through the narrow windows I could see the

wind twisting the ragged tops of the pines and firs flung with wild grandeur above the ravine on a level with the casements; I could hear its droning song.

I went down into the impenetrable darkness of the crypt. The red flame of a wax candle-end lit up the enormous marble sepulchres, the gigantic iron candlesticks and the golden mosaic in relief on the arches. The chill of the underworld exhaled from the tombs. Were they really here, those blue-eyed beauties who had reigned in the rooms of the palace? I could not reconcile myself to the thought.

I went up to the church again, and for a long time I watched the stormy, heaving agitation of the firs through the narrow windows. Behind me lay the church, sadly bright, forgotten by the sun, empty, forsaken perhaps for ever. The silence of death reigned within its walls, while outside the summer wind sang and whistled just as it did, exactly as it did, a century, two centuries ago. And I was alone, absolutely alone, not merely in this bright dead church, but, it seemed, in the whole world. Who could be with me? Among the multitude doomed to perish, I was, by some miracle, one of the few who survived, having lived through such a catastrophe as history had never before witnessed.

That was my last visit. I left next day.

And now, as you see, I am again in Moscow. Over a month has passed since I returned, but the deep, indeed the unutterably strange impressions I brought back abide with me. I think that they will never leave me. You see, all that I felt and understood so vividly, so acutely, during my expedition had been for ages evolving slowly in my mind. I do not foresee, indeed there cannot be, anything in the future to change the state in which I find myself. They—the people of the so-called new life—are right: there can be no return to the past, and the new holds undisputed sway—it has become ordinary, normal. I never lose consciousness of the fact that the last threads attaching me to the world around me are loosening, breaking; that I renounce it more and more, returning to that world of which I have been a part, not only since childhood, since infancy, since birth, but even since before birth. I return to the Elysium of my memories, of my visions, to a dream sparkling with the same glowing, impressive, living life as that in which lived the blue-eyed dead now cold in the empty palace in the forest.

You see, of course, that there has been a miracle. One who was rotting in an old grave was not so utterly destroyed as were those thousands of others who were thrown into it. Little by little, to his own great surprise, he recovered his senses, and eventually was able to raise himself and to return again to the world. He is now once more among the living; once more acquiring the habit of being—or at least of seeming to be—like others; once more he sees the town, the sky, the sun; once more he takes thought of food, clothes, work, position. But, my friend, can death, even temporary death, leave a man unscathed? Moreover, most important of all, how fabulously the world has changed, while we, so miraculously saved, have been lying in the grave. I repeat, such devastation, such a complete transformation of the whole face of the world in some short five years is unprecedented in the history of mankind. Imagine the almost instantaneous destruction of the old world and a few men buried under the ruins, under an avalanche of barbaric hordes. Suddenly they awake after two or three centuries; what must they feel? My God! Their first feeling is one of loneliness, terrible loneliness. For a long time I have been obsessed by the feeling that the more convinced I am of the reality, the actual reality, of my resurrection, the more overwhelming is the consciousness of the terrible change which had taken place. Of course I am not speaking of externals, though in externals we have reached an unheard-of pitch of abomination which centuries will not mend. . . . I look around me more and more carefully; I recall more and more clearly my life before death. . . . And the obsession grows: the old world to which I belonged is not, for me, a dead world. It is gradually resuscitating, and, inaccessible for others, it becomes the only, the joyful dwelling-place of my soul.

When I was leaving Moscow, as I drove through the streets, I felt more and more acutely what I had been feeling for a long time: how much I belonged to another period, another century, how alien to me were "navels" and the new creatures rushing about in motor-cars. Think of the station from which I started, the carriage in which I managed to get a seat, my neighbour drinking milk from a bottle. Remember the professor with his sacks and his scientific dreams, remember the forest path along which he trudged alone, so terribly alone. When the train stopped for a moment at the halt where he got off, I was greatly struck by the first, almost terrifying, impressions of silence, of forest depths, the scent of birch trees and flowers, the freshness of eventide.

My God! my God! Once more, after a thousand years of the galleys, once more this pure, sacred silence, the setting sun sinking behind the wood, the horizon, the arch of the forest path, the bitterish fresh scents, the delicious coolness of the gloaming—I felt how utterly alien I was to that world which had deprived me of all the things by which I lived and breathed; to the Soviet train in the corridor of which I was standing; to the peasant sleeping in it. . . .

So deep, so strong became this feeling of estrangement, that tears of happiness filled my eyes. Yes, I had survived; by a miracle I had not been destroyed as thousands of others had been destroyed: beaten to death, tortured, lost, leaving no trace, or dead by their own hands, shot, hanged—I was alive. I was even travelling. But what had I in common with that new life which had made the world a desert for me? I was alive—and at such moments as these I experienced exultant joy—but where was I living, and with whom?

And the night that I had spent on the inn porch was also a part of my resuscitated past. Had it been for me a night in June of the year 1923? No, it had seemed to be one of those earlier, unforgettable nights, the lightning, the thunder, the fresh breeze that preceded the storm were all of the past. And the impenetrable forest, the old manor—they took me straight back to the world of the dead, dead for ever and at rest now in the bliss of their unearthly abode.

And now, I have ever before me that sunny realm with its summer days and the wood in which the fairy palace is lost in slumber; the gateway with the lions and the tall grass on the top of the posts; the sombre fir avenues; the shallow ponds with many wagtails on their verdant banks; the lake overgrown with reeds; the for ever forsaken church; the glittering halls filled with the portraits of the dead. I cannot tell you how terribly alive to me all that is, I am obsessed by the amazing consciousness of its reality!

Do you remember those verses by Baratinsky, from which I have already quoted a few lines, and which harmonise so well with all that is of importance in my life to-day, all that is hidden in the innermost recesses of my heart?

Do you remember the end of that elegy which Baratinsky, burdened with sorrows and losses, dedicated to the Elysium of which he had a glimpse? There, in his devastated land, amid ruins and graves, "I feel," he says, "the invisible presence of a spirit, and he, this shade of Lethe, this phantom,

> "He solemnly foretells a land for me,
> A heritage of never-ending Spring;
> In which no trace of ruin I shall see,
> And, in the shade of oaks unfading, I,
> On banks of streams that flow eternally,
> Shall meet the spirit shrined within my heart."

The devastation which surrounds us is indescribable, the ruins and the graves are without number. What is there left for us but the shades of Lethe and that "never-ending Spring" to which they so " solemnly" call us?

Alpes Maritimes, 5/10/1923.

(II)

SUNSTROKE

(Translated by HELEN MATHESON)

L E A V I N G the hot, brightly lighted dining saloon after dinner, they went on deck and stood near the rail. She closed her eyes, leant her cheek on the back of her hand, and laughed—a clear, charming laugh—everything about this little woman was charming.

"I am quite drunk," she said. "In fact I have gone mad. Where did you come from? Three hours ago I did not know of your existence. I don't even know where you got on the boat. Was it Samara? But it doesn't matter, you're a dear. Am I dizzy, or is the boat really turning round?"

In front of them lay darkness and the light of lamps. A soft wind blew strongly against their faces and carried the light to one side. With the smartness characteristic of the Volga boats, the steamer was making a wide curve towards the small wharf.

The lieutenant took her hand and raised it to his lips. The firm little fragrant hand was tanned. His heart became faint with fear and ecstasy as he thought how strong and bronzed must be the body under the light linen dress after having basked in the Southern sun on the hot beach for a whole month. (She had told him that she was on her way from Anapi.)

"Let's get off," he murmured.

"Where?" she asked in surprise.

"At this wharf."

"What for?"

He was silent. She raised her hand to her hot cheek again.

"You are mad."

"Let's get off," he repeated stubbornly. "I implore you——"

"Oh, do as you like," she said, turning from him.

With its final impetus, the steamer bumped gently against the dimly lit wharf, and they nearly fell over each other. The end of a rope flew over their heads, the boat heaved back, there was a foam of churning waters, the gangways clattered. The lieutenant rushed away to collect their things.

A moment later they passed through the sleepy ticket office into the ankle-deep sand of the road, and silently got into a dusty open cab. The soft, sandy road sloping gradually up-hill, lit by crooked lamp-posts at long intervals on either side, seemed unending, but they reached its top and clattered along a high-road until they came to a sort of square with municipal buildings and a watch-tower. It was all full of warmth and the smells peculiar to a hot night in a small provincial town. The cab drew up at a lighted portico, behind the door of which a steep old wooden stairway was visible, and an old unshaven waiter, in a pink shirt and black coat, reluctantly took their luggage, and led the way in his down-at-heel slippers. They entered a large room stuffy from the hot sun which had beaten on it all day, its white curtains drawn. On the toilet table were two unlit candles.

The instant the door closed on the waiter, the lieutenant sprang towards her with such impetuosity, and they were carried away by a breathless kiss of such passion, that they remembered it for many, many years. Neither of them had ever before experienced anything like it.

At ten o'clock next morning the little, nameless woman left. She never told him her name, and referred to herself jokingly as "the fair stranger." It was a hot, sunny morning. Church bells were ringing, and a market was in full swing in the square in front of the hotel. There were scents of hay and tar and all the odours characteristic of a Russian provincial town.

They had not slept much, but when she emerged from behind the screen, where she had washed and dressed in five minutes, she was as fresh as a girl of seventeen. Was she embarrassed? Very little, if at all. She was as simple and gay as before, and—already rational. "No, no, dear," she said in reply to his request that they should continue the journey together. "No, you must wait for the next boat. If we go together, it will spoil it all. It would be very unpleasant for me. I give you my word of honour that I am not in the least what you may think I am. Nothing at all like this has ever happened to me before or will ever happen again. I seem to have been under a spell. Or, rather, we both seem to have had something like sunstroke."

The lieutenant readily agreed with her. In a bright, happy mood he drove her to the wharf—just before the pink steamer of the Samolet Line started. He kissed her openly on the deck, and had barely time to get ashore before the gangway was lowered. He returned to the hotel in the same care-free, easy mood. But something had changed. The room without her seemed quite different from what it had been with her. He was still full of her; he did not mind, but it was strange. The room still held the scent of her excellent English lavender water, her unfinished cup of tea still stood on the tray, but she was gone. . . . The lieutenant's heart was suddenly filled with such a rush of tenderness that he hurriedly lit a cigarette and began to pace the room, switching his topboots with his cane.

"A strange adventure," he said aloud, laughing and feeling tears well up in his eyes. " 'I give you my word of honour that I am not in the least what you think I am,' and she's gone. Absurd woman!"

The screen had been moved—the bed had not been made. He felt that he had not the strength to look at that bed. He put the screen in front of it, closed the window to shut out the creaking of the wheels and the noisy chatter of the market, drew the white billowing curtains, and sat down on the sofa. Yes, the roadside adventure was over. She was gone, and now, far away, she was probably sitting in the windowed saloon, or on deck, gazing at the enormous river glittering in the sun, at the barges drifting down-stream, at the yellow shoals, at the shining horizon of sky and water, at the immeasurable sweep of the Volga. And it was good-bye for ever and ever. For where could they possibly meet again? "For," he thought, "I can hardly appear on the scene without any excuse, in the town where she lives her everyday life with her husband, her three-year-old daughter and all her family."

The town seemed to him a special, a forbidden town. He was aggravated and stunned by the thought that she would live her lonely life there, often perhaps remembering him, recalling their brief encounter, that he would never see her again. No, it was impossible. It would be too mad, too unnatural, too fantastic. He suffered and was overwhelmed by horror and despair in feeling that without her his whole life would be futile. "Damn it all!" he thought, as he got up and began to pace the room again, trying not to look at the bed behind the screen. "What in the world's the matter with me? It's not the first time, is it? And yet—— Was there anything very special about her, or did anything very special happen? It really is like sunstroke. And how on earth am I to spend a whole day in this hole without her?"

He still remembered all of her, down to the minutest detail: her sunburn, her linen frock, her strong body, her unaffected, bright, gay voice. . . . The sense of ecstatic joy which her feminine charm had given him was still extraordinarily strong, but now a second feeling rose uppermost in his mind —a new, strange, incomprehensible feeling, which had not been there while they had been together, and of which he would not, the day before, have believed himself capable when he had started what he had thought to be the amusement of a passing acquaintance. And now there was no one, no one, whom he could tell. "And the point is," he thought, "that I never shall be able to tell anyone! And how am I to get through this endless day with these memories, this inexplicable agony, in this god-forsaken town on the banks of that same Volga along which the steamer is carrying her away?" He must do something to save himself, something to distract him, he must go somewhere. He put on his hat with an air of determination, took his stick and walked along the corridor with his spurs jingling, ran down the stairs and out on to the porch. But where should he go? A cab was drawn up in front of the hotel. A young, smartly-dressed driver sat on the box calmly smoking a cigar. He was obviously waiting for someone. The lieutenant stared at him, bewildered and astonished: How could anyone sit calmly on a box and smoke and in general be unmoved and indifferent? "I suppose that in the whole town there is no one so miserably unhappy as I am," he thought, as he went towards the market.

It was already breaking up. For some unknown reason he found himself making his way over fresh droppings, among carts, loads of cucumbers, stacks of pots and pans, and women seated on the ground who outdid each other in their efforts to attract his attention. They lifted basins and tapped them that he might hear how sound they were, while the men deafened him with cries of "First-class cucumbers, your honour." It was all so stupid, so ridiculous that he fled from the square. He went into the cathedral, where the choir was singing loudly, resolutely, as though conscious of fulfilling a duty; then he strolled aimlessly about a small, hot, unkempt garden on the edge of a cliff overhanging the silvery steel breadth of the river.

The epaulettes and buttons of his linen uniform were unbearably hot to the touch. The inside of his hat was wet, his face was burning. He returned to the hotel and was delighted to get into the large, empty, cool dining-room, delighted to take off his hat and seat himself at a small table near the open window. The heat penetrated from outside, but it was airy. He ordered iced soup.

Everything was all right in this unknown town, happiness and joy emanated from everything, from the heat and the market smells. Even this old provincial hotel seemed full of gladness, and yet his heart was being torn to pieces. He drank several glasses of vodka and ate a salted cucumber with parsley. He felt that he would unhesitatingly die to-morrow if, by some miracle, he could achieve her return and spend to-day, only this one day, with her, solely, solely in order that he might tell her and prove to her and convince her somehow of his agonising and exalted love for her. "Why prove? Why convince?" He did not know why, but it was more essential than life.

"My nerves have all gone to pieces," he said, pouring out his fifth glass of vodka. He drank the entire contents of the small decanter, hoping to stupefy, to benumb himself, hoping to get rid at last of this agonising and exalted feeling. But, instead, it increased. He pushed away the soup, ordered black coffee, and began to smoke and to think with intensity. What was he to do now, how was he to free himself from this sudden and unexpected love? To free himself—but he felt only too clearly that that was impossible. He rose abruptly, quickly, took his hat and his stick, asked the way to the post office and hurried off, the text of the telegram already composed in his mind: "Henceforth all my life, for all time till death, is yours, in your power." But on reaching the thick-walled old building which housed the post and telegraph, he stopped in dismay. He knew the name of her town, he knew that she had a husband and a child of three, but he knew neither her first name nor her surname. Last night, while they were dining at the hotel, he had asked her several times, and each time she had answered with a laugh: "Why do you want to know who I am? I am Marie Marevna, the mysterious princess of the fairy story; or the fair stranger; isn't that enough for you?"

At the corner of the street, near the post office, was a photo-grapher's window. He stared for a long time at the portrait of an officer in braided epaulettes, with protruding eyes, a low forehead, unusually luxuriant whiskers, and a very broad

chest entirely covered with orders. How mad, how ridiculous, how terrifyingly ordinary, everyday things appear when
the heart is struck—yes, *struck*, he understood it now, by the
"sunstroke" of a love too great, a joy too immense. He
looked at the picture of a bridal couple—a young man in a
frock-coat and white tie, with closely-cropped hair, very
erect, arm-in-arm with a girl in white tulle. His gaze wandered to a pretty piquant girl wearing a student's cap on the
back of her head.

Then, filled with envy of all these unknown people who
were not suffering, he stared fixedly down the street. "Where
shall I go? What shall I do?" The difficult, unanswerable
questions occupied both mind and soul.

The street was completely empty. All the houses were alike,
middle-class, two-storied white houses with large gardens,
but they were lifeless; the pavement was covered with thick
white dust; it was all blinding, all bathed in hot, flaming,
joyful sun which now somehow seemed futile. In the distance
the street rose, humped and ran into the clear, cloudless,
grey-mauve horizon. There was something southern about
it; it reminded one of Sebastopol, Kertch—Anapi. This was
more than he could bear. With eyes half closed and head
bowed from the light, staring intently at the pavement, staggering, stumbling, catching one spur in the other, the
lieutenant retraced his steps.

He returned to the hotel worn out with fatigue, as though
he had done a long day's march in Turkestan or the Sahara.
With a final effort he got to his large empty room. It had been
"done." The last traces of her were gone except for one hair-
pin forgotten by her on the table. He took off his coat and
looked at himself in the mirror. He saw reflected, skin bronzed
and moustache bleached by the sun, the bluish whites of the
eyes looking so much whiter on account of the tan, an ordinary
enough officer's face, but now wild and excited. And about
the whole figure standing there in the thin white shirt and
stiff collar there was something pathetically young and

terribly unhappy. He lay down on the bed, on his back, resting his dusty boots on the footrail. The windows were open, the blinds were lowered. From time to time a slight wind billowed them out, letting in the heat, the smell of hot roofs and of all the radiant, but now empty, silent, deserted Volga country-side. He lay there, his hands under his head, and stared into space. In his mind he had a vague picture of the far-away south: sun and sea, Anapi. Then arose something fantastic, a town unlike any other town—the town in which she lived, which she had probably already reached. The thought of suicide stubbornly persisted. He closed his eyes and felt hot, smarting tears well up under his eyelids. Then at last he fell asleep, and when he woke he could see by the reddish-yellow light of the sun that it was evening. The wind had died down, the room was as hot and dry as an oven. Yesterday and this morning both seemed ten years ago. Unhurriedly he rose, unhurriedly he washed, drew up the blinds and rang for a samovar and his bill, and for a long time sat there drinking tea with lemon. Then he ordered a cab to be called and his things to be carried down. As he got into the cab with its faded red seat, he gave the waiter five roubles. "I believe I brought you here last night, your honour," said the driver gaily as he gathered up the reins.

By the time they reached the wharf, the Volga was roofed by the blue of the summer night. Multitudes of many-tinted lights were dotted along the river, and bright lamps shone from the masts of the ships.

"I got you here in the nick of time," said the cabdriver ingratiatingly.

The lieutenant gave five roubles to him also, took his ticket and went to the landing-place. Just as it had done yesterday, the boat bumped gently as it touched the wharf, there was the same slight dizziness from the unsteadiness underfoot, the end of a rope was thrown, there was a sound of foaming and rushing water under the paddles as the steamer backed a little. . . .

The brightly lighted, crowded steamer, smelling of food, seemed unusually friendly and agreeable, and in a few minutes it was speeding forward up the river, whither in the morning she had been carried.

The last glimmer of summer twilight gradually faded on the far horizon; capriciously, lazily reflecting their varied hues in the river, making here and there bright patches on the rippling surface under the dim dome of blue, the gleaming lights everywhere sprinkled in the darkness seemed to be swimming, swimming back.

Under an awning on deck sat the lieutenant. He felt older by ten years.

Alpes Maritimes, 1925.

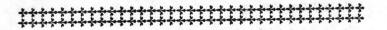

LEONIDE ANDREYEF

(1871–1919)

✣✣

THE LITTLE ANGEL

I

A T times Sashka wished to give up what is called living: to cease to wash every morning in cold water, on which thin sheets of ice floated about; to go no more to the grammar school, and there to have to listen to everyone scolding him; no more to experience the pain in the small of his back and indeed over his whole body when his mother made him kneel in the corner all the evening. But, since he was only thirteen years of age, and did not know all the means by which people abandon life at will, he continued to go to the grammar school and to kneel in the corner in the evening, and it seemed to him as if life would never end. A year would go by, and another, and yet another, and still he would be going to school, and be made to kneel in the corner. And since Sashka possessed an indomitable and bold spirit, he could not supinely tolerate evil, and so found means to avenge himself on life. With this object in view he would thrash his companions, be rude to the Head, impertinent to the masters, and tell lies all day long to his teachers and to his mother—but to his father only he never lied. If in a fight he got his nose broken, he would purposely make the damage worse, and howl, without shedding a single tear, but so loudly that all who heard him wanted to stop their ears to keep out the disagreeable sound. When he had howled as long as he thought advisable, he would suddenly cease, and, putting out his tongue, would draw in his copy-book a caricature of himself howling at an usher who pressed his

fingers to his ears, while the victor stood trembling with
fear. The whole copy-book was filled with caricatures, the
one which most frequently occurred being that of a short
stout woman beating a boy as thin as a lucifer-match with a
rolling pin. Below in a large scrawling hand would be written
the legend: "Beg my pardon, puppy!" and the reply,
"Won't! hang me if I do!"

Before Christmas Sashka was expelled from school, and
when his mother attempted to thrash him, he bit her finger.
This action gave him his liberty. He left off washing in
the morning, ran about all day bullying the other boys,
and had but one fear, and that was hunger, for his mother
entirely left off providing for him, so that he came to depend
upon the pieces of bread and potatoes which his father
saved for him. On these conditions Sashka found existence
tolerable.

One Friday (it was Christmas Eve) he had been playing
with the other boys, until they had dispersed to their homes,
followed by the squeak of the rusty frozen wicket gate as it
closed behind the last of them. It was already growing dark,
and a grey snowy mist was coming up from the country.
A lamp was burning with a reddish, unblinking light in a
low black building which stood fronting the end of an alley,
The frost had become more intense, and when Sashka reached
the circle of light cast by the lamp, he saw that fine dry flakes
of snow were floating slowly on the air. It was high time to
be getting home.

"Where have you been knocking about all night, puppy?"
exclaimed his mother, doubling her fist, without, however,
striking. Her sleeves were turned up, exposing her fat white
arms, and on her forehead, almost devoid of eyebrows, stood
beads of perspiration. As Sashka passed by her he recognised
the familiar smell of vodka. His mother scratched her head
with the short dirty nail of her thick forefinger, and since it was
no good scolding, she merely spat, and cried: "Statisticians!
that's what they are!"

Sashka shuffled contemptuously, and went behind the partition, from whence might be heard the heavy breathing of his father, Ivan Savvich, who was in a chronic state of shivering, and was now trying to warm himself by sitting on the heated bench of the stove with his hands under him, palms downwards.

"Sashka! the Svetchnikovs have invited you to the Christmas tree. The housemaid came," he whispered.

"Get along with you!" said Sashka with incredulity.

"Fact! The old woman there has purposely not told you, but she has mended your jacket all the same."

"Non—sense," Sashka replied, still more surprised.

The Svetchnikovs were rich people, who had put him to the grammar school, and after his expulsion had forbidden him their house.

His father once more took his oath to the truth of his statement, and Sashka became meditative.

"Well then, move, shift a bit," he said to his father, as he leapt upon the short bench, adding:

"I won't go to those devils. I should prove jolly well too much for them, if I were to turn up. *Depraved boy,*" drawled Sashka in imitation of his patrons. "They are none too good themselves, the smug-faced prigs!"

"Oh! Sashka, Sashka," his father complained, sitting hunched up with cold, "you'll come to a bad end."

"What about yourself, then?" was Sashka's rude rejoinder. "Better shut up. Afraid of the old woman. Ba! old muff!"

His father sat on in silence and shivered. A faint light found its way through a broad clink at the top, where the partition failed to meet the ceiling by a quarter of an inch, and lay in bright patches upon his high forehead, beneath which the deep cavities of his eyes showed black.

In times gone by Ivan Savvich had been used to drink heavily, and then his wife had feared and hated him. But when he had begun to develop unmistakable signs of consumption, and could drink no longer, she took to drink in her turn, and gradually accustomed herself to vodka. Then she avenged herself for all she had suffered at the hands of that tall, narrow-chested man, who used incomprehensible words, had lost his place through disobedience and drunkenness, and who brought home with him just such long-haired, debauched and conceited fellows as himself.

In contradistinction to her husband, the more Feoktista Petrovna drank the healthier she became, and the heavier became her fists. Now she said what she pleased, brought men and women to the house just as she chose, and sang with them noisy songs, while he lay silent behind the partition, huddled together with perpetual cold, and meditating on the injustice and sorrow of human life. To everyone with whom she talked she complained that she had no such enemies in the world as her husband and son, they were stuck-up statisticians!

For the space of an hour his mother kept drumming into Sashka's ears:

"But I say you shall go," punctuating each word with a heavy blow on the table, which made the tumblers, placed on it after washing, jump and rattle again.

"But I say I won't!" Sashka coolly replied, dragging down the corners of his mouth with the will to show his teeth—a habit which had earned for him at school the nickname of Wolfkin.

"I'll thrash you, won't I just!" cried his mother.

"All right! thrash away!"

But Feoktista Petrovna knew that she could no longer strike her son now that he had begun to retaliate by biting, and that if she drove him into the street he would go off larking, and sooner get frost-bitten than go to the Svetchnikovs, therefore she appealed to her husband's authority.

"Calls himself a father, and can't protect the mother from insult!"

"Really, Sashka, go. Why are you so obstinate?" he jerked out from the bench. "They will perhaps take you up again.

They are kind people." Sashka only laughed in an insulting manner.

His father, long ago, before Sashka was born, had been tutor at the Svetchnikovs', and had ever since looked on them as the best people in the world. At that time he had held also an appointment in the statistical office of the Zemstvo, and had not yet taken to drink. Eventually he was compelled through his own fault to marry his landlady's daughter. From that time he severed his connection with the Svetchnikovs, and took to drink. Indeed, he let himself go to such an extent that he was several times picked up drunk in the streets and taken to the police station. But the Svetchnikovs did not cease to assist him with money, and Feoktista Petrovna, although she hated them, together with books and everything connected with her husband's past, still valued their acquaintance, and was in the habit of boasting of it.

"Perhaps you might bring something for me too from the Christmas tree," continued his father. He was using craft to induce his son to go, and Sashka knew it, and despised his father for his weakness and want of straightforwardness; though he really did wish to bring back something for the poor sickly old man, who had for a long time been without even good tobacco.

"All right!" he blurted out; "give me my jacket. Have you put the buttons on? No fear! I know you too well!"

II

The children had not yet been admitted to the drawing-room, where the Christmas tree stood, but remained chattering in the nursery. Sashka, with lofty superciliousness, stood listening to their naïve talk and fingering in his breeches pocket the broken cigarettes which he had managed to abstract from his host's study. At this moment there came up to him the youngest of the Svetchnikovs, Kolya, and stood motionless before him, a look of surprise on his face,

his toes turned in, and a finger stuck in the corner of his pout-
ing mouth. Six months ago, at the instance of his relatives,
he had given up this bad habit of putting his finger in his
mouth, but he could not quite break himself of it. He had
blond locks cut in a fringe on his forehead and falling in ring-
lets on his shoulders, and blue, wondering eyes; in fact, he
was just such a boy in appearance as Sashka particularly
loved to bully.

"Are 'oo weally a naughty boy?" he inquired of Sashka.
"Miss said 'oo was. I'm a dood boy."

"That you are!" replied Sashka, considering the other's
short velvet trousers and great turndown collars.

"Would 'oo like to have a dun? There!" and he pointed at
him a little pop-gun with a cork tied to it. The Wolfkin took
the gun, pressed down the spring, and, aiming at the nose of
the unsuspecting Kolya, pulled the trigger. The cork struck
his nose and, rebounding, hung by the string. Kolya's blue
eyes opened wider than ever, and filled with tears. Trans-
ferring his finger from his mouth to his reddening nose he
blinked his long eyelashes and whispered:

"Bad—bad boy!"

A young lady of striking appearance, with her hair dressed
in the simplest and the most becoming fashion, now entered
the nursery. She was sister to the lady of the house, the very
one indeed to whom Sashka's father had formerly given
lessons.

"Here's the boy," said she, pointing out Sashka to the bald-
headed man who accompanied her. "Bow, Sashka, you
should not be so rude!"

But Sashka would bow neither to her nor to her companion
of the bald head. She little suspected how much he knew.
But, as a fact, Sashka did know that his miserable father
had loved her, and that she had married another; and
though this had taken place subsequent to his father's marriage, Sashka could not bring himself to forgive what seemed
to him like treachery.

"Takes after his father!" sighed Sofia Dmitrievna. "Could not you, Plutov Michailovich, do something for him? My husband says that a commercial school would suit him better than the grammar school. Sashka, would you like to go to a technical school?"

"No!" curtly replied Sashka, who had caught the offensive word "husband."

"Do you want to be a shepherd, then?" asked the gentleman.

"Not likely!" said Sashka, in an offended tone.

"What then?"

Now Sashka did not know what he would like to be, but upon reflection replied: "Well, it's all the same to me, even a shepherd, if you like."

The bald-headed gentleman regarded the strange boy with a look of perplexity. When his eyes had travelled up from his patched boots to his face, Sashka put out his tongue and quickly drew it back again, so that Sofia Dmitrievna did not notice anything, but the old gentleman showed an amount of irascibility that she could not understand.

"I should not mind going to a commercial school," bashfully suggested Sashka.

The lady was overjoyed at Sashka's decision, and meditated with a sigh on the beneficial influence exercised by an old love.

"I don't know whether there will be a vacancy," dryly remarked the old man, avoiding looking at Sashka, and smoothing down the ridge of hair which stuck up on the back of his head. "However, we shall see."

Meanwhile the children were becoming noisy, and in a great state of excitement were waiting impatiently for the Christmas tree.

The excellent practice with the pop-gun made in the hands of a boy who commanded respect both for his stature and for his reputation for naughtiness, found imitators, and many a little button of a nose was made red. The tiny maids, holding

their sides, bent almost double with laughter, as their little
cavaliers, with manly contempt of fear and pain, but all
the same wrinkling up their faces in suspense, received the
impact of the cork.

At length the doors were opened, and a voice said: "Come
in, children; but gently, not so fast!" Opening their little eyes
wide, and holding their breath in anticipation, the children
filed into the brightly illumined drawing-room in orderly
pairs, and quietly walked round the glittering tree. It cast a
strong, shadowless light on their eager faces, with rounded
eyes and mouths. For a minute there reigned the silence of
profound enchantment, which all at once broke out into a
chorus of delighted exclamation. One of the little girls,
unable to restrain her delight, kept dancing up and down in
the same place, her little tresses braided with blue ribbon
bobbing rhythmically against her shoulders. Sashka remained morose and gloomy—something evil was working
in his little wounded breast. The tree blinded him with its
red, shriekingly insolent glitter of countless candles. It was
foreign, hostile to him, even as the crowd of smart, pretty
children which surrounded it. He would have liked to give
it a shove, and topple it over on their shining heads. It
seemed as though some iron hand were gripping his heart,
and wringing out of it every drop of blood. He crept behind
the piano, and sat down there in a corner, unconsciously
crumpling to pieces in his pocket the last of the cigarettes,
and thinking that though he had a father and mother and a
home, it came to the same thing as if he had none, and nowhere to go to. He tried to recall to his imagination his little
penknife, which he had acquired by a swap not long ago, and
was very fond of; but his knife all at once seemed to him a
very poor affair, with its ground-down blade and only half of
a yellow haft. To-morrow he would smash it up, and then
he would have nothing left at all!

But suddenly Sashka's narrow eyes gleamed with astonishment, and his face in a moment resumed its ordinary expres-

sion of audacity and self-confidence. On the side of the tree turned towards him—which was the back of it, and less brightly illuminated than the other side—he discovered something such as had never before come within the circle of his existence, and without which all his surroundings appeared as empty as though peopled by persons without life. It was a little angel in wax carelessly hung in the thickest of the dark boughs, and looking as if it were floating in the air. His transparent dragon-fly wings trembled in the light, and he seemed altogether alive and ready to fly away. The rosy fingers of his exquisitely formed hands were stretched upwards, and from his head there floated just such locks as Kolya's. But there was something here that was wanting in Kolya's face, and in all other faces and things. The face of the little angel did not shine with joy, nor was it clouded by grief; but there lay on it the impress of another feeling, not to be explained in words, nor defined by thought, but to be attained only by the sympathy of a kindred feeling. Sashka was not conscious of the force of the mysterious influence which attracted him towards the little angel, but he felt that he had known him all his life, and had always loved him, loved him more than his penknife, more than his father, more than anything else. Filled with doubt, alarm, and a delight which he could not comprehend, Sashka clasped his hands to his bosom and whispered:

"Dear—dear little angel!"

The more intently he looked the more fraught with significance the expression of the little angel's face became. He was so infinitely far off, so unlike everything which surrounded him there. The other toys seemed to take a pride in hanging there, pretty and decked out, upon the glittering tree, but the angel was pensive, and fearing the intrusive light, deliberately hid in the dark greenery, so that none might see him. It would be a mad cruelty to touch his dainty little wings.

"Dear—dear!" whispered Sashka.

His head became feverish. He clasped his hands behind his

back, and in full readiness to fight to the death to win the little angel, he walked to and fro with cautious, stealthy steps. He avoided looking at the little angel, lest he should direct the attention of others towards it, but he felt that it was still there, and had not flown away.

Now the hostess appeared in the doorway, a tall, stately lady with a bright aureole of grey hair high upon her head. The children trooped round her with expressions of delight, and the little girl—the same that had danced about in her place—hung wearily on her hand, blinking heavily with sleepy eyes.

As Sashka approached her he seemed almost choking with emotion.

"Auntie—auntie!" said he, trying to speak caressingly, but his voice sounded harder than ever. "Auntie, dear!"

She did not hear him, so he tugged impatiently at her dress.

"What's the matter with you? Why are you pulling my dress?" asked the grey-haired lady in surprise. "Don't be rough."

"Auntie—auntie, do give me one thing from the tree; give me the little angel."

"Impossible," replied the lady in a tone of indifference. "We are going to keep the tree decorated till the New Year. But you are no longer a child; you should call me by name— Maria Dmitrievna."

Sashka, feeling as if he were falling down a precipice, grasped the last means of saving himself.

"I am sorry I have been naughty. I'll be more industrious for the future," he blurted out. But this formula, which had always paid with his masters, made no impression upon the lady of the grey hair.

"A good thing too, my friend," she said, as unconcernedly as before.

"Give me the little angel," demanded Sashka, gruffly.

"But it's impossible. Can't you understand that?"

But Sashka did not understand, and when the lady turned to go out of the room he followed her, his gaze fixed without conscious thought upon her black silk dress. In his surging brain there glimmered a recollection of how one of the boys in his class had asked the master to mark him 3,[1] and when the master refused he had knelt down before him, and putting his hands together as in prayer, had begun to cry. The master was angry, but gave him 3 all the same. At the time Sashka had immortalised this episode in a caricature, but now his only means left was to follow the boy's example. Accordingly, he plucked at the lady's dress again, and when she turned round, dropped with a bang on to his knees, and folded his hands as described above. But he could not squeeze out a single tear!

"Have you gone crazy or what?" exclaimed the grey-haired lady, casting a furtive look round the room; but no one else was present. "What is the matter with you?"

Kneeling there with clasped hands, Saska looked at her with dislike, and rudely repeated:

"Give me the little angel."

His eyes, fixed intently on the lady to catch the first word she should utter, were anything but good to look at, and the hostess answered hurriedly:

"Well, then, I'll give it to you. Ah! what a stupid you are! I will give you what you want, but why could you not wait till the New Year?

"Stand up! And never," she added in a didactic tone, "never kneel to anyone: it is humiliating. Kneel before God alone."

"Talk away!" thought Sashka, trying to get in front of her, and merely succeeding in treading on her dress.

When she had taken the toy from the tree, Sashka devoured her with his eyes, but stretched out his hands for it with a painful pucker of the nose. It seemed to him that the tall lady would break the little angel.

[1] In Russian schools 5 is the maximum mark.

"Beautiful thing!" said the lady, who was sorry to part with such a dainty and presumably expensive toy. "Who can have hung it there? Well, what do you want with such a thing? Are you not too big to know what to do with it? Look, there are some picture-books. But this I promised to give to Kolya; he begged so earnestly for it." But this was not the truth.

Sashka's agony became unbearable. He clenched his teeth convulsively, and seemed almost to grind them. The lady of the grey hair feared nothing so much as a scene, so she slowly held out the little angel to Sashka.

"There now, take it!" she said in a displeased tone; "what a persistent boy you are!"

Sashka's hands as they seized the little angel seemed like tentacles, and were tense as steel springs, but withal so soft and careful that the little angel might have imagined himself to be flying in the air.

"A-h-h!" escaped in a long *diminuendo* sigh from Sashka's breast, while in his eyes glistened two little tear-drops, which stood still there as though unused to the light. Slowly drawing the little angel to his bosom, he kept his shining eyes on the hostess, with a quiet, tender smile which died away in a feeling of unearthly bliss. It seemed, when the dainty wings of the little angel touched Sashka's sunken breast, as if he experienced something so blissful, so bright, the like of which had never before been experienced in this sorrowful, sinful, suffering world.

"A-h-h!" sighed he once more as the little angel's wings touched him. And at the shining of his face the absurdly decorated and insolently glowing tree seemed to be extinguished, and the grey-haired, portly dame smiled with gladness, and the parchment-like face of the bald-headed gentleman twitched, and the children fell into a vivid silence as though touched by a breath of human happiness.

For one short moment all observed a mysterious likeness between the awkward boy who had outgrown his clothes, and the lineaments of the little angel, which had been spiritualised by the hand of an unknown artist.

But the next moment the picture was entirely changed. Crouching like a panther preparing to spring, Sashka surveyed the surrounding company, on the look-out for someone who should dare wrest his little angel from him.

"I'm going home," he said in a dull voice, having in view a way of escape through the crowd, "home to Father."

III

His mother was asleep, worn out with a whole day's work and vodka-drinking. In the little room behind the partition there stood a small cooking-lamp burning on the table. Its feeble yellow light, with difficulty penetrating the sooty glass, threw a strange shadow over the faces of Sashka and his father.

"Is it not pretty?" asked Sashka in a whisper, holding the little angel at a distance from his father, so as not to allow him to touch it.

"Yes, there's something most remarkable about it," whispered the father, gazing thoughtfully at the toy. And his face expressed the same concentrated attention and delight as did Sashka's.

"Look, he is going to fly."

"I see it too," replied Sashka in an ecstasy. "Think I'm blind? But look at his little wings! Ah! don't touch!"

The father withdrew his hand, and with troubled eyes studied the details of the little angel, while Sashka whispered with the air of a pedagogue:

"Father, what a bad habit you have of touching everything! You might break it."

There fell upon the wall the shadows of two grotesque, motionless heads bending towards one another, one big and shaggy, the other small and round.

Within the big head strange torturing thoughts, though at

the same time full of delight, were seething. His eyes unwaveringly regarded the little angel, and under his steadfast
gaze it seemed to grow larger and brighter, and its wings to
tremble with a noiseless trepidation, and all the surroundings
—the timber-built, soot-stained wall, the dirty table, Sashka
—everything became fused into one level grey mass without
light or shade. It seemed to the broken man that he heard a
pitying voice from the world of wonders, wherein he had once
dwelt, and whence he had been cast out for ever. There they
knew nothing of dirt, of weary quarrelling, of the blindly-
cruel strife of egotism, there they knew nothing of the tortures of a man arrested in the streets with callous laughter,
and beaten by the rough hand of the night-watchman.
There everything is pure, joyful, bright. And all this purity
found an asylum in the soul of her whom he loved more than
life, and had lost—when he had kept his hold upon his own
useless life. With the smell of wax, which emanated from
the toy, was mingled a subtle aroma, and it seemed to the
broken man that *her* dear fingers had touched the angel, those
fingers which he would fain have caressed in one long kiss,
till death should close his lips for ever. This was why the
little toy was so beautiful, that was why there was in it something specially attractive, which defied description. The
little angel had descended from that heaven which *her* soul
was to him, and had brought a ray of light into the damp
room, steeped in fumes, and to the dark soul of the man
from whom had been taken all: love, and happiness and life.

On a level with the eyes of the man, who had lived his life,
sparkled the eyes of the boy, who was beginning his life, and
embraced the little angel in their caress. For them present
and future had disappeared: the ever-sorrowful, piteous
father, the rough, unendurable mother, the black darkness
of insults, of cruelty, of humiliations and of spiteful grief.
The thoughts of Sashka were formless, nebulous, but all the
more deeply for that did they move his agitated soul. Everything that is good and bright in the world, all profound grief,

and the hope of a soul that sighs for God—the little angel absorbed them all into himself, and that was why he glowed with such a soft divine radiance, that was why his little dragon-fly wings trembled with a noiseless trepidation.

The father and son did not look at one another: their sick hearts grieved, wept and rejoiced apart. But there was a something in their thoughts which fused their hearts in one and annihilated that bottomless abyss which separates man from man and makes him so lonely, unhappy and weak. The father with an unconscious motion put his arm round the neck of his son, and the son's head rested equally without conscious volition upon his father's consumptive chest.

"*She* it was who gave it to thee, was it not?" whispered the father, without taking his eyes off the little angel.

At another time Sashka would have replied with a rude negation, but now the only reply possible resounded of itself within his soul, and he calmly pronounced the pious fraud: "Who else? of course she did."

The father made no reply, and Sashka relapsed into silence.

Something grated in the adjoining room, then clicked, and then was silent for a moment, and then noisily and hurriedly the clock struck "One, two, three."

"Sashka, do you ever dream?" asked the father in a meditative tone.

"No! Oh, yes," he admitted, "once I had one, in which I fell down from the roof. We were climbing after the pigeons, and I fell down."

"But I dream always. Strange things are dreams. One sees the whole past; one loves and suffers as though it were reality."

Again he was silent, and Sashka felt his arm tremble as it lay upon his neck. The trembling and pressure of his father's arm became stronger and stronger, and the sensitive silence of the night was all at once broken by the pitiful sobbing sound of suppressed weeping. Sashka sternly puckered his brow, and cautiously—so as not to disturb the heavy, tremb-

ling arm—wiped away a tear from his eyes. So strange was it
to see a big old man crying.

"Ah! Sashka, Sashka," sobbed the father, "what is the
meaning of everything?"

"Why, what's the matter?" whispered Sashka sternly.
"You're crying just like a little boy."

"Well, I won't, then," said the father, with a piteous smile
of excuse. "What's the good?"

Feoktista Petrovna turned on her bed. She sighed, cleared
her throat, and mumbled incoherent sounds in a loud and
strangely persistent manner.

It was time to go to bed. But before doing so the little angel
must be disposed of for the night. He could not be left on the
floor, so he was hung up by his string, which was fastened to
the flue of the stove. There it stood out accurately delineated
against the white Dutch tiles. And so they could both see
him, Sashka and his father.

Hurriedly throwing into a corner the various rags on which
he was in the habit of sleeping, Sashka lay down on his back,
in order as quickly as possible to look again at the little angel.

"Why don't you undress?" asked his father, as he shivered
and wrapped himself up in his tattered blanket, and arranged
his clothes, which he had thrown over his feet.

"What's the good? I shall soon be up again."

Sashka wished to add that he did not care to go to sleep at
all, but he had no time to do so, since he fell to sleep as
suddenly as though he had sunk to the bottom of a deep
swift river.

His father presently fell asleep also. And gentle sleep and
restfulness lay upon the weary face of the man who had lived
his life, and upon the brave face of the little man who was
just beginning his life.

But the little angel hanging by the hot stove began to melt.
The lamp, which had been left burning at the entreaty of
Sashka, filled the room with the smell of kerosene, and
through its smoked glass threw a melancholy light upon a

scene of gradual dissolution. The little angel seemed to stir. Over his rosy fingers there rolled thick drops which fell upon the bench. To the smell of kerosene was added the stifling scent of melting wax. The little angel gave a tremble as though on the point of flight, and—fell with a soft thud upon the hot flags.

An inquisitive cockroach singed its wings as it ran round the formless lump of melted wax, climbed up the dragon-fly wings, and twitching its feelers went on its way.

Through the curtained window the grey-blue light of coming day crept in, and the water-carrier, benumbed with cold, was already making a noise in the courtyard with his iron scoop.

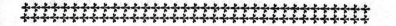

VALERY BRUSOF

(1873–1924)

✠✠

(I)

RHEA SILVIA

A Story from the Life of the Sixth Century

(Translated by Rosa Graham)

I

M A R I A was the daughter of Rufus the Scribe. She was not yet ten years old when on the 17th of December, 546, Rome was taken by Totila, the king of the Goths. The magnanimous victor ordered bugles to be blown all night, so that the Roman people might escape from their native town as soon as they realised the danger of remaining there. Totila knew the violence of his soldiers and he had no wish that all the population of the ancient capital of the world should perish by the swords of the Goths. So Rufus and his wife Florentia fled with their little daughter Maria. An enormous crowd of refugees from Rome left the city through the night by the Appian Way, hundreds of them falling exhausted on the road. The greater number, among whom were Rufus and his family, succeeded in getting as far as Bovillæ, where, however, very many were unable to find shelter. Many of them had to camp out in the open. Later on they were all scattered in various directions, seeking some place of refuge. Some went to the Campagna and were taken prisoners by the Goths, who were in possession there; some got as far as the sea and were even able to set out for Sicily. The rest either remained as beggars in the neighbourhood of Bovillæ or managed to get into Samnium.

Rufus had a friend living near Corbio. To this poor man, Anthony by name, who earned a living by rearing pigs on a small plot of land, Rufus brought his family. Anthony took the fugitives in and shared with them his scanty store. And while living in the swineherd's wretched hut, Rufus heard of all the misfortunes which came upon Rome. At one time Totila threatened to rase the Eternal City to its foundations and turn it into a place of pasture. But the Gothic king afterwards relented and contented himself by burning several districts of the town and pillaging all that still remained from the cupidity and violence of Alaric, Genseric and Ricimer. In the spring of 547 Totila left Rome, but he took off with him all the inhabitants who had remained in the city. For forty days the capital of the world stood empty: there was not a human being left in it, and along its streets wandered only frightened animals and wild beasts. Then, timidly, a few at a time, the Romans began to return to their city. And a little later Rome was occupied by Belisarius and was once more united to the dominions of the Eastern Empire.

Then Rufus and his family returned to Rome. They sought out their little house on the Remuria, which by reason of its insignificance had been spared by the spoilers. Almost all the poor belongings of Rufus were found to be intact, including the library and its rolls of parchment, so precious to the scribe. It seemed as if it might be possible to forget all the misfortunes they had undergone, as in some oppressive dream, and to continue their former life. But very soon it became clear that such a hope was deceptive. The war was far from being at an end. Rome had to endure another siege by Totila, when again the inhabitants died in hundreds from hunger and lack of water. Then when the Goths at length raised their unsuccessful siege, Belisarius also left Rome, and the city acknowledged the rule of the covetous Byzantine Konon, from whom the Romans fled as from an enemy. At

a later period the Goths, taking advantage of treacherous
sentries, occupied Rome for the second time: This time, however, Totila not only refrained from plundering the city, but
he even strove to bring into it some kind of order, and he
wished to restore the ruined buildings. At length, after the
death of Totila, Rome was taken by Narses. This was in 552.

It would be difficult to show clearly how Rufus managed to
live through these six calamitous years. In the time of war
and siege no one had need of the art of a scribe. No one any
longer gave Rufus an order for a transcription from the works
of the ancient poets or the Fathers of the Church. In the city
there were no authorities to whom it might be necessary to
address petitions of various kinds. There were not many
people, money was very scarce and food supplies scarcer still.
He had to make a living by any kind of accidental work,
serving either Goths or Byzantines, not disdaining to be a
stonemason when the town walls were being repaired or to
be a porter of baggage for the troops. And with all this the
entire family often went hungry, not only for days, but for
whole weeks. Wine was not to be thought of; the only drink
was bad water from the cisterns or from the Tiber, for the
aqueducts had been destroyed by the Goths. It was only
possible to endure such privations by knowing that everybody
without exception was subject to them. The descendants of
senators and patricians, the children of the richest and most
illustrious families would ask on the streets for a piece of
bread, as beggars. Rusticiana, the daughter of Symmachus
and widow of Boethius, held out her hand for alms.

It was not to be wondered at that during these years the
little Maria was left very much to her own devices. In her
early childhood her father had taught her to read both Greek
and Latin. But after their return to Rome he had no time to
occupy himself further with her education. For whole days
together she would do just what she thought she would. Her
mother did not require her help in housekeeping, for there
was hardly any housekeeping to be done. In order to pass the

time, Maria used to read the books which were still preserved
in the house, as there was no one who would buy them. But
more often she would go out of the house and wander like a
little wild animal about the deserted streets, forums and
squares, much too broad for the now insignificant populace.
The few passers-by soon became accustomed to the black-
eyed girl in ragged garments, who ran about everywhere like
a mouse, and they paid no attention to her. Rome became, as
it were, an immense home for Maria. She knew it better than
any writer who had described its noteworthy treasures of old
time. Day after day she would go out into the immense area
of the city, where over a million people had once dwelt, and
she would learn to love some corners of it and detest others.
And it was not often until late evening that she would return
to her father's cheerless roof, where it often happened that she
would go supperless to bed, after a whole day spent on her
feet.

In her wanderings through the town Maria would visit the
most remote districts on either side of the Tiber, where there
were empty partly burnt down houses, and there she would
dream of the greatness of Rome in the past. She would
examine the few statues which still remained whole in the
squares—the immense bull on the Bull forum, the giant
Elephants in bronze on the Sacred Way, the statues of
Domitian, Marcus Aurelius, and other famous men of ancient
time, the columns, obelisks and bas-reliefs, striving to remember what she had read about them all, and if her knowledge
was scanty, she would supplement it by any story she had
read. She would go into the abandoned palaces of people
who had once been rich, and admire the pitiful remains of
former luxury in the decoration of the rooms, the mosaic of
the floors, the various-coloured marble of the walls, the
sumptuous tables, chairs, candlesticks, which in some places
still remained. In this way she visited the ruined baths,
which were like separate towns within the city, and were
entirely deserted because there was no water to supply their

insatiable pipes; in some of the buildings could still be seen magnificent marble reservoirs, mosaic floors, bathing chairs, baths of precious alabaster or porphyry, and in places some half-destroyed statues which had escaped being used by Goths and Byzantines as material for hurling at the enemy from the ballista. In the quietness of the enormous rooms Maria would hear echoes of the rich and careless lives of the thousands and thousands of people who had gathered there daily to meet friends, to discuss literature or philosophy, and to anoint their effeminate bodies before festival banquets. In the Grand Circus—which now looked like a wild ravine, for it was all overgrown with weeds and tall grasses—Maria thought of the triumphant horse-racing competitions, on which thousands of spectators had gazed and deafened the fortunate victors with a storm of applause. She could not but know of these festivals, for the last of them (oh! pitiful shadow of past splendour) had been arranged once more in her own lifetime by Totila during his second sovereignty in Rome. Sometimes Maria would simply walk along the Tiber bank, sit down in some comfortable spot under some half-ruined wall, and look at the yellow waters of the river, made famous by poets and artists, and in the quietness of the deserted place she would think and dream, and think and dream again.

She became accustomed to live in her dreams. The half-ruined, half-abandoned town fed her imagination generously. Everything she heard from her elders, everything she read in her disorderly fashion from her father's books, mingled itself together in her brain into a strange, chaotic, but endlessly captivating representation of the great and ancient city. She was convinced that the former Rome had been in reality the concentration of all beauty, a marvellous town where all was enchantment, where all life had been one continuous festival. Centuries and epochs were confused in her poor little head, the times of Orestes seemed to her no further away than the rule of Trajan, and the reign of the wise Numa Pompilius as near as that of Odoacer. For her, antiquity comprised all that preceded the Goths; far away but still happy was the olden time, the rule of the great Theodoric; the new time began for her at her birth, at the time of the first siege of Rome, in the time of Belisarius. In antiquity everything seemed to Maria to be marvellous, beautiful, wonderful; in the olden time all was attractive and fortunate, in modern times everything was miserable and dreadful. And she tried not to notice the cruel reality of the present, but to live in her dreams in the antiquity which she loved, with her favourite heroes, among whom were the god Bacchus; Camillus, the second founder of the city; Cæsar, who had been exalted up to the stars in the heavens; Diocletian, the wisest of all people, and Romulus Augustulus, the unhappiest of all the great. All these and many others whose names she had heard only by chance were the beloved of her reveries and the ordinary apparitions of her half-childish dreams.

Little by little in her dreams Maria created her own history of Rome, not at all like that which was told at one time by the eloquent Livy and afterwards by other historians and annalists. As she admired the statues which still remained whole and read their half-erased inscriptions, Maria interpreted everything in her own way, and found everywhere corroboration of her own unrestrained imagination. She said to herself that such and such a statue represented the young Augustus, and nothing would then have convinced her that it was a bad portrait of some half-barbarian who had lived only fifty years ago, and had forced some ignorant maker of tombs to immortalise his features in a piece of cheap marble. Or when she looked at a bas-relief depicting some scene from the Odyssey she would create from it a long story in which her beloved heroes would again figure—Mars, Brutus, or the Emperor Honorius—and would soon be convinced that she had read this story in one of her father's books. She would create legend after legend, myth after myth, and live in their

world as one more real than the world of books, and still
more real than the pitiful world which encompassed her.

After she had dreamed for a sufficiently long time, and when
she felt tired out by walking and exhausted by hunger, Maria
would return home. There her mother, who had become
bad-tempered from the misfortunes she had endured, would
meet her gloomily, roughly push towards her a piece of bread
and a morsel of cheese, or a head of garlic if there happened
to be one in the kitchen, adding occasionally some scolding
words to the meagre supper. Maria, unsociable as a captive
bird, would eat what was given her and then hasten away to
her little room and its hard bed, to dream again until she
slept, and then dream again in her sleep about the blessed,
dazzling times of antiquity. On especially happy days, when
her father happened to be at home and in a good temper, he
would sometimes have a chat with Maria. And their talk
would quickly turn to the ancient times, so dear to them both.
Maria would question her father about bygone Rome, and
then hold her breath while the old scribe, led away by his
theme, would begin to talk of the great empire in the time of
Theodosius, or recite verses from the ancient poets, Virgil,
Ausonius and Claudian. And the chaos in her poor little
head would fall into still greater confusion, and at times it
would begin to seem to her that her actual life was only a
dream, and that in reality she was living in the blessed times
of Ennius Augustus or Gratian.

II

After the occupation of Rome by Narses, life in the city
began to take more or less its ordinary course. The ruler
established himself on the Palatine, some of the desolated
rooms of the Imperial palace were renovated for him, and in
the evenings they were lit up with lamps. The Byzantines
had brought money with them, and trade in Rome began to
revive. The main streets became comparatively safe, and the

impoverished inhabitants of the empty Campagna brought provisions into Rome to sell. Here and there wine taverns were reopened. There was even a demand for articles of luxury, which were purchased mainly by the frivolous women who, like a flock of ravens, followed the mongrel armies of the great eunuch. Monks went to and fro along all the streets, and from them also it was possible to make some sort of profit. The thirty or forty thousand inhabitants now gathered together in Rome, including the troops, gave to the city, especially in the central districts, the appearance of a populous and even of a lively place.

There was found at length some real work for Rufus. Narses, and afterwards his successor, the Byzantine general, received various complaints and petitions for the copying of which the art of a scribe was in request. The edicts of Justinian, acknowledging some of the acts of the Gothic kings and repudiating others, afforded pretext for endless chicanery and processes of law. Rufus sometimes had to copy papers addressed directly to his Holiness the Emperor in Byzantium, and for these he was comparatively well paid. And more important orders came to him. A new monastery wanted to have a written list of its service-books. A whimsical person ordered a copy of the poems of the famous Rutilius. In the house of Rufus there was once more a certain sufficiency. The family could have dinner every day and need no longer feel anxious about the morrow.

Everything might have been well in Rufus's home if the scribe, who had aged greatly in consequence of years of deprivation, had not taken to drink. Oftentimes he left all his earnings in some tavern or other. This was a heavy blow for Florentia. She struggled in every way to combat the unhappy passion of her husband and tried to take from him all the money he earned, but Rufus descended to every sort of artifice and always found means of getting drunk. Maria, on the contrary, loved the days of her father's drunken bouts. Then he would come home in a gay mood and pay no attention to the tears and reproaches of Florentia, but would eagerly call Maria to him, if she were at home, talk to her again endlessly about the old greatness of the Eternal City, and read to her verses from the old poets and those of his own composition. The half-witted girl and her drunken father somehow understood one another, and they often sat together till late in the night, after the angry Florentia had left them and gone to bed alone.

Maria herself did not change her way of life. In vain her father when sober forced her to help him in his work. In vain her mother was angry with her daughter for not sharing with her the cares of housekeeping. When Maria was obliged she would against her will sullenly transcribe a few lines or peel a few onions, but at the first opportunity she would run out of the house to wander all day again in her favourite corners of the city. She was scolded on her return, but she listened silently to all reproaches and made no reply. What mattered scoldings to her when in her vision there still glistened all the sumptuous pictures with which her imagination had been soothed while she had been hidden near a porphyry basin in the baths of Caracalla or had lain secreted in the thick grass on the banks of old Tiber? For the sake of not having her visions taken from her she would willingly have endured blows and every kind of torture. In these visions were all her life.

In the autumn of 554 Maria saw in the streets of Rome the triumphal procession of Narses—the last triumph celebrated in the Eternal City. The eunuch's troops of many different races—among whom were Greeks, Huns, Heruli, Gepidæ, Persians—passed in an inharmonious crowd along the Sacred Way, bearing rich booty taken from the Goths. The soldiers sang gay songs in the most diverse languages, and their voices mingled in wild and deafening cries. The general, crowned with laurel, drove in a chariot drawn by white horses. At the gates of Rome he was met by men dressed in white togas making themselves out to be senators. Narses went through half-demolished Rome, along streets in which the grass had grown up between the mighty paving-stones, in the direction of the Capitol. There he laid down his crown before a statue of Justinian, obtained from somewhere or other for the occasion. Then he went on foot through the town once more, going back to the Basilica of St. Peter, where he was met by the Pope and clergy in festival robes. The Roman people crowded into the streets and gazed at the spectacle without any special enthusiasm, though the chief actors had done their utmost to make it magnificent. The Byzantine triumph was for Romans something foreign, almost like a triumph of the enemies of their native land.

And on Maria the triumphal procession made no impression whatever. She looked with indifferent eyes upon the medley of colours in the soldiers' garments, on the triumphal toga of the eunuch—a small, beardless old man with shifty eyes—and on the festal robes of the priests. The songs and martial cries of the soldiers only aroused her horror. It all seemed to her so different from the triumphs she had so often imagined in her lonely visions—the triumphs of Augustus, Vespasian, Valentian! Here everything appeared to her to be strange and ugly; there, all had been magnificence and beauty. And without waiting to see the whole of the procession, Maria ran away from the basilica of St. Peter on to the Appian Way, to the ruined baths of Caracalla, which she loved, so that in the quietness of the marble hall she might weep freely over the irrevocable past and see it anew in her dreams, living and beautiful as it alone could be. Maria went home late that day and did not wish to answer any questions as to whether she had seen the procession.

At this time Maria was nearly eighteen. She was not beautiful. She was thin, her figure was undeveloped, and with her wild black eyes and the hectic colour in her cheeks she rather affrighted than attracted attention. She had no friend. When the young girls of the neighbourhood spoke to her she answered abruptly and in monosyllables, and

hastened to bring the conversation to an end. How could they
—these other girls—understand her secret dreams, her sacred
visions? Of what could she speak with them? She was
thought not so much to be stupid as to be imbecile. And then
she never went to church. Sometimes, on the deserted streets,
a drunken passer-by would come up to her and try to take
her arm or embrace her. Then Maria would turn on him
like a wild cat, scratching, biting, hitting out with her fists,
and she would be left in peace. One young man, however,
the son of a neighbouring coppersmith, had wanted to pay
attentions to her. When her mother spoke to her about him,
Maria heard the news with unfeigned horror. When her
mother became insistent, saying that she could not now find
a better husband anywhere, Maria began to sob in such a
desperation that Florentia left her alone, making up her
mind that her daughter was either too young to be married or
that she was indeed not quite in her right mind. So Maria
was allowed to live in freedom and to fill up her endless
leisure time as she pleased.

So passed days and weeks and months. Rufus worked and
drank. Florentia busied herself over her housekeeping and
scolded. Both thought themselves unhappy and cursed their
wretched fate. Maria alone was happy in the world of her
fancies. She began to pay less and less attention to the hateful
actuality of her surroundings. She went deeper and deeper
into the kingdom of her visions. She already held conversations with the forms which her imagination created as with
living people. She used to return home with the conviction
that to-day she had met the goddess Vesta or the dictator
Sulla. She would remember the things she had imagined as
if they had actually taken place. When she talked with her
father at nights she would tell him all her remembrances, and
the old Rufus would not be amazed. Every story of hers gave
him a pretext for being ready with some lines of poetry—he
would complete and develop the insane fancies of his
daughter—and as she listened sleepily to their strange

conversations, Florentia would sometimes spit and pronounce a curse, sometimes cross herself and whisper a prayer to the Holy Virgin.

III

In the spring following the triumphal procession of Narses, Maria was one day wandering near the ruined walls of the baths of Trajan, when she noticed that in one place, where evidently the Esquiline Hill took its rise, there was a strange opening in the ground, like an entrance somewhere. The district was a deserted one; all around there were only deserted and uninhabited houses; the pavements were broken and the steep slope of the hill was overgrown with tall grass. After some effort Maria succeeded in getting to the opening. Beyond it was a dark and narrow passage. Without hesitation she crawled into it. She had to crawl for a long way in utter darkness and in a stifling atmosphere. At the end of the passage there was a sudden drop. When Maria's eyes grew accustomed to the darkness she could distinguish by the faint light which came from the opening by which she had entered that in front of her was a spacious hall of some unknown palace. After a little reflection the girl considered that she would not be able to see it without a light. She went back cautiously, and all that day she wandered about, pondering on the matter. Rome seemed to her to be her own property, and she could not endure the idea that there was anything in the city about which she knew nothing.

The next day, having secured a home-made torch, Maria returned to the place. Not without some danger to herself she got down into the hall she had discovered and there lighted the torch. A stately chamber presented itself to her gaze. The lower half of the walls was of marble, and above it were painted marvellous pictures. Bronze statues stood in niches, amazing work, for the statues seemed to be living people. It was possible to distinguish that the floor, now covered with earth and rubbish, was of mosaic. After admiring the new spectacle, Maria was emboldened to go further. Through an immense door she passed into a whole labyrinth of passages and cross-passages leading her into a new hall, still more magnificent than the first. Further on was a long suite of rooms, decorated with marble and gold, with wall paintings and statuary; in many places there still remained valuable furniture and various domestic articles of fine workmanship. Spiders, lizards, sow-bugs ran all around; bats fluttered here and there; but Maria, enthralled by the unique spectacle, saw nothing of them. Before her was the life of ancient Rome, living, in all its fullness, discovered by her at last.

How long she enjoyed herself there on that first day of her discovery she did not know. She was overcome, either by her strong agitation or by the foul atmosphere. When she came to her senses again she was on the damp stone floor, and her torch was extinguished, having burnt itself out. In utter darkness she began gropingly to seek a way out. She wandered for a long time, for many hours, but only became confused in the countless passages and rooms. In the misty consciousness of the girl there was a glimmer of a notion that she was fated to die in this unknown palace, which was itself buried under the ground. Such an idea did not alarm Maria; on the contrary, it seemed to her both beautiful and desirable to end her life among the splendid remains of ancient life, in a marble hall, at the foot of a beautiful statue somewhere or other. She was only sorry for one thing—that darkness lay around her, and that she was not fated to see the beauty in the midst of which she was to die. . . . Suddenly a ray of light shone before her. Gathering up all her strength, Maria went towards it. It was the light of the moon shining through an opening like that by which she had entered the palace. But this opening was in an entirely different hall. By great efforts, scrambling up by the projections of the walls, Maria got out into the open air in an hour when the whole city was already asleep and the moon reigned in her full glory over the heaps of the half-ruined buildings. Keeping close by the walls, in order to attract no attention, Maria reached home almost dead from exhaustion. Her father was absent, he did not come home all that night, and her mother only uttered a few coarse outcries.

After this Maria began daily to visit the subterranean palace she had discovered. Little by little she learnt all its corridors and halls, so that she could wander about them in utter darkness without fear of losing her way again. She always carried with her, however, a little lamp or a resin torch, so that she could adequately enjoy the sumptuous decorations of the rooms. She learnt to know all about them. She knew the rooms which were covered with paintings and decorations in crimson, others where a yellow colour predominated, others which by the green of the paintings reminded her of fresh meadows or a garden, others which were all white with ornamentations of black ebony; she knew all the wall paintings, some of which depicted scenes from the lives of gods and heroes, some showed the great battles of antiquity, some showed the portraits of great men, others the ridiculous adventures of fauns and cupids; she knew all the statues that were preserved in the palace, both bronze and marble, the small busts in the niches, the glorious piece of sculpture of entire figures of enormous size which represented three people, a man and two youths, who were encircled in the coils of a gigantic serpent and were vainly striving to free themselves from its fatal embrace.

But of all the decorations in the underground palace Maria specially loved one bas-relief. It represented a young girl, slim and graceful, resting in a deep sleep in a kind of cave; near her stood a youth in warlike armour, with a noble face of marvellous beauty; above them, and as it were in the clouds, was depicted a woven basket containing two young children, floating on a river. It seemed to Maria that the features of the young girl in the picture were like her own. She recognised herself in this slim sleeping princess, and for whole hours she would untiringly admire her, imagining

herself in her place. At times Maria was ready to believe that
some ancient artist had marvellously divined that at some
time a young girl Maria would appear in the world, and that
he had, by anticipation, created her portrait in the bas-relief
of the mysterious enchanted palace, which must have been
preserved untouched under the earth for hundreds of years.
The significance of the other figures in the bas-relief was not
realised by her for a long while.

But one evening Maria happened once more to have a talk
with her father, who had come home drunk and in a gay
mood. They were alone, for Florentia, as usual, had left them
to their foolish chattering and had gone to bed. Maria told
her father of the underground palace she had discovered and
of its treasures. The old Rufus listened to this story in the
same way as he heard all the other stories of his daughter.
When she used to tell him that she had that day met Constantine the Great in the street and that he had graciously
conversed with her, Rufus would not be surprised, but he
would begin to talk about Constantine. And now, when
Maria spoke to him of the treasures of the underground
palace, the old scribe at once talked about this palace.

"Yes, yes, little daughter," said he. "Between the Palatine
and the Esquiline, it really is there. It is the Golden House
of the Emperor Nero, the most beautiful palace ever built in
Rome. Nero had not sufficient space for it and he set fire to
Rome. Rome was burnt, and the emperor recited verses
about the burning of Troy. And afterwards, on the space
that had been cleared, he built his Golden House. Yes, yes,
it was between the Palatine and the Esquiline; you're right.
There was nothing more beautiful in the city. But after
Nero's death other emperors destroyed the palace out of
envy, and heaped earth upon it; it existed no longer. They
built houses and baths on its site. But it was the most
beautiful of all the palaces."

Then, having become bolder, Maria told her father about
her beloved bas-relief. And again the old scribe was not

surprised. He at once explained to his daughter what the artist had wished to express.

"That, my daughter, is Rhea Silvia, the vestal virgin, daughter of King Numitor. But a youth—the god Mars—fell in love with the maiden and sought her out in the sacred cave. Twin sons were born to them, Romulus and Remus. Rhea Silvia was drowned in the Tiber, the infants were suckled by a wolf and they became the founders of the city. Yes, that is how it was, my daughter."

Rufus told Maria in detail the touching story of the guilty vestal Ilia, or Rhea Silvia, and he at once began to recite some lines from the *Metamorphoses* of the ancient Naso:

> *Proximus Ausonias iniusti miles Amuli*
> *Rexit opes . . .*

But Maria was not listening to her father, she was repeating quietly to herself:

"It is—Rhea Silvia! Rhea Silvia!"

IV

After that day Maria spent still more of her time looking at the wonderful bas-relief. She would take a scanty luncheon with her, as well as a torch, so that she might stay some hours longer in the underground palace, which she considered to be more her own home than her father's house. She would lie on the cold and slippery floor in front of the sculptured daughter of Numitor, and by the faint light of her resinous torch she would gaze for long hours at the features of the slender maiden in the sacred cave. With every day it became more apparent to Maria that she was strangely like this ancient vestal, and little by little in her dreams she became less able to distinguish which was poor Maria, the daughter of Rufus the Scribe, and which the unhappy Ilia, daughter of the king of Alba Longa. She always called herself Rhea Silvia. Lying in front of the picture she would dream that to her, in this new sacred cave, the god Mars would appear, and that from their divine embraces there would be born of her the twins Romulus and Remus, who would become the founders of the Eternal City. True, she would have to pay for this by her death—and be drowned in the muddy waters of the Tiber—but could death terrify Maria? She often fell asleep while musing thus before the bas-relief, and dreamed of this same god Mars with his noble face of marvellous beauty and his divine, consuming embrace. And when she awoke she would not know whether it had been dream or reality.

It was already scorching July, when the streets of Rome at midday were as empty as after the terrible command of King Totila. But in the underground palace it was damp and cool. Maria, as before, went there every day to muse, in her habitual sweet reveries, before the pictured Ilia, who lay dreaming of the god destined for her. And one day, when in a slight doze she was once again giving herself up to the ardent caresses of the god Mars, suddenly a noise of some kind forced her to awake. She opened her eyes, not understanding anything as yet, and glanced around. By the light of the little torch which she had placed in a cranny between the stones she saw before her a young man. He was not in warlike armour, but wore the dress usually worn at that time by poor Romans; his face, however, was full of nobility, and to Maria it appeared radiant with a marvellous beauty. For some moments she looked with amazement on the unexpected apparition, on the man who had found his way into this enchanted palace which she had thought unknown to anyone save herself. Then, sitting upright on the floor, the girl asked simply:

"You have come to me?"

The young man smiled a quiet and attractive smile, and answered by another question.

"But who are you, maiden? The genius of this place?"

Maria answered:

"I am Rhea Silvia, a vestal virgin, daughter of King Numitor. And are not you the god Mars, come in search of me?"

"No, I am no god," objected the young man. "I am a mortal, my name is Agapit, and I was not searching here for you. But all the same, I am glad to find you. Greeting to you, daughter of King Numitor!"

Maria invited the young man to sit down beside her, and he at once consented. So they sat together, youth and maiden, on the damp floor, in the magnificent hall of Nero's Golden House, buried underground, and they looked into each other's eyes and knew not at first what to talk about. Then Maria pointed out the bas-relief to the young man and began to tell him all the legend of the unhappy vestal. But the youth interrupted her story.

"I know this, Rhea," said he, "but how strange! The face of the girl in the bas-relief is actually like yours."

"It is I," answered Maria.

So much conviction was in her words that the youth was perplexed and knew not what to think. But Maria gently placed her hand on his shoulder and began to speak ingratiatingly, almost timidly.

"Do not deny it—you are the god Mars in the form of a mortal. But I recognised you. I have expected you for a long time. I knew that you would come. I am not afraid of death. Let them drown me in the Tiber."

For a long while the young man listened to Maria's incoherent speech. All around was strange. This underground palace, known to no one, with its magnificent apartments where only lizards and bats were living. And the obscurity of this immense hall, barely lighted by the faint light of the two torches. And this obscure maiden, like the Rhea Silvia of the ancient bas-relief, with her unintelligible speeches, who in some marvellous fashion had lighted upon the buried Golden House of Nero. The young man felt that the rude actuality of the life he had lived just before his entrance into the underground dwelling had vanished into thin air as a dream disappears in the morning. In another moment he might have believed that he himself was the god Mars, and that he had met here his beloved, Ilia the vestal, the daughter of Numitor. Putting the greatest restraint upon himself, he broke in upon Maria's speech.

"Dear maiden," said he, "listen to me. You are mistaken about me. I am not he for whom you take me. I will tell you the whole truth. Agapit is not my real name. I am a Goth, and my name is really Theodat. But I am obliged to conceal my origin, for I should be put to death if it were known. Haven't you heard, by my pronunciation, that I am not a Roman? When my fellow-countrymen left your city, I did not follow them. I love Rome, I love its history and its tradition. I want to live and die in the Eternal City, which once belonged to us. So now, under the name of Agapit, I am in the service of an armourer; I work by day, and in the evenings I wander about the city and admire its memorials which have escaped destruction. As I knew that Nero's Golden House had been built on this spot, I got into this underground palace so that I could admire the remains of its former beauty. That is all. I have told you the whole truth, and I do not think you will betray me, for one word from you would be enough to have me put to death."

Maria listened to the words of Theodat with incredulity and dissatisfaction. After a little thought she said : "Why are you deceiving me? Why do you wish to take the form of a Goth? Can I not see the nimbus round your head? Mars Gradivus, for others thou art a god, for me thou art my beloved. Do not mock thy poor bride, Rhea Silvia!"

Theodat looked again for a long while at the young girl who spoke such foolish words, and he began to guess that Maria was not in her right mind. And when this thought came into his head he said to himself, "Poor girl! I will never take advantage of your unprotected state! This would be unworthy of a Goth." Then he gently put his arms around

Maria and began to talk to her as to a little child, not contradicting her strange fancies but acknowledging himself to be the god Mars. And for a long while they sat side by side in the semi-darkness, not exchanging one kiss, talking and dreaming together of the future Rome which would be founded by their twin sons Romulus and Remus. At last the torches began to burn low, and Theodat said to Maria:

"Dear Rhea Silvia, it is already late. We must go away from here."

"But you will come again to-morrow?" asked Maria.

Theodat looked at the young girl. She seemed to him strangely attractive, with her thin, half-childish figure, the hectic flush on her cheeks and her deep black eyes. There was an incomprehensible attraction in this meeting of theirs in the dim hall of this buried palace, before this marvellous bas-relief of an unknown artist. Theodat desired to repeat these minutes of strange intercourse with the poor crazy girl, and he answered:

"Yes, maiden, to-morrow at this hour, after my day's work, I will come again to you here."

Hand in hand they went in the direction of the way out. Theodat had a rope ladder with him. He helped Maria to climb up the hole which served as an entrance to the palace. Evening had already fallen when they reached the streets.

Before they separated Theodat said once more, looking into Maria's eyes:

"Remember, maiden, you must not tell anyone that you have met me. It might cost me my life. Good-bye until to-morrow."

He got out first into the open air and was soon out of sight round a bend of the road. Maria went slowly home. It so happened that evening that she had a talk with her father. She would not tell him that at last Mars Gradivus had come to her.

V

Theodat did not deceive Maria. Next day, towards evening, he really came again to the Golden House and to the bas-relief representing Mars and Rhea Silvia, where Maria was already awaiting him. The young man had brought with him some bread and cheese and some wine, and they had their supper together in the magnificent hall of Nero's palace. Maria mused aloud again about the beauty of life in the past, about gods, heroes and emperors, mixing up stories of her own experiences with the wanderings of her fancy; but Theodat, with his arm around the girl, gently stroked her hand or her shoulder, and admired the black depth of her eyes. Then they walked together through the empty underground rooms, shedding the light of their torches on the great creations of Greek and Roman genius. When they parted they again exchanged a promise to meet on the following day.

From that time, every day, when Theodat had finished his dull labour at the armourer's workshop, where they made and repaired helmets, pikes and armour for the company of Byzantines who were garrisoning Rome, he went to meet the strange young girl who thought herself to be the vestal virgin Ilia, alive once more. There was an unconquerable attraction for the young man in the lissom body of the girl and in her half-foolish words, to which he was ready to listen for whole hours together. They explored together all the halls, corridors and rooms of the palace, as far as they could get; they rejoiced together over each newly-found statue, each newly-noticed bas-relief, and there was never a day but some unexpected discovery filled their souls with a new rapture. Day after day they lived in an unchanging happiness, enjoying the creations of Art, and in moments of emotion before a new-found marble sculpture, the work perhaps of Praxiteles, young man and maiden would lean towards one another and embrace in a pure and blessed kiss.

Imperceptibly Theodat began to consider the Golden House of Nero as his own home, and Maria became to him the nearest and dearest being in the world. How this happened Theodat himself did not know. But all the rest of the time which he spent on the earth seemed to him a burdensome and distasteful obligation, and only the time that he spent with Rhea Silvia underground, in the palace of the ancient emperor, seemed to him to be real life. The whole day the young man awaited in a torture of impatience the moment when he could at last leave the brass helmets and hammers and pincers, and with the rope ladder hidden under his garments run off to the slope of the Esquiline for his secret meeting. Only by these meetings did Theodat reckon his days. If he had been asked what attracted him in Maria he would have found it difficult to answer. But without her, without her simple talk, without her strange eyes, all his life would have seemed empty and void.

On the earth, in the armourer's workshop, or in his own pitiful little room which he rented from a priest, Theodat could reason sanely. He would say to himself that this Rhea Silvia was a poor crazy girl, and that he himself perhaps was doing wrong in corroborating her pernicious fancies. But when he went down into the cool damp obscurity of the Golden House, Theodat, as it were, changed everything—his thoughts and his soul. He became something different, not what he was in the sultry heat of the Roman day or in the stifling atmosphere of the forge. He felt himself in another world there, where in reality he met both the vestal virgin Ilia, daughter of King Numitor, and the god Mars, who had taken upon himself the form of a young Goth. In this world everything was possible and all miracles were natural. In this world the past was still living, and the fables of the poets were clearly realised at every step.

Not that Theodat believed in Maria's delusions. But when, before some statue of an ancient emperor, she would begin to speak of meeting him on the Forum and talking with him,

it seemed to Theodat that something of the sort had actually
taken place. When Maria told him about the riches of her
father, King Numitor, Theodat was ready to think that she
was speaking the truth. And when she had visions of the
glories of the future Rome, which would be founded by the
new Romulus and Remus, Theodat himself was led to
develop these visions, and to speak about the victories of the
Eternal City, its new conquests of territory, its new world-
wide fame. . . . And together they would imagine the
names of the coming emperors who would rule in their
children's city. . . . Maria always spoke of herself as Rhea
Silvia and of Theodat as Mars, and he became so accustomed to these names that there were times when he deliberately called himself by the name of the ancient Roman god
of war. And when both of them, young man and maiden,
were intoxicated by the darkness and by the marvellous
creations of Art, by their nearness to one another and by
their strange half-crazy dreams, Theodat almost began to
feel in his veins the divine ichor of an Olympian god.

And again the days went by. At the very beginning of his
acquaintance with Maria, Theodat had promised himself to
spare the crazy girl and not to take advantage of her weak
intellect and of her unprotected state. But with each new
meeting it became in every way more and more difficult for
him to keep his word. Meeting every day the girl he already
loved with all the passion of youthful love, spending long
hours with her alone in this isolated place, in the half-
darkness, touching her hands and shoulders, feeling her
breathing close beside him, and exchanging kisses with her,
Theodat was obliged to use greater and greater effort not to
press the girl to himself in a strong embrace, not to draw her
to him with those caresses with which the god Mars had
once drawn to himself the first vestal. And Maria not only
did not avoid such caresses, but she even, as it were, sought
them, leaning towards him, attracting him to her with all her
being. She lingered in Theodat's arms when he kissed her,

she herself pressed him to her bosom when they were admiring the statues and pictures, she seemed every moment to be questioning the youth with her large black eyes, as if she were asking him, "When?" "Will it be soon?" "I am tired of waiting." Theodat would ask himself, "And can it be true that she is crazy? Then I must be crazy too! And is not our craziness better than the reasonable life of other people? Why should we deny ourselves the full joy of love?"

And so that which was inevitable came to its fulfilment. The marriage chamber of Maria and Theodat was one of the magnificent halls of the Golden House of Nero. The resin twists, lighted and placed in ancient bronze candlesticks in the form of Cupids, were their bridal torches. The union of the young couple was blessed by the marble gods, sculptured by Praxiteles, who looked down with unearthly smiles from their niches of porphyry. The great silence of the buried palace hid in itself the first passionate sighs of the newly-wedded pair and their pale faces were overshadowed by the mysterious obscurity of the underground palace. There was no solemn banquet, no marriage songs, but long ages of glory and power overshadowed the bridal couch, and its earth and ashes seemed to the lovers softer and more desirable than the down of Pontine swans in the sleeping apartments of Byzantium.

From that evening Maria and Theodat began to meet as lovers. Their long talks were mingled with long caresses. They exchanged passionate confessions and passionate vows —in almost senseless speeches. They wandered again through the empty rooms of the Golden House, not so much attracted now by the pictures and statues, the marble walls and the mosaics, as by the possibility in the new room to fall again and again into each other's embraces. They still dreamed of the future Rome which would be founded by their children, but this happy vision was already eclipsed by the happiness of their unrestrained kisses, in whose burning atmosphere vanished not only actuality but also dreams. They still called themselves Rhea Silvia and the god Mars, but they had already become poor earthly lovers, a happy couple, like thousands and thousands of others living on the earth after thousands and thousands of centuries.

VI

Never, outside the hall of the subterranean palace, did Theodat try to meet Maria nor she him. They only existed for one another in the Golden House of Nero. Perhaps they might even not have recognised one another on the earth. Theodat might have ceased to be for Maria the god Mars, and Maria would not have seemed to Theodat beautiful and wonderful. Truly, after their union, the honourable young Goth had said to himself that he ought to find out the real relatives of the young girl, to marry her and openly acknowledge her as his wife before all people. But day after day he put off the fulfilment of this resolve; it would have been terrible for him to destroy the fairy-like enchantment in which he was living, terrible to exchange the unheard-of ways of the underground hall for the ordinary realities. Perhaps Theodat did not thus explain his delay to himself, but, all the same, he did not hasten to bring to an end the burning happiness of these secret meetings, and every time he parted from Maria he renewed his vow to her that on the morrow he would come again. And she expected him, and asked for nothing more; for her this visionary blessedness was sufficient—to be the beloved of a god.

"Thou wilt always love me?" Theodat would ask, pressing the lissom body of Maria in his strong arms.

But she would shake her head and say:

"I will love thee until death. But thou art an immortal, and soon I must die. They will drown me in the waters of the Tiber."

"No, no," Theodat would say, "that will not happen. We shall live together and die together. Without thee I do not wish to be immortal. And after death we shall love each other just the same there in our Olympus."

But Maria would look at him distrustfully. She expected death and was prepared for it. She only wished one thing— to prolong her happiness as long as it was possible.

The young man told himself that he ought secretly to follow Maria and find out where she lived—go to her real home and to her true father and tell him that he, Agapit, loved this young girl and wanted to make her his wife. But when the hour of parting drew near, when Maria, having heard Theodat vow that he would come again to-morrow to the Golden House, glided away like a thin shadow into the evening distance, the youth would once more postpone his action. "Let this be put off another day! Let us meet once more as Rhea Silvia and the god Mars! Let this fairy tale still continue." And he would go home, to the little room he rented from the priest, to dream all night of his beloved and solace himself with the new happiness of remembrance. And Theodat never asked anyone about the strange black-eyed girl, though almost everyone in Rome knew Maria. But in reality he did not wish to know anything about her except this—that she was the vestal Ilia, and that every evening she lovingly awaited him in the subterranean hall of Nero's underground palace.

But one day Maria, having waited till the evening, awaited Theodat in vain; the youth did not come. Grieved and disturbed, Maria went home again. Her mind had in a way become somewhat clearer since she had given herself to Theodat, and she was able to console herself with the thought that something must have prevented him from coming. But the youth did not come the next day, nor the next. He suddently disappeared completely, and it was in vain that Maria waited for him at the appointed place hour after hour, day after day—waited in anguish, in despair, sobbing, praying to the ancient gods, and using the words which her mother had once taught her: there came no answer to her tears and prayers. As before, an unearthly smile played over the faces of the gods in their niches in the walls; as before, the superb rooms of the ancient palace gleamed with paintings and mosaics, but the Golden House suddenly became empty and terrible for Maria. From a blessed paradise, from the land of the Elysian fields, it had suddenly been changed into a hall of cruel torture, into a black Tartarus where was only horror and solitude, unendurable grief and unbearable pain. With an insane hope, Maria went every day as before to the underground dwelling, but now she went there as to a place of torture. There awaited her the hours of disappointed expectation, the terrible reminders of her late happiness and her long-renewed inconsolable tears.

It was most terrible of all, most distressing of all, near the bas-relief which represented Rhea Silvia sleeping in the sacred cave with the god Mars coming towards her. All her remembrances drew Maria to this bas-relief, yet near it the most unconquerable grief would overwhelm her soul. She would fall on the floor and beat her head against the stone mosaic pavement, closing her eyes that she might not behold the radiant face of the god. "Come back, come back!" she would repeat in her frenzy. "Come just once again! Divine immortal, have pity on my sufferings. Let me see thee once again. I have not yet told thee all, I have not given thee all my kisses; I must, I must see thee once again in life. And after that let me die, let them cast me into the waters of the Tiber, and I will not resist. Have pity on me, Divine One!" And Maria would open her eyes again, and by the faint light of the torch she would see the unmoved face of the sculptured god, and then once more the remembrance of the blessedness which had suddenly been taken away from her would overwhelm her and she would burst into new tears and sobs and wails. And she herself would hardly know if the god Mars had come to her, if in her life there had been those days of perfect happiness or if she had not dreamed them amongst thousands of other dreams.

With every day her expectations grew more hopeless. Every day she would return to her home more anguished and more shaken. In those hours when there were glimmerings of consciousness in her soul she remembered dimly all that Theodat had once told her about himself. Then she would wander through the streets of Rome, and under various pretexts she would look into all the armourers' workshops, but nowhere did she meet with him she sought. To speak to anyone of her grief and of her happiness was impossible for her, and no one would have believed the stories of the poor crazy girl—everyone would have considered them to be new wanderings of her distorted imagination. So Maria lived alone with her grief and her despair, and her mother only shook her head dejectedly as she saw her becoming thinner and more wasted, her cheeks more sunken and her eyes burning more feverishly and with more strange and fiery reflections.

But the days passed by inconsolably—for the poor crazy girl, for the despoiled Eternal City, and for the whole world in which a new life was slowly coming to birth. The days went by: Justianian celebrated his final victories over the remaining Goths, the Lombards thought out their Italian campaign, the popes secretly forged the links of that chain which in the future would connect Rome with all the world, the Romans continued to live their poor and oppressed lives, and one day Maria understood at last that she would become a mother. The vestal Rhea Silvia to whom the god Mars had condescended from his Olympus began to feel within herself the pulsations of a new life—were they not the twins, the new Romulus and Remus who must found the new Rome?

To no one, neither to father nor to mother, did Maria speak of what she felt. It was her secret. But she was strangely quieted by her discovery. Her dreams were being completely fulfilled. She must give birth to the founders of Rome and afterwards await death in the muddy waters of the Tiber.

VII

Sometimes guests would gather together in the house of old Rufus—a neighbouring merchant who sold cheap women's finery on the Forum, the coppersmith's son who at one time had wished to court Maria, an infirm orator who could no longer find a use for his learning, and a few other poverty-stricken people who were dejectedly living out their days, only meeting one another to complain of their unhappy lot. They would drink poor wine and eat a little garlic, and among their customary complaints they would cautiously interpolate bitter words about the Byzantine rule and the inhuman demands of the new general who lived on the Palatine in place of the departed eunuch Narses. Florentia would serve the guests, and pour out wine for them, and at the speeches of the old orator she would quietly cross herself at the mention of the accursed gods.

At one of these gatherings Maria was sitting in a corner of the room, having come home earlier that day than usual from her wanderings. Nobody paid any attention to her. They were all accustomed to see among them the silent girl whom they had long ago considered to be insane. She never joined in the conversation and no one ever addressed a remark to her. She sat with her head bent in a melancholy fashion and never moved, apparently hearing nothing of the speeches made by the drinking party.

On this day they were talking especially about the severity of the new general. But the coppersmith's son took upon himself to defend him.

"We must take into account," said he, "that at the present time it is necessary to act rigorously. There are many spies going about the city. The barbarians may fall on us again. Then we should have to endure another siege. These accursed Goths, when they took themselves out of the town for good, had hidden their treasures in various places. And now first one and then another of them comes back to Rome secretly and in disguise, digs up the hidden treasure and carries it away. Such people must be caught, and it would never do to be easy with them: the Romans will have all their riches stolen."

The words of the coppersmith's son aroused curiosity. They began to ask him questions. He readily told all that he knew about the treasures hidden by the Goths in various parts of Rome, and how those of them who had escaped destruction strove to seek out these stores and carry them off. Then he added:

"And it's only lately they caught one of them. He was clambering up the Esquiline, where there is an opening in the ground. He had a rope-ladder. They caught him and took him to the general. The general promised to spare him if the accursed one would show exactly where the treasure was hidden. But he was obstinate and would say nothing. They tortured him and tortured him, but got nothing out of him. So they tortured him to death."

"And is he dead?" asked someone.

"Of course he's dead," said the coppersmith's son.

Suddenly an unexpected illumination lit up the confused mind of Maria. She stood up to her full height. Her large eyes grew still larger. Pressing both hands to her bosom, she asked in a breaking voice:

"And what was his name, what was the name—of this Goth?"

The coppersmith's son knew all about it. So he answered at once:

"He called himself Agapit; he was working quite near here, in an armourer's workshop."

And with a shriek Maria fell face downwards on the floor.

Maria was ill for a long while, for many weeks. On the first day of her illness a child was born prematurely, a pitiful lump of flesh which it was impossible to call either a boy or a girl. Florentia, with all her harshness, loved her daughter. While

Maria lay unconscious for many days her mother tended her and never left her side. She called in a midwife and a priest. When at length Maria came to her senses, Florentia had no reproachful tears for her, she only wept inconsolably and pressed her daughter to her bosom. Her mother-soul had divined everything. Later on, when Maria was a little better, her mother told her all that had happened and did not reproach her.

But Maria listened to her mother with a strange distrust. How could Rhea Silvia believe it, when she was destined, by the will of the gods, to bring forth the twins Romulus and Remus? Either the girl's mind was entirely overclouded or she believed her former dreams more than actuality; at the words of her mother she merely shook her head in weakness. She thought her mother was deceiving her, that during her illness she had borne twins which had been taken from her, put into a wicker basket and thrown into the Tiber. But Maria knew that a wolf would find and nourish them, for they must be the founders of the new Rome.

As long as Maria was so weak that she could not raise her head, no one wondered that she would answer no questions and would be silent whole days, neither asking for food or drink nor wishing to pronounce a monosyllable. But when she recovered a little and found strength to go about the house, Maria continued to be silent, hiding in her soul some treasured thought. She did not even want to talk to her father any more, and she was not pleased when he began to declaim verses from the ancient poets.

At length, one morning, when her father had gone out on business and her mother was at market, Maria unexpectedly disappeared from home. No one noticed her departure. And no one saw her again alive. But after some days the muddy waters of the Tiber cast her lifeless body on the shore.

Poor girl! Poor vestal of the broken vows! One would like to believe that, throwing thy body into the cold embraces of the water, thou wert convinced that thy children, the twins

Romulus and Remus, were at that moment drinking the warm milk of the she-wolf, and that in time to come they would raise up the first rampart of the Eternal City. If in the moment of thy death thou hadst no doubt of this, thou wert perhaps the happiest of all the people in that pitiful half-destroyed Rome towards which were already moving from the Alps the hordes of the wild Lombards.

(II)

THE MARBLE BUST

A Tramp's Story

(Translated by Rosa Graham)

H e had been tried for burglary, and sentenced to a year's imprisonment. I was struck by the behaviour of the old man in court and by the circumstances under which the crime had been committed. I obtained permission to visit the prisoner. At first he would have nothing to do with me, and would not speak; but finally he told me the story of his life.

"You are right," said he. "I have seen better days, and I haven't always been a miserable wanderer about the streets, nor always slept in night-houses. I had a good education. I am an engineer. In my youth I had a little money and I lived a gay life: every evening I went to a party or to a ball and ended up with a drinking bout. I remember that time well, even trifling details I remember. And yet there is a gap in my recollections that I would give all the rest of my unworthy life to fill up—everything which has anything to do with Nina.

"She was called Nina, dear sir; yes, Nina. I'm sure of that. Her husband was a minor official on the railway. They were

poor. But how clever she was in making of the pitiful surroundings of her life something elegant and, as it were,
specially refined. She herself did the cooking, but her hands
were, as it were, carefully wrought. Of her poor clothes she
made a marvellous dream. Yes, and the whole everyday
world, on contact with her, became fantastical. I myself,
meeting her, became other than I was, better, and shook off,
as rain from my clothes, all the sordidness of life.

"May God forgive her sin in loving me. Everything around
her was so coarse that she couldn't help falling in love with
me, young and handsome as I was and knowing so much
poetry by heart. But when I first made her acquaintance
and how—this I cannot now call to mind. Separate pictures
draw themselves out from the darkness. See, we are at the
theatre. She, happy, gay (this was so rare with her), is
drinking in every word of the play, and she is smiling at
me. . . . I remember her smile. Afterwards, we were together at some place or other. She bent her head down to
me, and said: 'I know that you will not be my happiness for
very long; never mind, I shall have lived.' I remember these
words. But what happened directly afterwards, and whether
it is really true that all this happened when I was with Nina,
I don't know.

"Of course, it was I who first gave her up. This seems to
me so natural. All my companions acted in this way: they
flirted with some married woman, and then, after a while,
cast her off. I only acted as everybody else did, and it didn't
even enter my mind that I was behaving badly. To steal
money, not to pay one's debts, to turn informer—this was
bad, but to cast off a woman whom one has loved was only
the way of the world. A brilliant future was before me, and
I could not bind myself to a sort of romantic love. It was
painful, very painful, but I gained the victory over myself,
and I even saw a *podvig* in my resolution to overcome this
pain.

"I heard that Nina went away afterwards with her husband

to the south, and that soon after she died. But my memories of Nina were so tormenting that I avoided at that time all news of her. I tried to know nothing about her and not to think of her. I had not kept her portrait, I had returned her letters, we had no mutual acquaintances; and so, little by little, the image of Nina was erased from my soul. Do you understand? I gradually came to forget Nina, forget her entirely, her face, her name, and all her love. It came to be as if she had actually never existed at all in my life. . . . Ah, there's something shameful for a man in this ability to forget!

"The years went by. I won't tell you how I 'made a career.' Without Nina, of course I dreamed only of external success, of money. At one time I had nearly obtained the complete success at which I aimed. I could spend thousands, could travel abroad. I married and had children. Afterwards, everything turned to loss : the works which I designed were unsuccessful; my wife died; finding myself left with children on my hands, I sent them away to relatives, and now, God forgive me, I don't even know if my little boys are alive. As you may guess, I drank and played cards. . . . I started an agency; it did not succeed; it swallowed up my last money and energy. I tried to get straight by gambling, and only just escaped being sent to prison—yes, and not entirely without reason. My friends turned against me and my downfall began.

"Little by little I got to the point where you now see me. I, so to speak, 'dropped out' of intellectual society and fell into the abyss. What place could I presume to take, badly dressed, almost always drunken? Of late years I have worked for months, when not drinking, as a labourer in various factories. And when I had a drinking bout, I would turn up in the Thieves' market and doss-houses. I passionately detested the people I met, and was always dreaming that suddenly my fate would change and I should be rich once more. I expected to receive some sort of non-existent inheritance or something of that kind. And I despised my companions because they had no such hope.

"Well, one day, all shivering with cold and hunger, I wander into someone's yard without knowing why, and something happens. Suddenly the cook calls out, 'Hallo, my boy, you don't happen to be a locksmith, do you?' 'Yes, I'm a locksmith,' says I. They wanted someone to mend the lock of a writing-table. I found myself in a luxurious study, gold all about, and pictures. I began to work and did what was wanted, and the lady gave me a rouble. I took the money, and, all of a sudden, I saw on a little white pedestal a marble bust. At first I felt faint. I don't know why. I stared at it and couldn't believe: Nina!

"I tell you, dear sir, I had quite forgotten Nina, and at this moment specially, for the first time, I understood it, understood that I had forgotten her. Suddenly her image swam before my eyes, and a whole universe of feelings, dreams, thoughts, buried in my soul as in some sort of Atlantis, woke, rose again, lived again. . . . I look at the marble bust, all trembling, and I say: 'Permit me to ask, lady, whose bust is that?' 'Oh, that,' says she, 'is a very valuable thing; it was made five hundred years ago, in the fifteenth century.' She told me the name of the sculptor, but I didn't catch it, and she said that her husband had brought this bust from Italy, and that because of it there had arisen a whole diplomatic correspondence between the Italian and Russian Cabinets. 'But,' says the lady to me, 'you don't mean to say it pleases you? What an up-to-date taste you have! Don't you see that the ears,' says she, 'are not in the right place, and the nose is irregular . . .?' and she went away; she went away.

"I rushed out as if I were suffocating. This was not a likeness, but an actual portrait; nay, more—it was a sort of re-creation of life in marble. Tell me, by what miracle could an artist in the fifteenth century make those same tiny ears, set on awry, which I knew so well, those same eyes, just a tiny bit aslant, that irregular nose, and the high sloping forehead, out of which unexpectedly you got the most beautiful, the most captivating woman's face? By what miracle could there live two women so much alike—one in the fifteenth century, the other in our own day? And that she whom the sculptor had modelled was absolutely the same, and like to Nina not only in face but in character and in soul, I did not doubt.

"That day changed the whole of my life. I understood all the meanness of my behaviour in the past and all the depth of my fall. I understood Nina as an angel, sent to me by Destiny and not recognised by me. To bring back the past was impossible. But I began eagerly to gather together my remembrances of Nina as one might gather up the shattered bits of a precious vase. How few they were! Try as I would I could get nothing whole. All were fragments, splinters. But how I rejoiced when I succeeded in making out in my soul something new. Thinking over these things and remembering them, I would spend whole hours; people laughed at me, but I was happy. I was old; it was late for me to begin life anew, but I could still cleanse my soul from base thoughts, from malice towards my fellows and from murmuring against my Creator. And in my remembrances of Nina I found this cleansing.

"I wanted desperately to look once more at the statue. I wandered whole evenings near the house where it was and I tried to see the marble bust, but it stood a long way from the windows. I spent whole nights in front of the house. I knew all the people who lived there, how the rooms were arranged, and I made friends with a servant. In the summer the lady went away into the country. And then I could no longer fight against my desire. I thought that if I could see the marble Nina once again, I should at once remember everything, to the end. And that would be for me ultimate bliss. So I made up my mind to do that for which I've been sentenced. You know that I didn't succeed. They caught me in the hall. And at the trial it came out that I'd been in the rooms on pretence of being a locksmith, and that I'd often been seen near the house. . . . I was a beggar, I had forced the locks. . . . However, the story's ended now, dear sir!"

"But we'll make an appeal for you," said I. "They will acquit you."

"But why?" objected the old man. "No one grieves over my sentence, and no one will go bail for me; and isn't it just the same where I shall think about Nina—in a doss-house or in a prison?"

I didn't know what to answer, but the old man suddenly looked up at me with his strange and faded eyes and went on:

"Only one thing worries me. What if Nina never existed, and it was merely my poor mind, weakened by alcohol, which invented the whole story of this love whilst I was looking at the little marble head?"

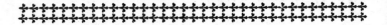

PANTALEIMON ROMANOF
(1884—1938)

✢✢

WITHOUT CHERRY BLOSSOM

I

I T seems as if there never had been so magnificent a spring before.

But, dear Verusha, I feel sad.

Sad, ill, as if I'd done something rather second-rate. . . .

I've a bottle with a broken neck in my window at the hostel, and a broken withered little branch of bird cherry in it. I brought it home last night. . . . And when I look at that bottle, somehow I want to cry.

I'll be brave and tell you all. I lately made the acquaintance of a comrade from another faculty. I am far removed from sentiment of any kind, as he would say; far from bewailing lost innocence, and even further from any gnawing of conscience over my first "fall." But there is something that rubs me up the wrong way, not clear, confused, ever present.

I'll tell you later, with "shameless" frankness, how it all happened. But first of all I would like to put some questions to you.

When you and Paul were united, for the first time, didn't you wish that the day of your first love might be to you a sort of festival day, somehow or other different from the everyday?

For instance, would it have seemed humiliating to you, on that spring festival day of your life, to go out of doors in dirty boots, or to wear a torn or soiled blouse?

I ask you because all my acquaintances, the folk of my own

age, look on the matter differently. I do not seem to have sufficient pluck to think and act just as I feel.

It needs a good deal of effort to go against the accepted opinion of those among whom one lives.

With us the accepted attitude towards the beautiful is one of youthful disdain, and it is the same with regard to any daintiness or correctness of attire or fastidiousness in the home.

Our hostel is all dirt, filth, disorder, tumbled beds. Cigarette ends on the window ledges, flimsy partitions between the cubicles all covered with torn placards and advertisements. There is not one of us who tries to beautify his dwelling, and as there is a rumour that we are going to be transferred to another building, the students are even more careless than they would be ordinarily, and frequently do deliberate damage to the place.

It is as if there were someone or other before whom we are ashamed to be seen occupying ourselves with such trifles as a clean and beautiful room and healthy fresh air in it. It is not because we have serious business on hand and no time, but because we feel obliged to despise everything connected with care for beauty.

That is the more strange because we all know that the powers that be, our poverty-stricken proletarian power, spend a vast amount of money and energy simply to make everything beautiful, putting flower-gardens all over the place, the like of which was unknown under the old régime of squires and capitalists, though they prided themselves on their love of an elegant, beautiful life. All Moscow gleams with stucco, and our university, which stood a hundred years looking like a tumble-down police station, has now been converted into the most beautiful building in Moscow.

And we . . . feel an involuntary pride in the fact that it is so beautiful. But for all that, our own life inside these walls, purified by our new government, our own life is dominated by filth and disorder.

All the girls and our men-comrades behave as if they were afraid of being accused of delicacy and good manners. They deliberately cultivate a coarse and debauched way of talking and slap one another on the hips. And when they refer to sex they make use of the most coarse expressions, the most disgusting street slang.

The most abominable epithets have with us full civic rights. And when some of our girls, I will not say all, a few, feel mortified, something even worse sets in. The rest try to accustom them "to the mother tongue."

Cynicism, the tone of coarse debauch and the trampling underfoot of all fastidiousness alone have success. Perhaps it is because we are a poverty-stricken lot, and having nothing to spend on dress, we just spit upon the whole business or like to pretend that we do. Or it may be that we think of ourselves as the soldiers of the revolution, for whom naturally sentimental notions and fastidiousness have no place. But if we are soldiers of the revolution we ought somehow to take an example from the power we have set up, and strive for beauty in life not simply for the sake of the beautiful, but for the sake of cleanliness and health. For that reason it seems about time that we decided to give up this exaggerated, over-emphasised barracks style.

But, you know, the majority like it. To say nothing of our men, our girls like it; it gives them more freedom and demands little exercise of will on their part.

But this neglect of the beautiful, the pure and the healthy leads to an appalling hooliganism in our intimate relationships. It begets a coarseness, a lack of ceremony, a fear of showing the least human delicacy of feeling or of sensibility or care towards one's woman friend or any of the girls.

It all comes from the fear of infringing the unwritten moral code.

Things are different with you at the academy. I am sometimes sorry that I entered the university. My mother, who is a village midwife, looks up to me with a sort of pious respect as to a higher being, but I often wonder what she would think if she saw the filth in which we live and heard the latest bad language that we habitually use.

For us love does not exist; we have only sexual relationships. And so, love is scornfully relegated to the realm of "psychology," and our right to existence is only understood physiologically.

The girls live with their men friends, and it is a small matter to go with them for a week or a month, or promiscuously, for one night only. And anyone who is trying to find in love anything beyond the physiological is laughed down as mental or a bad case.

II

What does he think he is? An ordinary student in high boots and a blue blouse unbuttoned at the neck. He always pushes back his untidy locks from his brow with his hands.

His eyes attracted me. When he is by himself and is walking along the corridors one feels a great seriousness and calm in his eyes.

But directly he fell in with any of his fellow-students he became, it seemed to me, exaggeratedly noisy, loose and coarse. The girls inspired him with self-confidence because he was handsome, the men because he was clever. He seemed to be afraid to lose the sort of leadership which he had.

I saw two men in him, one possessing a good deal of inner strength and seriousness of mind, the other a vulgar wag who irritated you by the way he had of showing off and impressing others with the appearance of being very coarse, much more coarse than, in fact, he is.

Yesterday at sunset we went out for the first time together. Evening stillness had settled on the city and the street noises were subdued. The air was fresh and there was a pleasant odour of the damp earth coming from the squares.

"Come along to my place, I don't live far from here," said he.

"No, I'm not coming."

"What's that? Etiquette?"

"It's not etiquette at all. That, in the first place. In the second place, it's very pleasant out of doors at the moment."

He shrugged his shoulders.

We walked along the quay and stood for a while at the drawbridge. A girl came selling branches of bird cherry blossom. I bought a spray of it and had to wait a long while for my change. He stood to one side, looking at me and frowning slightly.

"Can't you get on without cherry blossom?"

"I can. But it's better with cherry blossom than without."

"I manage always without cherry blossom, and somehow it does not turn out badly," said he, grinning unpleasantly.

Two girls were ahead of us. A whole crowd of students were mauling them, and when they tore themselves away the students burst into fits of laughter, stared after the girls and called out things after them.

"They've put the girls in a bad temper. Went to them without cherry blossom, and the girls took fright," said my companion.

"Why do you dislike cherry blossom so much?" I asked.

"Well, it all ends the same way, cherry blossom or no cherry blossom. . . . Why mince matters?"

"You speak in that way because you have never loved."

"Why is that necessary?"

"Then what is there in a woman for you?"

"Oh, drop this Chinese ceremoniousness and call me thou, don't call me you! As for woman, there is something there for me, and I dare say it amounts to a good deal."

"I shan't call you you. If everyone uses thou there is no pleasure in it."

We passed some lilac bushes. I stopped a moment to pin

the cherry blossom to my blouse. He made a sudden movement, pushed back my head and tried to kiss me.

I pushed him back.

"Don't want to; all right, don't!" said he calmly.

"I don't want it. As you don't love anyone, it's all the
same to you what woman you kiss. If instead of me it had
been someone else, you'd have wanted to kiss her just the
same."

"Quite right. A woman also kisses whom she wants to,
and does not confine herself to one. We had a little beano
lately, and the fiancée of a friend of mine who was there
kissed me with as much gusto as she did him. And if it had
been someone else near her, she'd have done the same by
him. And that couple are marrying for love at the registra-
tion office and the rest of it."

I was annoyed in the depths of myself when I heard him
speak thus. I had fancied that he was not entirely indifferent
to me. How many times had he sought my glance even when
I was in a dense crowd of other students! And why should
he spoil this delightful spring evening with licentious and
coarse ideas, when one craved tenderness and quiet conversation?

I hated him at that moment. We were passing a bench on
which a lady of a kind was sitting. She wore silk stockings
and her legs were crossed above the knees. She raised her
eyes whenever anyone went by.

My companion stared fixedly at her. And having gone on
a few steps he turned round and stared at her again. I felt
as if I had been stung.

"Let's sit down here," said he at the next bench. He
wanted to sit down there so that he could continue to stare
at her.

All at once I felt so upset that I felt I might begin to cry.
Fearing lest I should break down, I told him I did not want
to be with him any longer and said good-bye.

He was taken aback, and evidently bewildered.

"Why?" he asked. "Don't you like me to be sincere? Would it be better if I dressed my ideas up and lied?"

"I'm sorry you do not possess anything that does not need to be dressed up."

"Well, what are you going to do about it?" said he, as if not at first grasping what I meant. "In that case I'll be going also. Good-bye." He held my hand in his for a moment. "Only it's foolish, it's foolish," he repeated, and threw my hand down and strode away towards his home.

I also was taken by surprise. I did not think that he would go away.

I stopped on the corner of the boulevard and looked round. It was one of those May nights when you feel that the life encompassing you is for that night only and never to be repeated. The moon, with wisps of cloud about her, stood on high in a warm, cloudy yellow haze. The far-distant sunset tones were lost behind the roofs of many houses and the Kremlin towers. And the infrequent street lights were dimmed by the moonlight.

And there were gay crowds of young men and girls in the brightly lighted square in front of the cathedral, and loving couples on the garden seats under low-branching, close-cropped trees and lilac bushes.

There was a murmur of light conversation and laughter; one saw the glowing ends of cigarettes. Everyone seemed affected, intoxicated by the awakening warmth of the night and eager not to lose a moment of it.

But when such a night strikes no chord in your soul, when you are lonely and miserable and have no companion, you feel very sad, you could not feel worse.

A few moments earlier I had been indifferent whether he was with me or not. But the thought of his staring at that woman on the bench preyed on my mind. I felt a tearful anxiety, and I weakened to such an extent that I wanted nothing else in the world but that he should be with me.

In a word—don't condemn me—I could not bear to be

like one who has been expelled from the glad company, thrown out from the choir, this spring festival night.

And without considering what it might mean, I retraced my steps and hurried towards his house.

III

There was but one thought in my head: he might have gone out, I might be late, I might remain solitary. And then I reproached myself for breaking away from him so ridiculously without making the slightest effort to bring out the good side of his character.

I reflected that in this I had behaved in just the same way as those who shrug their shoulders at unpleasant conditions and do nothing to better them. It meant that I wanted to get something better without any expense of energy on my part.

I went under the gateway of the old stone house and felt the strange contrast of the air of the warm May night out of doors and the cold reek of unheated walls.

There are still many entrances like this in Moscow, with unwashed doors and rags of old advertisements hanging from them, filthy outer stairways scribbled over and unswept.

He didn't at all expect to see me again. Apparently he was about to sit down to work. There was a slight table that looked like a plasterer's trestles set up against one of the walls. An electric lamp bulb hung on a cord from the ceiling, but had been pulled over to the table and was fixed there by a nail.

"So, the heroine has returned!" he exclaimed. "Evidently thought better of it. So much the better."

He came up to me grinning and took me by the arm. Perhaps he was going to kiss me or stroke me, but he did neither.

"I was sorry we quarrelled and I wanted to put it right," said I.

"What was there to put right? Wait a moment, I'll put a notice on the door that I'm not at home. Otherwise someone may come."

He wrote out the notice, standing at the table, and then went out with it. Alone in the room, I had a look round.

This room of his had the same general character as that staircase. The walls were scrawled with telephone numbers; cigarette ends and scraps of paper littered the unswept floor. There was a tumbled, unmade bed alongside one of the walls, just as in one of our rooms at the hostel; dirty dishes on the window-ledge, empty bottles, butter-paper, egg-shells, cans.

I felt somewhat embarrassed and could not think what I would say to him when he came back. It would not be very wise to be silent, as that might be construed to mean something quite different.

Then it occurred to me to ask myself why he had gone out to fix that notice on the door. What if someone did come?

Suddenly I understood, and at the thought I went dizzy and caught my breath. With a beating heart I went to the window-ledge, having the intention of clearing away the bottle and cigarette boxes to make a place to sit down. I saw that my hand trembled. All the same I did clear the ledge and lay down on it on my stomach.

I had never felt before such an agitated tension of expectation as I did as I lay there listening for what might happen behind my back.

My only regret was that the best minutes of my life and happiness, perhaps of my first day of love, must be accomplished in the midst of the leavings of yesterday's food in this bespattered, dirty room.

That was why, when he came back into the room, I suggested we go out for some fresh air.

An expression of surprise and vexation flitted across his face.

"Why?" he asked. "Haven't you just come from out there?"

Then his voice changed.

"I've fixed it so that nobody is likely to disturb us. Don't talk nonsense. I'm not going to let you out anywhere now," said he hurriedly.

"I don't like being here."

"Ah, beginning all that over again . . ." said he crossly. "What's the matter? Where do you want to go to?"

His speech was choking and rapid, and his hands trembled when he thought to restrain me from going.

My hands also trembled, and my heart beat so violently it was dark before my eyes. A conflict was raging in my mind, the mood of surrender, the feeling that no one would disturb us, and the mood of protest, engendered by his thievish hurried whispering, his greedy haste and the loss of his calm and self-restraint. He seemed to have only one thing at heart, tó succeed before any of his comrades burst in upon him. He showed impatience and irritation at the slightest show of resistance on my part.

We women even in free love cannot look too squarely at the actual FACT. For us the fact is always at the end of the chapter, while at the beginning we are charmed by the man himself, his mind, his talents, his soul, his tenderness. We always begin by desiring something other than physical union. When this other desire has not been satisfied and a woman falls a victim to the momentary impulse of her senses, she experiences a disgust with herself instead of a fullness and happiness. She becomes hostile to the man as towards an accomplice in her fall, as towards a gross being who has forced her to have disagreeable and abominable sensations.

The unmade bed, those egg-shells in the window, the dirt, his furtive glances, and the feeling that things were not going the way they should, had already discountenanced me.

"I can't remain!" I exclaimed, almost in tears.

"Now what's the matter? Don't you like the furniture?

Not enough poetry in it? But I'm not some baron . . ." he cried with ill-concealed vexation.

I suppose the expression on my face changed at his shouting, for, as if anxious to undo the impression he might have made by these words, he began to calm me in hurried whispers.

"That's all right, dear, stop . . . it's quite true someone might come in."

I ought most certainly to have gone away then. But the fact of being alone with him there enkindled such sheer desire in me as in him. I chose to deceive myself and stayed on in the false expectation that something would intervene. . . .

"Wait, I'll make some poetry for you," said he, and turned out the light.

That was better truly, for one did not see the dirty bed nor the bottles nor the cigarette ends on the floor.

I stood at the window with my back to him. He came up behind me and put an arm round my neck while I remained looking out at the window. I could not see the expression of his face, but I was grateful to him for that embrace. I would have liked to stand there for a long, long while.

But his impatience got the better of him. He kept thinking that his comrades might come in. "How long will you stand there?" he asked, leading me away from the window with his arm.

When we got up he first of all turned on the light.

"Oh, I don't want any light," I cried in misery and alarm.

He looked at me with astonishment, and shrugging his shoulders, turned the light out again. Then he went back to the bed and began to tidy it.

"I must put my room-mate's bed straight, otherwise Vanya 'll guess right away that I've had a lady in the room," said he.

He was fussing around the bed and was on all-fours on the

floor, evidently looking for something. I was left alone. Presently he came up to me. Almost against my will I gave a deep sigh and turned my head round to see him. I was struggling with all my strength to overcome my feelings. He stretched out a hand.

"There," said he, "your hairpins. I crawled and crawled about the floor. Why must you be absolutely without light? You'd better be off now or somebody will be along. I'll see you out by the back way. The front door will be shut now."

We did not say a word to one another, and somehow seemed to be avoiding one another's eyes.

When I got into the street I walked some way mechanically, without a thought. Then suddenly I felt something metallic in my hand and I shuddered, remembering that it was the hairpins which he had put in my palm. I even stood and gazed at them. They were certainly hairpins, nothing more or less.

Still holding them in my hand, I staggered home. I still had that spray of crumpled blossom on my blouse, and it hung loose like a rag.

And the same wonderful night held sway over the town. The moon stood high over the masses of buildings, and the little clouds were like curling smoke. The same vague, misty horizon lay far away over the city.

And there was the same aroma of apple blossom, bird cherry and grass. . . .

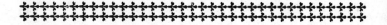

BORIS PILNIAK

(1894—1939)

++

HIS MAJESTY, KNEEB PITER KOMONDOR

I

"But the State, as the French teach, is the harmony of all
natural forces, not only of the physical but of the spiritual,
and I think that his Majesty Peter Alexeevitch did some harm
to the Russian State, for law-giving, that is, politics, is not
debauch. Having been many times in Venice, Paris and the
Low Countries, I cannot cease thinking of my own country.
Its history does not shine clearly, because the peasants and
the common people generally remain in their aboriginal
condition, and the nobility, pretending to study at the
Academy of Sciences and having their life regulated in all
sorts of ways, are nevertheless nothing more than a collection
of lovers and gallants, topers and profiteers, bruisers and
thieves and State embezzlers, for they have drunken away
their consciences and forgotten the traditions of their fathers.
The boy is torn from his mother's nipples to be trained as an
artillerist abroad, from his earliest years he is taught to drink
heavily, and at maturity all he has achieved is atheism and
clowning. Our Russia is in pestilence and famine, insurrec-
tions and disorders. . . ."

Thus Zotof, officer of the Guard, wrote in his diary, being
free for the time from his duties at the Admiralty fortress. He
was sitting in the office of the Admiralty College. The dark
stone room with its vaulted ceiling was bespattered and
filthy. Through the grimy little windows one saw heaps of
sawn logs, cord and bast. The smithy flamed on the left.
By the lower bulwark there was a flower-bed, and sentries

946

walked back and forth along the unfinished bastions. On the Neva itself there was a skeleton of a frigate looking like the frame of a dead mammoth exhibited in a museum. Beside the bastions and the frigate flocked the working rabble, driven thither from all parts of Russia—people of Tver, Vologda and Astrakhan, Kalmooks, Tartars, Little Russians in ragged jackets and bast shoes, some even without shoes. The snow lay in dirty heaps. The wind from the sea brought the thaw, the Neva ice had given in the night, but the grey clouds moved slowly—the March day was like October. There were rigid unsawn pine trunks in the ice just as at a river lumber camp. There were thickets of fir trees waving against the sky on Vassily Island.

It chimed seven from the Admiralty tower, and at the same time the creaking of the chains of the portcullis could be heard. A soldier entered and placed a dim oil lamp on the table. The clash of the bells, the creak of the chains, the bearing of the soldier, the raising of the flag—all spoke to officer Zotof of the temperament of the sovereign. And always when he thought of Peter he experienced a tense feeling of grief and pain. He was reminded of that grey January day when his father, the prince-pope Nikita Zotof, then eighty-four years old, arranged the marriage of a ninety-year-old priest to a woman of sixty, at Peter's orders. The wedding chariot of these "young people" was drawn by four bears, and a stag trailed behind. At the head of the procession was the chief executioner and Cæsar Romodanovsky, drunk as a lord. All the ministers, the great nobles, the foreign ambassadors, were present at this mockery. The bears, constantly beaten, growled and snarled ferociously. The prince-pope, half naked, in classic attire as priest, shuddered in the frost, shuddered and grinned, grinned to please the Tsar.

Peter had been at the office of the Admiralty College in the morning. Zotof was lying asleep on the table and a sergeant came and waked him. The Tsar was wearing his three-

cornered hat, green frock-coat much creased, tight breeches,
red stockings hand-knit by the Empress Catherine, and
trodden-over German slippers. His pockets were bulging
with various instruments which he always carried about with
him. He came, stooping but violent, waving his arms about,
striding and bending his knees out bandy-wise, imitating the
gait of a Dutch sailor.

His Majesty seemed to be in a good humour; Zotof had
shaken hands with him in the European manner. The bells
chimed a quarter to five. The gloom of fog before dawn
pressed on the windows. Peter made his usual improper jests
and guffawed, then went to the table and turned over some
of the papers there. After that he went to the secret document closet, which he unlocked with his own key, and
beckoned to Zotof to approach.

"It will not be possible for me to be present at the session
of the Admiralty College to-day, so I desire your Excellency
to eavesdrop it and make your report to Count Peter
Andreitch at the Secret Commission."

Never anywhere in the world was there such spying as in
Russia in the time of Peter. At the monarch's invitation,
Guard-officer Zotof, clanking his spurs, entered the cup-
board, and Peter shut the door on him and locked it.

Whereupon the monarch cried out in a lively voice: "I
have the honour to congratulate your Excellency upon
the opening of navigation. Your presence at the palace is
requested for to-morrow."

The closet smelt of Peter's sweat and vodka; it was dark
and stifling, but a faint light crept through a crack in the
door. Zotof lit his Dutch pipe, made a heap of papers to sit
on, and having smoked a little fell asleep. He was used to
sleeping in uncomfortable positions. At ten the members of
the college arrived, and Apraxin sent a sergeant for vodka.
Zotof wakened and listened. What he heard was familiar,
for all Russia was saying it. . . . Russia was ruined. . . .
The Kalmooks beyond the Volga were in revolt. . . . The

Don Cossacks were restless. . . . There was famine and pestilence in the villages. . . . Religious visionaries proclaimed
the discovery of Antichrist. . . .

Peter Andreitch Tolstoy, the head of the Secret Commission,
came at four o'clock and released Zotof from the closet.
And Tolstoy, who had destroyed a few hundred victims in
the torture chambers of the Admiralty and Petropavlovsk,
sat at the table with him and repeated the same gossip,
furtively, evilly.

"They've found a new martyr on the Kaivusari island;
he's in the torture chamber here. . . . All Russia seems
upset. Come to-night."

"May I ask your Serenity if you believe in him?" asked
Zotof.

Tolstoy glanced quickly round the room, then stared fixedly
at Zotof.

"He is full of faith," said he quietly.

It chimed seven and a quarter. Blear twilight settled on
the room. Lowering clouds driven by a wind from the sea
hinted of a river flood in the morning. Zotof strode about
the room in his big jack-boots, and stopping at the door he
read again the Tsar's order affixed there, already yellow and
fly-marked:

> "The great sovereign hereby proclaims, as was previ-
> ously proclaimed, that upon the ships and boats and
> likewise upon the galleys in the harbour of Sankt Piter-
> burg no fires may be lit and no tobacco smoked. For a
> first offence the penalty is ten strokes at the mast. A
> second offence will be punished by dragging from a
> ship's keel, a hundred and fifty strokes and penal servi-
> tude for life."

Having read that, Guard-officer Zotof filled his pipe and lit
it from the oil lamp.

At midnight, after another short sleep, he made the round
of the sentries. The sentries were on duty twenty-four hours

at a stretch and were beaten unmercifully if discovered sleeping. At midnight came the relief, and having seen the new sentries posted and transmitted his authority to another officer, he set off for his quarters in the Guards barracks away on the Moscow side. The rising water murmured in the canal, the gates of the drawbridge creaked. Zotof plunged into the gloom and the damp and his big boots dragged in the thick mud. A bell sounded on Kaivusari. Zotof stumbled upon building material lying in the way. A frightened prison sentry shouted in the dark. The Italian palace gleamed with yellow lights. In the German suburb, home of the many foreign adventurers, someone was striking heavy blows with a mallet. The wind was wet and rhythmical and persistent. Zotof felt seedy after his long sedentary duty; his eyes bulged, his body sagged. Drizzle. The officers' quarters at the barracks were noisy; there was a din of instrumental music, shouting and singing. The officers were just back from the Assembly, where they had danced and got drunk. The young crowd had dragged a young *danseuse* into the orderly room.

Guard-officer Zotof took out his day-book, wherein he recorded the progress in the building of Peter's "paradise," Sanktpeterburg, that dreadful city on the quaking marshes, city of rotting mists and fevers.

Through a war accidentally begun, and everything that Peter did was accidental, finding himself accidentally near Nienschanz, Peter accidentally decided to build the fortress of Petropavlovsk, without a thought of this "paradise." That was in 1703, and only ten years later did he begin to build Sankt-Peter-Burkh, and build it violently, wildly, cruelly, as he did everything else.

The chief problem in building the "paradise" was to keep it different from Moscow. Sanktpeterburg must be of stone. No stone was allowed to be carted anywhere in Russia except to Sanktpeterburg. If a house were of wood it had to be painted to look like brick. After the Turkish war there was a severe shortage of working hands, so towns, suburbs, villages, estates were ordered to send their official quota, a man from every nine houses. People were driven north with cudgels or brought in chains. Every workman must also bring his tools and his axe, each foreman his chisel, rod and auger, and all must bear as much food as possible. The workmen famished, rotted, died in epidemics; few lasted longer than a year. Every twelvemonth perished some hundred thousand of them. The foundations of the city were human bones. There were not enough barrows; they carried the earth in the folds of their shirts. Their bark boots wore out; they went barefooted. They worked up to the waist in water. They dwelt in filthy mud huts. Some fled; some mutinied; some became highwaymen. They caught them and hung them in tens on the ramparts of Petropavlovsk.

All the workmen were ordered to cut off their beards. There was much swindling, and Peter admired a clever swindler. All could be arranged by bribes. Peter called bribery "craftiness." He wrote: "Twenty thousand roubles are in default from the government of Kazan. We are astonished that our affairs should be overlooked to that extent," and he threatened the whipping-post. The navvies were buried where they fell. Ragged, starved, scurvy-stricken, crazed with fear, with suffering and non-comprehension, the working populations toiled on. You could not appeal to the gentry without permission. Sticks were put up on all official roofs to indicate the time by hours. The controller of the city was Prince Menshikof, general-governor of Ingermanland, lieberkinder-Sasha, as Peter called him.

At dawn they sounded the tocsin. There was cannon fire from the fortresses of Petropavlovsk and the Admiralty. Officers and men flocked out on to the drill square of the barracks, the men fixing bayonets on the run. There was a hubbub of bugling and the regiments went into formation. It was a dirty daybreak. The wind, which had risen in the

night to become a gale, whistled through the three remaining
fir trees of the barrack yard. Flood threatened. All the supplies of sawn timber on Vassily Island had floated off. Guard-
officer Deryabin had been drowned. The swollen Neva
rolled forward in a foam of rushing blue-green water. There
was a steady cold drizzle from the sky. There was a clatter
of little bells from the city belfries. Further cannon salutes.
At the word of the general in command the other officers
marched their units off the square in the direction of the
Italian Palace. The morning was dull and cold, damp and
dirty.

A mounted orderly galloped up and met them on the way.
As he raised his hat the wind blew away his wig. He shouted:
"His Imperial Majesty has cancelled the drill in the name
of the first of April and the opening of navigation. He now
invites all to the palace to make merry!"

The soldiers shouted back their military greeting to the
Emperor; their officers commanded "about turn" and they
all marched back.

II

Wolves had been appearing in packs, attacking people and
cattle, and the high water had trapped a number of them on
the Mistula–Elagin island. Peter took a hundred men and
went off to capture some wolf-specimens for his natural
history museum. The day was dull and wet.

On Kaivusari among the dreary tents of the Kirghiz and
Kalmook workmen a man had been making strange speeches.
He was a barefooted tramp. His long grey hair and beard
waved in the wind. His severe countenance was that of an
ascetic. He wore a fairly decent monkish coat. The old man
had said that Peter was the Antichrist and that he was going
to put his mark on the people. Whoever did not bear the
mark would be denied bread. He declared that the Neva
would rise and destroy the new accursed city. He showed the
Kalmooks his beard licence, a metal disc stamped with the

double eagle, a print of a man's mouth and beard and the words *tax paid*. Soldiers of the Semenovsky regiment had set upon the old man with sticks and beaten him. He took refuge in a tent, but they caught him. Peter, returning from the wolf-hunt, took part in a hunt of a different order. The unfortunate victim was ordered to be taken to the dungeon of the Admiralty. Since the murder of the Tsarevitch Alexis in the Petropavlovsk fortress, Peter had given orders that in future prisoners be put to the question only in the torture chamber of the Admiralty dungeon.

When the old man was brought in to the torture chamber he was met by Count Tolstoy. He stood facing the count erect and motionless. Tolstoy smelt of vodka; the old man smelt of onion and radish.

"What's your name? Where d'you come from?" asked Tolstoy.

"Christened Tikhon. From the parish of Belokolodezhsky in the district of Kolomna."

"You belong to the triple alleluia and two-finger blessing persuasion, eh?"

"To them," answered the old man after a moment's silence.

"Come closer, you son of a bitch!"

He came near, and as he did so the count gave him a kick in the stomach.

"Prophesy! When's the great flood coming?"

"When the flood will come the God of Sabaoth alone can tell. I am not yet able to foretell it."

"Make your prophecy."

There was no reply. Both were silent.

Then the old man began to speak.

"Listen . . . count! There is justification for most things, but not for ruin. . . . What do you hear everywhere? Wailing, moan and universal weeping. Only foolery and showman's stuff succeeds. The whole people goes naked, conscience is for sale everywhere, truth has been shut away. Oh, Russia! The show! . . . My son has become an old man,—

and it is all the war, the Germans have overcome. The Tsar goes about with pipe in mouth, dressed like a foreign sailor, like a German, drunk as a fiddler, swearing by the Mother of God like a Tartar. . . . Tsa-ar! . . . Why, Count! grasp this: our Tsar is a substitute; the Germans sent him. When he went with his friends into the Swedish countries and found that Tsaritsa-slut he met another girl called Ulrica who took him to bed and enchanted him. Her navel was hot as a frying-pan. She substituted a new nature in Peter Alexee-vitch, so that when he waked up he wanted to cut off beards and shorten cloaks and bring in two-wheel carts. Bread is going to be sealed; the seals have been brought. They've started counting the years a new way. Heretics are abroad preaching schism, papists, Lutherans. And when it was the name-day of the Swedish girl Ulrica the nobles and boyars went to her and asked her in honour of the day to release the Tsar from the spell, but she made a mockery of it . . . all is mockery and show-man's stuff. . . . Open your eyes, Count! . . ."

The oil lamp burned dimly and smoked. Drops of moisture hung from the walls and the ceiling. The damp was pene-trating. Tolstoy sat watching the old man, his eyes asquint but unmoving. The old man babbled on, afraid to stop, afraid to be silent. The lamp began to splutter.

"Come here, you son of a bitch! You've said enough of that."

"I am called an elder. I've had three sons killed in the wars. . . ."

"When do you prophesy the flood?"

"God alone knows when the flood will be, but it will be."

"Come here, son of a bitch! Do you know what the post is for?"

An iron door opened suddenly and Guard-officer Zotof entered. He staggered to a stool, collapsed on it and laid his head on the table. Then he pulled a square bottle out of the top of one of his big boots and guffawed.

"What now?" asked Tolstoy.

"There's just been a fine to-do in the Senate. Yaguzhinsky and Skornyakovy and the most serene Alexashka Menshikof have been hitting it up, pulled the over-procurator by the hair, Shafirof, Golovkin and the most Serene himself called thieves! . . . Hubbub. Case for impeachment! . . . Menshikof ran off to the Empress to complain, in the old style. The Court was mighty rowdy after the merry-making. Ober-fiscal Myakinin made a report to the sovereign. He turned to Catherine and said: 'That Menshikof was a bastard; his mother bore him in sin, and he is finishing his days in buffoon-ery. If he does not mend his ways he will find himself without a head.' But the debauch went on. Alexashka is now weeping at the Tsaritsa's feet . . . smelling them."

Zotof guffawed again and rolled his head on the table.

"Blockhead!" exclaimed Tolstoy. "Don't you know that monster has the Tsar's ear?"

Zotof's bloated drunken face paled for a moment and he pulled himself together. Zotof stood up and faced Tolstoy. The count smiled pusillanimously.

"While your Excellency . . ."

Zotof interrupted him in a tremulous voice. "Your Serenity . . ."

Tolstoy turned furtively to the door, rang a bell and called a soldier.

"Carbine," cried Tolstoy, and turned to the old man. "Come here, you son of a bitch! When . . .?"

Zotof interrupted him.

"Come on, tell us something," he squeaked, and struck the old man in the face.

Zotof's shaved lips quivered.

The soldier came in with his gun and faced the prisoner. Then the old man fell on his knees and crawled to Tolstoy's feet like a dog and whined. The lamp guttered and stank.

"Little son, Count, have mercy, do not shoot. . . ."

Tolstoy drew back, frowned, ordered:

"Fire!"

The old man howled and crawled into a corner. The matchlock in the soldier's hands flared, then exploded with the sound of a cannon. Smoke filled the room; the lamp went out. The voice of the old man ceased. His neck and ear were broken; only his feet twitched convulsively. Tolstoy averted his eyes from the spectacle and said calmly:

"Take his body to St. Thomas Island and hang it in the place where he was caught, for a lesson."

Tolstoy and Zotof left the dungeon together, and when they had crossed the bridge, Tolstoy whispered the news that a letter of General-Admiral Apraxin had been intercepted by the Secret Commission. Apraxin had written words which amounted to insubordination and mutiny:

"We are quite lost; we wander about helplessly like the blind. Everything is in complete disorder and we have no idea what to do next. The whole business of the State is coming to a standstill. . . ."

There was a thick fog in Petersburg. Somewhere beyond the river, probably at the Astoria, there was a clash of music. Zotof lost his way and spent the night at a wayside hut. He felt sick and melancholy.

In the morning he received command to go to the Kolomna district of Moscow government and make a "good *anstalt*" there. Zotof went drunk three days, then got on a horse-dray with the Tsar's letter in his wallet. Any method of getting to a place was justifiable as long as one did get there—when one was on the sovereign's orders.

III

At Tosnoi, eighty versts from Petersburg, Zotof crossed the river on the ferry. Then he felt that he was entering Russia, the real authentic ancient Russia. He grasped that it was the season of Lent and that the gentle, bountiful Russian spring was giving its blessing to the land.

The road from Petersburg to Tosnoi had reminded him of a military road, littered as it was with the bones of horses and human skeletons, with broken wagons and torn-down trees. On the Tosna river the ferryman talked of gangs of bandits who attacked convoys in regular formation, and Zotof could not make out whether they referred just simply to robbers or to the Tsar's soldiers. On the further shore in a field beside a tavern a forcible shaving of convicts and workmen was going on, so that they might not by chance come before the eyes of the monarch bearded. There was a tavern here, and Zotof had Lenten soup. There was a gentle sunset and the spring air caressed the sweet-smelling earth. A Lenten chime was sounding from some church, and at the tavern window someone sang a song in melancholy strains:

> "Peter the nut-cracker
> Took a hundred roubles from each prince,
> Fifty from each boyar,
> Five roubles from each peasant.
> From him who has no money
> He takes the child.
> From him who has no child
> He takes the wife.
> From him who has no wife
> He takes his head! . . . "

It was a clear and gentle evening and the martins dipped in the blue waves of the river as they flew.

It was spring and Lent, but Zotof felt keenly that while Sanktpeterburg, with its debauch, peculation, swindling and cruelty, with its mists and fevers, was trying, though stupidly, to look like Europe, away beyond Sanktpeterburg in immense Russia there was nothing but strife, disorder and absurdity. The local authority twice changed, the impositions, the head-taxes, the quartering of regiments upon villages, the requisitions, the collections, camp-life in the home—thought of these things were all mixed and doubly mixed in the popular mind. Rural and military commissaries, Baltic officials, *Landrats* and *Landrichters*, quartermasters, governors, voivodes, with varying and confused scope of authority and jurisdiction, rushed from district to district and province to province, subjecting whom they could to their power, exacting, flogging, hanging—clean-shaven, obscene, more obscene than the most foul-mouthed Tartar tax-gatherers. The peasantry were afraid of this new clean-shaven bureaucracy which was always drunk and spoke in a mixture of German and Russian, afraid as of the plague. A new generation had come into being, having the constant knowledge that Russia was always at war—at war with the Turks, with the Swedes, with the Persians, with her own people, with the Don, with Astrakhan, with Trans-Volga. Recruitment followed recruitment, taxes were added to taxes. They pulled down the bells from the belfries of the churches; they put taxes on horse-collars, bath-houses, hives, coffins, souls. There were defaulters, absentees, famine. Deserters from the wars brought back syphilis; they came back drunkards or physical wrecks. Enraged by the life they had led, many took to the forests and lived by robbery. The wise old Russia with her legends, songs, monasteries, treasures seemed to have hidden herself away for two centuries to come.

At one village as Zotof's conveyance rolled through a peasant woman came out, screeching wildly, and almost threw herself under the cart-wheels.

"Oh, I'm sick of it all," she cried. "Sick of this newfangled shaving and their making my son a laughing-stock for the unclean. . . ."

"What are you yelling, you shaggy monster?" cried Zotof to her.

"Drive over my breasts, over my eyes if you like, but give me back my child," she cried from the mud. "May my words become a mountain in your track, may they weigh more than gold and be harder than the stone of Alatyr. . . . Dreadful devil, storm and blizzard, one-eyed forest demon, raven-wizard, Koshtchei-Yadun,—ferocious Antichrist Peter! . . . But your mortal hour is coming!"

This was in the Valdai Hills, and the village was among maples on the side of a hill. It was midday, and the thatched roofs were warming up in the spring sun. Larks were singing in the sky above, crows also were calling. In the evening one would hear the cry of the moor-cock and the owls and the singing of the village girls.

The peasant woman's imprecations followed Zotof as he left the village behind and drove towards a five-domed monastery on a height. Forests and fields were built up in front of him to the sky.

Arriving at the district of Kolomna, Zotof first galloped to the Passion Monastery and then to the district office. On Holy Thursday in the evening he put up at the local military headquarters at Biely Kolodez. Certainly the peasants and soldiers must have expected him, for they met him with a fanfare of drums. The soldiers gave an account of their duties, and the peasants brought bread and salt and a petition. The peasants seemed greatly scared. Guard-officer Zotof was of a mind to begin his inquiry at once, but a priest accompanied by a local noble, Viliashef by name, came and invited him to vespers and to share the evening meal with the priest.

The white limestone church stood on a hill over the Oka; there were forests behind it, meadows and a far horizon. The little mica windows peeped at the earth; on the walls were the dark severe faces of the saints. It was a long time since Zotof had been to church. In Sanktpeterburg going to church was a jest. He was struck by the severity, simplicity and order of the place. He stood motionless with his candle in his hand. All about him ragged, destitute peasants prayed ecstatically and noiselessly. The candle lights were dim under the shadow of the vaulted roof; the service was long. When they came out of the church it was already dark, and thousands of stars shone in the vast sky. A young bear could be heard in the river meadow; the corncrakes were settling down for the night; the moor-cock still called in the thickets. The priest's cottage was lighted by a small lamp. The walls were covered with clay. He brought in honey and black bread and spring water, and sat down in front of them arranging his beard. Zotof remarked that his face looked tired. There was an expression of grief in his eyes, pain and—faith. The priest was tall; he was no longer a young man and he held himself sternly and calmly. Viliashef, who was also bearded, wore a uniform and he stood by the stove in the shadow.

"What good news have you?" asked the priest. "In Sanktpeterburg there must be many novelties. . . ."

Zotof put his sword in a corner, bowed and sat down.

He had not much to say.

"Leaving the paradise, I am astonished by the misery I see around me. The land resounds with grievance, extortion and debauch."

"That's so," said the priest and Viliashef together.

"His Majesty has been made emperor. We have had celebrations of victory. The old nobility is quite bereft of power and now merely looks on when decisions are taken. His Majesty governs without reason and at the whim of his bizarre fantasy."

"That's so. . . . You speak darkly. . . . That's so."

The priest drew his dark cloak about him and straightened the cross on his chest.

"Taste the honey," said he. "Is it true that the Tsar carries on like a religious freak and uses a pipe-stem instead of a cross at the gatherings of his church of drunkenness and mirth? Is it true that he took the cast-off mistress of Menshikof to wife and now has a harem in the Turkish style? . . . Do you know that the soldiers quartered upon us in the village beat up all the peasants in a quarrel over a trollop of theirs? . . . Learn about it!! Wait. Do you know what they sing here? It's not two beasts come together, the nation

is singing it—truth and falsehood have fought together and
falsehood has overcome. Truth has gone to heaven, but—
but falsehood roars on with ugly German face. . . . Learn
about it! . . . Learn that it's not a Tsar we have but
Antichrist . . . an epileptic German . . . who puts tax on
cottages, baths, graves, horse-collars!"

"I cannot listen to such dishonourable things said about
my sovereign," said Zotof somewhat irresolutely.

The priest prevented him saying more. He stood up, holding
his cross in his left hand and raising his right.

"One moment," said he. "My father lately set out for that
marshy city to seek the truth. Have you by chance heard
anything of Tikhon Startsef? He is my father!"

"I cannot listen to dishonourable things said about my
sovereign," repeated Zotof with severity.

But he went red and his fleshy face swelled. There was
perspiration on his shaven upper lip. He stood up, clenching
his fists.

"I cannot listen . . ."

"Tikhon Startsef . . . Startsef—haven't you heard of
him? If you live with the wolves, don't you howl with
them?"

"Don't you howl with the wolves?" repeated Viliashef.

Guard-officer Zotof, putting his huge fists behind him,
stumbled towards the door, seized his sword and went out
hurriedly, bumping his head on the beam as he crossed the
threshold.

"Like the wolves, what?" they cried after him.

The red and mournful disc of the Easter moon gleamed
dimly over the horizon. It was quiet and dark. The bear
still cried from under the Oka cliff. The church was like a
cross in the sky. Zotof filled his pipe and got a light. His
mind surged with confused recollections of his own father
and his rôle in that church of drunkenness and mirth, and
with thoughts of Tikhon Startsef, also a father, and with
thoughts of Peter and Russia, that Russia which he loved as

a mother lost in childhood. And he had found something
that he had not yet written in his diary . . . that he was
fated to howl with the wolves, yes, to whimper like the wolves
that Peter went to trap on Mistula-Elagin island.

The night of Gethsemane came on.

IV

A man the joy of whose soul was in action. A man of
genius. A man who was abnormal, always tipsy, a syphilitic,
a neurasthenic, suffering from psychic disorders and fits of
melancholy and violence. One who murdered his son with
his own hands. A monarch who had no power of restraint
over himself, who did not even understand that he ought to
control himself, a despot. A man absolutely without sense
of responsibility, who despised everything outside himself,
never to the end of his life understanding the historical logic
or national physiology of life. A maniac. A coward. Frightened in childhood, he hated the old Russia into which he
was born, turned blindly towards novelty, lived with foreigners; he took the easiest way, had a barracks education
and took as his ideal the life of a Dutch sailor. A man who
to the end of his days remained a child, loving play more
than anything else in the world,—and playing all his life:
playing at war, at ships, at parades, assemblies, illumina-
tions, playing at Europe. A cynic, despising mankind, both
in himself and in others. An actor, an actor of genius. An
emperor who loved sexual debauch more than almost anything else; one who married a prostitute, Menshikoff's harlot,—a man with barrack ideals. His body was immense,
foul and very sweaty, clumsy, bandy-legged, spindly, ruined
by alcohol, tobacco and syphilis. As he advanced in years
his red peasant-woman's face sagged and his red lips withered.
His red syphilitic eyelids dropped and yet would not tightly
close, and from those eyelids he looked out with insane, wild,
drunken and childish eyes, with such eyes as a child's when

he looks at the cat he is sticking a needle into, or at a pig while putting a red-hot iron on its toes. But he had no choice —he did not understand what he was doing when he killed his own son. He fought for thirty years, played his game of senseless war, only because his amusement regiments of childhood had grown up, and the Moscow river was too small for his toy fleet, the Preobrazhensky Lake too confined. He never walked anywhere; he always ran, waving his arms, straddling with his bandy knees and imitating the gait of a Dutch sailor. His clothes were dirty and in bad taste, and he disliked changing his linen. He took pleasure in over-eating and ate with his hands. His immense hands were greasy and calloused.

In Sanktpeterburg on Easter Eve at four hours after midnight a rocket was sent up from the Winter Palace, and at that signal the cannon of the fortresses of the Admiralty and Petropavlovsk were fired. On Kaivusari Island, in the Trinity cathedral, they began to ring for early vespers and the organ was played. The sovereign, the empress, the ministers and the notabilities all met Easter, according to regulation, at the Trinity cathedral. Peter wore a black frock-coat with horn buttons. He stood in the choir in his jack-boots and sang in a slender baritone. The first vespers had been delayed because the Tsar had been asleep. When the moment came when the clergy start in procession about the cathedral with crosses and banners, Peter went out to look over the fireworks. Ober-firewerke-meister Demidof lighted a lamp under an immense double eagle. From the eagle a rocket shot out and hit a lion, setting it afire. The lion roared dully and exploded in small pieces, signifying that the eagle, the Russian power, had overcome the lion, Sweden, its ancient enemy, destroying all its leonine intentions. The cannons fired again. The night was dark and windless; it drizzled. Away beyond the ramparts the Kirghiz and the Kalmooks lay on the earth, scared by the eagle and the lion; they lay beside their tents, beside the dead man hanging on the willow tree, and trembled. The cannon continued to give salvos throughout the night. The Imperial standard was raised. Men gave one another the Easter kiss upon the lips; women were ordered only to give their hands to kiss. Immediately the liturgy in the cathedral was concluded, the trumpeters and oboists and drummers formed up to regale the sovereign with martial music and lead a procession to the Neva and be ferried to the Summer Garden on the Peruzina island, where the Easter festival was to be held. The Neva, which had swollen and rolled forward in white ripples, was free of traffic. On the standing ships there were lighted lanterns which glowed dimly. The watchmen whistled to one another to prove that they were not asleep.

The Tsar had spent the evening before at the Italian Palace in his working cabinet. At the height of a man's head there was stretched across the room a low covering of canvas; for Peter could not tolerate a high ceiling. Candles burned on his table. There was a wretched light; the place smelt of sweat, vodka and damp. All sorts of instruments and tools lay in odd corners of the room: globes, astrolabes, matchlocks, ship's models, boots; there was a joiner's bench covered with shavings and looking like an uncomfortable mattress. On a shelf near by were various jars containing specimens, human and animal monstrosities preserved in spirit, carefully collected by Peter for his natural history museum, collected by order. His ukase was headed: "Concerning the bringing in of horn monstrosities and sports of Nature, whereas it is known that these occur in the human race, it also happens that animals and birds bring forth monsters."

Peter was sitting at a table, leaning on one elbow and copying from a book of compliments the correct Easter salutation to send to Romodanovsky in Moscow. He was wearing a nightcap and his undershirt, all patched and sweaty at the armpits, and he sat all hunched up. Gentlemen-in-waiting stood at the door looking away from him like side horses.

The Tsar wrote:

> "Highly respected sir,
>   In fulfilment of my filial duty, I must not omit to wish you every blessing at this time of God's mercy, holy Easter, and to hope that not merely in this year, but in many years to come, you, sir . . ."

The Tsar did not finish the letter, perhaps taking into consideration that there was a copy of the book of letters in Moscow. And he signed himself:

> "Your Majesty's most humble slave,
>   Kneeb Piter Komondor."

A cuckoo clock struck the hour. Peter threw his head back.

"D'ye hear?" he asked.

Poluboyarinof, who was in waiting, went out of the room and returned with a glass of vodka, gherkins and some pickled cabbage on a tray. Orlof set the chess pieces and moved his king's pawn, that Orlof through whom Peter's mistress Mary Hamilton perished.

Peter was not jealous, and willingly shared his mistresses with his friends. The "fraulein-hussy" indulged herself with the Tsar's gentleman-in-waiting, Orlof, but she was in love with Peter and he had her executed. He came to the scaffold, said good-bye and kissed her again. She was in a white dress tied with black ribbons. When the executioner struck off her head, Peter lifted it and gave a discourse on the anatomy of the human neck, then he kissed the dead lips somewhat otherwise than he had kissed them earlier when she was a little girl, crossed himself and went away. He ran off to the wharves, bandy-legged, waving his arms, hatless as always in hot weather.

The Tsar drank the vodka, ate a gherkin and also advanced his king's pawn. The game proceeded rapidly and the Tsar managed to place his knight so that he could take either his opponent's queen or his castle, and he laughed loudly. But he did not finish the game; he was interrupted by the entry of one of his financial idea men, the writer Mitukof. He stood in the low doorway in a hired dress and with his red hair showing under his wig, and bowed unctuously.

"Guten abend!" said Peter.

Mitukof was bowing like a weathercock when the wind has hit it.

"Take laplace," said Peter. "Take a seat."

Mitukof sat down on the edge of a chair and pulled up some dirty linen putties from his high boots, which were someone else's and two sizes too big. ·

"Tell us what you have on your mind."

"Your Tsarish Majesty! Ever ready to serve thee . . ."

"Not me, but the State, as I myself have served it since I fought ás bombardier in the first Azof campaign. Give us the sense."

The wretched peasant sighed deeply.

"Since various sorts of taxes have been imposed on the people, collar taxes, hat taxes, hive taxes, taxes on baths and beards, I have thought why not have a tobacco tax. Fine everyone who does not smoke and let him pay according to his rank and position."

Peter leaned over towards Mitukof, staring at him with wild distraught eyes, guffawed loudly and called Orlof.

Orlof stood up at attention.

"Put this man in a closed room and see that a pipe is given him and that he smoke all night without stopping. Have a watch kept. If he gets sick, have him shaken by the collar and administer twenty strokes with the rod. If he goes through the ordeal successfully, give him paper in the morning and ask him to set down his project in writing for my approbation on the following evening."

Mitukof collapsed and fell on his knees. Orlof took him by the shoulders and led him out by a secret door. Peter, with his arms folded behind him, laughed gaily, accompanying the couple as far as the doorway.

Poluboyarinof brought more vodka, and the Tsar drank it. He sat at the table and read. The candles burned feebly and smoked. Peter's immense calloused hand like a hoof lay on the dirty table among scraps of food, tobacco ash, papers, chess pieces. Peter himself was in shadow. Orlof soon came back with a report.

"Mitukof is vomiting, your Majesty."

Peter did not answer. Orlof peered at him. The Tsar had rested his greasy shaggy head with its peasant-woman's cheeks on an arm of his chair, and with half-shut eyes was staring glassily in front of him—he slept. Orlof stood at attention and quietly dozed. The quiet of the room was only broken by the monarch's heavy breathing. And down below somewhere in a cellar Mitukof was vomiting convulsively.

There was a pallid dawn, dreary and empty as an autumn morning. There was merry-making in the Summer Garden on Peruzino Island. The Tsar had been drunk for hours. By his orders sentries had been placed at the gates with orders to let no one out till midnight. The garden had been laid out in the foreign style, with pavilions over the Neva, with fountains, with avenues of sickly-looking trees, with hunting lodges and little Dutch houses with pointed roofs. A dry, cold, dreary day ensued. The Easter banquet was to be given in the open air. The marshal of the feast was to be the Tsar himself. Guardsmen were trailing up and down the avenues with buckets of corn-brandy and baskets of coloured eggs. The Tsar's Easter congratulations were accompanied with the present of an egg and a spoonful of vodka. The gentlemen sat at long narrow tables near the main pavilion; the ladies were accommodated separately beside the fountain of the Alley of Statues. The Tsar ate and drank standing, and poured the leavings of the dishes upon the head of the prince-fool Golitsin. Drunkenness came on rapidly. The ladies were not behindhand with their liquor. Suddenly a squeal was heard. It was the Empress, in a paroxysm of tenderness (was it tenderness? was it hate?), tickling the new Imperial flirt, the Fräulein wench Rumiant-seva, who kicked and squealed, while the other women giggled. Some of the ladies were dressed in ill-fitting expensive clothes which neither resembled Russian nor foreign fashion, unless they were like the clothes of the wives of Dutch parvenus, or of sailors' wives out on a spree without their husbands. Their hair got out of curl; their fat faces perspired; their bodies, swollen with eating, burst their lacings. They sang shrilly and deafeningly, like peasant women in a cabbage-field. The Tsar, fuggy with drink, noticed that the old man Prince Trubetskoy was quietly helping himself to a second portion of sweetmeat, and he shouted to the guards to seize him. The old man's mouth was forcibly opened and jelly was forced down his throat till his eyes started out of their sockets.

Then the orchestra struck up and the officers dashed to the women's quarters to seek partners for the dance. The ladies in a confused mob screamed and laughed, and the gentlemen played with them and pushed them about and grabbed them straight by the breasts, to stamp in a drunken minuet. Yaguzhinsky, the French gallant, started to fight with his new wife. At the men's tables some of the old men had fallen asleep and slipped down to the ground. Priests smelling of pickled cabbage quietly disposed of the heel-taps. Buturlin, the new patriarch of mirth, at his post in the smaller pavilion, blessed an eagle of wine with his cross. Peter ordered the lackeys to prepare a cold buffet and bring buckets of water to restore the dead drunk to consciousness. His own new black coat was long since messed up. Then Peter went to Buturlin and drank the eagle of wine and thereupon joined the dance.

His dull eyes lighted upon Rumiantseva, and a boisterous

expression came into his sagging cheeks and a smile flickered
on his faded lips. He ran to the girl, picked her up in his
arms, throwing off her skirt as he ran and rending her
under-linen. He went to a hunting lodge and put off with
her in a small boat, calling out to the Empress:

"Katka! Little fool! Be an example! I command silence."

Rumiantseva returned in a few minutes red and flustered,
arranging her dress again and looking like a trampled hen.
The Empress came up to her and whispered something.

Peter invited Tolstoy to come over and talk with him
on the lake. He sat on a table with his feet on a sofa,
his frock-coat cast aside, and he smiled feebly. Tolstoy
stood in the doorway of the house and squinted cautiously
around.

"Petka. Your Excellency. . . . Rare specimen! . . . We
all know that Ivashka Musin-Pushkin was my father's
son. My father was not able to acknowledge it, so they
say. Tikhon Streshnef or the doctor knew. Now, since you
are the head of the Secret Commission, I want you to set
other matters aside and find out the truth of this without
fail."

"I will obey, *batushka*."

"What's that? Keep your distance! Not *batushka*, but Emperor. . . . Do you understand? . . . You've no other business on hand except the work of your office, which you
must not neglect; for if you do you will answer for it before
God, and you won't escape judgment here either. . . . Ah,
wait a minute. There was an old believer caught on St.
Thomas island. He foretold the flood and my downfall.
Where is that old believer?"

"Executed, your Majesty."

"By whose orders? What circumstances? When did he say
the flood would be?"

"He did not say, your Majesty. Guard-officer Zotof was
present and was annoyed by what he heard. Shot. . . ."

Those unwinking eyes of Tolstoy winked rapidly.

Peter stood up, convulsively straightening himself. He flung his right foot back; his face became contorted; his chin turned towards his left shoulder; his eyes stared wildly, helplessly, insanely.

"By whose order? Under what regulations? Mutiny! I'll quarter you; Zotof for the knout!"

Tolstoy rushed out at the door, and, seeing no boat, flung himself in the water and called to the Empress:

"Little mother, he's sick!"

Catherine took a boat and came to Peter. He was standing waving his arms; his twisted chin rested on his left shoulder. His eyes were wild as those of a frightened child. Catherine alone could soothe him at such times. She took his head in both her hands and put it against her breast and gently scratched his ears. She sat down and nursed his head in her abundant lap, and the Tsar fell asleep helplessly like a child.

On the cold and empty flood of the Neva sailors were sailing little yawls. There was a faint clamour of little bells. Away on Vassilievy Island where those few pines still waved in the sky the working people were singing and dancing.

It began to rain. The Court hid in pavilions and summer-houses; for the sentries still stood at the gates and it was forbidden to go away till midnight. The river was ruffled, blown by a cold damp wind. Thus passed the grey, damp, marshy Sanktpeterburg Easter Day.

Nikola on the same day enjoyed warm and joyous breezes. The village girls sang their spring song, and sang it all day and all night, till a new sun came. The morning beams were clad in red sarafans; the evening beams went down in a marshy bath. And thus they sang:

> "I am dressed in my dresses,
> Girdled with red dawn,
> Surrounded by bright moons,
> Jewelled with separate stars;
> My light is the red sun.

> Oh, Thunder, strike, let loose thy fires,
> Warm with thy thund'rous bolt
> Our old mother, Mother-Damp-Land."

The village girls sang then so that they might sing for two centuries. They were singing of the 17th of October throughout all time.[1]

[1]The 17th October was the date of the Soviet Revolution.

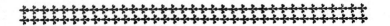

ISAAC BABEL

(*b.* 1894)

++

LIFE AND ADVENTURES OF MATVEY PAVLITCHENKO

(Translated by JOHN HARLAND)

C O M R A D E S, countrymen, my own dear brethren! In the name of all mankind learn the story of the Red general, Matvey Pavlitchenko. He used to be a herdsman, that general did—herdsman on Lidin's farm, working for Barin[1] Nikitinsky and looking after the barin's pigs till life brought stripes to his shoulder straps; and then, with those stripes, Matyushka began to look after the horned cattle. And who knows, if Matvey had been born in Australia, he might have risen to elephants—he'd have come to look after elephants; only the trouble is, I don't know where they're to be got in our district. I'll tell you straight—there isn't a bigger animal than the buffalo in the whole of our wide region. And the poor chap wouldn't get no comfort out of buffaloes —it isn't any fun for a Russian fellow to get a laugh out of a buffalo! Give us poor orphans something in the way of a horse for keeps—a horse, so as its mind and ribs can work themselves out at the far end of the fields.

And so I look after my horned cattle, with cows all round me, soaked in milk and stinking of it like a sliced udder. Young bulls walk round me—mouse-grey young bulls. Open space round me in the fields, the grass rustling in all the world, the sky above my head like a harmonica with lots of keyboards—and the skies, boys, in the Stavropol district are very blue. Well, I looked after my cattle like

[1]*Barin*—sir, the master.

this, and as there was nothing to do I used to play with the winds on reeds until an old gaffer says to me:

"Matvey, go to Nastia," he says.

"Why?" I says. "Or maybe you're kidding me?"

"Go," he says, "she wants you."

And so I goes.

"Nastia," I says, and go black in the face, "Nastia," I says, "or maybe you're kidding me?"

But she won't hear me out, but runs off away from me and goes on running till she can't any more; and I run along with her till we get to the common, dead beat and red and puffed.

"Matvey," says Nastia to me then, "three Sundays ago, when spring was in the hedges and the fishermen were going along by the river bank, you also went with them and hung your head. Why did you hang your head, Matvey? Or was it some notion or other that was heavy on your heart? Tell me——"

And I answer her:

"Nastia," I answer, "I've nothing to tell. My head isn't a rifle and there ain't no sight on it or chamber either. As for my heart—you know what it's like, Nastia, there isn't nothing in it, it's, as you might say, just milky. It's terrible how I stink of milk——"

But Nastia, I see, sort of goes back into her shell at my words.

"I'll swear by the cross," she says, and bursts out laughing with all her voice over the whole steppe just as if she was beating the drum. "I'll swear by the cross that you play about with the girls."

And when we'd talked a lot of silly rot for a bit we got married soon and I began to live with Nastia for all I was worth, and that was a good deal. We were hot all night; we were hot in winter and all night long we went naked, rubbing our hides raw. We lived hellishly well right on till up comes the old 'un to me the second time.

"Matvey," he says, "the barin touched your wife a bit everywhere, yesterday. He'll get her all right, the barin will."

And I:

"No," I says, "if you'll excuse me, old 'un; or if he does I'll nail you to the spot."

And sure enough off goes the old chap, and I did twenty versts on foot that day, covered a good piece of ground, and in the evening I got to Lidin's farm, to my gay barin, Nikitinsky. He was sitting in a room upstairs, the old man was, and he was taking three saddles to pieces—an English one, a dragoon one and a Cossack one—and I stuck to his door like a burr, stuck there a whole hour, and all for nothing. But then afterwards he looked my way.

"What d'you want?" he says.

"A reckoning."

"You've got designs on me?"

"I haven't got no designs, but I want straight out to——"

Here he looked away and spread out some scarlet saddle-clothes on the floor. They were brighter than the Tsar's flags, those saddle-clothes of his were, and he stood on them, the little old fellow did, and strutted about.

"Freedom to the free," he says to me and struts about. "I've tickled all your mas, you orthodox peasants. You can have your reckoning if you like, only don't you owe some little trifle, Matvey, my friend?"

"Hi, hi," I answers. "What a nerve you've got, and that's a fact. Seems to me as it's you as owes me my pay."

"Pay!" The barin lets go then, and he knocks me down on my knees and shuffles about with his feet and boxes me on the ears for all the Father, Son and Holy Ghost's worth. "Your pay! And have you forgotten the yoke you smashed for me? Where's my yoke?"

"I'll let you have your yoke back," I answer my barin, and turn my simple eyes upon him and kneel before him, bending lower than any earthly depth. "I'll give you your yoke back, only don't you press me with debts, old fellow; just wait a bit."

And what d'you think, you Stavropol boys, comrades, fellow-countrymen, my own dear brethren—that barin kept me hanging on like that with my debts for five years, five lost years I went to pieces, till at last the year eighteen came along to visit me, lost bloke that I was. It came along on lively stallions, on its Kabardin horses, bringing along a big train of sledges behind it and all sorts of songs. Eh you, little year eighteen, my sweetheart! Can it be that we shan't be walking out with you any more, my own little drop of blood, my year eighteen? We've been free with your songs and drunk up your wine and made out your laws, and only your chroniclers are left. Eh, my sweetheart! It's not the writers as rushed about over the Kuban those days, setting the souls of generals free at a distance of one pace. And Matvey Rodyonitch was lying in blood at Prikumskoie at that time, and there were only five versts of the last march left to Lidin's farm. Well, I went over alone, without a detachment, and going up to the room I went in quietly. The estate owners were sitting about there in the room upstairs. Nikitinsky was carrying round tea and billing and cooing to them; but on seeing me, his face fell, and I, I takes off my Kuban hat to him.

"Good-day," I says to the folks. "Good-day, and it please you. Are you receiving visitors, barin, or how's it going to be between us?"

"It's all going to be quite quiet and honourable between us," answers one of the fellows then—a surveyor chap, I notice by the looks of him. "It's all going to be quite quiet and honourable between us, but it looks as if you have been riding a good way, Comrade Pavlitchenko, your face is all splashed with dirt. We, the estate owners, dread such looks —Why's that?"

"It's because, you cold-blooded estate owners," I answer, "because in my looks one cheek has been burning for five years—burning in the trenches, burning in action, burning with women, and will go on burning at the Last Judgment. At the Last Judgment," I say, looking at Nikitinsky jolly-like, but he's no eyes by this time, only balls in the middle of his face, as if they had rolled down those balls into position from under his forehead. And he was blinking at me with those glassy balls, also jolly-like, but very horrible.

"Matyusha,"[1] he says to me, "we used to know each other some time ago, and now my wife, Nadejda Vassilievna, has lost her reason because of all the happenings of these times. She used to be very good to you, wasn't she? And you, Matyusha, you used to respect her more than all the others, and you don't mean to say now you wouldn't like to have a look at her now that she's lost the light of reason?"

"All right," I says, and I go out with him into another room, and there he begins to touch my hands, first my right hand, then my left.

"Matyusha," he says, "are you my destiny or not?"

"No," says I, "and stop jawing like that. God has gone and left us blasted slaves, our destiny's no better than a turkey-cock, and our life's just about worth a kopeck, so stop jawing like that and listen if you like to Lenin's letter."

"A letter to me—to Nikitinsky?"

"To you," I says, and takes out my book of orders, opens it at a blank page and read, though I can't read to save my life. "In the name of the nation," I read, "and for the foundation of a nobler life in the future, I order Pavlit-chenko, Matvey Rodyonitch, to deprive certain people of life, according to his discretion."

"There," I says, "that's Lenin's letter to you."

And he to me: "No! No, Matyusha," he says. "I know life has gone to the dogs and that blood's cheap now in the apostolic Russian Empire, but all the same, the blood due

[1] *Matyusha*—diminutive of Matvey.

to you you'll get all the same, and anyway you'll forget my look in death, so wouldn't it be better if I just showed you a certain bit of flooring?"

"Show away," I says. "It might be better."

And again I went through a lot of rooms with him and went down into the wine-cellar; and there he pulled out a brick and found a casket behind that brick, and in the casket there were rings and necklaces and orders and a holy image done in pearls. He chucked it at me and went into a sort of stupor.

"Yours," he says, "now you're master of the Nikitinsky image. And now, Matvey, back to your lair in Prikumskoie——"

And then I took him by the trunk and by the throat and by the hair.

"And what am I going to do with my cheek?" I says. "What's to be done about my cheek, kinsfolk?"

And then he laughed out, much too loud, and didn't try to get away.

"Jackal's conscience," he says and doesn't get away. "I'm talking to you like to an officer of the Russian Empire, and you blackguards sucked the she-wolf. Shoot me then, damned son of a bitch!"

But I wasn't going to shoot him. I didn't owe him a shot anyway, so I only dragged him upstairs into the parlour. There, in the parlour, was Nadejda Vassilievna clean off her head, with a drawn scimitar, walking about in the parlour and looking at herself in the glass. And when I dragged Nikitinsky into the parlour, Nadejda Vassilievna ran and sat down in the armchair, with a velvet crown on, trimmed with feathers. She sat in the armchair very brisk and alert and saluted me with the scimitar. Then I stamped on my barin Nikitinsky, and trampled him for an hour or more. And in that time I got to know life through and through. With shooting—I'll put it that way—with shooting you only get rid of a chap. Shooting's letting him off and too damned easy for yourself. With shooting you'll never get at the soul, to where it is in a fellow and how it goes and shows itself. But I don't spare myself, and I've more than once trampled an enemy for over an hour. You see, I want to get to know what life really is and how it is inside us——

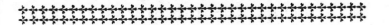

MICHAEL ZOSCHENKO
(1895—1958)

✤✤

AN EVENING OF CULTURE

I HAVE always been a sympathiser with the point of view of
the Centre.

When militant communism was compromised by the introduction of the New Economic Policy, the NEP, I did not
protest. We are going to have the NEP; well why not. But
all the same the introduction of the NEP did cause a desperate tugging at my heart strings. I foresaw that it would mean
some nasty changes in our way of life.

What freedom we had in the old era of militant communism!
In all the things which make for civilisation and culture we
had freedom. In those days you go to a theatre and sit down
without first removing your great-coat. You could take your
place in just the same rig-out as that in which you had been
walking in the street. That was freedom achieved.

But nevertheless this culture question is a bitch of a question,
even considered from the point of view of what you wear in
the theatre. Of course there's no doubt that the public
without great-coats looks much better, is better sorted out,
more charming and elegant. But what is fine in bourgeois
countries may be a bit out of place with us.

Comrade Loktef and his lady friend Nusha Koshelkova
met me one evening lately on their way to the theatre. For
my part 1 was merely taking the air, or I had stepped out to
moisten my throat—I forget which.

They fell in with me as I was walking along and persuaded
me to accompany them to the theatre.

"Your throat may be dry but it won't run away from you"

979

said Comrad Loktef. "Your throat you have always with you and another time you can go and give it a gargle. This evening, come with us to the theatre and see *Greeka*".

To be brief they persuaded me to go with them and spend a cultured evening. Of course they bought my ticket; thirty *rouble* tickets. We walked in together up the main stairway. Suddenly some shouted after us—"Great-coats off! Your overcoats, take them off!"

Loktef and his lady at once began to take off their cloaks. For my part I hesitated. That evening, going out for a drink, I had slipped into my trousers, but I still wore my night-shirt. I wore neither waistcoat nor jacket, and brothers mine I felt awkward about taking off my great-coat. "An offence against decency can now easily take place" I reflected. Not that my night-shirt was so to say dirty. It was not specially dirty. But of course it was just a plain ordinary night-shirt. Big buttons; broad hem. I felt it would hardly be considered decent and proper walking through the foyer in such large buttons.

"Comrades" said I to Loktef and lady. "I hardly know what to do. I'm not particularly well-dressed today. It's a bit awkward for me because if I take off my coat my braces will be visible, and my shirt, I must say, is very plain."

"Well, show me" said Comrade Loktef.

I unbuttoned.

The lady of course also took a squint. "Now I'd better go right back home" she exclaimed. "I cannot be seen in a theatre with a man in his night-shirt. I wonder you didn't come with your drawers over your trousers. The idea of coming to a theatre in such a get up. You do feel embarrassed, don't you!"

"When I set out I had no idea I was going to a theatre" I answered her. "You don't think I wouldn't have worn a jacket. Perhaps you think I haven't one. Or I am saving my jacket for another occasion?"

Well we stood there on the stairs, thinking it out. Then

Loktef, the hound had a bright idea. "I know what" said
he. "I'll take off my waistcoat; you put it on and you march
bravely into the auditorium, looking as if you had taken off
your jacket because you found it too hot in here".

Loktef began fumbling under his coat, intending to unbutton his vest, pull it out and hand it to me.

"Oh gracious mother" he exclaimed. "I haven't put my
waistcoat on today. Perhaps I could give you my tie instead.
That would look more decent. Run it round your neck
and march in as if you felt hot".

"No, my God, better I go back home" said the lady. "One
gentleman in little more than his drawers; the other wearing
a tie instead of a jacket. Why doesn't he ask permission to go
in in his overcoat. Perhaps they would make an exception.

We went and begged and implored the management to
allow me to go in in my great-coat but they showed us the
Soviet book of rules and regulations. It was not allowed.

"It's not 1919 now. You can't sit in a theatre in your overcoat" said they.

"Well then, there's nothing for it but for me to return
home" said I.

But I reflected that they had paid thirty roubles for me and
I just simply could not desert them. My feet refused to budge.

Then Loktef the hound made another suggestion. "Unbutton your braces" said he "and let Nusha carry them in
her hand as if it was a hand-bag. Then you roll in your shirt
as if you were wearing a summer blouse, *apache* style, and all
the whole look as if you were oppressed by the heat."

"All the same, I'm not going to carry any braces" objected
Nusha Kolenkorova. "I don't go into a theatre in order to
carry intimate objects of the masculine toilet. Let him carry
them himself, or stuff them into his trousers' pocket"!

I took off my overcoat and stood in my shirt looking like a
dog's aunt.

And it was absolutely dog cold in the theatre. I shivered.
My teeth chattered.

People began to stare at us. "Well you scoundrel" said the lady. "You may as well help me unbutton my cloak. It will stop people staring at us. Oy-oy, by God, I'd better have gone straight back home!"

And it was not easy to unbutton her. It was so cold. My fingers being cold could not get round the buttons. I did a few exercises, opening and shutting my hands so as to bring the circulation into my fingers. At last I got her unbuttoned. We disposed of our coats. All was in order and we went in to see the show.

The first act went by without incident, only I was very cold and performed gymnastic exercises all the while.

Suddenly in the entr'act our neighbours behind us were heard raising objections. They called the stewards and pointed at me.

"Ladies do not like looking at night-shirts" said they. "It shocks them. More than that the son of a she dog keeps on twisting and turning all the time".

"I twist because I'm cold" said I. "Let some of you sit here in your shirts! You can take it from me brothers, I'm no more happy about it than you are. But what's to be done?"

They hauled me off to the manager's office and wrote everything down. Then they set me at liberty.

Some time afterwards I had to pay a fine for this. There's a stinker! You never can guess from what quarter some unpleasantness will arrive . . .

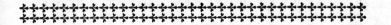

GLEB ALEXEYEF

✛✛

DIPHTHERIA

(Translated by LEONIDE ZARINE)

S H E was brought to us one Monday—and, you know, on Mondays we are rushed off our feet. The real thing to blame, I tell you without attempting to hide anything, was parental love. I know there is nothing more beautiful than parental love, but for the children in our diphtheria ward it is more harmful than hatred. By the hospital rules parents are allowed to visit the ward once a week, and all the week the children behave very well, they do not become peevish, and do not scream. But on Sundays the parents trudge into the ward—tearful, suspicious mothers, glowering, silent fathers. Under cover, as you might say, they stuff the children with all manner of sweets, nougats, fruit drops and the like, and secretly they all meanly tip us with sixpences that we shall give better attention to their own children, as though all patients are not the same to us; they kiss, cuddle and torment their children, and when, having almost satisfied their insatiable love, they at last depart, the children yell after them, and for two days we can do nothing with them, half of them have a rise in temperature and there is pandemonium in the ward.

During such days I run about mechanically, taking the place of a mother, and the children, jealous lest I should stay at the bedside of one longer than at another, yell hoarsely, and the disturbance is more difficult to deal with than the malady itself. So, on one of these crying days, I was called out by one of the attendants: they had brought in a girl choking in an advanced stage of diphtheria.

"Well," I said to her, "I will take her in at once. Have you seen Maria Alexandrovna?"

She said that Maria Alexandrovna was on her rounds, but that Zinaida Borisovna was in the operating theatre.

"Nevertheless, we will wait for Maria Alexandrovna. . . . You see how my little ones are yelling, they won't let me leave them." . . .

And, really, the moment I made a step towards the door those two dozen angel hearts set up a chorus of yells, choking with resentful childish anger; but I went into the reception room and saw: a man in a cap standing, with miserable little beard, trousers bulging at the knees like balloons, shoes quite dusty from the dirt of the roadway—some sort of clerk, no doubt—and in his arms a child enveloped in a dirty blanket. He held it closely but aloof, just like we women hold cats, as though afraid that the child might bite him or jump out of his arms. I moved the blanket and examined the girl; her throat was much inflamed and swollen twice as thick as normal, it was covered with pus and the larynx was almost entirely closed. What was necessary was quite clear; a tube would have to be inserted in the throat so that the girl would not choke, and perhaps an incision of the throat would have to be made, a serious operation even in these days of medical wonders. Such an operation is one which no doctor has the right to refuse to perform. I quickly weighed up the situation; the child could not live more than half an hour, she must be taken from her father and Maria Alexandrovna must be found.

"Give the child to me!" I said to the father.

He only pressed the gasping bundle more tightly to himself.

"What are you afraid of? . . . You know that you are in a hospital, don't you?"

But he seemed as though he had turned wooden in his grief; he clung to the child like a treasure which could never be replaced, and somehow I felt in my heart a regret that on Mondays I could not think a good word of parents. Perhaps to a man the most precious thing is the embodiment of his life in another—take away this treasure and what would remain of this one, for instance, but sagging balloons of trousers and dirty boots? I went over to him and put my hand on the blanket, but he raised his eyes to me, the glassy eyes of a man who in his despair sees nothing.

"Come, come," I said, "we want to save your little girl. Is she your only daughter?"

"The only one," he acknowledged bitterly.

"Then you must be glad that you have come in time; we shall have to put a small tube in the throat, as it is quite choked up . . . you can hear how she breathes."

But when I mentioned "tube" he staggered back as though he had been struck, a clammy perspiration rose on his forehead and his eyes became a staring white, as though bleached. I have seen many parents. It is true that mothers show great sorrow, they are ready to fly at your throat as though you are to blame for the illness of their children. Fathers are generally silent, sometimes indifferent; perhaps it is because the parental feeling only comes to a man later when the child begins to assume individual human traits, or because a child is not the only thing in life; but this man standing before me showed all the signs of a mother, he was just as suspicious, opened the blanket like a mother: it was all very sad and yet very funny.

"Do you hear me?" I said, "my good citizen . . . if you go on in this way you will kill the little girl . . . if we don't operate immediately she cannot live more than half an hour . . . you are not a peasant woman!"

He began to rush about the room and, like a frightened bird, he tried as he ran round in circles to get further away from me, then he suddenly stopped dead and handed the child to me.

"Take her! . . . here you are . . . take everything!"

"It is not I, but science who takes her from you to save her life," I answered.

I took the child, and he breathed deeply and closed his aching eyes as though relieved of an unbearably heavy burden.

"That's right," I said; "you wait here . . . have a smoke . . . everything will be all right."

"Very well, I will smoke," said he.

I took the child away quickly so that he should not change his mind and call me back. I opened the door of the operating theatre, and on the threshold stood Zinaida Borisovna, wearing a white overall and rubber gloves.

"Operation?" she inquired.

"No, intubation," I replied.

She nodded, and it seemed that by her nod she gave me an order. Could it be possible, I wondered, that she would make this intubation; would she dare, not having done it before? I must tell you frankly that I had no faith in her. She was young, having finished at the university three years before, and since then had served her term with us. According to the general view she was a capable doctor, clever and with plenty of self-assurance. I wonder if you will understand me? You see the doctor making the incision in the throat, you see the naked windpipe, and over it the knife, one false movement of which costs a human life! At such moments I felt an exalted veneration for those skilful magic hands. But on a piano, for instance, one person can play with wonderful technique and yet the music does not appear wonderful, whilst another will go down the keyboard irregularly and yet tear your very heart-strings.

I had held the hands of both of our doctors. Zinaida Borisovna had the strong hands of a healthy peasant girl, wide-boned, almost mercilessly sure in every movement; sometimes she would take up a crying child, and the child would quieten immediately under the touch of those merciless hands. She would take a bandage from a throat, not roughly, no, just as it ought to be done, but how one breathed with relief when it was over! "Thank God everything was all right that time!" Perhaps it was just this that put me on my guard with her. I did not feel in her that all-embracing devotion to the work which there was in Maria Alexandrovna. Zinaida Borisovna would not stay half an hour in the ward when her work was finished; she would not show any unnecessary interest, she would not come in during the night as Maria Alexandrovna did to see if all was well with a serious case; she was more abrupt, more severe, only allowed the patients to have what was prescribed, and she had no smile, no joke, no kind word . . . she had no sympathy in the performance of our work. She saw in our work of relieving human suffering just duty which had to be performed honestly, that was all.

"Prepare for the operation," said Zinaida Borisovna to me.

"I have already sent for Maria Alexandrovna," I said, and I approached the table and laid down the little girl.

She flushed to the roots of her hair, but her eyes remained bright and cold and her voice as hard as steel:

"There is no time for waiting . . . you can see yourself . . . please prepare the instruments."

"Very well," I answered, and I hastened to prepare the bandages and instruments, but my hands trembled, and as though purposely for some reason or other I could not find one thing nor the other. And the child on the table began to turn blue and I saw that it was impossible to wait longer. But what could I do if I had no faith in her?

"What are you doing? What is wrong with you? Are you delaying purposely?" asked Zinaida Borisovna. From where did I gather courage at that moment? Perhaps it was because I was not one of those happy ones with children of their own, and towards every child I felt a little as though it was mine, and I seemed to think, "What if it was my daughter lying at death's door and we were quarrelling, not I as myself but as a mother? . . ." and then it seemed that my thoughts of the parents were heartless and unjust.

"I have no faith in you!" I answered.

"Ah, is that so?" she almost shrieked, and she moved towards me with that involuntary movement, chest thrust forward, with which an angry woman moves when she can find no words. "I order you to prepare everything immediately for the operation. Do you hear? Otherwise you will be responsible."

Having received the order I dared not answer. It was my duty to obey the doctor, and in this case she was right, not I. If every worker in such work as ours (and this applies to work in general) began to be guided by her inner convictions, what would be the result? Also it was impossible to wait any longer, the face of the child was burning and there was already a submission in her movements, she did not throw her arms about but lay stretched out on the table, and I knew what such submission meant.

"I obey you," I answered, and in a second I had prepared everything.

In my bosom everything was on fire, I could hear nothing but footsteps; would there be none in the corridor? Once, even, I imagined I heard, and rushed to the door, but it was the ward-maid passing. . . . Oh, how strongly Zinaida Borisovna and I hated each other during those moments . . . and what is remarkable is that in herself Zinaida Borisovna was a very sympathetic being, her strength and self-assurance attracted one to her, her every movement was masterly, not because she was a doctor and occupied a good position, but because of her inborn character. People such as we on the forty-rouble rate of pay have to go through life protecting ourselves as the people in the Moscow tramcars do with their elbows, as you may have seen. With our forty roubles we protect ourselves from hunger, from ridicule and weariness by love of our neighbours, from emptiness of heart by a burning desire to perform great deeds as did Maria Alexandrovna, in our smallness we did not want to quit the world without leaving some trace behind . . . but there was none of this in her; perhaps that was why I didn't believe in her, why I never experienced any griefs or pleasures or doubts with her as I did when I worked with Maria Alexandrovna.

I prepared the little girl and laid out the instruments in the order in which they would be required, then I took up my position at the table, and only then did I find relief from my thoughts; it is always necessary at operations that the sight should become more certain, the hands more skilled, and that one should become a machine whose movements are timed to the second. My duty was to hand the instruments as required, to take them back and put them down, to follow the movement of the doctor's hands with my own, but never to touch them; it is exceedingly dangerous if an unskilled nurse touches the hands of a doctor with her own during an operation.

"I am ready," I told her quietly.

"Now that is excellent," answered Zinaida Borisovna, and she approached the table.

Then she began to make the intubation; and my premonitions, my bitter premonitions were realised! She choked the child by inserting the tube unskilfully. She choked the child, and in me—how strange the human being is ordered—there rose, not pity, not despair, but some sort of gloomy, wicked triumph. "Look now, all of you, wasn't I right!"

Just then Maria Alexandrovna entered the operating theatre. Her footsteps were always unheard: we medical people become accustomed to moving about silently, like mothers, but this one rushed in like a tigress seeking her cub. Her grey hair hung dishevelled over her face and her hands trembled; she didn't ask me anything; everything was obvious without a word being spoken: the blue face of the child, the eyes, from which even death had not extinguished pain, open like empty windows. Both Zinaida Borisovna and I moved away from the table to make room for her; she felt the pulse and moved in silence towards the wash-basin. I followed her movements from the window, but dared not raise my eyes higher than her feet. I was afraid to hear the truth, but I noticed that her boots were quite worn and dirty, and thought to myself, "How can one wear such worn boots!" When she had washed her hands Maria Alexandrovna went out of the operating theatre silently, as only mothers walk, or people when there is a dead body in the room.

"Go and tell the father," said Zinaida Borisovna.

At first I didn't even grasp her words. Her face was composed; only her well-shaped eyebrows were raised guiltily over her brow, a movement which is only known to doctors through whose hands a person who has recently died has passed.

"Tell the father!" she repeated.

"You killed her, so you can go and tell him," I answered.

She lowered her eyebrows threateningly and said:

"What goes on in here is secret . . . you understand that!"

But I only smiled in answer to her: "You are afraid! Probably you are afraid that you will lose your position!"

We were talking in whispers and grasped the meaning of the words rather than heard them, but it seemed to us that we were screaming at the top of our voices.

"You are afraid to lose your position," I repeated, moving nearer to her and looking her over as though seeing and understanding her for the first time. Perhaps it was so. You can live with a person a lifetime and not know what sort of person he is, what is the colour of his eyes; then suddenly comes a moment when the man seems to remove the cover from his heart and the naked heart pulses on your open palm. I understand now how small and mean I was then, playing by means of my stupid words as with a ball with her heart in my hand.

"You think now about duty! Ah, is that so? Why didn't you think about it before the operation? This isn't employment—almost everything on earth can be called employment, but a human hand armed with an operating knife cannot be employed—such a knife in a human hand calls for heroism."

"What then," smiled she bitterly, "must one face damnation?"

"Yes, damnation!" I seemed to shriek. "The knife in your hand means service, not employment. . . ."

"Nonsense, that is your stupid idealism . . . and that . . ." and she indicated the child, who seemed to me as though she turned her little blue face on the table as though trying to hear our duel, "that is only a passing event, and, maybe, an experimental lesson. . . . Go to the father!"

"I will not go!"

"I order you to go!" she said, with the quiet command of a doctor asking for a bandage to be passed. At that moment I seemed to discover in her something which she dare not look for in herself. Which of the two of us was right? Who dare decide this? Perhaps with my hasty words about service I was trying to throw off the blood on my hands on to those of my neighbour? Perhaps after all the scalpel had not to be an incense-burner in the hand, but a finger which became a part of the body and did not tremble, for although Maria Alexandrovna was a very experienced doctor, her hands always trembled during an operation, as though she was finding the required nerve, not with her eyes but with her heart. Did I not in myself, when the time came for an operation to be performed, feel that there was not a human being but an object before me? Only then did I control myself and become precise like an instrument in my movements. Service and employment fight for supremacy within all of us; was it then the fault of Zinaida Borisovna that one had reached such a limit that the other had to be dispensed with?

"Now go to the father," she said tenderly, as though to a small child, and I went out meekly. I knew exactly the scene which would ensue: the father, smoking as he awaited the news of the death, would start running about the waiting-room and, ashamed of his tears, would shout and threaten; and the more he threatened the more profusely would flow the offending despised tears. Then he would fall prostrate on a chair and his face would become the vacant face of a man who had just been told that the world had come to an end. I knew all this by bitter experience, and thus everything happened. With professional reserve I waited until he had had his say and became exhausted, choking with impotent anger. It was my duty to ask him certain questions which were necessary on the death of a child:

"Do you desire a post-mortem, or will you remove the child for burial?"

And, as often happens with parents, he understood "burial" but not death; he understood at once from his innermost heart, and dropped on the floor the cap which he had just been waving like a dagger. The falling cap awoke again in me a feeling of pity for him and a sense that we were to blame for his distress, and I nearly went to pick up his cap, to comfort him somehow with this human movement. This is true—our professional coldness is most terrifying to the parents, they cannot understand it, but if they did they would not place their children in our wards and they would die, fed with sweets and choked with caresses and loving tears. And then once again, for the last time in that terrible day, the other sense came to the top and I forced myself submissively to carry out the order of Zinaida Borisovna. I informed him with polite coolness:

"You must ask in the office for information regarding the death."

I knew that with this official phrase I was ending my relations with him (and not only mine, but those of the hospital which I represented); but as I uttered this cruel phrase I heard, for the first time in my life, the sound of my own words, something which one generally never hears.

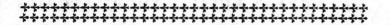

A. OKULOF

✢

THE UNEXPECTED MEETING

I

I t was a joyous and glittering May morning, and the sunlight poured in at the window of a little wooden house and fell in bright splashes on the freshly-planed flooring.

Troops were passing in the street. The brass bands played martial music, evoking the joy of battle and the thought that we must go eternally—forward. Forward, forward, forward, thumped the band's Turkish drum. . . .

The old grey-haired mother was scolding her boy Alexis.

"What is there for you to rejoice over or to refuse? Regimental commander in the Red army . . . I'll say that's fine! . . . What an honour for you, for Alexis Skobeyef! Forgotten your father, I suppose? Forgotten everything, eh?"

No, Alexis had not forgotten his father. That father of his had been a rich man, a business organiser, promoter, and had gone over to the Whites, to be lost sight of from that day on. Alexis often grieved about it secretly, and the thought hung over him like a threat or a shame. No, he has never forgotten and never will forget.

But his mother goes on reproaching him endlessly.

"You're not twenty yet, you're still a boy. Think of your father. He is the head. He knows everything, understands everything, he's not like you and me. Why don't you go seek him and forget your swelled head? He is saving his country and his religion. . . . What are you doing here? Only learning in the Red army how to kill the protectors of your country. I can't think who you take after in our fine old family."

These conversations frequently drove Alexis to the limits of his patience, and then he would quarrel bitterly with his mother.

But to-day the sun is shining too brightly, the music of the soldiers in the street is too gay. The bright blue sky reminds him forcibly of distances and open spaces. He has no idea of quarrelling; he is resting a few minutes before going on duty again.

His younger brother is playing with his sword and causing the bright, glittering steel to reflect the sunlight in the room.

"If I hit you with this thing right on the brow, what then? Wouldn't there be a lot of blood? You'd bleed a long time, eh?"

The little boy did not wait for an answer, but put the sword back in the scabbard, sighing.

"But I'm going to be a commander too . . . absolutely. I've made up my mind. But you, what do you think?"

And suddenly, unexpectedly, Regimental-Commander Skobeyef jumped from his chair and got on to all-fours on the floor.

"A-rr-r, a-rr-r!" He arched his back and made a noise like a bear. "I eat all little boys, a-rr-r!"

Then he began to play round on the floor, upsetting chairs and making a good deal of noise, while mother, unwillingly silenced, continued to grumble under her breath. Then he rolled over on his back, pawing the air with all-fours.

Sister Olga came in, and her muslin skirt played the air on his face as she passed.

Alexis grabbed at her slender body and held it with his strong hands like a reed. "A-rr-r, and I'll eat you too!" he cried.

Olga did not like it particularly.

Hunchbacked Matriona looked in from the kitchen through the open door.

"Barin, barin . . . there's a message come for you."

"Where from? Who brought it?"

"A soldier gave it in."

Alexis read the notice. It was an army order. It stated that after the retreat of Kolchak some hundred thousand dead bodies remained on the Barabin steppes in a state of putrefaction, threatening serious danger to the health of the local population. "To remove this menace an Extraordinary Commission for the destruction of corpses has been organised, the E.C.C. . . . to which have been assigned . . . regt. commr. 2nd N.N. inf. . . . who will hold themselves in readiness within twenty-four hours. . . . The well-being of the republic demands that this work be done quickly, with every means at its disposal. . . ."

Alexis at once began to think out the practical details : what clothes and weapons and ammunition he must take with him, and how to make the greatest haste to the scene of action.

At that moment Natasha Shaposhnikova came in and asked where Olga was, and whether they had had breakfast and what was going on. And with Natasha came joy.

Alexis smiled and said: "In the first place, it is quite possible that we have not had enough breakfast; in the second place, Olga has gone out somewhere in a hurry and I never interfere in her affairs; in the third place, Mamma is huffed and has gone into the yard to look after the chickens; in the fourth place, I am going away."

"Where?"

"I've received an order to go and shift the dead."

"What dead? Going for long?"

"Don't know at all how long it will take to tidy up a battlefield; to tidy it up, tidy it up, tidy it up. . . ."

Alexis wanted to play at bear again and began roaring and tumbling about. Natasha took some wood and lit the fire in the old stove.

"Mamma is angry, heh? I'd better get you boys something to eat."

Alexis sat and watched her, but suddenly started up and

asked her if she did not think it fine that he should get a change of air. "That's a good thing for a man, to go to the wilderness for a while, don't you think so? Come on, tell me, tell me sincerely." He put his arms round her and held her and pestered her to say she approved.

And the fire burned up, and when he released her she decided to make an omelet for the family, an omelet from three eggs. Then Olga came in, disturbing them.

"Olga, I'm ordered away on special duty to-morrow. Get some linen ready for me."

Olga said there was almost nothing clean. "Well, put in what is clean!"

The omelet burned underneath and filled the room with smoke.

"Well, Natasha, I'd like to say good-bye to you before I go, only not here. Tell me when and where."

"Come and see me to-day. I'll expect you." That was all she said. The omelet got in their way, like Olga.

II

She was washing one of her two chemises in a wash-basin when he appeared in the doorway.

"Why don't you come in?" she called out, laughing and showing her white teeth. "Come in! Excuse me doing this, I shan't have any time later."

Alexis looked at her quickly-heaving bosom, at her feet in their worn-out slippers, at her old skirt hanging from her famished body, at the beads of perspiration on her brow.

"How is it you never receive anything anywhere—rations, clothes and so on?"

"I've no patience to wait; always bread lines, and lines for other things, lines, lines, lines. . . . You have to wait a long time. I can't."

"Others seem to fix themselves up somehow. They have enough to eat and clothes to wear. There ought to be someone to look after you, just to see you don't die of cold and hunger, or if you die to see that you don't die naked."

"Oh, has anyone time to look after everybody?" said she, and laughed gaily. "But see what I've cooked for you . . . just the most delicious stewed pears. Just a moment, I'll put the pot on again."

She wiped her red hands, swollen and cut with washing.

"I know where you got those pears; from the soldiers' rations as a worker in the Voenkom. God! you'll never boil these pears to make them soft. I could not crush them with my heels."

And thinking of the sort of compote they would make, he laughed heartily. But when his eyes rested on her torn stockings and the holes in her heels he frowned and grieved, from the love he bore her.

Natasha caught the direction of his glance, bit her lip and felt confused.

"Don't think I like to have potatoes in my stockings. I feel so upset not to be able to dress myself properly; it's because of that you'll get tired of me. Oh, don't say you are a revolutionary and the rest of it. . . . All the same you'll fall in love with pretty women. And being well dressed means a great deal. You don't know how good it is to wear nice clothes, of course you could not understand. I do want a little happiness, Alyosha. Is that wrong, from a revolutionary point of view? Why are my hands so helpless and weak? I don't do my work well in our Voenkom. I dislike clerking there. I'd like to be with you, at the front. Is there anything wrong in that? I am for the revolution; but I am also a woman, that's what's bad."

He looked from her to the clock and fingered the military order in his pocket. He took her red hand, worn with washing, in his hand, worn with hard work in the ranks. He caressed her hands with his rustling palms.

"All the same, I am leaving to-morrow, Natasha. Who knows what may happen? But I love you. I cannot take you with me. But, all the same, I love you. Do not be angry with me for going away at once. I have to put the regiment in readiness. Don't fear, we'll meet again."

III

At home, mother and sister are getting ready his linen. Alexis must go and say good-bye to his other friends. Plunging through the mud and dirt and dust of the Omsk bazaar, he comes to a wooden shed where his Esthonian acquaintance, Otto Karlovitch, sells tea, coffee, pies and stolen Government spirit.

"Hey, hey, our infantry general has arrived. . . . What shall we give him, a pie?"

Alexis stood at the door of the shop and looked into its smoky depths, where at three plain tables some Korean cigarette hawkers were sitting, carriers of cigarettes and opium. There were also some cattle-dealers connected with the commissariat and some soldiers belonging to Alexis' command. At a fourth table were his friends, those for whose sake he had come.

Truth to say they were not exactly friends, but schoolmates; he had no friends and had never made any. But these people occupied the place of friends in his soul.

There was Korovin, a worker in the Gub-Zem-Otdel; and Sokolsky, son of a director of the school in old days. It was to meet these he had come for lack of others.

"Otto Karlovitch, give me a pastry!"

Alexis spoke to Otto Karlovitch in a gentle, almost tender voice, but he for his part was deep in converse with a Caucasian acquaintance.

"Waige hai. . . . Mamenka, get one out of the basket."

And he went on talking, with his lips close to the Caucasian's ear.

". . . That's what happened. It's the truth. The commissar came to me every day, almost every day. He took spirit, he took money, he took various things. Eh! I just can't tell you all he took; he simply robbed me. And he robbed all the neighbours. Your friend from the Caucasus was living next door. And I tell the truth when I say that life became unbearable. But the Caucasian did the job well. He invited the commissar to come and drink vodka with him. Funny! He put arsenic in it. Funny, wasn't it? I gave three milliards towards the funeral. All the neighbours subscribed, and didn't we have a fine funeral? Weren't there musicians? . . . Waige hai?"

And Otto Karlovitch laughed long and loudly with his friend.

Alexis raised a glass.

"Otto Karlovitch, don't you hear? I am drinking your health. Hey, Otto Karlovitch, I am leaving the town to-night."

But Alexis' old schoolmates at the other table interrupted him and prevented his making a speech.

"Don't act the idiot in front of us. You've become a Red, haven't you, brother? So, tell us without joking how that came about."

The childish gaiety faded from the eyes of the young man and his face puckered up with doubt. He fidgeted with his cap, he almost choked, finding words.

"How I became a Red, how it's done; wait a moment, I'll tell you."

He felt he could not tell them about that. He could speak of anything else under the sun, but not of that. But after a moment's hesitation he began to tell them calmly and reflectively.

"How one becomes a Red is clear enough for myself, but it's hard to explain. Any kind of irregularity in life; for instance, that one man should have a good time and another not; that some should die in work and others in idleness. There's filth everywhere, bestiality of all kinds. . . . It is difficult to live in all this, but how arrange things differently?

As for the revolution, you cannot escape from it. . . . But don't you like it? Be patient, mates, it can't be avoided. What else? There's little to add. Every man thinks about things in his own way. You declare that the working people are rabble. Perhaps that's right. But what would you answer if I said that those who do not work are rabble also? Surely you remember how they carried on in the Tsar's time, and how, but lately, the Kolchak crowd carried on with all their officers and generals? Did they not behave worse than all the ignorant, terribly ignorant peasant partisans put together? Did they not go one worse? But why waste words, mates? It is difficult to explain why the revolution is so dear to me. But that does not matter. My life belongs to it, and that's all that matters."

The Caucasian was telling Otto Karlovitch another story.

"You see, when one commissar dies another takes his place. The next one was drunk twenty hours a day. When he had sobered up a little in the fresh air he would begin arresting others for drunkenness; drank for twenty hours and arrested people for drinking for four hours; a big work, very fine. We had some jolly fights—no one knew who was hitting the other and why."

"All the same, I drink to the revolution," said Alexis, raising his glass. "The revolution at any cost, even if I have no friends. . . . Farewell. I am leaving to-morrow—to go and bury enemies. . . . It will be fine on the Steppes in the spring. We shall bury, but we won't let others bury us. Farewell!"

IV

Alexis entrained with his regiment, and lying down on the floor of a goods wagon, was soon asleep. Sounds and voices mingled in his dreams, the locomotive whistling, the long-drawn call of some locomotive replying from somewhere, the ringing of station bells, shuffling of soldiers' feet, a conversation.

"But why not let me go?" says a whining voice. "I have a bride waiting for me, and where's the sense in going to bury corpses for me? I'll make it all right for you, honest I will. Let me go and get married. One does not get married every day in the year, you can understand that for yourself."

"Clear off or I'll report you."

Another conversation entered his drowsy consciousness.

"The revolution was quite a simple matter: the people wanted to eat."

"That's wrong: they wanted to live."

Then Alexis fell into a happy dream of the magnificent things he would do in life, crowned with fame, enveloped with love, and of the things he would have to overcome and would most certainly overcome as soon as possible. Falling off into a soldier's sleep, always ready to wake, he vaguely remembered that he must get up at one of the small stations and speak to a signalman with whom he was acquainted, a duty that was not official but connected with Natasha. He was up ten minutes before the train arrived.

A pale dawn threw a green light on the station buildings. The signalman was there, a worn-out man with hollow cheeks and eyes red from sleeplessness; he had been in his box sixteen hours on end. He was a solitary figure on the empty platform and was looking about him in an official way.

"Trifonof?" inquired Alexis in a sleepy voice. "Pavel Petrovitch? . . . Comrade . . . will you send my mother and the Shapovnikofs in Omsk a pound of flour each? . . . I'll pay out funds. . . . Can you? Hey, can you? Here it's easy to buy."

"I'll do it."

"What are we waiting for?" asked the station-master of the guard. "Give the whistle."

In the silence of the night the locomotive roared wildly forward like some great beast; the brakemen blew their squeaky horns and the smoke and heat of the locomotive were wafted backward. The wheels rumbled along the lines over the damp earth, through the sparse woodland and the undulating country. Alexis lay down again on the floor of the train and fell asleep. And again he dreamed, dreamed of love that was uncommonly sweet, of unheard-of glory and of unsurpassed behaviour on his part.

At a halt the local station-master, out of ennui, came alongside and talked to Alexis.

"Comrade commander, you're going to bury the corpses, are you?" said he.

"Yes, for the Extraordinary Commission for the disposal of the corpses."

"Jolly sort of job. Begins about ten versts from here, and goes on for about sixty, and all corpses. . . . Coffins. . . . I suppose if you were to do it in the Russian way, the orthodox way, you'd have to make coffins for the lot, and that would take you about twenty years. You can see for yourself it is Steppe country, there's little wood. Where would you get the wood to do it? The Steppe all around is almost quite bare. . . ."

"And what's a coffin, if I may be permitted to ask?" said a gay young fellow, the station watchman. "It's all the same, you rot in the earth, coffin or no coffin. They say all goes to dust the same way. But perhaps that's incorrect. You know best."

The station-master gave a big puff from his cigarette and the smoke slowly dispersed in the morning air.

"Yes, our Steppe will soon be covered with spring flowers," said he. "But we have dreadful winters. They got caught in the midst of it, in a howling wilderness, and a blizzard came on. There was no way of escape. . . . When you get about ten versts away from the place you begin to smell the fresh spring air, but if the wind happens to be coming from that direction, spring ceases, and you have a stench of death. You cannot imagine what it is. And to think that all these were once people."

The watchman looked at Alexis with questioning eyes and then set his lips.

"What do you think, comrade commander? Perhaps they

were people. But I ought to tell you how those Kolchaks travelled. The common soldiers were dying like flies, dying of typhus. But the Kolchaks went off in the Imperial train with music and embracing their madames. . . . I got well again, I have a strong heart. . . . But you can judge for yourself the sort of people they were who died. Somehow it wasn't right. Of course all people are sinners. All the same it was bad. They did not live properly, and after death they made a stench all over the countryside. They changed into a dangerous carrion."

Alexis's light-hearted mood passed as he listened to these words.

"Well, let us get on. You say it is only ten versts more. What are you holding us back for?" he asked.

The train moved on, and in a few minutes the regiment of Alexis entered into the realm of the E.C.C.

The snow was melting on the rough surface of the Steppe and trickling away. Here and there human bodies were being released from the drifts, here a pointing arm, there a leg stiff from the knee, there a bare back with torn shirt. Emaciated bodies with all the ribs showing lay all over the Steppe, abandoned, dreary.

Crows circled in the air above the scene and called to one another, fluttering against one another's wings, some rising upward on the wind, others suddenly descending to the fields of carrion, settling upon the dead and fanning them with their wings and ceasing to call to one another. The day was cloudy. There was silence.

The crows settled unhurriedly on the tumbled dead, pecking persistently at uncovered faces, spluttering over rotting cheeks and picking out the eyes from the eye-sockets, looking up with reasonless animal eyes at the sky, at the passing train, at the engine-smoke. . . . Alexis watched them from the window of the train.

The wind had scattered torn and crumpled papers over the Steppe, perhaps the military orders of the lost army.

At last the troop train stops at the E.C.C. base. In the cold early morning air Alexis sees a number of men working, shovelling and clearing or leaning on their shovels.

"Devil take this mother earth of ours, it's still frozen stiff," says one. "Our shovels are not much use here . . ." says one of the workers.

There were explosions and bursts of coffee-coloured smoke in the near distance. Holes were being blasted for the heaps of dead and the corpses were being burned in them.

Someone came to Alexis and inquired if he were giving orders to the regiment to detrain. His mind was back in Omsk with Natasha and the spring; he was thinking of Omsk and of the spring sun and larks and of people, yes, of those who had been people, the corpses they were destroying. He made an effort and replied to the questioner: "Yes. . . . Fine. I'll go and report at once. And I'll find out where exactly we are supposed to start."

V

Alexis sat beside a blazing bonfire outside his tent; the wind was rustling and murmuring over the plains, making the embers of the fire glow and glow again. He sat, embracing his knees with his hands. It was his first night in the realm of the E.C.C., the realm of death; and death was blood, filth, stench and decay.

He saw his dreams and his thoughts in the fire, all the strange mixture of light and gloom, fire and darkness, hopes and recollections, grief and joy. He sat there by his camp fire amid the shadows of the vast Steppe, shadows that wavered, shadows that shuddered in the withered masses of last year's grass, shadows that climbed on to every mound and tussock of the dark plain, and through the murk he overheard the conversation of the workers sitting round the neighbouring fire.

". . . When the Kolchak generals took our village they plundered all the houses, burned some of them for an example . . . spoiled our girls, upset the women . . . rotten business."

". . . This corpse destruction is getting too much for me. I've broken my nails on the hard earth picking them up. And how the living can turn out the pockets of the dead I don't understand, it's disgusting. . . ."

Alexis dropped off to sleep and dreamed of his father, dreamed of a far-off voice of childhood's days, which said to him: "Take care of yourself, my son, don't trust others. Others are all thinking of themselves first. Don't bother about their affairs."

Then in his nightmare he seemed to be calling his father.

"Come, papa, just come and see what you have done; come, come."

Spring. . . . The E.C.C. . . . Sunshine, odours and stench. It was suffocating; it was impossible to sleep. One's chest was being crushed. He suddenly sat up and looked around him. The night had passed and sunrise was dispersing all dreams and visions. The fire was out. A new day of burying had commenced. His mind turned from his dreams to the thought of the tens of thousands of dead and their monstrous fate. Some, of course, had gone consciously and shamelessly into the adventure, a mere few, but the others, the vast majority, blindly, without volition of their own. Why had it been necessary for them to go thus to torment and death?

VI

"Comrade-commander, don't you want to wash?"

Anisyef, his favourite lieutenant, was calling to him. Some of the workers had fetched a bucket of water for him. Alexis washed the sleep from his eyes in snow-cold water. That done, Anisyef handed him a telegram:

"You are ordered to proceed with all haste in the work of clearing up the corpses. Every day's delay constitutes a new danger for the troops and the local population. All means should be used to get the task done quickly."

"Well, let's get on with the digging, comrades," cried Alexis. And he and all his men turned to at once to uncover the dead in the melting snow.

They turned up the grey school uniform of a boy who must have been still at the high school. When they pulled at a boot sticking out of the half-frozen snow the leg of the boy came away in their hands. At another point they uncovered trousers that had broad red stripes on them, the sign of general's rank. A general! The old man's beard was frozen in wisps to his uniform. But the corpses were not only of soldiers. Here and there were women, old and young, with children close to them, women with pinched noses and long tresses which fell away from their scalps at the slightest tug. And then soldiers, soldiers, soldiers, hundreds and hundreds, thousands and thousands, rank after rank, heap after heap. They kept on uncovering them from morning till evening, at every foot, at every yard, all in the same monotonous grey uniforms, in the same ragged overcoats; the same yellow-green faces, fallen brows, gleaming, grinning teeth.

"Comrade-commander, we're tired. Can't we take a rest?"

"No, dig on!" said Alexis, biting his lips and frowning.

"But all the same they will never be able to destroy such a great number of bodies."

"How they'll destroy them is not our affair. Dig on!"

His head swam from the stench; at times he almost choked. And he was utterly miserable in mind and soul. The workers smoked; someone asked for a match. Alexis for a moment looked over the dismal scene, the wide plain with its patches of deep snow, the gloomy clouds lowering upon the wide wilderness, the birds near the clouds flying in long tenuous streamers north to south. Explosion followed explosion at the scene of the dynamite operation, and the smoke of many pyres hung heavily upon the distant regions of the Steppe. A hysterical feeling possessed him, and he wished to stop working and seize his temples in his hands. "What a frantic crime, and no one punished for it," he reflected. "For the chief villains got away." He tried vainly to excuse it and see the whole calamity as a matter of history, the struggle of the classes, something inevitable. He felt he could trample on the body of a dead general without a squirm, but not on the mass of peasants and workmen, even workmen, in soldiers' uniforms. He was horrified by the useless death of all these. "The mercilessness of history . . . let it go at that. Yes, if it was necessary for the revolution, I make no objection!"

He went the round of his Red Army men, all busy with their shovels.

"Faster, faster!" said he. "We've been ordered to make haste. We must get on with it."

He saw Anisyef and three of his men struggling with the body of a bedraggled old man in an even more bedraggled overcoat. Anisyef smiled up at Alexis in a tired way and pulled at the dead body.

"Pull, brothers! Let's send this merchant to the general factory."

The soldiers jested.

"He's got a bit wet. We'll soon have him dried."

Alexis looked at the pitiful bedraggled old man, on his side-whiskers which had grown down to his chin, at his grey locks all dirty and tangled, and then at the collar of his blouse made by a familiar firm in Omsk—and his heart suddenly trembled.

Yes, he recognised all that, the side-whiskers, the grey hair, the blouse. A blinding memory; the last days at home. . . . "Take care of yourself, my son, don't show yourself," . . . and then, "Remember my testament, son. Do not betray your country. . . ."

The soldiers round about were already talking of something else, of another corpse they were unearthing. "Pity they killed this one, look at his rags. How poor! . . . They didn't kill him. He froze. . . . Well, what's it matter? Off with him to the incinerator."

Alexis breathed convulsively and tears trickled down his face. A lump came in his throat.

"Father . . ." he whispered. "So that's what's happened? This is where you are. . . ."

He stood some minutes licking his dry lips.

"That's how it ended. . . ."

Bitter sorrow cut him to the heart. The Steppe swam round his tear-stricken eyes. A flood of memories rose in his soul : the first caresses, the first pleasures, the first impressions ; his father teaching him, taking him shooting on the Steppes, his walking with him through the thick green grass.

Alexis leaned over the dead body and tried to lift it with his hands, but the rotten fur cloak split from shoulder to shoulder, disclosing his coat, which was also falling to pieces. The contents of his pockets fell out on to the snow and the mud ; Soviet money, Kolchak money, receipts, old letters, a railway ticket. . . .

With trembling hands he gathered them all together, and amongst the papers he found the old man's last letter home, unposted, a letter to mother together with newspaper clippings in which Kolchak's retreat was explained and the speedy victory of the Whites said to be certain.

Alexis looked around him in a dazed way. Victory of the Whites . . . the Steppe sown with the dead. . . . But what would it have meant if the Whites had actually won? The earth in blood, cities, towns, villages . . . a million men tortured, executed. . . .

He wiped his eyes with a dirty rag which served instead of a handkerchief. But still he could not control the muscles of his face.

"Comrade Anisyef, help me," he said.

Anisyef approached.

"How can I help you, comrade-commander?"

"The fact is, this is my father. Give him a proper burial! But we must get on with the work. I'll come back presently when you have dug a grave."

VII

The work of clearance went on accompanied by explosions, and still the evil odour rose on the wind. But with each day the Steppe seemed to grow younger and to rejoice. Day after day the work went on, and sunshine and spring were allowed to have their victory over the dead. The Red soldiers, anticipating the conclusion of their heavy task, went laughing and jesting about their work.

The expression of Alexis did not change.

"Lively!" said he. "Get on with it! It's time we had finished."

His face was set, his gaze was steady. He seemed filled with heroic determination, a will towards struggle and victory.

"Faster, comrades!"

But with each day the bright light of youth seemed to fade in his soul. A pallor settled on his cheeks. At night, when the others slept, he lay awake thinking of the world, and a great pity for humanity filled his heart. "People are just naughty children. . . . And how difficult it is, how painful, to try and make things a little better . . . to make it better for everyone!" . . .

He recalled the great feeling of responsibility which he had had when undertaking this task.

They gleaned the last dead bodies out of the new green grass under the spring sun while the crows cawed and fluttered away over the plains. The last morning came and Alexis was wakened by sunrise. He dashed the sleep from his eyes and went out to meet the dawn. Where the rosy light was reflected in the puddles of the Steppe, life was going on. At a hundred yards from the army tents the wild ducks were calling. They dared; there were no hunters about. Some long-legged birds whose name he did not know were wading in the water and cleaning their feathers with their beaks. The mighty stream of life was rolling on along its appointed way, tirelessly and unwaveringly—ever onward and further.

Alexis sat down and watched the sunrise warming the clouds with rosy flame.

He had ceased thinking of anything. He was content to observe and listen. And then it was some blight from the past seemed to fall from his soul. Solitude, morning and youth forced him to get to his feet, straighten himself and strike himself resoundingly three times upon his chest—one, two, three.

"We are going to live, and if in order to live it becomes necessary to fight, we will fight."

VIII

In answer to his report that the work was done, Alexis was ordered to return to duty at Omsk with his men. That was an order which was happily fulfilled. The troop train filled with singing and jesting soldiers, and they moved slowly from the field of the dead to the strains of a concertina. They passed slowly by the scene of their labours, the pits and the mounds.

Alexis stared for a long time at a white cross slowly receding as the train went away, the cross on his father's grave.

He was sorry about his father, but something stood in the way of his sorrow. The thought that his father had belonged to the past and that he hated the future had intervened. And he knew he was going to have great difficulty in telling his mother and sister the circumstances of his death and burial. He knew how they would grieve. . . . He supposed they would demand that the body be brought to Omsk and interred in the city cemetery. He would have to seek permission for that, but would the authorities grant it? He began to reproach himself a little for being so indifferent, and to reflect that perhaps a certain shabbiness of mind at this point reflected a shabbiness of soul in him. But when he closed his eyes the events of the last few years surged up before them: the defeats of the Soviet army, the bloody and drunken debauch of Kolchak, his father joining the Kolchak standard, his own awakening to common-sense and reason, his joining the Reds, victory, the feud with his mother, his iron devotion to the revolution. . . . What a whirl of events and what changes! Then, most important of all, the choice—victory or death, the *yes* or *no*, *for* or *against*, without hypocrisy or chatter. Destiny at the point of the bayonet.

Whenever the train stopped one heard the concertina and the songs of the soldiers.

At night, when the compartment was lighted by one pale candle and shadows danced upon the floor and the wooden walls, he heard Anisyef snoring vigorously, and his thoughts turned again to life and youth. He had a sudden realisation that the days of death and decay and the burial of the malodorous past were definitely over. The real situation was this, that he was going back to duty at Omsk and to his kindred, and that Natasha was waiting for him there.

He laughed gently to himself and turned round into a sitting position.

"Hey Anisyef . . . friend . . ."

But Anisyef went on snoring.

"Sleeping? Ah, well, it does not matter."

He lit a cigarette in the half-dark, and its dulling, glowing end was like a promise, now fading away, now shining clear again.

IX

When he arrived at Omsk he decided to keep the news of his father's death to himself for a few days so that he might prepare his mother and sister for it. More than that, he was driven by some inner necessity to take a little spiritual rest, if only that the fumes of the death kingdom might somewhat evaporate. He wished to occupy his mind with something else and confirm the thought that joy and spring were real.

When he came to Natasha again her girlishness came as a surprise, her slender breast so tiny and quick-breathing. It was strange to see her as before with her old skirt hanging from her starved hips, with her threadbare stockings and the holes in the heels. Yes, just the same . . . even the tender look of love in her eyes . . . she was just as she was.

But death breathed on his brow.

He looked upon Natasha.

Poor helpless human love, fragile and unprotected! It flickers in life like the flame of a little wax candle blown this way and that by the wind, seeking calm and always likely to go out. Grief may come, but while there is this wavering flame of love, unextinguished, it will lighten and warm individual life.

"Well, tell me, Aloysha, tell me all about it."

He began to tell her, but the need of the present continually interrupted his story of the dead past. He is tired and worn-out. Life keeps intervening. And Natasha ran from him to attend to the teapot. She told him to go on, but she was not listening.

When the tea was ready he sat down beside her, quite close to her, and looked into her eyes. There he read a calm and unwavering faith in the future.

"My friend," said she, "I like life . . . and you. I want to live at all cost, and most of all with you. Whether you conquer or are conquered, it's all the same to me. I want to live with you to the end. . . . Oh, don't think that other men have not taken a fancy to me. But they were uninteresting, they knew nothing and wished nothing and were afraid of everything. . . . You are not that sort. . . . As for me, let me be with you in action, wherever you may be."

He looked on her and reflected.

"There are women and girls aplenty," was his thought. "But there is only one love."

And putting the thought of her aside for a moment, he thought of another thing.

"So it is with the revolution in my life: it is the one thing. I am ready to sacrifice everything for it—without any reservation."

VALENTINE KATAEV

(b. 1897)

✠

"THINGS"

(Translated by L. Zarine)

G E O R G E and Shurka, under the influence of a passionate mutual love, were married in the month of May. The weather was beautiful. After listening impatiently to the brief congratulatory speech of the registrar of marriages the newly-married young couple went out of the office into the street.

"Where shall we go now?" asked the lanky, thin-chested and quiet George, looking sideways at Shurka.

She, tall, handsome and hot as fire, pressed herself to his side, tickling his nose with a twig of the lilac which was entwined in her hair, and dilating her nose, passionately whispered:

"To the bazaar. To buy things. Where otherwise?"

"You mean to buy our furniture?" said her husband, smiling stupidly, and straightening his cap on his head as they went along.

A dusty wind swept through the bazaar. Thin coloured shawls floated over the stalls in the dry air. Shrieking gramophones played one against the other among the music stalls. The sun shone on suspended mirrors which swung in the wind. All kinds of fascinating stuffs and wildly beautiful articles surrounded the young couple.

A blush spread over the cheeks of Shurka; her forehead became quite moist; the lilac fell from her dishevelled hair and her eyes became large and round. She seized George by

the elbow with her burning hand, and biting her thick
cracked lips dragged him along the bazaar.

"Eider-downs first," she said chokingly, "eider-downs
first." . . .

Deafened by the shrieks of the stallholders, they hurriedly
purchased two square patchwork covers, heavy and thick,
too wide but not long enough. One was a vivid brick-red,
the other a funereal lilac.

"Now goloshes," she muttered, her warm breath suffusing
the face of her husband—"with red linings and lettering so
that no one can steal them."

They bought goloshes; two pairs, ladies' and men's, with
crimson lining and lettering. Shurka's eyes became almost
glossy.

"Towels! . . . with embroidered cockerels . . ." she almost
groaned as she put her burning head on her husband's
shoulder. In addition to towels with embroidered cockerels
they also bought four blankets, an alarm clock, a piece of
fustian material, a mirror, a small carpet with a tiger design,
two handsome chairs with brass nails, and several balls of
wool.

They also wanted to buy a bedstead with large nickel knobs
and a number of other things, but there wasn't sufficient
money. They returned home loaded. George was carrying
the chairs and supporting the rolled eider-downs against his
chin. His wet hair was sticking to his white forehead and
perspiration covered his thin, flushed cheeks. There were
violet shadows under his eyes. His half-open mouth showed
unhealthy teeth and he was inclined to dribble.

Back in the cold lodging he threw off his cap with relief,
and coughed. She threw the things on his single bed and
looked round the room, and in an impulse of girlish modesty
smacked him lovingly between the ribs with her big red
fist.

"Come, now, don't cough so much," she said with pretended severity, "or you'll soon die of consumption, now that

you have me on your hands . . . that's a fact!" and she rubbed her red cheek against his bony shoulder.

In the evening the guests arrived and there was a wedding feast. They looked over the new things with respectful admiration, praised them, ceremoniously drank two bottles of vodka, ate some pie, danced to the strains of the harmonium and soon departed. Everything was just as it should have been. Even the neighbours were astonished at the quiet decency of the wedding, with no excesses.

When the guests had gone, Shurka and George once again admired the things, and Shurka covered the chairs carefully with newspapers and locked the other articles, including the eider-downs, in a trunk, arranging the goloshes, with lettering uppermost, at the top and fastened the lock.

In the middle of the night Shurka awakened in an anxious state of mind and roused her husband.

"Do you hear, George. . . . Now, George dear," she whispered warmly, "wake up! We were wrong, you know, not to take the canary-coloured eider-down. The canary-coloured one was much more interesting, I am sure we ought to have had that one. And the goloshes had also the wrong lining; we didn't guess. . . . We ought to have had them with a grey lining. They would be so much better than the red ones. And the bed with knobs . . . we really didn't consider that enough." . . .

In the morning, having despatched George quickly to his work, Shurka hastened to the kitchen to discuss her wedding impressions with the neighbours. Having talked for five minutes for decency's sake about the delicate health of her husband, she led the women into her room, opened the trunk and exhibited the things. Taking out the eider-downs, with an audible sigh she said:

"It was a mistake that we didn't take the canary-coloured one . . . we didn't think to buy it. . . . Ah . . . we didn't consider." . . .

And her eyes went round and dimmed.

The neighbours praised the things. The wife of the professor, a good-hearted old woman, added:

"This is all very well, but your husband seems to cough very badly. We can hear everything through the partition. You will have to pay attention to this, otherwise, you know . . ."

"Oh, that's nothing, he will not die," said Shurka with deliberate roughness; "and if he does, that will be all right for him and I will find another man."

But suddenly her heart trembled.

"I will feed him with hamburger. He must stuff himself!" she said to herself.

The couple were hard put to it to exist till the next pay-day. But then they went at once to the bazaar and bought the canary-coloured eider-down, also many articles indispensable to the household and other absolutely beautiful things: a clock that chimed, two pieces of beaver fur, a small stand for holding a flower vase in the most up-to-date fashion, men's and ladies' goloshes with grey lining, six yards of plush, an amazingly splendid plaster dog covered with spots of various colours, a woollen shawl and a small greenish-coloured trunk with a musical lock.

When they returned to their home Shurka put the things neatly in the new trunk. The musical lock played a scale.

During the night she awakened, and laying her hot cheek on the cold, perspiring forehead of her husband, said quietly:

"George! Are you asleep? Don't sleep! George dear! Do you hear? . . . There was a blue one . . . what a pity we didn't have it. It really was a nice eider-down . . . somehow glossy . . . we did not think." . . .

Once during the middle of the summer Shurka entered the kitchen very gaily.

"My husband," said she, "is going on holiday. They have given everybody a fortnight, but he has a month and half, I give you my word. With an allowance. We shall go at once and buy the iron bed with knobs, that is quite certain!"

"I would advise you to arrange for him to go to a good sanatorium," said the old wife of the professor meaningly, putting under the tap a sieve of steaming potatoes, "otherwise, you know, it will be too late."

"Nothing will happen to him!" answered Shurka angrily, thrusting out her arms akimbo. "I can look after him better than any sanatorium. I will fry hamburger for him and let him stuff himself as much as he likes!" . . .

In the evening they came home from the bazaar with a small handcart loaded with things. Shurka walked behind the cart and gazed as though enchanted at the reflection of her flushed face in the nickel knobs of the bed. George, puffing heavily, could hardly push it. He had a sky-blue eider-down pressed up to his chest under his pointed chin. He coughed incessantly. A dark bead of perspiration gathered on his sunken temple.

During the night Shurka awakened. Intense, devouring thoughts would not let her sleep.

"George dear!" she began to whisper quickly, "there was a grey one left . . . do you hear? . . . What a pity we didn't have it . . . oh, how nice it was. Grey, grey, and the lining wasn't grey, but rose-coloured. . . . Such a lovely eider-down."

The last time George was seen was during a morning in the late autumn. He moved awkwardly down the little side street, his long, transparent, almost waxen nose thrust in the collar of his well-worn leather jacket. His sharp knees stuck out and his wide trousers flapped against his long bony legs. His small cap hung on the back of his head. His lank hair came down on his forehead, wet and dark.

He walked unsteadily, but carefully avoided the pools in order not to wet his thin boots; a weak, happy, almost contented smile played on his pallid lips.

When he got home he was obliged to take to bed, and the district doctor came. Shurka hastened to the insurance office to claim the sick benefit. She had to go alone to the bazaar, and returned with a grey eider-down, which she put away in the trunk.

George soon began to feel worse. The first snow—wet snow —appeared. The atmosphere became a foggy blue. The professor and his wife whispered together and another doctor soon appeared. He examined the patient and went out into the kitchen to wash his hands with antiseptic soap. Shurka was standing with tearful face in the midst of a cloud of smoke; she was frying large hamburger cutlets with garlic on the stove.

"Are you mad!" exclaimed the professor's wife in amazement. "What are you doing? You will kill him. Do you think he can possibly eat hamburger cutlets and garlic?"

"He can," said the doctor dryly, shaking the water into the basin from his white fingers. "He can have anything now."

"And what harm could cutlets do him?" shrieked Shurka, wiping her face with her sleeve. "Nothing will happen to him."

During the evening the sanitary attendant came in his white cotton overall and disinfected the general rooms. The smell of disinfectant pervaded the corridors. During the night Shurka woke up. An inexplicable sorrow was tearing her heart.

"George!" said she with an impatient whisper. "George, now, George dear, wake up! I tell you, George . . ."

George did not answer. He was cold. Then she jumped from the bed and lumbered heavily in her bare feet along the corridor. It was nearly three o'clock, but nobody in the place could sleep. She ran to the professor's door and fell down.

"He is gone! Gone!" she was screaming in terror. "Gone! My God! He is dead! George! Oh, George dear!"

She began to wail. The neighbours peeped from their doors. Blue wintry stars glittered on the crisp frost behind the dark windows.

In the morning the pet cat approached the open door of Shurka's room, paused on the step, peeped into the room and suddenly its fur bristled. It fuffed and backed out. Shurka was sitting in the middle of the room, and with her face bathed in tears was saying angrily to the neighbours, as though she had been affronted:

"And I was saying to him, Stuff yourself with cutlets! He didn't want them. Look how many there are left! What can I do with them now? And who have you left me to, you wicked George! He has left me and wouldn't take me with him, and wouldn't eat my cutlets! Oh, George dear!"

Three days later a hearse drawn by a grey horse stopped outside the house. The main doors were opened wide and an icy draught went through the whole building. There was a smell of pine. George was taken away.

During the funeral feast Shurka was exceedingly gay. Before she had eaten anything she drank half a glass of corn brandy. She became quite red, her tears began to flow, and stamping her foot she said in a broken voice:

"Ah, who is there? Come in all of you and be merry . . . all who wish. . . . I will let in everybody except George. . . . I won't let him in! He refused to eat my cutlets, definitely refused!"

And she fell heavily on the new trunk and began to beat her head on the musical lock.

After that everything in the lodging went on as before, quite orderly and decently. Shurka took up again a post as servant. Many men came during the winter to propose to her, but she refused them all. She was waiting for a quiet, kind one, and these were all bold fellows attracted by the things she had accumulated.

Towards the end of the winter she became considerably thinner and took to wearing a black woollen dress which even added to her good appearance. In the garage in the yard there was a certain chauffeur named Ivan. He was quiet,

kind and thoughtful. He was consumed with love for
Shurka. During the spring she also fell in love with him.

  The weather was beautiful. After listening impatiently to
the brief congratulatory speech of the assistant registrar of
marriages, the young couple went out of the office into the
street.
  "Now where shall we go?" asked the young Ivan shyly,
glancing sideways at Shurka.
  She pressed to his side, tickled his red ear with a twig of the
overpowering lilac, and dilating her nose, whispered:
  "To the bazaar! To buy things! Where otherwise?"
  And her eyes suddenly became quite large and round.

2681